Stoker

Evolution of a Vampire

A historical novel fusing the life and times
of an author, prince, and legend

CALVIN CHERRY

PAGE PUBLISHING, INC.
New York, NY

First originally published by Page Publishing, Inc. 2018

ISBN 978-1-64138-906-8 (Paperback)
ISBN 978-1-64138-907-5 (Digital)

Printed in the United States of America

Every writer has an inspiration.
Every icon holds a story.
Every legend hides a dark side.

In loving memory of the talented Abraham Stoker. He may be gone, but his Count lives on . . .

Foreword
A Note for an Undying Breed

Though I do not recall the exact moment or age when I was first introduced to the supernatural, I do fondly remember receiving a set of illustrated comic book-like classics for Christmas when I was around seven years old. There were four in all: *Moby Dick, Dr. Jekyll & Mr. Hyde, Frankenstein,* and *Dracula.*

I vividly recollect the latter of the four striking my interest profoundly; and by the age of ten, I somehow managed to trade something for an abridged version of Bram Stoker's masterpiece. Even though I did not completely understand and recognize the significance of the work until I was much older (since then I have read the unabridged version countless times), this early fascination spawned a whirlpool of trips to the school library to borrow books about ghosts, movie monsters, werewolves, and of course . . . vampires.

Flash forward several years. Now at age forty-seven, this unique hobby is still a big part of my leisure time. From vampire books to vampire films, I have experienced them all, and as with anything else, I have my favorites: Anne Rice's *The Vampire Lestat* and Joel Schumacher's *The Lost Boys* (just to name a few). Through everything, however, I have wondered what it would be like to have been a fly on the wall during the period leading up to—and including—the penmanship of *Dracula. It* has always amazed me how little the world knew of the historical Dracula and how interesting it would be to merge the two figures together into a historically based prequel to one of my all-time favorite novels. This book is the outcome of this dream, and its purpose is threefold: to entertain and educate the horror fan, to explore the taproots of where the genre was born, and to pay tribute to a remarkable writer and brilliant work.

This concept had been filed away—but frequently pondered—in my brain for nearly a decade, and it took less than a year to complete a draft. Though this is my first book, I found it very easy to develop what I trust readers will find to be an interesting (yet hopefully scary) plot centering historic characters and vampiric folklore that were already intriguing, infamous, and colorful respectively. Like Joel Schumacher set out to accomplish in his famous film, I wanted to keep to the roots of the folklore and spirit and style of *Dracula* while expanding upon concepts Stoker introduced (i.e., the Scholomance) while offering a unique twist to the legend. For example, why was Vlad buried on a desolate island surrounded by a lake?

Nevertheless, less than a few weeks after beginning my writing, my ex-wife began to notice a strange phenomenon in the master bedroom of my previous home in Kennesaw, Georgia. There was a stone figure of Vlad Tepes as a vampire bat that we had mounted to the wall opposite our bed. It hung upside down (such as that of an actual bat) with its head pointed to the floor. Directly over its heart was a hole for a second piece, a stone cross/stake that attached and doubled as a candleholder.

With this said, between the hours of noon to 5:00 p.m., Lisa was home with our son Jacob (who had just turned two) and began to discover that randomly, components of—or even the entire figure—would fall off the wall! This had never happened before though the decoration had been hanging there for about seven years! Some days, the candle would be under our bed, while other days, the cross would turn up missing. On several occasions, Vlad himself would be found on the floor, and on one particular disturbing instance, she found him hanging right side up with his head pointed to the ceiling! To make the ordeal even more interesting, she never heard or witnessed when any of the paranormal activity actually took place, and after about five encounters, we discovered a revelation: the pattern seemed to revolve around me completing an additional chapter in this very book! Though these experiences seemed to have continued all the way up to the completion of my novel, we never found a logical explanation. Vlad now hangs in the foyer of my current home in Hiram; but since the publication of *Stoker*, the figure of Vlad has stopped misbehaving. But the cross/stake candleholder has been missing for years.

But enough about my influences and onward to the man of the hour: Mister Abraham Stoker. So what contributed to this well-educated Irish theatre critic/manager in writing about the supernatural? In a Freudian-like answer, his mother. Certainly, Charlotte Stoker was a flamboyant character. For an Irishwoman in the early 1800s, she was a social crusader for female rights—something considered scandalous in the least, if not downright controversial for her time. She married Abraham Stoker Sr., a civil servant at Dublin Castle, and when she was not making speeches at the Statistical and Social Inquiry Society or volunteering at workhouses, she was busy being a mother of seven, the third eldest being Abraham (Bram) Stoker Jr.

Charlotte Stoker loved the arts. She attended every new production that came to town and educated herself with different cultures. She was also quite the storyteller and doted on Bram every opportunity she had. Whether it was travel, art, food, literature, or politics, she made sure to pass these passions on to Bram at an early age.

Being eccentric, she was also captivated by the supernatural and the bizarre. Bram recalled that his mother's favorite pastime was when she sat by his bedside at night and retold countless stories and myths of old Ireland. Often the tales included spirits, rotting corpses, or premature burials. They were always fascinating and were guaranteed to be unusual.

Likewise, his mother filed away in her brain numerous historical accounts of the famine and disease that she witnessed in life and would recount her own memories of surviving the cholera epidemic during the mid 1800s. In his adulthood, Bram recalled one such story in disturbing detail: "Day after day and night after night a priest sat with a horsewhip to prevent those wretches [doctors] dragging the patients down the stairs by their legs with their heads dashing on the stone steps, before they were dead," he wrote.

"By twos and threes our dead neighbors were carried away," she had told him, remembering the devastation cholera had left behind, "until two-thirds of the population were buried."

Though ghost stories and recollections of the macabre were Bram's way of gaining his mother's utmost attention, they were also a way of learning early on to celebrate both life and death; and in doing so, his overactive imagination was born—including the ghastly decomposing bodies that often hid under his childhood bed. Indeed, Charlotte Stoker was ahead of her time, and her influence continues to haunt the very masterpiece of horror that is known today as Bram Stoker's *Dracula*.

Yes, we all know the name Count Dracula. Many of us have read the book and have seen at least one of the many movies; however, few people know about the man behind the novel and the historical character from which the name was derived. Digging further, nevertheless, even fewer members of our society know about Bram's employer, actor Henry Irving, who likewise fit the physical traits and dark, somber personality in the famous text. Yes, as you may soon inquire, there was a Henry Irving; and positively, there was a Beefsteak Room (though it was said to be a hidden chamber off from a rear stairwell of the Lyceum Theatre). And oddly enough, the actor was actually more famous than Stoker, who failed to reach his appropriate fanfare until after death.

Nonetheless, the two were inseparable in life, and we know the Queen of England in fact knighted Henry as the first honorary actor before dying several years before Stoker. However, it has been said that Bram was so much a part of Irving's controlling and dismal life that Abraham suffered two strokes, partially due to the stress and separation of their peculiar relationship. In researching this topic in preparation for my novel, I could not help but see a connection between the author and his employer to Renfield and that of Count Dracula. In the pages ahead, I make an attempt to explore these same relationships by introducing a fictional Slovak (Nicolae), whom a friend of mine referred to as a "Renfield to the extreme."

Indeed, there is a fine line between history and fiction, and the book you are holding crosses the threshold that will probably tease many readers and leave them wondering "Was this really how it was?" No doubt, thus is where the power of literary license is most brilliant and will hopefully persuade the readers to beg for more. But in all fairness, I will clear up what I believe will be some of the misconceptions right away: Abraham Stoker never set foot in Transylvania, and though despite many Dracula loyalists' disappointment, there is no proof that Vlad Dracula was of the Un-Dead—that is, vampirically speaking!

Notwithstanding, perhaps the greatest difference between Stoker's masterpiece and this novel is the fact that I have merged the life and times of Vlad the Impaler in with the plot of the story that is loosely based on Bram Stoker's life (yes, he was an invalid until age eight), the vampire myth, and the creation of his famous work. The absolute carnage I suggest the historical prince practiced is from known events that have put him beside those of the likes of Adolf Hitler and Attila the Hun. We know his birth house in the town of Sighişoara, Transylvania, (now known as northern Romania) still exists and is toured frequently; in fact, the second floor has actually been remodeled into a restaurant! And the castle in Poenari is still visited today, though it is in ruins due to several earthquakes. Interestingly enough, the Romanian people view Vlad as a great warrior due his courage of standing up against the Turks, and consequently, a bust was resurrected in the courtyard of the city as a memorial and tribute to his powerful ruling. And rest assured, many of the vacationers that gaze upon it cannot help but think of the fictional Count simultaneously.

Perhaps Vlad's gravesite at the Snagov Monastery (Bucharest) is as intriguing as the historical leader himself, for century-old myths proposing that the Impaler's remains were moved, stolen, or never buried there at all led to excursions that revealed a gaping grave with a few animal bones. In the 1930s, a similar excavation to answer the lore that his cadaver was actually buried elsewhere in the monastery (a hidden tomb near the front door as opposed to under the main alter) unveiled a decapitated body, richly dressed. However, before adequate research could be conducted to identify the carcass, the dead body was stolen. Nevertheless, formal tours are given across

Vlad Dracula's stomping ground today (visit http://dractours.com), which are a peculiar makeup of historians, Bram Stoker fans, gothic enthusiasts, vampire cult members, or the dark and curious.

In addition, despite the misconception that the great man who brought the vampire myth and the renaissance of Vlad Tepes to the forefront of the gothic world, it could be said that Abraham Stoker was far from being as wealthy and famous as one of today would expect. Like Edgar Allen Poe, he would not live to see the literary impact his novel would have on our society and the movie industry as a whole; of course, after its first publication in 1897, it has never been out of print, and second to the Holy Bible, *Dracula* has sold more copies than any other book in modern history. Though Abraham Stoker did not have much faith in seeing his book take to the stage—let alone invade Hollywood—Count Dracula has been portrayed on the big screen more than any other character in the era of film.

However, when Bram died on April 20, 1912, and less than a year after publishing *The Lair of the White Worm* (with a disappointing result, I might add), the widowed Florence Stoker lived another twenty-three years and was able to see her husband's legacy flourish to new heights. Along with this notoriety came the publication of *Dracula's Guest* (which was to be believed to be Chapter 1 of his novel that was pulled at the last minute due to length and bits of which I also weave into the plot of *Stoker*) and lawsuits that, with Noel Stoker's council, kept the film industry from using his psychologically thrilling tale or characters without sufficient rights or permission. She died in 1935 a few years after Bela Lugosi became a household name—one that would forever be associated as the ultimate Count and the supreme visual image of the man "clad all in black."

Not all was a calamity or setback in the Stoker family. Noel, who married and became a successful attorney, had one daughter and lived long enough to see the true import of his father's work, which set the stage for the genre to follow, until he joined his parents in 1961. But as a boy, as depicted in the pages to come, I would like to add that it had to be interesting, being raised by such a unique and eccentric father. There was the occasional pass down of ghost stories of three generations and instances where actor Henry Irving frightened the young boy in various costumes. Furthermore, impromptu trips to Cruden Bay were common. Yes, at Kilmarnock Arms, the remaining chapters of *Dracula* were completed (some even suggest Slains Castle was used as an inspiring model for Castle Dracula), and Noel's description of his mother's gracefulness causing men in public to "stand up in chairs" to have a better look said it best and told of her amazing attributes that attracted high society. We know through diaries, letters, and written accounts that Florence's good looks did not bring with it a life of heavenly blitz—she was often alone, bored, and unhappy. Ironically, her secret admirer's most famous work (referring to Oscar Wilde and his novel *The Picture of Dorian Gray*) preaches vanity has its price. And certainly for a woman who struggled to maintain her graceful youth even into her senior years and long after Bram's death, one could create a symbolic connection by seizing the opportunity as an open invitation to a vampire.

It is also a fact that the Stoker's dined often with the "bigwigs" of their time and that others in Bram's profession not only admired him as a man but also respected him as a scholar and an inspiring writer. Certainly, all these factors, people, and places must have played an important part in his creative proceedings. I took this into careful consideration while writing this novel. Several of the connections I reference are known fact while some have been the object of speculation. And then there are some fresh influences that are there due to literary appeal. In other words, it makes for a good story!

But undoubtedly, it was not just the people in Stoker's life or Le Fanu's *Carmilla* that influenced his famous work, but it was also the love for the theatre. For example, the dark, foreboding castle in Macbeth is recreated in *Dracula*, in addition to the three dark sisters, an impeding sense of doom, and a taste for blood. It the famous scene where Lady Macbeth washes clean the gore on her hands, the feeling of being "unclean" is foreshadowed when Mina Harker wipes Dracula's carnage from her lips. Likewise, Abraham Stoker was said to have had a keen peculiar interest in the supernatural. In fact, many even suggest that a nightmare resulting and accompanying a severe case of food poisoning brought about the plot of his story. In my tribute to the man, I play on such urban legends throughout my text as I honor his heritage by using the Celtic crucifix as the weapon of choice in his search, seizure, and slaughter of the King Vampire.

Moreover, just as Abraham Stoker paid tribute to his close colleague Oscar Wilde (by using the word *wild* frequently in his work) and by borrowing first and surnames from real persons, I too have taken such literary license: Sea Captain Oscar (Wilde) (Walt) Whitman and fictional character Jonathan (Harker) Watts, just to name a few. Furthermore, I would also like to note that my take on the characters Professor Abraham Van Helsing (Doctor Van Zant) and Lord Godalming (Old Man Godalming) share in this prequel in a reverse sort of way. For example, in Stoker's classic, Lord Godalming is a secondary character that we know little about and walks in Van Helsing's limelight as a student as opposed to a teacher. However, I have swapped places and have Old Man Godalming as the instructor and main character while, rather, Doctor Van Zant is the nonbeliever who is educated through trial and peril.

Indeed, Stoker's model has stood the test of time as with Vlad's legend and the ever-popular vampire myth. Their almost cult-like following is as true to life and popular today and could not be so eloquently proven by the internationally celebrated convention of Dracula's 100th birthday in 1997 hosted across various parts of the globe (i.e., Los Angeles, California, USA; Whitby Bay, England, UK) and as with the opening of *Dracula: The Musical.* And the obsession does not show any sign of stopping. A few years later, Anne Rice's *The Vampire Chronicles* was taken to the stage (with a soundtrack written by Sir Elton John and his long time lyricist Bernie Taupin), and rumors of a full-blown Dracula theme park is said to be under development and to be located in either to be opened in Vlad's birth town of Sighişoara or near his burial site at Snagov Lake. And if that is not enough, a recent website I visited suggested there is another attempt to find/exhume Vlad Dracula's body and to actually "clone" Vlad to fight what is being referred to—or suggested as—a vampire-like disorder (what?). Finally, there are many more vampire films in the hopper, which will be sure to entertain or annoy (for who can beat Lugosi's portrayal?) the die-hard fan. So Un-Dead Heads . . .

stay tuned! For the purposes of my novel, I felt like it was critical to research how modern society has strayed away from the original myth, having been strongly influenced from Hollywood's spin and modern vampiric literature. As we know from Stoker's own notes, he researched the vampire myth thoroughly, and I wanted to write a book that explained the evolution of the myth (something usually reserved for a subject matter book as opposed to a story), I felt it made sense for me to trace the author's steps by making references to these texts, and in some cases (for not all of his reference material is still in print), I almost recreate his notes for the reader to learn from.

In conclusion, as I have suggested that Abraham Stoker's mother and Henry Irving were a piece of his literary work, here I pose that Vlad the Impaler was part of *Dracula* too. But the reality is this connection is up to the reader to decide for himself. Indeed, it is fact that the link between the historical and fictional Dracula has been in debate for years and somewhat ambiguous to prove based on Stokers notes, which are on display in the Rosenbach Museum in Philadelphia. Fact: We know one of the books he used in his research of Wallachia mentioned Vlad Dracula. There is also a strong possibility that Arminius Vambery, a Hungarian folklore expert he met in 1890, shared details of the the Impaler. But just how much Bram Stoker knew of Vlad is a riddle experts have been chasing for years. And to what extent his fictional character was influenced by this knowledge is left up to our imaginations. On the other hand, no Dracula enthusiasts can dispute the origin of the name, for there is, and will always be, one true Dracula: Vlad the Impaler. Indeed, we can't argue where the name came from. And certainly the rich history the vampire reveals to Jonathan Harker in Chapter 3 almost appear to be excerpts from the Prince's biography: "When was redeemed that great shame of my nation, the shame of Cassova, when the flags of the Wallach and the Magyar went down beneath the Crescent, who was it but one my own race who at Voivode crossed the Danube and beat the Turk on his own ground?" We can prove that around the same time Stoker was researching material for Dracula, the British Museum had purchased one of the German pamphlets printed in 1491, which related atrocities about Dracula. Possibly Stoker discovered it there on his own or had been directed to it by Vambery. In addition, we have Van Helsing's statements such as, "I have asked my friend Arminius, of Buda-Pesth University, to make his record; and . . . he must, indeed, have been that Voivode [Prince] Dracula who won his name against the Turk." Though Bram Stoker never set foot in Castle Dracula physically, one might argue that he was taken there in a spiritual sense. Indeed, such statements seem to foreshadow Vlad Tepes's life and cannot be mere coincidence.

So what reason is there to explore this riddle and test our imaginations? Because if we all reach deep into the darkest chambers of our souls, do we not all have an essence of the man inside us we all love to hate and fear? He is the demon that perches itself on our shoulder as a child when contemplating on telling a lie. He is the inner voice that talks an adolescent into committing a heinous crime. He is the hardened part of a husband's heart that suggests he commit adultery. As a result, the bridge between fact and fiction becomes unclear, the fine line between good and evil becomes clouded, and the overpowering horror that continues to terrorize young and old alike surfaces to a new level of madness and cruelty.

So finally, I bid you adieu on what I hope you will find to be a pleasant and dark journey, and upon its conclusion, when you turn out the light at night and are afraid to confront the face that might appear in the bedroom window, remember there *are* such things— and they *are* far worse than death. They are *Un-Dead* . . .

Author, Calvin H. Cherry, 2017

Letter from Abraham Stoker to Florence Stoker—found unopened by his widow two weeks after his death.

St. George's Eve, 1888

My dear Florie:

It is with superstitious and unnatural terror that propels me to write this letter—if for no other reason than to quiet my frantic heart and untamed nerves after the peril that befell these eyes tonight has reeked havoc on thy own brain and has remained unchecked. Henceforth if it may come to pass your own precious orbs set their sight on these words so alarming, then honor and preserve my name and sanity—for this I have surely been reduced! Whence all things that seem as they may abruptly uproot themselves and leave a man questioning events and facts that he would not bare to his own soul, then how shall he ever sleep thereafter? Alas, but forgive me. I am somewhat previous.

I resolved to venture out tonight with the underlying reason to critique a particular performance for my column. Notwithstanding, it 'twas what would occur afterward that continues to chill my heart to the core. As I left my fly at the curb of the theatre, the midnight blue sky was beginning to cast a patch of shifting clouds over the landmark. From the onset of the evening, I found it to be a gloomy one. I stood silent for several minutes, unmoved as I stared upward. The smoky abyss almost appeared to be a pair of massive, claw-like hands that lashed out and placed a chokehold over the fair prism of light that modestly lit a portion of the roof and front of the structure. This peculiar effect transitioned me into a morose disposition whilst I witnessed the few people, whom were also arriving to join in on this midnight mass, approach sporadically, out of tune with another. This lapse between entering guests might have appeared to the average onlooker to mean absolutely nothing—that is to say, totally normal. But to another with a keen eye and skeptical nature, the embarking few could be arriving in secrecy—as acquaintances, in fact, as opposed to perfect strangers. Their oncoming dark shadows descended upon the ground like extensions of something far from the semblance of man but rather something supernatural. With the exception of an occasional whisper of a fellow society member exiting a horse drawn carriage or taxi, only the sounds of crickets summoned the air.

Once isolated and secured inside the edifice that harbored our affairs like an un-kept wavering spouse, we proudly announced our kindred unity: "Hail to the Masonic society! Hail to the Hermetic Order of the Golden Dawn!" Hitherto, my intrigue toward the western esoteric tradition had captured my interest in the philosophical, spiritual, and psychic evolution of humanity. And as my growing interest in the principles of occult science, systems of mysticism, and applications of Egyptian ceremonial magic brought me to the group, it was something much darker that caused me to flee from it!

The room that doubled as the Osiris Temple this terrible night contained a total of seven members, including myself: Sir Richard Burton, J. W. Brodie-Innes, Pamela Colman Smith, Arthur Edward Waite, Arthur Machen, and the remaining spectator—a friend who has requested to remain anonymous. We gathered in this medium sized chamber set forth to practice the ancient art of necromancy.

Sister Pamela, who had previously explained to all of us that witches are astrologers by heart, were, and for the sake of the new coven, still are women of science, picked this exact night and hour to contact the dead for grave purposes. For she boldly stated, "On the eve of St. George the moons of the universe are precisely aligned and in perfect harmony with the spirits that have crossed over—or, in any respect, those that are trapped between the physical and spiritual world hereafter. "The physical body," she went on, "which has long rotted away in the molded grave, has mated with the maggot and has established kinship with the moth and the beetle." The others looked on at her with unsettled glances of wonder and amazement. "But the soul . . ." and here she paused and held up her left index finger which was bejeweled with a large onyx, "the soul's eternal place of rest is determined by a twist of fate we can command; and therefore we should look to the stars for inspiration and guidance!"

"Ah! The human soul," Burton said with a wry smile, "a gift we hope to give back to the almighty if not ruined foremost by the wrath of man! Nay, time does not alter our appearance to a sight of ugliness; nor does age harden our hearts to one of wickedness. This, my friends, is brought on by the rude work of humanity gone astray!"

To this we all nodded our heads in agreement. We checked the time. It was a quarter of an hour shy of midnight. By and by, I broke the awkward silence that was solely masked by the ticking of the clock. It was apparent we all fell into a sort of state of introspection. "Alas," said I, "the greatest work of mankind started in the brain; however, pride, greed, and unwanton curiosity shall always spark a thought which questions our motives and level of our own intelligence at such a profane time. Let's pray this is not such an occurrence!"

"Amen" was the anonymous words that chimed the chamber. And with mechanical nods resembling those of seven synchronized marionettes, we began the ritual that would reshape all our lives.

"It is midnight—the eve of St. George—the witching hour, when we mystics assert that all spirits are without rest and when necrosis is at its prime," explained the witch. "What say you . . . shall we prepare?"

We all motioned with various gestures and gazed speechless as she donned the mysterious garb of a sorceress: a heavy black, felt cloak, fastened at the neck by a remarkable amulet of a pentagram which connected to a golden chain that shimmered against the super sensitive skin. This spectacle added even more wonder to her dress; for though it was soothing to the eye, it made me shudder all the same. In the center beheld a great ruby—of immaculate color, as bright as blood—whereon the luminosity shineth. At first glance it was the priceless antiquity of the object which drew my attention to its radiance, for no doubt, the worth of such a huge jewel would bring a fortune to a collector of precious stones. Nevertheless, it was rather the strangeness and resemblance of the accompanying gems that caused me to start back in fleeting paralysis: by the flickering flame of a candle our sister hostess had since lighted clearly revealed seven stars, each containing precise seven points. I then recounted the number of us in the room and let out a low intake of breath and suffered in silence as all color left my face.

"The stars summon us!" Pamela cried. The ominous calm we all seemed to share was suddenly replaced by a vague, overpowering sense of morbid resonance as our host lifted off a jewel studded cloth from atop the table revealing a glass ball made of beryl. We all drew back in breathless bewilderment mingled with a nebulous feeling and look of consternation about the object, the woman, and what they each represented: the unknown; the suspense; the recklessness abandonment.

As we all clasped hands and cleared our minds in complete quiet, our goddess of misrule placed her hands over the object and began to slowly speak. As she addressed the crystal, it caused my breath to stand still—for it was the result of months of diligent study that we sought for: an Egyptian Sorceress that commanded a society with a power—a being whom was too well advanced and abhorred in her day—one we all wanted to communicate with; to learn from her; and like elementary pupils fancying a well-versed instructor, Queen Tera had seven disciples tonight.

As our coven joined a chain, the corresponding seven stars seemed to illuminate one by one as our hands touched. The sight of that wondrous ruby, now noticeably ancient in the bright radiance, caused my mind to drift hastily to my fond, ubiquitous comrade, Sir William

Wilde or Merrion Square, in my native Dublin, whose excavation In Saqqara, Egypt, dug up the mummy which told of the identity we quest to reach tonight. "For William," I thought to myself as the clock on the nearby mantelpiece struck twelve.

And then we quickly labored to make contact. How shall I even begin to tell such a queer experience? My heart raced without harness as the perspiration began to collect and drip from my brow and the end of my nose. My nerves quivered. Hitherto, the voice of the witch spoke in a manner that caused my nerves to contract; however, her body soon grew lithe and agile, and from that point forward, the manner of her speech changed to resemble that of another – one much deeper, like that of a man – which made my limbs twitch and tighten to whence I was frozen in fright.

And then the unexpected happened.

My dear, Florie, 'tis true there are some abnormalities in human nature that are so strange that one must pass through them to fully comprehend. Insomuch a shadowy pall obscured a great deal of the details that followed, I will my mind and gall to record everything that I can recollect of that heinous night. Indeed, her very personality seemed to become absorbed by another of a malignant nature—for her mannerisms and tonal quality of her voice transitioned as words flowed in a pitch of untellable pathos. At once the witch's speech broke off in mid syllable; and her eyes became a dull yellowish tint, as one would witness in a corpse that 'twas longing for the ground.

She gasped . . . but only once.

And with a gaping mouth and an everlasting stare of unbounded horror, she fell back in her chair lifeless. As she did so, I stood spellbound on that wondrous ruby, so too those with me, as it darkened harshly around her skinny neck. At last, her final words echoed in my ears for several minutes, "Bagali Laca Bachale!"

The remaining six did not know what to think of this. Notwithstanding, we did not comprehend the sequence of events—that is, as those of reality—until the violent hands of time proved we were not to be awakened. Henceforth, a strange fear gripped us like a boa constrictor by the throat. We looked at one another . . . dumbfounded in a half shock half frightened sort of way. Hitherto the ball began to glow like a blue flame whilst an eerie semblance of foreign matter—such as specks of dust—fixated itself around the table in the form of a circle. A seething horde of spirits seemed to conjure up from the matter and began to swarm the object to which we all were obsessed with now lackluster eyes.

As I felt all of the rosiness escape my cheeks, I sensed a new form of intelligence had entered the room. Shapeless shadows blasted from the crystal, splitting it into hundreds of minute, shattered fragments. One of the members let out a shrill shriek as the largest piece struck him in the center of the skull with the immense velocity of a bullet. A raging stream of blood flowed freely from the wound. Three others fled the place in states of indescribable trepidation. So strong was the feeling to hurry from the place myself, only believing that running from the specter could only increase my plight of danger, I remained.

And mustering all the bravery I could, I finally addressed it point blank:

"Queen Tara! Is it you?" I whispered to the glowing object that seemed to almost leap and became animated like a living ember. At this moment I experienced a quick rush of wind pass through me like an apparition. Along with this peculiarity, I instantly became light headed and almost sickly to my stomach. And surely if I was not already seated, I would have joined Sister Pamela on the cold, hard floor. Alas, as I sat gazed and overwhelmed by the conglomerate of these baffling sensations, her still body, which was already showing a degree of stiffness and chill, merged with the feelings of uncertainty and danger, caused a neurotic condition that shot a bolt of panic throughout my system. This spout of dread and lack of self control must have left me in disarray for a short while as my next recollection 'twas only to discover another member had disappeared from my group whilst the remaining personage, whose identity I must holdback, lay too on cold floor, breathing stutteringly, with a look of madness across the face.

The shriek of terror that communicated that I was, indeed, utterly alone in this threatening séance started yet provoked me to redouble my efforts; and I commenced shaking my unconscious friend to almost violent proportions. The result was disappointing, for my efforts were in vain. Kind wife, ne'er had I been abandoned in such a bleak state of distress! What was I to do?

The blood that gushed from my companion's head wound seeped across the deck, under the back of the aforementioned, and beside the head of the woman. But it was not 'til the amulet that lay next to it suddenly changed to a matching horrid hue that I was thunderstruck by a feeling of uncraven horror.

"Holy Virgin!" I croaked. "Queen Tara?" I repeated with a breaking voice. "Did you do this?"

Henceforth the matter, whence seemed to float downward and circle the table like a cocoon of death, began to shine an even more lurid blue as the center of the crystal darkened in contrast. And in a fleeting moment, I thought I saw the image of a tall, richly dressed figure flit past my eye and then fade to black. My eyes closed in wild confusion. And, as I did so, out of a secret hiding place crept my soul. I watched in helpless anticipation as it lingered in the air of corruption all around me. This horrible feeling lasted for at least half a minute. And then joltingly, an ear piercing bellow that originated from the pit of one's stomach called my name. But from whose voice it belonged, I do not know. Nevertheless, I felt the severe awareness of evil mixed with a curious desire to listen. My uncertainty was then coupled with an insatiable appetite for something that I could not comprehend. All these terrible shocks, fantastic sensations and overbearing fears became too much for one human frame to withstand. I closed my eyes and fell into a stupor . . .

And now . . . here I sit in my own study. How I found my way back to my humble abode unharmed, I cannot fathom. Is it that the spirit of Tara thrives on my mixed emotions? Only she and the almighty can speak of this, and neither has answered my query. Though the thought of finding even small elements of pleasure in such a place and time repels me as I recall this nightmarish ordeal, I can't help but think logically that when one unlocks his chamber and spills the secrets of his soul, that it not be looked upon by man as a false pretense but by the father as a forgiven repentance of sin. It is true that the remarkable night was over, but the mystery of it lingers: Did two die to give life? And if this notion rings true, whose life was resurrected? And finally, 'twas this frightening night only the revolting prelude of hundreds to come?

As I tax my brain with these and other stimulating questions, something deep within my darkest corner of my soul seems to know these answers and I shudder to write of them. Just as my studies of Egyptology took me to faraway places that were close to my heart, this phantom somehow affected me in a way that altered my own spirit and redirected my purpose henceforth. I feel myself morbidly enthralled about something I cannot possibly understand; yet in this same thread of thought and analogous breath, I cringe in horror. I feel corrupt and accursed for surrendering.

Lovely wife, can it be the bane of man's existence haunted me tonight? Has an omen from beyond merged with the dim and jagged edge of my core? Or am I suffering from delusions? I sense that through my unknowing, its life altering influence is planning to taint the world with a torrent of blood and reap sorrow, pain, and eternal fear in exchange for fame. Yet I feel hopeless in stopping it and quite bewildered to conjure up such an incredible idea. Notwithstanding, I cannot shake this melancholic unraveling of thought. This night I feel the purpose of my life was renewed: I was introduced to an alternative motive and a new manner has been beset before me to be explored.

My dear Florie, my conscience is telling me its story has become my story - that the fiber of my essence divulges my tale has become its medium for survival. Unless the facts of tonight that I have so fully unburdened prove to be fancy, promise me you pray for both of us and for our son's safety. Thus, if proven true, this story will be like none other ever told; and there is forbidden danger in writing such an outrage on humanity. Nevertheless, whatever my fate will be, I know there is no escaping it. For one thing is certain: once you have had a glimpse of the dark side, it stays with you to the end.

Your loving husband,
Bram

Prologue

The cold rain clattered on the windowsill of the modest upper level flat. The apartment's address was 7 South Hampton Street, which happened to be located on the west end of town in the noisy market district of Covent Gardens and walking distance of London's main shopping, dining, and entertainment hub. Though old English tulips surrounded the apartment at the ground, in contrast, other areas were not projecting the elegance it so desired for the residence was beginning to show signs of age: the worn roof needed repairing, and several windowpanes were broken. Nevertheless, it was home to a middle-class aspiring aristocrat and his Victorian family. As the droplets fell harder, the wind joined the crusade, blowing feverishly—almost howling like a wild wolf ready to jump on its prey. A small puddle of water formed in the floor of the study of Abraham Stoker, a theatre critic by trade and a theatre manager by profession. As he sat under a desk staring at the cracked glass and then into the orange flame of a candle that rested to the left side of his work, his wife, Florence, rested soundly two rooms over, as did his son, Noel, across the hall.

As the man snatched a paper from a new typewriter, which was positioned in the direct center of the desk, he finished editing his latest stage review. After sealing it in an envelope he preaddressed, at once, he cast it aside and immediately begun to adjust a table of numbers to close out the quarterly expense ledger for the Lyceum Theatre. In time, his eyes began to see double digits; consequently, his mind began to wander and he yawned resignedly. By and by, the writer rested his elbows on each corner of the desk, cupped his head in his hands, and began to eyeball the room.

The study doubled as a library. Thus, his vision sporadically fell upon a mass of papers that sat next to an entire row of books on Egyptology on the top inter-most shelf, next to the door of the room which exited into the hall nearest the two bedrooms. The papers were an unfinished handwritten draft of a novel titled *The Jewel of the Seven Stars*.

Stoker frowned. It was evident to himself his work at the theatre was preventing him from turning out a book every other year. And coupled with his column in the Dublin Express, he overheard Florence Stoker's powerful words that described his vocation: "A ministry of absence."

With a sad look upon his face, Bram shifted his work to the left of his desk and opened the top drawer, revealing a diary that he placed in front of him.

The journal was opened to a page dated April 16, 1897—an era in which a great upsurge of the Victorian class stood bewildered whilst mechanization and invention led to England becoming the workshop of the world. Despite this twentieth-century pressure, the scribe was written close to an Old English calligraphic style at the top of the paper. The rest of the diary was completely full of various handwritten notes. But almost hidden from sight, opposite the machine rested a thick manuscript, bundled together with a several pieces of string as if pending an editor's analysis.

As soon as Abraham's sockets fixed upon the sight, he immediately turned away in breathless horror. As if it were some omen of torment, he grew nervous and feverish from the mere sight of the completed novel. As he protracted backward in his chair, he looked down at his feet and said with a quivering lip, "You are my creator, but I will become your master!"

It was just after midnight—the "witching hour," his mother would have called it—and with the exception of the pelting rain and the occasional burst of wind, which would lunge itself against in thrashes as if in some mad fit of rage to get inside, a feeling of melancholic desolation weighted down the study like a foreboding sense of gloom and compelling eeriness. The author shook away his apprehension, and in a stoat-like fashion, he looked at his latest project with both abhorrence and praise and thought to himself, *It is a montage, a whirlwind, a dream, a life, and a nightmare all in one.*

His sight finally left the manuscript keenly, and with a tear in his eye, which could be classified as one partly, derived from a terse form of gladness and a weary sense of exasperation, he let out a prolonged sigh of agony.

"This . . ." he whispered aloud as he placed his hand on the final draft of the book, "this motley tale of unbridled terror has become the scourge of my existence!"

Alas, it was a strange internal struggle indeed when a person's vocation becomes an avocation. And due to the thick of pain and boundless grief, which, consequently, lived out every word of his most recent work, Bram's lifelong passion for literature was certainly being tested. This scuffle was likewise occurring at a time in his life when he was finding it difficult to make an earnest livelihood as a result of it. The author gleamed at several published articles of his such as *The Duties of Clerks of Petty Sessions in Ireland* to short fictional stories such as *The Snake's Pass* on a nearby shelf with pride, although the royalties from the moderate success of such works required him to supplement his income by maintaining his job at the theatre.

As he sat stock still on the wooden bench with his rough hands over his distraught face, he contemplated if this next novel would thrive any better. After all, it would no doubt be received as a more gothic-like, frightening and physiologically compelling tale of terror for anyone that dared to pick it up. But despite Stoker's belief that his novel would come across as a great scare for many, he knew firsthand that its development was not without a steep price. The author wanted it to bore a hell within the soul of every reader only to pine for the pilgrimage to extinguish it by his destruction—*its* destruction. Undeniably, it was a sore trial to write, and hitherto, Bram thought transcribing his madness to paper would somehow keep him quiet and liberated from the dire ordeal. On the other hand, it had proven to take the opposite approach.

Such irony, he thought to himself. *It all comes rushing back when the moonbeams flood my pupils, and the dark chambers of my core awaken once more!*

Similar to the Greek *Katharsis*, any self-purification or revitalizing in writing this story resulted in a sudden emotional breakdown that aroused in the author overwhelming feelings of fear, anguish, and melancholy.

"By God's cross—the climax is over! Henceforth, deliver me spiritual peace!"

For a native Irishman of forty-three years of age, he looked to be at least a decade older. His burley stature was discounted by his tired eyes and shown premature lines on his bold forehead. Hitherto, the malevolent events that led to his latest creation had caused the writer's bushy ginger hair to begin to recede. His beard was unkempt. As a boy who could not walk until age seven, his then invalid legs seemed to be cursing him now—as if forcing him out of bed each night to perform a midnight watch. As Bram's quick and neurotic glances toggled back and forth between the broken window and his desk he began to write: "It has been seven years—seven long years since the dream awoke me with a feeling of such an unspeakable horror. I now pray for my sanity every time I close my eyes . . . I fear *it* might return." Little did Stoker know that the beast he was meant to write about would forever be entwined and associated with the man—the author—of whom he wrote, for just like Victor Frankenstein's monster, the reanimated corpse was forever *his* burden; and it was *his* own creation that led to *his* demise.

Suddenly, the sound of a dog barking in the distance caused Abraham to leap from his chair and dart to the window with pulsating, piercing eyes. The Irishman wiped the foggy residue off the pane with his right hand and suppressed a shutter as he cursed at the howling creature.

"Bah! To hell with the hounds! How dare one creep upon me! Bother the accursed beasts! Night's forsaken children!"

Then he slipped the large typed manuscript into a black leather bag thrice its size. The stack of paper was swallowed up in the black pit as the man patted the traps saying, "Godalming, your handbag of horrors continues to serve a purpose . . . this one is you, mate."

As he stared into the flickering flame that continued to dance wildly, projecting all sorts of queer silhouettes about the ceiling, he added "Finis!" to his diary, put out the flame in between his right thumb and index finger, and left the study to join Florence in hopes to find comforting sleep. But never in his wildest dreams did he realize that his own nightmare would be haunting those of others an entire century later. The Irishman's gray eyes closed as he reclined against his pillow while his thoughts drifted back to seven years earlier: the origin of a myth, the rise and fall of a Wallachian Voivod, and the birth of a monster. And just as Mother Nature's cycle of season's transition from sunshine to briskness to snow, at the autumn of one's life, a higher power finds it appropriate to escort man back to the beginning to retrace his path. Regardless if one's choices were of benevolence or cruelty, in the end we must go there again before the judgment.

Whatever the case may be, if those steps trailed in life were of radiance or obscurity, they are our own to justify. Indeed, life can be fuller and brighter to walk alongside the righteousness of the Father's angels; however, as the soon-to-be acclaimed author reflected, it is those walks with the Devil's demons that tempts, tries, and challenges our character by forcing us to make a stand for what we believe in.

For Abraham Stoker, this year was 1890 . . .

CHAPTER 1

A Close Encounter

> There are bad dreams for those who sleep
> unwisely.
> —Dracula to Jonathan Harker

𝕴t was a typical Sunday evening at the Stoker household: Bram,
who was seated at the kitchen table, held up the *Dublin Evening
Mail* insomuch it concealed his entire face from his family. His nostrils flared and his brow contracted in heavy wrinkles while his eyes
darted over every headline. Seeing his father's focus was concentrated
on the words of the paper, Noel Stoker decided to disrupt the silence
by making some of his own.

"Papa," the young lad yelped as he tugged harshly at his elder's
trousers, pulling himself up into his lap, "May I have permission?"

The boy's eyebrows gathered together impatiently when he
received no response and he began groping his way up the chair,
reaching for the paper that stood in the way between father and son.

Florence Stoker, who was not used to having her husband home
from the theatre this early on a Sunday, motioned Noel down from
the chair with an imploring wave of the hand as she began to clear
the supper table.

The Irish author, who invariably maintained a faraway look
in his steely gray eyes, had lowered his face over the paper and was

oblivious to all other causes. His dour characteristics and disproportional features were profoundly noticeable at the moment: his wide forehead, which centered itself above his otherwise small almond-shaped orbs and revealing curious visage. Likewise, Mother Nature had granted him a queer large bump over his eyebrows—a birth feature he spent his entire lifetime in embarrassment of—and he stroked it discreetly with his left hand as he flipped pages with his right. His thick reddish beard seemed to be an indicative symbol of his scrutinizing study and rendered him in control of the table before him.

"Papa!" Noel called out again, this time with a higher and louder pitch tone that resembled the sharp pang of a whistle. Bram slowly lowered the news to his eye level, and without words, his intense look communicated the message he wished not to be disturbed at the moment. Feeling dejected, Noel shifted his energy to his mother's attention, which jumped from beverage preparation to her son as he tugged impatiently at her dress.

"I want it, Mama," Noel Stoker pleaded, with scowling face and wrinkled nose.

"Noel, please . . . not now," his mother interjected before her husband rose from his chair.

Florence, who was born Anne Lemon Balcome, looked on as she poured herself and her husband a spot of tea from the fire. She was a frail and small woman but managed to hold court wherever she was. At five feet eight, she was delicate where her husband was hardy, she was chatty where he was reticent and she was inquisitive where he was unconcerned.

She sat at the kitchenette wearing an English bonnet and day dress, quietly sipping a cup of hot tea. And seeing that Bram was reading his own review of *Hamlet*, being another great follower of the cinema and the work of William Shakespeare, she lifted the paper from under her husband's hands in complete silence. The writer watched his spouse's face as she quickly read the piece and could tell from her beam she was so enthralled by what Abraham had written analyzing the performance of Henry Irving as Hamlet for the Theatre Royal.

"I do believe your stamp of approval gives Mr. Irving's ability the credit he so desires and deserves," Florence said cheerfully.

Bram grunted in a neutral sort of way that caused his wife's mood and tone to drop to a laconic manner. He took another sip of his tea before taking the paper back from Florence. Out of the corner of his eye, he saw his son begin to climb up on of the chairs and reach for something that was on the top shelf of the cupboard.

"Alas," Florence continued, "I would fancy to accompany you on the opening of *Faust* if Mother minds Noel for a night—as it would be such as the lovely evening we met!" She said this in a dreamy sort of way that made Bram smile as if he recalled that evening too. "Can we not be fellow spectators for one night only? I do get awful weary of you keeping up the front of the Lyceum and wish you in the audience with me."

"A genius! Autocrat! The man was better than ever," her husband replied as she looked up in a distraught sort of way. "Henry's portrayal of the wild, fitful, irresolute, mystic, melancholy prince that we know in the play was spot on, but given with a sad, picturesque gracefulness which is the actor's special gift—"

"Did you not hear a word I just said?" Florence interrupted bitterly.

Indeed, now working also as Irving's agent and acting manager at London's Lyceum Theatre, Stoker's time was divided, and on occasion, Bram and Florence found themselves somewhat estranged. The emotional distance between the three family members was so thick in the room at that very instant that it was only ironic when Noel, who suddenly leapt from the cupboard with a dagger, began to make pretend stab marks at the air asking, "May I take it to school for show?"

"Are you daft? What would the headmaster say to this?" Florence Stoker replied crossly, looking like a half-concerned mother and a half-astonished Victorian princess. "Can you believe such nonsense, Bram? Taking a butcher like that to class would be absolutely dreadful!"

Like Florence, Irving Noel Thornley Stoker was a talkative lad; thus he seemed to get along and relate to his mother better than his father whom was absent a majority of his early childhood. In contrast to his father, the lad had grown up to loathe the theatre, comparing it to a thief that stole his Papa's days and nights. Noel's most frequent contact with his father was mainly watching the elder dress in making ready to spend long hours at work whilst he listened to the retelling of Charlotte Stoker's tales, Stoker's own stories of Irish pixies and supernatural horror myths that would become the center of several of the author's works.

Bram Stoker, who was a large, burly man, was once referred to by his son as a "red-bearded giant" who used to "lie at full length on the drawing room carpet, and let me climb about his chest" after his father would come home at night for a solitary late supper that would be warmed on the kitchen coals. But even though Noel was raised in solitude and was somewhat deprived of fathering during his formative years, the Irishman did not refrain from making comments about his son's peculiarly handsome looks.

"Look at the little chap, Florie! He resembles a cupid with his arrow!"

Master Noel held up the impressive blade to his father, who in turn placed down the news. Abraham pointed the knife toward the ceiling of the kitchen as if it was an object of study. "You acquired this at Godalming's shop, I presume? Excellent craftsman work, but alas . . . no doubt you somehow talked the Old Man out of it without his approval. Nay, it be certainly not for classroom show-and-tell. And certainly not at your age! You better get along without it!"

"Humph," sighed eleven-year old Noel as he lowered his head in disappointment.

"Mind your father. He knows best," Mrs. Stoker pleaded as she placed the dagger back in an aged brown leather bag and secured in the cupboard.

Having been born into a military family she was socially ambitious and frivolous all the same. Though she was eleven years younger than her husband, this did not make her any less courageous than he, and if Abraham considered himself the most masculine man, then Florence Balcombe was indeed his grand feminine counterpart. Despite the fact she was penniless when they met, she was born into the Victorian era and she fit the description well. She was strikingly pretty—one that loved to test wits—and was considered admirable by everyone she came in contact with. And even though her beauty attracted too many promiscuous gazes for Bram to deal with, she thrived on these reactions. For all intents and purposes, she could have been classified as a lady-in-waiting, but tonight, she was pleased that her husband was home.

"Now bugger off to bed, little man!" the writer said, swatting his son on the bum.

As Noel inched out of the room, Florence Stoker hesitated a moment and then whispered assertively in Abraham's ear. "No more bloody stories!" Florence insisted. "He probably feels he needed to purchase a knife for protection from all the ghosts and ghouls that your mother poisoned you with . . . 'tis no wonder you have been waking up every night for the past week in cold sweat! Stop this madness now before you spread your night terrors on to the rest of the household!"

The author stood up with a sigh and then walked to the front window and looked out upon the ray that was sinking fast. The residence, which overlooked a private garden, featured a setback that allowed hansoms and broughams to drive to the front door. The man studied it as if he expected company. Though Florence felt this orchestration suggested a high-class level of importance, she secretly loathed when unwanted visitors would call on her husband, especially Henry Irving, for he would call on him all the time and at the most inopportune moments.

"Now really, Florrie, the lad is just being an eleven-year-old, and I am sure some chap at school had one like it," the Irishman answered. "I think it is more of him wanting to fit in than protecting himself on my account from the fiends that could be haunting his nightmares."

Florence Stoker was commonly referred to one of the three most beautiful women in all of London (Lady Hare and Marie Spartali Stillman being the other two) and was nicknamed the Beauty by several. However, whenever Bram called her, he simply referred to her as Florrie. The nickname came about soon after he met his wife in 1876 shortly after becoming employed as a theatre critic for Dublin's *Evening Mail*. The two made a striking couple and together longed to go to the theatre with fellow Victorian couples. In addition, they were equally unhappy with their social standing at the time, and so, on December 4, 1878, in the harsh but in vogue St. Ann's Protestant church on Dawson Street in downtown Dublin, nineteen-year-old Florence Anne Lemon Balcombe wed thirty-one-year-old Abraham Stoker. But in setting precedence, Henry Irving called her husband away immediately after their wedding, canceling any chance for a honeymoon in lieu of business.

As Bram stood at the window reflecting on these days of old, he watched the assembly of people proceed past the window and neighboring streets while Florence stood at a distance, pondering if her husband was hoping Irving was amongst them.

"'Tis a new season at the Lyceum—opening night is upon us!" the manager said as if he were disclosing a terrific secret his wife did not already know. In return, she nodded silently to appease him. After all, he had been away every evening for the past month and a half for its preparation.

Being the positively feral lady she was, Florence was enough of a pragmatist to make the most of things occupying the evening hours in other ways than being in her husband's company. And she prohibited to allow marital negligence turn her into a withering psycho-neurotic that often plagued live-in servants of the time. Therefore, she used her husband's notoriety to surround herself with popular people and resurrected herself beautifully by having and attending to formal dinners, often escorted by someone other than her husband. She remained intact, refused to be soothed by laudanum, and strategically saw that her entourage was not made up of one boring individual.

As the thespian couple had many dealings that had befallen them in their respective spheres of life, the events, peril, and stress collectively worked themselves up into a collection of conflicting turmoil that kept both of them quite worked up and often prevented time to dwell on the mundane tasks and trivial details others appreciated in a common family life.

"Perhaps you could join me for the premier act?" asked Bram. She hesitated for such past occasions had proven to be awkward, where they did not arrive together, sat together or left together;

and Noel's dislike of actor Henry Irving—coupled with his juvenile impatience—planted second thoughts in Florence's head.

"We will see," was Florence's neutral laconic answer. "Good night . . . I suggest you not stay up too late."

On this particular night, after spending most of the day handling the paperwork of Irving's affairs at the theatre, he retired to his bedroom exhausted. In two days, the Lyceum's production launch of Goethe's *Faust* would prove most eventful, and he was looking forward to writing what he anticipated to be a positive review for his column in the Dublin's *Evening Mail*. Not only would his employer star in the show, Stoker would up the ante by writing what he expected to be a rave review of the play.

Theatregoers will be cueing for hours opening night! he thought to himself as he as undressed and laid down next to his wife. As he overheard the occasional carriage or passer by project, the silhouette of a horse or English gentleman on the wall of the room, he thought about how it was always a challenge not to be biased when critiquing his own client's work. Times were good, and he expected that the staging would embark on another six-month tour of America. The last time this happened Florence and Noel left their London flat to send the summer months with Grandmother Balcombe in Dublin and Noel missed his father terribly. However, Abraham did not reflect on this thought long, and within moments, his eyes grew delusional from fatigue and closed while his thoughts drifted back to his own less pleasant memories and strange world of his youthful straits.

* * * * *

Charlotte Stoker leaned over, gently pressing her lips quietly on the cheek of four-year-old Abraham Stoker after carrying him to his nursery. Consequently, she stepped back and stared at the lad with grave worry. Having grown up in times of desperation, famine and epidemic fear herself, the lad's mother was deeply concerned about the outcasts of society, and she remained secretly afraid her invalid son was on the verge of joining the ranks of Dublin's misfits. As a result of an unknown infirmity—a childhood condition that often brought young Stoker to the point of death—Abraham was usually the center of attention and constant worry of a family of seven.

Young Bram's tiny bedroom on the third floor of the modest Georgian terrace house overlooked Dublin Bay. His almond-shaped eyes were weary after watching the stormy high tides lick the roadway long into the evening. This fantastic view was everything to him: a secret world especially built for a sickly child—one with a keen sensitivity to nature's unexplained wonders. Whilst his older brother and sister ran about the house or played games in the sprawling leafy park outside his window, Master Abraham remained in bed daydreaming about the great unknown. Between extreme spells of introspection, his mother would check up on him as the periods of silence disturbed her; so she would often pick him up and carry the child from room to room.

One could say his inability to walk isolated him from the womb and this unspoken discrimination brought about a secretive nature in the boy that fed an indulgent supply of dark thoughts. Indeed, his solitude ordained his intelligence as the undefined illness confined him to the room, which furnished his mind with an assortment of fears such as death and abandonment.

On this particular night, young Stoker set his mind on William Stoker, his father's older brother, who was associated with Dublin's Fever Hospital and House of Recovery. And like other doctors of the time, this uncle practiced the art of bleeding as a cure for organic diseases.

"Will Uncle William bring on the leeches?" asked the boy quietly with a startling glare in his now saucer-like eyes.

"Good heavens, certainly not!" his mother sharply responded without hesitation, though the man seldom hesitated to take blood freely on a whim in hopes to cure his nephew with no advance warning. "Your uncle has yet to prove this theory does anything but alarm you, weaken your body, and shake your spirits! And I dare to say, your father is in agreement!"

Abraham Senior was a civil servant that drudged away in the parliamentary section at Dublin Castle. Though he provided a middle-class income to his family, they were not isolated from the hard times that lurked outside their home. After all, young Bram was born during the nightmarish years when crops failed to the point that many assumed that the whole food of the country was gone. There were riots, looting, and marches that took place below his son's window, and the sounds of landlord's evicting tenants too weak to tend their crops wrung his heart. Overcrowded poorhouses locked out the homeless, and the distant cries of starving families roaming the countryside would sometimes lull him to sleep at night.

Charlotte, who was a determined-looking Irishwoman with a round, quizzical face, put out the wick of a lantern positioned on an English oak stand next to the door. She wore a traditional native bonnet framed by a definitive visage and lighted by a suggestion of a smile. Positively, she provided the flamboyant genes in the Stoker family, and she presented herself with an independent stature and an intimidating quality that caused some folk to question her motives or avoid her altogether. Likewise, she was intelligent, hardworking, and literate—well read for an untutored Sligo girl.

"Bless you, child," she whispered in a soft, comforting voice as she peacefully sat out to leave the room.

Having been born into a family consisting of constables and military members that went back three generations, Charlotte saw that her seven children—consisting of five sons—were weaned on the rough and tumble. As all of Bram's siblings, including himself, were bore in a ten-year span. If it were not for Bram's unique and puzzling disability, his parents' attention would have been more diversified; however, it was not until Abraham was seven years old until he knew the true import of being able to stand upright and the everlasting consequences of being the household's main event. Indeed, in all sense of fairness, he was outright negated the paramount rites of passage from infant to child. He never crawled on the parterre to retrieve a toy, never pulled himself up using a piece of furniture or wobbled his way in the direction of his mother's outstretched arms. In contrast, he discerned the distress in her voice when the doctor came to examine him.

Having lived through the cholera epidemic that beset the West Country population, one of Charlotte's worst fears was losing her eyesight and being forced to dwell out her senior years in utter darkness. This thought terrified her, and she was equally concerned about Bram's wellness, having vowed to Abraham Senior that all her children would attend Dublin's acclaimed Trinity College with the "sons of the aristocracy."

"Tell me about the sickness," the half-awake young Irish boy called out to his mother, as she was about to crack the door. She turned and smiled in his direction and then paused before answering.

"Alas," she sighed, "more than one and a half million people died from starvation and disease while an equal number immigrated. It was said to have come from the east, rising out of the Yellow Sea, growing nearer and nearer until it was in Ireland. And Mrs. Feeny, a very fat woman who was a music teacher, was buried an hour after, and men looked at each other and whispered 'Cholera,' but the whisper the next day deepened to a roar . . . for in many houses lay one—nay two or three—dead! One house would be attacked and the next spared! There was no telling who would go next, and when one said 'goodbye' to a friend, he said it as if forever."

She then pulled the bedsheets tightly up close and around his neck and continued, "Now that is all for tonight, my dear. Those terrifying days are far behind us . . . good night and pleasant dreams."

As his mother left the room, a worried look fell about his innocent face as he turned over on his pillow toward the window and looked out at the quiet November sky of Clontarf, Ireland. He stared at the twinkling stars outside hovering over nearby Dublin. Within minutes, his gray eyes began to grow tired and the orbs seemed to glow brighter. He gazed at two stars in particular and became fixated with them, as they appeared to outshine all others. He thought to himself that these two objects were actually guardian angels of Ireland, protecting everyone from the famine and diseases of yesteryears. This was not an unusual assumption, considering Bram had developed an overactive imagination—a trait he no doubt inherited from his mother, who was the most elaborate storyteller of the unusual and bizarre of anyone around Clontarf and beyond, from days lying in bed with only his imagination for comfort.

Drifting in and out of consciousness, he saw the two lights began to evolve from a bluish haze, transforming shape and changing colors from white to yellow and then from yellow to red Abraham continued to peer out from under his blanket, letting the images lull him peacefully to sleep.

Suddenly, his breathing alluded to heavy, strenuous gasps as young Stoker became still with fright under the realization that the lights were directly outside his window. Stricken with horror and unable to scream, the lad began to shake uncontrollably as he watched two eyes stare back at him, illuminating a deep hypnotic red.

The phantom shape outside focused on the boy for what seemed several minutes until finally the young invalid was able to muster up enough courage to grab hold of the string that was attached to a bell above the bed. This homemade contraption was the handy work of Abraham Senior who assembled it to primarily alert family when the handicapped boy was in trouble. Master Bram rang it wildly; and almost immediately the rampant sounds of footsteps filled the home. As the door to Junior's room flew open, the glowing eyes outside had disappeared, and only the calm star-filled sky was there, the occasional gust of wind and the distant sounds of Dublin's streets.

* * * * *

Abraham Stoker was abruptly awoken from his sleep in a cold sweat. Indeed, childhood fantasies bred adult nightmares. But seeing he was in his London flat lying next to his beloved, he inhaled and exhaled quick, short breaths for several minutes until full control of his respiratory functions returned and his nerves fell back to regularity. *By God's cross!* the man thought to himself, sitting up in his bed broad awake. *Can it be a terror I imagined as an ill young boy be making a cruel attempt to steal my mental health as a full-blown man?* Concluding several efforts to revert back into a slumber in vain, he stole remotely to his study where he decided he would write in his diary again, expecting that the act would quiet him and soothe his mind into a more pleasing dream in time.

"This psychological connection from youth is a manifestation of our own fears within," he began. "The city sleeps—wharves, ramparts, and bridges are masked by the miasma that has crept up from the deep, the brazen filth of the remote streets is engulfed in the bluish mist, but above them and shadowy against the sky, the castle extends its arms as if for some monstrous hold."

Such a recollection of Dublin Castle connected him immediately back to his childhood paralysis, forcing him into an almost powerless state of being. However, seeing himself outwardly as a muscular Irishman, he chuckled at the absurdity of such a train of thought. By and by, he placed his pin back in the ink jar and approached the window of the study. It was now 1:00 a.m., and still slightly shaken from the nightmare recalling this terrifying childhood experience, he watched the blinding rain fall harder. The darting sound, however, shrouded the presence of a creature on the rooftop. A mysterious animal spread its cape-like wings, shielding the fitful rays of the moon the rain had not already claimed. The night turned completely dark as the apparition flapped its way into total blackness.

But the author was unawares of such a presence, and regaining his composure, Bram returned to his desk and reclaimed his space in his diary. Dunking his pen in the ink jar, his thoughts shifted to a more recent and even more horrifying account of what was yet to pass. And the beast lurked night after night thereafter; whence it would soon begin to invade his dreams henceforth. Someone—or *something*—would cause the writer's every childhood fear to surface once again. Indeed, the aspiring author was being admired from afar by his most livid nightmares. But without his conception, an underdeveloped mutual attraction was transpiring: Stoker was attracted to this monster—for the very strength it possessed back then, a young invalid prayed years for and the grip it held this day, a detached husband and father was striving to overcome.

CHAPTER 2

A Doll of Crimson

Listen to the children of the night. What
wondrous music they make.
—Dracula to Jonathan Harker

April 18, 1888, was an eventful evening for Abraham Stoker. Though every opening night of a play spawned excitement, the debut of *Faust* was particularly special for three reasons: he managed the leading man, he was a colossal disciple of Goethe's work, and Bram himself was asked to critique the premiere for Dublin's *Evening Mail*.

What a bloody honor, the Irishman thought to himself.

It 'twas no secret that the author was exulted in having his name and picture in the newspaper, and he had an odd infatuation with men of power. Noel recalled how his father's sentimental idolatry allowed for opportunities to rub shoulders with the great: from poet Walt Whitman to James McHenry, an Anglo-American who amassed a fortune from the Lake Erie New York railway, such adulation stroked his own ego while gaining benefactors to the theatre. Though this obsession was doubtless aided by his growing insecurity over Irving's affection—or lack thereof—the fledgling writer anticipated adventure; and his coming 'twas like a charge of cavalry whose intelligence and insightfulness placed him at the social nexus of Victorian society.

Though Irving failed to consistently express his own appreciation for his employee's faithful and loyal service—for his overwhelming demands accounted for countless days and nights away from home with little or no monetary return or personal accommodation—society as a whole respected his position at the Lyceum and fellow novelists, playwrights, and poets alike, crossing all genres, were in awe of his ability and overtly courteous and gallant demeanor.

The attendance that night broke all recent records, and Irving gave an award-winning performance as Mephistopheles. Florence and Noel conveniently stayed home for Mrs. Stoker swore to it that Noel was not feeling well. Despite the fact that the boy had matured amidst a backstage of elaborate props and Shakespearean costumes, over the years he did frequent and while away many hours in the Lyceum's painting room, which had become a fantasy nursery where the lad helped Joseph Harker paint scenes and gold leaf on drop curtains. Noel kept company that night with his mother.

Though mother and son were well (that is, in the sense they were spared of any physical ailment), they were hurting emotionally due to excessive loneliness. Evening after evening, the two waited keeping each other company while Bram attended to the theatre. The family maintained an outward appearance of closeness in public; however, within the confines of their own home, the truth was apparent by emotional distance. Indeed, Florence was not all together truthful with the people she chose to surround herself with, including her own mother. In fact, she became so bored with herself when Noel would be at school, and Bram would take to the theatre that she took singing lessons as a fashionable escape from her desolation. However, in a letter to her mother, she said, "[The] master describes me as 'earnestly progressing;' it is nice to find oneself appreciated. It's the only amusement I indulge in as I have so much to do now for Bram." On the contrary, she was eagerly filling a full social calendar, often escorted by W. S. Gilbert, a popular playwright, who shared in her dislike of the overconfident actor who engrossed her husband's time and energy with an iron fist. Ironically, it would be true to state that while Irving was controlling Abraham Stoker, his wife was beginning to join forces with the English female by beginning to rally one another to break free from the chains of a male-dominated society and advocate for the "new woman," in addition to speaking out at public meetings to improve economic issues surrounding immigrants, poverty, and overpopulation.

Consequently, these same conditions were beginning to produce a wave of crime, which led to gender- and stereotype-based crimes, and as of late, promiscuous women were often the target audience. Indeed, for weeks an unknown killer, deemed "Jack the Ripper," had been brutally slaughtering prostitutes in the White Chapel district. Albeit Abraham felt that his review of the Lyceum's latest production might be overshadowed by the ongoing saga, he proceeded and hoped his client would engulf enough acclaim to see a successful run that could lead to greater promising stage opportunities and funding for the theatre. Notwithstanding, the Whitechapel investigation plastered the main headline and kept the community up in arms, suggesting women to stay inside at night.

"Wherefore this rogue shall indeed take feign stabs at future receptions!" Stoker wrote. "For every murder, there is at least three score in missed attendance that are shut in—afraid to leave their abode for weeks on end!" Furthermore, there was an unspeakable perception that men who left their wives alone at home—at night, for that matter, and without a man's protective hand—were considered ungentlemanly and outright cowardly. In any event, Noel was once again in the position of being the defender of the Stoker domicile while Irving kept Abraham immersed in other affairs.

Henry Irving, a tall, dark-haired, dignified Englishman, fifty-two years of age, carried a wealth of knowledge about many topics. Wherever he seemed to go, the spotlight somehow always managed to shine in his direction, and he had an intrinsic need to always be in control of the situation. Though he seemed to always be the dominating presence when in a room full of people, he was actually reserved when amongst a crowd but always quite theatrical in one-on-one conversation. Moreover, there was a macabre aura of mystery and loneliness about the man, which often caused him to come across in a cold and harsh sort of way, resulting in many actors' retaliation. But as time proved to show, Bram wrote more about this peculiar man in a separate diary—one which was often higher priority than his own journal, providing more detail than he did about his own wife and son.

Noel, who was born Irving Noel Thornley Stoker, actually dropped his first name in his maturity, saying he resented Irving for having monopolized his father for years on end. Recalling his father's special diary, he commented by saying, "It is, I think, another sign of his love and devotion for his friend, that however long had been the day—or night—the record in that diary was never deferred."

On this particular opening night as acting manager of the Lyceum, Bram lingered an hour after the show to total up earnings and to discuss business with Irving. Since the high-strung actor was always excitable after a show and thrived on audience reaction, the man who was the center of attention preferred discussion, recognition, and feedback in lieu of sleep. Thus, Stoker, who was his own center of attention in youth—though by chance and confined to home by fate—understood this, and it was not unusual for them to visit after shows to discuss finances, current affairs, or their careers.

The actor socialized backstage with a few of the lingering patrons and cast whilst the Irishman tallied up the revenue for the evening. As everyone left the building, Irving poured two glasses of wine and handed one to his manager.

"By Jove, we took in about three thousand pounds tonight, sir!" stated Abraham, who was in the process of retrieving his overcoat to exit the theatre for the night.

"Aye, and you were quite impressive tonight," he quickly added. "The acting, wardrobe, props, makeup . . . they were all remarkably astounding!"

"Nevertheless, we seek our reward in the approval of audiences. I trust the public will harmonize with your testament," Irving answered.

Though the Irishman wanted to be a literary man, still in his forties, money and loyalty bound him to Henry Irving. But this did not seem to discourage Bram from handling his employer's affairs in the most professional way possible. In fact, despite Irving's often unreasonable and sometimes outrageous demands, it could be said that the fledgling writer went above and beyond any rational person's expectations: every well-received speech the actor ever presented was written by Stoker; every major investment and ledger transaction was well researched and double-checked to prevent error or a negative repercussion. And with similar anal qualities, the two men seemed to feed off of each other's insecurities as well while also sharing weird interests, mystical beliefs, and a fondness for each other's solitary nature—a trait that seemed to gel when the theatrical gatherings had died down. Indeed, while abroad in the United States, their pastime was often spent visiting the local mortuary together where they would study the faces of death and even take bets with each other on how the corpses expired before reading the fresh tag which hung on a cold foot. They preferred to celebrate this pleasure in each other's company, and Abraham saw Irving as a sycophant and friend whilst the actor genius saw himself simply as an autocrat with a hypnotic power over others. Indeed, H. J. Loveday, the Lyceum's stage manager, never once tried to abate Irving's spending on spectacular productions, and when the three men would chat late into the night, wags would often refer to the talking heads as the Unholy Trinity.

"Far be it from me to make little of life in Dublin or the advantages of it, but I predict our current project and your sensational review might rouse another welcome there!" winked the actor.

Stoker flashed a broad smile for he knew Irving's self-interest-driven agenda usually meant another lofty venture was on the horizon. "London in view!" the writer exclaimed jubilantly. "Chanting students will pay tribute and chair you through the streets—a time-honored tradition, though neither comfortable nor safe."

"How so?" Henry asked.

"You might fall face forward being carried aloft, so always entwine your fingers in the hair of the bearers on either side to prevent them moving in opposite directions . . ."

Deftly, the master stroked the servant's own vanity by stating "Ah, your accuracy and wisdom is always spot on! But enough for tonight."

"Goodnight, Sir Henry," the Irishman said, touching his right hand to his large hat.

"Cheerio, Stoker!" said the actor, smiling. "'Til tomorrow!"

* * * * *

It was after midnight when Bram caught a ferry across town. Though he had a custom-made bicycle that he ordered to accommodate his grand stature, he preferred to ride it home during the warmer months. Tonight, he decided to walk, believing the cool nighttime air would do him some good. But as he placed his hands in his pockets to warm them, prior to setting off in his direction the sound of a dog howling in the darkness startled him.

How odd such a night creature would tarry so close to the city, he thought to himself.

The author looked around to see if anyone else heard the moaning. He realized he was alone, but a sort of melancholy feeling began to swoon his body as the thick London fog started to surround his feet and crawl slowly up his legs toward his knees. He quickly proceeded to walk toward home when suddenly, out of nowhere, a man stepped out of the fog and began to gaze at him from head to toe.

At first the writer was frightened and then horrified, thinking it was Jack the Ripper in all his infamous glory; however, he let out a relieved sigh when he saw it was a homeless man—possibly in his sixties—whom was wandering around the Thames ferry in search of food. But when the vagabond saw the author approach, he grew quite bewildered and nervous.

"Are you all right, dear sir?" Abraham asked.

As the Irishman confronted the vagrant, as if to hand the man a shilling or two, the fellow glared at him in a most unusual fashion that was both surreal and mind-boggling to watch. A look of terror seemed to spread across the man's face as he bellowed out, "I see the eye—the evil eye! Right here! And it is upon you!"

The dog howled again in the distance; only this time, it appeared at closer range. In reaction, the man grew more apprehensive at the noise.

"He is coming for you! Aye, might God have mercy upon your very soul!"

"Who?" Bram asked, "*Whom* do you speak of? *Who* is coming?"

"Look for yourself!" the man said in a low, raspy whisper—as if a third party might eavesdrop on the conversation. At this moment he placed his left hand on Stoker's shoulder and pulled the Irishman toward him. And with his right hand, the stranger took up Bram's right. In the moonlight, a passer-by could have mistaken them as a couple dancing; however, a closer glance would reveal a gentleman and an unfortunate both seemingly terrified of the other.

"Look for yourself!" the man repeated as the strands from his shattered split-ends, cascading down his grimy face, were brushed back from his eyes. "He was watching you then, and he is watching you still!" At this, he gripped the author tightly by the head, covering each ear with a calloused hand, and met him eye to eye.

"Look!"

The vagrant's eyes seemed to flash like an eclipse from the sun while they released an energy force, which magnetized the writer completely, leaving him totally helpless and vulnerable. And then a scene was reveled before Abraham Stoker from long ago, one that was set in his native soil while he was still in the womb—a tragedy that he learned of through second or even third-hand murmurs, a travesty that he often tried to forget . . .

The Stephensons, who lived on a Dublin farm about a quarter of a mile from the Stokers, went though a devastating and terrorizing trial while Charlotte was in labor with Bram. The wood that surrounded their country farm also posed the dilemma of roving woodland creatures that were equally ravished. Thornley, Bram's older brother, frequently visited to play with their son Jack of the same age. Early evening on September 10, the Stephensons placed their two-year-old daughter, Emily, down for a nap while Neil Stephenson went into town in search of affordable food. Jack, who wanted to be the first to bite into a currant bun, tagged along to keep his father on the straight and narrow. Indeed, it had been several days since the family had sat down for a decent meal, and Emily, especially, was weak and fatigued. It was that same evening that Sarah Stephenson closed the screen door to the kitchen and stepped outside to the back of the house with a laundry basket in hand.

With the full moon illuminating the backyard, the frail woman unclipped garments on a long piece of cord strung between two hardwood trees. She hummed softly to herself for several minutes to pass the time and to ignore the hunger pains that were beginning to claim her body. As the sun sank down into the valley behind her, a sinister silence seemed to settle in the air around her. And in a matter of seconds, a sort of paranoia began to take control of her faculties. She became increasingly frightened—first worried about her husband and son returning safely with food, and then an immediate concern for her own safety and that of her daughter. Sarah quickly unclasped the remaining garments to the lengthy narrow fiber and then shuddered slightly as she gathered her basket and turned abruptly to walk back inside.

Suddenly, she froze in fear as a low growl came from behind her. Clearly, it was a snarl of danger, and Sarah slowly turned her head to view the silhouetted profile of what appeared to be a large malnourished dog through a piece of clean white linen flapping in the wind. The beast circled Sarah, dripping what was seemingly fresh blood from its mouth.

It continued to bellow an ominous gnarl, snapping and champing its razorlike teeth together like a malevolent hungry fiend as it thrashed its head side to side causing droplets to fly, soiling the clean, dry linen that was waiting to be reclaimed.

And then Sarah's own life's blood rushed to her head as she came to the ghastly realization of the horror that was unfolding before her very eyes. Her sight became dizzy, her limbs became weakened, and her mind swam wildly as she dropped the laundry basket, causing the contents to scatter about the ground.

"*Emily!*" she screamed.

With the sudden outburst, the dog trotted off toward the woods while Sarah Stephenson raced inside. Her weakened, trembling legs must have been a bad omen passed down in Charlotte's delivery; for the frantic mother tumbled to the grass numerous times as her legs became numb and weighted down while she gasped away the feeble breaths that somehow continued to mobilize her body toward the house. With every occasion, she forced herself up from hands and knees until she was at the entrance of the back porch.

The screen of the kitchen door had been ripped to shreds. She swallowed hard as her heart began to race, and at last, a shrill cry escaped her mouth as she noticed the animal's red footprints that winded their way from the direction of the bedrooms, through the kitchen, and out into the back lawn. The woman's eyes bulged into a fit of nervous fear as she shook rashly and followed the trail of blood through the kitchen and hallway, onward to Emily's room, where she finally fell to her knees and saw the ghastly, disturbing sight.

Pieces of her daughter's body were scattered about the room that was in complete disarray. A small rocking chair was turned over on its side and was covered in gore. Next to the wooden legs laid a girl's baby doll. The clothes it wore were mangled, and the gold locks of yarn were frosted crimson. A pillow sat in a large red puddle that stained the floor in front of the small iron bed. The wall behind it was smeared with vital fluid and what appeared to be part of a small arm was jutting from the corner of the blood-soaked frame.

"*No!*" Sarah Stephenson sobbed.

The poor woman fainted on sight; nevertheless, she was awakened several minutes later by her husband who was in the process of ordering Jack to say outside with a loaded shotgun.

"Shoot only if you are in danger!" Mr. Stephenson called out to him.

Sarah had fallen upon the bed in a helpless gesture as the tears began to stream down her face like a heavy rainfall. Her husband gathered her up in an awkward form of comfort as they shook uncontrollably in each other's arms.

A blinding flash caused Abraham to whence, thus releasing him from the drifter's haunted glare. The Irishman fell back in fear. Shaking and wild-eyed, he gathered himself up from hands and knees, sweating profusely as he managed to speak in broken gasps.

"By God's holy cross! What in the blazes did you just show me? Who in the devil are you? And how do you know of me? Speak to me, man!"

Suddenly a low, lengthy, familiar howl—one extremely close in proximity—caused the stranger to abruptly turn and face the landing. Starting back, he trembled at the knees and blurted out excitedly: "Heed the nocturnal melody of beast! Repent of your contact! And save thou soul whilst time allows! I must free myself from him . . . just as she!"

Stoker was thunderstruck at what happened next. The man sprung to the ledge of the ferry and flung himself feet first as if it was the only recourse of self-protection. "I was simply bewildered by the entire ordeal," the author explained in his journal. "The whole predicament happened so quickly, and in such a time that light was scarce, that I even wonder now if what I witnessed was not some trickery of the moonlight: for the silhouette of the drowning victim appeared to be that of a female—a woman with long, flowing dark locks—but as I grew closer to the water's edge and gained a better view, I saw only a helpless unfortunate, raving about 'The eye—the eye!'"

Immediately, realizing that the beggar was unable to swim, the writer jumped after him and pulled the drowning man to safety, fighting in protest every inch of the way. The cries alerted a patrolling officer who took a report of the event and followed up the next day by notifying the Royal Humane Society. Although the strange rescue awarded the author with a bronze medal for saving the suicidal victim, it was the weird last words of the vagabond that struck a cord with the hero:

"Beware, mate . . . he was the Prince of Evil. Now he is a king— the King of the Un-Dead!"

* * * * *

It was a brisk ten-minute walk home before Abraham could escape out of his wet clothes. The household was asleep, but he was distressed over the disturbing affair and the odd words and puzzling reaction the man demonstrated. On conclusion of dining late on a hearty crab dinner his Mrs. Stoker left on the hearth, the writer turned in quietly hoping not to disturb Florence, who would have surely been alarmed by the event, as was the patrol officer. This ordeal, coupled with the nightmare from several nights ago, caused Bram to have difficulty falling asleep. Recalling his juvenile encounter with a creature with beady red eyes and the screaming drowning man—who seemingly was more frightened by the author than the deep water—the Irishman's restless mind lapsed into a vivid, livid recollection of everything that had been.

He was watching you then, and he is watching you still. These mysterious words of the vagrant suddenly struck a cord with the Irishman. "Ohhhhhh!" Abraham Stoker screamed, awakening his wife. "It 'twas not a dog at all! Nay, it was a monster—the same monster! The same red eyes!" he cried out to anyone who could hear. "Aye, I witnessed the entire horrid act like I was actually there!"

He thrashed wildly.

Noel, who was awakened prematurely from the sudden outburst, also rose and burst into the room as Florence was placing her arm around Bram and whispering words of comfort. The writer had beads of sweat covering his brow, and it was all too clear for him to doubt what killed poor Emily. And realizing that those same lurid eyes would haunt his own bedroom window years later set his teeth on edge. The pieces were slowly beginning to fit. Notwithstanding, how could a creature disappear and return many a passing year but with unexplained gaps that questioned and failed to account its own demise?

Great Scott! Stoker thought to himself. *When the drifter spoke of repenting of my contact, was he referring to that godforsaken séance?* His racing mind blasted his thoughts to the dreadful piece of correspondence he had hidden from his wife and vowed to never revisit. *Could there be some form of diabolical connection to all of these harrowing events?* "At that moment, the serenity of conscience propelled me headlong into a state of clarity and relentless torture," the Irishman described.

The flaring nostrils and contorted brow informed Florence her companion's heart was sickened about something; however, his words were driving her into a world of confusion.

"Bram! Come to at once!" Florence shouted. "You are distressing me! From the perplexed look upon his face, she expected he was confused and bewildered by a vision he had just witnessed so profoundly in his sleep. His reaction was as dreadful as if witnessing a live murder while involuntarily relinquishing all personal means to prevent it. Realizing the scene was no place for a child, Florence signaled Noel to go back to his room.

"Mother always said it was someone's famished dog . . . but I tell you, Florrie, I looked into its awful eyes! It was the devil in wolf's clothing!" Stoker cried. "You should have seen what he did to that innocent, tiny girl!"

As Florence had taken to socializing with the wives of the tycoons of Colmman's Mustard, Bovril, Horlicks, and Coats Thread, the thought of such outlandish nightmares and horrors—ones that the writer accepted as fact intertwined with supernatural hype— would prove to be a source of scandalous gossip that could damage her own social standing. Thus she quickly decided to dismiss the event as a multitude of false beliefs prompted by food poisoning.

"Dearest husband, it was another dream, and Charlotte was not there! Neither were you for that matter, " Florence said reassuringly. "She should never have told you such stories . . . and for the love of God! You must quit eating shellfish in the evenings! The food must be contaminated, and it is poisoning your stomach and your brain!"

The woman's attention was diverted to an awkward Noel, who was still positioned in his parents' doorway, rubbing his eyes aimlessly as if part asleep and part giddy by his father's raving and his mother's firm tone at such an knotty time in the night. She was equally perturbed by this event, and with rolling eyes, she waved her left hand in a motion to suggest disapproval.

"You fail to understand, Florie," explained the writer. "I rescued a man tonight after he showed me a vision! Nay, it was no dream— for I have yet to fall asleep this night in lieu of dwelling and pondering over its dire significance!"

Florence Stoker was at a loss for words. Suddenly, another voice broke the silence.

"What is wrong, Mama . . . Papa?" the boy asked wearily, shifting from side to side in his nightgown. The author did not have the wherewithal to even notice his son, let alone answer his call. On the other hand, Florence quickly sent him back to his room with a firm order to cease and desist.

"Shush! Haven't I told you that little boys should be seen and not heard?"

Food poisoning or not, to Abraham Stoker his vision was as real as the hell that the beast had come from. Nobody could convince him otherwise; and deep within the recesses of his mind, he feared it would return again. Though it was not clear when it would happen, what it was, or what its exact mission was, to him two things were for certain: it had something to communicate and it was, indeed, baneful beyond all human consideration and lacked respect for anthropological life.

"Your interpretation is nothing more than fancy puffed up from lack of sleep, being overworked, and an overindulgence of excitement and seafood!" Florence demanded. "Enough of this for now. Rest presently, and we will further discuss it in the morning." Abraham Stoker sighed and said nothing in return. With a slight pause, he complied. But as the night drew onward, there came a low, gruesome growl out of the still of the night—an evil, fierce yowl that was as real as the tightness that had developed in Bram's chest and as cold as the blood that curdled in his veins. He sank down in his bed next to his sleeping wife, pulling the covers tightly around his throat, and remained stock awake until morning.

The fear that was building up within Abraham caused him to dart his eyes at every shadow that surfaced, and though the howling subsided into the early morn, the Irishman had a sinking notion that the source of the noise had not escaped him—that the same two glowing red eyes were watching the writer's every move. It felt like an Un-Dead spirit, suspended in time, cursed to live in utter darkness.

CHAPTER 3

A Mysterious Quest

Welcome to my house. Come freely. Go safely; and leave something of the happiness you bring.

—Dracula to Jonathan Harker

The next several days were difficult for Abraham Stoker. Though he was able to fill his time with management work at the Lyceum Theatre, periodically, his thoughts were brought back to the same amoral ruby orbs that first came to him in the form of the amulet used in Golden Dawn's séance and then as the ravenous wolf—years before Bram was even born—or as the creature that lurked outside his bedroom window when the boy was just a young invalid. And more recently, the same pair seemingly provoked the vagrant's strange behavior, resulting in the drifter catapulting to his death off the Thames Ferry. To the writer, he was encompassed about with peril for it appeared as if the burning eyes were haunting him to no avail.

"The vagabond spoke with so much terror and passion in his voice that I genuinely believe now that he actually feared for his life! It was as if whatever he was afraid of was somehow working its way though himself by the likes of me!" the Irishman wrote in his journal. "Could it be that the homeless fellow was reading my dreams—that the 'evil eye' is real—that he had a vision of consternation that was to appalling to speak of?"

Still unable to sleep soundly, the fourth night found the author up and about the study, watching the rainfall and beginning another piece for the *Dublin Evening Mail*. However, at the stroke of midnight, the sound of the rain pounded even harder on the roof of the South Hampton flat and distracted his concentration. A gust of wind outside the window interrupted Bram Stoker from his writing, and he hesitated in his chair for a moment, collecting his thoughts.

The Irishman began to think about the Yorkshire location of Whitby—a medieval fishing village that that had grown into a Victorian resort. The creepy atmosphere of the study at the witching hour, coupled with that of the fleeting storm, provided a dreary and melancholy effect on his usually set of iron nerves. The lingering aftermaths of the numerous nightmares combined with the earlier event at the ferry caused him to long for the misty, mystical port where he and his family would sometimes go on holiday for up to three weeks at a time.

The writer's reverie was roughly disturbed by the draft from the broken windowpane, which caused the candle flame to flicker. After dancing madly for a few seconds, while projecting vast exaggerated shadows across the study, it commenced to glow a bright orange, illuminating the several paragraphs Abraham just authored. He baptized the end of his ink quill in the black jar, just before pushing himself away from his desk in complete awe.

Something did not feel right.

The man's heart began to pound in his chest as he watched the puddle of rainwater that had been collecting on the floor directly under the window suddenly begin to evolve. He slowly approached the substance and kneeled down to place his finger in the transformed vile matter. To his disbelief and frantic horror, the cool rainwater was now warm blood. He fell over backward, slipping in the fluid, while grabbing hold of one of the wooden legs of his desk chair. Attempting to stand, plasma began to flow freely from the cracks of the windowpane, down the adjacent wall, and onto the floor beneath. Collapsing into his chair, the legs snapped, and Bram's grand frame struck the deck with a mighty thud.

As the vital juice continued to stream out of the window seal, the red pool grew and crept closer to Abraham. He closed his eyelids is disbelief, and when he opened them again, the matter was gone.

"I simply slipped in a puddle of rainwater that collected on the floor—nothing more, nothing less . . ."

The writer's diary recounted, "I lay hushed and motionless on the divan, closely mimicking the decisiveness of a corpse, as I harkened attentively to the chorus of the night. The breeze outside coiled and buffeted its current off the windows; thc only ray of light came from a single sconce that hung adjacent to the pane. Every few seconds, the force of the bluster against the glass caused the flame to vibrate—casting a series of ghoulish shadows that seemingly crawled across the floor, lengthen in height, and sprouted arms and hands with dagger-like talons that reached out and vanished as the candle flickered again.

"As this panorama played out repeatedly over the course of half an hour, the light eventually grew dimmer, and then the entire room was swallowed in complete blackness. This pitch left my senses to home in on the beating of my heart, and with every gust of wind, the dull, steady pounding in my cheat would quicken and swell to an almost deafening volume.

"According to my internal clock, at least an hour had past since I lay down, and my thoughts had been racing with images of mystery and horror. Nonetheless, after a few more minutes, my tired mind and overwrought body began to drift into delusions of fear until I succumbed to sleep.

"Before I fell into total reverie, however, I was jerked abruptly awake as an icy cold sensation froze my body to an immobile state of terror: a draft suddenly passed over my body—much like a front door that had been swung open and only to be quickly shut again. My breathing became intensified, and my bulging eyes darted about the obscurity of the room.

"I was not alone!"

A sudden rustle on the roof then startled the Irishman, and he could see a large dark shape flying swiftly toward the window.

"Heaven help me!" Stoker cried out loud helplessly, making the sign of the cross about his chest. At length, a white mist began to fill the room, surrounding Bram's tumultuous body. Suddenly the author heard someone call his name from outside the window.

"Abraham Stoker."

Silence.

The writer turned his head toward the window, squinting through the London fog. Slowly taking his arm behind his back, he felt a leg of his chair and grabbed it firmly. Breathing with stutters, he commenced to crawl toward the direction of the window. Lubricated from the liquid on the cold wood floor, he took each step sluggishly, careful not to slip.

"I trust thou have been expecting me, Lord Stoker," the distinct voice from outside said in a thick Romanian accent.

As sweat dripped into his eyes, the Irishman grabbed hold of the windowpane with his right hand and pulled himself up, facing the mysterious voice. With the leg of his chair still clutched in his left hand, he wiped the salty residue from his eyes with the sleeve of his nightshirt—now streaked in red like a painter's palette. The author felt as if his mind was playing tricks on him for he could neither identify the voice or where the gore was coming from.

"I bid thee a good evening . . . Gentleman Stoker."

"Do I know you, sir? Show yourself!"

Bram peered through the mixture of fog and rain outside in what he thought was the direction of the voice.

Was it coming from the roof? he thought silently. Bram gripped the leg of his chair with all his might.

Again . . . utter silence.

Stoker gasped in sheer fright, taking notice to the reflection of the candle in the window. The sight of his own reddish beard resembled the wild, freakish hairs of a beast when aroused through anger. He reeled back in alarm. Still unable to locate the source of the voice, he held up the candle, following the path of light with darting glances to and fro. By and by, he turned and once more gazed into the flickering flame and waited cautiously in a peril of extreme panic.

"Abraham Stoker," the voice spoke solemnly, "I honor your appeal and cometh forth as it be your will."

The orange light turned red, and Bram's heart quickly surfaced to his throat when he realized the voice must have been coming from inside the study all along. Within the glowing red ember, a dark shadow of a man emerged—a figure that cut at Stoker's very soul.

And then the candle went out.

For a brief moment, nothing was visible, and all that could be heard was his own heavy breathing and the pounding of his own heart—but only one heart. At length, a tall, unlit shape stood in the corner of the study. A small beam from the full moon projected its ray of light on what once again seemed to be a blood-drenched floor at the foot of the window. This small gleam assisted Bram in determining the distinguishing features of the mysterious stranger erected before him.

"My un-welcomed guest stood about six foot tall and was clothed in a thick crimson cloak of silk brocade with large round silver buttons linked to a filament cord," wrote he. "About his waist he wore a large buckle decorated with golden threads. And on his cranium my visitor donned a crown worked in cloisonné, with terra-cotta-colored claws, all holding a turquoise stone."

I hazard that such grand attire, in no doubt, dated back to the middle of the fifteenth century, as I have witnessed similar garments on display at the British museum, thought the author. Though his face was still hidden in darkness, Abraham could tell his company had long, wavy jet-black hair. He faced his host studying him in utter stillness. Clenching the piece of broken chair behind his back, the man of the house cleared his throat in nervous apprehension and mustered up the courage to address the intruder.

"Who are you?" Abraham Stoker demanded. "What do you want from me? Why do you impede on me and my family at such an hour?"

The lofty stature approached and replied, "Thou hast seen me and knowest me, dost thou not remember?"

"No, sir . . . I know you not."

There was something unusual and very unsettling about the figure, yet his voice carried a vaguely familiar tonal quality to it as one might associate with a faraway dream.

Standing up, Bram stepped back from the man, never taking his eyes off him.

The Irishman leaned against the side of his desk waiting for further dialogue with the leg from his chair glued to his right fist. The shape before him smirked with a courtly bow. Still hiding his face in the darkness, the guest answered in the same thick Romanian tongue:

"Ye maintain ignorance of my acquaintance, therefore, I approach thee as a foreigner and shall telleth of my history. My formal name is Prince Vlad Tepes Dracul—of Sighişoara, though most countrymen calleth me The Impaler. Whenceforth, I am now of the gangland, and whosoever I shew myself to proceedeth thenceforth by christening me Son of the Dragon."

Bram was taken aback by this enigmatic answer, and his expression changed to one of consternation and total astonishment. With rolling eyes and flapping jaw, courageously, yet cautiously, he took a step toward what he perceived to be a dangerous warrior of old royalty. Though there was something slightly familiar about the visitor, the Irishman could not pinpoint why. Perhaps this voice spoke to him in one of his visions or nightmares. The author simply could not place it at the present as his thought processing was clouded by fear and alarm.

"I say unto you, behold! I am the dark presence in your soul that arouseth the precarious nature of life. I am the thirst for power you so coveteth," the tall man went on proudly in a strict tone and askew demeanor. "When the night comest alive, I am where ye long to hide!"

"I do not understand, man! What do you want from me!" an aloof Stoker asked again, only this time with more emphasis.

In the meantime, as this strange exchange of dialogue continued, an almost smoky scent had filled the study—that is, much like an aged article of clothing that had been released from a musty trunk where it had been treasured and housed prisoner for several hundred years.

"Take heed and be aware: ye are the chosen one, my friend," replied Dracul. "It is due to your belief I cometh and likewise you come hither unto me! But before I shall telleth why I seek ye this night, I shall foremost teach thee of where I have been."

Abraham Stoker took another step closer to the monstrosity he was conversing with and could now make out the peculiar features of his face: the man appeared to be around forty-five years of age and had a pale, gaunt visage. He wore a dark moustache that curled slightly at the ends—one that swept against both sides of his emaciated cheekbones—under a thin, aquiline nose. Even though the politeness of his guest hitherto was of a manner of which certain to gain trust and comfort, these tactics might begin to wear thin or transgress at his student's slightest resistance. Though the writer feared such opposition might unmask a being of a baleful kind, he could not masquerade his discomfort any longer and imagined Florence and Noel would dash into the room any instant distressed and worried.

"Forgive my lack of hospitality, dear sir, nevertheless, I hold no stock in where you have been! And I wish you gone . . . this very instant!" insisted the host, now making out two claws which were connected to a dragon positioned in the center of the star on his headdress.

"Alas, dear sir . . ." the warrior replied. "I will surely leave in my due time, however, not one moment sooner—not before thee hear me out. And thou *will* hear me out! Harken and understandeth ye shall! My friend, history is foundeth on truth and deception—one of both light and darkness—and somewhere hidden deep within lay a secret: a story worth to be told that is far greater than any thou could be imagined!" These compelling words were spoken with a surly nature and of a man of great imperious command as he continued, "Alas, life 'twas the prelude of my demons whilst death remains the insurrection of my doom! Aye, Wallachia 'twas under my rule; and as a warrior prince, blood and death became a strategy for survival—if not other armies would taketh away that I so protected for my countrymen! Yet when I asketh if God had a place reserved for me in paradise, notwithstanding the many victims I had sentenced to death, I was denounced from the church and condemned to hell!"

"One day, I invited an ecclesiastic by the name Hans the Porter to my throne room and confideth, 'Sire monk, tell me truly, what will be of my fate after death? Could one in the eyes of God be considered a saint, if one has shortened the heavy burdens of so many unfortunate people on this earth? Might after death the expiation of what some considers sin could be declared as good works?'

"To this the monk boldly replied, 'Great pain and suffering and pitiful tears will never end for you, since you, demented tyrant, have spilled and spread so much innocent blood. It is even conceivable that the devil himself would not want you. But if he should, you will be confined to hell for eternity. You are a wicked, shrewd, merciless killer; an oppressor, always eager for more crime; a spiller of blood; a tyrant; and a torturer of poor people! What are the crimes that justify the killing of pregnant women? What have their little children done . . . whose lives have you snuffed out? You have impaled those who never did any harm to you. Now you bathe in the blood of the innocent babes who do not even know the meaning of evil! You wicked, sly, implacable killer! How dare you accuse those whose delicate and pure blood you have mercilessly spilled! I am amazed at your murderous hatred! What impels you to seek revenge upon them? Give me an immediate answer to these charges!"

The intimidating Impaler paused his tale, which he had begun in an awe-inspiring and shocking way. His fierce movements animated his anger, and his extraordinary words both amazed and enraged Abraham Stoker. Indeed, as gruesome and malevolent the accusations were, Bram could not conceive of a single person committing such heinous acts. "What was your reply to the monk's allegations? Go on, sir . . . please continue."

"I will reply willingly and make my answer known to you now. When a farmer wishes to clear the land, he must not only cut the weeds that have grown but also the roots that lie deep underneath the soil. For should he omit cutting the roots, after one year he has to start anew, in order that the obnoxious plant does not grow again. In the same manner, the babes in arms who are here will someday grow up into powerful enemies, should I allow them to reach manhood. Should I do otherwise, the young heirs will easily avenge their fathers on this earth . . ."

His wide-eyed listener cut him off, abruptly exclaiming, "You cruel oppressor! The monk spoke the truth—you are a bloodthirsty madman! How can you pardon yourself of such evil acts you pass as chief leadership? Your actions clearly defy the commandments of the Father of the Lord Jesus Christ!"

There was a long pause before the Count spoke again, which was like the silence of the grave. The author witnessed the stoic stare that towered in front of him and began to fear his quarrelsome response might have invited fury. At last Dracula responded calmly, "Wherefore thou God when evil was inflicted upon me and my family? And wherefore thou father when Turkey unleashed complete wrath upon my country of Wallachia? Nay, I was forsaken as 'twas my master was forsaken ages before me! Be ye not unwise in thou faith, alas, wherefore He when thou canst walk or whence thou friends were molested or killed by spirits and wild beasts? And where 'tis He now whilst whores are being murdered in thou White Chapel district and the mud of London are committing suicide out of fear of what will pass?"

To which the author replied forcefully, "To all things God holds a purpose; and through patience, prayer, and holy works will our faith be answered!"

To this the dark prince's facial expression changed from a haughty countenance to one of a complete paroxysm of rage. With dull hard eyes and stiffened stance, he shouted in a fierce tone: "Thou speaketh with a fools tongue! Thy own mother was stricken with hunger as she witnessed a country be plagued with disease! Nay, he abideth not and worketh not in my own labors, for with my father administers power within me to take such vengeance upon man's world myself! Being cleansed by the blood of Christ may giveth eternal salvation when your body ceases to be, but being washed by the blood of the beast straight away provideth immortality herewith."

"Your wicked words entice me not! The holy word speaks the truth!"

"Truth 'tis relative. Oh ye hypocrite! Men and science challenge thou faith to new levels daily, and pretendeth not that thou own curiosity eateth away at your soul as a worm lays an egg within an apple and devours it from the inner core! Aye, I can see from your visage that you are torn by my words. And how can thou calleth thyself a believer of the modern age of man whilst following such beliefs without drowning in your own peccadillo? I say to you: are you not forsaking one master over another?"

The Irishman was a Trinity man; therefore, he was schooled at the art of debate. And with his flair for the theatre, Abraham Stoker had a talent for resolving confrontation and carried a sharp skill at influencing others. Indeed, his father figures—which included such poets as Alfred Lord Tennyson and Walt Whitman—considered their pupil a talented one, and persuading total strangers to see his point of view or to make monetary donations to the theatre made him a dynamic presence. However, this asset did not seem to be of any assistance when testing his wits against a supernatural force. Therefore, he said nothing as Vlad went on.

"Ye, the church banished me whilst the enemy heldeth me prisoner and wiped out my family. When I gaineth control a second time, it was only to find my own army plotted to overthrow and kill me! No amount of faith caused your God heed answer to these claims; wherefore, solely the fallen one answered the hatred I felt. And it 'twas through this entity a monster was unleashed in me—one which I knoweth thou can feel in yourself also. Oh, ye pride-forsaken wretch! Why locketh these thoughts and feelings when both masters knoweth thy are consumed within and hideth them not? Free thyself from the mortal chains that bind you, and let me showeth the way to the ultimate state of liberation!"

Bram Stoker could not listen to such blasphemy any further. Indeed, his guest had long worn out his welcome, and without thinking clearly, the host lunged at the Count with the leg of the chair with the intent to bury it deep within his chest. Vlad immediately threw out his right arm; however, it was not in an aggressive way intended to knock his aggressor back several feet and to the floor; but instead, it was in a welcoming fashion—as if inviting further rogue force. "Alas, feel the winter of thou heart, oh man of foolish nature! Relinquish the repressed conviction you feeleth and keep bottled throughout your wretched life!" the Impaler said in a tone that was almost genteel.

The odd scene set before any onlooker would have resembled a burly, red-bearded giant, untidy in appearance with an upset temperament, colliding against an even taller man—though thinner in stature—whose calm and collected countenance would have one questioning which being was, in fact, the actual monster.

Thus, seeing his efforts not only were in haste but also was like to a bird buffeting against a windowpane, the author fell back from Dracul in total exhaustion. The brute approach used in striking the man with fist and force was to no avail. At last the Irishman succumbed to defeat and stared at his mysterious guest in silence, breathing heavily, with a look of astonishment upon his disappointed face.

"The man seemed insistent on spinning upon my brain a yarn of conviction which schooled my nerves, challenged my moral compass, and taxed my wits whilst trying my sanity—all at once!" Stoker wrote. "For what seemed several long minutes, he and I confronted one another on all accounts of what one would consider human dignity and honorable character. I pined over my strong beliefs as a respectable citizen with a protestant upbringing until his immoral jabs penetrated the elixir of my very soul! And then something around the fiend's neck sparkled in the moonlight and suddenly caught my eye. My vision became fixed upon the source as I realized it was a necklace: a gold chain, which, at first sight, resembled that of a pentagram. And then upon shifting my focus to the center of the object, I was blindsided by the large ruby connected to a star of seven points."

It was Sister Pamela Coleman Smith's amulet.

"You accursed fiend!" the author stammered out through quivering lips. "How did you acquire—?" At that moment, all forms of apathy rushed from the mortal's body while feelings of rage and vengeance took full control of all mental and physical faculties therein. Augmented by blind notions of shock and fear, the writer came at his visitor again with renewed and unbridled force.

"Ah, the jewel of the seven stars—you believeth I stole it from someone thou held dear? Nay, its rightful owner only reclaimed it!"

This time, the force of the writer's plunge took the Count off guard. A glimpse of surprise dashed across his façade before his eyes flashed like lightning between a contorted brow and flaring nostrils. "Dost thou not comprehend whom you are dealing with?" the untouched being snapped in a grisly pitch. His cruel mouth sneered as he actually chucked at his thug. "Foolish man! I am the King of the Underworld! I cannot be done away with so easily!" As if he was defending himself against a man of straw, Vlad struck back with little effort and unmatched resistance. Within seconds, Abraham Stoker was lying on the wet floor, totally on his back, helpless, and unable to move. The abstruse of a man stood over him as if inspecting his prey before devouring its meal. While his assailant let out a faint chuckle, Bram was finally able to look directly into its eyes: the pupils were startling, totally black and projected a hypnotic stare. Soon the Irishman found himself quickly falling into a trancelike state.

Within seconds, the azure glow that formed from the blue mist around him recalled stories of the blue flame which formed from the cobalt haze.

"You were there too! It has always been you!"

The writer quickly turned away, breaking whatever spell he was being drawn into. *If I am unable to kill this beast on my own accord, than maybe I could succeed with luring some help from others!* the author thought to himself. Thus, he immediately remembered his family in the other room. *But Great Scott! How have they not been awakened by the commotion in the study?* However, before he could speak out or call upon them, the Prince reacted with a silvery, mechanical laugh and said, "Alas, so if thou cannot kill me, ye wish to delegate the task to your family? Nay, they cannot hear us—likewise, Madame Stephenson heard not the cries of her own daughter. The mere wave of my arm commandeth your wife and son to sound and undisturbed rest."

What the writer saw just seconds before in the Un-Dead trance was just reinforced by its own words. This additional intelligence spared a new flight of fury, which rose the man off the floor and into another attack on the monster. "Murderer! Cold-blooded savage! Be gone from this house at once!" an angry Stoker shouted as he lunged again at the fiend full force, only to be struck down a third time by an invisible shield. This latest attempt sent him back to memories and feelings as a young child, huddled fearfully in an immoral state in his bed, unable to walk. Darkness. Alone. Looking for a bell to ring . . .

"I told ye once that I am already gone from this world! I wisheth not to harm thy family in our agreement, but I suggest thou retreat and listen attentively! I dare you that my patience hangs by a thread!"

Having been amazed that the monster that stood before him had read his thoughts, Abraham now feared not only for his own life but also of that of his family. Half standing, he listened intimately to what the warrior needed to say. Vlad Dracul continued, "Before I was cast into the netherworld, I was a Machiavellian fifteenth-century leader. I launched a campaign against the entire Turkish Army and fought bloodthirsty battles to preserveth the country of Wallachia. However, the Turkish and Hungarian empire curseth and defieth me."

"Nevertheless, why do I need to know this?" Stoker asked, trembling from anxiety and uncertain what kind of response this question could trigger. Bewildered and frightened, whilst the writer awaited an answer, his arms searched the floor for anything to protect himself with. "The blood baths I coveted as a man came to me at a steep price," explained the Impaler. "Though I have been able to seeketh my revenge on the mortals that brought harm to me and my earthly family, I have since been condemned to spend eternity in the dark with the Un-Dead. And for over four hundred years, I have been damned to feedeth on the blood I so craved as Prince Dracul."

The ruthless barbarian overlord flashed a ghastly smile that revealed his odd teeth, which appeared curiously pointed and gleamed as the moonshine glistened upon their whiteness. *Was this some weird trickery of the moonlight?* the Irishman asked himself.

The tall man continued, "I telleth thee all this because I have summoned thou to communicate my history to the world."

"But . . . why me?" questioned a contentious Bram. "What I know of you is far from flattering! Do you not have someone of your own kind to carry out such a request of colossal gall?" Here he annunciated the word *own* whilst pointing to the night sky to suggest his teaming minions from the pit. The Prince, who was now standing directly in front of Abraham Stoker, was within inches of his apostle. His breath carried a pungent stench of death that made the writer lightheaded and caused his stomach to churn uneasily.

"Thee, my dear sir, are an aspiring writer and holdeth the ability to understand the supernatural, hence thou are my link between the living and the dead. I know about the Order of the Golden Dawn and how ye have always been in touch with darker impulses of your mind. Alas, as a boy, you were raised by your father to believeth there are more things in heaven that will save thee than those found on earth, however, 'twas your mother that tuned thou to the physical, the spiritual, and the power of immortality which cometh from the beyond! My friend, I am one of these great mysteries! Verily, I say again unto you that I am cursed to liveth in the darkness between both worlds, and it is thou gift that I shall useth so others may partaketh of my legend and to finally understand its true import." The Impaler delivered this last line with a pale, cold laugh.

Abraham, concealing a slight morsel of interest, looked at the man curiously.

"Go on," he said.

"My friend," Vlad continued, "the underworld is not permitted to reveal themselves to mortals unless to feedeth or to pass on the black offering. When ye be permitted to telleth my word it will expose my presence, breaking the dark curse forever, and I will finally cross over into the afterlife!"

"If breaking the spell of eternal damnation is merely repenting you sins to a mortal, why has it taken you centuries to do so?" questioned an argumentative Stoker.

"For the reason that it has taken four hundred years to findeth the right person. I repeateth, we cannot expose ourselves to mortals.

And though ye are human in a physical sense, thou spiritual being and soul are kindred of the outer realm. Such connection breaks the mortal decree and, therefore, relinquishes me of this Un-Dead curse!"

To Dracul's host, the story being told was almost like a lost Shakespearean play he was being requested to conjure up from the ages and act out before mankind. In listening to the dramatic scene that was unfolding before him, Bram lapsed quickly into memories of his own acting days at Trinity. Stoker had abandoned acting and altogether gave up auditioning for minor parts in university productions to linger around backstage—to learn how the gaslight men created chiaroscuro moods, to watch artists paint scenic drop cloths. His anticipation for adventure, along with his sense of belonging, was finally fulfilled with the arts: he discerned unseen critical wisdom and felt important delivering fatherly advice to apprehensive young actresses. However, this night his security was stripped bare.

"Who is providing guidance to whom tonight?" Bram asked his unsure self. "Assuming that I believe what you are telling me is factual, you have shown yourself to me this evening. I see you have not perished; nevertheless, do I hear you say you desire to? Moreover, I ask does this not contradict the plight of your existence? Insomuch that your supernatural powers—your immaculate strength, insatiable thirst for blood and the gift of immortality will come to an brusque end—that is, once the world learns of your chronicles?"

"Nay, it be a vex I wisheth not for—rather it 'tis one others felt I so deserved," explained the King of the Underworld. "I was destined to be the Blood Prince, as I cometh from a long line of warriors that practiced unlawful evil that finally helped form the Order of the Dragon. But alas, I feel I have paid the price for my carnage, and now I seeketh peace."

"And you feel my ability to dream and write theatrics can set you free of a four hundred year old spell?"

The Prince smiled. "Ahh! Aye, ye are elite—that is why thou are not considered a *mortal* by standard definition thyself! There is a keen, morbid interest and ability within you that driveth you to write and think unorthodox notions. There has always been something at work in your soul thee have never understood; yet I do appreciate such eccentricity on thy behalf. Indeed, you are the closest connection to the Un-Dead without actually being true dead; and this is the prudent reason why I recruiteth you—thy . . . my dark medium! Will thee not alloweth me to translate? Nay, more importantly, let me *show* ye my anecdotes!"

"And the crux. . . ? That is, what do I, or what will I and my family, gain from this . . . this unconventional experience?" Abraham asked in a manner that did not appear too avaricious.

Vlad Dracul smiled again. "Knowledge," he answered with a sly and frank snarl. "Notwithstanding, thou family shall be spared in this journey . . . ah, ye will go it alone, my friend."

"And if I don't?" Stoker asked boldly and even more quarrelsome than before.

The Impaler appeared to be angered by this question and grabbed Bram by his nightshirt, the writer recognized the dark look, which set upon his stoic face before he spoke the chilling words, which set his teeth on edge. The Romanian lifted him off the floor to eye level and stated harshly, "Thy shall be mournful thou spake such words, for the gates of hell will swing open wide for you and your kin!"

The fiend's flesh was cold to the touch, and the author shivered in protest—with an eerie utterance, shocked at the man's prodigious strength.

"Moreover," the warrior added, "thy soul will die with you. On the contrary, if thou abideth by my wishes, thee will live and ye character will flourish with new insight on the Old World and the powers that reach beyond man's fragile existence!"

With a sharp turn of his body, the tall man abruptly took hold of his dark cape and advanced a pace toward the window.

"And now, friend Stoker, I bid thee farewell. Alas, thou shall heareth from me again, and when ye do, I will make my expectations fully transparent."

The host lifted his torso off the soaked floor. Having fallen against a shattered piece of glass, Stoker revealed a streaked portion on the deck where he had momentarily lain in a small pool of blood. The cut on his arm and sight of the fluid seemed to pull the guest toward him for a brief moment. A look of wild fury blazed in Dracula's eyes for a split second. Indeed, the author witnessed the color of his pupils transform from red to black. But then the man turned away as if he was staring directly into the brightness of an eclipsed sun.

"Goodbye, Prince Drac—" a besieged Bram broke off, trying to speak yet trembling from shock and horror.

"You may call me Count Dracula," the intruder said smiling, fully exposing his teeth again, portraying objects, which closely resembled canine tusks shimmering pearly white in the twilight of the full moon. The dreadful confirmation drove the writer to his defensive manhood—this was his home, and a man's home is his castle, regardless whether man or beast invades its walls.

Abraham Stoker realized he now had two pieces of the chair in his hands and positioned them together to form the sign of the cross. Expecting the Prince would hiss like a serpent in reaction to the symbol of Christ's passion and cower back in repulsion, the author was bewildered when the monster's beastly eyes began to glow red—two amoral ruby orbs. Bram's senses became unleashed with a Pandora's box of fear. Dropping the cross, a floodgate of shuffled grisly images and terrorizing memories impeded upon his brain to the deafening sound of a chorus of screams from Sister Pamela, Emily Stephenson, and the Londoner vagabond. Flailing his limbs in fear meaning movements, the writer shrieked aloud as those same engrossing five words of the vagrant fell upon his ears again like the weight of the world: "The evil eye is upon you!"

The Irishman recognized that this was the same beady pair of eyes he had witnessed outside his childhood window thirty-nine years earlier. Indeed, it was also the mad dog that had murdered Emily Stephenson. He knew for certainty now the homeless man spoke the truth. And to Stoker, the truth petrified him with dismay.

The evil eye stood before him.

"Like electric shocks on aching bone, all my senses were elevated to an extreme level of alertness," the author wrote. "All at once, I found myself frozen in a state of nervous arousal. I trembled with apprehension as the sick feeling of nausea began to quickly envelop the pit of my stomach.

The capped figure before him began to transform and took shape of a large gray wolf. The animal, which was even more horrible in the flesh, sniffed about like a wild beast as it quickly planned its exit. And Bram, a full-fledged man by his own right, reeled from the inconceivable shock and its reverence thereto. He shuttered at the thought of how the young and helpless Emily Stephenson must have felt as it descended upon her. The grotesque image of the girl's body lying in a heinous, mangled state became transfixed in his brain, and the pungent stench of acrid blood invaded his nose like wind and sand in a desert storm.

Abraham Stoker was accustomed to the unusual combinations of smells; however, the powerful ones from that terrible night were both vile and harrowing to imagine or rationalize. "As an Un-Dead man, the ghastly stench was all too rank, but as an Un-Dead animal? Faugh! How can one find the right words to describe such an odor?"

Though Abraham Stoker's pastime was his writing, he was an avid reader too, and in seeing the tall man before him transform to all fours, the author could not help but recall Polidori's horror tale and questioned its authenticity. Until now, it did not seem possible to conceive such fright and unspeakable dread. Indeed, the Irishman had only lived out such terror in books and on the stage. And he enjoyed inhaling the biting sensations intertwined with the perfumed—the aged paper and withering velvet curtains matched against the freshly leather-bound spine and the ivory face makeup, the mildewed covers or the vinegary seafood dinners in contrast to the new ink or the cosmetics of jonquil and jasmine. Moreover, with his love of literature and the stage, he formed relationships with other literary men and discovered a backstage family with whom he felt important and accepted—sometimes more so than that of his own.

And now this . . .

"On the other hand, that night, I mustered the realization that my faculties were up for a rude awaking. And I had a sinking feeling that my families tied by literature, theatre, and blood would soon be pulled out from under my feet; and the most powerful debate or acting sequence could neither alter its untimely coming or its bitter outcome," the author wrote.

The hound howled and crashed through the study window, shattering pieces of glass in all directions. As it absconded into the inclement weather and the treacherous darkness of the night, it left a cool bluish glow about the room that lingered for several minutes before evaporating to dust. And while it hovered, it left a soothing yet melancholy effect as of a drowning victim whose last glimpse was that of the city of Atlantis before the echoing peel of that final gasp when the heart beats no more.

CHAPTER 4

The Gothic Letter

> My Friend . . . I am anxiously expecting
> you . . . I trust that your journey from London
> has been a happy one, and that you will enjoy
> your stay in my beautiful land.
> —Letter from Dracula to Jonathan Harker

The dim gray light of morning cast its rays over the Stoker household the following dusk. When the family gathered to breakfast, to his amazement, Abraham concluded that his family had heard absolutely nothing during their sleep but the rain pelting against the rooftop and the roaring of the wind. Likewise, to his dismay, there was no tangible evidence of the visitor or of the struggle that had taken place just a few hours before in the study—one room over from where they were discussing the outlandish events from the night before. The Irishman was bewildered to see the blood had totally vanished from the windowpane, wall, and floor as if to blatantly mock him and present his plight to Florence and Noel that the entire ordeal was a complete figment of his overactive imagination. Bram's nightshirt was soiled from perspiration—not vital fluid. And the only reminder of the grim encounter was of a shambled desk chair positioned in the middle of a pile of shattered glass.

Abraham Stoker sat across from Florence and Noel with his head between his hands in utter silence. He had not slept in over forty-eight hours, and the preceding week 'twas a compilation of implausible, ill-fated jitters. After the monster's dramatic exit several hours earlier, Stoker remained in the study—standing post in case it returned for a curtain call targeted for either him or his family.

There was no doubt that Abraham Stoker loved his family dearly and made sure they were provided for. However, having a father that spent countless hours toiling as a civil servant at Dublin's Castle, this sometimes destructive work ethic was passed down in the family genes resulting in similar consequences. Indeed, Abraham Senior spent his entire adulthood trying to make a name for himself, only to find that the position he attained for many long years was as far as politics would allow him to excel. As a result of this disappointment, the stress he brought on himself affected his well-being. His health began to fail him at an early age, and some suggest he worried himself to an early grave.

Like his father, Bram put extra pressure on himself; and just like Charlotte had to deal with an ailing husband, Florence had to step aside and let her husband dream. It was a fact that Charlotte Stoker shepherded her family from one place to another when Abraham Senior's heath required medical attention from Switzerland or France, and due to her husband being forced to retire before his prime left the family with only a modest pension requiring frugal meals.

This somewhat embarrassing situation caused Bram's parents to be equally worrisome about the theatre manager/fledgling writer's own path to fame:

"I am glad to hear you have some amusement with your hard work," responded Charlotte sarcastically when learning of her son's life choices, "but [work as] a manager to a strolling player?" She huffed in a voice of disapproval.

However, his father bluntly referred to his son's aspirations as a "moral infection," classifying his fellow actors and journalists as "rogues" and vagabonds." Like similar middle-class parents of their era, Charlotte and Abraham Senior looked to the professions, not writing or theatrics as rightful careers choices. They both complained of Bram's intentions through recalling stories of rowdy, uneducated louts writing their way to the poor house, and the theatre was no better, overflowing with immoral temptations and frivolous behavior. But in the end, Bram proceeded with his soul and only worked harder to succeed and earn his parent's acceptance. Many years went by, and in his adulthood he wrote them exuberant letters, and in their shabby sitting rooms, Stoker knew his parents worried he was jeopardizing his civil-service career with what they felt to be a superficial fantasy.

Whether Noel Stoker knew of his own father's physiological desire to make his parents proud or of the self-worth complex which drove his father's ambitions to sometimes ridiculous heights was clear or not, this particular morning it did not seem to matter. Indeed, Noel's driving thoughts centered around the English muffin he was eating and appeared to be eyeing a second that remained on the center plate. Florence, sitting down her tea, broke the hush.

"Pray tell you walked in your sleep again, eh, Bram?" she commented, exasperated. "The last time you pulled a bloody stunt of the sort, you hurt yourself something terribly."

Abraham did not look up or respond.

Florence Stoker had an unusual way of dealing with problems: changing residences and unnecessary shopping. During the run of their marriage, they did not stay at the same residence but a couple of years, and with every relocation brought about a more spacious and luxurious home, which only furthered the requirement for additional purchases. On the outside, this Victorian persona fit her personality well and was a way she could escape her demons of loneliness and marital neglect. But on the other hand, she found that no matter what house she was living in her husband's life was out of balance. And regardless of the number of ball gowns she picked up in Paris, Amsterdam, Italy, Switzerland or Vienna, Henry Irving remained the "real" man of her home.

The woman looked at her husband intensely when her son reacted to her last statement.

"Yay . . . Papa walked right into the door of the loo and broke his bloody nose!" smiled Noel, swiftly capturing the last muffin while the adults were disengaged from eating.

"Noel, mind your tongue!" Florence warned and quickly turned back to her husband. "Obviously you were walking the floors again whilst in slumber and picked up the chair and then smashed it into the sash! Of all the foolish rubbish . . . the sight of the candle and the sound of the rain outside must have confused you into belief of a fire."

"Bloody well right," Noel agreed forcefully. "You were smoldering!"

"Pipe down, lad!" Florence scolded.

Noel quickly acquiesced, but with a slight grin, and stayed in the room to digest a dose of melodrama before joining his friend Jonathan for a morning stroll to the schoolhouse. Though Noel had acquired his father's thirst for knowledge, he was also developing an aura of adventure and sense of stubbornness that would occasionally clash with Florence's personality. And like his mother often found herself just wanting to be noticed, her only son likewise shared with her this desire and her talkative nature.

Bram Stoker pushed himself away from the table with the assumption that what he witnessed during the late hours was, indeed, a bad dream. Though he was having trouble rationalizing the damaged window and chair, he convinced himself into believing it had nothing to do with the horror of "Dracula."

Perhaps Florence is right, he thought to himself. *I have been speaking folly. Alas, the lack of sleep has embellished my imagination . . . I was deranged last night and attacked the bloody window.*

Stoker sent Noel off to school while Florence cleared the breakfast nook and cleaned up the aftermath in the study: a sole dilapidated chair. Abraham finally put last night's events behind him and chose to instead concentrate on the piece that he had yet to finish scribing for the forthcoming edition of Dublin's *Evening Mail*.

Removing a chair from the kitchenette, he transported it to the study recalling Henry Irving's profound performance as Mephistopheles. He would explain in his critique how the immaculate costumes were going to be the rave of the country and that Irving's red devilish ensemble was the first of any of its kind and would surely send shivers to anyone bold enough to look his character in the eye.

Indeed, it seemed that Irving's best performances consisted of him portraying eccentric, villainous roles where he scared the audience into loathing him but then formed some sort of odd individual connection with the viewer, pulling them back into a realm of pity. He would rave about Henry by writing, "He carries the talent of playing those character's the audience loves to loathe and possesses the unique ability to act as his own makeup artist—a skill that is completely unheard of and shocking to the acting community."

Having fully regained his composure, Bram collected his thoughts toward the grand opening of Faust. Seating himself at his desk, he reached down to claim a piece of paper out of his supply drawer used for his writing. Shuffling the other items on the countertop aside, he submerged his pen into his bottle of purple ink and began to write:

"April 18, 1890, Lyceum Theatre, London, England. 'A historical night it was . . . an absolute pleasure' was the familiar words coming from the lips of those lucky theatre goers who experienced opening night of Goethe's production of *Faust* starring Britain's own Henry Irving."

As his right hand feverishly went to work, his elbow bumped a foreign envelope that somehow got tucked inside his diary, marking where he left off the night before. It fell to the wooden floor beneath him like a light feather.

"Mr. Abraham Stoker." His name was handwritten by what appeared to be a distinguished gentleman's hand in the center. Stoker ceased construction of his piece, and subsequent to becoming quite bewildered, he reached down to pick up the strange, unknown piece of correspondence.

How in the devil did this get here? he thought to himself with a glare of skepticism. In total apprehension, the writer looked about the room in every direction.

There was absolutely no being at hand.

Alas, he was completely alone—that is, with the exception of Florence, who was busy dressing in her bedroom across the way.

Why had not Florence noticed this when she was tidying up earlier?

The study grew morbidly silent and cold. The anxiety building within the author continued to swell until finally, Bram Stoker took a gold-plated letter opener that resembled the shape of a Celtic cross and neatly sliced through the envelope.

As he opened and unfolded the letter, his heart sunk deep within his cavity. A bitter chill swept down the entire length of his spine as he let go of the paper and watched it glide to the floor in suspended slow motion. It read as follows:

April 19, 1890

Dear Mr. Stoker,

I trust thou have given much thought concerning our council last night about my request. Having redeemed you a gentleman, I expect ye to leaveth immediately by locomotive to the coast of England. Thither you shalt travel by vessel to the seaboard of Romania where thou wilt find a coach that will take ye to the town of Sighişoara. Thou pilgrimage will continue to the city of Brasov thitherto the village of Transylvania. Afterwards, my kind friend, you will knowest Curtea Domneasca in Bucharest and Castle Bran; whereat you depart to the Snagov Monastery.

I believeth ye will find the currency in your pea coat more than sufficient to cover your troubles and expenses for your travels to come. Finally, the diligence will start at noon tomorrow. I bid thee a fond farewell and pleasant journey.

Yours truly,

D

And then there came a delay that lasted a few seconds, which was proceeded by the ringing echo of a name . . .

"*Florance!*"

* * * * *

Florence Stoker rushed to her husband's side to find him leaning over his desk as if he had just suffered from a terrible stroke. He was breathing harshly and was unable to formulate any words for a several minutes.

Abraham Stoker reread the letter, with the sparse belief that his eyes deceived him at first glance. However, his worst fears were, indeed, true, and the reality of the situation had to be reasoned with utmost care—Count Dracula was a cunning, dangerous brute. In effect, he was more lethal than the Irishman had knowledge of at the present and would only become deadlier if his wishes were not carried out to the meticulous detail.

"How is this possible?" the writer asked his wife dubiously, who was in the process of reading it in its entirety for the third consecutive time.

Florence was well into her adulthood, having experienced and shared many moments of eerie fright. Most notable was an experience she shared only a few years earlier with her son and companion, Mrs. Casaan Simpson, whilst Bram was touring America with Irving. The unthinkable occurred on April 13, 1887, when the three left Newhaven on the steamship *Victoria* en route to Dieppe. There were 120 passengers and crew on board, and these three were planning to catch a train in Dieppe to go shopping in Paris. At precisely 3:00 a.m., approximately an hour before arrival, a dense fog obscured a risky line of rocks under the lighthouse at Cap d' Ailly, a bluff nine miles west of Dieppe. Due to the lighthouse keeper falling asleep, the passengers, who were awake and preparing to disembark, heard no foghorn. A fire for the steam-powered light did not get underway until 4:00 a.m., but by that time, it was too late.

As Florence held Dracula's letter in her hand, she felt the same tenseness of nerves and feeling of alarm she remembered securing her luggage as the *Victoria* crashed into the rocks, ripping open the bow, flooding the forward cabins. In only two hours, the ship was sunk and twenty had drowned, fourteen in the panic of lowering the first of only four lifeboats, each built to hold eight or nine. Florence, Noel, and Mrs. Simpson made it into the third, but the hysteria of the experience was hard to forget. But through it all, she remained focused and thought logically of the outcome.

But the fact of the matter was the letter she was holding perplexed her beyond reason. Coupled with the incredible tale her husband relayed over breakfast, the piece of paper she held in her trembling hand sent an accursed reaction like none other she had ever felt. Even during the darkest hour of being shipwrecked, she took comfort in the crew that diligently worked to save them, and by and by, Florence kept her eyes affixed on the lifeboats being lowered into the water. But who was looking out for them now—the apparently wicked Count Dracula she knew absolutely nothing about?

The woman was engrossed with terror, and she could feel the perspiration escape her clammy skin. But in an attempt to not upset her husband any more than necessary, she took a deep breath in a prudent effort to calm herself and regain what sense of nerves she could remuster in the process. When she finished rereading, she looked at her husband kindly and slowly spoke in a most serious tone: "My dear Bram, this must be a prank of some kind. Perhaps Noel is upset at you for not permitting him to take that accursed scalpel to school?"

"Not possible, Florie," Stoker retorted. "He could not have been able to pull off a hand like this . . . he is a horrible scribe!" The author paced the floor for several moments. Thereafter, he walked toward the coat stand to the right of the front door. In the meantime, however, Florence's mind continued to spin aimlessly in all directions.

"Then he put one of his no good cronies up to it, dear husband! There must be a logical explanation to all this madness! This will no doubt blow away—pay it no mind and carry on as usual." His wife's higher-than-usual pitch depicted an immediate prayer and plea for some normalcy; nevertheless, Florence knew she was preaching to deaf ears. The mere thought of her husband's time being called away on another man's mission rung at her already bleeding heart that seemed to have turned into a dark diamond though years of separation and disconnect. The woman looked on as Abraham Stoker searched his pea coat frantically.

"There is but one way to tell if this Dracula is a man of his word!" he bravely exclaimed. As her husband repeated Dracula's name, Florence gasped nervously, realizing the conversation had evolved from Dracula being a figment of an imagination to a living, breathing person whose trustworthiness was being called into question.

Out of his right front pocket, Bram found a stack of currency one thousand pounds in total. Both sets of eyes glared at the bank notes as if they were thieves on the run. Abraham counted it first, and then a confused Florence took the notes and counted them suspiciously. They both stood at the front door in complete amazement for a matter of several minutes. She could tell from the dire consternation in his eyes that her husband's mind was at work, and suddenly she feared for the safety of those she loved.

The frigid pair lingered silent for a long, long while. Many that knew Florence well gossiped that she was not content with motherhood, yet she was adamant that her son would have a reputable education. In fact, she set her sights on Winchester but shunned from the needlework and other motherly qualities that accompanied feminine parenting techniques. Notwithstanding, in the coldness of the moment, she reevaluated her life and became distraught at the fact her husband was actually thinking of leaving his family—to venture hundreds of miles away in an unknown land to write about a mysterious stranger.

How will Noel and I survive? What if Bram does not return? she thought to herself, growing more noticeably excitable. *Noel will have to learn to work!* Suddenly she had a hint of compassion toward the vagrants that huddled like cattle amidst London's notorious slums and the unfortunate Whitechapel women that a man named Jack (as he so confidently called himself) had suddenly taken an infamous interest in.

Finally, Bram broke the quiet and addressed his wife with a look resembling a soldier who had just been ordered by Elizabeth I to do battle.

"Florie, I am afraid I must go," the writer said, taking Florence in his empty arms. "Otherwise, I have a compulsive fear that horrible things will happen!"

* * * * *

Abraham Stoker was a widely educated man—and on a broad range of subjects, for that matter. Therefore, the speculation that a fiend had been indirectly haunting him since his youth and had suddenly begun to entertain him directly now, by making inquiries and ordering his cooperation, would not come too lightly.

The man quickly seeded the advice of others and was careful in every respect. Though it seemed he had no choice but to agree to Dracula's not-so-uncertain terms, before setting off on such an odd excursion the Irishman wanted to know more about the forces he was to reckon with.

Consulting with other intellectual giants was quite simple for a man who began so at the tender age of twelve. For he spent those next four years studying under the great Rev. William Woods at Bectue House College in Dublin's Rutland Square. Thitherto he matriculated at Trinity College where he studied mathematics and was invited to join as president of the Philosophical Society and the Historical Society—two of the most prestigious student organizations of the time. There he spent countless hours debating such topics as "Sensationalism in Fiction and Society."

It was during this time a growing interest in writing exploded, and despite his childhood disability, Stoker had grown up to be a very strong man attracting comparable strong personalities. However, he had never been absent of his childhood demons. For when he finally gained mobility at the age of seven, his subconscious feared his self-made prison would return; therefore, he chose to join their rugby team and excelled in long-distance walking events. Thus, such notoriety was excelled by force rendering a degree of popularity for a man who was already standing six foot two inches tall. During this period of his life, he weighed in at one hundred seventy-five pounds, and despite his childhood condition and lumpy facial features, he managed to become quite the athlete and ruggedly handsome.

The Irishman's days at Trinity were a blessing in disguise. The leg irons he was born with had seemingly disappeared from his feet. And the young author was meeting many interesting people that would ultimately influence him for life. Hence, this star-struck inspiration, coupled with being a product of his raising, he loved to challenge himself to new heights. And he was certainly not one to be easily defeated—as he indirectly described in a letter to his hero Walt Whitman—which eloquently suggests that the weight of the world kept him motivated whilst praying upon the counsel of the "masters": "You have shaken off the shackles and your wings are free. I have the shackles on my shoulders still—but I have no wings . . ."

Though the fledgling writer's taste in literature was as vast and eccentric as the Irishman's knowledge of the world, the information he was seeking to join him on his tour of Romania was conclusive to the man and country that summoned him. In the early days of the author's formative writing, his interest in the Romantic poetry of Byron, Keats, Shelley, and Whitman was highly recognized amongst the institution and everyone that was lucky enough to get to know Stoker. Likewise, he cultivated the theatre during his education and made many friends in doing so. When in doubt, Bram looked to this alliance with other colleagues for spiritual and professional support, and through this bond, he continued to seek advice.

Prior to taking a carriage to the Lyceum, Bram sent a telegram to another close friend, Arminius Vambery, a Hungarian professor at the University of Budapest, for some information about Vlad Tepes Dracul. It read as follows:

ARMINUS, COULD THE ASSOCIATION OF THE WORDS *DRAGON* AND *DEVIL* IN ROMANAIAN LANGUAGE EXPLAIN AN EARLIER LINK BETWEEN VLAD TEPES AND VAMPIRISM? BRAM.

"*Vampire* . . ."

The nervous man pondered over this word intensely. He had read the popular "Vampyre" by John Polidori, the first vampire story in English published in the April issue of *New Monthly Magazine* in 1819, followed by the enthralling many adventures of *Varney the Vampyre,* or *The Feast of Blood,* a nineteenth-century British novel written by James Malcolm Rymer. But it was undoubtedly Sheridan Le Fanu's wonderfully written *Carmilla,* published in 1872, that had inspired his interest in the occult. And now he found himself hesitant regarding his curious destination, which was undoubtedly somewhere amidst the Carpathians, shrouded in mystery and overrun with such supernatural beliefs.

It was amusing to him to think that his next telegram would go to America, clear across the globe from the Carpathians.

The land beyond the forest, the reluctant traveler thought to himself. *A dangerous place, indeed! And if at any time I am in need of words of wisdom, the time could not have been any more blatant!*

Despite the fact that his own novice writings had not received stellar acclaim, he continued to hold the attention of American poet Walt Whitman. Though Whitman's health complicated Stoker from meeting his idol face-to-face, they carried on a relationship in the post that continued until Whitman's death in 1892. They discussed the anatomy of their work, and Whitman's mesmeric mastery in poems such as "I Sing the Body Electric" and "The Sleepers" hinted of the hypnotic nuances that Count Dracula tried to compel Stoker with the night before. And in wiring his master the day of his amazing journey to Transylvania, the response obliquely encouraged him to dump his shackles and sprout his wings for what could become a life altering event.

"The man, you repeat, fulfills the boy. I value your good will highly. Thou seem to have remained of the same mind, mainly, in substance, as at first . . ."

In addition, the Irishman's youthful ambitions were shared frequently with the likes of the Oscar Wildes, Henry Jameses and the Mark Twains of the literary universe. Yet he was sometimes criticized for neglecting his own writing, crowding even more into his daily schedule by studying the law. Indeed, pressure from Florence for him to become a barrister added to his internal struggle, and when discussing his new opportunity with the "seasoned ones," he was fondly encouraged to move forward with any experience independent of Irving's shackles and the Lyceum's ball and chain.

Though the writer had many acquaintances, he could count his closest friendships on one hand. Among these select few was none other than actor Henry Irving, regardless of the restrictions his employer forced upon him and the often one-sided conditional relationship.

Abraham Stoker was loyal to Henry Irving and for many personal reasons, for not only was he his best mate but he was also his employer—and an extremely talented man that he respected. After all, Abraham Senior raised his sons up to honor this relationship amongst all others; correspondingly, his friend had flourished and mastered the art he so longed to be a part of in his youth.

Indeed, Irving was Britain's best leading actor during the prime of his life, and having always wanted to be an actor himself, Abraham Stoker looked to Henry as a mentor. "[My] host's heart was from the beginning something toward me, as mine had been toward him," Stoker once commented, recalling his close relationship with Irving.

But on the evening of April 19, 1890, Abraham Stoker set out to visit Henry with a serious, stern demeanor that spoke of something grave and apart from all typical conversation. His intention would be to confide in him, to explain what he had witnessed the evening prior and where he would be the next thirty-plus days. Someone else would need to step in and take care of the bookkeeping at the Theatre, and he would need to correspond with Henry through the post.

When Abraham's carriage arrived at the London's Lyceum Theatre, it was six in the evening and the cast was arriving and getting in costume and makeup. Bram met Henry in his dressing room where he made the bold announcement. Henry listened attentively while applying his satanic shades of red and black to his face, glancing to and fro between his own reflection and that of Abraham Stoker in a powdery-looking glass. Being the dramatic being Irving was, the Irishman had expected a more alarming response. A skit perhaps . . . after all, a call such as this would certainly qualify for something out of the ordinary.

"Bram, my good friend," Henry started, "go do what your heart tells you; however, on the account of the personal safety of you and yours, do go quietly and carefully!" he said sincerely.

The author nodded understandingly. Then Irving went on, "Keep in mind that there are dangers in this world that man cannot alone explain. And some of them God would rather us leave be. Nevertheless, the persisting interest that troubles mankind must continue to search for answers. So—go it alone, if you must—but take the good Lord in spirit, and know that I will watch over your family and trust in the business we have created together 'til you return." At the close of these words he stood up, almost equal in height with his employee, and made a half bow. Stoker returned the gesture.

"You are a fine man and my fond friend," answered the author respectfully. "And I intend to do as you suggest. And I very much appreciate you keeping this establishment going for me in my untimely absence."

"One other substantial matter, Bram," Henry added. "This Dracula sounds cruel and reproachful. Henceforth, I would not go and venture off of the path he has recommended." He stated this with a concerned look, returning the letter to Stoker. "In all uncertain terms, you are not going on holiday! But proceed with caution, learn what you will, and perhaps, who's to say you will not come back with the literary accolades you have so long yearned for?"

The two men smiled at each other and exchanged handshakes. The writer then returned to his South Hampton flat to pack some clothes and personal items. But by way of it all, little did Abraham know the following day, he would begin the incredible adventure that would alter his life permanently and become the premise of horror that would go down in popular literature forever.

CHAPTER 5

The Feast of Blood

It is out of the lore and experience of the ancients and of all those who have studied the powers of the Un-Dead. When they become such, there comes with the change the curse of immortality; they cannot die, but must go on age after age adding new victims and multiplying the evils of the world; for all that due from the preying of the Un-Dead become themselves Un-Dead, and pray on their kind.
—Dr. Abraham Van Helsing

As Bram approached the British Museum the following morning, the intense foul, vulgar odor of wine, grease, vinegar, and beer caused him to hold his breath until he was well clear of the overflowing street gutters of London's notorious slums. Peddlers, pickpockets, prostitutes, and porters all suspiciously lingered in the passing alleyways like common criminals. Stoker, who preferred to almost speed-walk to most of his destinations, was very accustomed to the gazes of the many unfortunates and conditioned himself to respond with apathy.

Of a population of about three million, about eighty thousand transients found shelter nightly in commercial lodging houses—

known for its unsanitary conditions and loose morals. Child abuse was a major problem; however, due to infamous personas like Britain's own Jack the Ripper at large, authorities were frequently too busy with what they considered more pressing matters of the sort.

The author carried with him an immense sense of compassion for the sick and hungry. Indeed, understanding on a personal level years of being restricted to a bed, unable to walk, caused his heart to ache as he reached into his trouser pocket, pulled out a shilling, and handed it to an old man dressed in a tarnished pinstripe suit that was ripped at the left leg and write arm. The man, who was unable to pick himself up off the ground, smiled—thus, exposing a mouth full of broken and missing teeth. His skin was gnarled and dirty, and wiping his long, tangled hair out of his face, he looked up at the writer. Then removing the shilling from Stoker's hand, the unfortunate looked at it graciously and replied in a course yet gratified voice, "My indebtedness to yeh guv'nor!"

Bram nodded politely and walked onward. Upon taking notice that the man's sunken face and baggy clothing were visible signs of prolonged hunger, the memory of Charlotte Stoker's recount of his own family's hardship resurfaced as he continued to walk briskly away from the homeless district.

The potato famine of 1846 had left many families in Dublin wondering how they were going to survive the crop season. Hundreds of families starved to death whilst many more relocated. Though Bram was not born until the following year, his mother told him how she once extracted a pint of blood from the main artery of the family cow with a blood transfusion instrument and consumed it, as it was the only nourishment available.

"The number of deaths due to starvation brought the cries of a banshee to my ears," she told Bram. "Malnourishment—coupled with disease—was the most frightening way to suffer, because secretly, we knew that the well Sligo townspeople were terrified by them, and they were pushed with other stricken travelers into pits and were buried alive. The clergy fled, doctors died, and drunken prostitutes cared for the dying when the last nurse collapsed."

Thus, Charlotte acquired the dreadful fusion device from one such doctor, and when her family feared such a ghastly end would become their own, she finally—but regretfully—called upon the veins of their family cow to keep them alive.

The famine was especially tough on animals since anything their owners were able to grow or purchase went to their immediate family. It was just a matter of time livestock and pets alike would turn up sick and often die from disease or starvation.

"We reluctantly drank her blood for several days until food became available. However, during these distressing hours the slow ticking of the clock and the frail thumping of our hearts became increasingly muffled and in sync. Thus, our demise seemingly rung loud in our ears, much like the gong of death's bell."

Likewise, during this grievous hardship, Charlotte knew of a husband who carried his wife to the hospital on his back with a red handkerchief wound tightly around her waist to stop the pain. "When he returned that evening, he was told she was in the house of the dead, a makeshift barn where hundreds of bodies were thrown on top of the other," she explained to her young son. "He rushed there, searched frantically, and in the dimness, glimpsed the red cloth. He carried his wife home where she lived many more years."

But the horror haunted Charlotte, who began to loathe the town and fear for her family's future. Following Bram's birth, the Stokers fled to Clontarf, known as the location where King Boro defeated the Dancs in 1014—where the conditions were somewhat better. After reliving his mother's bizarre account of blood letting the bovine, the author's own breath tasted rank and fetid from ingested blood.

It began to spit rain as Abraham walked by a young boy playing hopscotch with his nanny. He smiled and nodded at them as thoughts of his mum resurfaced—in particular, the memory of her explaining the "legend of the vampire" one dismal afternoon. The specifics flooded his thoughts as if it had happened only yesterday:

"Where do vampires come from?" Bram had asked whilst his mother prepared stew and potatoes for her husband and family of seven. Though young Stoker's Anglo-Irish literary legacy was enhanced with the birth of Wilde, Shaw, and Yeats, his mother's fascination with other cultures flourished through the writings of Abbe Evariste Huc and Richard Francis Burton. And as a middle-class reformer, Charlotte took what action she could to help Ireland overthrow its feudal past, though the mythology of the Crescent and its neighboring villages would never be forgotten.

"Today they are still deeply rooted in the Balkan region," she said in a staunch voice. "Though there have always been vampire-like creatures in the mythologies of many cultures, some are monster-like—such as a demon, whilst others appear in the form of beast or of man—such as Varney, the penny dreadful!"

Varney the Vampire: or, *The Feast of Blood* (1847) by James Malcolm Rymer was published the year of Stoker's birth. It reaped of exotic, gloomy settings that allowed the reader's dreams and imaginations to shudder from dismay as Sir Francis Varney, a Restoration nobleman (the first vampire to wear a black cape), went on a lengthy blood feast—an epic saga full of haunting and carnage. No doubt this fascination stirred Charlotte's mind, packing it full of fearsome images. However, it was Polidori's *The Vampyre* that grabbed and spooked the young enthusiast and prompted him to wonder about life's "real monsters" years later.

Stoker knew that the vampire, as it became known in Europe and, hence, America, largely originated in the Slavic and Greek lands of Eastern Europe. Ireland at large, including his mother, was particularly captivated with the folklore; and suddenly, Bram had followed suit. He felt like he had met one face-to-face—the "lord of the vampires," to be precise—less than forty-eight hours ago, and he developed and insatiable appetite for any and all information he could find on the fiend. Indeed, he was on a quest for ammunition, and to do battle with the Un-Dead required a belief in the occult.

As the nineteenth century receded, Victorians turned to seances, extrasensory perception, mesmerism, palm reading, and crystal gazing for answers. It was also during this period of Bram Stoker's life that table-rapping fortune-tellers prospered. And though such contradictory approaches came across as being irrational choices to firm believers in a lucid science, his artistic friends such as Dickens, Tennyson, Carlyle, and Yeats were impressed observers—and even the occasional practitioners—of what many referred to as picayune quackery.

Stoker himself was readily drawn to the controversial ideas of the occult, Egyptology, Babylonian lore, celestial prominence, and magic. Likewise, he had always been intrigued by phrenology, and his eclectic library supported these interests holding many books on these vast topics, including a chronicle of the Ku Klux Klan and the five volumes of J. C. Lavater's essays on the physiognomy, published in 1789.

Arminius Vambery replied to Abraham Stoker's telegram early that morning and directed the writer to the British Museum, where a book and a package would be awaiting him in their research department. The Irishman, dressed in a brown wool overcoat and Shelby hat, closed his umbrella while stepping out of the English rain. Shaking himself off, he advanced up a flight of about fifty steps and then approached a deserted counter. Removing his hat and seeing no bell to ring, the author cleared his throat.

"A-hem!" he exclaimed in a meager attempt to call the attention of anyone within earshot. In a matter of a few seconds, a portly middle-aged lady appeared with a look of surprise across her face. Sitting down a set of books she was in the process of arranging, the woman eagerly advanced in Bram's direction.

"Excuse me, Madam," he said respectfully, "can you please assist me?"

He politely handed the museum's librarian the telegram.

"I would like to pick up a few items that have been set aside for me, please," Abraham Stoker stated quickly and firmly as if in a hurry.

"Ahh, yes, Mr. Stoker. They are right here," the woman replied, looking at him behind a set of thick spectacles, which made her perplexed baby blue eyes appear magnified three times their normal size. Her tonal quality hinted of a keen sense of interest in the exchange. She handed the writer a book titled *The Land Beyond the Forest* (1888) by Emily Gerard and a package which contained an inscription:

PERSONAL FOR—PLEASE DELIVER
TO ABRAHAM STOKER.

Stoker smiled politely, collecting the merchandise, as she handed him a separate note.

"*An Account of the Principalities of Wallachia and Moldavia* (1820) by William Wilkinson is available at the Whitby Public Library," she explained, pointing to the memorandum. "Are you a historian, sir?"

Abraham was familiar with the research of Emily Gerard, for she had written an essay in 1885 called "Transylvania Superstitions" which had caught the Irishman's curiosity. Gerard, who was married to a Hungarian officer, lived in Transylvania for two years. And being so overwhelmed by the colossal volume of queer stories, she began to write them down—eventually tracing their births to what she believed to be the root cause of a "bewildering variety."

"No," the author replied distractedly to the librarian, "just traveling."

Bram had failed to gain an opportunity to read the book that evolved from Gerard's research, but opening up the book, his interest was soon rekindled:

"Demons, pixies, witches, and hobgoblins, driven from the rest of Europe by the wand of science, had taken refuge within this mountain rampart, well aware that here they would find secure lurking places, whence they might defy their persecutors yet a while."

Would Abraham Stoker be the one to test their wits and drive them out?

The Irishman gave the librarian a thankful yet puzzled look as he took the novel and read the note from his adventuresome friend:

April 21, 1890

Bram:
    Yes, a connection is present; and it is one as ancient as the legend of the vampir itself. As the Bible foretells of the Second Coming of Christ, Satan's Armageddon will come to pass when his sibling's evil has inherited the earth and hell runneth over with his Un-Dead army.

Beware, my good man, of Vlad's lies and may these books prepare you for what could very well be the saving grace or the violent end to mankind!

May God's power keep you in the light and compel you homeward though his son's saving grace.

Your friend,
Arminus

Vambery, who was also a scholar of ambiguous languages, had the notorious habit of sometimes communicating in riddles. The writer fidgeted with the note for several seconds before he folded it in half.

"What is the connection?"

Transferring the paper to his front pocket of his overcoat, the author's hand shook slightly as he mustered up a half grin for the woman standing across the counter.

"Thank you very much," he stated with a nervous smile, placing his hat back on his head. And quickly as he could, Bram made his way back through the misty London streets and on to his home in South Hampton.

* * * * *

As the train pulled out of Penington station at approximately 7:00 p.m., Abraham Stoker continued waving to his wife and son until their forms were no longer visible. Whitby Bay was a distance of approximately 331 km away from London, but with the hour delay taking off (due to engine trouble), it would be early morning before he reached the Count's private ship, which was scheduled to take him across the English Channel to Le Havere, France.

Roving past a boxcar partially filled with supplies being shipped to Holland, Bram claimed a seat in a passenger car and settled down for his journey. Only the green pastures and meadows shined in his path as he chugged and rumbled along peacefully across Britain's countryside to its North Sea border. A medium-sized suitcase and book satchel were his only traveling companions.

The haze gray compartment came complete with very little: a small wood burning stove, a bench, and a reading lamp. Anything beyond this inventory was left up to the traveler's imagination. The sole seat, which doubled as a bed, contained a hard cushion that was not even long enough to support the Irishman's height. The back of the caboose was full of cargo—crates and boxes of various shapes and sizes—and next to the heat source stood a bin waist high full of kenlin. The small lantern that hung on a latch directly over the bench undoubtedly was to be used as a light source when the sun or the stove was on strike. All in all, the environment delivered a very rustic, uncomfortable, and lonely feeling that probably made the most rugged passenger miserable.

Not even an hour into his journey, the oncoming darkness and drop in temperature initiated the need for more logs to be added to the fire. Bram did this himself, lit the lantern, and then curled up on his bench using his coat as a blanket and his traps as a pillow. The splendid sunset dropped with such velocity that a part of him felt as if he was watching the change in scenery in fast motion concurrent with that of the speed of the car.

By and by, he reached into his bag and pulled out *The Land Beyond the Forest* and proceeded to read of Gerard's historic account of the vampire myth from its birth in Indian mythology to its later incarnation in Europe. Here she suggests that Dark Age superstitions had run rampant through Europe during the 1800s, and the "vampir"—rooted from an Ancient Indian myth—swept through the eastern world beginning in the late seventeenth century and continued through the eighteenth century.

Without advance warning, a sudden and quick vibration of the train compartment ended with the novel being jolted—almost completely out of the writer's hand. The Irishman, startled and partially alarmed by the movement, gazed out into the dim blankness. He listened attentively for any new sign of engine trouble.

All he heard was the muffled low screeching of the locomotive beyond the walls of his compartment. Unsure what it was exactly that interrupted his reading, he peered out of the window. The sun was almost completely set. At length, seeing that he would probably never know what caused the abrupt noise, Bram regained his place inside the book. And upon hearing or seeing no further signs of disturbance, he felt satisfied that normalcy had won and continued further reading in his selected text.

Gerard's recap of the vampire lore was quite extensive and helpful—if not forthright necessary and instrumental—to comprehend the true import of his own mission in Romania. For example, the author discovered about the Carpathian type, which were subject to progressive madness; the Incubus, who were sexual and demonic in nature and could take on the appearance of other persons while attacking during intercourse and in dreams; and the Lamia, a Greek quadrupedal vampire which had an animal body and female head; the Nosferatu ("that of the devil"), a Nigerian vampire with fangs and possessed superhuman strength; and the Baital, an Indian vampire which are reputed to be half man, half bat—just to name a few.

Such reading was engaging but mysterious, nonetheless. But he continued to read on as the eerie images—coupled with the mystery of the night—made the desolation of the train creepier than he ever imagined plausible.

Nonetheless, Stoker read on to find out what deterrent methods could be useful. *"Could there actually be vampires amongst us?"* the Irishman thought to himself. For reading about the occult and folklore for interest sake seemed far easier suddenly now that Dracula was forcing him to accept myth as fact.

Gerard suggested that some types could be discouraged with salt, holy water, or fire while others could be turned away with garlic, wolfsbane, or mirrors. And even though there were variations between myths, there was a common thread between similarities: they all preyed on the blood of the living, victims could ward them off with sacred items, and vampiric powers deteriorated during the day. Abraham made notes as he turned pages; and as he read on of the vampirism folklore of Arefyu, he was amazed to learn at how townsfolk were absolutely terrified of such creatures and were almost obsessed of their downfall. Indeed, paintings, drawings, and stories of men, woman, and children alike existed in history of being sentenced to death or mysteriously drowned, burned, staked, or decapitated due to an association of what was often a misconceived vampiric association.

Nosferatu. Bram wrote and underlined this word in his notes. "So this is the creature that has summoned my aid?" he questioned silently to himself. Growing cold, Stoker got up and fed the fire further kindling and adjusted the lantern for additional light. Looking out his window, he noticed it was completely invisible now, and only the sound of the fire kept the Irishman company. He continued reading about methods of destruction: Sunlight or a stake through the heart could kill some types, whilst others referred to water or an arrangement of stones being placed on its gravesite.

The roaring of the train seemed to become less and less audible in the traveler's ears until everything was mute but the sound of his own brain working.

What could Vlad had done to deserve such a curse to be put on him? He pondered this to himself for quite some time. *True . . . vampires are loathed for their horrible acts, but were they given any alternate choice? Is vampirism not a curse forced upon the victim? Are the vile acts not a product of the creature's nature?*

Though the solicitor's popular adage was that the client is always innocent until proven guilty, this concept was rarely taken seriously and often ignored in an ever-growing society that seemingly enjoyed stringing any and everyone up by a noose. However, this gentleman's Irish blood and English heart stood by a fair trial. And even after reading Arminus Vambery's unsettling letter, the author did not want preconceived assumptions or myths of vampirism to cloud his judgment or to stand in his way of the absolute truth.

Florence's pressure for her husband to become a barrister eventually forced the writer to be initiated into the Inner Temple, one of the four Inns of Court, when he was only thirty-nine. Naturally, she was proud Bram was called to the bar just a few weeks before Dracul's visit, but many felt she was gravely disappointed she would never see him practice law or try a case in a higher court. Instead, she found her dream of being married to an attorney would be lived out vicariously through his writings. Certainly, he frequented the Inner Temple's library, but 'twas to take notes and only incorporate law into his stories as the counselor outlined his plots. And any true exposure Florence gained as the companion of a legal professional was acquired secondhand by her often attentive escort, W. S. Gilbert, whilst her husband was called away by Henry Irving. Indeed, it was Gilbert's own certification that prompted the Anglo-Irish educated acting manager to become a lawyer when Florence's interest in Gilbert prompted a touch of jealousy.

At around 11:00 p.m., Abraham's eyesight began to set adrift from the pages and waned toward the rapid movement of the shadowy countryside that flashed quickly before him, now dimly illuminated by the moonlit sky. With *The Land Beyond the Forest* still in his hand, he reclined back in his seat and shut his eyes as superstitious visions and myths of the old world engulfed his mind like an abyss of steel.

* * * * *

It was twilight when a band of four gypsies parked their covered wagon alongside of a rural off-beaten path in Arefyu. A bristly, bearded old man dressed in a native gown and turban jumped off the driver's seat and made several hand gestures whilst he impatiently waited for others to join him on the ground. A middle-aged man and woman slowly climbed out of the wagon, carrying a much younger pregnant girl that appeared to be having mild to medium contractions. As the old man rattled off instructions in his native tongue, he gathered rocks and sticks from the edge of the woods. The younger man and woman were left to set up camp. Through this process, the girl sat down with her back against a large tree, reeling in pain and discomfort all the while.

Within a matter of minutes, the girls' moans turned increasingly extreme as the contractions became closer together and more intense. By and by, the gypsy couple moved the girl inside a primitive tent and placed her on several blankets arranged on the ground. With her eyes closed and teeth clenched, she proceeded to wail holding what was a monstrosity of a swollen stomach. Soon a worried look spread across the young girl's face as if implying something did not feel right.

Tears began to roll down the girl's face whilst her mother whispered unrecognizable words of reassurance and comfort into her right ear. The expecting father took a rag and gently patted away the perspiration that collected on his wife's forehead and then proceeded to wipe clear of the streaming beads that had collided with her painful signs of weeping.

"The time is at hand," the older man said in Hungarian as the temperature outside began to fall rapidly. For a brief moment, he stood stock still, looking up into the starry night and listening to the wilderness. A coyote sounded his call of the wild from what was seemingly a mountainous range a short distance before them.

Outside the tent, the old man piled up a combination of sticks, brush, and lumber inside a circle of rocks and generated a spark that quickly converted into a blazing fire. He stepped back from the wigwam as the flames began to spread and grew even higher. Within minutes, he heard the cry of a baby and rushed to the tent flailing his arms in excitement.

But something was horribly wrong.

Quickly the cries of joy transformed to shrieks of terror as all looked upon a male that was born with reddish skin and a full head of dark hair. All at once the grandmother's pallor turned a waxen hue, and her visage convulsed with horror as the infant felt her fear and answered by his own despairing cry, displaying a set of prominent incisors that gleamed like ivory against his carmine skin.

The mother's shrieks of pain transformed into screams of consternation as her eyes met her child's. She began to push her entire weight backward from the infant, unawares that the umbilical cord was still attached, until she isolated herself into a corner of the tent. She then looked away from it, closing her sobbing lids tightly in a hysterical form of indigenous prayer.

Seeing that the grandmother was about to drop the infant, the boy's father quickly sliced through the umbilical cord with a hunting knife he brandished from his pocket. He then snatched up the baby while noticing that the infant was likewise born with dark eyebrows that met in the center of its tiny nose. Much like her daughter, the gypsy woman then crawled on all fours to a corner of the tent and rocked back and forth in a fetal position, screaming uncontrollably with her hands and covering her face as if guarding herself from an enduring form of evil.

The older man blurted out several words—words that were whispered as if they were forbidden—before crossing himself in a look of hysterical terror. The young mother, still reeling in pain, was now crying profusely and refused to look up until the child was out of sight. The two men exchanged a few distressed sentences. And then with sideward glances of mutual understanding, the old man carried the boy outside the tent and hurled him into the open flame.

As the coyote howled louder, the glowing fire jumped to the sky in a celestial light. The newborn child acted as an organic source of fuel that spread its sudden—but finite—elevation of heat rapidly around the small group. With the agonized screams of the tiny baby came the even more appalling reactions from the band of gypsies as they urged the campfire to burn even higher, hotter, and faster—as if the current exertions were failing to yield their desired intent.

The two men stood back listening to the infant whine and then squeal in sheer agony until all outcries ceased. With this sudden silence, instead of reactions of guilt otherwise came sighs of relief. And as the four adults fled the clearing, the howling of the coyote passed and the night fell shamefully quiet. Indeed, all that remained of camp were smoky embers and the carcass of what was just moments before a helpless newborn human child.

* * * * *

In a wake of sheer horror, Stoker raised off the passenger bench, screaming to the terrible stench of what he sensed to be burning mortal flesh. Alarmed at first, his attitude shifted to that of extreme outrage, and then, realizing that the queer, repulsive smell was coming from the stove, he eventually regained his sense of awareness. As the journeyman recollected his whereabouts, his panic subsided and he was left alone with the solemn tears of utter sadness.

Holy virgin! It was another bloody dream! he told himself as the train stopped in Portsmouth to pick up some cargo. *So real, so vivid . . .*

"Never could there have been a more grisly or gruesome sight to behold upon the meek than at that single ghastly moment: through the blazing flames came the painful cries of a tortured baby that called out for its mother, who shun away from its unconditional love thus rejecting her parental responsibility," wrote the author. "And delegating her unjust plea of demise to her spouse, the newborn's father and grandfather shown no mercy nor sorrow, cursing its very presence and feeding the fire through unjustified fears of impeding terror."

Was this unlawful act of carnage a harrowing vision of what superstitions and brutality I will face on this foreign soil I so seek out of the darkest shadows of my soul?

Visually shaken from the gypsy's actions, Stoker made an immediate choice to desist his reading until the following morning. Upon reaching for his bag, the odd silhouette of a hairy creature projected off a moonbeam and onto the floor in front of the Irishman. The author jumped back in his seat in complete and utter awe, recoiling from the sight he so loathed without knowing.

On the floor before him was a large rat equivalent to the size of a domestic feline. It seemed unusually old, as the thing's body hair was gray and vastly worn. Bram sat crunched in his bench frozen from any and all movement. He thought to himself there was something profoundly weird and not quite right about the vile animal, and the writer refrained from gazing at it directly except out of the corner of his eyes.

Suddenly the air in the passenger car grew cold and death-like—the exact same melancholy feeling that Abraham Stoker had felt two nights earlier in his study when he was summoned to Vlad's beck and call.

"What do you want?" Stoker asked, frozen from fright.

The creature remained fixed, staring his audience down with glaring black eyes. Slowly, Bram raised his right leg two feet off the floor as the animal stood up on its hind legs, like a begging dog, sniffing the air with an alertness of danger. The Irishman's foot then came down with an abrupt swiftness, almost crushing the rodent's grotesque, irregular skull. Squeaking like a rusty door hinge, the thing quickly scurried clear of Stoker's foot and next looked back at him with a burning stare.

The door of the boxcar opened as a burly cargo handler carried in a massive crate. The rat brushed past the man's legs and disappeared down the train track.

"Zounds!" the man said. "How peculiar! That be the second stinkin' vermin I have seen on this 'ere train today! It must be some spoiled cargo somewhere. Loomin'! I'll be sure to check out the hold, sir . . ."

Stoker said nothing but shook his head up and down twice as in agreement.

"E-gad! But from this awful stench I do believe one crawled up in the kindling hold! Here, let me take a quick look, will ye please, mate?"

As the traveler could not help but admire the man's enthusiasm at a time when other humans present seemed inviting, he shook his head and grumbled a word of acknowledgment. But when no dead rodent turned up, the man backed away and scratched his head in mystery. And then seeing the smoldering fire, he looked at the passenger with a sort of sheepish look.

"I don' see no such animul in the hold," he said worriedly, sniffing the air like a dog. "I'm 'fraid the ruddy pest must've got passed as fuel to the fire!"

The fellow then backed away and brought the crate along toward the back of the boxcar and sat it down on top of a larger item.

"Just going to set this down in the corner, mate," he said, changing the subject.

The Irishman sighed and checked the time on his pocket watch. A perplexed look fell about the author's face as he realized it reflected the exact time the train left Paddington Station.

"Something wrong, mate?"

Abraham thumped his watch several times before making a reply.

"My time is wrong," the writer answered with a look of surprise, striking the glass case with his thumb and index finger repeatedly to no avail. This was a brand-new watch, and it had been fully wound prior to departing Pennington station. "Any idea when we will reach the coast?"

"Oh, we should be leaving for Whitby Bay in about . . . ehhhh . . . ten minutes," the man said, checking his wrist. "We should arrive at Whitby station no later than one o'clock a.m."

Placing his gold chain that was attached to a belt loop back in his right pocket, the Irishman politely thanked the gentleman and leaned forward till he was on the edge of his seat. Though it appeared to the journeyman he was being tested by something far greater than himself, he sat perched as if he was a man on his dignity, proudly watching his own back in a way that would have caused Scotland Yard's own Sherlock Holmes to grow green with envy.

CHAPTER 6

A Ship of Lost Souls

The searchlight followed her, and a shudder ran though all who saw her, for lashed to the helm was a corpse, with drooping head, which swung horribly to and fro at each motion of the ship. No other form cold be seen on deck at all.
—Bram Stoker's Dracula

The *Citadel* was a typical Bulgarian schooner that was built in 1870 for a wealthy retired mariner who longed to spend his remaining senior years fishing in the Black Sea off the coast of its homeport in Varna. But alas, the gentleman's untimely death in 1876 forced the boat to go up for auction, and Prince Vlad seized the opportunity for a considerable sum, using the repurchased ship for transporting goods around Eastern Europe.

"Despite its age, my first glimpse of the grand vessel was a splendid and slightly intimidating sight to behold," wrote the author. "With its five masts standing high in the Whitby air—all of equal height, with the exception of the aft sail being faintly taller than the rest—its LOA registered at approximately 55.3 m and thus controlled the harbor. However, there seemed to be a morbid aura about it that puzzled me in a queer and alarming sort of way: the terrorizing feeling of death and gloom hung in the air like a vague curtain, and

I found myself quickly sinking deep into its shadows—almost as if the sun was abruptly set on my life. Thus, adamant to not give in to what I considered at the time to be a lack of sound sleep, I quickly pulled away and alluded my attention to other matters: the library."

She was bald-headed and with gaff-rigged oyster dredge. Her construction was oak on oak—wooden planks lay on frames of the same sort, as was the tradition in Slovakian-built vessels. She had relatively light scantlings—no knees and no horn timber—also characteristic of boats built in this era and region. Indeed, with a rig height of 70 feet and a sail area of 3,562 square feet, the 57-ton vessel was worthy of a sharp salute.

Whilst three strong men brought supplies onboard Dracula's private boat that was docked at Whitby Bay, Abraham Stoker sped walked to the public library. Since it was shortly after 1:00 a.m., he handwrote a note and left it in their post in an envelope with three quid:

TO WHOM IT MAY CONCERN: I WILL BE TRAVELING BY TRAIN TO ROMANIA FROM LE HAVRE, FRANCE. PLEASE SHIP RESERVED WILKINSON NOVEL TO THE MUNICH STATION. EXPECT TO ARRIVE THERE IN 7 DAYS. B. STOKER

The *Citadel* got underway at approximately 2:10 a.m. With all sails set, the schooner left the pier quietly and began to make good distance quickly down the English Channel. Leaving the port, the captain gleefully announced, "A-hoy crew! It is 555 km to Le Havre France. If weather permits, we expect to set dock 8:00 a.m. . . . just in time for breakfast!"

Bram was at the aft of the vessel looking up at the stars when a short seaman dressed in dirty dungarees and fishing hat approached him at the mast. The man spoke with a Hungarian accent.

"The boss wants me to escort ye to your cabin below deck."

The squat man, who stood around five feet and weighed in around one hundred twenty-five pounds, appeared to be humbled standing before the journeyman who stood at six feet, two inches tall and weighed twelve stone. The seaman analyzed the writer for a few seconds before saying anything further. The author stood watching the man intently, which caused the massive bump over his eyebrows to gather in the middle of his face, which only intensified his less-than-average looks. However, the effect likewise produced a strong, determined look upon his face, which caused the other man to appear intimidated for he broke his concentration and moved toward his guest.

The sailor took Stoker's suitcase from him, and they went through a hatchway and down a flight of steps to a group of quaint cabins.

"This one here is yours . . . mate," the man stated, flinging open a door marked with the numeral three on its facing.

For such a lofty man to say the cabin was small would be an understatement. On the other hand, it contained the essentials: a bunk, a small wardrobe, a table and chair, and a washroom. Abraham made his toilet, rested his suitcase on the mattress, and sat down at the table with his satchel. He pulled out the envelope that Arminius Vambery had given him and placed the contents on the tabletop.

The sound of the English Channel swished against the side of the boat peacefully as Stoker glanced over the information he had been given. The data included a historical background of Dracula and his strict moral code, an explanation and origin of his name, and an intriguing hypothesis in his colleague's hand suggesting that Vlad III was cursed to an immortal hell of vampirism. Bram proceeded to read the material beginning with the meaning of the infamous name itself:

> Vlad Tepes (pronounced *tse-pesh*) intermittently ruled the Wallachia region of the Balkans in the mid 15th century. Tepes translated into English means "impaler"—a method in which he frequently punished his enemies and transgressors. Likewise, this public propensity was also coined an unpopular means to frighten and chastise those thinking about switching sides.

Though a sudden movement of the boat caused his resources to slide across the table, he seized them before they were beyond his immediate reach. Stoker immediately picked up his reading again, taking various notes and memorandums along the way.

> *Drac* in the Romanian language translates into the English word *dragon; ul* is the definitive article. Thus, Vlad III's father became known as Vlad Dracul, or Vlad the Dragon. The translated Romanian ending *ulea,* means "the son of." Therefore, Vlad III consequently became Vlad Dracula, or "the son of the dragon." Notwithstanding, the word *drac* is synonymous with the word *devil* in Romanian. The sobriquet, henceforth, took on a double meaning for enemies of the notorious ruler and his father alike.

Abraham Stoker turned to some documentation that explained the political forces that were present at the time to Dracula's life. Stoker then summarized what he learned in his notes:

> To gain appreciation and understanding of Vlad III's position in life, it is equally essential to recognize the social and bureaucratic factors that existed during the fifteenth century: the determined struggle to seize control of Wallachia, Romania, a southern region of the Balkans, which resided between the two powerful forces of Hungary and the Ottoman Empire.

The writer rested his eyes and hands for a moment and looked down at his watch. It was still not working. The reaction on the man's face was one of sudden shock, validating that it was fully wound.

What is the meaning of this? he thought to himself. Considering the author's anal character of always winding a well-working watch before setting off for bed, this bizarre discovery annoyed him greatly.

For the writer had made a life habit of keeping good time, and furthermore, being on time whenever and wherever he was required to be was a fundamental business requirement in his intrinsic code of work ethics.

Upon seeing that the time still remained frozen to the exact second the train left Paddington Station, a look of consternation swept across his face, and the disappointment left him perplexed and disgruntled.

It is practically a spanking-new watch!

After pining over the odd malfunction for several minutes, the exasperated Irishman finally continued his scribbling . . .

> Constantinople had stood as the protecting outpost of the Byzantine or east Roman Empire for nearly one thousand years and blocked Islam's access to Europe. Notwithstanding, during this period, the Ottomans succeeded in penetrating deep into the Balkans, and with the fall of Constantinople in 1453 under Sultan Mohammed the Conqueror, all of Christendom became threatened by the armed might of the Ottoman Turks. Assuming the ancient mantle as defender of Christendom, the Hungarian kingdom to the north and west of Wallachia, also reached its zenith.

Bram took his eyes off his writing and research material and glanced toward a porthole that reflected the midnight darkness outside. How strange it was, he thought, to be writing research for something other than a theatrical review. Even though his first novel, *The Snake's Pass*, was just published—a documentation of how the farmers of rural Ireland suffered under the English landlord system—he was still not acknowledged as being an original writer. With the exception of a handful of friendly colleagues in the field, his talent was overlooked or underestimated. Perhaps this will change one day.

The wind outside began to let out a fierce roar. The flame lighting his study almost gave sway, causing the darkened room to cast all sorts of ugly shadows that instantly posed quakes from every angle. As the Irishman watched and listened with nervous anxiety, he realized his eccentric readings had begun to feed his imagination. Soon his overactive thoughts triggered fear, followed by the onset of panic. And then the small room began to pick up a mixture of spooky images and unclear thoughts that made the brave man cower back like a child. Nonetheless, after several false alarms and jumps, the Irishman smiled in his own embarrassment and regained control of his faculties. Henceforth, his breathing returned to normal, and his note-taking continued . . .

"The Wallachian dictators were compelled to appease the north and the west to maintain an existence. Dependent upon what served their self-interest at the time, alliances were forged with one or the other. Albeit for a short period, Vlad III was considered a hero by the Romanian people for his leadership and standing up to the encroaching Ottoman Turks and founding relative independence and sovereignty."

Abraham Stoker momentarily stopped his reading. After a slight pause and weary sigh, he thought how we wished he were at the round reading room of the British Library; for there is where he normally conducted research for his novels. And he was very accustomed to the perks and commodities of the place: every reader had a chair, folding desk, and small hinged shelf for texts; pens, ink, blotting pad, and a hat peg. Bram fancied being amongst so many books, and the accommodations brought comfort to his work. Indeed, he was becoming lost in an absorbing reverie.

The boat began to rock back and forth, in a similar fashion such as a mother lulling her infant child to sleep. The motion was making the journeyman slightly queasy, and he silently wished the movement to settle off. Abraham flipped the page of his notes and read on:

> The means of succession to the Wallachian throne was an additional factor influencing political life. Indeed, the throne was hereditary, but

not by the law of primogeniture. The wealthy land-owning nobles, known as boyars, had the privilege to elect the *voivode* (warrior-prince) from among various eligible members of the royal family. This process allowed for succession to the throne through violent means. Hence, assassinations and other aggressive overthrows of reigning parties were rampant. Both Vlad II and Vlad III assassinated competitors to attain the throne of Wallachia.

The rocking of the ship became more intense, and it was about 4:30 a.m. when Abraham became unusually fatigued and heavy-headed. He quickly packed his study materials away and assumed position on his rack to commence sleep. The author soon fell into slumber without dreaming, but at approximately 5:10, a shout woke him from topside. Thus, he quickly got dressed and proceeded to the forward part of the ship to see what the commotion was about.

The first mate, which was visibly and almost violently upset, was addressing the commanding officer whom had been discussing the ship's movement alongside a steersman. A dead body lay in the passageway between the quarterdeck and the captain's cabin. The skipper was documenting the discovery in the ship's log while making fruitless attempts to calm the first mate down. Stoker walked over to the still-warm body and recognized the man as the same one who had helped him to his quarters just a few hours ago.

"I tell yer, Cap'em . . . it was 'im! He must 'ave been lurkin' 'round the engin' room as Nigel was leavin' to 'it his rack. Not 'ong afterwards, I heard this mad 'owlin' of a dog! When I rushed 'opside to check on things, 'e was already dead!" stated the first mate excitedly, trembling from fear.

A bolt of absolute horror shook throughout the writer's large frame, jarring him broad awake in an instant. Surveying the area in what little light there was happened to be more than sufficient to glean the realization that the whole area was spangled with blood.

"The horrible aftermath before me made me doubt humanity and question what wreckage might be in store for me in the weeks to come," recalled the journeyman.

"It was *'em!*" repeated the first mate in mortal hurry.

"And exactly whom is the *he* you are referring to?" Abraham asked boldly, though turning his eyes away from the massacre before a sickened feeling came over him.

"Did you see a person or a dog? Whichever the case may be, the canine or brute would still have to be on deck somewhere as there is nowhere else for the monster to go—lest it jumped overboard!"

There was no reply from either the captain, steersman, or the first mate. Only a look of grave hopelessness.

The body had been drained of almost all its blood. It was already growing stiff, and on the sailor's doomed face was the frozen expression of a paralysis of horror. There was a repulsive matter under his fingernails such as an integration of dried blood, chipped wood, and animal hair. The follicles resembled that of a large dog or coyote. Though it was in vain, there were scratches and indentions on a nearby wooden flagpole—one that the man desperately tried to climb to no avail. There were two tiny prick marks on the left side of man's neck, precisely on the jugular vein.

Nosferatu, Abraham said to himself as a horror of great darkness descended upon his living soul.

At that second in time, the true meaning of the curse of the vampire ravaged the Irishman's mind and body like the wolf form that had its way with Nigel Henley. The grisly carnage on deck resembled that of a calf attacked by a pack in the night. Only the role of man and beast was grossly switched, and the terror of this realization made the writer question the intent of the man—that is, if he could even be considered a man—that carried out the heinous act.

The world seemed so unbearably cruel at the moment that the infestation took everyone's breath away. And though the light of the full moon partially hid the revolting nature of the sight by the veil of the night, the simple fact that there was no sign of movement in the man brought everyone close to tears. And the writer's towering presence spoke volume as the shadowy beams struck his reddish beard in a weird trick of the night that seemed to make the course hairs appear darkened of gore.

"What ruthless villainy!" shouted the commanding officer.

"Th' 'oor bloke made an earnest attempt to climb his way out of danger," stated the first mate. "Up the bloody flagpole!" He crossed himself ceremoniously and went on in a more morose and slower, respectful tone. "I bid ye fair winds an' followin' seas, Nigel."

The three men stood around trembling in a state of fright, disbelief, and sadness. Following this bizarre marriage of emotion, there came a moment of desperation coupled with logical thought. Caught up in the stress of the ordeal, they did their best to hold back tears as the captain suggested the other two conduct a thorough search of the ship forward to aft.

"I will mind the helm. Now go arm yourselves before you search . . . but don't wake the rest of the crew," he ordered.

Though they followed through with the order, there was no discovery of a dog—living or dead—onboard the schooner. Notwithstanding, all was not back to normality for at precisely 5:30, an overwhelming feeling of solemn, gloomy despair suddenly took control of the ship—almost as if a complete change of atmosphere fell about the vessel. The sleeping crew began to be aroused from horrible nightmares and was next awakened by hideous laughter.

Simultaneously, a massive rolling cloud overhead had all but covered up the full orb above; and the boat was lighted only by a fraction of a moonbeam. Henceforth, a whirlpool of feral shadows of all sorts and sizes danced about the deck. This surmised the entire crew to a feeling of utmost unease. The Irishman recognized this as the same melancholy feeling he had experienced twice before.

At once, all three men's attention was shifted from the stiff corpse to the sudden rapid stirring that came from the mast of the *Citadel*.

"Hark! Who goes there!" shouted the captain.

His burly stature was tense as if the wrath of Thor were about to be unleashed. The trio raced to what appeared to be a figure of a tall, grotesque shadow of a man dressed in dark clothes. His exact identity could not be bestowed from where they were standing; however, as the men made preparations for an ambush, the crew found themselves lost in a world gilded between that of fog and mist. The sound of diabolical cackling fell all around them—yet they were blinded in all directions. The distorted sound continued to echo and manifested itself like a plague, growing louder and louder as it traveled up and down the entire length of the vessel. Stoker suddenly recalled the distant memory of his younger self huddled fearfully in his bed as a rush of wind and a skirl of laughter coursed through the night as his legs failed to take action.

The evil noise exposed the remainder of the crew who unwillingly and unknowingly joined the others in what was becoming a living ring of terror. The unusual grandeur of fog and mist swept past every corridor and compartment of the ship. The *Citadel* and its entire troop alike froze suspended in the English Channel completely victimized by the bizarre power that had them under total control. Unable to see and coupled by the fear of falling overboard—or even worse, devoured by the source of the devilish laughter—everyone remained stock still in the morose horror of the moment. The harrowed torment lasted for what seemed several minutes of maddening blackness.

My beloved Florie and dear Noel, how I resent not taking you both to America! the author thought remorsefully, recalling his family's own misadventure at sea. *The fear . . . the suffering you both must have suffered as the rescue team worked their way onward! How I wish I could hold on to you both now—as you must have clung to one another—until at last your rescue boat was lowered whilst you watched the entire ship go under! Oh, woe! Alas, how could I have let such a sore trial pass by without even the minimal amount of adoration, recognition, or regret?*

The grim chuckle continued and began to ring in everyone's ears. There was only a crew of fifteen to twenty on board, yet the festival of laughter boomed of that of a great concert hall for an audience of several thousand. It was not an ordinary sound of glee, but to the contrary, it was one of purest, devious evil. The tone was dark, mysterious, and unrecognizable to that of any living thing one might encounter on earth. This sent chills to the crew members, forcing them to screw up their ears with both index fingers in a means of protest or retaliation.

"Will this moment never end!?" the writer screamed aloud.

And then a sort of wild feeling came over the crew, and if it were not for the thick combination of fog and mist that concealed everyone from one another a terrible outpour of insanity—soon followed by rage—might have been expected to occur: crew member against crew member, a bloody annihilation, self-mutilation . . .

But right before dawn, the obscurity passed. The figure had vanished. And the crew was instructed by the captain to lock themselves in their rooms until a second search of the ship was made. The skipper, too, withdrew himself in his cabin carrying the ship's logbook. Locking the door behind him, he made a 6:30 entry that read, "Tonight, my crew and I experienced the nethermost hell as of yet. I pray to God for the safety of the rest onboard and that we make it to our final destination with no further wicked occurrence."

* * * * *

The brilliant sunrise glistened warmly against the cool waters of the calm North Sea. However, what was usually a soothing and tranquil gift of nature almost seemed surreal or 'twas instead a rude awakening to a rather horrid night.

As the morning broke off, the coast of France the atmosphere of the ship had changed dramatically, although the mood of the crew had not. With a grand horizon and French setting as a distant background, a solemn burial at sea was conducted for the seaman.

"Within half an hour, the deck was quickly transformed and covered with a rich, velvet pal, bordered with white sarcenet and satin," the writer recalled. "The body of the deceased was laid out on the half-deck on trestles and sewn up in his hammock which became his shroud. A couple of thirty-two pound shots were enclosed, next to his feet, to bear the body down to the depths of the ocean. The remains of Nigel were then covered over with the union jack. The crew respectfully lined up on both sides of the body and fired several shots into the still air. Oh, how unusual and melancholy the entire ordeal seemed opposite such a gruesome night!

"All was still, almost as death itself, as several low voices sounded around me. As it came to the close of the service, eight bells were struck, and at the words 'We now commit this body to the deep,' the captain and first mate reverently raised the corpse. And then there came a dull splash in the water. All that was the mortal of their deceased shipmate was gone to its long home. The rest of the crew advanced to the gangway and fired a treble salute over the grave of the departed."

The celestial light from the freshly risen sun did not appear to brighten the crew's spirits or lift their sinking hearts that seemingly grew heavier and darker with each word of remembrance.

The ship then braked for coffee and a quick breakfast—not because they wanted to but because their sleepless and ravished bodies called for them to. Bram joined the almost silent ritual, but nothing could curtail the sorrow that festered behind their complacent faces. Though he made several attempts with crew members to entertain the possibility of a vampire being on board or for their explanation of the previous night, it was almost as if they were afraid of being overheard by the very air they breathed and had been sworn to utmost secrecy:

"I dare not speak about it. I must not talk bad of the 'boss' . . . You don't know what you are asking!" were the common replies the author learned to expect.

Though Abraham Stoker felt he knew the truth behind the culprit that was to blame, he eventually refrained from consulting with the crewmates and decided to keep this disclosure to himself.

But the howling . . . that same melancholy feeling . . . the same tall, gaunt figure . . . the same wry laugh," the journeyman thought abstractly. *How can all this evidence be a coincidence?*

Around 7:15, the port of Le Havere was visible on the horizon, and the captain announced a dock time of approximately 7:45. However, before Stoker left the ship, the commander of the vessel motioned him into his private cabin and shut the door in utter silence.

The commanding officer was a strong man of medium build dressed in a dark wool ensemble, typical of a mariner with anchors on every snap and button, topped off with a commander's cap to suit. His bushy graying hair stuck out wildly from the scrambled egg-like brim and was partially wet from perspiration. It was clear the stress from leading what was no doubt a rambunctious crew, coupled with a rough lifestyle, had worn away at his appearance: hard seagoing days turned into years of hard lines, and an early life of loose liberty and strong drink led to a middle-aged man that was aged beyond his actual years.

This morning, he looked at Stoker with weakened eyes that foretold of stress and worry. His glare spoke of important but unsaid things, and his eyesight glanced about the small quarters as if he was not sure how to begin the conversation. Abraham noticed the man looked tired, disturbed, and unwell, but his stern focus and commanding presence captured the writer's attention full throttle.

"I feel the need to talk about last night," Bram finally said invitingly. "Captain, please permit me to be very candid, for I believe I know the identity of the enemy that commits such acts of bloodletting, commands the fog at a whim, and transforms himself into a vicious wolf whenever he so wishes."

"I know you do," the skipper shockingly replied. "And that is why I have called you in my cabin."

Bram Stoker was bewildered and was for a loss of words. He stood in front of the man, stunned with a look of confusion and astonishment on his face.

"Though I dare not speak his name, we refer to the same person," began the skipper in a hushed tone. "Indeed, I am afraid my second mate is no longer with us because he spoke unwisely of the boss. You must be careful and be aware of what you say and do at all hours—especially during the night, for that is when he is most powerful."

"I can't believe what I am hearing!" denounced the Irishman confusingly. "You live in constant violation of the safety of your own existence and that of the crew? Yet you work for the very man that you fear most?"

"And do you not, as well fine sir?" replied the captain directly.

Abraham fell silent and thought about his last statement for a moment. Next, the captain leaned forward, as if making preparation to foretell some scandalous secret.

"As long as I and my crew carries out his wishes, we feel safe. However, few know of the true terror or understand the monster that employs us. The legacy he and his father left his countrymen was one of great bloodshed."

"Tell me more," replied Bram curiously. "Why don't you and your men fight to end this madness?"

The commander of the vessel seemed thunderstruck by such an extreme and outright notion of defiance and replied gravely, "We are dealing with something much more powerful than us! He was a great and powerful tyrant as a man, and he has become even more powerful as a monster! I dare not curse or stand in the path of his destruction—lest I too become destroyed!"

The captain continued surreptitiously, "The brute we speak of is credited with impaling close to one hundred thousand men, women, and children on stakes, and he is known more than anything else for his inhuman cruelty. And impalement, mined you, is one of the most gruesome ways of dying imaginable. It is a slow, painful death! My shipmates know not of what I tell you, for they would panic at such revelation. Surely they would tremble with fear if they ever learn of such horrors! And fear leads to panic, and panic provokes foolish mistakes! I cannot afford such errors on my watch—not at the expense of my crew!"

Stoker swallowed hard for this was valuable information to consider as he continued to embark upon a path of what was beginning to resemble a road to enduring evil. And as they talked over the Count in secret council, the writer began to understand how the envied life of a Prince Vlad had its fair share of success and disappointments.

"Indeed, here was a man that lived beyond one's inspired wealth and had more fame, power, and fortune than the average man could imagine," replied the officer of the deck. "Yet for every person that bowed to him in favor, another elsewhere feared and loathed him. Until finally, murder became the answer. And as brutal death became the resolve! And as brutality became his trademark vengeance, his horror would ultimately become immortalized and strike terror in the hearts of all ages to come."

But before the writer could respond to Vlad's sad and terrible life story, the skipper brought the conversation around to the *Citadel*.

"This ship has become one of lost souls, and it is I that has been cursed to steer it wherever the master commandeth," the sea captain continued sadly.

"However, my dear sir, you still have the opportunity and hope to save yourself as you have yet to reach his country! It is in his very kingdom where his strength and power are two folds. Please consider this, my kind friend . . . turn back before it be too late!"

Abraham Stoker was confounded once more into a state of utter silence.

"I am afraid I cannot tell you any more,"—the commander went on crossing himself—"as I fear I would be putting the lives of myself and my crew in jeopardy. However, go smartly as you leave this boat and proceed with caution!"

The officer placed a small item in Stoker's overcoat pocket and backed away reservedly. But in a gentlemanly gesture—and one of not appearing to be rude—Bram politely waited to inventory the contents until his feet were back on dry land.

And then at last, the ancient mariner raised his hand and touched the brim of his hat as if honoring the writer a sharp salute. The journeyman gathered his things and threw up his hand in friendship as he swiftly left the boat, unable to overhear the captain's short prayer:

"May God carry you safely along your pilgrimage as the devils of the pit will be upon you where you walk."

CHAPTER 7

The Dead Travel Fast

> You cannot deceive me, my friend; I know
> too much, and my horses are swift.
> —The Coachman to the English Herr

braham Stoker had approximately an hour to dine on a spot of hot tea at a nearby French bar prior to boarding a train departing Le Havre Station and heading east to Munich. As he sipped his beverage, he recalled the small object the sea captain had placed in his overcoat pocket and fancied the opportunity to identify its contents. To his dismay, it was a small phial resembling what appeared to be a clear, mundane liquid.

Of all the colossal gall, Stoker thought to himself. *How am I bloody well supposed to protect myself with an ounce of water?* He then noticed an inscription on the bottle that read, "SAVE YOUR SOUL. SAVE YOUR HONOR." Bram taxed his brain for several minutes to grasp the meaning of the bottle, its contents, and the mysterious message and came to the conclusion that the captain must have been experiencing some level of religious mania. But as the foreigner thought about the land he was traveling to, including the level of superstition he had been reading about, good reasoning—or should we say, an "alternative form" of reasoning sense—began to sit in.

Folkloric accounts have noted that "water" (in several different forms and types) can deter a creature of the night. For example, Eastern European vampire experts have determined that the Un-Dead can only pass running water at the slack or flood of the tide, whereas Russian legend holds that a supreme way to keep a suspected vampire from changing was to throw the corpse into a river, under the belief that the earth could not tolerate the presence of a revenant. The Germans treated suicide victims in similar fashion but also poured water on the road between the grave of a potential vampire and his home as a barrier to prevent his return. And in Prussia, the *leichenwasser*, the water used to wash a corpse, was saved and used in this manner.

But the power of water did not stop with the small quantity that Abraham Stoker held in his palm, and as the determined Irishman gazed upon it a second time he recalled the Greek study told of a mysterious island of Therasia, in the Santorini group, that was said to have been infested with vampires. According to the Greek storytellers, they had been banished to that island because of the prayers and exorcisms of a pious bishop on the island of Hydra, where they had previously been located. Importantly, he noted that according to the myth anyone venturing near the shore of Therasia would hear the noise of the vampires who walked along the shore in an agitated state because they could not cross saltwater.

Apart from its appearance in lakes, rivers, and oceans, water was a course of cleansing and purifying agent. Like fire, it had taken on a number of sacred and mythological connotations: It was often used in religious initiatory rituals such as baptism and in ablution rites such as the bathing that occurred before a Muslim prayed in the mosque. Moreover, within Christianity in Europe, in the Roman Catholic Church and the Eastern Orthodox churches, practices had developed around blessed water, generally referred to as "holy water," that gave the full sway to a number of supernatural or magical meanings and uses. Originally considered of symbolic cleansing value, it came to be seen as having an inherent sacred quality because it had been consecrated for religious use. Indeed, holy water was used in the funeral services of both churches and thus often was present when the bodies of suspected vampires were exhumed and killed a second time.

Remembering everything that he had read concerning ancient and tribal beliefs, the journeyman's stern face relaxed to a gentle and solemn expression. And then he griped the vial tightly, and after kissing it, he slipped the divine object quickly—and ever so gently—back into his coat pocket.

* * * * *

As the time to aboard the train lessened, an odd degree of heaviness came across the author's spirits, which hitherto had been so unaccountably raised. Bram sensed as if the shadow of some coming evil were resting on his soul—as if a sort of momentous calamity were preparing for him, wherein the lot would be enough to drive the man to madness and irredeemable despair.

Undoubtedly, Abraham Stoker was a courageous gentleman, but the overwhelming fears that were beginning to oppress his being to no end unconsciously betrayed this redeeming quality. The true nature of his worse forebodings would soon be at hand. Upon realizing this, the writer took heed to his own self-introspection and internal warnings, and soon he found himself denouncing his qualms — swearing evil did not need his disordered fancy of fears—and the journeyman channeled his nervousness to the best way he knew possible: by writing . . .

"Alas, it has been four full days since I have last written in my journal," Stoker recalled, "and though much had happened since my last entry, almost all of it I wish could be derived as one continuous nightmare." The Irishman wished to his very essence of his being he could pass off everything that had happened to him thus far as dreadful ravings brought on by sleepwalking or hysteria. However, he continued to pinch himself to find he was not asleep; hence, it must all be true. In any circumstances, the series of mishaps felt very real, nonetheless, and he decided to use his diary to record the events of his travels abroad henceforth, as he expected they would quiet him and "assist in making sense of what has been thus all but dark and horrid nights."

The bold journeyman could not help but to question his destiny and doubt if the Count would hold true to his word. And soon the utter feelings of guilt began to cloud his sense of reason and judgment.

Oh, Florie! What have I agreed to do? he thought to himself. *Just as Victor Frankenstein chose to forsake the ones dear to him and reject spiritual enlightenment in lieu of science, my feet have been deep in muddied waters, molding the career of my own monster: one Henry Irving!*

His overridden resentment began to show in his own sympathetic, overpowering words, which were heavy-laden with an aura of sadness and suffering.

"Once the heart hardens, the soul becomes detached; and the monster flourishes, the evil festers within, and in due time, the end result of such an unfortunate endeavor gives rise to the grim realm of demons—in and through which the solo investigator may experience and be subjected to variant levels of fear," wrote the author. "The monster becomes in control of its creator!"

Indeed, just as Dr. Frankenstein lost power to his creation, actor Henry Irving had long seized ruling over Abraham Stoker's life, and now the unthinkable has occurred: the gathering of evil forces had multiplied in the form of a vampiric visitor, and this monster seemed to have been summoned to drain the Irishman of what life he had left.

As Abraham Stoker sat solemnly writing an entry after take-off, he traveled by boxcar to Munich. Bram expected to arrive in Sighișoara about twenty-one days from departure, and he described the events of his trip as follows: "The journey I have embarked upon has commenced to be a grand, dark, and extremely odd one."

Even though the writer was somewhat disconnected and used to being away from his wife and son, a sense of loneliness and a foreboding longing fell over him—despite the fact the passenger train was filled with about fifteen energetic people. They were mostly middle-aged German peasants, and Stoker was delighted to practice his language skills and associate with some regular townsfolk that did not involve talk of queer sightings, raging dogs, or the walking dead. At least for the present moment, he felt relieved to rest his mind of such weariness and disturbing thoughts much less he swoon himself into a coma.

For several days, the company Abraham Stoker kept was of fantastic host, and he learned much of the French and German culture. The food served onboard was of finest quality: baked fish, roast pork, loin, and mutton. The author was likewise overjoyed to understand the train was ahead of schedule and expected to arrive in Munich earlier than originally planned—perhaps as much as one full day. The train felt like it was flying off its tracks, though the oak and elm trees passing by the lucid windows were curiously distinguishable. And if the journeyman's mind was not distracted by other pressing matters, it almost might have seemed the leaves were actively changing color and texture before his very eyes.

* * * * *

The locomotive arrived in Munich twenty-four hours early. Four of the passengers jumped train to head north to Bavaria. Though Stoker's translation was less than superb, he made out key phrases to determine they were destined to tour Chateau Neuschwanstein.

While in Munich, Abraham was able to locate the parcel delivery desk and picked up the package (a reserved novel) that was sent by the Whitby Library. The book was average size, medium weight, and was wrapped up in a coarse parchment paper with burlap string. Bram claimed it gladly with a smile; however, when he returned with it to the boxcar, something did not feel right. Though the man could not point the cause, it was an eerie, foreign feeling that came over the entire train—somewhat like a chill but unusually different. The journeyman decided to postpone reading the new book until the following day in hopes he would feel better therewith. He decided to retire early and get some much-needed rest.

For several hours, the weary-headed author rested with a blank head and perplexed expression on his face, and when he awoke, it was with an urgent sense of unusual excitement he could not explain. "Foremost, I feel some better; nevertheless, I have awakened to find myself filled with uncanny anxiety, yet I have no idea why this be," the Irishman noted in his journal.

Then he began to read the Wilkinson account of Wallachia and Moldavia and found the text both fascinating and intriguing—an unquestionable indication that he thought the book to be an important text for his research. As the writer read, he took many copious notes from the 1820 source, noting the call number and capitalizing certain words on the page for emphasis.

In doing so, he learned more about the Wallachian Voivode from the fifteenth century that fought the land against the territorial Turks. Highlighting a reference to the word *devil*, the author sat back and thought about the possibility of a connection between his newfound enigma and the ancient one.

At the pace I am going, I should have the book finished by the end of the day, he thought to himself. *And it is so strange . . . it feels like the train has left its tracks, though my eyes tell me my mind is deceiving me.*

A slight chill still lingered over Stoker's body, and the nervousness was no better. Moreover, he felt as if he was not alone: "Though I am the only person in my seat, I feel another immediate presence—yet nobody is around. I see passengers on the other side of the train; notwithstanding they are remote in distance. The combination of these feelings has me severely fretful, though I mask my condition as the other passengers could mistake me for being mad. I will pray and hope this sort of calamity will pass soon," he described. And until this stress subsided, he was unable to read or concentrate on anything else.

By the following afternoon, the author had convinced himself *it* was *He*.

"For whatever the reason be, He—or should I say, 'the vampire'—choose not to disclose himself, possibly because of fear of being noticed by other passengers." This thought scared him severely and drove Stoker to a new height of worry and uneasiness. Though afraid, he eventually forced down dinner and decided to retire early. The conductor communicated they will be in Vienna in six days . . . again, earlier than expected! This was comforting to Bram as he was getting weary of his ride including the constant gyrations associated with it. Likewise, he was beginning to feel claustrophobic, and the nine remaining passengers begun to agitate him—constantly jabbering in languages he did not understand. The clackety-clack of the locomotive was growing to an unbarring decibel to his ears.

Despite the Irishman's overwhelming fears, his sleep was deep and almost completely undisturbed, consisting of images of himself curling up next to a warm fire and a book on Egyptology with Noel in the near vicinity and with sounds of Florence preparing tea. However, unbeknownst to Bram, the vile of liquid that was tucked away in his pocket began to change, slowly heating up and glowing a slight scarlet hue.

* * * * *

The following morning, Abraham Stoker awoke abruptly to the call of his name but mysteriously found nobody at his side. After a brief spell where he shook away the lingering effects of sleep, he differentiated the alarm to what he believed to be a false reaction to long hours of rail noise. Thus, he continued his reading of some of the atrocities of Vlad Tepes as he decided it might take his mind off of the overwhelming unease, yet he came to a particular picture of the man that shocked him immensely.

Vlad Dracula was drawn feasting amongst a forest of stakes and their grisly burdens outside Brasov whilst a nearby executioner cut apart other victims. As he studied the wood-cut image with such grave agony, his concentration was interrupted by the sound of droplets splashing about the page. Two drops fell on Vlad himself; and the substance glowed bright red, turning his eyes a shocking crimson color such as that of a demon. A mad rush of horror rocketed through the journeyman's body when he dipped his finger in the element and pressed it shakily to his lips.

The fluid was blood, and as it fell upon the dreadful scene, the excess matter trickled down the page of the book, leaving a ghastly smeared trail. The same disheartening voice whispered his name again as a disturbing flashback of terror froze still in his brain:

"Woe to the dying! He soaked his bread in their blood and then . . ."

Abraham Stoker shuddered.

Soon the sight before him resembled a pail of crimson paint that was steadily poured over the area of the boxcar where the journeyman had begun reading.

"I believe I must have flown into some sort of fit of rage as I flung the book across the floor of the boxcar and gasped in what I prayed was an outburst of delusion! I put my hands up to my face in disbelief when a nearby passenger observed that the blood was actually mine! My nose had begun to bleed," Bram Stoker recorded in his journal. "I made my toilet at the back of the train and within a matter of minutes was able to get the matter under control. However, I was deathly pale. I felt faint and extremely sick to my stomach. Perhaps it is motion sickness, as I continue to feel we are traveling much faster than normal speed."

Two noble German women insisted that the author lie down and that the baked chicken he had eaten for lunch was the cause of his taking ill.

"It was not fully cooked," the eldest said to the other in their native language. Indeed, Stoker was deeply touched by their tender solicitude, and when the younger lady suggested that it was prudent to rest the remainder of the afternoon, he kindly obliged. However, as Abraham was waiting for sleep, the conversation drifted off the topic of chicken and seemed to become controversial and deadly. As he slowly drifted, he watched as their facial expressions changed dramatically from the sweet, hospitable overtones to ones of grave concern, fear, and pity. There the journeyman decided to translate some of the conversation he overheard as the two women discussed his condition. It was troubling to his soul as he heard words such as *supernatural*, and the older lady whispered, "Loathing devil."

When Bram woke for dinner, he immediately discovered the two women had hung a crucifix above where he had slept. He was not fretful of this because his nap was actually the most pleasant sleep he had experienced in several weeks. After eating a bowl of porridge for his evening meal, Stoker sat and observed the scenery, sipping a glass of port wine. Though he could not explain it logically, Abraham could not shake the feeling that the entire atmosphere was changing the further east he traveled. He could neither describe it fully nor place his finger on it. "I continued my reading and prayed we would reach Romania soon for I felt like I was becoming a wreck of my old self."

* * * * *

A full day early, the train arrived in Vienna, and once again, Abraham Stoker was overjoyed, as he needed some fresh air and a change of scenery. The passengers had about an hour and a half to stroll the train station where Bram picked up some breakfast and a local newspaper. His brain was full of cobwebs from his bizarre ordeal, and though he could not make out every headline of the paper or of the events in their entirety, the break—albeit a short one—offered a good dusting.

As the journeyman sat and watched the passersby, it felt as if he caught them staring at him nervously or purposely found a way to avoid his presence. However, the writer did not have long to dwell on the matter before the boarding attendant called for a reload.

"I have set off again, this time for Budapest," Abraham Stoker wrote in his journal. "Though I write this with a touch of sarcasm, full speed ahead!"

Indeed, the final hours he would spend on the rail before reaching Hungary would be almost unbearable—the noise . . . velocity . . . exasperation . . .

"As I get closer to my final destination, the company I have kept on the boxcar has dwindled down to just myself and one other. It is as if I am plummeting into the bowels of hell, and I must withstand the heat solo," Bram wrote. "Could this desolation be just another link in this chamber of horrors that seems to be enclosing in on me like a fortress of intolerable doom?"

The driver sent word that the train would reach Budapest in two days, and for this Bram was thankful. Stoker was about at his wits' end and had lost all stock in the locomotive. His days were getting to be merged into one continuous, freakish reverie and there was no one to talk to—only one tall man that came and went from the box car at random without saying a single word.

The man always looked the same: dressed gaudily in black with a large rimmed hat pulled down concealing what he believed to be a harsh and abrasive face. The unfamiliar person made the Irishman very uncomfortable, and he, Bram, considered informing the train attendant if this lurking should continue.

Since Abraham had the boxcar all to himself, the feeling of claustrophobia subsided and was replaced with a "quite lofty" feeling as he calmly described. The afternoon hitherto arriving in Budapest, the author sat down for noontime tea and cake; however, he once more sensed the feeling he was not alone and the terrible ordeal of the previous week flashed before his eyes. The journeyman's skin grew cold and began to tighten as his hairs tingled at their ends. His palms and face turned clammy as he forced himself to slowly turn around in his seat and look over his shoulder.

There stood the train attendant.

The reaction in both men seemed to be one of collective, sudden alarm. Although the servile one was aware of Bram's presence, it seemed he was not prepared for such an unnatural greeting.

"I beg your pardon, sir, I did not mean to scare you!" he said apologetically.

As the uniformed man fetched the passenger's utensils and placed them on a tray, the writer told the gentleman about the mysterious roaming alien.

"And in telling of the man I found the air that circled around me grew bitterly dank and cold—like a dead man's hand when left in the mortuary's icebox overnight," the journeyman wrote. "And though I was outwardly appalled to learn that no one of that description had bought a ticket, I somehow internally knew—"

"It must be some bloomin' vagrant that needs to be dealt with," grumbled the attendant, disrupting his patron's thoughts. Then the assistant vacated the car as quickly as he had come and left an infuriated Abraham Stoker to his own devices.

The night before arriving in Budapest, the dark phantom intruder fancied another visit. Stoker was again reading silently to himself but was interrupted by a strange sensation as if being closely watched.

"As the regularity of my breathing grew heavier, my heart quickened along with the pace of every footstep—paces that I was only taking in my mind—which abruptly stuttered with every few feet as my quivering limbs and darting eyes projected quick glances of consternation to the eerie, dull pounding of a kettledrum that I found to be my beating heart," recalled the writer.

He found the darkness of the night was endless and still but lurid and vividly alive with diabolical sights and sounds of unthinkable horror that could drive the weak to the grave.

Bram looked up to justify this feeling, and as he eluted, there stood the trespasser.

"He was clothed completely in black. The hair that was visible underneath his hat was profuse, his eyebrows enormous and shaggy, and he had a heavy moustache that had grown wild under his beaky nose. His skin was as pale as ever; and as he held up his right hand— as if to greet me—I trembled at a strange revelation: he actually had hair growing in the palm of his hand!"

Most noticeable to the author were the brilliant extended canines that protruded over his lips when the mouth was relaxed. Though his eyes were gray, they flashed red as he approached. And as his long, extended fingernails curled up around the Irishman's clasp, the interloper's poignant, rank breath almost caused Abraham to fall faint.

The unusual man stood about a distance of three feet in front of Stoker. And after a clever smile, he finally spoke, and Abraham was thunderstruck as he immediately recognized the voice as that of Count Dracula.

"I see ye have schooled thyself of my native land including that of my reign and my families' history. Though I accept this as a flattering testament, understand there are facts that you knowest not, and the events ye fathom as devious horrors are somewhat misleading to a mortal's morality."

The journeyman's reaction was one of intrigue and surprise, but the hypnotic development that somehow had begun to creep into his body unexpectedly was equally appalling, and he sunk down against the vibrating bulkhead as the vampire continued.

"My dear old fellow, herewith is only part of my story," the Count said pointing at Wilkinson's *An Account of the Principalities of Wallachia and Moldavia.* "In time, ye will knowest the truth and 'ere understandeth."

As soon as he spoke those words, Stoker noticed the Count seemed startled by an object. Bram followed Dracula's eyes and noticed Vlad was looking at the crucifix that was hung by the two German women. The monster took two steps back, and yet the hat he was wearing shadowed his face, the Irishman could see his eyes blazed of hellfire. After a slight pause, Dracula chucked a good Flemish laugh and again spoke serenely.

"Alas, I seeth others try to amuse ye with such trinkets of faith and comfort; but I warn you, my friend, Stoker, though thou cross might bringeth tranquility, it does not terminate the endless, awful cries one such as I am damned to hear! Though there are slight pauses of utter silence, the void is even harder to bareth—as the scheme of murder haunts the very night I am cursed to walk!"

And then the vampire vanished into the thin air and tiny particles such as that of dust floated about the boxcar. *The dead travel fast, as does this cursed train,* Bram thought to himself. *For when your own footsteps stirs a jolt of fright and your own shadow and gasps cause you to look over your shoulder in fear, one cannot possibly know or understand the true import and meaning of sheer terror, and it is this degree of philological calamity that slowly eats away at a person over a level of time and launches an otherwise sane person into utter peril and madness.*

At this precise moment, the author's face was fixed with an expression of unreserved terror for he was convinced that the fiend was watching him like a rabid dog at all times to ensure he was obedient to the monster's wishes. The writer then fell over in his seat short of breath, wheezing like a beached fish gasping for air. The only sounds were those of the journeyman's panting and of the long, black train as it continued to bolt down the dark path before him.

"Dear God in heaven," Stoker shouted out loud, placing the crucifix directly over his expeditious beating heart. "What have I agreed to do? Christ, please forgive me! End this dire nightmare, and have mercy on my tortured soul!"

But something told Stoker that the outlandish dream was terribly real, and as he had lapsed into a spacey, dreamlike state, a moment later, Bram bolted out of bed broad awake, dripping wet from perspiration. The uncanny presence of a mysterious form seemed to lurk beside his rack—traces of a tall, dark, image that hovered for a short moment and then disappeared in a sort of mist that left a foreign residue and a feeling of wickedness about the boxcar.

CHAPTER 8

The Order of the Dragon

> Here I am noble; I am boyar; the common
> know me, and I am master. But a stranger in a
> strange land, he is no one; men know him not –
> and to know not is to care not for.
> —Count Dracula to Jonathan Harker

The next several days onboard the rail were uneventful, and the Irishman reached Romania without any delay. To Abraham Stoker, the town of Budapest seemed quite Christmas-card romantic, mountains rose all around, and the squalor was softened by the presence of a surprising number of churches, Christian and Orthodox, most of them built in the days of the Austro-Hungarian Empire. Grubby-looking shepherds dressed in flowing cloaks guarded pastures and stables. Some bowed at Stoker—in an almost courtly fashion—as he passed by; whilst others remain fixed on the sheepfold and failed to take any notice.

During his short stay in Hungary, Abraham dined on bors (sour soup with a lot of vegetables), and snitel-breaded escalope (grilled veal) at a local restaurant while waiting on his coach to transport him to Romania. Through Bram stood out boldly as a tourist, very little spectacle was made of his presence—that is until his coach arrived.

About 6:00 p.m., Vlad's carriage parked in front of the quaint restaurant where Stoker had enjoyed a peaceful and relaxing dinner. "At almost an instant, all of the passers-by scattered as if the angel of death had arrived and commenced boarding prodigal sinners," Stoker wrote in his journal.

The four-hour-long carriage ride from Budapest to Sighişoara was as eccentric and mysterious as all other encounters and events leading up to this juncture of his journey. The gothic coach Count Dracula provided had arrived several hours late, and it was practically nightfall before Bram began to make his ascending climb through the Transylvanian alps and to the country once known as Wallachia, home of the infamous Vlad Tepes III.

The driver neither got up nor spoke but motioned the author to climb inside the ride. The rather creepy carriage man 'twas dressed from head to toe in solid black, resembling the legendary ferryman that carries unfortunate passengers down the river Styx to an eternal and fiery doom. His face was concealed with a large-rimmed hat, similar to the same one Dracula had worn the previous night onboard the train. He watched his passenger carefully whilst loading his self and belongings.

Hitherto, the irregularity of the situation 'twas not singular to the eccentric cabbie; in particular, the two horses were of reddish color and of the oddest breed. Their eyes appeared to be black as soot, and the manner of the mares was almost savage like, snorting what was seemingly smoke as would be exhaled from a dragon. They were restless during their brief stop, but the driver held them at bay with stern gestures. Their unusual massive teeth gleamed pearly white, and they were obviously very strong, though in an odd sense of the word, this comforted Stoker as he imagined the ride before him would require animals of diligent vigor to complete the trip. Within a few minutes, the driver cracked a massive leather whip . . . and they were off.

Whilst waiting for transportation, the journeyman looked up some historical information on Transylvania and noticed that several races inhabit the land. According to Gerard, Romanians, Hungarians, and Saxons are the most populated with gypsies, Jews, and Armenians followed with the least. It was interesting to notice that the province was thinly populated. Gerard explained that this was arranged on purpose to resist attacks from without.

Despite Abraham's strong and inquisitive desire to see his surroundings, the later part of the journey up the rough terrain was in complete darkness. But based on the writer's daytime view of the remote land, he hazard an assumption that the countryside was absolutely breathtaking—that the picturesque peaks, valleys, streams, rivers, and mountain ranges were all blessed with the majestic beauty of spring—that the elms, oak, beach, and perch trees complemented the landscape with utmost splendor.

"I could make out the silhouettes of many striking plains, narrow winding valleys, and emerald mountainous torrents breaching over gray boulders," the writer recalled. "The cliffs were seemingly heaped so high and so near around me that I had to extend my entire head out the carriage window and crane my neck to steal a glimpse of the darkening sky."

But oh, how the foreigner wished Florrie, of whom he made the habit of calling his loving wife when he missed her so deeply, could have experienced the bits and pieces of his travels abroad that were not shrouded in the otherwise supreme gloom and relentless despair.

The horses climbed up and then even higher. The coachman continued to enforce this behavior for what seemed to be several hours. And as they ascended, the sun continued to set, and eventually, Bram could see nothing but faint shadows illuminated by the moonlight. This created a dire eerie feeling, and considering he was in a strange land, anything out of the ordinary would appear to be exaggerated, nonetheless.

The average altitude of the high mountains was around 1800–2300, and as the driver went around the steep slopes and sharp ridges, the rocky scenery likewise seemed dangerous. Stoker leaned in the direction away from the steep cliffs in hopes to make the breathtaking view less of an uncomfortable sensation.

As the coach progressed, the mountains became wider and rounder. The hill-like points became even rockier with piercing ridges. Though quite hazardous to someone not accustomed to rallying such terrain, the journeyman thought to himself, *In the sunlight, these mountains must have picturesque glacial valleys, wintry lakes, as well as endless forests at the bottoms. But at dusk . . . they become alive with the unknown!*

The brilliant moonlight streamed its luminous rays on everything in its path—much like a promise of new hope or peace—casting oblong, supernatural-like shadows that seemed to reach out and grasp those that have refused to take an appreciation of such things.

The landscape varied from fertile plains, where cereals and vegetables were grown, to smooth hills covered by orchards and vineyards. As tranquil the world around him seemed at the moment, the sudden howling of wolves and coyotes quickly offered an alternate viewpoint as the full moon had crept up fully behind Bram overlooking the high mountains and deep forests.

"The moonlight must have had a strange effect on me as I drifted off into a comatose-like slumber," Abraham Stoker noted in his journal. "Though the howling of dogs continued in my dreams, I question the validity of the encounter, for if they be true, it had to be packs of them all around the carriage."

After riding in a train for the first piece of his journey, Bram was well accustomed to the bumps, sudden shifting, and gyrations of travel; therefore, it was not unusual that the widest turn on the steepest mountain peak did not stir him from sleep. Notwithstanding, the Irishman awoke and cursed himself with the sharpest of tongue—for he fathomed that by virtue of sleep, he presently had no recollection of the route just taken. It was the feeling one must suffer after being hypnotized and to awaken unable to recap whence he came from, what just happened or where one be at present. Could the truth suggest that the Count decided to play out the Hansel and Gretel images of the Three Brothers Grimm? Indeed, there were absolutely no crumbs left for the author to find his way back.

* * * * *

At half past midnight, the coachman parked in front of a residence in the city of Sighişoara, the only medieval citadel in Europe still inhabited. The lamps of the carriage shone, thus illuminating a rather old, rustic structure that appeared off-putting for a prince.

"The dwelling was a three-story stone composition of dim yellowing hue with a tiled roof and scores of small windows and an opening suitable for a small garrison," wrote Stoker.

The coachman jumped out of the driver's seat and waved for Abraham to go through the middle archway on the lower level of the house. Carrying his bags, the writer entered and walked up a set of steps, which led to a moderate sized sitting room. It was obvious that no one was currently living in the quarters; however, someone of significant royalty once occupied the domicile. Though very aged and unkempt, the furniture, draperies, and artwork were of the finest and most noble quality.

Bram stood in the middle of the flooring for several minutes familiarizing himself with what he described in his diary as "fantastic chattels and furnishings" when the touch of a hand suddenly fell upon his right shoulder. It was the carriage driver, but he appeared out of nowhere as Stoker was facing what he thought to be the only entrance.

"Do ye approve of my old home?" asked the man in a genial tone. The foreigner was baffled as he immediately recognized the voice of the Count. Being a man of true grit, he withheld his sudden feeling of nervous hysterics—laughter, crying, and every motion that is in between.

The bloke is all over the bloody place! the journeyman thought to himself. *I can't escape his presence, yet if these escapades continue, my mind will come off its hinges!*

Not knowing what to say, the Irishman stood silent, thus when his nerves subsided, he bravely collected all his thoughts and addressed Count Dracula in a most professionally disguised voice:

"I hazard a guess as to why you have brought me to what I assume is your birthplace. Is this true? Are you prepared to weave me a good story tonight?"

"Ahhh, my friend Stoker, yes, thou are correct on both accounts and speak of my diligence with such a cynical overtone!" replied the Count politely. "Please, I bid thee welcome. Go make your toilet whilst I poureth ye a glass of wine. Alas, we have much to discuss this very evening."

When Abraham Stoker returned, Vlad handed his guest a glass of port and looked him directly in the eyes. Within a few seconds, the author fell himself falling into a deep trance. He let go of the wine and fell back into a high back chair, ornately decorated with inner gold leaves and the finest red velvet.

Dracula spoke with a gleam in his eyes and a stern, earnest look about his face. And then, after a short pause, the Count began his unusual and remarkable story . . .

"Friend Stoker, Wallachia was foundeth in 1290 by Radu Negru, a man who was also known as Rudolph the Black. Hungary dominated my homeland until 1330, when it became independent. The first ruler of the new country was Prince Basarab the Great, an ancestor of my dear father. My Great Grandfather, Prince Mircea the Old, reigned from 1386 to 1418 until the House of Basarab was split into two factions: my great-grandfather's descendants, and the descendants of another prince, whom we knowest as Danest." The Count broke off and stepped close to Abraham with a sigh followed by a slight pause. His listener raised an eyebrow as if keen with interest and as to motion for his host to continue.

"This—that very separation, my friend Stoker—is what initiated the struggles to assume the throne during my families reign, and it was between these two competing factions which triggered much of the battles and bloodshed that was to come upon me, my family, and my kingdom's people." Dracula backed up and seated himself. He pointed to what appeared to be an aged yet beguiling mural, depicting three men and a woman, painted in neo-Renaissance style. The innermost figure was that of a fairly rotund man with a double chin, stretched well-waxed mustache, an olive complexion, oval-shaped eyes, arched eyebrows, and a finely chiseled nose.

Vlad Dracul? the writer thought to himself. *The uncanny similarity of the oval almond-colored eyes!*

The mural painted the Count's father wearing a white Oriental turban and a loosely fitting gown of central European style, with broad sleeves fastened by a massive amount of cruciform clasps.

Significantly, he held in his left hand a staff of office, while his right griped a golden cup.

The author was alarmed to see what resembled the formation of a tear swell up in Dracula's eyes. His host must have recognized this for he quickly turned away. And with a look of grief—one hitherto completely unbeknownst to Bram—sustained his story.

"I was born as Vlad Tepes in 1431, in this very fortress of Sighişoara, Romania," the Count said, slightly striking the armrest of the chair in which he was seated at present. "My father, Vlad Dracul, at that time appointed military governor of Transylvania by the emperor Sigismund of Hungary, who came to be the Holy Roman Emperor in 1410, had been inducted in to the Order of the Dragon about one year hitherto. The Holy Roman Emperor and his second wife, Barbara Cilli, originally created the order, which could be compared, to the religious society, in 1387. The main goals of such a secret fraternal order of knights were mainly to uphold Christianity—to protect the interests of Catholicism. Alas, my father sworeth to defend the Empire and to crusade against the Ottoman Turks. Its emblem was a dragon, wings extended, hanging on a cross!"

Dracula, now seated, was dressed in the Order's official attire: a black cape over a red garment. He pointed to the headdress, which was to be worn only on Fridays, or during the commemoration of Christ's Passion. Stoker looked on, dazed, star-struck, and still in a trance.

"Thou already knoweth how my name came to pass—therefore, I will not explain again. But note my father was admitted to the Order the year of my birth because of his bravery in fighting the Turks. He proudly woreth this emblem of the order and later, as ruler of Wallachia on his dress and on his coinage," explained the Count fondly. Dracula stood up proudly and stuck out his chest, much like a peacock on the strut or a general of war marching back from victory. Vlad looked out the window into the nocturnal sky and Stoker followed him with glassy, roaming eyes. With his own eyes still peering into the midnight abyss, the vampire went on . . .

"In 1431, King Sigismund also made my father the military governor of Transylvania, a region directly northwest of Wallachia.

However, my father was not content to serve as mere governor, and so he gathered supporters for his plan to seize Wallachia from its current occupant, Alexandru I, a Danesti prince. In 1436, he succeeded in his plan, killing Alexandru and becoming Vlad II."

The Count could tell that Stoker looked confused as to why such assassinations were necessary.

"Ahhh," Dracula stated very cunningly, "ye question why such aggression was redeemable as thou are such a noble gentleman yourself. But trust me, friend Stoker, it was required . . . there was such purpose!"

"I will continue. My childhood," Vlad III stated, "was of a typical one for that of the sons of nobility throughout Europe. My early education was left in the hands of my mother, a Transylvanian noblewoman, and her family. But after my father succeeded in claiming the Wallachian throne, my real education began. I had an elderly boyar as a tutor who had fought against the Turks at the battle of Nicolopolis, and in my apprenticeship to knighthood, I learned the skills of war and peace that were deemed necessary for a Christian cavalier."

Dracula began to pace the floor in excitement, pretending to draw an invisible sword as he commenced his story of his father's throne:

"For six years, my father, Vlad Dracul, attempted to follow a middle ground between the two powerful neighbors! The current prince of Wallachia was officially a vassal of the King of Hungary, and my father was still a member of the Order of the Dragon and sworn to fight the infidel! At the same time the power of the Ottomans seemed unstoppable, my father was forced to pay tribute to the Sultan, just as his father, Mircea the Old, had been forced to do."

Stoker noticed that the black eyes of his speaker were beginning to glow red and the razor-sharp teeth protruding over his bottom lip seemed longer and even more horrifying to look at. The writer tried to stand, but it was as if some kind of enchantment had him glued to a chair like a marionette on strings, and it was Dracula who was the puppeteer.

"Alas," the Prince picked up again, "in the winter of 1436, my father, Dracul II, became Prince of Wallachia, one of the three Romanian provinces, and took up residence at the palace of Tirgoviste, the noble capital. I followed my father and lived six years at the princely court. Nevertheless, in 1442, my father attempted to remain neutral when the Turks invaded Transylvania. The Turks were defeated, and the vengeful Hungarians under John Hunyadi, the White Knight of Hungary, forced my family to flee Wallachia! It was during this time my younger brother Radu and I were taken hostage by the Sultan Murad II to Adrianoples."

Dracula paused, and his blood-stained lips appeared unusually cruel and morbid. It appeared his canine teeth had split his bottom lip open—presumably out of anger—and the result landed in a fresh trickle of blood that seeped down his chin, creating a ghastly appearance that caused the Irishman to cower back in revolt and fear. Vlad grew irate, and his bushy eyebrows curled like a winged spread bat over his blazing eyes that seemed to project sparks of hellfire about the room.

"By political force, I was incarcerated for four long years by the cursed Turks, whilst my brother Radu was forced to remain until 1462! My father was unable to intervene unless he surrendered his good faith. Oh, how this wicked captivity played upon my young and mortal brain and such boyar upbringing! To see such conditions put upon my own father and brother and to not adopt a cynical view of life? *Damn them all!*"

The Count paused and looked at Stoker furiously, who was finally allowed to speak, though he did not move from his chair.

"Whatever did you do during this time? How did you keep up your strength?" Abraham asked. The Count thought for a minute before giving a reply.

"I strategized," he answered. "And it was the thought of revenge for myself and my own family that carried me though until I again saw the light of day and . . . eventually beyond," said the Count dreamily.

Dracula paused a short while to gather his thoughts and once more looked out the window as if he were back in incarceration, searching for the sun; however, he let out a groan and winced, recalling it was nightfall—a time he had been restricted to for over four centuries.

"Indeed, the Turks set me free only after informing me of his father's assassination in 1447! Alas, how I remember being overjoyed—to finally be enabled to witness the brightness of the sun but to only become heart-wrenched to learn that my father was dead! *Curse the Turks to the bowels of hell!*"

The Count went into some sort of frenzied fit of range, flailing his arms about his head like a madman, knocking over pieces of furniture throughout the room. He resembled a veritable red-eyed, unrestrained demon that was set free from the pit to take over the world.

"The assassination was organized by Vladislav II, but he did not stop there, defiled man! Upon release from captivity, I also learned about my older brother's death, Mircea, and how he had been brutally tortured and then buried alive by the boyars of Tirgoviste! The fools! They had no recollection of whom they were dealing with," he shouted angrily.

At that point, Dracula took a brief pause to regain his normal sense of composure—that is, whatever the case, there is such a normalcy of an Un-Dead presence—and then backtracked his story. The journeyman seemed touched by the chain of events and to gain an increasing sense of grief for the Count.

"What a brutal path of destruction that was bestowed upon you and your family—indeed, it is much more bereavement than one family should be asked to bear," replied the author in earnest.

"I thank you . . . and please forgive me, my dear Stoker, as I am getting ahead of myself. In 1444, Hungary broke the peace and launched the Varna Campaign, led by John Hunyadi, in an effort to drive the Turks out of Europe. Hunyadi demanded that my father fulfill his oath as a member of the Order of the Dragon and a vassal of Hungary and join the crusade against the Turks, yet the wily politician still attempted to steer a middle course, and rather than join the Christian forces himself, he sent my oldest brother, Mircia. I believed my father hoped the sultan would spare the lives of my youngest brother and myself and release us from captivity—to this, I cannot say for certain—hitherto the Christian army was utterly destroyed in the Battle of Varna. John Hunyadi managed to escape under inglorious conditions. From this moment forth, John Hunyadi was bitterly hostile toward my father and my oldest brother! Hence, my father was assassinated, and the boyars and merchants of Tirgoviste tortured then buried Mircia alive! And so Hunyadi placed his own candidate, a member of the Danesti clan, on the throne of Wallachia."

Abraham stopped the Count fully interested in the development and interjected, "Were you then released from captivity in order to do battle against this aspirant?"

The Count flashed a suspicious smile and sat back down in his chair. He sighed and placed his hands behind his head, thinking. The foreign guest noticed the long, sharp nails protruding at least an inch beyond his host's cold, pale fingertips. The nails on the Count's hands were like ten implements of war that could slice open a flesh wound upon demand. Vlad leaned forward in his chair and pointed his index weapon at his listener as if to render some kind of destruction.

"How correct you are, my dear friend Stoker," the Count softly whispered. "And that is when life became hell on earth!"

It was not long before a cock crowed in the distance and the Count quickly cut short his conversation with Abraham Stoker. Bram left the room to tidy himself only to come back to an empty chamber. However, adjacent to the sitting room was a dining area with a table already prepared with breakfast.

The writer ate a hearty meal and then walked about the house to see what was of interest to him. The other chambers had furnishings of similar quality to that of the sitting room and other quarters he had entered, and every wall was decked with renaissance artwork by the likes of the masters such as Da Vinci, Michelangelo, and Rembrandt.

As the writer walked about the floors of the house, which was located in a prosperous neighborhood surrounded by the homes of Saxon and Magyar merchants and the townhouses of the nobility, he came to the startling conclusion that there was absolutely no exit!

Though he clearly recalled just hours before coming up a flight of stairs from a ground floor entrance, that flight of stairs had suddenly up and disappeared!

"Good God!" Stoker shouted out loud. "I am now the prisoner!"

This sense of entrapment, clearly enforced by the Count, caused Bram to fly into an escapade of furious running and sheer panic. For nearly a full hour, Stoker scurried from room to room with frenzied vigor to find freedom. However, with every attempt, he came to the same conclusion: there were no doors leading out to the city below him.

Resembling a lab rat suffering from exhaustion after making repeated rounds in its cage, the Irishman finally sat himself down to think.

The bloody windows! he thought to himself, suddenly bubbling like a well of good spirits.

Abraham knew every floor contained at least four windows, and though he had not looked out one just window yet he distinctly recalled the Count standing at a pane in the sitting room during their conversation just hours earlier.

The house where Vlad took up his headquarters was located in the main square near the Councilmen's Tower. The numerous windows in the abode were openings for defensive purposes such were customary in the Middle Ages, when street brawls were frequent.

Upon jetting back to the sitting room, the journeyman's sudden spark of liberation reverted back to one of sheer disappointment and captivity.

The beast boarded the damn windows! he said to himself gravely. As the foreigner walked through every door, which only took him into another room of the house, he confirmed again and again every single window about the residence had thick black iron posts covering the only opening, which all seemed to tease Stoker by taunting his falsified independence and hopes of prevailing freedom.

It was around noon when Abraham surrendered and came to the realization that there was nothing he could do but sit and wait for the Count's return. He could see no living being from his place of dwelling, and his sense of forced anxiety had swoon himself into a state of total desperation. In due time, he found a dark bedroom and sat down, holding his face in his hands.

"God help me bear my sorrows!" the journeyman shouted, shuttering until the bed beneath him shook himself into slumber.

* * * * *

At dusk, Abraham Stoker was awaked by the voice of Count Dracula.

"I awoke, praying the entire ordeal was a nightmare, but there he was again, the Count, standing before me with what appeared to be fresh blood on his lips inviting me to dine. It was too hideous to believe it was all real! I would rather believe this diary to be that of a madman than a sane one as the former is lighter on my heart and soul," Stoker noted in his journal.

After Bram freshened up, Vlad sat in the dining room and attentively watched his guest eat a grand dinner of stuffed quail, assorted vegetables, bread, and port wine.

"I trust ye had a good day's sleep and that thou accept my apologies for keeping you up so late," the Count said in an earnest tone, as if he were completely unawares that his guest was incarcerated. At this, the author placed his fork down and balled up a fist that he used to strike the table.

"Why do you keep me held prisoner?" Stoker boldly asked. However, almost immediately, the writer realized his anger and reeled it back, pouring another glass of wine. "Why carry through the unjust, cruel act of me that you loathed so much yourself in youth?" he calmly asked the vampire.

The Count sat silently, perhaps taken aback by the question. But soon afterward, the familiar suspicious smile returned to his face, and he spoke what seemed to be words he chose carefully:

"My dear friend Stoker, you have my promise that ye will leaveth this place when your work here is done. Thou agreed to come to my home to perform a task at hand, is this not so? Would it not be rude of a guest to break his word and up and flee without cause or explanation whilst his host is out conducting business? Ahhh, my dear sir, unlike my incarceration, you are not held up, secluded in a dark room! No, ha! Ye have full reign of my home, its comforts, and everything therein! Do not consider yourself a prisoner, for that you are not, but rather understandeth thou are in a foreign land with extraordinary people. I intend to protect you from our strange ways and your own ignorance! In time, my dear sir, you will seeth for yourself, and as you abide time in my land—unbeknownst to you—you will comprehend my logic that you resent at present."

After hearing the Count's response, the guest suddenly felt ashamed and slightly embarrassed from his outburst, but the author still could not shake something of his coldness and very intimidating presence. There was a sense of uneasiness about the Count's story that drove Bram to a level of discomfort and a cynical mind-set about the entire ordeal.

"Come, come . . . enough of this, please finish your dinner," curtailed the vampire. "We have lots more to talk over!"

As the Irishman concluded his meal, the Count soon thereafter picked up where he had left off the night before in similar form and fashion:

"On receiving news of my father's passing, I was released by the Turks, and they supported me as their own candidate for the Wallachian throne. I managed to briefly seize sovereignty, yet within two months, Hunyadi forced me to surrender and I fled to my cousin, the Prince of Moldavia. My successor to the throne, however, Vladislov II, unexpectedly instituted a pro-Turkish policy, which Hunyadi found to be unacceptable. He then turned to me, the son of his old enemy, as a more reliable candidate for the seat! In turn, he then forged an allegiance with me to retake the throne by force, but in doing so, I was obligated to denounce my religion of Catholicism and convert to the Greek Orthodox faith. I received the Transylvanian duchies formerly governed by my father and remained there, under the protection of Hunyadi, waiting for an opportunity to retake Wallachia from my rival!"

The Count stopped briefly and once again confirmed he had gained his guest's interest.

"I was only seventeen years old, yet I was supported by a force of Turkish cavalry and a contingent of troops that was lent to me by Pasha Mustafa Hassan. It was at this time I made my first major move toward seizing the Wallachian throne. However, by another claimant—no other than Vladislav II himself—I was defeated only two months later. In order to secure my second and major reign over Wallachia, I waited and plotted out my victory!"

The writer did not want to appear to praise the man that became a fiend by carrying out his own savage and ruthless atrocities, yet he felt for his own sake he needed to interject a statement of praise, for obviously, the Count had a touch of vanity—even after death.

"You seem to have been a man of utmost persistence and energy. For this I must commend you as I have seen many a noble gentleman give up and grieve over spilt milk and desperate times that come along with all walks of life. Please continue . . . I believe the year was 1453?"

"Ahh, yes, the Christian world was shocked by the final fall of Constantinople to the Ottomans. Hunyadi thus broadened the scope of his campaign against the insurgent Turks. In 1456, Hunyadi invaded Turkish Serbia while I simultaneously invaded Wallachia! In the Battle of Belgrade, Hunyadi was killed and his army was defeated. I coincidentally succeeded in killing Vladislav II and taking the Wallachian throne," stated Vlad III triumphantly.

Dracula took off his headdress and placed it in Stoker's hands to see it close up as if a prize won for the most bloodshed. Abraham inspected it whilst the vampire turned his aquiline nose up to the ceiling and sniffed the air. He then continued, "The sweet smell of victory! How I plotted and schemed for so long, but finally I intercepted what was rightfully mine for the taking! Hark . . . hark! Waiteth until July of 1456, when I finally was able to attain the satisfaction of obtaining my vengeance against those that slain my father and tortured my brother to death—to seek my revenge on the men that likewise defied me!"

The Count let out an evil-sounding laugh toward the window as if announcing his testimonial to the world outside. For a moment, it seemed he had had forgotten his sole audience. The Prince hesitated and then looked at his guest who appeared to have just a moment before heard a joke and was lingering on—still waiting for the punch line to be delivered.

"What happened next?" the journeyman asked. "Please continue, tell me more!"

"I will do more than that, my dear friend. Indeed, I will show you! But here I must stop for the night, as I must depart and do not want to keepeth ye up through the night as before. Tomorrow we will travel to Tirgoviste, my capital city, to my castle some distance away in the mountains near the Arges River."

* * * * *

The Count vanished without warning, and Abraham Stoker was left to roam freely over the three-story fortress. Once more he took to being a caged rat in a maze, darting about the place but was again unable to find a way out. He gathered a few books from Dracula's study. Among them were: *The Book of the Courtier* by Baldassare Castiglione, *The Prince* by Niccolo Machiavelli, *The Praise of Folly* by Desiderius Erasmus, and the *Complete Works of Shakespeare* by William Shakespeare.

As excess adrenaline restricted him from sleep, Bram decided to read for several hours and then wrote some in his journal about the conversations he had with the Prince. The sun was coming up over the Transylvanian Alps when he realized Vlad had again left breakfast on the table. The Irishman dined on cascaval, telema (various cheeses), pastries, and cirmati (sausage), and strong coffee.

Though the author's watch was still in decommission status, it seemed like 9:00 a.m. After dining, Stoker's thoughts returned to home, and subsequently, he decided to pen Florence a letter. Hence, he retrieved a piece of parchment and a quill and ink out his bag and scribed the following note:

> My dearest Florrie,
> Certain things are rotten to the core, and I am in the midst of one of them. As I write I am somewhere in the Transylvanian Alps, I believe Sighişoara, and the Count—though providing

me the necessities of food, shelter, and clothing—has me held captive. Though my host has not harmed me per se, I can see the hostility that glares from his eyes when he looks at me. Although he assures me safety, he will not permit me to leave—under any circumstances! Lest he speaks of Great War stories with such deadly earnest that I fear what might come next! The Order of the Dragon is upon me, and "it"—or shall I say "He"—will materialize again at dusk.

Hitherto, the atmosphere that surrounds this very place is an odd one; it is not so much as one of that of home, when an occasional depressed vagrant jumps from the Thanes River bridge, but rather one of constant gloom and utter disparity, such as a massive funeral parlor after a terrifying battle of immense bloodshed! The longer I stay here, the colder and darker the residence becomes, and I feel it closing in on me like a deadly vice!

Florie, my loving wife, how I miss your ethereal beauty and sweet blue eyes and fine brown hair! How I would give my life this day to hold you in my arms! My dear, you might have noticed I did not date this for post as my pocket watch has failed me, and I am not aware of the day nor month. I have been reduced to the life of such a creature as Dracula comes to me at night only to leave me to my own devices to sleep during the day. It is all like a horrible dream, and the events are all mixed up like a whirlpool of endless nightmares! Woe is me! Oh, the horrors and bewilderment I have borne have been more than I dare to disclose in this mere letter and wish to burden you with, but please promise me—my darling, my love—that you will keep me close in both thought and deed and pray for my safety and sanity whilst I work and attend to the monster's filthy wishes and desires.

Your loving husband,
Abraham

P.S. I now go and hide this letter whilst I strategize a way to post it without the vampire's knowing, as I cower its discovery would anger him gravely—that is to be made aware of my communication with the outside world and such an exchange of fears!

CHAPTER 9

The Intruder

> The last conscious effort which imagination
> made was to show me a livid white face bend-
> ing over me out of the mist. I must be careful of
> such dreams, for they would unseat one's reason
> if there were too much of them.
>
> —Mina Harker's journal

Τ he top floor flat at 7 South Hampton Street was of convenient
location for the Stoker family. Not only was it very close walking distance from the Lyceum Theatre, it was on the periphery of
Covent Gardens. The bustling, noisy market area made it quite the
spot to take up residence for someone who enjoyed shopping and
entertaining, such as Florence Stoker.

Abraham Stoker did not seem to mind his wife spending an
immense portion of his twenty-two-pounds-a-week salary, which was
considerably more than what many of the three million Londoners
were making—half of which migrated from Ireland, Scotland, or
Italy due to agricultural failure. Not with standing, many still could
not get ahead and were eventually driven to a life of poverty. The
Stoker's, having migrated from Dublin, were among the "fortunate."

Though Florence's 5'8" patrician profile would have produced
many a customer in a So-Ho back alleyway, everyone that knew

her would have agreed she was too much of the aristocratic class. Moreover, the likelihood of finding a drunken Bram Stoker washed up out of the Thames River would have never happened in a million years. For after all, he had too much to write about, and Florence usually kept quiet, regardless of the time this meant he had to be away from home. Simply put, he managed and wrote; she mothered and entertained.

Indeed, Abraham Stoker's life's blood was spent with the Lyceum; however, his first and foremost ambition was to be a seasoned writer. Though Florence did not fancy the idea of her husband working for free, her spouse's unpaid position providing his service as a drama critic for Dublin's *Evening Mail* was both homage to his heritage and delivered writing samples to the public at large. Whereas most of the family's primary income originated from the Irishman's position as acting manager at the Lyceum, it was seldom enough to satisfy the lifestyle in which they wished to live: Florence wanted to add a new bonnet to her wardrobe; Bram wanted to add a new book to his library.

Because of the Stokers' aspiration of spending, it was not unusual for the author to write editorials and short stories to supplement his income. Hence, this overtime resulted in even longer hours apart from his family. And when Florence felt lonely, well . . . she would just go and throw another dinner party.

Despite the fact their rent was a mere one hundred pounds a year, the journeyman was always writing on demand to pay debts—whether it was the result of Florence's frivolous spending at home or Henry Irving's excessive demands at the theatre. This endless cycle of financial carelessness and bad decision-making lasted most of his adulthood, and oddly enough, many of his novels were spawned under pressure and were quickly written for one hundred pounds to keep the theatre in sound operation and his family well fed and nobly dressed.

In a tight-laced corset, complete with bustles and high heels, Florence Stoker stood in front of her dressing mirror late evening, preparing for bed. Though she was not sleepy as of yet, her habitual act of combing out her long, fine brown hair was of a means to keep her quiet and while away the hours until she was succumbed by sleep.

A poor lady cannot rally over her husband's work, but his long absence with no word has me filled with utmost concern and dreadful worry! Florence said to herself removing her summer bonnet. *Nevertheless, one such as I cannot stay willed in sublime misery either at the thought of no news from her husband.*

Mrs. Stoker placed her hat on a wooden nightstand close to the mirror where she sat. After hesitating for a few seconds whilst she searched for her brush, her thoughts kept drifting back to Abraham and how peculiar it was for him to tarry so long without posting a letter or wiring a telegram.

How foolish of me, though as I am sure the Count has him awful occupied, and as his wife, I should not think so selfish things but instead muster enough patience to wait. I know . . . I will have Henry Irving over for noon tea tomorrow! What an entertaining man and good friend of my dear husband he is!

Florence uplifted her own spirits by producing a mental list of other guests to invite from the theatre as she brushed her hair in her usual most graceful fashion until every single tangle was at least thrice removed.

And as for that young son of mine, well . . . I shall call upon his chums, and perhaps, even their parents and summon them all for dinner the evening after next! But only if Noel assures me he will stay well behaved at school and cease defying authority! she thought to herself. *And he must make promise he will stop playing so rough with knives and the sort!*

As she combed, she looked at herself in the mirror. Having been eleven years junior to her husband, she felt it important to preserve her youthful vanity the best she could as she saw fit. Though soaps, creams, and powders did not act as magnets to her husband, in a queer kind of way she expected there would come a time in their relationship—when the hustle of London life settled—their marriage could pick up as it started, slow-paced and loving attributes all restored with a youthful appearance.

Certainly times have not been easy for the couple. And as the lonely bride sat pondering over her plight, she soon forgot about her husband when she thought she found several graying strands of hair that pulled out from her comb.

"Mercy me, what an unfortunate lot!"

This often-quick obsession with eternal beauty was forever more a pattern or state of comfort that she would drift into when faced with trial or tribulation. Indeed, shipwrecked Florence Stoker noted in a letter to family henceforth that "I was dripping wet; my dress torn, and trailing—my hair over my face. Of course, my dresses were spoiled by salt water, half my linen stolen, and everything of value gone." When she, Noel, and Mrs. Simpson were put in a lifeboat, she made comments about being none to happy with her bloated figure. In sum, it seemed she was more worried about appearance than survival.

As Florence's strokes of vanity continued, her mind eventually drifted back to the year she and Bram first met in Dublin and how they both fell passionately in love with each other. *What a splendid courtship!* she said to herself as she curiously reached to unlatch the crucifix that stared back in the reflection before her.

The estranged wife of author Abraham Stoker looked at its presence in the looking glass with a perplexed stare and baffled reaction. For not only did she not recall hanging the object about her neck that morning, bur she also did not recall a piece of that kind in her jewelry box.

As she touched her hand up to her throat, a reaction of alarm and breathlessness consumed her. And then suddenly she shifted into a mode of panic as she began to grope the area of about her neck wildly—as if searching frantically for something lost of great importance. Something was not quite right.

There was no crucifix.

Florence's heart sank in her chest, and the overwhelming feeling of fear and urgency took over her body. She dropped the brush to the floor, and with shortness of breath, Mrs. Stoker leaned closer and stared back at the now apparent foreign image reflecting back to her in the mirror.

The weary wife drew back shaking in horror with eyes pierced of terror. Though the person on the other side resembled a striking image of Florence, something was terribly different and unsettling about it. Florence was not wearing a crucifix at the present and was dressed in a dark-colored corset. However, the person in the mirror was wearing a white dressing gown and wore a cross around her neck. And Florence's long brown hair fell about her shoulders, but the person in the mirror was wearing her hair pinned up underneath a veil. The face in the reflection was ghastly pale, such as that of a corpse, and she gazed as if studying the life form on the other side with a look of doom and disparity.

After a prolonged acute stare, it was obvious that the woman in the glass was not a complete likeness but 'twas rather someone who once upon a time resembled Florence Stoker from the great beyond.

"I ask who is calling unto me?" she whispered nervously to the object in the mirror. "From whence you came?" Florence waited anxiously, but there was no response.

"What dost thou want? And why dost thou torment me so?"

As Lady Stoker reached down to pick up anything to defend herself with, the image on the other side lunged forward. And with transparent outstretched arms—ones that projected clearly outside of the looking glass—the lady of the mirror repeated in a grave, melancholy tone that was filled with pain, which seemed to take the last breath out of her:

"I say unto you, beware of evil spirits and he of unclean blood!"

A jolt of fright elevated inside the living woman as she exceedingly let out a blood-curdling scream. Florence then took the metal brush and smashed the mirror with her right hand. The object crashed, splitting into hundred of small pieces that scattered all about the room. Consequently, countless shards of glass caught her hand and arm in different places leaving cuts and gashes that reached all of two inches below her right elbow. Blood poured from the wounds as she ripped a piece of linen from her bed to dress the damage, never taking her eyes off of the mirror. Through the gaping, broken object that remained intact, all that Florence could see beyond was her own self, holding her mangled arm and the reflection of the bedroom opposite her through what resembled a cob web of shattered glass.

A noise of abrupt unsettledness then came from the other side of the house.

"Mum!"

As Noel called to his mother from directly outside the room, a gust of wind blew the door closed. The strong breeze came from the bedroom window that unexpectedly opened like a fierce storm though the weather was presently peaceful and quiet. Noel continued to beat on the bedroom entry screaming to his mother with the likes of "Open up!" and "Who goes there?"

Florence struggled to free up the door from her side; however, the entrance would not budge. It was as if an invisible force unexpectedly guarded the chamber.

And then, without warning, the temperature of the bedroom dropped by at least twenty degrees. Simultaneously, a gray mist manifested outside the window and began to flow from the open sash and traveled down the windowsill and concentrated in the middle of the room.

"Good heavens!" she yelled astonishingly as she ran to the window to guard it henceforth. "Noel, please go back to your room and lock the door! Go now! And make certain your window is locked as well! Quickly . . . go! *Go!*"

Mrs. Stoker approached the window and peered beyond the immediate mist and wind and noticed nothing that would logically warrant such conditions of storm or fog directly outside her house.

"Dear God, Bram! What dire straits have we surmised ourselves to?" she called out fearfully to the elements. "The most secret chambers of my soul are not prepared for such scheme of horror that is afoot tonight!"

As Florence reached to close the window, she witnessed directly in front of her—not even an arm's length away—the hazy outline of a tall, thin figure that stirred amongst the fog. Without haste, forcing the window to with every ounce of strength she could muster, she let out a petrified wail and collapsed on the floor.

* * * * *

Noel Stoker locked himself in his room and walked the floor in fidget apprehension. Despite the fact he was in his nightclothes, he had not slept at all. Since sundown, he had felt a queer feeling which provoked a sense of restlessness. It was particularly cold in the room; however, it was midsummer outside, even in the coldest of summers Noel had never experienced a chill in his room at this time of year that merited lighting a fire! He had been hovering by the hearth in his bedroom when he heard his mother scream and asked him to go back to bed. Noel acquiesced; however, he could not shake the sentiment that something unpleasant, unkind, and unloved had somehow been invited into their home.

Good riddance! Noel said to himself disapprovingly as he walked back to the fire from his bedroom door, confirming it was locked.

"Papa goes on holiday, Mum screams for me to go lock myself in my room, and I must stay in here with the willies and take a chill! Has the entire universe gone daft?"

Indeed, Irving Noel Thornley Stoker was no longer the "little man" in his father's eyes but rather the head of household. And it did not take long for the young chap, by virtue of his inquisitive nature, would be challenged to stand in his father's stead. And by what better way to try a new role than by breaking into rare form during a crisis situation?

The flames flickered various shades of bright orange, red, and yellow as Noel paced back and forth in front of the warm colors in an uneasy manner with hands deep in his pockets, shivering with every step.

Noel was an exceptionally bright child for his age. He was also taller and more broadly built than other boys in his age group. Not only was he book smart, he had common sense to couple with this knowledge, and his reddish hair set him apart from the average Londoner aged twelve. This winning combination of the like in other kids his age group separated him. His peer group envied the lad because he seemed to be blessed with every kind of positive intelligence and physique. Noel was strikingly handsome and always the leader in class. Many of the popular, jealous kids eagerly—but secretly—wanted to learn from him the skills they had yet to master themselves while the less fortunate went to him for protection. On the other hand, however, he was still a young boy; hence, the Stoker parents have been battling an overload of curiosity, which yielded trouble in the class room and at home. In sum, he was growing up too fast, becoming a man in a child's body. Noel had the intellect and personality that was not going to accept an answer from an adult if he could not follow the logic. This defiant and often argumentative nature would persevere when Noel thought he was correct, and in many cases, he outwitted his own parents.

"Mum! Are you sure you are okay?" he yelled blindly but loudly to where his mother could overhear him in the other bedroom.

There was no answer.

"I'm coming out now, Mum . . . it is chilling in here and I fancy another log on the fire . . ."

As Noel placed his right hand on the door to unlock it, the flames in the fireplace seemed to come alive and growled and unearthly sound. Simultaneously, two conflagrations extended and formed demonic-like arms that glowed red with hands outstretched to grab him. The boy's face turned to one of extreme distress, and he lurched backward in dread, discovering the hairs on the arms were black in color but appeared to be singed from excessive heat. The devilish objects reached out closer to Noel as he struggled to open the door. As the lad worked the latch in nervous apprehension, the claws on the snatching arms came closer. There was no denying the fact they were razor-sharp and resembled talons such as those belonging to a falcon. The thing continued to let out an unearthly growl and then clearly called out his name in a hellish-sounding tenor. Within a moment's reach of him, Noel bravely pushed open the door and fled down the corridor to find his mother.

The hallway was now full of mist and fog that slowed down all diligence. It was unlit, without warmth, and dismal. All visibility had been raped from the corridor; however, Noel was quite familiar with his own house and felt along the walls just the same.

"Mum! Answer me! Where are you?" he shouted anxiously as he approached her closed bedroom door. The door was locked from the inside, but not giving up hope, Noel recalled the location of a spare key.

"Father's desk!" he said out loud.

As the young boy felt his way to the study, various objects darted out into his path like a roaring tornado as if to stifle his passage: heavy dining room chairs, large coffee tables, and curled-up rugs—amid other inanimate objects—materialized and imposed war amongst the thick of fog. All at once, pictures began to fall off the walls as Noel felt his way down the corridor to the study, dodging the sordid obstacles with an arm over his head in self-protection.

A brushstroke portrait of Charlotte Stoker flew by and crashed into the back of her grandson's head like a battering ram. The adolescent was stunned for several seconds and braced himself against the archway in front of the study with his head swimming from pain. For a brief moment, he thought he heard his grandmother calling to him.

"Leave this house at once!"

Covering his ears he denounced the voice. And as the effects of the impact settled, he continued to make his way to the study where the desk was turned over on its side. In no time, Noel found the drawer and let out a breath of hope.

The key was there.

"Thank you, Papa!"

Upon retrieving the means of entrance, Noel made his way back to the bedroom in similar fashion as before and hastily unlocked the door. At first it resisted—seemingly by something that 'twas placed against it on the opposite side—but kicking in the sentry with all his force, Master Stoker freed it ajar.

When Noel threw open the door, he entered into a domain where angels would have feared to tread. The entire room was one of infinite mist and made the young boys flesh creep up in knots as he stood in what was once his mother's room but was now the lair of some deathly peril. The fog twirled around such as a graveyard inhabited by a population of lost souls, wailing like banshees amongst the grim and grisly ranks of the undead. The temperature was that of an icebox, and the smell of demise was in the air. Noel covered his nose and resisted in regurgitating his dinner. In the corner of the room was his mother's bed, which contained her unconscious body. But the spectacle of what her valiant son saw next caused his skin to crawl right off his bones.

Florence was not alone.

Kneeling above her was the rude figure of a tall, dark, thin man that looked upon Noel with full disgust.

"His eyes glared scarlet with a horrible vindictive stare," the boy later recalled as a grown man, "that was connected to a distorted face full of fury, hate, and evil. And my heart immediately grew cold and bloodless as a low groan sprung from the depths of my soul!"

The sinister phantom that was holding his mother's right arm gleamed at Noel with reddened eyes and contorted brow through the dense fog. Next, it sneered angrily, displaying its canine teeth and a lolling red tongue under an aquiline nose, reeling in the vile, diabolical madness it had created before him. And like a shot being propelled out of the mouth of a gun, the monster disappeared into the mist and dissolved through the chase of the window.

"Mum!" Noel Stoker shouted, frantically slapping his mother's right cheek. "Mum! Wake up, please *wake up!*"

About four minutes after the fiend and mist had leaked out of the room, Florence Stoker awoke in a state of confused misadventure. She did not remember anything, yet her quarters laid in a status of complete disarray—there countless pieces of broken glass scattered all over the floor, her bed linen was torn, all the furniture was tossed about, and numerous marks were all over her right hand and arm. There was no sign of blood anywhere, yet the abrasions that was visible all up and down her right hand and arm were clearly fresh.

Florence did not recall ever falling asleep; notwithstanding, she felt like she had awoken from a long, exhausting dream that had taxed her brain immensely and had taken the last ounce of life from her body.

"Mum! Are you okay? What is wrong with your arm there? Do you remember nothing?" questioned Noel.

"I cannot recall anything at all," she replied perplexedly. "I was combing my hair . . . and then . . . the next minute I am here and you are violently shaking me!"

The son looked at his mother warily as if to unfold the roots of mystery and fear lying deep within human nature.

His mother continued, "It is all such unsettling to me . . . and I reflect, the only feeling that I can remember is this dank sensation on my arm followed by a curious lapping that seemed to last the duration of my sleep—similar to what a kitten would make tidying one's self."

CHAPTER 10

Forests of the Impaled

We are in Transylvania and Transylvania is
not England. Our ways are not your ways. And
there should be to you many strange things.
—Count Dracula to Jonathan Harker

On St. Bartholomew's Day of 1459, the common peasants of
Brasov woke from their beds with expected plans to celebrate
Easter Sunday peacefully and quietly among family and friends. For
the Boyar class and their respective families, however, the new Prince
of Wallachia had announced a grand feast to commemorate the holiday and his recent rise to power. For the nobleman and common
person alike, it was talked of to be an event to be remembered.

Directly outside this Transylvanian city, there stood a large
clearing resembling that of a massive battlefield. There, upon a hill
overlooking the city, one could partake of an immaculate view of this
picturesque countryside, which had been gracefully touched by the
rites of spring.

Abraham Stoker, dressed in his traditional English suit of tweed,
was seated on the hill looking toward the beautiful sky that seemed to
negate the horrible experiences his Romanian fact-finding pilgrimage
had imposed on him thus far. Though Bram was not sure when,
where, or how the Count had let him out of the Sighişoaraian for-

tress, he was thankful to see the sun after so many hours of darkness and captivity.

Stoker spent what he believed to be well over an hour that afternoon enjoying the breathtaking bird's eye view of this town on Saint's Day, but the mood of the day suddenly dramatically changed to one of dire loathsomeness, prevailing evil and unwelcomed fear.

The clear skies seemed to shift unexpectedly and began to glow a vastness of somber scarlet. Simultaneously, the Irishman noticed what appeared to be hundreds upon hundreds of people being led out of the city into a clearing. It did not seem natural—almost as if it was an act of brutal, aggressive force—and the cries and shouts that could be heard from the valley below sent a chill to his very bones.

A sense of overwhelming suspicion bewitched the writer, and he left his hillside post to venture down into the town to identify why everyone had begun to pile out in droves as if participating in an emergency evacuation. But what the journeyman stumbled upon immediately turned his blood ice cold and made his knees buckle in sheer horror. Without warning, the Irishman's heart, mind, and soul were catapulted into an unholy world whence the light of day failed to pass illuminating a path of escape. And at that moment, all hope turned up lost in carnage of bloodshed, and the love of the almighty became forsaken. With eyes not transfixed into a status of antediluvian terror, Stoker lamented in his diary:

"How can I even begin to describe what was taking place before me in mere words? Nay, I have ne'er ever witnessed such an evil picture of cruelty, bloodlust, and depravity! Even in my darkest nightmares, I could claim some element of light, glean of strength, or sound reason. However, the scene unfolded before me was of utter despair—as if our creator had abandoned all hope and Lucifer himself had made his hell on earth!"

Men of free peasantry and middle class were executing thousands of Boyars and their families by the grisly act of impalement. As if he were invisible, Bram walked amongst the disheveled, alarmed crowd who paid him no notice—but who rushed by gnashing their teeth and wailing in an absolute state of desperation.

The author immediately came upon an elderly nobleman who had a horse attached to both legs. The doomed man appeared to be praying silently to the heavens with a look of extreme fear and panic upon his face whilst an oiled, sharpened stake was gradually forced into his body. Abraham perceived that the two middle-aged peasants performing the atrocity were taking orders from a senior boyar who seemed to be communicating in Romanian that the stake "shall not be too sharp," lest the victim might die "too rapidly from shock."

To add auxiliary dread to the breathing fright-mare, the man's wife looked on in tears as a palisade was inserted into her body through the buttocks. Two different men—who appeared to be more experienced with the heinous task—pushed the instrument of torture through her helpless form until it emerged from her mouth.

Oh, merciful lord, Bram said to himself. *What could these people have done to deserve such inhumane torment?*

Other victims were being impaled through remaining bodily orifices or through the abdomen or chest. One screaming infant was impaled on a stake forced through her own mother's chest and was left to hang upside down. A dead faint came upon the writer for the baby died as a despairing cry escaped its tiny mouth whilst the mother continued to linger on, convulsing in extreme pain, as the salty mixture of tears and blood drowned her blinding eyes and parched mouth.

Oh, woe to those that are men of God for thou service to the Lord has been brutally punished, and may we have mercy upon those that are men of the world as such unlawful carnage will great you thereafter in hellfire, where the wailing shan't be silenced!

With a face transformed with utter grief and sorrow, Stoker collapsed to the ground in front of another woman who was in the process of having her breasts removed by an executioner as a second man prepared a red-hot stake. Reeling in agony, the sordid pole was plunged through her vagina and out her back, snapping her spine in the process.

"Alas, I surrender!" Bram cried out on his knees. "For the sake of the Almighty, I beg you to relieve me of this unbarring terror and restore my sanity whilst it is not too late! Has all of earth's hatred conglomerated into this oh-so-sad place? Has all of man's evil ways been fulfilled by atrocities in such of a repugnance of unspeakable sin?"

This sudden outburst by a conspicuous-looking Irishman all at once caught the attention of a head boyar who seemed to be supervising the hellish event. Very rapidly, the sweet spring air was being laden with the putrid stench of miasma.

"What tyrant is responsible for this butcher work?" the journeyman pleaded to know.

"Kaziglu Bey [the Impaler Prince]!" screamed an elderly lady nearby who was having her sexual organs mutilated.

Ripping off the author's jacket, the team leader dragged Abraham to a clearing where he abruptly dropped him. Bram struck his head on a rock, causing it to bleed, whilst the boyar motioned for a second man to procure another fresh spike. But just as an unimaginative rush of consternation overwhelmed the body of the hostage—and exactly as the two executioners were about to plunge the instrument of torture through Abraham's frame—a powerful command was heard by all:

"Stop! This man is mine!" a vociferous, intimidating voice shouted from behind with a distinct sneer and tonal accent that the foreigner knew all too well.

Nodding in acknowledgement, the boyar instantly released Abraham who fell to the ground in front of a long table, which was arranged for a massive feast.

The sole person seated at the center had a familiar cold, terrible appearance that made the Irishman's heart sink; he had that same strong, aquiline nose and swollen nostrils . . . that haunting, thin pale face. Abraham looked up and cried into the large, wide-open ebony eyes, which smiled cunningly in return.

"I implore you—by all you hold sacred, by the sparse of kindness and hope that exists in you—please set me free of this madness! Let me go! Oh, hear me, man, *let me go!*"

His host's nonchalant and unresponsive reaction to what must have been perceived as pathetic ravings caused the writer's blood to bubble over with an irate hatred for the ruler. And after a passing moment in exchanging intense glances and jeers, the master spoke serenely to his captive.

"Verily I say unto thee, cometh, sit down and sup with me," Vlad Tepes stated cordially, motioning for a nearby boyar to bring a second chair. "Surely thou knowest there is a method to what you refer to as my madness."

Dracula, banqueting amongst the grove of stakes, proceeded to explain how they were being arranged in various geometric patterns.

"They are placed in a ring of concentric circles, friend Bram! Dost thou see the height of the spear indicates the rank of the victim?" questioned the Count. His thin black eyebrows made his already sinister stare and stoic expression appear even more cruel and threatening than ever.

Having no other alternative choice, Abraham Stoker seated himself at the ghastly table. Directly behind him were several executioners that proceeded to scalp, decapitate, skin, hack, and cut off the noses and ears of other helpless victims.

"Is there no end to your horror?" wept the writer. But after a delayed response, his desperate question was answered by an even more appalling action. In order that the Prince might better enjoy the results of his orders, he had commanded that his dinner be prepared outside in plain view and that his boyars join him for a feast among the woodland of impaled bodies.

Confounded and speechless, Abraham watched Dracula dip his bread into an ornate goblet, which appeared to be the blood of one—possibly even a squalid combination of several thereof—decaying corpses that stood before them.

The air was now wholly burdened with the bitter offensiveness of fresh gore, and coupled with the heat from the sun, the vile, vulgar reek was too much for anyone with sound human characteristics to withstand. Flies and other insects buzzed around the field, landing on limbs, wounds, and plasma that had splattered on the ground.

The foreigner covered his mouth in disgust in an effort not to lose his last meal. "Great Scott! How could you! How do you account for such a criminally induced massacre? How do you sleep at night knowing you are responsible for such contemptible acts of evil? As a mortal—a ruthless ruler—not yet a creature of the night, what instigated your heart to frost over, founding you to reject your own Orthodoxy faith?"

Stoker waited for a reply as he watched Vlad cut into a mysterious piece of rare meat that turned Abraham's stomach sour. Unable to contain his composure any longer, the Irishman lowered his head to the ground and emptied the undigested contents of his system.

"Ah, so ye are not hungered, friend Bram," stated Dracula calmly, taking a garment from his lap and proceeded to wipe away several red droplets that clung to the long, thin moustache that curled slightly at the ends against his cheeks. Looking to the ground beneath his guest's stance, he saw pieces of baked kidney and chunks of potatoes that resembled a hodgepodge that was once a shepherd's pie. When the author backed away from it, his left shoe clung to the mass.

The Impaler's eyebrow rose to his forehead, and then he spoke crossly at the journeyman as if he was offended or angered at what had just occurred, saying, "Thou were displeased with the English meal I labored to prepare? I am gravely disappointed. Dost thou knowest one's supper is supposed to stick to your ribs—not your boots, friend Stoker?"

At this the author stood to his full height and shouted wildly, shocked and outraged at his host's complacent demeanor. "Can you not see I am sickened to death? Woe is me! I entreat you, Dracula! Why commit such crimes? Do you not tell you have me fighting for my life and core? Answer me, man! Where lies the guilt? Your heart has been hardened as a man and your mind lost into an abyss of darkness. Your body has become a slave to evil, and your soul now belongs to Satan himself!"

The Count stopped eating and looked Abraham Stoker directly in the eyes. Stoker immediately noticed that Vlad's temples seemed to swell, which increased the bulk of his head, which was connected to a bull's neck. His black curly locks hung on his wide shoulders, creating a domineering and mean presence.

"Alas, I just cometh unto reign, my friend, and what thou first signify as an act of cruelty is actually a tactic to solidify my power!

Moreover, what ye mistake as butchery is motivated by a desire for vengeance!" said the Count serenely.

The writer looked on and continued to listen amongst the screaming and slaughtering that continued to take place in the midst. Many of the ill-fated victims did not die instantly—but were rather forced to slowly drown by the own internal bleeding. Though many were unable to respond to stimuli or communicate effectively, numerous were able to live long enough to witness their own family members being executed near by.

"Look!" the foreigner cried now frantically, now pointing with his right index finger. "Innocent women . . . children! What say you?"

"Ah, this fantastic act of revenge is aimed at the boyars of Tirgoviste for the killing of my father and brother Mircea!" explained the Prince sharply. "Why should I treat their families any different? Indeed, in memory of my fair bride, why should I be challenged to differentiate between crushed bones? Whether it 'tis done through a vast plunge off a tower or a sharpened pole, death becomes her! No! I do not act in haste; for surely I was well aware that many of these same nobles were part of the conspiracy that led to my father's assassination—including the burying alive of my elder brother! Many also played a role in the overthrowing of numerous Wallachian princes!"

The man actually loved? the author said to himself. *He actually took a wife?*

As Dracula continued to dine, Vlad suddenly noticed that one of his boyars was holding his nose in an effort to alleviate the terrible smell of clotting blood and emptied bowels that was strewn about infinite field. To Stoker's astonishment, the Prince ordered the sensitive nobleman to be impaled on a stake higher than all the rest so he might be above the horrible and offensive stench.

The journeyman shuddered and looked on in a state of dismay as the deafening wailing continued. And as if the terror being carried out before him bore a resemblance to attending a theatre, the Count continued to watch they play and went on coolly:

"This morning, I dined with my noble guests and asked them how many princes had ruled during their lifetimes. I already knew that all the nobles present had outlived several princes, for none had seen less than seven reigns."

"So you immediately had all of the assembled nobles arrested?" asked Bram hotly.

"I am the *true* Prince," Dracula replied agitatedly, "and I chose not to give them further capacity to plot against me!"

And so as it was, the day lasted, and by nightfall, Count Vlad Tepes Dracula III had impaled thirty thousand of the oldest boyars and their families on the spot. The near death and rotting corpses were left up for months as a warning to those that remained of what could occur if loyalty to their new prince was broken and to the invading Turkish armies.

* * * * *

Abraham Stoker awoke in a foreign bed in a state of mass confusion. He felt as if he had been emerged into a pool of deep, dark water, and the peal of a bell suddenly sent his body bolt upright. Though he immediately recognized that he was not in the fortress in Sighişoara; hitherto, he did not recall leaving. But he alarmingly found himself in the same suit that he had worn in his dream—only with several noticeable alterations: his jacket was gone, the ghastly smell of dried blood reeked in his clothes, and his shoes were soiled with the combined residue of dirt and vomit. Moreover, coupled with the revolting scent, the back of his head ached terribly. With his right hand, Bram felt for the place where he struck a rock after the boyar dropped him on the ground. As he feared, the place was there . . . exactly as it was in his nightmare.

The Irishman's body shivered in response and miserably cried, "It is all bloody real! This immoral, heinous act actually happened to me!" Then Stoker paced the floor endlessly. And though the time was less than a few hours, the minutes aged him several years and seemingly lasted a lifetime.

The bedroom he was in was much more immaculate than the one at Sighişoara; it looked newer, it was better preserved, and the chamber was heavily decorated in what appeared to be a combination of artifacts from the late fifteenth through the nineteenth century.

The author immediately noticed a window in the corner of the room and raced to look out. The opening was without bars; however, the sheer distance from his view to the ground below was breathtaking and caused him to make a step back and gasp.

Abraham believed he recognized the ostentatious structure. It was apparent from the scrutiny that the fortress was built on the side of the Poenari Mountain that overlooks the Arges River and the distant city of Tirgoviste. Seeing his belongings on a nearby bench, he rummaged through the contents until he found the book he borrowed from the Whitby Library. Bram opened up the text to a particular photo and carried it back to the window that presented a side view of the wing he was in, in addition to a different annex in close distance and several towers of medium proximity. Then he compared history with reality.

Dracula's castle, Abraham Stoker said to himself.

The antiquity of Vlad's castle was, indeed, a grim story on its own accord. After the thirty thousand were murdered on St. Bartholomew's Day, the horror did not cease but continued for the remainder of Dracula's rule. From the Transylvanian City of Brasov, the younger and healthier nobles, merchants, boyars, and their families were forced to march north from Tirgoviste to the capital town of Poenari. According to Bram's research, this was a grueling fifty-mile trek, and those who survived were not permitted to rest until they reached their destination: a fortress on the ruins of an older outpost in the mountains overlooking the Arges River.

As the writer recalled this ruthless account of compensatory toiling, he could almost hear the cries of the beaten down townspeople and the salty, bitter taste of their blood, sweat, and tears. For the enslaved boyars were forced to labor for many long months rebuilding the old castle with materials from a nearby ruin. They were obligated to continue working naked after the clothes fell off their bodies and very few survived to see what became known as Dracula's castle.

"My God!" Bram, repulsed, cried out loud. "I sleep on the very ground they labored on the outskirts of death! Vlad succeeded in creating new nobility and obtaining a fortress for future emergencies!"

The journeyman continued to read further about Vlad's brutal punishment techniques. Although impalement was clearly Dracula's preferred method of execution, it was by no means his only hellish tool of torture. According to historical evidence, the cruel prince often ordered people to be boiled, blinded, strangled, hanged, burned, roasted, nailed, decapitated, skinned, buried alive, stabbed, and exposed to the elements or to wild animals.

You wild, bloodthirsty man! the foreigner said to himself.

Abraham Stoker was revolted over the Count's sadistic actions and felt an extreme sadness toward the victims and their families who had suffered by his hand. As the sun began to set in the window behind him, the author said a silent prayer and continued to make an attempt to comprehend the historical figure and how he earned the infamous nickname Tepes, "The Impaler."

Bram learned that it was this same technique Vlad Dracul III had used in 1457, 1459, and 1460 against Transylvanian merchants who had ignored his trade laws. The raids he led against the German Saxons of Transylvania were also acts of proto-nationalism in order to protect and favor the Wallachian commerce activities. Throughout his reign, the Count continued to systematically eradicate the old boyar class of Wallachia and was determined that his own power be on modern and thoroughly secure footing. In the place of the executed boyars, Vlad promoted new men from among the free peasantry and middle class—men who would be loyal only to their prince.

Stoker's skin crawled and began to feel clammy as he learned anecdote after anecdote about the philosophy of the menacing Vlad Tepes Dracula. And when accomplished, the foreigner slammed the text shut in an utter state of fear—afraid that he, Stoker, would never be able to sleep soundly again.

"How can I possibly write a book about a man so feared and so hated?" Abraham noted in his journal. But as there was nothing else to do but dwell on his precarious plight, Bram regained his place in the dreadful text and read on as scornful darkness and brilliant moonbeams began to seep into the bedroom.

The Count was known throughout his land for his fierce insistence on honesty and order. Almost any crime from lying and stealing to killing could be punished by impalement. And being so confident in the effectiveness of his law, Dracula placed a golden cup on display in the central square of Tirgoviste. The cup could be used by thirsty travelers but had to remain on the square. According to the available historic sources, it was never stolen and remained entirely unmolested throughout Vlad's reign, and merchants who cheated their customers were likely to find themselves mounted on a stake beside common thieves.

Bram paused from his reading to light a candelabrum that hung on the wall opposite the window which projected the ray of a full moon. The echoing howling of wolves sounded in the distance, and the river's peaceful sounds of running waters could be heard slightly below him.

In time, the cooling effects of the rushing stream worked the man into a condition of dreariness, and the journeyman found himself getting droopy. Fearing what might happen in his sleep, his self-consciousness went into protective overdrive, and Stoker jumped to in a full fit of trepidation and anxiety. But suddenly, as he turned from the window with a tensed face full of worry and tension, the foreigner was completely startled at a different sight. For there, standing in the middle of the room, was the figure of a woman, dressed in a white gown and a veil covering her face! How she entered the room was a total mystery as the door to the chamber was old and bulky and would have made some sort of noise to announce her presence.

An icy sentiment sailed up Abraham's spine as he stared at the woman closely, although he found himself turning away in disbelief before mistaking her for what he thought was his own wife, Florence, but only from a different world. Her long brown hair and fair skin were of radiant proportions. She had delicious ruby red lips and ethereal brown eyes that were intriguing to look into.

"Forgive me Madame, but you startled me . . . I did not hear you come in," said he hesitantly. The woman did not speak but seemed to look through Stoker with a sense of heartache or vexation.

"Please let me introduce myself. I am Abraham Stoker and I am here as a guest of Count Dracula. Are you also visiting, or do you work here in the castle?"

The author noticed that the woman was wearing a cross around her neck and seemed to glide rather than walk across the floor. She did not speak but continued to study the Irishman in every detail with a glare of deep sorrow and bereavement.

"Who are you, Madam? Do you need help?" Bram asked the woman awkwardly in an almost nervous tone.

In a soft, feminine voice, she replied: "I am the truth."

Abraham Stoker thought he was dreaming. For surely the woman that so much resembled his wife was clearly an apparition that manifested itself out of a dream brought on by angst and lack of sleep. Notwithstanding, with every retake—after a self-pinch and rest of his eyes—the woman remained fixed, almost hovering slightly above the cold stone flooring several feet from the heavily bolted door.

"Let me out of this horrid place at once!" Bram screamed to the top of his lungs. "Please . . . I beg of you! My sanity is hanging by a mere thread!"

The woman approached Abraham and tenderly motioned for him to sit down on a gothic sixteenth-century bench that was married to a nightstand missing its mirror.

"I come to not harm you, and this you can be sure of. Rather I seek you out to provide memoirs of the man you fear and for very good reason," the woman whispered passionately.

Abraham seated himself and looked into the lady's eyes with sudden keen interest. Like the vagrant man back home by the Thames River, he could almost see through them into another place in time, but for some mysterious reason, her presence comforted him and all his fears and bad memories seemed to disappear for the duration of her visit. And as she began to speak, a great sense of peace and hope motivated him to begin scheming a plan of escape.

"The atrocities of Vlad Tepes were much more severe than what you have learned," stated the visitor. "Dracula was also very concerned that all his subjects work and contribute to the common welfare of the community in a productive manner. He looked upon the poor, homeless, cripples, and beggars as thieves. He once noticed that this population had become very numerous in his land; consequently, he issued an invitation to all the poor and sick of Wallachia to his princely court in Tirgoviste, claiming that no one should go hungry in his land. As the poor and crippled arrived in the city, they were ushered into a great hall where a fabulous feast was prepared for them. Whilst the guests ate and drank late into the night, Vlad himself then made an appearance and asked them, "What else do you desire? Do you want to be without cares, lacking nothing in this world?" When they responded positively, Dracula ordered the hall to be boarded up and set on fire. No one escaped or survived the flames."

Bram's face returned to one of total alarm and dire foreboding and said, "The infidel! What an amoral misdeed!" After a brief moment of silence, Stoker asked offended, "What on earth was his reasoning behind this harrowing course of action?"

She severely replied, "Vlad explained his action to the boyars by claiming that he did this in order that they represent no further burden to other men and that no one will be poor in his realm."

Indeed, it was beginning to appear the man of scorn was spawn from evil and thrived on performing acts of cruelty that were in complete defiance to the word and teaching of Christ.

"The Devil!" exclaimed the journeyman under his breath as the woman continued.

"But Dracula's torture against the people of Wallachia was usually as a means to enforce his own moral code upon his country. Maidens who lost their virginity, adulterous wives, and unchaste windows were all targets of his malice. Such women often had their sexual organs cut out. On one occurrence, he executed the wife of a Boyar who was thought to have been unfaithful. She was impaled on the square in Tirgoviste with her skin lying on a nearby table."

Abraham Stoker was speechless and appalled at the thought of one vindictive human being, spilling such a wrath of iniquity over a country. These acts of savagery make London's own Jack the Ripper to be almost generic in nature.

"What an odious act of callousness!" Bram cried out sternly, shaking his head in disbelief.

"Alas," the woman said wearily, "it was only the beginning. In 1462, the Impaler launched a campaign against the Turks along the Danube River. It was quite risky, the military force of Sultan Mohammed II being by far more powerful than the Wallachian army. However, during the winter Vlad was very successful and managed to gain many victories. To punish Dracula, the Sultan decided to launch a full-scale invasion of Wallachia. His alternate goal was to transform this land into a Turkish province, and he entered Wallachia with an army three times larger than his enemy. Finding himself without allies, Vlad, forced to retreat toward Tirgoviste, burned his own villages and poisoned the wells along the way, so that the Turkish army would find nothing to eat or drink. Moreover, when the Sultan, exhausted, finally reached the capital city, a most gruesome sight confronted him: thousands of stakes held the remaining carcasses of some twenty thousand Turkish captives, a horror scene, which was ultimately coined the 'Forest of the Impaled.' This terror tactic deliberately stage-managed by Dracula was definitely successful; the decaying corpses were left up for months and the invading Turkish army turned back in fright. The scene had a strong effect on Mohammed's most stouthearted officers, and the sultan, tired and hungry, admitted defeat. Even Victor Hugo, in his *Legende des Siecles*, recalls this hideous incident."

The foreigner had heard enough, and any pity he had felt toward the man had been lost in a world of violence.

To communicate such a fantastic story of gruesome death to the world at large would certainly be a scandal of shock and controversy, Abraham Stoker thought to himself. *Yet it is what the Count is demanding of me.*

"Forgive me, Madam, I am awe-stricken and traumatized by your recollections. Must you carry on?" asked Bram.

"Please hear me out," pleaded the woman. "In time, you will understand."

Unable to fathom where the peculiar lady was going with her story, the man fell silent once more as she urged herself onward.

"Mohammed II, the conqueror of Constantinople, a man not noted for his squeamishness, returned to Constantinople after being sickened by the sight of twenty thousand impaled Turkish prisoners outside of the city of Tirgoviste."

Abraham noticed that through the veil, it looked like the woman had moved herself to tears and retelling this story was painful but somehow important and necessary to her.

"Woman, why tell me of such horrible things that trouble you so?"

The visitor quietened herself for a spell and looked intently upon the foreigner's pale face before replying, "You need to understand his evil. For only then can you truly protect yourself from it, and if ever there was a man of God that needeth protection, it is you at this, oh, sad hour!"

The Irishman's heart seemingly fell to his feet like a heavy stone, and he began to tremble in the foul-smelling shoes that lobbied in the bloodshed he so loathed to sit in judgment. It was then the writer realized he was somehow part of this fantastic but gruesome heritage and 'twas becoming perilously intertwined his world of a vampire. Swallowing hard, he wiped the sweat of trauma from his brow.

"Please continue, Madame," he said in a voice that broke in apprehension.

"Nevertheless," she began again, "following his retreat from Wallachian territory, Mohammed left the next phase of the battle to Vlad's younger brother Radu, the Turkish favorite for the Wallachian throne. At the head of a Turkish army and joined by Vlad's detractors, Radu pursued his brother to Poenari castle on the Arges River."

"So his own brother joined the Turks to trap and seize him in this very castle?" Bram questioned.

She nodded her head in acknowledgment. "The end of Vlad was very near, and its ending warrants my earnest warning to you. Dracula loved the sweetness of the earthly world much more than the eternal world, and he abandoned Orthodoxy forsaking the eternal light for immortal darkness. A lance riddled, headless corpse that was once buried at the Snagov monastery will complete your excursion. However, prepare now and go armed to do battle with the incubus."

"Immortal darkness?" the writer asked. "Do you mean Nosferatu?"

Alarmed and confused by this statement, Abraham excused himself from the conversation and chose to retrieve the vampire book he had in his bag. When he had located it, Bram looked back to the woman for further clarification and questioning. However, to his bewilderment, the woman had vanished without warning.

* * * * *

The following morning, Stoker rose to the sound of voices coming from the courtyard of the castle. He raced to the tower window in a sort of crazed excitement to discover several Slovaks laboring below dressed in working attire. The men wore vests with lace-up shirts and wraparound dungarees whilst the women wore light skirts and headdresses. Many carried bundles of what appeared to be sticks on their backs that were sent off down the Arges River.

Abraham yelled out the tower to an elderly lady that seemed stunned to see his presence in the window. He proceeded to describe the lady that had visited him the night before and asked of her current whereabouts. The woman cocked her head back several times as if put out by what her ears were hearing. Mumbling things that brought a look of extreme worry to her visage, she at first pretended to not understand English. Though distressed throughout the entire exchange, she took pity upon the captive, and as the ordeal went on and became more desperate, the author could tell from her facial expression she seemed to understand him but did not know how to communicate back in English. At last she crossed herself and motioned to a man that was working nearby to translate.

"Is there a way out of here?" Stoker yelled, hoping that one of them would be able to unlock what he imagined to be a series of bolted doors between him and the main entrance.

As the older lady was getting the gentleman's attention, the journeyman remembered the letter he had written to Florence and decided now would be the opportune moment to see that it got posted. He rummaged through his bag and luggage to no avail. It was as if his correspondence to the outside world had up and disappeared with no logical explanation.

An agitated Bram returned to the tower window to witness both the man and woman conversing erratically with numerous hand jesters, pointing up to his window during moments of intensity.

"Please! Help me," the captive cried out hysterically. "I am being held prisoner!"

The man's face turned grim, and he too crossed himself. Finally, the man called up to Stoker in broken English.

"The woman you described is that of Countess Dracula. Out of respect we are not permitted to enter her wing of the castle. She leapt from the window in which you stand in 1462."

"Pace voua, morti nostri [Rest in peace, our dead]," the old lady stated crossing herself in an odd manner that demonstrated an outwardly expression of nervous excitability. And the author's tired, bloodshot eyes immediately sunk back into his suddenly lightened head as he fell to his knees, wailing his beloved's name, which echoed unheard down the desolate halls of the ruined castle.

CHAPTER 11

Murder outside the Lyceum

> Never did I see such baffled malice on a
> face. The beautiful color became livid, the eyes
> seemed to throw out sparks of hell-fire, the brows
> were wrinkled as though the folds of the flesh
> were the coils of Medusa's snakes, and the lovely
> blood-stained mouth grew to an open square as
> in the passion masks of the Greeks and Japanese.
> If ever a face meant death—if looks could kill—
> we saw it that moment.
>
> —Dr. Seward's diary

The Lyceum, a 1,500-seat theatre a block between Wellington, Exeter, and Burlegh street downtown London, England, was the premier place to be on a weekend night in the late 1800s. Regardless if one fancied Shakespeare readings, quality stage performances, or simply enjoyed witnessing the state-of-the art costumes, lighting, and effects, the Lyceum provided it all for a cost of a few pounds per ticket. It was not unusual for non-theatregoers to make the occasional attendance just for the sake of the experience, and the likelihood of rubbing noses with the notoriety class was enough for attention seekers to queue for hours.

Though the theatre drawn the likes of the royal family, celebrity status, and political officials—not to mention the aristocratic crowd that just wanted to flaunt their wealth or were looking for companionship—many, on the other hand, flocked to pay reference, or perhaps up close abhorrence, to a man whose offstage antics and public speaking became almost as entertaining as his stage presence. Truly, the Lyceum was the hot spot of the town, a place of action, and the home of its lordship, actor Sir Henry Irving. And being the egotistical person he was, the man savored the position as master of ceremonies.

Indeed, believing that his profession was a true form of art, he often addressed the skeptics boldly:

"I trust with all my soul that the reform which you suggest may 'ere long be carried out, and that the body too is justly entrusted our higher moral education may recognize in the stage a medium for the accomplishment of such ends," he once said importantly at a Trinity sponsorship. "We seek our reward in the approval of audiences and in the tribute of their tears and smiles, but the calm honor of academic distinction is and must be to us, as actors, the unattainable, and therefore the most dear when given unsought."

Henry Irving controlled the Lyceum with a rod of iron. His declaration was law both on stage and off, and he brooked no opposition. Though a gallant man whose code of honor was to answer insolence with the point of a sward, Irving specialized in villains and was especially known for his makeup wizardry. But he was also unique for he believed romantic acting was dependent on flamboyant gestures, movements, and phrasings. Sir Henry carried the power to make the onlooker a part of the character, to share in the suffering, to make audiences think and feel, not just react. Undeniably, Abraham Stoker was drawn to this interior expression on the future of drama and believed his employer's performances had bite and ridicule.

"If you do not pass a character through your own mind, it can never be sincere," the Lord of the Lyceum once told the Irishman he often labeled "an uncommonly useful man." Notwithstanding, the eccentric actor carried with him a sense of humor—or sardonic, grotesque, fantastic humor. Likewise, he had an incomparable power for eeriness—for stirring a dim sense of mystery, and no less masterful was he in evoking a sharp sense of horror. This latter gift most certainly attracted Bram, who wrote that Irving was a "histrionic genius" and deserved "not only the highest praise that can be accorded, but the loving gratitude of all to whom his art is dear!"

Even though Henry Irving was at his prime of his career in the 1890s—for not only was he the most popular British stage actor of his generation, the supporting cast working for the Lyceum were amongst the highest paid in England—the actor's dark side haunted him deeply, kept him melancholy despite his tremendous success, and followed him wherever he would travel. To add to the theatre's hype, cutting-edge productions such as *Faust* and *Macbeth* were in high demand to go on tour as far north as the United States, but turmoil and behind-the-scenes dynamics were often rampant.

"We shall be all right," he would often answer a fellow actor or actress who would nervously request to rehearse their scenes with him. "We're not going to run the risk of being bottled up by a gas man or a fiddler," referring to what he believed to be rehearsal dangers. He demanded spontaneous performances and often ignored supporting cast members in such regards. Never a mentor or a teacher, he certainly believed others in his profession were pale copies of him and therefore must not develop distinctive styles. And despite his sincere desire to elevate acting as an art, Irving curiously never felt a responsibility to give something back to the next generation. It was this attitude that frustrated more than one talented performer.

What was Irving—who had reasons for all his machinations—plotting? To answer this inquiry, at present Henry was anxiously waiting for Stoker to return from his hiatus to sort though the red tape and paperwork to take the most successful shows on the road. Nevertheless, on this particular night, it would be another spectacular delivery of Faust, and concluding four more performances as Mephistopheles, the theatre would than close for a month whilst work commenced to revamp a second season of *Macbeth*, with Irving starring as the leading character: a king who gained and maintained the throne through bloodshed before being assassinated by one of his own men.

Once having the ambition himself to take to the stage, Abraham Stoker respected Irving's acting ability. Though their professional relationship was sometimes strained due to financial vision differences, they were inseparable friends, with the Irishman often spending more time with the actor than his own family.

"We understood each others nature, needs, and ambitions, and have a mutual confidence, each toward the other in his own way, rare amongst men," stated Bram. "I cannot honestly find any moment in my life when I failed him, or when I put myself forward in any way." And indeed it was so, for not a week went by without some kind of Irving caricature being published—an act that was often solicited on behalf of his devoted friend.

But despite the author's temporary absence from the theatre, Henry managed to somehow promote the remaining performances of Faust while an assistant stage supervisor managed the books.

Nevertheless, on this Saturday night before a packed house, Irving recited his lines as the devil as cleverly as ever—his dark saturnine eyes engaging scholars, including those that felt his profession still considered to be on the fringes of proper society. And complete in dark makeup and creepy costume, he addressed the lovely Gretchen, who listened attentively in the garden:

"You do not appear to me in vain, as I at one time thought. I have learned the error of my way of approach to you. You have given me, through life and particularly through love, that which I wanted, a sense of communion with the universe. I, who sought to know what it is that holds the world together, who contemplated the active harmony of the macrocosm through its symbolical representation and demanded to experience all things human, pain and joy alike, have learned to understand the real meaning of your words."

After the final curtain, his lordship returned to express his gratitude. The whole house rose simultaneously. He did not attempt to quell the demonstration: he relished adulation; humility was not in his lexicon. "When I think that you, the upholders of this classic in every age," he intoned, "have thus flung aside the traditions of three centuries and have acknowledged the true union of poet and actor, my heart swells!

Continuing to bow before the standing ovation for some time, then as if on an invisible cue, the audience sat down, and the actor presented on of his trademark farewells. "Every fiber of my soul throbs, and my eyes are dim with emotion as I look upon your faces and know that I must say goodbye. Your brilliant attendance on this performance sheds a luster upon my life!"

Sir Irving retired to his dressing room in usual fashion to consult with the cast for several minutes hitherto his removal of makeup and wardrobe. But as it often came to pass, he felt some were unable to do justice—either to themselves or to their parts—and because of this stance, his savageness became unleashed like a wilder beast:

"It is absolute rubbish! You must reach for a bauble consciousness and be alert for every detail of this method called acting! How do you expect a full house to queue to see a performance when they can't bloody well hear the likes of you?" Irving shouted angrily to a young girl filling in for leading lady Ellen Terry, whom had taken ill. She stood stock-still, red-faced from embarrassment.

"Don't ye think, guv'nor, a few rays of the moon might fall on me—it shines equally, ye know, on the just and the unjust?" the girl asked feebly.

"Actors who bring feelings to a part excel over those that imitate emotions based on observations and the feelings of others," his lordship answered coldly.

"I am truly sorry, sir," she at last replied apologetically. "Indeed, I suppose I did not expect an assembly quite so large."

"Well, by Jove . . . you best better pipe up tomorrow night— that is, if you wish to continue with this 'ere cast! Polonius said, 'To thine own self be true.' But I argue that a man cannot be true to himself if he does not know himself, if he mistrusts his own identity, if he puts aside his special gifts in order to be an imperfect copy of someone else!"

The girl nodded in a sense of shame, and without saying a single word, she exited the dressing room, but not before pausing suddenly to take notice of an older blond woman standing directly outside. She was dressed as if belonging to a wedding party of some great importance. As the inspiring yet humiliated actress passed the beautiful lady, who continued to linger on, the latter caught the door. And silently forcing her head in intrusively, she silently stared at Irving removing his makeup.

The observer was dressed in an elegant royal-blue corset with sequined fills carrying a matching handbag. Henry caught a look at her in his mirror and turned to acknowledge her.

"Well . . . well . . . would you like me to autograph your program, Madame?"

"Oh, bravo! Please do, I would be so delighted!" she said, answering the actor enthusiastically without remote hesitation. He tone was like that of a child when she spoke, and she stood rubbing her hands gleefully as she handed over the parchment.

As Irving signed the document, the woman looked at the Lyceum lord, radiantly causing him to smile back in return with his usual clout of vanity.

"I assume you were pleased with tonight's performance?" he asked in a way that seemed to be more of a confirmation than a question.

"Oh, indeed! I was," the lady replied in an almost frantic sort of way, as if she was astonished to be asked such a comically charged question. "It was so lovely! Your rendition this evening reminds me so much of my favorite Bible story from Genesis . . . you recall the scene in the beautiful Garden of Eden where Eve is seduced by Lucifer, heaven's fallen angel. In fact, I believe I will go and purchase Goethe's poem immediately!"

The actor looked up at his devoted follower slowly. And wiping his oily hands on a cloth, he smiled like a Cheshire cat. His face was blank of makeup and beamed of perpetual blitz. But then he hesitated for a brief moment as if in deep thought and finally replied, "I didn't know that the devil expected to be an instrument in the revival of trade, but the many forms of honest industry which he has been the means of stimulating are quite bewildering," he responded enigmatically, catching the woman by surprise. A perplexed look fell about her face, as if studying his words carefully. At last she answered, "Well . . . you act the part with so much zeal and emotion!"

Fussie, the snappy and alert terrier that accompanied the actor at all times, suddenly thumped his tail on the ground to express his portly pleasure. Taking notice, his lordship reached out his arms in a loving gesture and responded as if he were the proud and giddy parent of a newborn child. It appeared all the intimacy Irving withheld from people he instead lavished on his dogs that became the sole critical link between him and humanity.

"Come, let me clutch thee!" the actor exclaimed, reaching out for the dog with a longing that would have made the biblical father welcoming home his prodigal son less than earnest. And upon soaking a piece of biscuit in a glass of champagne someone had left him after the performance, he reached down and handed it to the mutt. The animal ate it out of its owner's right hand, licking his fingers and jumping about its legs in heartfelt gratification to its owner. They all three smiled and were happy in each his own way. For a split moment, the actor actually forgot he had a visitor, and clearing his throat in slight embarrassment, began to speak as if already in the middle of conversation:

"I embraced acting as an antidote to a lonely and restrictive youth," he told his audience with passion. "I devoted myself to the stage from the early age of twelve and conquered a disabling stammer; yet when I changed my clunky name at age eighteen for the role of Romeo, the devotion returned twofold as a gift that has abounded great rewards and has become my life's work!"

Indeed, the man born John Henry Brodrilb of Somerset chose to first honor writer Washington Irving and than made history acting and reciting those whom he felt were the true pioneer artists of the world.

As the minutes fleeted by, Henry and the lady talked for nearly an hour before he finally excused himself to change clothes and retire for the night.

Motioning to his private exit—a door located directly outside his dressing room—the actor stated, "My dear, I did not mean to keep you so late. I'm afraid I must beg you to curtail our lovely conversation and permit me to offer you a rain check for our next performance!"

"Oh, that would be absolutely splendid," she said, overjoyed.

"And since it is so belated, may I suggest you use my passage, which will take you immediately behind the theatre. Wellington is the next street over, which leads into the main stretch of road still somewhat occupied and patrolled at this hour."

"Thank you so much," she replied. "And I bid thee a good night."

"I do hope to see you again," Irving said smiling, nodding a cordial farewell. Delighted, the woman curtsied and spoke in an almost subservient tone:

"Forgive me, I am Miss Mary Dickinson, and I do hope to call on you again soon," she blushed, holding out her left hand. Irving quickly obliged by gently cupping it in his own and softly pressing her soft skin to his pursed lips.

Thenceforth, as she turned and walked away, it seemed the departing gesture was meant to resemble a kiss of death for soon he returned to the solitary tormented soul that longed for something more: something romantic, something mysterious and with edge—something much like the leading men and those poetic lovers in which he acted out onstage. But with the complicated and unusual arrangement he had formed with his own Mrs. Florence Irving, everyone who knew felt the drama was as theatric exit center stage.

"Fussie, my dear boy . . . come let me clutch thee!"

* * * * *

Leaving the theatre, the woman placed her autographed program in her bag and stood at the back alleyway. Any remaining shade of the evening had long melted into the darkness, and the traffic on the busy streets were beginning to dwindle to only a few coaches as pedestrians quickly making their way to their overnight destinations. Due to the Whitechapel murders, the entire city was overly cautious about being out past dark, and for very good reason. After all, safety was prudent, especially amongst women traveling alone.

Preparing to cross, she checked the time and noticed it was approaching the witching hour. The nighttime air felt good on her face and lungs, but she could not help but notice it was unusually quiet for a Saturday evening. The alley was shadowy. And the clustering buildings, which in the uncertain tremulous light that fell from several adjacent street lanterns, made it somewhat of a challenge to distinguish any shape or form, clearly hampered the view. All around the woman, the wind howled like a banshee, causing her to take on a jaunty impudence and the feeling of intolerable solitude. Shaking this sentiment off as nothing to ponder over, she crossed Wellington Street. The moon shined overhead, and with the exception of the slight street noise in the distance, all she heard was the heels of her shoes clopping like horse hooves on the pavement below. Observing that there was not a soul in site, she proceeded to head toward Exeter.

Lady Dickinson was not a verbose woman. At times, she fit the cold-natured description of her idol, which often maintained a cheerless, disheartening, melancholy demeanor. Yet her talkative spirit of late was readily overcome by the bereft of vitality of London's pan alleys and dive bars. In time, the soundless gloom of the night became more dreadful and soul killing than she ever thought imaginable. Miss Mary carried her short, slender frame with purpose, walking heavily and swiftly. Her stride picked up, as so did the city fog, and it did not take long until her usually regulated breaths became noticeably unstable and heavy—shrouded in hints of tense discomfort that often accompanies the likes of oncoming fear. She diffidently made her way across the alley whilst the woman was overcome by an anomalous feeling, as one would sense being watched or followed. Turning around abruptly, she spotted no one—the dead, London air was silent. She pointed her nose up to the sky in a strange likeness, as if she were a bloodhound in check, and awkwardly shifted her stance from side to side and impatiently waited.

There came a rustle—some sort of slight noise around her but more like above her—that caused the woman to hesitate and look about fearfully. With much perturbation, her nerves contracted as she apprehensively called out into the blackness. "Who's there?"

There was no answer.

Now feeling severely uneasy, she stood still quietly listening for several seconds, seconds that appeared to be many minutes to her before proceeding down the dark alleyway.

In an attempt to regain her composure, she made another few paces. The echoing of her steps sounded loudly to her ears—almost magnified several times but muffled as if in slow motion.

As she made her way to Exeter, the harrowing, unwanted feeling unexpectedly returned. The fleeting glimpse of grief and demise pulsed through her overtly charged brain. Gasping for breath, she paused to cross, but the woman's face turned to stone when she continued to hear the low dull sound of footsteps, although her own feet were firmly planted on the dusty pavement.

"Please answer me! Who's there?" she cried again in an extremely anxious and unsettling tone.

Still there was no reply.

Now terrified, Madame Mary began to tremble as she walk briskly to the corner of Burlegh Street, hoping that she would run into a crowd of folk—possibly a patrolman that could assist her in catching a cab. Her face turned pale, as the approaching footsteps seemed to also pick up in the rhythmic stride of her own. She was now in an almost state of alarmed panic and continued to look behind her every few seconds, but as with every glance as before, nobody—or nothing—was remotely visible.

"Why are you following me?" she cried out loud. Her voice was shaking with unholy terror. "Whoever you are, please show thyself!"

In a state of hysterics, she stood stock still, listening attentively. Her mind went racing as she was preparing to take off her heeled shoes and run wild into the thick of the fog, banking on the notion she would be concealed from danger and far gone before any nemeses would hit upon and tackle her bounds. However, at that moment, a universal apprehension clung to her that would have caused the strongest man to gnaw his tongue with pain.

Suddenly, a cold, heavy hand fell on her shoulder. She turned about carefully and then stood quietly, completely paralyzed in fear! The low, dull sound resurfaced; notwithstanding, this time, it was her heart. The tall cloaked figure of a man stepped out of the shadows and looked down on her with controlling, hypnotic eyes. It was an iron look on a face of immorality—one she harshly disliked from commencement.

"Y-you!" she cried, but her voice was broken and faint from dread. Indeed, she could barely get out any recognizable word, let alone a group of them to perform a coherent sentence structure.

She turned to run, but the blazing pupils drawn her in, burning the woman and forming immediate mutilations to her face. Quickly, Lady Dickinson drifted into a coma induced from a terrible horror—a fright that was like none other she had ever known.

The woman dropped her bag, covered her visage, and tried to scream; hitherto, the man held up his hand to silence her cries. The assaulter took her by the waist as if to dance with her in the moonlight. Twisting aimlessly, as if attempting to break free, the female found all her efforts were in vain. There was no escaping the fiend's clutch; she was too trite and scared to scream—too alone and powerless to solicit aid.

His foul breath reeked of the odor of stale blood, causing the woman to make a feeble attempt to look away. Nonetheless, the alluring eyes stigmatized her and any attempt to defy the monster— in any shape or form—was to no avail.

Holding her waist with his left arm, he ran his long, pointed fingers through her hair with his right. The drawing down of his grisly brow and the stern set of the mean jaw presented a death mask of enduring cruelty. And with eyes continuing to glow a fiery light, she said with an unyielding, hungered tone that was vexed with evil:

"The vital fluid of life is finite, my dear, and you will now replenish me!"

Shuddering in trepidation, she finally collapsed in his arms. And supporting her back with his left arm, the creature grabbed the bulk of her hair with his right, reclining her while exposing her bare neck in the process. The horrid eyes blazed even deeper than before. Looking up toward the moon, its mouth spread back—gruesomely in full form—displaying its sharp, white fangs that resembled the teeth of a savage carnivore. In a quick blood-frenzied movement, he lurched forward and sank his incisors deep into the flesh.

She screamed . . . but only once.

The woman groaned, but with each swallow of blood being drained from her body, her delayed reaction became more and more subdued and her breathing eventually became shallow.

Now clawing at her neck, the vampire continued to drink for several seconds until her breathing was almost nonexistent. Recognizing that the woman was on the verge of death, the leech ceased its feeding. Pulling back with bloodstained lips, he hissed, "Now, sweet child . . . drink from your maker!"

Resembling a bat protecting its young, he threw open his flowing, black cape and brought her inside. And then, in a matter of seconds, he had bled her body dry and then consumed her soul.

It has often been told that when extreme shock, sadness, or tragic event occurs in one's life that the world around them grows queer and dreamlike. In Miss Mary's final minutes leading up to her repugnant attack, the fleeting passage of death and destruction hung over her like a weighty raincloud, one that was full and reddened of blood. Though the morose image seemed surreal, the nightmarish vision exploded. And as her life quickly seeped out of her body, Miss Mary Dickinson's essence floated slowly above her person, watching the murder replay in slow motion. And as her heartbeat ceased, she heard the pure spirit whisper, "The bitter curse never prevails upon a stainless heart!"

* * * * *

The passing hours that eventually brought sunlight to the awful scene did not change the dark reverie or spectrum of stillness that seemingly captured the crime panorama like a lifeless dome. Finally, the onset of dawn unexpectedly broke the lurid spell. An elderly gentleman stumbled upon the body at daybreak whilst going for a morning stroll. Recognizing the heap as a human form, the old man gawked in disbelief, and concealing his face partially with his worn-out hands, he turned and fled the area in an overly anxious manner, calling out, "Councilor!" Then the elder immediately began to patrol the area, continuing to beckon for law enforcement in an ever-growing raspy voice:

"Councilor! *Councilor!*"

Within minutes, he located a uniformed Bobby who sounded his whistle for appropriate backup. Soon additional officers were on scene, followed by a medical examiner and then several gathering onlookers. Within a short while, a team of at least twelve surrounded the body as if it was some great mystical entity.

The shell of the woman rested on her back in gothic proportions—one arm outreached in an attempt to protect her neck while her other limbs were twisted as if in a struggle to find liberation. Her face was rigid—frozen in a look of terror with numerous mutilations present. Her neck was mangled, and the corners of her mouth were stained scarlet.

"Poor old girl . . . some sick bastard sure had a blood feast with her!" said one officer to another.

The medical examiner spoke as an assistant recorded, "Female Caucasian . . . approximately fifty-four years old found lying on her back on the corner of Wellington and Burlegh, a short distance behind the Lyceum theatre. Several deep mutilations are present upon her face. There are proportional deep lacerations across the neck, severing the carotid artery and the internal jugular veins. The tissue borders are frayed . . . the carpal bones are crushed. Directly over the jugular vein are two medium-sized bite wounds. The pricks are partially clogged by the dried flow of blood, and the surrounding areas of the openings are slightly inflamed, resembling an allergic reaction to a drug. There are perforations of the esophagus, coupled with multiple lacerations—"

"Her body appears to have been drained of blood," added the medical examiner.

Detective Inspector Cotford, who had arrived on the scene earlier with physical research agent Singleton, had been searching for clues or hint of identity.

"There is no identification on the woman and no known witnesses to the crime," stated Cotford.

"Very odd," answered Singleton. "It is obvious by the remains of the dress, this woman was of money. Hence, she likely was toting a handbag of the upper-class society."

"Indeed," replied Cotford. "In all plausibility . . . her attacker absconded with it!"

And in the victim's right hand, in place of the blue purse, were a few stands of black mane.

"May God have mercy on her . . ." cried a bystander, "for her throat has been ripped out!"

CHAPTER 12

The Labyrinth

I am awe in a sea of wonders. I doubt. I fear.
I think strange things, which I dare not confess to
my own soul. God keep me—if only for the sake
of those dear to me.

—Jonathan Harker's journal

When Abraham Stoker realized that the letter he had written to his wife, Florence, had vanished, he flew into a fit of rage. He proceeded to turn the entire contents of his chamber upside down, to no avail. The correspondence was nowhere to be found, and the entire ordeal seemed to question—or hitherto mock—Bram's sanity. His feeling of entrapment within the castle walls only enhanced his reoccurring bloodstained nightmares. Coupled with a recent visit from a ghost of a victim of suicide, his only thread with the outside world and his family was in that letter.

"I expect to open my eyes any minute to find myself in a sanitarium bed donning a straight waistcoat," wrote the Irishman in his diary. "Though my expectations are rejected time after time as I recognize my surrounding as of those of the Count's hideous castle of evil and darkness—one that I loath and reject as my personal house of pain!"

To the author's surprise, the door to the bedroom of Countess Dracula must have been unlocked during her visit. This sudden discovery and spit of freedom sent a jolt of excitement through his body as that of a lunatic being released from his padded cell.

"God bless you, miss!" he said as the heavy door creaked open wide, displaying a long, cold, corridor of stone pillars and tapestries. "May your soul find peaceful rest!"

With his bags in hand, the journeyman cautiously made his way down the massive hall that was dimly lit with a few torches mounted on each side. He was surprised to find many of the rooms unlocked; however, none proved to be a way out. It appeared many of the chambers had not been lived in for years, and there was no sign of life anywhere within this tower or wing of the castle. Cobwebs were everywhere, and reeds, bones, and scraps of decayed food were scattered about the floors. The quarters reeked of the dampness and the stale smell of environments that had not seen the light of day for centuries.

After several minutes of exploring, the writer stumbled upon a passage that revealed a spiral staircase. He seized one of the torches off the neighboring wall and onward descended. Down, down, and further down he went until he began to feel as if he was due to burst into flames at any given moment.

As he plummeted, Bram noted the sides of several of the steps and adjoining walls dripped a murky liquid and that many of the bricks being submersed by the foul-smelling substance were eaten up by mold and algae growing into oblivion. Abraham covered his nose to squelch the odor and proceeded to go downward. Stepping on many crawling insects in his path, he came to an archway, which emerged an immense door. Throwing his entire weight against the entrance, Stoker forced it open and instantly noticed he was now in an entirely different wing of the castle. The harsh wind outside blew against the ancient castle walls violently as the foreigner gathered himself for what he hoped would be the means of a grand escape.

Recognizing immediately this part of the fortress was more preserved and ornately decorated, he hid behind a stone column and listened attentively. The Irishman gazed nervously all around him, searching for any exit to the outside. The room before him resembled that of a great hall consisting of many wooden benches and large tables made by laying wood planks across other benches.

But as the author stood stock-still, broad alert, and attentive, he peered into the unfamiliar territory and feverishly tensed as the pores on his face opened and unleashed the residue of nervous perspiration. The sound of wind became a low, dull noise and continued to evolve until Abraham realized he was actually hearing approaching voices! Upon this unexpected realization, he turned to duck out of plain view. And clenching his weighty bag in his arms—the only means he had as a weapon—he waited as the now distinct whispers echoed around the corridor in his direction.

The shadow of Stoker's bag cast an unusual appearance before the wall in front of him. As the tremulous dark mass remained fixed, the mundane object became very mean, almost as if it towered over the man holding it. And then suddenly, the image sprouted arms and lunged forward. He plummeted directly into another person. Caught totally off guard, Bram dropped his torch and stumbled to the stone floor.

"Aieee!" the elderly lady screamed, equally startled to see someone else milling about the castle.

Picking himself up, Stoker realized it was the same Slovak he had called out to for help from his tower window.

"I am very proud to meet your acquaintance," the writer said earnestly.

She studied him for several minutes whilst the other gentleman, the translator from the courtyard, approached, equally as startled from behind.

It was clear to Abraham now that the two of them were married and were employed by the Count to see to his home. However, they were obviously thunderstruck to see how he had managed to free himself from a section of the castle that was off limits to them.

Suddenly the woman let out another scream, pointing to an object that had fallen out of Bram's bag and onto the floor in front of them. It was a picture of Florence Stoker.

The woman's husband took his anxious wife into his arms and in broken English asked, "Did you take this from her?"

"Take what from whom?" Abraham asked unknowingly. "This is a picture of my wife, Florence Stoker of London, England. I hired a photographer to take it months ago."

The couple gazed at it in complete amazement and then back at Abraham curiously—almost as if in state of utter disbelief.

"She reminds us of someone who used to live here," the man said as his wife began to gently weep. "The Countess . . . she looks like the Master's dead bride! We not see that picture before. My wife think you took from her room and now we are cursed!"

Stoker looked at his new friends sweetly and touched both of them on their shoulders and replied, "On the contrary, I believe the ghost of this fine lady has assisted me in my quest for freedom. And now, my counterparts of late, will you kindly please show me the way out of this haunted, dreadful place?"

Though the male seemed to stress several times that they had by no means complete access to the castle grounds, the couple took the journeyman on what seemed to be a long-winded excursion of the fortress instead of a direct path to freedom.

As they proceeded, Bram learned that the Slovaks were hired by Count Dracula to maintain the castle and its accompanying grounds in exchange for food and shelter. They seemed very nervous to speak of their employer, but when the author asked about the circumstances of the Countess's suicide, he got a queer reaction: neither the old woman nor the man would look him directly in the eyes and seemed to change the subject. Only the man said something to the effect of "Ottoman Turks after Vlad Tepes" and "many bad things happening."

"We passed through imperial gates, boundless impressive courtyards and mazes of galleries, spiral stairways, gothic vaults, low dungeons and dark halls," Abraham described in his diary. "Nevertheless, everywhere seemed to be tainted—polluted by history—adding its gruesome reek and a layer of dust to the castle's aura of death."

Upon entering what appeared to resemble a grand dining room, Bram paused for a moment and motioned for the old lady and man to wait as he stood awe stricken by a painting mounted on an immense wood-burning fireplace. It was a portrait of Countess Dracula; however, looking at her as she appeared in life form was a new and quite breathtaking sight. The Irishman moved closer and closer as tears began to dwell up in his eyes.

"She was the spitting image of my wife, Florence, I tell you! Those same delicious eyes and ruby red lips! The likeness is uncanny to fathom!" he said to the others. "Oh, dearest Florrie! I love you with all the moods and tenses of the word! How I miss you so!"

Holding back tears, it suddenly donned to Bram that there could possibly be a grim connection between his being held prisoner and Florence's letter missing in action. Could Dracula strategically be splitting them up whist he preyed on her life?

All at once Abraham looked at the Slovak pair with eyes raving like a maniac.

"Whilst I fondly appreciate the grand tour of the residence you share, I demand to be on my way this very instant, lest I make haste, I fear some foul thing of the night will find my Florence!"

The couple leapt back away from the journeyman's immediate reach as if his glare and sudden outburst had frightened them. Looking at one another sheepishly, they exchanged several words in their native tongue and turned to stare at Bram with looks of utter hopelessness. With sweating palms, he realized he needed to bottle his emotion and rethink his plea in simpler terms they could understand. Taking a death breath and wiping his brow, Abraham Stoker picked up his bags and gazed at the Slovaks with a longing expression.

"Kind friends, you are my only hope. Please . . . help me find a way out! I beg of you! If I stay, I will surely die here."

It was vivid to Bram that the recent additions to his alliance were not comfortable discussing certain things. Though friendly and honest natives they were, it seemed to manifest out of some sort of fear for their own wellness that challenged their consciences. This was evident when the man said, "Front entrance forbidden! I show you secret path!"

Using a candelabrum for lighting, the three crept along a secluded hall to a larger complex structure the nobles referred to the

Court of Tirgoviste and down a deep path of stairs. The only sound coming from the ancient ruins were their shallow breaths—though the couple consistently looked behind them with every turn and each passing step.

They proceeded to climb the Chindia Tower, which was built by Vlad Tepes as a watchtower and was commonly referred to as Dracula's Palace. Abraham was fascinated that it seemed to be filled with all sorts of historical information. Via the window. one could see a breathtaking view of the Poenari Mountain and miles ahead in the distance. Stoker took watch for several minutes, imagining Dracula gazing from the same exact spot strategizing his brutal attacks and escapes from Turkish seizure.

The old woman looked nervously at her husband and crossed her chest as he rolled back a table and uncovered a heavy Persian rug—one that produced a cloud of smoke integrated with the dirt of ages, which all but disintegrated at the touch of humans being.

"Here!" the man said, almost whispering to Bram.

"My apologies," Abraham said, somewhat dazed and confused. "What do you wish of me?"

"Help me move stone," replied the Slovak.

The two of them lifted back a large square tile at the edge of the floor that displayed a hidden stairway. The man likewise crossed his chest and said, "We cannot go with you, but may God keep you safe."

Abraham tore a portion of a portly, ornate drape covering the window at the front of the tower to fuel the candelabra and light his pathway to independence. As he fondly bid his farewells, he commenced his travel down the steps simultaneously bowing to his cohorts. The man all of a sudden appeared to be old and haggard by the ordeal, whilst the elderly woman chanted something over and over that the writer would not be able to translate until later: "Even a man that is pure of heart and says his prayers by night may become a wolf when the wolfsbane blooms and the moon is shining bright."

* * * * *

As Abraham proceeded down the mysterious forbidden stairs, the sound of the heavy sandstone being positioned back in place within the floor above brought shivers down his spine. It reminded him of his mother's stories back in his native Ireland of victims being buried alive. The similar thought made his blood turn cold and his hands grew clammy.

There is no turning back now! Stoker thought to himself apprehensively.

Each movement produced a haze alongside the imprint of his foot amongst mounds of soot that clung to each step. With every descending pace, the temperature of hole plummeted. To ease the distress of the event, the Irishman pictured himself in the living room of his English home sitting at a cozy fire, writing peacefully near his family. As he approached the bottom of the stairwell he made every effort to keep this thought alive; nevertheless, he was all but prepared to encounter the calamity therein.

The staircase ended at a tunnel, resembling what he thought to be a cave. The flooring was all dirt, and the ceiling was barely high enough to where Bram did not have to duck to keep himself from striking his head on the stone roofing. He proceeded forward several steps, shining his lighting in every direction. Even with the flame lighting the way, it could not mask the bitter coldness of the damp place.

Abraham continued to walk in the only direction of the tunnel without vision or sound of any evidence of life form along the way. Nothing unusual struck him about the cave with the exception of the smell.

"It was as if happening upon a butchery that had shut its doors in mid-operation and remained sealed for years to come," the author recalled. "The repulsive stench of decaying remains and musty molds coupled with fermented earth and stagnant waters were all the perdition one gentleman could withstand. And to be alone is to be left with one's personal fears and alarms."

Small- to medium-sized pools of liquid were in random corners throughout the cave. The contents of these puddles appeared to be aged water that had collected over extreme periods, spawning biological growth. As he walked deeper into the cavern, insect life seemed to materialize there, and Stoker found himself stepping on all kinds of arthropod larvae and crawling species—both alive and dead.

As the tunnel wound on, the journeyman noticed the air in the cave became denser and his flame flickered wildly. He was now far away from the sealed entrance, and breathing was becoming more of a laborious challenge.

Suddenly, his attention became invited to some images on the cavern wall. As his eyesight focused in, he lighted one particular area. Bram realized it was human writing! Most of the carvings were written in Wallachian and Hungarian languages. However, deeper into the cave, he recognized several other messages scribed in Bulgarian and Turkish tongues. Though the foreigner's translating skills were not advanced, he wrote down several that stuck his interest while recognizing many reoccurring words and phrases along the way: *doom, Impaler Prince, dragon, evildoer,* and [the] *end is near.*

As he walked even deeper into the cave, the temperature seemed to grow even colder until his own breath in front of him seemed to freeze upon contact. Within a few hundred more yards, he stumbled upon a fork with a tunnel leading to the right and left respectively. After deciding to head left, he suddenly fell upon a mass that cluttered the cavern's floor. "The prayer of a righteous person has great power as it is working—healing, holiness, and deliverance. I prayed to find a way out—however, I was not the only one needing healing," the writer recorded. Picking up his torch, he gasped to see the remains of what was once an Ottoman Turk. Its uniform fell to pieces upon the writer's touch, and the expression of the figure seemed to be from that of starvation coupled by a lack of oxygen. The soldier seemed to cry out for a proper burial after left rotting unnoticed for all of four hundred years.

And as the man held his torch up steadily high above the floor, what happened then caused the blood pumping through his veins to halt and congeal suddenly.

In craven horror, Bram wearily came to his feet and started back in utter disbelief. He had stumbled upon a discovery too shocking to describe in mere words. And to say that the Turk was not alone but rather had plenty of company to while away the centuries would have been a grotesque understatement. For what the journeyman was standing in was an entire room full of mummified bodies! He gasped for breath as his shaking hand caused the flickering flame to dance wildly upon the various faces of death.

"Father, please! I implore you! Deliver me from the evil that haunts this living nightmare from dusk till dawn!" Stoker cried aloud, his voice echoing as it ricocheted off the damp cavern walls.

Abraham stood bewildered for many minutes in a state of complete uncertainty. There was clearly at least six hundred bodies in that room alone, and he was not sure what was in store for his discovery beyond the threshold of his path.

Bram brushed the ashes of the man that had dusted his own disheveled red beard and came to the realization the only way to get by was to climb over the bodies. After mustering up enough bravery, Stoker proceeded. The carcasses beneath him crunched as he walked over them and crumbled into particles of fine powder that created an eerie frozen vapor that clouded the cavern floor.

The tunnel took another sharp turn into an additional long stretch that consisted of further writings, though seemingly more desperate in nature than the latter. Some of them were in languages Abraham had little difficulty translating, and nearly all of them contained reference to Vlad Tepes Dracula. Likewise, one particular writing referenced the Count's liberation from the Turks in 1462.

Great Scott! Abraham said to himself. *Vlad escaped through this same secret cave and fled across the mountains into Transylvania where he appealed to Matthias Corvinus for aid!*

Moreover, other writings mentioned the king immediately had Vlad "arrested and imprisoned in a royal tower" whilst others—ones that had to be translated later—referred to bodies being "hacked into pieces like heads of cabbages" and the "voivode [Vlad the Impaler] roasting the children of on-looking mothers and [afterwards] they [the mothers] had to eat their own." Abraham wrote many of these passages down in his notebook.

"The marvel on the vista of my enterprise cannot be fathomed: I am exploring wild, mysterious lands to unravel the thread of disquieting secrets that have already begun to work some sort of dark magic in my soul—one of which I dare not hazard. I tremble as I set these words to paper with a partial impression of curiosity and adventure and a semi-harrowing effect for what I may discern. Intertwined in these unvisited regions, I sense a story that is screaming to be heard. Nevertheless, heaven watched over me as Vlad sets out to crown his wretched testimonies! Indeed, only one being touched by the hand of God can penetrate the soulless and cage the unresolved will of a vampire!"

The piece of cloth on the torch was quickly depleting, which made the Irishman extremely worried. The tunnel before him seemed to be closing in on him, causing the oxygen intake to grow dense, thereby making it more difficult to breathe. Coupled with the ghastly smells and already dimly lit light, something needed to happen soon.

Within moments, he found himself back at the fork—only this time he exited the tunnel that he originally came to on the right side. Upon realizing this, Abraham began to panic, almost unable to breathe. Simultaneously his torch burned out, and he fell to his knees. As he was overcome with horror, he collapsed on the cavern floor in total darkness.

* * * * *

Hours turned into days; and days turned into weeks. Shrouded in complete and dismal blackness, Abraham Stoker drifted in and out of consciousness for what seemed to him to be a lifetime of unspeakable terror. For extremely long periods, he lay on the cold, hard, damp dirt cave floor, a surface that at times became completely infested with insects that crawled over his entire body. Though the bugs managed to act as a blanket to sustain warmth, the pests crept through his clothes, facial hair, and even his bodily cavities. In extreme hours of desperation and hunger, Bram consumed those that squirmed though his lips to maintain some means of nourishment.

During short times when outside air managed to filter in through crevices in the Poenari mountain, Stoker managed to slowly feel his way around the cavern; however, with each attempt, he found himself going in circles—as if the tunnels were a roundabout that always brought him back to the same familiar fork. After nearly one hundred failed tries, Abraham fell amongst the head of corpses to say a silent prayer for his family and was prepared to join the mummified soldiers in their quest for eternal rest.

The fool says in his heart there is no God, yet creation shouts God's existence. And to say that creation was self-originating contradicts the law of cause and effect. Therefore, as a believer, I pray to my maker: please release me from this presage of horror!

Suddenly, at the Irishman's dimmest hour of need, a ray of light came into the room and fell upon a rock twenty-four feet above the flooring. The odd sight almost blinded Bram, as it had seemed an eternity since he had witnessed the light of day. As the beam continued to shine on this area of the cave that had yet to be explored, his eyesight gradually adjusted; and Stoker realized the glow was coming from the ghost of the Countess.

Abraham mustered the strength to smile and eventually whispered, "God bless you, sweet child," as he forced himself to his feet, feeling like he had regressed to his youth—early years spent as an invalid learning to walk.

The spirit continued to light the way, an opening of a crawlspace that was only attainable by climbing up and over several bulky stones. This task was no easy challenge for the weak, malnourished Stoker, but after several hours and countless misses, he found himself at the mouth of the opening.

The voice of Countess Dracula then spoke to him: "There are far worse things in life than death itself; sometimes it can be knowing dreadful frights that are too gruesome and evil to believe or understand. On the other hand, it can be the infidel that rejects the truth only to be doomed to eternal darkness."

Abraham Stoker looked at her earnestly, hoping that she will direct him on to what he prayed to be his path of freedom. She continued, "Alas, it was not the Turks that I feared . . . nor of the possibility of being captured by the Ottoman Empire, but instead it was my husband: the man that he was becoming—the midnight crusader that he would evolve into which I had to free myself from."

The hovering ghost floated down beside Bram and perched itself on the edge of the rock before him. She looked at the Irishman passionately with the same longing expression that seemed to beg for spiritual release.

"If I had not jumped, Dracula would have brought me into his dark world with him. So I bid thee farewell . . . go now and find your own freedom."

"Kindred spirit, what could I ever do to repay you for saving my life?" Abraham asked with utmost earnest and desire.

The Countess looked at him quietly for several minutes and said, "Release my own grimly, tainted soul from captivity and cease the horror and vile darkness Vlad Dracula has brought to thousands over centuries and the thousands more to come lest he be stopped! Only then will my spirit be able to rest peacefully."

With those words, the ghost disappeared, and Abraham Stoker was once again left in the cold and gloomy solitude of the labyrinth-like cave of death.

"No! Do not leave me . . . please!" the author shouted desperately as he stood up.

With the outburst came sudden rustling of movement from overhead. Excited that it was perhaps the ghost again, or better yet, she was preparing a means for escape, the man beamed the first time in what seemed to be a lifetime of drudgery. As he stood back and waited, the overhead rafter seemed to project a warning of danger or aura of uneasiness that sent a chill down his spine. And what immediately followed resembled the flapping of large wings. Then without any warning, the entire cave all at once came alive with giant vampire bats! There were thousands of them in total—all flying toward the sound that disturbed their sleep: Stoker's voice.

As they buffeted and ricocheted off of Bram's body, he immediately covered his face in reaction and proceeded to fall to the ground for protection. For several minutes, the journeyman rested in a puddle of mud listening to the heinous, loud screeching of the foul beasts overhead, circling wildly as if on a savage blood hunt. And then, as suddenly as they appeared, they were gone

The writer's brain quickly went into action. Considering they all had flown away into the night, he realized there had to be an exit near. This thought gave him a sudden burst of vigor as he peered in the direction of the distant sounds of the bats. A gleam of outside light shown up ahead, thus he quickly followed it.

A few hundred yards in front of him, Abraham discovered an underground mountain spring, where he passionately quenched his thirst after a long spree of dehydration. Afterward, he dunked his entire head in the steam to assist in washing off the mud, insects, and decomposed ash that had taken up residence on his visage and facial hair. This activity somewhat refreshed the still visually shaken and ill Stoker, but taking a deep breath, he set forth a constant stride to the direction of the outside ray of light that was less than one quarter of a mile ahead.

With every pace, the light grew larger and larger until Bram could clearly see an opening at the lower north side of Poenari Mountain. With a gasp of restored fresh air, the free man laughed in a half-wary, half-manic fashion and then fell on the grass-covered hillside, kissing it like a sailor returning home after being lost at sea.

"Oh joy! What rapture! Woe are my weary, sun-deprived eyes! Do not deceive me in my plight to freedom!"

* * * * *

As Abraham Stoker continued to frolic in the grass his mood abruptly changed to one of utter terror.

"How does one prepare himself to witness the ultimate horrible shock of wickedness?" Bram wrote in his journal. "For one with reasonable state of mind could never image such fierce and glorified acts!"

For though his escape was no hallucination, he wished the scene that was set up directly outside the cave's exit was an optical illusion. Indeed, about three hundred feet toward the right of the mouth of the cavern was a great pot with two handles filled with boiling water, which rested upon a grand wood burning fire. Over the kettle was some sort of queer staging device with wooden planks that secured the body of an elderly woman. With a look of horror, Abraham gasped as he recognized the clothes of the Slovak from the castle, a melancholy structure now perched high on the mountain overlooking him with watchful eye. Adorning the end of the trap was a hole that was made to allow the head of the victim to fall through it.

Her head was missing.

Directly to the right of this scene of torture was an even more grisly sight—for there was a small table, set up as for an elaborate meal, and seated in a high-back chair directly in the center of the table was the Slovak's wild-eyed husband, digging savagely into the contents of the woman's decapitated head, which had been boiled in the pot and slit open and arranged on a plate in front of him!

Stoker wailed madly, calling out to the man; nevertheless, he continued to feast as if in some sort of brainwashed resonance. The Slovak was delusional to the degree he was not even aware of the Irishman's presence.

"Is this the end?" an exasperated Abraham called out to the night. "Has it come to this!"

At that same moment, a sound of an approaching horse was heard. Ahead in the distance there was a destrier, a sixteen-hand warhorse bred for battle. Riding in its saddle, with his legs straight, balancing a sword and shield as if practicing for war at the tilt, was Dracula. And then suddenly, the Count's voice whispered in a cold, harsh, demonic tone like he was standing directly over him in the author's left ear: "Oh, what gratefulness they exhibit! Do not defy me, friend Stoker, otherwise thou must answer to what becomes of Miss Florence if thee do not heed my warning! Recall I summon ye to learn of my story and to write it for others. Do not judge me or get involved lest you invite destruction upon your own household!"

Without even pausing for a reply, Vlad Tepes rode off into the night leaving the foreigner with a headless corpse and a flesh-eating lunatic that was once his comrades. Looking up at the full moon, Abraham howled as he was once again overcome with grief and terror. As his heart sank even further in his chest, he feverishly cried, "Behold my ravaged, gutted body and heavy soul, for I am half the man with half the brain—only a poor, faint shadow of my past existence! Indeed, everything I once believed in has been challenged—

completely reshaped into a hellish, horrific, walking fright mare!
Alas . . . the night! Dusk truly is nature's coldest, darkest hour. Hark!
Thine is the lowest of late!"

CHAPTER 13

Sleepwalker

> Suddenly I became broad awake, and sat up, with a horrible sense of fear upon me, and some feeling of emptiness around me. The room was dark, so I could not see Lucy's bed; I stole across and felt for her. The bed was empty.
> —Mina Murray's Journal

Ancient folklore about vampirism dated back to the earliest Indo-European nomadic civilizations that emerged from the steppe land north of the Caspian Sea approximately 3000 BC. The Terrifying Sovereign, god of death, magic, and mythology that enforced the belief of battle between good and evil led to the tribal and warrior elite's to feat the European forests that were claimed to be at one with the dead and haunted by prowling wolves. This origin evolved through ancient culture and linked the undead and wolf, which became known as the lycanthropic vampire of Eastern Europe.

The demon that Noel witnessed in his hearth several nights before had been doing some haunting of its own as his dreams had been turned into invariable nightmares. He could not help but ponder if there were some connection between the fiery fiend and the mystifying monster that had preyed upon his mother. Moreover, he was beginning to think his father's wild tale of a vampire running wild through the streets of London, England, was no longer a psychotic episode to him at all, nor was it a far-fetched cry from the reality of the situation.

Seated at the dinner table with his mother, his best mate, Jonathan Watts, and several other friends of both his parents, Noel's thoughts centered on the topic of the supernatural and became similar to a giant Chinese proverb. Noel was questioning everything out of the ordinary, and though his mother planned an elaborate dinner party to mask the situation, Noel found the socialization distracting and hurried to finish his meal.

"So how is my dear old girl getting on?" Oscar Wilde inquired of Florence Stoker as he leaned over in a Chippendale chair and across the dinner table.

"Poor O . . ." Florence immediately answered while pouring him another cup of tea (as this was what she nicknamed him as he could not seem to keep himself out of scandal, lawsuits, and incarceration). "How kind of you to ask. I am doing very well—in good spirits and fine health indeed! Here . . . have another spot of tea!"

Noel Stoker winked secretly at his friend Jonathan Watts, who was seated directly across from him in a tweed Knickerbocker, flannel shirt and jacket, as he knew his mother was bluffing. Jonathan, a lad two years Noel's junior, winked back at his chum as they knew one another all to well and found themselves manifesting the same thought: something foul was in the air, yet the adults appeared to be oblivious to it or were in complete denial. It seemed these two adolescent boys were left to sort it out.

"Mum, do you believe we really have souls?" the boy asked unexpectedly. "Do you think they live on past death?" His mother grew very quiet as a look of astonishment fell across her face.

"Yes, son," she answered politely. "I believe our souls are an extension of ourselves in our truest—as God sees us as opposed to how we believe to be."

As she said this, Oscar Wilde immediately joined in the conversation by adding philosophically, "I view the soul as an animated corpse—material death in its very ability to inspire both allure and revolt ion, desire and horror. It is the embodiment—sometimes beautiful, sometimes hideous, but always fascinating—of the persistence of the object and the perilously permeable line between life and death, being and unbeing self and other."

The two boys seemed to cringe in their seats at this answer as Lady Stoker made a gesture to the author as if to change the subject lest he might frighten the youngsters. However, as his mind continued to work deep in thought, he failed to notice her.

"You see," he said continuing as if he did not pay notice to Florence's protest, "we fear our souls because we are reminded of the dark side of ourselves. As Lucifer knows our hidden, ferocious, repressed quality, and on the other, he panders to man's morbid excitement at the prospect of sadistic pleasures. The transgression of the boundaries exposes repressive aspects within a society by making visible the culturally invisible, by tracing the unsaid and the unseen, that which has been silenced, made invisible, made absent."

"O," Florence shouted abruptly, "please!"

"So you think the devil is after our souls?" Noel said, interrupting. As everyone looked at the boy smiling, Jonathan took his last bite of fish and pushed his plate away, gawking at his friend.

Oscar Wilde placed his hand on the lad's shoulder and sighed a wanton breath and said delicately, "Sir Richard Burton—alas, for he is no more—once asked if someone could be born without a soul or perhaps lose theirs along the walk of life. Truly, man has descended their lack of soul and their heightened erotic instincts. Evolution was not necessarily progressive, but could be retrogressive. I believe Satan's role is to present an extension of feudal rights founded on systematic exploitation. The world today is on the point of being reversed, colonized by demons expressing both fear and guilt. The fear is that what has been presented as the 'civilized' world is on the point of being colonized by 'primitive' forces. Thus the colonizer finds himself in the position of the colonized, the exploiter becomes exploited, and the victimizer victimized."

Everyone seemed to ponder over this powerful statement as the light of numerous candles reflected off the eighteenth-century silver that was ornately displayed on a mahogany credenza. It created a calming yet eerie mood about the room as Noel too hurried to clean the remainder of fish and chips that were settled on his plate.

Henry Dickens, son of well-known British author Charles Dickens, suddenly took center stage.

"Oscar is correct," he agreed importantly. "As divine creations, man sometimes fails to consider the morality of his own encroachment on other species. In considering the food chain, we see humans reign supreme: we are the ultimate carnivores, domesticating and consuming other creatures. But should we not consider Satan himself to be a predator? Do his demons not prey on humans? As Darwin recently proposed in *The Descent of Man*, any species faced with a new predator will have it numbers depleted: 'Man may be excused for feeling some pride at having risen, though not through his own exertions, to the very summit of the organic scale and the fact of his having thus risen, instead of having been aboriginality placed there, may give him hope for a still higher destiny in the distant future.' Hence, I believe the exertions of men have helped us to rise to the top of the food chain. However, I feel it is foolish and pretentious to assume we will always be there. Our Victorian sensibilities show that God and the old ways must not be forsaken in favor of modern science."

"That is precisely what Mary Shelly was driving at," shouted Wilde. "The two systems can, and should, exist together, and it is up to humans to decide how best to mingle those narratives!"

"To be triumphant over our own demons will eliminates the immediate fear, but never the fear itself," Dickens retorted. "And the blood of all of our fears is in our children. If humanity is to continue to flourish through our offspring, we need to become heroes and face the enduring evil that can pray upon our souls."

The two young friends seemed to turn a shade lighter as Florence jumped up from her seat. Seeing the topic was frightening her, he quickly redirected the topic of conversation.

"And how is that husband of yours getting along?" Henry Irving politely asked. Noel gave the man a look of complete disgust as the actor rounded on his mother. "You said he traveled to Romania some time ago to do research on his next book? There is nothing that interests you that is not of importance to me, so please . . . do tell!"

Once again, Florence lied and put on a brave face for her visitors. "Abraham is faring well in his travels, and in his absence, I have been at my wits' end this season and receiving lots of attention from both sexes, theatres and parties and dinners thrown in, but I enjoy every moment with zest!"

For the truth of the matter was Bram Stoker fled London under precarious conditions and had not been heard from hitherto, and Florence was in a state of desperation—coupled with extreme loneliness and worry. To keep from going stir crazy, she kept herself busy by surrounding herself with friends and entertainment; however, when alone with Noel, she became sad, and her son could often hear her at night, crying softly from her bedroom door. Likewise, after his mother's encounter with the strange man, she had been acting queer, often standing by or staring out her bedroom window, sometimes pacing to and fro as if expecting something to happen or awaiting the arrival of someone or something.

Author George Morre, who arrived late to the dinner party in his usual fashion, balanced his chair on its hind legs in a manner to either entertain or irritate, depending on one's current mood. The other guests began to laugh, but Florence did not seem to notice. She gave Noel a look to signify a commitment of silence.

"May I beg to be excused, Mum?" Noel asked, placing his dinner napkin down next to an empty plate. Jonathan quickly followed suit.

His mother nodded courteously to both of them and waved the two onward to Noel's bedroom, where they immediately began to discuss a conversation they had started silently over dinner. As they left, Morre brought the conversation back around to the earlier conversation: the human soul.

"Splitting of the scientific endeavor from the Word of God gives rise to the realm of demons, in and through which humanity may experience and be subjected to variant levels of fear. Our conscience is the essence of our soul, and when society conspires against his right to die—when it experiments with its bones, its muscles, its sinews, its blood—it thus digs deep into the yawning mouth of its own wounds! And through helpless openings we force ourselves into the secret places of a forbidden body. We plunge deeper and deeper to find further discoveries, and to the shame of the havoc of its limbs, we add the insult of our curiosity and the curse of our purpose: the purpose to remake him. And we lay odds on our chances of escape, and in doing so, we combat with death, our only savior."

There was a long pause between them all. And then the hostess jumped to her feet and gave a trying grin. With a wan-looking expression and a trembling hand, she held up a teapot.

"Does anyone fancy for another spot?"

* * * * *

"There must be a common link to all of this!" Noel said to Jonathan after they retreated to his room.

Jonathan, who nodded his head in agreement, was a few inches shorter than his friend with sandy-blond hair and deep-blue eyes. Even though Noel had an advanced puberty advantage over Jonathan by a couple years, his best mate's intelligence and aptitude skills were in no way inferior to Noel's.

He spoke with a thick English accent: "Do ye fash the bloomin' creature that's scarin' ye Pop mightn't be the bloke that was after ye Mum? An' it be the auld thing ye saw in the fire?"

"It is possible," Noel answered. "Vampires are shape shifters."

The two enthusiasts took turns analyzing Abraham Stoker's incredible encounter with the undead, followed by Florence's visit and then finally Noel's rendezvous with an incubus.

"Dad mentioned the creature that came to him fled the study in the form of a wolf!" Noel exclaimed. Without Florence's knowledge, Noel had transcribed a copy of his father's diary prior to his travels abroad.

In Eastern Europe, the vampire was closely connected with the werewolf. Thus, it was believed wolf men would become vampires unless they were exorcised. Though werewolves were not known to change shape other than from a man to a wolf, vampires were infamous for their shape shifting into many forms—all nocturnal creatures: bat, owl, rat, and wolf.

"An' ye Pop had nigh' dreams an' visions of wolves attacking!" Jonathan added.

They proceeded to formulate a strategy of how to ward off the beast, followed by a plan for disposal.

"Silver!" they cried simultaneously. "Werewolves are allergic to silver!"

Exorcising the curse of the werewolf prior to the transformation to vampire was commonly done by precious metal. The most prevalent form was by a silver bullet through the heart. Thinking on his feet, Noel reached under his mattress and pulled out the knife that his mother had sharply disposed of in the kitchen cupboard. The two friends had acquired the knife at a nearby shop they often visited, operated by Old Man Godalming, as they frequently called him. The back of the shop was a bazaar of the bizarre—so to speak—as the owner, David Godalming, specialized in collecting artifacts of the macabre all the way back to the fifteenth century. The two had visited the shop only days after Florence Stoker's room was invaded, and Noel sought confidential advice from the man he so trusted.

Though the knife was not silver, it would have to do until they could come up with something more practical. The two boys felt somewhat reassured knowing the knife was there, but for extra security, Noel hung a crucifix on the headboard of the bed.

"Mum!" Noel said. "We have to also protect Mum!"

The two concluded that the man that terrorized both Bram and Florence Stoker was, indeed, the same man, yet myth stressed that the undead cannot enter one's home unless invited during the initial visit. Though this confused both of them and pondered further thought—for they could not fathom how Abraham Stoker had been tricked into giving initial permission—their hypothesis remained the same: the Stokers were dealing with one mighty vampire.

Old Man Godalming told the boys that ancient cardinal belief stated that the vampire casts no reflection because its image is an affront to God. Though Noel had not proven this folklore with the man identified as Dracula, he recalled how his mother's vanity mirror was ironically smashed just moments before the Count's grandstand about her bedroom.

Likewise, he stated that his father's trip to Romania struck another connection with belief in vampirism for on St. Andrew's Day, 30 November, the townspeople smeared their window and doors with garlic to ward off the children of the night. Moreover, other civilizations believed that stuffing garlic cloves down the mouth of a vampire would keep it from rising and attacking again.

"Salt!" Jonathan shouted whilst recalling a statement Godalming had referenced, "They loath commin table salt!

Though the Stokers were without garlic flowers, they had plenty of salt to spare. While the dinner party continued on late into the evening, the two lads snuck into the kitchen and fetched a box of salt and formed a trail clear around Florence Stoker's quarters. For safe measure, Noel decided to do the same in his own room and then promptly returned the box to its rightful place without detection from anyone.

It was a few minutes shy of 1:00 a.m. when all of the dinner guests went home, and Florence, who swiftly shot back into "mother mode," stuck her head in Noel's room to bid them both a pleasant night and peaceful dreams.

"Jon dear, I have told your mother that you will sleep over tonight, but don't stay up too late lest you want to cause me trouble overseeing to her wishes!"

Upset and unnerved, the two boys changed into a pair of Noel's dressing gowns and continued to talk by the firelight until it completely died. The flickering coals glowed deep red, resembling fireflies in the moonlight, and despite the topic of conversation, the sight was calming to their anxiety. Both of them began to yawn and crawled up in bed gazing at the embers and then to each other to recap their plan of action.

"Tomorrow morn' we aught to visit auld bloke Godalming again. Nay, we shan't tarry . . . me sense th' pang of death!" said Jonathan matter-of-factly.

As the two lads rolled over in opposite directions, they both recognized silently that time was of the essence. However, little did they know that with each passing sunrise and sunset times would become all too harrowing to bear.

Old Man Godalming had preached that some variations or forms of vampire were notorious for being compulsive creatures, and some were anal counters or obsessive knot undoers.

"Stories of pouring stones over a vampire's grave after dusk will keep the creature counting until dawn, thus self erupting into flames at sunrise," he had told them. "Likewise, hanging a bloody object full of tangled fibers over one's drape or bedpost was said to keep the fiend occupied whilst the victim sought a more meaningful weapon of destruction."

However, no matter the means to ward or exterminate could outsmart the undead if the prey got lured in by its trance, for most forms of vampiric creatures carried a strong hypnotic power.

"Simply looking into its eyes too long could cause someone to be victimized by its spellbinding stare —making it all too late for the prey to grab a crucifix or a wreath of garlic flowers!" explained Godalming.

Noel witnessed this strange capability on two occasions: when he gazed upon the vampire in his mother's bedroom, and secondly, the hideous sight of the demonic face that appeared in the hearth. In both cases, the red eyes beamed of pure evil and sent out sparks of hell fire in all directions. Each creature seemed to want to captivate Noel's attention by swooning him into a helpless trance. Drifting off into slumber, he lay on his pillow, staring at the last flickering ember in the hearth that crackled and glowed the same ghastly crimson hue.

As Noel and Jonathan fell into a deep sleep, the last image Noel had before dreaming set in was the feeling of violation: the amoral, blaring eyes and the malignant face bending over his mother. For now it seemed to him the grisly, malevolent image would eternally haunt his dreams and shut out all memory of sunshine and happiness. Since that horrific night, both the vampire and demon would not escape his thought and became integrated into one grotesque orb—almost as if they had been spawned from the same fiery chasm.

Noel's rest was strangled by his many overwhelming fears for he tossed and turned relentlessly several hours before finally sitting upright in bed with his eyes fixated on the fireplace that was completely dead of activity. In a sleeplike, trance he studied it for several minutes whilst Jonathan snored aggressively on the other side of the bed, thus totally oblivious to his mate's odd behavior. It was about 3:00 a.m., and all was quiet about the house

Noel kept staring into the darkness in the direction of the hearth as if he was listening attentively for some pressing answer or calling. And then he rose. Ever so softly, to not disturb his houseguest, he crept slowly across the floor of the bedroom still dressed in his nightgown. When he got about twenty feet in front of the fireplace he stopped, and without taking his eyes off it, he proceeded to get down on all fours! He hesitated for a brief moment, as if waiting for further directions from an invisible and inaudible source, and then commenced crawling toward the hearth like a large dog sneaking up on its prey!

When Noel was about ten feet away from the hearth, all at once, the dead furnace became full of life—self-igniting into a wild burst of dancing flames! The sudden flash of light caused Jonathan Watts to awake abruptly and quickly rolled over, rubbing his eyes in the direction of the source.

To his utter horror, he saw his friend, who was only a mere few feet from the flames, crawling toward his demise like an infant unaware of any sense of danger. Shaking uncontrollably, his mate cowered in a paroxysm of fear and cried out, "Noel! Stop!"

Realizing that his friend was asleep, Jonathan rushed to him, calling his name again—only louder than before.

"Wake up, Noel!" the lad shrieked in a soul-sickening manner.

The sweltering heat from the inferno was singeing Noel's hair and eyebrows when Jonathan snatched him back by the shoulders and rolled him out of harm's way. In an instant, the fire disappeared like the blowing out of a candle. Noel jumped back, returning to his senses. He then looked at Jonathan with a perplexed expression.

"Mother! Is Mum all right?"

* * * * *

The following morning, it appeared the trail of salt had kept at bay any vampiric or unwanted spirits from invading Florence Stoker's room as she was in perfect rare form over breakfast. It was Saturday, and though Noel had tried to explain what he and Jonathan believed to be true, his mother would not hear of any of it. Her memory of the man hovering over her like a wild animal was fragmented, and what she could recollect she passed off as fever.

"Off with you both to Godalming's if you so fancy, but promise me, lads, no more knives! That is what is wrong with society. I am weary of hearing of the likes of Jack the Ripper hacking up woman and of the sort! And you two going on about vampires and monster men! I am full up of such talk! Now bugger off, both of you, but be back by noon empty-handed! Adieu!" she said with finality.

The brisk walk to old man Godalming's knife, gun, and archery shop that same morning was an opportune moment to clear the air. Both were fully dressed in baggy dungarees, long-sleeved work shirts laced up the center and brown burlap vests that helped keep off the wind and misting rain. Any onlooker would have mistaken them for two castaways looking for trouble. And with a listless look, Jonathan exclaimed, bemused, "Whut in the bloody blazes happened last night, mate? Hell, if I hadn't snatched, ye would have crawled right up into the damn hearth!"

"I don't remember . . . it is all a sketchy haze," replied Noel with a yawn, rubbing his eyes. "But I am certain it has something to do with that demon that I saw the night Mum was attacked. The bastard kept reappearing in me dreams!"

The nights afterward always started the same way. As Master Stoker would fall asleep, soon he would see the vision of the monster, rising over the back of her boudoir—a distorted face, red, and the mouth open and wet. It closed in on her as she snatched at her own eyelids. The teeth would bite down against her naked throat as the long fingers raked across the sensitive skin. In the shadow, he appeared to have draped half his face with a dark cape that was lined on the inside with scarlet satin. He then gave a high, rattling laugh. The sorrowful echoes of Florence sobbing went on endlessly as she made a feeble attempt to tear him off—her tears meeting blood, blinding her. The sheet that covered her bosom had rolled off, and his mother laid helpless, cold, and barely dressed on her back. And in the bright light of the moon, it appeared that a whole pail of crimson paint had been dashed across the woman's left side of her face, neck, and chest . . .

It was approaching 9:00 a.m. when the boys turned the corner of Hampton Street.

"Are ye sayin' this devil lulled ye to the fire himself?" Jonathan asked energetically.

"I . . . I don't know. But I am certain I did not feed the blasted inferno—in fact, 'twas completely dead once I fell asleep."

Within an hour, they came to Godalming's shop. It was a small, modest, rustic-looking building that was converted some twenty-five years ago from a one-room log cabin. By outside appearance, one would mistake it for the home of a junkyard dog, but on the inside, it correlated to the equivalent of a Pandora's box. Both Noel and Jonathan found the place to be a whirlpool of fascinations and mystery and Mr. Godalming to be an interesting man and a dear friend.

Every weapon imaginable was meticulously displayed, and with each piece came a story that only Old Man Godalming himself could deliver with a gentleman's absorbing and humorous appeal.

"A top of the morning to ya, boys!" he said gleefully as they entered through the front door.

Godalming was a burly, portly Englishman about six feet tall with a bald head. He was about sixty-eight years old, and sitting high up on his wrinkled face was a pair of round spectacles that were held up by a piece of black roping that was supported by his reddish, leathery neck.

"So . . . you lads ready to catch a vampire today, are ya?" he said with a wide smile and slight chuckle. He bent, as if in a stiff bow, woodenly at his thighs.

They all quickly seated themselves, and Noel and Jonathan each proceeded to tell him their own version of what happened the night before. The man was silent, supping on tea whilst igniting a fat cigar, and gave them both an inquisitive, firm look. And then, when they concluded their stories, he gestured as if to say "Wait a moment."

The old man wandered off toward the back of the store, and through a curtain that separated itself from another room, a far-removed place that Noel liked referring to as the voodoo shop. The curtain seemed to suggest that the room be forbidden, as it was unbeknownst to many and not open to the public. "It is only available to those that have the need to know," Godalming once said, and though Noel and Jonathan had seen it only once, it frightened them both; thus they waited patiently out front for Godalming's return.

The back room was completely filled with a collection of odd and rare artifacts of the bizarre—in fact, it was more of a museum of the freakish of nature than a shop. There was an Egyptian coffin that housed a real mummy, several shrunken heads, a witch's cauldron, several books of spells and magic, instruments of torture, and many jars containing the anatomy of infamous victims.

Dom Augustin Calmet, a prolific writer of the Benediline order, published the most authoritative eighteenth century work on vampires in 1746. His *Traite sur les Apparitions des Esprits et sur les Vampires* examined the horrid attacks of the undead and described the traditional methods of killing them. Godalming owned a copy of the first edition, and having read it himself several times over, his knowledge of the subject was always well reinforced.

Godalming returned in a few minutes with a large empty jar and black leather bag about three feet in length and a foot and a half deep. He sat the objects on the table before them, and with a stern, grave facial expression, he spoke.

"This very jar was said to have once contained the skull of Prince Vlad Tepes Dracul! After he was assassinated in 1476, he was decapitated by one of his own soldiers, and his head was sent to Constantinople, where it was boldly presented to the Sultan and displayed publicly as proof that the Impaler was, indeed, dead."

The two boys looked at each other with an expression of shock and bewilderment.

"Count Dracula?" Noel asked.

"Th' bloke who sent Noel's Pop away?" added Jonathan.

"Yes, Dracula . . . known as the great Impaler," Godalming continued. "Legend has it he returned from the grave soon after as a creature of the night—a vampire, one of the undead. However, you are not dealing with any ordinary vampire. No, Dracula was said to have been conceived by the devil himself! As a mortal born into royalty, he was upheld by his old country as a hero. Nevertheless, throughout the rest of the world, he became a legend as the one of the most bloodthirsty madmen in all history! And to the underworld, he is the king of all vampires!"

The boys looked at the large leather bag and then back to Godalming.

"Ah, for this very reason you need the greatest protection."

Godalming pushed the tote in a forward direction to where it was in front of the two children for formal inspection.

"My dear, young friends . . . you can plainly see the jar is empty. Thus, Vlad Dracula reclaimed his head. Now if you want to set things back the way they were . . . well, you will need what is in this bag!"

CHAPTER 14

Deliverance from Evil

He has had some fearful shock—so says
our doctor—and in his delirium his ravings have
been dreadful; of wolves and poison and blood;
of ghosts and demons; and I fear to say of what.
Be careful with him always that there may be
nothing to excite him of this kind for a long time
to come; the traces of such an illness as his do not
lightly die away.

—Letter, Sister Agatha, Hospital
of St. Joseph and St. Mary, Buda-
Pesth, to Miss Wilhelmina Murray

A whirlpool of violent, dark images flooded Abraham Stoker's
mind for what appeared to be an endless time of torture and
unspeakable terror. Through the ordeal of bodily unconsciousness,
a subset of his mind questioned if these events were, indeed, so, or
were they only lurid thoughts he dreamed up whilst his body recovered from the terrible trauma he had undertaken? Whatever the case,
fact or fiction, the end result would be an answer all too frightening
to bear. If the representations were true, how could one berserker of a
man—that is, if Prince Vlad could even be referred to as a man—be
capable of performing and delighting himself is such ruthless car-

nage? This caused the Irishman's blood to turn cold in his veins. And secondly, if these thoughts were instead only the fragments of Bram's overactive imagination, than this would suggest his conjuring up of such crazed, neurotic dreams a sign of abnormality of the mind.

Moreover, the author's body was in poor health after the long, dismal, treacherous entrapment period in the Poenari Mountain. His body was malnourished; and coupled with the horrors he had suffered since the night before leaving London, the combination of consternation and ailment had swoon himself into a psychosomatic state of shock. He was unsure how long he remained unconscious; however, between episodes of mass murder, dark captivity, and savage beasts, he began to feel he was losing his grip on reality. For the first instant in his life, he was questioning his own sanity.

"How grueling the passage of time can be when one is so far removed from loved ones!" Stoker wrote. "Assailed by agonizing disappointment and severe iniquity, I have resolved to commit my thoughts to paper as I am utterly unaided in my strange quest. Without rashness, I alone must arm myself from danger and prove persevering in a foreign, untamed element."

"I think a great deal—in fact, likely too much—for my daydreams invade me with vague fears, whilst my nights blast me with horrors so unlike anything of earthly significance could surmise. Alas, this constant state of melancholy, terror, and solitude may, by and by, take a brutal blow to my disposition if left unchecked. Of the few folk the Count has graced my spirit to encounter they have only been at a distance or of an acquaintance that spoke a language I could not understand. The barriers this embarkation has rendered me are becoming dreadful, and oh, how I long to talk to someone other than he! Though Dracula's words are astonishing and equally intriguing, they fall on one's ears as drops of poison. Nay, I cannot describe or fully comprehend the long-term damage without comparing his terms to that of the art of ancient Chinese water torture—where the water in truth be droplets of contaminated blood!"

As the writer tossed and turned on the rocky ground, a thunderous, frowning sky with rolling clouds lofted over what looked to be Castle Dracula, only centuries younger. In the courtyard stood two men dressed in Turkish garb that suggested a status of nobility or boyar quality. Vlad Tepes, donning his princely attire, gave them each a polite bow and bid them inside gratefully.

This image was immediately merged into a darker frame, which resembled some sort of dungeon filled with overturned earth. A massive octagonal box with a heavy lid sat on the dirt floor; and with a mighty thrust, the top slid back, revealing a scathing, bloodthirsty Count. The corners of his mouth were smeared crimson, thus lying there, he closely resembled a tick fully gorged with blood. The vampire was more horrifying and revolting as ever. Clad all in black, he shot out of the coffin like a madman with blazing red eyes that raged with fury. Then he leapt out a window and evolved into hundreds of ghost owls that emitted loud, spine-chilling hisses.

The light-colored animals resembled a sky of sinister phantoms that glided silently but wildly through the writer's mind, with wingspans up to about fifty inches. They soon returned to the castle courtyard where the bodies of the two Turkish men lay—alive, but in distress. The men previously entered the castle with their headgear on to discuss tactics of war. This insulted Dracula, and when they did not uncover immediately upon his request, the Prince became outraged and had two guards drive several metal spikes into the heads of both that they may keep the hats on permanently.

In a flight of peril, the birds circled and then flew down upon them in raptor fashion, hen-pecking the nails and gouging at their eyes—snapping at the skin on their visage—until their faces were nothing more than bloodied-up skeletal figures, resembling walking zombies that had been enveloped in flame. As the men were being attacked, their arms flapped fiercely about their foreheads and eyes wailing for many minutes until they vanished. When the vision faded, the journeyman saw the two men topple over in great heaps in the corner of the courtyard where they were left alone to die.

The grim facial expression of one of the men turned away from Abraham, and then suddenly, the features darkened and became unclear. They all at once began to change and transformed into that of a troubled female who seemed to be sleeping wearily in a bedroom. Though the scene was hazy, Stoker subconsciously felt there was something familiar about the room. The face of the woman was not visible, but the vile thing that crouched over her was undeniably that of the Count. He was paler and more horrid-looking than ever. The grim sight of him bending down over the helpless woman, focusing in on her throat like an untamed animal eyeing a piece of raw meat, was sickening to watch and was repulsive to his soul. The filthy ghoul leached over and placed his cold left hand under the woman's head. Turning her neck to her side, his long razor-sharp nails tingled amongst her dark hair that was spread out over her pillow-like angelic wings. As the face of the woman became noticeable, the Irishman's eyes flew open wide, and he sat up broad awake, screaming in terror.

It was that of Florence Stoker.

* * * * *

Flailing his limbs wildly, Bram came to and looked all about realizing he was in what appeared to be a modest country cottage unrecognizable to him. He was lying on a small hard couch with his head propped up somewhat by a flimsy pillow. He noticed that the couch, though it seemed to be very clean and kept, was very old. Being the tall man that he was, Abraham's stockinged feet hung off the end of the sofa, and his shoes had been taken off and placed on the floor beside him.

His red beard was untrimmed, and his ruddy complexion was tempered somewhat by the wide-open fully gray eyes that gazed so frankly into the unknown. He stood up, holding on like grim death, shaking like an earthquake—dreadfully frightened.

The room he was in resembled a family den or living quarters that also doubled as a dining room, for there was a table in the corner set for four people. Opposite the table was a hearth—fully lit and roasting what appeared to be a small piglet. Underneath the broad iron roaster, directly over the fire, sat a kettle that projected the smell of cooked vegetables, such as those of an assortment of peppers.

Mounted on the wall on the left side of the fire hung the skin of a great wolf. On the other side of the room, there was very little—

only a medium-sized rocking chair surrounded by several family-like oil-on-canvas paintings and portraits that were tacked to the wall.

As the author surveyed his surroundings, his eyes became affixed to an outline that rested in an oak rocking chair. With a look of horror transcending upon his face, he came to the realization he was not alone. The figure of an old man—absent of all movement and signs of life—rested in the chair. The spectacle startled the foreigner so severely that he nearly jumped out of his skin.

"The sight of another human being brought comfort but also a shock of terror to my aching bones. To wake up amongst the dead after such a journey of threat 'twas a grueling thought," described Stoker. "And as I approached the worn-out body, with ironic instinct, I armed myself with a rod iron pot that was positioned on a resting table. But as I found myself standing in front of the geezer, he let out an unexpected long-winded, powerful breath that caused the vessel to drop from my hand like it weighed ten and twenty stone."

The old man shot forward in the chair like a cannon as the writer reeled backward. Seeing now that his mystery host was only deep in sleep, the two were taken aback by the sight of the other. The wide-awake men eyeballed each other like two strangers in an odd land. And quite literally, this was, indeed, the atypical situation at hand.

"Where am I . . . who are you?" called out Bram, springing up from his feet again with a fist prepared to fight.

The man was dressed in loose clothing, which consisted of homemade trousers and a shirt with full white sleeves and a large black leather belt which met in the middle, holding both garments in place. The local national answered something back to Abraham in Wallachian and continued his rocking movement pointing toward the adjacent room of the cottage. Not understanding what was said, but seeing the man was quite harmless, the writer relaxed his stance somewhat and toward him thinking he might be hard of hearing.

"I am Abraham Stoker. How did I get here?"

The old bloke said absolutely nothing but nodded with a smile and continued to sway forward and backward. As Abraham got closer to the man, he realized the fellow had to be close to one hundred years old and felt foolish for contemplating a struggle. He rocked barefoot, and it was apparent his skin was sun-beaten due to many long and hot years toiling in the sun. His face was gnarled, and his eyes looked tired.

Wishing not to appear rude, the journeyman smiled back and proceeded to call out to the rest of the house, for the meal being cooked smelled fresh, and he assumed the elderly gentleman had not prepared it, and thus was not living on his own accord. But there was no answer.

Bram walked to a window that was located directly behind the old man and looked out in an effort to make some kind of attempt to scope out his whereabouts. Beyond a small immediate yard, which consisted of merely a well and a clothesline, were rows and rows of grapevines. They were many deep and continued for what seemed to be miles. Peering far beyond the vineyard and toward the horizon, the Irishman got a glimpse of what appeared to be the Carpathians. Looking in the other direction, however, Abraham was able to disclose his locality with a look of fright. On the west side of the house, though many, many miles in the distance, was Poenari Mountain, and high above the Argnes River was Castle Dracula.

Upon seeing the ghastly sight, Stoker through the curtain back in horror. The lurid intimidating presence seemed to sit there, mocking his very existence.

"I must be in the village of Tirgovistc," he stated aloud to himself.

And then—without warning, as if it came out of nowhere—a raspy voice answered him.

"Yes, but beware how you gaze because the hills have eyes."

The author was instantly startled and completely taken unawares by the response. The old man had answered him in German, and even though the foreigner's unkempt appearance of late might not have suggested the true Irishman he was, his reddish hair was an obvious sign he was not German. Furthermore, he had already attempted to communicate in English. German must have been the only other language the fellow knew.

"Vlkoslak," the writer replied.

The word meant *vampire*.

The old geezer seemed to jolt a bit and sat up in his chair as if he became suddenly scared. His entire countenance changed dramatically. Next, he made the universal sign of the cross over his chest and pointed again toward the window—as if he were heeding a dire warning.

Abraham pulled back the curtain once more and 'twas alluded this time not to the castle but instead to a short thin woman, about sixty years of age approaching the cottage with a load of firewood in hand. He noticed she had some of the same features of the old man, and the journeyman recognized her from what must have been a much younger family portrait that hung on the wall. As Bram did not know Wallachian, he turned and posed the question "Your daughter?" in German. The elderly bloke immediately perked up, nodding his head, and pointed to the table spread for four.

Four? the former thought to himself. *I only count three. To whom does the fourth setting belong?*

The woman was dressed in a flowing white dress that appeared aged and tarnished with a dark substance that resembled that of grape juice. Around her waist were several strips of fabric that formed a belt and hung down, flapping about in the wind. Underneath her dress, she wore a petticoat, and on her feet were thick brown leather boots that were covered in mud. On top of her head, she donned a blue bonnet that tied under her neck and shielded her face from the hot sun that shined on through the abundance of clouds and pounded down on the thirsty land. By the looks of the blooming flowers, fruiting trees, and marmalade skies, it had to be late summer.

My God! Bram exclaimed silently, *It was April when I left England!* It was paramount that he returned home quickly, for the longer he stayed abroad, the more demoralized he was becoming. He was surely in the toils and gathering wrath that was slowly surmising his self to atrocious, unbearable suffering.

"Welcome to our home, dear sir," the woman said with much feeling in perfect English but with a strong international dialect. "My name is Barbola Hupnuff, and it appears you have already met my father, Ioan." She sat the load of firewood down next to the fireplace.

"I am very pleased, madam," the Irishman said, kissing her hand with a courtly bow. "Abraham Stoker . . . of London, England."

When the woman took off her bonnet, she revealed a pretty, but somewhat haggard, face—one that seemed taxed by many years combating cruel elements and dire straits. Her dark hair was shoulder length and fell about her slightly wrinkled face. Brushing the locks back from her equally dark eyes, the author could tell she was a lady . . . graceful but strong.

"My brother, Janos, is out in the vineyard working; but he shall be in for dinner soon. Though I have kept your lips moist with water, I am sure you suffer from terrible thirst and hunger. You have been sleeping for close to a week. Why don't you go freshen yourself in the lavatory, and then we eat and talk."

After the guest made his toilet, he returned to find the brother, a forty-year-old barbarian-like man dressed in high boots, dirty dungarees, and cowboy hat, had joined the others at the supper table. He was clean, with the exception of his long brown mustache that sat atop a stern upper lip, and had a flat nose and floppy ears that had long graying whiskers protruding out of them. His skin was dark and rough—apparently from toiling in the sun—and he reeked of wine. If Stoker did not know better, he would have passed him off as a "sot" or "flunky" of his native land. The two shook hands, and everyone sat seated themselves to sup.

Since only Barbola spoke fluent English, over dinner, she remained busy translating almost everything that was said. Indeed, it was late August, and Abraham was discovered six days ago, staggering out in town raving about awful things that did not make sense to anyone. Barbola believed he had been spotted at least three days prior to her bringing him back to the cottage and that he must had suffered a terrible shock of some sort as he was hysterical and seemed scared and frightened. He was very week and trembled uncontrollably.

"My heart could not leave you there . . . as I could see you were a foreigner that somehow had gotten lost and was experiencing ill health."

"I think I must have expressed my utmost gratitude and love for this fine family a million times over as I can only imagine how I must had appeared to be a suspicious Irishman down on my luck and off my head," Bram recorded in his journal. "Though I have plenty of the money Count Dracula left me on my person, they did not take any of it and turned me down when I offered them 20 pounds for their trouble. Hitherto, they are, indeed, the kindest people of most honorable and noble quality I have met."

They dined on the roasted pork loin, which was done up in vegetables of all sorts that had been seasoned and cooked in the pot between the fire and the swine. Janos brought out several bottles of homemade wine and poured glasses for everyone. The writer was ravished, so he had seconds, followed by thirds, of everything.

Conversation turned from the meal to the weather and then to the family. The Hupnuffs owned a wine vineyard that was inherited down from Ioan's father. Ioan had operated it for over forty years until his wife passed away about twenty years ago and he became too old and poor health to do so. Janos, who had been following in his father's footsteps, took control while Barbola replaced her mother with the housework and became a nurse to her father.

The foreigner sat attentively and listened for some time about the secrets of wine making. Indeed, all varieties of grapes are mixed indiscriminately; in other words, no care is taken to separate the overripe and those yet green from the others. Then a group of almost naked men are placed in a large number of tubs for the pressing process. There they danced barefooted with all their force, to the music of the bagpipes, on the heaps of fruit which the carriers throw into them.

Though it was a picturesque, extraordinary scene, by British standards, the entire process seemed rather dirty and careless, the writer kept to himself.

The family's open and airy quality made the Irishman feel right at home and quite cozy. After several glasses of wine, Stoker felt comfortable enough and decided to turn the conversation around to himself and the events—of what he could recall—that led up to his being rescued.

The candid reaction was both interesting and unusual to watch; upon the very mentioning of Dracula's name, the daughter's good spirits changed. She almost immediately fell back into her chair into a mood of morbid melancholy and began to fidget with her clothes. Then she began to translate to her brother and father who reacted almost in the same peculiar way; and then all three of them began to converse—talking over one another is a state of nervous excitement.

Words such as *vrolok*—werewolf, *voivoid*—warrior, and *Ordog*—Satan, were repeated numerous times, and when they were done, they all looked at Bram with gazes full of pity and grave concern.

The son and father were terribly distraught and made their earnest attempts to communicate all kinds of information in English or German; however, in their state of anxiety, their translations got mixed up in several different languages and vernaculars, but very few words were understandable to the Irishman.

Barbola decided to retire to the living room whilst Janos opened another bottle of red wine. In the interim, Ioan calmed his nerves, and the daughter began to go into detail about Count Dracula. As she talked, the entire cottage seemed to reek of panic, superstition, and fear.

"Vlad Tepes was a hero to Wallachia for he was successful in prevailing against the Turkish Army. But everyone, including his own people, feared him. He singlehandedly committed more acts of cruelty in his lifetime than all his predecessors combined, and Dracula's punishments were more brutal than anything imaginable in the worse level of hell," said she.

"No one was immune to Vlad's mania as his victims included woman and children, peasants and great lords, ambassadors from foreign powers and merchants. However, the vast majority of his casualty came from the merchants and boyars of Transylvania and his own Wallachia."

The son returned with a fresh bottle of wine and again poured everyone a hearty glass. He sat down on the floor in front of the sofa next to his sister. The author sat attentively on the other side, and the old man rocked to and fro in his chair, listening to his daughter's telling of the old country's history, seemingly to the rhythmic pattern of his own heartbeat.

She continued, "Many have attempted to justify Vlad Dracula's actions on the basis of nascent nationalism and political necessity. Legion of the merchants in Transylvania and Wallachia were German Saxons who were seen as parasites, preying upon Romanian natives of Wallachia. The wealthy land-owning boyars exerted their own capricious and unfaithful influence over the reigning princes. Vlad's own father and older brother were murdered by unfaithful boyars. However, many of Vlad Dracula's victims were also Wallachians, and few deny that he derived a perverted pleasure from his actions."

At this, the elderly man began speaking very rapidly to his daughter and ranted for several minutes at which Abraham looked on and finished off another glass of wine. Soon the brother joined in, and it was apparent the journeyman's discovery of the bodies in Poenari Mountain were troublesome to the men and perhaps had opened up some old wounds. The men pointed to the direction of the castle and then proceeded to cross themselves whilst the daughter explained that her father's great grandfather had been seized by the Prince as a laborer when the castle was being built. He was never heard from henceforth, and his body was never recovered.

"Although Vlad III experienced some success in fending off the Turks, his accomplishments were relatively short-lived. He received little support from his titular overlord, Matthius Corvinus, King of Hungary, and Wallachian resources were to limit to achieve any lasting success against the powerful Turks. Turkeyland finally succeeded in forcing Vlad to flee to Transylvania in 1462 when he escaped though the same secret passage that you journeyed through Poenari Mountain—and possibly even fell upon my great ancestor! Dracula then absconded across the mountains into Transylvania and appealed to Matthias Corvinus for aid. The king immediately had Vlad arrested and imprisoned in a royal tower."

Abraham was fascinated by these revolutions and stopped to query her.

"How long did he remain imprisoned? Whilst he was there, did he undergo any changes or continued his schemes of villainy?" he asked abruptly.

After consulting a few minutes with her father and brother, she again responded, "Russian pamphlets indicate that he was a prisoner from 1462 until 1474. However, during this period, he was able to gradually win his way back into the graces of Matthias Corvinus. Though even in captivity he could not give up his favorite pastime, he often captured birds and mice and proceeded to torture and mutilate them. Some were beheaded or tarred-and-feathered and released. Most were impaled on tiny spears," she said sadly with a look of disgust upon her face.

At this thought, the author was speechless and fell back on the couch in a catatonic, mind-boggling state of bewilderment. He shook his head in a solemn manner and motioned the woman to go on.

"In 1476, Vlad was again ready to make a bid for power. Vlad Dracula and Prince Stephen Bathory of Transylvania invaded Wallachia with a mixed contingent of forces. Vlad's brother, Radu, had by then already died and was replaced by Basarab the Old, a member of the Danesti clan. At the approach of Vlad's army, Basarb and his cohorts fled. However, shortly after retaking the throne, Prince Bathory and most of Vlad's forces returned to Transylvania, leaving Vlad in a vulnerable position. Before he was able to gather support, a large Turkish army entered Wallachia. Vlad was forced to march and meet the Turks with less than four thousand men."

The Irishman was impressed by the Count's courage but at the same time was disgusted by his savage and bloodthirsty approach. He ran his fingers through his bushy reddish beard and inquired enthusiastically, "Was this ultimately the end of his reign of terror?"

To this she responded, "Vlad Dracula was killed in battle against the Turks near the town of Bucharest in December of 1476. It was reported he was assassinated by disloyal Wallachian boyars just as he was about to sweep the Turks from the field. His body was decapitated by the Turks and his perfumed head was sent to Constantinople where the sultan had it displayed on a stake as proof that the horrible Impaler was finally dead. He was reportedly buried at Snagov, an island monastery located near Bucharest."

Whilst Barbola cleared the table, Janos lit a pipe and offered one to his guest. Abraham turned it down, indicating that he did not smoke, but proceeded to ask questions about Vlad after his death. Stoker could tell immediately that this made all three of the family members a bit uncomfortable. The daughter gave a hiss-like gasp from the kitchen. The son's dark skin turned several shades lighter. And the old man's hands began to tremble, reaching out to refill his glass of wine. In lieu of this queer reaction, Bram did not risk his company's hospitality by pushing the subject.

Janos assisted in refilling his father's glass and offered to do the same for the journeyman. The writer politely declined, stating he had already had too much as he was beginning to feel a bit light-headed.

It was approaching eleven when Barbola helped her father to his bedroom. Within thirty minutes, her brother bid his foreign guest a courteous good night and followed suit, leaving Stoker and the daughter alone to converse.

"Father has had an exciting day as we rarely have company," she said. "Janos gets up before dawn to cut firewood followed by any work that must be done in the vineyard before the heat of the day is before us."

The Irishman and the Romanian woman talked quietly amongst themselves until about one thirty in the morning. Considering Abraham's long period of sleep, he was not very tired, and being in the company of a traveler such as Stoker was exciting for Barbola and initiated a mass of conversation.

After several minutes of discussing British culture, Romanian life, London customs, and Transylvanian traditions, there was a long pause, and Bram noticed the daughter's expression changed to one of utmost seriousness and grave concern.

"You asked about life following Prince Vlad's assassination," she said to him with a tone of sternness. "Though many feared him then, even more people fear him now . . . and it is worse! Much worse!"

She got very close to her guest, and by and by, looking over her shoulder occasionally—as if expecting to be invaded by Dracula's army—continued to tell her story from earlier:

"Dracula being dead was too good to be true! And though the land was free of his brutal wars, unworthy arrests, mass impalements, and savage tortures, we dare not repeat his name! We risk not for it is said that those that conjure him up pay ultimately with their souls. Indeed, he is believed to be 'undead.' People have claimed to see him in the night in the form of a vampire, and he feasts on the blood of those that fail to worship him as the true and only Prince of Wallachia."

"Has anyone tried to stop him?" Abraham asked of her.

"Every century henceforth, a few have tried but failed miserably. It is believed he is powerful now and has all the reinforcement of hell behind him! They claim he carries the strength of twenty men!"

Stoker shook his head in agreement as he recalled the night in his study when Dracula picked him up by one hand and threw him across the floor like a kitten.

"Kind woman," said the Irishman wholeheartedly, "though what we discuss in outrageous and unbelievable to fathom, I believe you. And as you, too, believe the stories I share of my incredible journey thus far, I want to thank you again from the depth of my troubled heart." He covered his chest with his right hand and looked at Barbola sweetly with idolatrous beaming eyes.

"For when a man begins to think his mind has become unhinged and feels the world he is a part of is a horrible place, he soon experiences a loss of hope. And not only have you given me a ray of renewed confidence, but you have also accepted my thesis as truth and that there are good people left to live for."

He kissed the woman's hand, and she blushed radiantly.

She then looked at him with an abundance of earnest and said, "I believe I found you not by my own doing but by some higher power that I cannot explain. When we pray for help, God sends help."

By this there was a moment of prolonged silence. And then they both conversed and plotted out what they knew had to be done.

It is said that vampires are weakest during the day and that they must rest in their native soil," claimed the daughter. "In daylight he must sleep at his mortal burial site in Snagov, forty kilometers north of Bucharest."

Bram placed his hands over his face and thought of what he should do. He cowered for his life and shuttered at what might happen if he tried to stand in between Dracula's quest for blood, yet he feared something grave for his own family back in London if he did not take appropriate action. Likewise, he knew he needed to work in haste, but he needed a clever strategy. The two of them talked over a plan of attack for the following day.

Barbola and the author decided that he and Janos would visit Vlad Tepes's resting place at dawn and would resume his remains. Since the monastery is a historic shrine and a public site protected by the Romanian government, one would need to stand guard whilst the other committed the grim act of disposal. However, they would not go empty handed.

After a few hours of sleep, Stoker and Barbola would get up with her brother before dawn, and Janos would whittle one of their vineyard posts into a long wooden stake to drive through the creature's heart. Whilst her brother remained busy with his handy work, she would dig up the roots of an ancient plant that grew behind the cottage to stuff down its mouth and throat.

Indeed, the genus *Aconitum*, which is commonly referred to as monkshood or wolfsbane, contains some very easily grown plants. The common wolfsbane is one of the most poisonous, yet it is one of the most handsome of hardy plants. In the past, the root was now and again mistaken for horseradish and eaten with fatal results. The plant, which produces blue-green foliage, has a smooth texture that blooms mid-late summer through early fall. Moreover, the blooms produced are an impressive and beautiful blue-violet, but more importantly, however, their scent and root are known to be toxic and even deadly to werewolves . . . and vampires.

Abraham would locate a shovel and go dressed as himself—the tourist—whilst Janos would dress as his self, a groundskeeper, and carry the shovel on his person. Finally, Barbola would stay behind and tend to their father and pray for their safe return.

Retiring to his bedroom, Stoker felt in his jacket and located the vial of holy water that the Captain had given him on his voyage over. It was a comforting thought to know it was still there, and he placed it under his pillow and clenched it throughout the rest of the night.

＊ ＊ ＊ ＊ ＊

It was nearly 3:00 a.m. when Abraham had finally drifted off to sleep. Though he was not tired after his long spell of unconscious dreaming, he was quite weary of what the sleep produced. The weird nightmares had taken toil on him, and the thought of sleep again disturbed him. Thus, he lay awake thinking.

What does all of this mean? he thought to himself. *Why am I of such humble and modest nature chosen to embark on such a grim and wild adventure?*

Bram wrote, "Though I dream of such supernatural affairs of things that have happened or events that may be or will come to pass, no man should have to bear such a horrible burden that tears at the very thread of one's being and is at constant conflict with his own sanity! May God protect us and give me supreme strength whilst committing the dirty work that is before mankind!"

The Irishman did not dream of sinister castles, bloodsucking bats, or anything of the kind that night; instead, his thoughts were of back home—and in particular, pleasant thoughts of his dear wife Florence. In his scattered dreams, she was in gay spirits and perfect health, darting about their flat in London. And though it was only a few hours until the Three Musketeers rose to prepare for their conquest, his dreaming spree was short and perhaps cut off more so than usual. The only unsettling thought that came to mind when he awoke was that there was always someone else in his dreams with Florence. Oddly enough, it was not Count Dracula but his employer and good friend Henry Irving. Bram thought this was a little odd and a bit uncouth, but in the excitement of the day, he brushed it off deciding that the good fellow was only checking up on her whilst during his own travels abroad.

Abraham was knocked up at 4:30 the following morning and everything was set out as the two planned. When he rose, Janos was already outside the house performing his morning chores before fulfilling his new obligation as "stake suitor." Barbola could be heard in the kitchen preparing coffee and striking up a fire for their morning breakfast.

Stoker made his toilet and dressed himself, and as he was walking into the kitchen to greet his alliance, something dreadful happened. From the room, there came a cry of despair so intense that the air seemed to freeze over. And upon hearing the morning silence awfully broken by the disheartening groan, the writer leapt into the room, calling out to Barbola. The woman suddenly began to shriek something terrible as if experiencing a horrible fit of unimaginable pain. Despite his body's bewildered state, Stoker ran to her as fast as he could and found her lying on the floor, moaning in a way that was too painful for anyone with a pure heart to watch.

The woman had dropped the cups of coffee that had crashed on the floor, and he found her lying in the mist of the scattered pieces of neutral clay and black liquid. She held herself as if she was in the mid process of giving birth, yet the Irishman knew the woman was not expecting—for neither did she mention it or show any signs of pregnancy. A startling feral scream escaped her lips like none other the writer heard before.

"Barbola!" Abraham cried helplessly. "What on earth is the matter?"

Stirring in the corner of the entrance hobbled the girl's elderly father, who stood in complete awe at what was happening. For 'tis only when a man is face-to-face with his own worst nightmares than one can truly understand their utmost significance and importance—for his daughter was being ripped wide open from groin to her breasts by some invisible entity.

Evil again had full sway.

The two men were thunderstruck at what was witnessed. The woman's dressing gown became soaked as it turned red in color, and as the deep cuts tore into her body splicing through her abdomen, chest, and spleen. Warm blood began to pour out of her like a running stream that seeped clear across the wooden floor. She gasped and twisted like a fish out of water; her eyes rolled in a way that was too terrible to begin to describe.

"My God in heaven! What is doing this!" the journeyman screamed. And unsure of what to do, he took the vial of holy water out of his pocket and tossed it all over her.

Indeed, there was absolute havoc about the room. The sound of a loud thud was heard behind Stoker. As he continued to douse the water about the wailing body of the old man's daughter, Abraham looked over his shoulder and saw that the elderly fellow had grabbed his heart and fell to the floor, hitting his head on the corner of the kitchen table in the process.

"Leave her be, you foul beast from the pit!" the author shouted aloud belligerently, striking and cursing the space around them. His warm breath escaped into the bitter air, causing a cloud to linger and eventually dissolve into a ghostly evaporation.

And then the holy water seemed to produce a queer reaction as the cutting ceased and a hissing sound seemed to come from the cold atmosphere followed by a sizzling and elements of steam that rose from the body. The array of noises escaping the woman, spirit, and old fellow was a queer and powerful combination that seemed to awake every deafening echo imaginable—in hell and beyond.

At length, the woman stopped her groping, and the horrendous, endless cries turned into faint moans that faded within seconds, too dead silence. Her chest soon failed to rise and lower.

The poor woman was dead.

Her mangled body lay motionless on the floor in a coil-like position with her bulging eyes fixed in a state of distress and utter terror. The geezer had expired as well, for he apparently had a condition of the heart and the sudden shock that transpired from the sight exhausted it to an untimely end. Moreover, the strike to the head resulted in a slight concussion, and within a matter of minutes, his heart ceased to beat.

A pool of fresh blood had manifested from both bodies—tainting the once brown floor into a sea of scarlet.

"O gracious and dear God! What am I to do now?" Bram shouted apprehensively.

The sound of a cockcrow was heard in the distant as Abraham covered up both bodies with the tablecloth and a look of utter defeat and sorrow upon his face. Though unwilling to surrender, he slumped down in a chair between them and looked at the ghastly scene before him as if to validate it was, indeed, real and not some awful nightmare.

Stoker rose and through opened the sash of the kitchen window and called to Janos.

"Danger! Come quickly!"

There was no answer.

Followed by a slight pause, the Irishman quickly called again, only this time a degree louder.

"*Janos! Hurry!*"

The writer sat docketly at the window and waited with beating heart but to no avail. Again, there was no reply.

The cries were deplorable and the sight before him too appalling to stomach, but the dead silence surrounding the cottage was even more dreadful to bear.

The journeyman wrote in his journal, "Is this newest tragedy and desolation yet another scheme of ruthless villainy? O woeful sorrow! Her cries wrung my breaking heart; and I sit abound to all the violence and extravagant emotion one man can possibly attain!"

At last he stole back to his chair and collapsed. The author plummeted over with his hands in his face and began to sob desperately for a prolonged period, followed by several more minutes of deep thought.

Then Stoker repeated the Lord's Prayer.

CHAPTER 15

The Becoming

> She was ghastly, chalky pale; the red seemed
> to have gone even from her lips and gums and
> the bones of her face stood out prominently; her
> breathing was painful to see or hear.
>
> —Dr. Seward's Diary

Abraham Stoker once said to his wife, "It would be a mistake to turn back the leaves of the book of our past when the present can be so interesting." Indeed, during her husband's absence, Florence needed to fill her days and nights with plenty of exciting things lest she plummet into a sea of speculation and worry about his condition and safety. Thus she continued to uphold her Victorian aristocratic image to the tilt; she appeared at ballrooms with her long hair up—where she would undoubtedly be photographed and noticed by everyone.

Noel Stoker described his mother as an "an ornament not a woman of passion." For even in her final years of life, he often made remarks about her voluptuous appearance she proudly carried and the reactions of those that coveted her.

"People used to stand on chairs to look at her. She was still a very beautiful woman in middle age and when she was seventy-five," her son stated. Certainly other women were envious of her beauty and the attention that she stirred, and the fact that she could even arouse the interest of married men —or even those whose sexual preference was in constant speculation—only fed her ego and vanity complex, which was elevated considerably without her husband's presence.

Even years after she and Bram were married, former suitors continued to daunt on her and openly expressed their sentiments of fondness. Florence's long-ago and brief courtship with poet and author Oscar Wilde, then a footloose undergraduate, who was also was a close friend with her husband, evolved into a strange friendship initiating an array of notes, flowers, trinkets, and whispers that lasted for years well into her marriage and his prison term. Florence could have been seen as a consummate soul who enjoyed the reflected celebrity of her former suitor's growing cult.

Popular playwright W. S. Gilbert seized on her anxiety about being alone and harbored her constant need to be surrounded by people. And not far subsequent to the latest events described in this chapter, he went as far as giving Mrs. Bram—as he affectionately called her—a Madagascar lemur to keep her company and fully entertained. The unusual monkey was trained to rest sweetly on her shoulder as she would flit about the flat, talking to it all the way as if 'twas a human being.

But for Noel, his father's frequent absences working, touring, holidaying—or whatever the case happened to be—meant that he was left in charge. And for a preadolescent boy, part of his childhood was sacrificed to a need to become a man before his time. Indeed, there was no doubting that he was fond of his mother; and as to his own interest, looking after Florence during his father's travels abroad was of greatest priority.

Though Noel and Jonathan sealed off her room repeatedly with a trail of salt, they both knew that it was not going to be the ultimate closure to their troubles. There was much work to be done; however, unlike his glamorous mother, the pending tasks were loathing and ugly—work he knew his mother could not possibly understand.

Until of late, Noel had passed off his father's claims as fiction brought on by a combination of food poisoning, flagrant night-mares, and an overactive imagination. Moreover, they had received no word from Abraham Stoker since his leaving London, and Master Stoker felt that adding to his mother's stress by rallying evil spirits would prove to be only malignant to her well-being. Thus, after much thought, he and Jonathan would instead carry out their plan secretly. It was just going to take longer than they anticipated.

Old Man Godalming asked twenty pounds for the black leather bag; but hitherto, they could only scrape together five between the two of them. Thus, the lads were in the process of carrying out another plan of action to conjure up another fifteen whilst Florence continued to stand watch at her bedroom window and cry herself to sleep.

Noel feared if this repugnant behavior continued much longer, it would only escalate in time and might even emerge into something of graver nature—perhaps even fatality—with or no vampire. This particular evening was no different.

It was half past eleven o'clock when the young master elapsed into what was first restless but eventually sound asleep, and his mother, dressed in a house coat over her dressing gown, sat herself down at her vanity in habit-like fashion to begin her nightly ritual of combing out her long, dark locks.

She was utterly sick with apprehension, and the numerous weary days and sleepless nights had begun to take their toll on her otherwise youthful and radiant face. As she brushed the mass that fell from her head, there was a long spell of silence about the house. It was lonesome without her husband, yet still there was no word from him, nor was there any way for Florence herself to make contact. His locality was unbeknownst to her—or to anyone for that matter.

"Oh, what a sore trial of late!" she said to her reflection exhaustedly as the lemur jumped to her shoulder to recline for a stay. "Alas . . . this lingering mystery continues to creep in and devour my soul, yet it seems to have no end in sight!"

Her head became filled with a whirling school of doubt and dread regarding her husband's mysterious circumstances. The endless questions troubled and agonized her spirit into one of fear: Was Bram dead? Could he be in dire need? Had he have found someone else to love?

At this thought, she noticed the effect of this pain on her facial features and coiled back in wonder. First she covered her visage in embarrassment and then began to cry as if a broad aching void had consumed her.

"Certainly a man does not want to return home to a sniffling, haggard wretch! I must regain my composure at once!"

To hide the sight of her reflection, she quickly removed her housecoat and covered the looking glass. As the monkey sat peacefully dragging its tail repeatedly across the back of her neck, its owner's countenance became one of faraway sadness overshadowed by morose and melancholy. For a long spell, she seemingly sunk deeper and deeper into the gloom simultaneously as the haunting moon replaced the setting sun. And at length, she began to weep again.

At this sight, the unique pet began to grow restless. It proceeded to pace back and forth on Florence's shoulders and sporadically stare back at her reflection with a different kind of temperament – one of fear or threat. As she continued to sit crying softly, there suddenly came a noise that startled Florence; thus she rose up in reaction. It was a sort of buffeting sound that would beat against her window every few seconds such as that of a child casting stones at the house for a prank or attempting to gain one's attention in an unorthodox kind of way.

"Noel?" she called out reluctantly. "Is that you?"

Then the lemur became increasingly untamed and finally jumped to the floor on its hind legs, screeching loudly. Florence pressed her left index finger up to her lips in an effort to calm the distraught monkey to no avail. And after hearing no reply to her call, she took several nervous paces toward the noise and paused. She listened attentively, and there came the noise again.

She quickly walked over and benignly perched herself at the window—just as she had done many nights hitherto—and watched and waited patiently.

The noise ceased as she opened the sash and peered her head out into the cool night air. She gazed downward and saw that there was no visible person on the ground; however, assuming it was one of her son's friends, she called to the street below, "Jonathan? Are you up to mischief?"

There was no answer.

"Cease this behavior at once! You alarm me so!"

Only the faint chirping sound of the crickets filled the night, and her expression changed to a placid one as she leaned back in deep, introspective thought.

At the sight of the open window, the primate's feral state worsened. Unlike the endearing gentle pet that Florence had grown fond of, it turned unexpectedly into a vicious beast. Its sudden change of demeanor was disturbing to see or hear and its reaction horrified her. And she backed away from the animal in a status of fear as it bounded to the casement in attack fashion. A sense of terror began to develop in her heart as she witnessed the wild look of danger its eyes. Then it proceeded to shine as if the very air outside was its native jungle in complete distress and total violation.

"Woe! My dear, dear . . . oh, poor fellow . . ."

And then there came a glimpse that brought her thoughts of love, pity, and hope to one of merciless loathsomeness, incomprehension, and despair. Momentarily the shadow of something stirring in the distance caught Florence's attention. Mistaking it as a crow or black bird at first, she looked again. As the shape came closer, she found it to be one of a black bat that circled and whirled about the area. Upon this realization, she assumed she positively identified the source of the earlier noise. Nonetheless, there was something peculiar about it that troubled and scared her severely. It was much larger than any other bat she had seen before, and it appeared aggressive and diligent—like it was there for some grave purpose.

Indeed, as she stood watching the foul beast, it would have been labeled an unusual observation for any spectator: a true battle of intelligences between Victorian wits and rodent intimidation.

With the exception of a few rare cases of vampire bats attacking livestock in the rural country, bats are usually passive creatures that distance themselves from human beings. They tend to fly in a scattered kind of pattern with no direction or grace, but this mammal was the exception. It was as if the creature had a mind of its own like no other dumb animal of its own kind. It seemed to hover in a sort of unclean, unholy savage delight and had a reason for its mission—though unaware to any mortal's reasoning.

A piercing shriek burst from the primate's lips as it flailed its limbs and leapt off the window ledge and onto the chamber floor. On all fours, it hurled itself into a corner of the boudoir by a half running, half jumping motion where it sat wide-eyed, shaking as if in a convulsion of terror.

Florence spoke not and became goose-fleshy. For several minutes she supervised the window and its movement and by and by became strangely and utterly horrified of its presence despite the fact that it was just one of God's common beings. But to Florence, unless her mind was playing tricks, it stared directly back at her with beaming eyes of red that illuminated the passing hours of darkness. She closed hers for several seconds and then looked again and found this to be so: it undoubtedly focused its sight on her and continued to flap about wildly as if staking out her window.

She wished it to be gone and ultimately decided to throw a random object at it, but to no avail. It took a downward dip as if diving for a mouse on the ground and then returned to its non-faltering plight.

Upon witnessing its stamina, she had another idea.

"The lamp! It is attracted to the light in the room!" she whispered under her breath.

Thenceforth, she blew out the lantern that rested near the window and waited patiently a few minutes. Upon creeping back to the sill, she glared in the direction of where the bat seemed fixed. In the distance she saw nothing, and with a calm sense of relief, she turned her head to look up at the moon.

At that precise moment, the provoking stillness and blackness of the chamber caused and extremity of fear to come across her. Even the lemur, which up to that time had been extremely vocal, fell deathly quiet, as it lay crouched in a heap in a bend of the room.

But then a kind of horror grabbed Florence, which almost made her knees buckle beneath her. She was instantly thunderstruck. For the creature was hanging upside down atop the windowsill! It stared

directly at her and snarled its mouth back as if about to communicate. It let out an unusual high-pitched screech as Florence bolted
backward and slammed the pane shut with a mad sense of urgency.
She then waited with beating heart. Her face had turned an awful,
ghostly pallor, and she began to tremble with fear.

"Heavenly Father . . . please protect me this night!" she prayed
with breaking voice.

Without prior notice, Florence's thoughts went blank, and she
began to feel dizzy. Soon the woman emerged into a somnambulistic
trance, and by and by, Florence found that she must had fallen asleep
as when she came to she started up in her bed. To her astonishment,
she found the window was wide open. The small monkey remained
in a silent and motionless heap in a bottleneck of the chamber. And
there . . . there hovering in the middle of the room in front of her
bed was the bat! It was watching her with the same wicked eyes that
beamed with sparks of hellfire.

Florence reeled back in her bed and held the covers up over her
face to suppress the shriek that was dwelling up inside her lest she
send the angry animal into attack mode. As her eyes peeped up over
her blanket, she realized the true size of the immense creature—it
was the length of a widespread bald eagle! With each flapping of its
diabolical wings, there came thrusts of wild wind that propelled cold
chills throughout the room.

Her heart sank as she watched the beast before her begin to
change. The width of the wings grew smaller and downward into
a cape-like canopy, whilst the length of the thing sprouted until its
form touched the wooden floor. The hair seemed to grow back into
the flesh as the bat-like features evolved, 'til . . . until they began to
resemble the features—the ghastly features of a man!

* * * * *

Florence was about to let out a blood-curdling cry when an arm
of iron nerve rose up from the mass and silenced her instantly. At the
wave of the hand, the woman fell back in the bed powerless. As he
approached her, the soft beams from the moonlight illuminated his
appearance, and she was able to get a long, hard look at his likeness.

Though the thing before her looked like a man, it was clearly not human.

His eyes were very large and mean—such as those of a dragon—and appeared as giant rubies radiating the worse level of Hades. His long, dark hair hung in heavy curls well beneath his bold shoulders, and his thin narrow nose seemed to disappear at the base in the luxuriant mustache that almost swallowed the distended nostrils. His temples were also swollen, and his complexion was livid and pale—such as one of a cold corpse. His cheeks were broad and high and rested on a strong jaw. In the center were thin, cruel bloodstained lips.

Florence noticed his clothing 'twas of that of a noble man—possibly even that of medieval royalty. He wore a black fur-edged robe with a high gilt and encrusted collar, and atop his head donned a crimson velvet cap augmented with rows or pearls, a gold star, and an upright ostrich-feather plume.

He was intriguing yet a horrifying specimen to look upon, but somehow the figure preyed upon Florence's mind. As baffling as it seemed to her, she felt as if she knew of him. The creature within the resemblance of a man seemed to encircle the poor woman with his hideous embrace, and when the thing drew closer to Florence's bed it delivered a silent sinister smile that revealed the long white canine teeth that were dangerously sharp and equally repulsive.

Oh may heaven have mercy in my hour of need!

The wife of Abraham Stoker lay terrified as she somehow recalled in her distant memory of seeing the capped thing in front of her before; nevertheless, the details were foggy and fragmented. Underneath her sheet she grabbed at her own flesh, expecting to awaken from a lingering nightmare. Her immediate reaction to the pain proved her wrong. He was very real. It was all happening to her.

"Stay quiet, child," an Eastern European voice said as the tall figure emerged from the darkness. "I am Count Dracula, and I bid ye not to be afraid."

The beaming eyes consumed Florence as she waited with devouring anxiety. She began to shake with emotion and quickly began to escape further into a dreamlike state.

"May God bless me and keep me . . ." she replied in a laconic tone as she reclined firmly against the headboard of the bed with chained will.

Bram, darling . . . where are you my love?

At this, the Impaler seemed to be struck down with a keen feeling of annoyance. Having been able to read his victim's thoughts, he replied, "Ha! I pity not those who let the muster of love taketh a strong hold on the weak and passionate heart!" He muttered this diabolically with a concentrated look of hatred upon his face. "I carry no stock in human affections and am absent of all gain that humanity provideth on earth. Alas, I am a predator—not an inhabitant of this world—who is empty of kindness and expects no love in return. However, it will come to pass when mankind will bow down before the underworld, and those that believeth not in me will be devoured by the fear that will swell in their hearts! Aye, thou will surely become slaves to me and my maker, and thy cries of pain will be music to my ears!"

And then he approached the bed of the sleeping Florence Stoker. But after two paces, he stopped and hesitated, looking fondly upon her radiant and angelic face. Though it only lasted a split second, for the first time in four centuries, he felt human compassion and was void of all evil and abhorrence. The Count stood over her, and she could feel his breath close to her neck as he rolled his head such as that of a dog sniffing out a bone or a monster preparing to bestow the kiss of death.

"Ah! Indeed, how long it has been—an entire century four times over—since I have looked upon a human's face as beautiful as your own!"

The fate that was building up in Florence was suddenly pressing for she was completely captivated by Dracula's stare. For some time, the two remained affixed and gazed silently at each other, and for a brief moment, she experienced a sense of longing and hollow desolation in the vampire that sent a momentary lack of reasoning to her brain. A feeling of pity digested her as she felt his lips kissing and flirting all over her throat. She quivered in languorous ecstasy.

Vlad rose back and looked at her with the most earnest glance a creature of the night could muster and said, "The night was made for lovers, but alas, for those that loveth not spend their lives in solitude and sadness forever searching aimlessly. The nights turn into months and then years—and in my cursed state, even lifetimes of dark loneliness! Hence, when King love cometh may no man stand between I and the ardor worth preserving, for it is the very essence of my yearning fight . . . and for me time remaineth still!"

His bruising weight suddenly fell upon her body and she fainted whilst the hypnotic power of the monster upon her seemed to flow throughout her entire body. The final words she could remember in her dream was the Count saying, "For the blood is the life! And the youthful blood ye crave shall be yours for the taking! It is the gift of eternal juvenility! And it is I that can provideth this to you!"

The livid white face and red eyes sprung back, revealing the white fangs that in seconds pierced the skin of Florence's jugular vein. A shock of sudden pain filled her body, causing her to shake with emotion until tears begun to fall down her cheeks. And then a sort of placid feeling came over the woman as the Count latched on with drawing consumption and she could feel the vital fluid of life flow out of its shell. As if in protest, she reached out toward Dracula's chest. Her touch found the necklace hanging around his throat, and he fingers latched on to it as she gave an absentmindedly gentle and benign smile.

Though Florence could not recall the events of that remarkable night for a lengthy time henceforth, when the memories eventually resurfaced in vivid reveries, she described them as a paradox of mixed emotions—ones horrible yet pleasurable: "I sensed a peculiar turbulent exhilaration that 'twas gratifying, ever and anon, fused with a indistinct awareness of trepidation and revulsion. I was mindful of a love mounting into reverence, and also of abomination."

This sensation continued for over half a minute until the fiend abruptly pulled back. Simultaneously, he ripped open his shirt and held up the nail of his right index finger, which resembled more like a claw of a raptor. Ready to make an incision over his left breast, he hesitated and then looked upon the sleeping face of Florence Stoker.

Though she was partially drained of blood, she lay peacefully in a solemn, weakened state of elegance with her perfumed hair spread gracefully about her pillow. Seeing this the Count instantly pulled back.

"No, it is all too soon!" he said divergently.

He quietly gazed at her for some time with eyes that seem to have softened. There were vast areas of white on each side of the dark iris that made him resemble somewhat as he appeared in his mortal state: Wallachia's bold Prince. He drug his tongue over his bloodstained lips such as that of a forklike serpent after gorging itself. Standing erect, he displayed several red beads of blood that had freshly fallen from the corners of his gore smeared mouth staining his fair ruffled shirt. Florence's breathing was shallow but steady as he watched her linen nightgown rise and fall in quiet fashion in sync with her resting diaphragm.

"Sleep well, my child, and do not scare thyself of the dreams ye manifest as the horrors I knowest will soon be mingled into your own. And the memory of tonight will be a strewn dream of distant images by the time thou awaketh. For soon thy will be my bride, and until we meet again, I keepeth ye with watchful eye and mind."

After kissing the woman's voluptuous lips, the vampire vanished in the lingering dank, foul air that chilled Florence Stoker's chamber well into the night.

* * * * *

Normally, Florence Stoker was always up bright and early preparing breakfast every morning; however, the following day she was not in the kitchen, and the absence of pots and pans knocking about was missing from Noel's accustomed ears. The peculiar stillness worried the lad; henceforth, he entered his mother's boudoir to query the reasoning behind this strange desolation and was shocked at what he found—his mother was still in bed . . . ill-looking . . . nonresponsive.

"Mum! Are you all right?" he called out to her.

She answered not.

Her complexion was of a ghostly pallor and slightly drawn. Her breathing seemed difficult, and her lips appeared unusually pale.

Noel rushed over to her side and began shaking her violently in an effort to wake her.

"Mum! Wake up! Wake up!"

After a few additional attempts, she began to moan quietly and started to stir. Upon this Noel noticed two small indentions on her neck directly over the jugular vein. They were fine and slightly swollen at the edges such as that of a bite from a small animal. Noel jumped back in astonishment and cried out, "No! It can't be! How did this happen?"

His mother must have gone on a tidying spree of some sort because the trail of salt he and his friend Jonathan had left was gone entirely. This was indicative of the higher supernatural power that seemed to haunt their very world.

Within a few minutes, his mother gathered what wits she was able to muster, and began talking to her son in a dreamlike state. She was lethargic and appeared frightened by something, yet she could not remember why or any of the details from the prior evening.

Noel noticed something glisten in his mother's right hand. As she approached closer and studied the object, he recognized it as a beautiful necklace with a broken gold chain. Master Stoker had never seen anything in his mother's collection before, for if he did, he would have surely remembered its uniqueness. Florence saw the confused look on her son's face, and upon gazing at it herself, she too looked perplexed.

The centerpiece was a kind of amulet with an unusual giant red stone in the middle of what appeared to be a pentagram with seven points connected to seven stars that lined up perpendicularly.

"Mum . . . where did you get this?" Noel asked urgently.

"I . . . I do not recall," his mother responded hesitantly. "Perhaps your father left it in my jewelry box as a surprise before he left, and I just discovered it last night."

Noel eyed his mother suspiciously as he took the object from her hand and sat it on her dressing table. And then the two of them noticed the diminutive mass of black, white, and grayish fur curled up in the corner of the room.

"The monkey!" Noel shouted.

"Bother! Have pity on the creature!" Florence followed.

But the poor lemur was cold. Though its heart ceased to beat somewhere in the night, it was apparent it died in a state of absolute fright; its eyes were still wide open and wild with frenzy.

"Say it is not so!" the woman cried as her son took a sheet and wrapped up the stiff animal. "What did this, Noel? Did you hear it cry out in the night?"

"No," he answered hesitantly. "But that is the way *he* wanted it."

"Who?" Florence answered with a puzzled look on her face. "I fail to recall any disturbance or alarm, though I feel as if I have dreamed for an eternity . . ."

His mother concluded she would call on Mr. Gilbert to dispose of her pet in the garden that morning and to investigate into replacing it with another exotic species—a chimpanzee, perhaps?

While Florence was left to her own devices to retrace her actions and memories from the previous night, Noel proceeded to prepare breakfast for three as his mate Jonathan would be coming by soon to join him on his walk to school. But all along the way, the former kept prying at his mother's memory until she was able to shed some light and detail of her condition. Though Noel hazarded a guess, the grim reality was somewhat unbelievable, nonetheless, and he required all the information she could provide as he and Jonathan still needed to locate and stomp out Dracula's lair. Furthermore, Noel had to somehow convince his mother that his Dad was not speaking folly, and there was, indeed, serious purpose for his travels abroad. The Stokers were all in grave danger, and Noel sensed this shadow of dread. However, to uplift and cast it out, there was plenty of dirty work to be done.

About the time Noel brought their food to the table, there came a knock at the door. Upon seeing it was his friend Jonathan Watts, Noel rushed him up and the former joined the others in the kitchen. Entering with textbooks in hand, the younger lad had a look of amazement upon his face, for not only was his best mate cooking, he was doing it on a school day! He cheekily smirked at the sight and a slight laugh followed, but upon seating himself at the table, he glanced over at Noel's mother.

"Limey! Whut in the 'ell happn'd to ye, Mrs. Stoker?" he asked with utmost surprise. "Ye are wan-lookin' this morn!"

Florence was beginning to break out of her funk after putting away a cup of hot tea and a muffin. After patting Jonathan on the head, she answered him in a quiet tone, "I must have fallen asleep at my window and left the sash open in my carelessness. Though I do not know how long I slept this way, somehow during the night, I must have found my way back to my bed—as this is where I was when Noel awakened me. It was all quite mysterious for I seemed to dream about it over and over during the night—this . . . this flapping . . . and buffeting of the sort—and then I woke up very late but still feeling extremely tired and sluggish. And there lay my poor, pitiful, little pet lemur on the floor . . ."

"Daid?" Jonathan blurted out with a surprised look of speculation.

Noel gave an affirmative nod and caught his friend's attention by discretely pointing toward his mother's neck without her noticing. Jonathan reeled back in his chair with a short gasp. Florence picked up on this reaction.

"Though I do not fancy the thought in the least, I believe a bat bit me during my watch at the window! Tho' I am quite embarrassed by it all, these marks must have come from such an animal and explain the queer noises I heard in my sleep. And then too I vaguely remember seeing such an animal outside my window . . . in the short distance! It is all very odd, I know . . ."

Noel and Jonathan looked at each other, and without saying a word, their hearts sank in their chests and their countenances changed to ones of dismay.

"What else do you remember, Mum? Do tell, please, as it is all very important!" exclaimed Noel.

His mother looked at him curiously. There was a long pause as Noel and Jonathan sat staring at Florence with spellbound looks. And then she finally shook her head in despair and waved her hands at them wearily as if giving in or giving up on the matter.

"Nothing at all! My mind is bloody well blank of it except for what I already told you both!" She quickly changed the subject and passed it all off in a stern manner when she followed up her speech by saying, "Fiddlesticks! Now bugger on off to school and think no more about it! I am going to wire Doctor Van Zant to inquire about a rabies shot, and if I keep having spells of restless sleep, I may entreat him for a mild draught . . . now off, you two!"

Starting up from the table, they each picked up their books and began to walk toward the door.

Then Jonathan paused and looked at his friend's mother as if suddenly recalling something important.

"Might ye recall an odd bloke in ye dreams—say, 'bout yea tall and pointed nose—such as that of a beak?" asked Jonathan.

Upon hearing this, Noel peered at the boy with a disheartened stare, and Jonathan then realized himself how strange and pathetic it probably sounded. Florence's reaction was none different.

"For God's sake! Heavens, no!" she replied. "What an asinine question!"

She waved them on toward the door, and Noel glanced back with a saddened look of despair and disappointment.

"Mum, we made a trail of salt about your room, but now it is gone. Though it seems very strange to you, it is important you leave things as they are in your room hereafter. Please promise me of this! If not for your well-being for mine and Papa's sake!"

She watched him with confused expression; however, Noel said this with such earnest affection it deeply moved his mother. She quickly altered her tone for normally she would have answered such a statement in a condescending way.

"Noel, quite frankly, I do not get your drift at all, and I am in no state to worry with such unusual matters right now with your father being absent. But I promise you as soon as I am feeling better, we will talk about what is troubling you."

At this, Noel felt best to end the conversation and to meet his friend out on the street. Finally, he thought for a moment and looked at his mother again, but this time changed the subject. Though it was only indirectly, his mother was not aware of this.

"Can I borrow the necklace you woke with this morning?" he asked kindly.

Florence's eyes widened. "What on earth for?"

Noel quickly dreamed up an excuse to satisfy her and answered, "For school—you know, show and tell?"

Florence looked at him with a half-stern, half-doubtful look but saw that he was quite serious about the request and stepped off toward her bedroom. She quickly returned with the piece of jewelry in her hand and held it out for the taking—pointing her left index finger at him as a warning before letting it go.

"You better mind this for safekeeping!" she insisted. "I expect it back when you are through with it!"

He smiled and put it in the front pocket of his trousers and shook his head in silent agreement. Then he turned and proceeded to meet Jonathan below when one final thought came to his mind. Once again, he paused and looked back over his shoulder at his waiting mother for a last time.

"Now what is the matter?" Florence Stoker sighed in exasperated fashion.

"Mum . . ." Jonathan was serious when he asked his question. "You see, there is this tall, thin man . . . all pale and dressed completely in black!"

Her mood quickly changed to one of agitation and she quickly answered in an excited way with frustration in her voice.

"The same bloody man your father claimed to see? Now you too! Hush this talk! Noel, my dear boy, your overtly ambitious will and intrusive, curious nature will one day get the best of you! And naughty children with poor judgment do not foster well in today's society of a strict British moral upbringing! Off with you for good this time! Go on! Or you will be late getting to the school house!"

Her son's acquiescence was acknowledged by his remote silence, but his mood spoke greater volume. The lad hung his head in disappointment, and then he retreated to join his mate outside. But as the two boys walked away, Florence watched them through the kitchen window; and without even realizing it, reached for the two tiny prick marks on the right side of her neck. There was something odd and unsettling about their conversation, and replaying the entire incident in her mind, her head began to ache horribly.

Concluding the cause of her condition was brought on by the bite—possibly even by a rabid bat, she feared—Florence hurried to the hall mirror and looked at the marks carefully for the first time. The puncture wounds were now slightly swollen around the edges, and the clotted blood in the middle seemed to tighten against the sensitive skin, causing it to throb. As she examined herself, the red areas appeared to suddenly radiate a crimson color that stood out dramatically against her fair pallor.

Without warning, a sense of nervous apprehension and urgency stole over her entire body and she collapsed on the floor in a frightened state. Though she could not understand it, there was something about the lesions on her throat that was disturbing. By and by, she sat against the wall in the hallway and scratched her head in deep concentration. She felt like a hospital patient awakening from an acute case of amnesia.

How peculiar? she thought to herself. *Somehow these wounds almost glow in a way that is distantly familiar in a dreamy but nightmarish sort of way . . . it is as if . . .*

Her mind went empty once more. Though her son and his friend had left and were by this time at school, she felt like she was not alone in the house. And then suddenly out of nowhere, the sound of the flapping and buffeting against her windowpane came back to her ears—first softly, but then the racket escalated into a loud, offensive tone.

In total paranoia, she was succumbed with fright. The woman closed her eyes tightly and screwed up her ears with both index fingers. After numerous attempts to calm herself and block out the noise, Florence took a deep breath and made yet another attempt to jar her memory bank.

"The noise . . . the whiteness . . . the glowing red dots . . . they are all . . . Oh! What do they matter?" she sobbed uncontrollably.

As she lay emotionally beating her fists on the cold wooden floor weeping, the small puncture wounds expanded slightly and a glittering droplet of blood trickled down from each against her pale neck, almost resembling a set of livid orbs on a thin, pale face, crying amidst her grief.

CHAPTER 16

Forked Tongues

Come to me, Arthur. Leave these others and
come to me. My arms are hungry for you. Come,
and we can rest together. Come, my husband,
come!
—Lucy Westenra to Arthur Holmwood

hen Jonas failed to reply to Abraham Stoker's despairing
shouts from the kitchen window, Bram felt an aloof gloom
come over his entire body that reeked of sudden fear and unfriend-
liness. The writer then dashed through all the rooms in the house
as he continued to call his name again and again—louder with each
and every attempt. Lastly, he positioned himself at the front door
and hollered out, thinking the man might have been in the small tool
shed that was in close proximity of the front porch. Jonas answered
not, and the Irishman felt his heart sink deep within his chest but
decided to venture out bravely into the vineyard—fully prepared for
the worse and the unexpected.

However, all the self-talk and mental conditioning in the world
could not have made Abraham ready for what he stumbled upon:
"My worn-out body and weary mind were growing accustomed to
the shock and horror that seemed to thrive in Vlad's country, but
the vital difference in what I found in the vineyard is Dracula's evil

was now becoming personal. And the absolute fright that gripped my flesh and scared my bones to stiffness awoke the true meaning of terror in my pulsating veins. For there, deep within the vineyard, was Jonas impaled on a pitchfork."

Bram was thunderstruck for the man was speared back first, thus the poor fellow's spine had to have been shattered in numerous places. Indeed, the monster that committed this diabolical act of carnal cruelty had to possess incredible strength; therefore, the ghoul had to be none other than Vlad the Impaler. Though the poor Irishman had not been harmed directly by the Count—that is, in a physical sense due to his testimonial promise—he was uncertain of how much more emotional and indirect suffering his body and mind would be capable of enduring without severe and lasting damage.

"Oh, merciful God in heaven!" the author cried. "My heart is sickened and the serenity of conscience has blasted me into a state of relentless torture! Hear my prayer and put an end to this madness! Free me now of this devil from the netherworld!"

Jonas was plunged though the spikes at an angle; therefore, two escaped through his lower and upper abdomen respectively, one through the center of his chest and the last through his heart. The handle of the instrument was submerged deep into the ground so far as resembling the display of a scarecrow sent up from hell. And above in the red sky, several large onlooking vultures and buzzards had begun to circle—cawing and battling each other out to make a claim for its supper.

What an ironic end, Abraham thought to himself. *To the bloke who was preparing the stake that would impale though HIS undead heart, 'twas the very monster that ended his own life—in an even crueler fashion!*

Jonas appeared to be looking up to God in prayer with a wild, helpless, glazed-over stare fixed upon his face. A shining stream of blood covered the ground below him where flies buzzed about, landing and taking off aimlessly, wading their feet and wings in the scarlet substance.

"Woe is I! Alas, another travesty in this symphony of horrors that seems to cling to this voyage like a repugnant nightmare of the damned! Aye, my body, mind and soul have suffered long, enduring lashes—beaten and stricken with spouts of paranoia and the paranormal; nevertheless, I shall go it alone and hunt down the fiend and stomp him out to his real death . . . even if I become a martyr by my own accord!" Stoker wrote.

With a heavy heart, the downcast journeyman lowered the body. Next, he built a kind of altar out of an assortment of brush that he located in the work shed. Though it was locked, he quickly found the key on a ring that he rescued from the old man's body. Whilst Abraham was in the shanty, he likewise found the wooden stake Jonas had made that very morning and placed it in a large bag along with a pickaxe and shovel. He also discovered a bicycle in the building which he tied the bag to its rear axle along with his traps. Then wrapping the other two bodies in a table linen and curtain, he quickly transported them out of the house separately and placed each upon the altar.

Concluding the recital of a silent prayer, the Irishman lit the brush and watched the flames quickly devour the Hupnuff family. The terrible sight was one that would linger in one's most disturbing nightmares without end. The trio of bodies soon began to produce a thick, smoldering, reeking cloud that was sickened with the foul stench of burning flesh. It quickly suffocated the crimson sky, where the mixture of cooked tissue and smoky bone created incense so unpleasant that the sky seemingly grew an even darkened hue of blood red. But even still, the birds of prey continued to circle. And though the foreigner could not view them clearly through the bellowing smoke, he heard their maddening squawks all the same. And in a daring act of intimidation, the eyes in the back of the author's skull could identify they were drawing nearer and nearer for their grisly afternoon meal.

Crossing himself, he burst into tears followed by boisterous, uncontrollable laughter. Stoker then threw himself to the ground; and whilst the writer was upon his knees, he held his arms up toward the heavens. The air was becoming overwhelmed by the foul, vile stench of human skin.

"I will never forget the awful stench of burning, decomposing, liquefying flesh!" he later recalled.

Bram was choked with emotion, repulsion, and a touch of insanity that one might feel after being denounced by his creator. Indeed, he felt as if his faith was being tested with numerous setbacks, long periods of gloom and countless spouts of desperation. If more than human consideration was not required of him, he would not have been able to continue to carry out such a cruel and dreadful task. He laughed until he cried and then cried until he laughed and continued this pattern in repeating intervals for several moments until he was empty of any feeling whatsoever. His internal state was becoming a numb, aching void that was hardening with every step of the way. This did Abraham much good for the emotion in him had ballooned to a point of overwhelming and overbearing grief.

"Save our souls! Give us peace! May the father, the son, and the Holy Ghost help a true and honorable gentleman perform his duty for the sake of mankind!" Stoker shouted, looking up to the universe through the now-burning inferno.

The Irishman returned to the house one last time and rummaged through Jonas's wardrobe until he found a suit of common work clothes that somewhat fit. Unlike his English suit—one that had grown both worn and soiled throughout his tour of the "land beyond the forest"—the tourist felt he needed a more discreet set of attire that did not label him as an outsider. The end result was a set of aged trousers, though about a half inch too short, and a neutral shirt that made the man feel a bit too clumsy about the waist, despite his extensive weight loss while trapped in Poenari Mountain.

Upon dressing himself, the sight of a book lying alongside of Barbola's bed caught the visitor's attention. Abraham realized it was a journalistic account for the words *Agatha Hupnuff* were handwritten on the first page. Striking his interest, Bram decided to read bits and pieces he was able to make out or translate by the use of his polyglot dictionary he always carried on his person while traveling abroad. Quickly seeing it was the personal diary of the mother, he became intrigued and hopeful it would explain her death of some twenty years past and would provide some additional clue to the underlying mystery of Transylvania and his grotesque mission at hand:

The Diary of Agatha Hupnuff

April 26—Vineyard very dry. Pray for rain, but none came.

May 15—Still very little rain and crops did not flourish. People becoming desperate for food.

June 6—Famine hit city of Tirgovsite. I pray for family as we still in good health, but still no grapes. Tonight awakened by noise from shed, but looked out window . . . see nothing.

June 8—Famine worsened and many people were sick. Awakened again by noise from shed. Thought to see movement of dark shape but then vanished. Possibly animal Jonas can slay for supper!

June 9—Look everywhere on grounds for animal to no avail. Several people in city die today, and I cannot sleep from these thoughts of terror. God keep my family safe! Saw from window small amber lights coming from shed. Set out to find cause, but they too vanished in film of vapor and fog mist that enveloped the building.

June 10—Family found me this morning asleep in front of shed. This puzzles them all, as they did not hear me leave the house previous night. I have no remembrance of the outcome, only that I set out to find the source of the same red lights.

June 12—Some rain come but not enough to yield crops. People continued to get sick and die. In desperation, men are slaughtering their own sick animals for food . . . even children's cats.

June 13—Woke up again in front of shed. Family worried sick and seem concerned for my safety. Ioan plans to sleep in chair next to front door beginning tonight.

June 15—Dreamed voice came from shed. The tongue seemed evil to me though it promised family would be blessed with bountiful crop. I felt it was deceptive, as there have been none of late. Sense as if I am getting sick as other townsfolk. May God keep me strong until this passes!

June 20—Woke up again in front of shed. Must have crawled out of bedroom window and scratched myself on nails during process as neck is scarred with two wounds. Feel terribly sick and family very anxious about me. May God continue to keep them safe!

June 22—Could not sleep for soon, we will run out of food from cellar. Do not have much money to buy any and townspeople have seldom to sell. During the night, saw red lights again coming from shed. I must have passed out. Barbola claimed she stopped me from climbing out of window once more.

June 28 –Family hungry and many feeding off of blood of livestock. This news is frightening for I had dreamed of doing the same—only it was no goat or sheep but an ugly, unbeknownst wolf-like beast that appeared frail-looking and actually spoke to me in the voice of a man! Oh! But of what cunning tongue it was! I suspect it is the same voice from shed as it promised me rain, though I dare not tell family of this for I wish not to worry them more at present. May the good father preserve my mind, as I am weary and think such very bad things!

June 29—Much joy . . . but not all joy, as I still believe dark cloud over me. It rained today but the marks on my neck are of grave concern as they are more prominent and ugly to study. During the day, I feel deathly ill and sleep for hours, but at night, I come alive again! Son sent for doctor but none came due to much sickness from famine. Must wait turn. So I wait . . .

July 1—More rain! But family behaves strangely around me and speaks superstitious thoughts in private. There is nothing to eat so family drinks wine from cellar. I do not drink and family imprisons me to my own room at night. My mouth and skin feels unusually different. I dreamed of the two lights again, and they speak of a fruitful crop to pass.

July 2—I am stricken with fear and grief and find it difficult to write such blasphemous words about my own actions! Barbola tells me I attacked my husband last night! She believes it was out of hunger! I then jumped from window, and Jonas said he followed me without my knowing and claimed to find me on the throat of neighbor's only living cow. I do not remember anything and pray it not be. My family says it is *all true*! So I dare not call them liars. I am afraid . . . terribly afraid!

July 3—What is happening to me? Doctor came and fled house in fear of something yet he says nothing! Ione insists I look at him strangely . . . daughter away all-day and brought back wolfsbane plant that I fear has made my condition worsen. Though dark times, some happiness came to us today . . . Jonas out tending to vineyard as I write. Signs of growth have sprouted. Hope is all we have! Oh, have mercy upon my soul, dear Father! I feel as if the end is near!

July 4—My hearing has somehow grown to that like a dog! I hear them scheming to move me to the cellar to where they will bolt the door until they find a cure. I must not let them do this, but I am too weak to get out of the bed during sunlight. Father forgive me! What have I done? I hear them coming! They are at the door now . . .

Abraham felt the hairs on the back of his neck jet straight out like sewing needles pricking against his bare skin. His beating heart raced for several seconds and then unwound to what seemed a grinding halt. The room was deathly quiet, and all was still with the exception of the Irishman's mind racing wildly over every detail he had read. In every sense of the word, he was dumbfounded. For this meant the mother had not died of natural causes—as he had been so led to believe. She had become undead! And the extreme ghastly shock of this discovery was to reveal that the family was now true dead whilst she must still be counting the days confined to their own cellar! Furthermore, as of late, they had been feeding her blood— actually keeping her alive by bringing her living animals—until they could rid the earth of the very creature that had transformed her!

In short, the journeyman was absolutely flabbergasted by this revelation. And the more he thought about it, the more his equilibrium became out of balance. "Mine God!" Stoker said out loud in complete awe and amazement. "This explains the wolfsbane that Barbola planted clear around the entire shed! It tells of her eagerness to rescue and nurse me back to health—to help plot out a plan of destruction for Dracula! They desperately wished to somehow reverse the transformation and to save their dear old mother!"

The man had been pacing the floor but finally became too dizzy to stand. The room spun around like a comet. And though the very thought cut him to the quick of his soul, he knew there was only one answer to this discovery. And it was in the cellar.

* * * * *

It was approaching noon when Abraham Stoker once again mustered the strength of a great Irishman and made his way to the shanty. Along the way he gathered up a handful of fresh aconite—commonly known as wolfsbane or monkshood—and was quickly able to locate the cellar entrance hidden underneath a heavy piece of wood that was concealed by a grand trunk filled with all sorts of weighty objects. A large golden crucifix was placed over the door that was also locked by a thick chain. Within several seconds, he found the key on the ring carried by the old man and quietly raised the trap.

A low, dull moan could be heard from underneath, which brought about a tremble of terror throughout his body. The vulgar stench that escaped from the pit below caused him to hesitate and reel—almost falling backward—and to flee out of sheer horror and vileness. After reclaiming his courage, Bram lit a piece of candle he acquired from the house, and after crossing himself, he proceeded down a dark set of steps.

The groaning became more profound, and with every release of the cries came a burst of air that seemed consumed by a filthy mass—reeking of evil proportions—that clung to the hole, waiting to attack each breath as an infectious disease that tramples upon a living cell.

As Stoker descended further the foul, loathsome air became stagnant, and the reeking odor caused him to shutter to an utmost degree of nausea. The malodorous atmosphere became fainter, and soon he saw a small area that once may have resembled that of a woman's boudoir: there was a nightstand with a broken mirror directly across from the stairwell pushed against the wall. The room was covered in dust, at least an inch deep, with masses of cobwebs thick in every corner whilst others were scattered upon the ceiling.

The author could no longer hear the dreadful sound of the deadened moaning, and this thought brought about an immense feeling of discomfort that was even more harrowing than if the groans had continued.

It knows, the Irishman thought to himself. *It smells my warm life blood pumping in my veins!*

Because there was absolutely no light in the place he stood motionless . . . listening . . . and then with trembling hand, he proceeded to shine his candle in all directions.

Suddenly, he thought he heard heavy breathing and saw a quick glimpse of what appeared to be a shadow of an object dart by a medium-sized cot that was pushed up against the corner of the cellar. In fearful reaction, he immediately pointed the light of the candle back in that direction, but then the form was gone.

A few seconds passed as the iron nerves of Abraham Stoker began to collapse all at once. And at last, without any warning, there came a loud wailing—such as that of a wild beast under attack—and the figure of a raving woman lunged forward at the intruder, grabbing for his throat with razor-sharp claws. In retrospect, she could have easily been called a specter of the tomb than a woman.

The journeyman started backward just as the creature jerked and fell face forward on the dirt floor that was covered with pieces of tattered, rotting cloth, and animal bones. The writer gasped a sigh of relief when he noticed a large chain was bolted to the fiend's left leg that restricted it from reaching the staircase. He eyeballed its entire length, following the pieces of cold metal to the other end where it was mounted to an iron loophole that was built into the adjacent wall behind the bed.

Abraham swallowed hard. He expected the thing below was not actually the sweet, middle-aged woman that was gleefully displayed on the family's living room painting but rather a wretched nightmare of her and one of the Count's undead abominations of God.

Though he was prepared to discover an unsettling sight, he had not expected in his most horrifying dreams to encounter the scrutiny that was lying before him.

"The woman lifted herself with hands and knees drooling like a rabid dog. She appeared to be around fifty-five years of age, yet her waxen pallor and dirtied, brittle hair made it difficult to hazard a sure guess. Her eyes were blazing like a mad lunatic gone berserk, and they burned into me—like hot poker on a block of ice! With every exhale, it delivered the surrounding air a gust of a pungent, vile smell that would cause the squeamish to regurgitate their last meal! Auuughh! To think of it sickens me!" the author recorded in his journal.

"Her once-attractive dressing gown was now in rags and was soiled all over with scarlet stains that resembled that of arid, dried blood. She champed her fanged teeth together so fiercely that it caused her mouth to bleed, producing a trickle of gore that ran down the corner of her bottom lip and chin."

Her sight repulsed Abraham, yet he felt for the woman's soul all the same.

This . . . this very creature was Barbola's mother! he thought to himself.

"Good God!" he sobbed out loud, unsure of whether his emotion was predominated by that of sadness, rage, pity, or terror.

Then the creature spoke. "They normally bring me a live animal," the woman sneered grimly with a sinister stare. "But with their forgetfulness comes a splendid reward! I will gladly accept thee instead!"

In an instant, the thing bolted forward in the Irishman's direction, practically snapping the chain in two. Seeing that her next effort might yield a more gruesome result, Bram reached into his pocket and produced a handful of wolfsbane. Holding it with outstretched hand, the woman's reaction was both startling and equally peculiar. Almost instantly, her wild behavior became tame, like a zoological attendant giving a sedative to a raving animal. Her face fell, and her nostrils twitched nervously as she backed away.

Again she spoke, but this time with an almost pleasant tone that caused the journeyman to believe it was a different voice altogether.

"If it is not food you come here with, then why do you come?"

Abraham hesitated for a moment, looking into the woman's eyes. They now appeared to be gray and almost human. Almost . . .

"With deepest regret, I bear news that your family is dead," said Stoker.

The moment the creature comprehended these words, it seemed to go through some kind of physical change—almost a complete metamorphosis—that was both shocking and pitiful to watch. Her hard lines and cruel features of her face seemingly disappeared as she fell onto the musty mattress in an utter state of despair. All the horrifying vampiric traits supposedly escaped her body though the paleness remained, albeit now lessened. She then began to sob, and as the writer approached her in reserved, cautious fashion, he was amazed to see the stream was actually tears of blood! After a brief moment of silence, she looked at her visitor crestfallen and solemnly asked, "How? How did they die?"

Not exactly prepared for this question, the Irishman was hesitant to answer at first; however, feeling that the creature would know if he were inventing a reason, he decided to answer truthfully.

"Dracula . . ." he replied. "They were all murdered by Prince Vlad Tepes of Wallachia."

As of late, Abraham had witnessed the creature turn from a vampire into a woman and then from a woman into a mother. Notwithstanding, he was not quite sure what the thing before him had become after hearing his last response.

She seemed to cry out in a sort of deep, emotional pain that struck the bare bone of her unrestful soul. Her eyes became fixed and blackened, and suddenly, it appeared that an empty shell of a woman sat wailing in pain. Hitherto, the distress turned to resentful anguish, followed by a sense of numbness that caused Stoker to grow nervous. By and by, she looked up at him and finally said with what seemed to be of the most earnest, extreme emotion: "It is all over now. If I stay here, I will surely vanish without blood. But if Dracula becomes true dead, what will the rest of my mortal existence be like in your world without my family or purpose?"

The author said nothing as the woman stood up and walked toward him. As the two strangers from different worlds stood there studying each other intently, it was as if a destiny of death 'twas keeping one of them from leaving the cellar.

But which one?

And as their heads worked up each one's scam to fool the other, one could almost hear the cool, morning drop of dew fall from a leaf and splash against the ground above. The Irishman cowered back, guarding himself with a hand full of wolfsbane clinched in his pocket. But the poor soul that stood before him seemed to plead desperately, begging for physical and spiritual liberation. The man's heartstrings tugged hard at his conscience and convinced him that the aconite was required not. And as the foreigner placed the strong plant back into his pocket, the dark prisoner spoke to him once more: "I can see in your mind you are planning to seek vengeance against the maker of all this evil, but before you do, I beg of you to set me free! It has been two and twenty years since I have seen the light of the sun! Please give me the key to this chain!" she said, holding up the lock that bound her to the black hole. "In return, I give you my word that I will not harm you! I want to see them one last time before my heart burns to ashes and my soul is released from this misery!"

Bram stood still with a look of deep thought upon his face. He was in complete awe of this change of behavior over the woman. Still seeing he was not totally convinced, she continued, changing her demeanor to an even higher degree of desperate tone and trusting nature.

"I implore you, sir! Please let me go! Oh, woe is me! I promise you no harm! In exchange I will give you some information on the Master that will help you in your mission! Please! I beg of you! Show some pity on me, man! Can't you see? Don't you understand what you would do to me—by keeping me here to die?"

She was down on her knees, pounding her fists to the floor in short gasps of breath. This latest development struck a chord with Abraham Stoker. He hesitated for a moment, as if unsure, and then the writer approached the stairwell with a countenance of sorrow and melancholy.

The thing behind him began to moan again in even deeper desperation as the journeyman proceeded to climb the gloomy staircase. And upon pausing a second time half way up, he turned and looked back at the emotional wreck of the creature over his right shoulder.

Stoker than flung the set of keys to the woman, and suddenly, there was a wild dash followed by the clanging nose of iron chains and the rustling of heavy locks. Nevertheless, the Irishman was not totally up the stairs when he felt two hands grab hold of both his ankles and bolted him backward, causing Abraham's body to fall, hitting himself headlong down several steps.

With grinding eyeteeth, the woman lunged in a hellish panther-like movement. The blood in Bram's veins froze as two orbs blazing with fury fixated themselves on his bare throat.

"Damn your forked tongue!" he shouted angrily. "And to think I pitied you! Turn me lose, you wretched woman!"

Stoker kicked and pulled himself up two sets of steps until his eyes could see the flooring of the shed above him. The vampire was weakened by her evident hiatus from feeding, and the author continued to latch on and pull both their weights upward to the shanty. Along the way, the thing hissed and laughed and cunningly spoke: "The thirst for human blood is a lust like no other foolish man! Never believe the words of a fasting child of the night! *Hah!*"

The foreigner reached for the heavy, wooden door of the cellar, and as the creature's head appeared in plain view, he freed his right arm. Finally, with all his strength, he slammed the door back, striking the thing hard on the top of its head. It stammered back with the blow and cursed madly. As it gathered its wits, the Irishman used these few seconds to pull himself all the way up and crawled across the floor of the shack.

The vampire continued to approach him chuckling under its breath. The building in all its total blackness was absent of any windows, so thinking on his feet, Abraham Stoker positioned himself boldly in front of the entrance.

Within less than a minute, the thing crawled out of the pit and stood up—hovering over him, smiling with a sinister stare that could only mean death . . . and in this case, something even worse lay beyond.

"Say your prayers, brave Irishman," the creature said slyly, "for I can see your fear, feel your weakness, and smell the blood that flows freely in your veins! But . . . bid your farewells, because soon your life will be mine! And then you too will see what it is like to be imprisoned for eternity!"

With those words, Abraham flung open the door to the shed, entirely exposing the room to the brilliant rays of the sun. Shrieking wildly, the thing in front of him covered its face as the pale, chalky skin began to melt and peel away. And as time elapsed next, it seemed to go into a fit of convolutions and rage as it fell to the ground. Stoker watched in amazement as it tumbled into a smoking heap and crawled aimlessly upon the floor.

It then seized a blanket of some sort that covered a trunk or wooden box in the corner of the room and flung it around her body, wailing and shrinking back in sheer, unsung agony. Crossing himself, the writer took hold of her legs and began to pull with all his strength. In the vampire's weakened state, he found the creature to be of lightweight and nonresistant as he proceeded to drag her body outside. To an onlooker, the hideous scene would have appeared to be of an animal control person who had caught a mangy dog that was being hauled off to an unpleasant end.

Though the thing under the covering flailed its limbs, it was too weak to fight as the Irishman had expected. Within minutes, they were upon the altar Stoker had built, and bravely picking the thing up, he hurled the swoon on top of the still smoldering bodies that was once Agatha's immediate family.

"May God's will be done!" shouted the author, crossing himself once more.

With this came a prominent blood-curdling scream so intense and painful Abraham had to cover his ears. It did not take long for the smoking embers to inflame the blanket, devouring the creature in a holocaust of infernal heat. Though he was not certain if the cries were from the woman—hitherto recognizing the corpses of her mortal family—or of her unbeating vampiric heart as it was cooked to an ember.

The last coherent words of the monster came through so plain and recognizable that Bram could swear they were the words of a woman—a wife, a mother—and not those of an undead bloodsucker:

"Unclean snatcher!" cried Agatha Hupnuff. "Beware of the thieving cadaver and he who has more than one resting place!"

The journeyman pondered these puzzling words for a brief moment until his thoughts were interrupted by an ear-piercing screech that lasted for almost an entire minute.

"The short time seemed an eternity," the foreigner wrote. "And then the wailing became a faint groan, and all was calm but the popping and crackling of ashes. Nonetheless, that despairing shriek still rings in my ears, and I am afraid it will stay with me until the judgment day."

CHAPTER 17

Tragic Telegrams

6 September—Terrible change for the worse. Come at once. I hold over telegram to Holmwood till have seen you.

—Telegram, Seward, London,
to Van Helsing, Amsterdam

"Behold where stands th' usurper's cursed head," stated MacDuff, Thane of Fife, dressed in complete Scottish attire. "The time is free."

Picking himself up off the floor, a simulated decapitated and heavily garbed Henry Irving looked at the young actor with a state of mediocrity and boldly stated, "Need I remind you this 'ere play, in all sense of the word . . . is 'bloody', hence your lines should be spoken as if you have tragically arisen from the inability of the doomed, escaping an evil destiny!"

Indeed, when it came to rehearsing, Henry Irving was known to throw himself into the role to where his skin would contract and his eyes would shine.

"His lips grew whiter and whiter and his skin more and more drawn as the time went on, until he looked like a livid thing," leading lady of the Lyceum Ellen Terry once recalled. Likewise, the actor demanded accuracy in every detail, no matter how trivial. Stoker once recalled a practice of a scene where Hamlet's mother, Gertrude, drank the poison and Hamlet grasped the goblet to prevent Horatio's drinking from it. When Irving flung the cup down, it rolled to the footlights; he watched it curiously and then ordered the prop man to have it fitted with bosses below the rim so it would not roll. Moreover, the actor ordered that the wine should not spill; colored sawdust would be substituted.

"There is a sort of fascination in the uncertain movement of an inanimate object," the author remarked. In sum, Irving could not allow a rolling cup to divert the audience from him.

Amidst three weird sisters being helped into gothic costume came a shout, "Telegram for Mr. Irving!"

"I'm Henry Irving!" said he, dusting himself up off the floor. Taking the telegram, he signed for the delivery and thanked the messenger.

"That will do for now . . . break for tea but be ready to deliver your part afterward with more emotion! These characters are deep and mysterious and should be able to materialize in the psychology of the viewer!" exclaimed Irving, addressing the nobleman.

MacDuff nodded and walked off into a large set that resembled a desolate, brooding castle to which an unsuspecting stranger is lured and then visited in his sleep: Shakespeare's immortal Macbeth. Henry Irving, the Lyceum's owner, was anxious to get the fall season underway with himself as the lead role where the foul contagion of evil is seen as an infectious plague to be destroyed by teamwork. However, a lack of cooperation could prevent the play from getting underway due to Irving's numerous frustrations doubling as stage and box office manager. Nevertheless, the other employees secretly wondered if Bram Stoker's prolonged absence would shed a deeper respect and appreciation for the man that Irving so egotistically pushed and bossed around. Indeed, Abraham wrote an average of fifty letters a day for his boss to ensure the theatre's patronage did not dive into the red. And coming from a man who had also skipped his own honeymoon to prevent the Lyceum and its Lord's needs from falling behind, Stoker's prolonged absence spoke volume to all.

On this particular afternoon, actor Henry Irving was in an even gloomier and shorter mood than usual, and his crossness had made the cast and crew apprehensible. For the previous night, a carpenter had thrown his coat with a ham sandwich in the pocked over an open trap. Nosing and nudging for the food, his dog fell through and was killed instantly. Appearing to be overtly saddened by the ordeal, the actor carried Fussie back to his dressing room, where Ellen Terry witnessed him talking to the terrier as if it were still alive. And it was only this morning the actor had the dog's head stuffed and the remains buried in the Hyde Park Dogs' Cemetery. Nay, the plump, self-indulgent Fussie would no longer sup on terrapin and other delicacies in Irving's sitting room where they had always sat opposite one another simply adoring the other. Fate had it that the actor would need to find a replacement—a new companion—and his best mate, Abraham Stoker, was nowhere to consult the matter.

With the unread telegram still in hand, Henry made his way to his dressing room, passing by numerous actors and actresses out of character discussing various topics, none relating to protagonists, motivated by power and ambition. Upon seeing the man, they quickly curtailed their private conversations and immediately began to rehearse his or her parts on the sidelines. Noticing this behavior, Irving gave a crooked smile under his pointed nose and reinforced his stern policy with theatric flair and macabre humor: "Hark! Opening night beckons, thus be prepared . . . lest we too shall expect to receive the curse of immortality from a covenant of supernatural forces and die with our throats slashed!"

Indeed, Macbeth was by far Irving's favorite production and he expected only the best. Likewise, he fancied himself in the leading role, and though the honorable Hamlet was appealing and the public loved the evil Mephistopheles, it was always Macbeth that ceded the utmost internal reward and personal satisfaction.

The actor had a niche for playing characters who were mysteriously thrilling—those that people secretly known to them in childhood dreams by enacting a life in which terrors are as fascinating as delights, ghosts and death, agony and sin, became like love and victory phases of an accountable ecstasy. Stage villains such as Mathias,

Mephistopheles, and Iachimo—not to mention the squat Emperor Napoleon—all became a sinister caricature of his own stage characters as mesmerist and depleter, an artist draining those about him to feed his ego. In retrospect, somewhere along the journey, Irving found he had lost himself along the way. Indeed, a consistent feeling of happiness was a far cry away, as was an internal sense of peace.

As Irving made his way backstage, he paused for a moment to read the telegram:

> YOUR PRESENCE IS NEEDED AT THE STOKER RESIDENCE. FLORANCE IS IN GRAVE HEALTH.
> —DR. VAN ZANT

Henry Irving stood motionless in the corridor when behind him approached his good friend and stage dresser, Walter Collison, an older gentleman with bald head and frail face that seemed very happy to be there. His eyes bugged with excitement.

"Ma lady is ready for her sleepwalking scene, gov'nah!" he said, interrupting, failing to notice Henry's mind was preoccupied by more important matters.

Henry disguised the emotion the wire had surfaced in him and gave a halfhearted smile at Walter that probably would have appeared forced if Walter had not been so overzealous at the present time.

"You sweat twice as much in that [role]!" the later said, gallantly touching the shirtsleeve of Macbeth.

"Thank you, Walter," said he, nodding, "but I am afraid that you will have to keep things moving without me. Something unexpected has come up that will require me to be out the rest of the afternoon."

The man's face suddenly fell but then nodded in full conformity and bowed out of Henry's way. Folding the telegram in half, the actor placed the paper in his front pocket and walked in the direction of his dressing room.

Upon entering his quarters, Irving realized he was not alone. Standing in the corner, gazing at several Kodak photos of recent performances tacked to the wall was an Englishman, probably in his late thirties, about six feet, smoking a cigar.

"Are you the owner of this theatre? Irving, is it?" the man asked, nodding as Henry entered.

"Indeed so, and who are you, kind sir?" replied the actor.

The man flashed a badge that he pulled from his navy-blue overcoat. "Inspector Cotford," he answered.

The man was dressed in a pair of light-gray slacks and scuffed-up brown loafers with a white dress shirt and paisley bowtie. His skin was fair, and with his swept-back brown hair, his presence made him look more like a door-to-door pen salesman than a detective.

"I am pleased to make your acquaintance," Henry politely answered. "May I offer you a seat and a glass of brandy?"

The man sat in a guest chair that was positioned directly across from the actor's makeup mirror.

"No, thank you, I never drink on duty," replied the man.

Henry poured himself a glass and, after taking a swig, walked to his wardrobe and removed a set of street clothes.

"My apologies for omitting all formalities, but I beg you to get directly to the point of your visit. You see, I have an emergency to attend to . . . and if you do not mind me changing whilst we talk . . ."

"That is quite all right," the inspector said, talking to the door of Henry's closet. "I have come to ask you about a woman that was found a short while ago not far from this theatre. She was murdered shortly after midnight."

There was a slight pause of silence from both sides. Finally, Henry's voice came from inside the wardrobe. "Yes, how can I forget such a horrible incident—especially when it hits so close to home. I believe it was a Saturday night . . . the closing night of *Faust*?"

Inspector Cotford stood up and pulled a Kodak from a briefcase that had not escaped his left hand.

"Perhaps this picture will refresh your memory even more as I have reason to believe she spoke to you after the performance."

Henry recalled the young girl that had stood in closing night for the female lead that had taken ill. He recollected that night the extra had seen the fan waiting outside his dressing room as he reprimanded the actress for her meek delivery. Realizing the inspector must have interrogated a sampling of cast and crew members from that evening's performance, he thought carefully for a moment before choosing to speak again.

"Please, may I have a look . . . as in all modesties, I have many fans that drop by for autographs and it is hard to say for certainty."

Emerging from the wardrobe wearing a fur-collared overcoat and black wideawake hat, Henry took the picture and proceeded to study the photo.

The dead woman's middle-aged face was pretty—just as he had remembered her; however, the lovely blue dress was completely splattered in gore. Her neck was mangled as if a mad dog had attacked her . . . or a wild man had torn her throat open with a butcher's knife.

Henry nodded as if to recall the woman's visit but articulated his reaction and response with precision. He wanted to ensure anything that he said matched up against what the young actress had shared. Moreover, it was paramount that he be careful not to disclose anything that would elude suspicion or could be taken out of context.

"Yes, I remember her vaguely. She waited outside this very room as she wanted to commend me in person for a successful show and to solicit my signature," said Irving.

"What did you autograph?" asked Cotford. The actor looked at the ceiling as if searching for a visual representation for an answer.

"Ahhh . . . a program, I believe. Yes, I am quite certain it was a program," he finally replied. "But, dear sir, why do you ask something so trivial?"

"Because there was no program found on the scene. No means of identification was on her person when her body was discovered. Did she tell you her name?"

"No."

"Did she mention where she lived?"

"Certainly not."

"Perhaps where she was going?"

"Negative!"

This back-and-forth exchange lasted for some while, and recalling the urgency of Dr. Van Zant's telegram, the actor decided it was time to end the conversation.

"Inspector Cotford, please excuse my frankness, but I really have nothing further that might be of any benefit toward your investigation. She told me absolutely nothing but that she enjoyed the play; then I courteously let her out the back door into the alley."

Irving reached for a furled umbrella that hung from a stand next to the door. The inspector took this as a clue to be on his way.

"To me it sounds like the Whitechapel murders have begun to spread to the West End, so unless I am a suspect for Jack the Ripper, I really think you are talking to the wrong man. Furthermore, I need to excuse myself as I must catch a cab to South Hampton to assist a friend in emergency."

Cotford stood with his briefcase in hand. "If you can think of anything after the fact, please be sure and contact me at headquarters," said the detective inquisitively.

The man bowed and thanked Irving for his time but, upon leaving, turned back one last time with a puzzled look upon his brow.

"This is like no Ripper murder that Inspector Abberline or I have witnessed! This crime does not match his style—she was not an unfortunate, there are no missing organs, and there is an unusual loss of blood. Plus Research Agent Singleton found a hair sample . . ."

Henry Irving's ears froze.

"But there must be something wrong with the lab analysis. As farfetched as it may sound, it suggests she was slain by a corpse! When the medical examiner made an attempt to collect another follicle from her fingernails, it was discovered the body was missing from the morgue!"

* * * * *

Hydrophobia, or rabies, is an acute and deadly viral infection of the central nervous system: a disease that is perhaps one of the most terrifying known to man. Caused by a virus that dwells in the saliva of an infected animal—some that may serve as natural reservoirs of the virus—it is commonly transmitted by bite wounds.

In the United Kingdom, there have been situations in which a person had close contact with a contagious animal and had not known it, as when a sleeping person awakens to find a bat in the room and can't see a bat bite or scratch or unaware of mucous membrane exposure. Florence Stoker reported that just within just a few hours of awaking to find the bite wounds on her neck, she had begun to suffer from a loss of appetite, nausea, tiredness, headache, restlessness, stiff legs, and an unusual sensitivity to sound, light, and changes in temperature.

Dr. Van Zant swiftly administered a passive immunization, an anti-rabies vaccine that was first given on a human subject less than a decade earlier by French scientist Louis Pasteur, which was a very important step forward in the field of bacteriology. By injecting antibodies or disease-fighting proteins into the patient, the human rabies immunoglobulin shot commences the body producing its own protective antibodies within a few days; however, if left untreated and the patient is left to their own devices, the treatment had been proven to not react to individuals as they progress in the advanced stages of the infectious disease. Florence Stoker was quickly beginning to show mixed signs of the mid- to late-stage symptoms of rabies, in addition to some other signs Dr. Van Zant had never seen before: episodes of irrational excitement which alternate with periods of alert calm, followed by convolutions and extremely painful throat spasms; a fear of liquid, particularly blood; and a great loss of blood that could not have been the result of a "common" vampire bat.

Based on the fact that advanced symptoms of the disease were beginning to materialize, this suggested that Florence Stoker's body was not responding to treatment. Since the final stage of the disease involves the victim usually dying from cardiac or respiratory failure within a week after the appearance of rabies symptoms, while the excited state is most prominent, it was critical that appropriate action be taken. If the patient survives this stage, muscle spasms and agitation stop, only to be replaced by a growing paralysis leading to death.

Around 6:30 p.m., a cab pulled up and parked in front of 7 South Hampton Street. With the engine still running, Henry Irving jumped out and handed the driver a pound note without standing by for returned change. He proceeded to rush up the drive, and as someone from an upper window must have seen him coming, he did not have to knock and was thus immediately buzzed upstairs.

The ambience and peculiar scene he instantly encountered as he walked into Florence Stoker's bedroom was one of most funereal fate and disturbing proportions. For lying in the center of her bed was something that moderately resembled the wife of Abraham Stoker, but somehow, she had been robbed of her natural beauty. She was thin, languid, and appeared to be almost bloodless. She lay in a contorted position, partially on her left side, with one arm hanging on to the headboard—as if the bed were going to consume her at any moment—whilst her other arm was lying palm up hanging off the edge of the mattress. Her legs were widespread with both feet dangling as if preparing to give birth at any moment. Her complexion was a radically ghostly pale, and she appeared to be in some sort of stupor. She mumbled something under her breath that seemed to contain the word *drink*, but then her eyes shot wide open as if experiencing a sudden image of terror. She jumped maniacally as if suffering from convulsions to where her buttocks actually left the bed for a fraction of a moment. Finally, she seemed to faint and swooned herself into a restless sleep, gasping for air every several seconds.

"For the love of our God and Savior! What has happened to her?" Henry Irving said desperately, almost forcing the words from his pursed lips.

A man was at the back of the room pacing back and forth, stopping every now and then to gaze out the window. The actor's sudden outburst startled the man, for the latter jumped back into reality from an otherwise session of the brain that was devoted to science. He stood approximately five feet tall and had bushy salt-and-pepper hair that was not combed in any particular way and resembled an unorganized mass, which had just surfaced from a sandstorm. He wore a set of small round spectacles that sat high up on his flat pug nose, and above his bright-blue eyes was a pair of equally bushy graying eyebrows that were always arched from a wrinkled brow— indicative of a man deep in thought. His bold forehead was also lined from age and signified the wisdom of a scholarly English gentleman of about sixty years of age. Dressed in a brown suit with a matching waistcoat and conservative ascot, he had been so occupied analyzing his patient's condition that he had practically forgotten that he had let Irving up; moreover, the former began to blush from embarrassment for not taking notice of his caller's presence.

"Good evening. Henry Irving, I presume?" the man said, holding out his right hand. "I am the Dr. Van Zant that telegrammed for you. I must apologize for such clumsiness and not introducing myself sooner. As you can see here," the doctor said, waving his right arm in the direction of the ailing woman, "Madame Florence's status of health has me both intrigued and baffled! I hope you do not mind me calling on you, sir, as I understand her husband is out of the country, and though I made an earnest attempt to identify his whereabouts from the Mrs. I was unable to make any sense out of her. Noel told me that you are the man's employer, and perhaps you are aware of where Abraham should be telegrammed? Eh?"

"Where is the boy?" Henry immediately replied, removing his hat.

"I did not feel right by him seeing his mother in such a miserable state as this, so I asked him if there was anyone he could stay with until her health improved. He mentioned the Watts family about three blocks away, I believe? Eh?"

Before the actor could respond, Florence suddenly gave a great gasp, which alarmed both men to the point of rushing to her side. She seemed to struggle for breath for several seconds as sudden short wheezes caused her diaphragm to flutter. The Doctor bent over and propped up her head with a pillow whilst Irving looked on in wild wonder. By and by, her breathing was regulated again and her chest rose and fell in customary fashion. Pushing the centerpiece of the round rims toward the base of his nose, the eldest continued, "I have diagnosed the Mrs.'s condition as an unusual form of the *Rhabdovirus*. This is a progressive neurological illness characterized by an ascending paralysis—usually starting in the feet and working upward—but in Madame Stoker's case, it is even more severe!"

"Are you saying the old girl is rabid?" Henry asked appallingly.

The doctor shook his head and then motioned for the actor to step toward the window where he began to speak in a whisper.

"Look at the paleness! Eh? Her limbs are cold to the touch as if she is suffering from postmortem! I'm afraid that if the diagnosis of rabies is confirmed after symptoms began to develop, there is no cure for active disease and the prognosis is ultimately fatal. Though she was treated immediately with an anti-hydrophobia injection, her body seems to be rejecting the drug! Therefore, I administered a human diploid cell vaccine followed by a RVA right after I telegrammed you and must now sit back and observe! I pray it attacks the *Rhabdovirus*."

"And if it does not?" Irving reluctantly asked.

Hearing this question, the man of science seemed to stammer for several seconds. His countenance changed to an even more serious and graver expression as he finally murmured his final answer into the actor's ear in an almost scary and suspenseful tone.

"The name *hydrophobia*, meaning 'fear of water,' was given to rabies because the ancient Greeks observed that rabid animals were averse to water, but actually, the truth is that they cannot drink because of throat paralysis, eh? The infection starts with a 'prodromal period' that usually lasts for one to four days. This period can include fever, headache, malaise, muscle aches, and loss of appetite, nausea, vomiting, sore throat, cough, and fatigue. I am afraid the patient has shown or complained of all of these. Infected people may also experience a tingling or twitching sensation around the area of the animal bite. Did you notice the two wounds on the side of her neck? Eh?" Van Zant asked, pointing to the patient. "They appear to be enlarged, mangled, and irritated as if she has clawed at them in her sleep or state of confusion!"

As Henry took off his overcoat and placed it over a chair in the corner of the room, the doctor went on. "The second stage begins with symptoms that look like those of an encephalitis or inflammation of the brain. There may be fever with symptoms of irritability, excessive movements or agitation, confusion, hallucinations, aggressiveness, muscle spasms, abnormal postures, convulsions, weakness or paralysis, and extreme sensitivity to bright lights, sounds, or touch!

Madame Florence insisted today that the drapes be pulled back and was already showing signs of uncontrollable rage. She seemed to calm down soon after I met her wishes, but I cannot surmise if it was the actual light of the sun that agitated her so or perhaps a hallucination of a bat, eh? You see . . . the attack seemed to frighten her, so I believe this is why she sleeps so restlessly! Indeed, she has experienced a great shock, and I must not leave her alone in this condition. However, I need for you to wire her husband as I hope for the best but fear the worse! We need to be ready, just in case!"

With his head tilted down slightly, the physician stared at the Lord of the Lyceum through the thick round frames intently, which were again resting at the end of his pug nose.

"Just in case? Doctor, I don't understand!" shouted Henry Irving. "Is there something that you are not telling me? Are you saying she is dying?"

Van Zant held up his index finger and made a "tsk-tsk" sound as if relaying the other to lower his voice or take back the question. "Sufferers also experience and increased production of saliva or tears and there can also be an inability to speak as the vocal cords become paralyzed," continued the scientist. "I am afraid she is beginning to show signs of this development. The last stages of rabies produce symptoms that reflect the infection's destruction of many important areas of the nervous system. There may be double vision, problems in moving facial muscles, abnormal movements of the diaphragm and muscles that control breathing and difficulty swallowing. It is the difficulty in swallowing—combined with increased production of saliva—which leads to the 'foaming of the mouth' usually associated with a rabies infection. Finally, the patient can slip into a coma and stop breathing. Without life support measures, death usually follows within four to twenty days after symptoms begin. But I cannot predict nor prevent such a travesty without successfully deriving with a proper diagnosis, eh? This is why I cannot leave her! To study her, my friend, is the madam's best hope! But there are other things that concern me!"

His look fell from that of an experienced doctor to a doubtful man that seemed to be in the center of solving the darkest secrets of the universe.

"Go on, please explain!" said Henry, urging him on.

"Her condition also seems to be integrated with that of a wasting disease—such common to that of consumption or tuberculosis. Though I am still waiting for lab results, if I am correct, this makes the lady's condition ever more grave! Eh? Likewise, she seems to have lost a great deal of blood! I have ruled out anemia as a prognosis as that condition targets only the loss of red blood cells, whereas my tests show a loss of whole blood. What baffles me is, where did the loss come from? Eh?" And taking hold of the right, wired earpiece of his spectacles with the same hand, he repositioned them before as he continued: "A common vampire bat bites and licks—typical of a cat lapping up a saucer of milk. The bat that preyed on Madame Florence would have needed an entire colony of friends and would have had to lap feverishly all through the night and way into the morning to steal only a fraction of that much blood! Eh? There are many pieces to this strange puzzle . . ."

At the precise moment the doctor said the word *blood*, Florence suddenly jolted up in the bed and back down again, gasping and rocking—wheezing as if to catch her last dying breath. The two men raced again to her side, and Van Zant wet her lips with a moist towel. In about two minutes—a moment that seemed to the men to last several hours—the restlessness passed, and she fell back into a slumber. However, Van Zant's expression fell to one of acute alarm and sternness.

"Quickly! Roll up your sleeve whilst I get out the instruments! It is far worse than I expected!"

Unsure of what was happening, Henry began rolling up his left sleeve reluctantly and asked in a very direct way, "What kind of operation are you performing here? How in God's name can you expect help from an actor who knows little to nothing about medical science?"

"Hurry! Hurry! There needs to be an immediate transfusion of blood, and I need a donor! Her body has not been able to replace the blood she lost from the bite because of her wasting condition and the wild attack to her nervous system, eh? Her heart rate is very weak! We have no time to lose, my friend. We are in a mortal hurry!"

Though this operation was still revolutionary, 'twas far from being the first case tried. Indeed, in 1818, James Blundell, a British obstetrician, performed the first successful transfusion of human blood to a patient for the treatment of postpartum hemorrhage. Using the patient's husband as a donor, he extracted approximately four ounces of blood from the husband's arm and, using a syringe, successfully transfused the wife. And also devising various instruments for administering such operations, he assisted in performing the first successful whole blood transfusion in 1840 to treat hemophilia. The device, named an *impellor*, provided blood under pressure to the recipient, whilst the gravitator, a gravity-fed apparatus, was to help in this last extremity by transmitting the blood in a regulated stream from one individual to another, with as little exposure as may be to air, cold, and inanimate surface. Ordinary venesection—being the only operation performed on the person who emitted the blood—and the insertion of a small tube into the vein usually laid open in bleeding, being all the operation which it is necessary to execute on the person who receives it.

As Henry sat on the edge of the bed, he watched the doctor set up the surreal procedure in a frantic pace with deadly earnest. He was hard at it, and although the description of the instruments appeared complex, their use was simple: after applying an antiseptic to control infection, a needle was inserted into the main artery of Florence Stoker's left arm whilst she slept soundly on the bed with her back arched and head resting upward on her pillow against the headboard. Next, a supporting device clamped the instrument in place that was attached to a channel, by which blood was expelled, that was adjoined to a double-way cock that connected the valve to a syringe. Then the doctor tied a snug piece of cloth a brief distance above Irving's right elbow and finally proceeded to insert a needle that fed to a valve that entered the cup.

"Are you ready to begin? Eh?" asked Van Zant to the distraughtly awaiting Henry.

Seeing the actor nodding in acknowledgement, the doctor turned a plug on the double-way cock a quarter degree, which began to channel the blood from Irving's arm into the head of the syringe, and gradually began to fill the cup. In a regulated stream, the gravitator begun its remarkable work, and a steady flow of blood soon filled the device and made a direct path to the sick woman's arm and began to fill her veins.

With an extended arm, Henry towered directly over her, watching the entire process unfold as every ounce of man in him stood out bravely in rare form and zeal. Van Zant watched keenly too as to observe that the cup never emptied itself entirely; otherwise, air might be carried down along with the blood. Likewise, he eyeballed the transfusion carefully to ensure that Irving's plasma—which was issued by dribbling from his right arm—might not be admitted into the receiver, as its fitness for use was doubtful. Moreover, he managed the accumulation of fluid in the receiver to prevent its rise above the prescribed level, and he supervised with attention the countenance of the patient to guard against an overcharge of the heart. This latter cause was of great importance.

Within about ten minutes, the ghastly procedure was over with. As Van Zant was putting away the instruments, he continued to monitor Florence's condition. Her body had regained some of its fullness, and her breathing was more regular. The paleness of her skin soon turned several shades darker, and the haggard and wasteful look was gone thus replaced by her youthful and natural beauty.

"Incredible!" the doctor whispered under his breath. "I have never seen anything like this! Eh? Her heartbeat is growing stronger, and her body seems to be fighting off the advanced stages of the bite in such a rapid fashion! Indeed, it is a true marvel of science!"

The doctor suggested that Henry lie down after drinking something to rehydrate his system and rest his body from the procedure; however, the actor denied both requests, claiming he had business to attend to.

"Young man, your body must be weak from this ordeal, and your system needs to revive itself before you go your way. Please, I insist! A glass of fluid and a few minutes' rest will help regain your strength. Your body needs to replace at least a fraction of the blood you lost before any strenuous activity . . . eh?"

"On the contrary, I shall be fine," Irving firmly replied. "I rally your concern—nevertheless, this sudden tragedy has set the theatre back a rehearsal, and I have a prudent errand to run before I head back to the Lyceum. Through all the excitement, I have lost track of time and did not realize it was so late. I am certain the employees are on pins and needles!"

The doctor saw the actor was persistent and was amazed at his diligence despite the pang the operation had to have evoked on his body. As he watched Henry retrieve his overcoat and hat, the Doctor stood back and looked at him closely. Though they had just spent an evening together, the time had been preoccupied in such a mad state of affairs Van Zant had yet had a moment to study Irving's appearance and character closely.

He was unusually tall and lanky, and considering the amount of blood that he just disbursed, the Doctor was bewildered that his complexion had not changed the slightest degree. His skin was before—as it was then—the color of parchment. And his shaggy eyebrows and his trionic mop of graying black hair mussed the pincenez slightly askew on the famous aquiline nose; deep furrows bracketed the thin, stern mouth. Indeed, he seemed strong as an ox and a fine but certainly uniquely eccentric specimen of an Englishman.

As Van Zant watched the actor put on his wide-awake hat, he recalled the main reason why he had summoned Irving there in the first place.

"Please, sir, wire her husband and ask the gentleman to come at once! I know this is a lot to ask, but until he returns, I need for you to help stand watch, as the lady should not be left alone . . . eh? I will stay the night but must be back to my office in the morning to think and to read up on some of the latest medical journals for some clue as to what just happened here. Furthermore, I want to contact a few collogues of mine and a particular specialist that deals in rare blood diseases to search for some answers!"

Henry nodded in acquiescence and said, "Kind doctor, it is the least I can do on behalf of the Stoker family. I will be back in the morning by seven o'clock. Again, I can't thank you enough for treating her. You are, by every definition of the word, a true and honorable fellow!"

As Henry Irving approached the door, he turned and looked back at the woman—now breathing in a regular, rhythmic pattern—and saw very little sign now of the unnatural, agonized woman that wildly took command of the room less than an hour before. If it were not for the two marks that still dominated the left side of her neck, he would have had to fathom whether it all was just a demoralizing, atrocious dream.

* * * * *

The sun was about to set as Henry Irving left the Stoker residence. Unable to find a cab or coach anywhere, the actor decided to walk a few blocks over to the Covent Garden Market district and take Charles Street to the telegraph office. He passed several groups of people cluttered together like packs of wolves shopping whilst several soloists walked by hurriedly as if rushing to catch a train that was steaming up to leave its platform.

As he made his way up Charles, he thought about how unusual and powerful—yet horridly fascinating all the same—the evening's events had left him. How unconventional it was to know that the blood that had left his body willingly was now flowing in the veins of Florence Stoker and aided in keeping her alive to fight off her peculiar illness. Next to living out his fantasies on stage, it was a power rush like no other he had ever felt before. He also pondered over what his counterpart, Abraham Stoker, would think of the act of generosity—if, for the very donor was still unsure at the moment, he chose to tell him.

When the Lord of the Lyceum was four blocks from the telegraph office, a feeling of uneasiness hit him all at once. It was like a sensation that animals are rumored to feel right before an earthquake. Irving's head began to swim wildly, which caused him to stop and grab hold of the base of a street lantern to retain his balance. Several passers-by slowed down to take notice. In particular, one man pointed Irving out to a young lady that was attached lovingly to his arm whilst another woman in a white petticoat carrying a ruffled umbrella as a walking stick grabbed her young son, covering his eyes as if he had just been exposed to a leper.

The dizziness lasted for some time as beads of sweat formed on his face and palms. A man approached him and asked, "Art' ye all right, mate?" but the actor spoke not and took no notice. Indeed, he felt too ill to speak. But instead he closed his eyes tightly, thinking that he ought to have obliged to the Doctor's wishes to drink and rest until his body was replenished.

When the strange episode had passed him by, he picked himself up and quickly made his way to the telegraph office to send a wire to Abraham Stoker. Upon entering, he found the place was empty with the exception of what must have been an eighteen-year-old boy operating the front counter.

"May I help you, sir?" he said quickly but in a suspicious tone as if he had been dosing on the job.

Irving shook his head as he took a form off the counter and wrote out a message that read:

FLORENCE HAS TAKEN ILL. YOU ARE NEEDED AT HOME. RETURN TO LONDON ON THE NEXT TRAIN LEAVING BUDA-PESTH.
—HENRY

Addressing it to Abraham Stoker at Castle Dracula, Poenari, Romania, he began to hand the paper off; however, after thinking for a moment, he hesitated. After dating it, Henry motioned to the boy he was finished. The former handed it to the lad along with some currency without saying a word. The teenager wrote something at the bottom of the form for the dispatcher and then walked toward the back of the room, to where several men of various ages were seated, punching out Morse code. However, in a few seconds, the boy came back with a perplexed look upon on his face.

"Excuse me, sir, but you wrote the twelfth on the form," the lad said as if confused.

"Yes, that is correct," replied the actor in a pompous tone. "Now can you kindly give me my change back as I must be on my way?"

"But . . ." began the young attendant as if unsure how to respond, "I assume there is some mistake. I hope you don't mind, but I did read your message. Please forgive me if I appear too forward, but do you intend to postdate a telegram such of this nature? You see, it is only the fifth, sir."

Henry Irving gave the boy an impatient glare that suggested further annoyance and that he cough up his change and say no more regarding the matter. Taking the pound note and few coins from the youngster, he said snappily, "Child, thou art quite inquisitive for a youthful chap of your age. I am fully aware what day it is, thus the date I wish the telegram to arrive at the Transylvanian Alps is precisely what I have asked for. Now I suggest you take your meddlesome charm elsewhere!"

The actor left the office in a huff and decided to catch a cab back to the theatre, but because it was approaching ten o' clock, he would have to walk toward Piccadilly square to flag one down.

Many a person considered then—as many still do—a walk along the River Thames as a relaxing way to unwind at the close of an eventful day. For centuries, its current had winded its way through downtown London and carried on for two hundred miles capturing over two thousand years of history. It harbored such world heritage sites such as Hampton Court, the Tower of London, Big Ben, and the Houses of Parliament. Though the mighty river had contributed to such positive land-breaking events such as the boarding of the pilgrim fathers on the Mayflower, it also had a dark side, and it had even been dubbed, at times, a River of Death. Indeed, it had witnessed many wars and battles, and the secrets that took place in the Bloody Tower were meant to stay buried deep in the red waters that, over years, cleansed themselves just in time for other disasters.

When Irving was just a small boy, the combination of foul smells and diseases linked to insanitation forced commissioners to comply with Mosaic Law and employ a team of engineers to revamp the cities drainage system. And until late, the river had been known as London's sewage quagmire. Because the Thames ran through a low-lying valley throughout the centuries, the river had burst its banks, swamping riverside settlements and causing death and destruction mixed with garbage and human waste. It was unquestionably Mother Nature's own flood plain. For the reason that riverside properties had always been desirable, Britons ignored the lessons of the past and continued to build on the highly desirable riverside land. High embankments and flood alleviation schemes were often seen part of man's fight against nature, and for the dejected, the Thames Ferry was the precise place to jump to one's death. Moreover, throughout the ages, countless bodies of murder victims had washed up along the shores. And from time to time, an unfortunate—one who made his home under a bridge or along the banks—would hit the bottle a little too hard and slip. Indeed, the cold waters shocked many back to sobriety, and may God show mercy on the poor blokes that could not swim.

On this particular night, however, there was not a soul in sight. As Henry Irving walked along the walkway, the moonlight was bright enough on the water to cast a rippling effect that seemed to dance off of a large sheet of glass. The actor stopped for a moment and gazed over the south bank and the green and leafy islands along the side of the riverbank. Looking down at the water for a brief moment below, he stared at his own reflection. Though the night was peaceful and the waters appeared calm and clear of mystery, the image of the Lyceum Lord appeared to foretell a different story. The faintness he experienced earlier began to return again. Keeping his footing as to not fall headlong into the river, he waited a moment for the uneasiness to pass. And then seeing he was alone with his God, he reached into his coat pocket and pulled out a blue purse that contained a brush, a looking glass, and a hand fan. Taking the bag in his right hand, he flung it over and watched it land directly in the moving water. After stalling a brief spell to witness the sinking current carry it downstream and out of sight, he spotted an unoccupied cab within his distance driving slowly up the street. Waving both his arms over his head, Henry walked swiftly in its direction. The driver soon stopped and rolled down his window.

"To the theatre, my dear fellow . . ." Where there were other bitter waters to explore.

CHAPTER 18

A Pact with the Devil

The Draculas were, says Arminus, a great
and noble race, though now and again were sci-
ons who were held by their coevals to have had
dealings with the Evil One. They learned his
secrets in the Scholomance, amongst the mountains over Lake Hermanstadt, where the devil
claims the tenth scholar as his due. In the records
are such words as *stregoica* (witch), *ordog*, and
pokol—Satan and hell; and in one manuscript
this very Dracula is spoken of as *wampyr*, which
we all understand too well.

—Mina Harker's journal

As Abraham Stoker walked away from the cremation of the entire
Hupnuff family, he felt bewildered, deadened, and hollow
inside. His face was ashen gray, and at that particular moment, he
sensed within him a mood so deep as death than if the weight of all
the earth's soil had him entombed six feet under.

"How shall I recollect the solemnity of such a moment of gloom,
sadness, and horror that invokes such a travesty of the heart—to
unveil the blackest things that the world or netherworld could stand
to bear? How shall one begin to fathom such absolute terror, know-

ing all good and well that it is only a prelude of what is left to come?" Stoker wrote in his journal. "Such active thought causes my bones to shake with fear and my blood to run ice cold! But . . . alas! I must not shrink or falter! There is dirty work to be done! Notwithstanding how grueling the passage of time can be when one is so far removed from loved ones! Assailed by agonizing disappointment and severe iniquity, I have resolved to commit my thoughts to paper, as I am utterly unaided in my strange quest. Without rashness, I alone must arm myself from danger and prove persevering in a foreign, untamed element.

"I think a great deal—in fact, likely too much—for my day-dreams invade me with vague fears, whilst my nights blast me with horrors so unlike anything of earthly significance could surmise. Alas, this constant state of melancholy, terror, and solitude may, by and by, take a brutal blow to my disposition if left unchecked. Of the few folk the Count has graced my spirit to encounter, they have only been at a distance or of an acquaintance that spoke a language I could not understand. The barriers this embarkation has rendered me are becoming dreadful, and oh, how I long to talk to someone other than he! Though Dracula's words are astonishing and equally intriguing, they fall on one's ears as drops of poison. Nay, I cannot describe or fully comprehend the long-term damage without comparing his terms to that of the art of ancient Chinese water torture—where the water in truth be droplets of contaminated blood!"

Upon seizing a bicycle in the Hupnuff shanty, with his bags and tools abound, the Irishman sat off and followed the sometimes-confusing road signs until he reached the intercity of Tirgoviste. After a slight communication breakdown with a station attendant, he reserved a seat on a noon train that would land him in Snagov, a city located 40 km north of Bucharest, by 1:00.

Whilst he waited, Abraham's stomach gave in and he decided to lunch. Though Stoker found himself too distraught to eat, he did so anyway to keep up his strength. He located a quaint restaurant two blocks from the station that served him *Tochitura*, roast pig done up with red potatoes, purple cabbage and a pickle dish known as *polenta*.

The waitress, a supremely happy woman who appeared to be in her early fifties, raved about her homemade *zacusca* and was insistent that the author try some at "no cost." Not wanting to appear rude, he did so as she stood over him with her hands on hips, tapping her foot patiently for some kind of response.

The dish resembled a sort of relish made of bell peppers, onions, and tomato juice, almost too salty for his taste. But Bram smiled politely in approval, and this gesture triggered an immediate dance of gayety in the waitress. This slightly amused the writer, who could not figure out how she was able to shake in such movements wearing a dress that fit way too tight for modesty.

When the entertainment was finished, the journeyman turned back to his plate to see a heaping spoonful more had found its way there, but upon hearing the oncoming train, he quickly washed all of it down with several glasses of wine, paid his bill, and reclaimed his bicycle parked outside. Deciding to ditch the bike, the Irishman boarded the train with his traps and tools in hand and found a comfortable window seat. In less than five minutes, the train left the platform, and he was on its way.

Though the outside appearances of the land were inviting to Abraham Stoker, he knew all too well that looks could be deceiving and that his destination—in all probability—would be perhaps the closest he would ever be to hell on earth.

Notwithstanding, Romania was one of the most fascinating, beautiful countries the foreigner had ever seen, and despite petty details of modern commerce and efficiency, this seemed somehow appropriate in a land that inspired thoughts of music and poetry. As the train steamed its way southeast a visual of fertile plains and soaring mountains attacked the passenger's eyesight in all directions. Indeed, Romania was a feudal land. Its people, gifted artistically, tended otherwise to be somewhat inefficient and unhurried. The country was an anachronism in this busy century, as its workmen could spend fifteen years with picks and shovels digging a tunnel under the railway tracks at the main station in the capital. This amusing thought made his native Dublin seem like the capital of modern industry.

As Stoker rolled onward, he passed several quaint towns and villages that were surrounded by friendly brooks and fragrant meadows. Colorfully clad peasants and musically gifted gypsies seemed to jump out of them amidst a colony of hay carts surrounded by giggling naked children. Closing his eyes, the author heard their gay songs, and his head was filled with laughter.

Oh, what I would not give for a dreamless state of sleep—for a deep faculty of slumber wrought by their resident voices that seem isolated from the evil Dracula has plagued me with! Bram thought to himself.

These folk were his first contact with the subtly subjective moods of the Orient that, he had learned from Barbola, were reflective in many aspects of life in Romania. As she had explained, for centuries, the land had been under Turkish rule. Now a proud and upcoming Western nation there still clung to her something of the aura of the mystical east. And though Romania was still a little country, though independent in spirit, the Irishman noticed its peoples had a less exalted image of themselves: at a time when Cuba was fighting Spain for its independence and H. G. Wells was writing *The Time Machine*, a Romanian beekeeper sold his honey on the side of a dirt road less traveled, and at a time when art nouveau was becoming the predominant art style in Europe, Romania was taking its inspiration from the Baroque period, and while Petipa Ivanov's *Swan Lake* had just delighted an audience with a first performance at London's symphony hall, a colony of gypsies could be heard conversing, singing, and playing a sad haunting melody on the violin during an evening in Snagov—a refrain that spoke of a people forever outcast from their true Indian home.

The writer listened to the soft violin that continued to play to his ears, and within a few minutes, he was lulled into the beginning stage of restful sleep.

"What occurred next must have been a queer energy dream," the writer recounted. "I was falling into a cold, dark abyss. My vision suddenly became impaired and my hearing muffled. But some while after my senses adjusted, I satisfied my reasoning by concluding I was in water. The ambient noise caused my hearing to grow restless, so I looked around in consternation as I adjusted to my surroundings.

Suddenly, the sharp peal of what appeared to be a bell of some sort was coming from ahead of me, but the murkiness of the water would not permit me to identify the source for sure."

But it was not the unusual ringing sound that caused Stoker to bite his lip to suppress a scream; rather, it was the sudden, shocking visual of bones which exposed themselves to his immediate right that caused him to shudder in fear. The writer tried to swim away, but his reverie forced him to remain stationary in the same vulnerable spot. By and by, the muddiness of the deep was blinded by a bright blue light that revealed the remains to not be human after all but rather those of an animal. Indeed, by what the author could tell by studying the bone structure closely, the skeletons of many oxen rested at the bottom of this lagoon.

"I was gladdened at this latest discovery; whilst hitherto, my dreams seemingly have been paved as a stony road to hell!"

After a few passing seconds, Bram's eyes caught the blue light as it began to dim in intensity and followed it through the cloudy darkness to what resembled an ancient structure at the floor of the mere. The light was actually a blue flame that shone through the opening in what was unmistakably a thirteenth-century Orthodox Church.

Instinctively, the foreigner felt a sudden compelling rush to swim to the flame for somehow he knew the light was giving away the location of Vlad Dracula's ill-gotten loot; however, the ember faded as quickly as it appeared, and the voice of Countess Dracula spoke: "Do not be deceived. The love for fortune comes with its price, and its temptation is only a deterrent from what our heart truly desires."

As her voice broke off the sight of Florence Stoker lying on her bed with a pale, haggard countenance flashed in the writer's mind, causing him to jump wide awake. His mind then darted immediately to an early memory of a conversation with his mother, Charlotte Stoker: "Deep within the mountains and unexplored caverns of the old country are rumored to be inhabited by a coven of evil spirits. And on the eve of St. George, they grow restless. For it is said that on this night, all the witches meet and hold court at the Gania Drakubiy. Any mortal that has ever found this devils' garden is said to be sacrificed in a great feast to Satan himself! Since I was a little girl, every fifth of May we protested the dark influences and burnt offerings that the Sabbath worked to conjure up by placing square-cut blocks of green turf in front of each door and window."

"What will this do?" young Stoker asked.

"It bars their entrance to our home and stables and protects us and our sleeping cattle. But do not fear, for this same night, legend holds one could grow rich for all the treasure buried in the ground to escape the clutches of enemies gone by begins to bloom and reveal themselves by giving forth a color of wine to serve and guide favored mortals to their place of concealment. Earthen jars, old Dacian coins, and golden ornaments have been unearthed when a distant bell toils and the bluish flame is revealed. But alas, ye must be quick to mark the sight for the glow will disappear as quickly as the peal of the bell is silenced, never to be revealed again until a year later."

"Why would spirits want to give away their treasures?"

"Some are benevolent, while others are of a pernicious nature. So you must go carefully!"

* * * * *

A clock at the station in Snagov indicated it was a quarter past noon when Abraham Stoker reached its platform. As there was no other obvious means of transportation available to him, he began to walk aimlessly around the station. After several disappointing attempts, he was able to cough up a few quid to get precise directions to Dracula's tomb, and having wasted nearly an hour, he was then on the correct path to Lacul Snagov.

The journeyman set off down a long country road with traps and tools in hand, and it did not take long for him to see that Snagov was a charming and serene place. "It seemed at every turn, I met up with a dancing gypsy and her minstrels stationed next to a wagon with a sackcloth top and a goat tied to its side," Stoker recalled. *Oh, how I long for dancing, loud noise, and free air—nevertheless, the ironic timing of the occasion would be the equivalent of a man at death's door being thrown a birthday celebration!*

After about a two-kilometer hike past numerous small country cottages, Bram stopped at the top of a dirt path leading toward a crude wooden dock on a freshwater lake. There, about a quarter of a mile across the water, he could make out a small isolated island. Overlooking—but nestled in an imposing forest—the stout brick spires of Snagov Man Stirea protruded amongst a foggy mist and an abundance of wild drooping reeds that seemed to suffocate the fourteenth-century edifice.

Dripping from perspiration, Stoker approached a wiry young man that exchanged him a small wooden rowboat for a few coins. Using two planks of wood as oars, Abraham proceeded across the water.

Water . . . the writer thought to himself, recalling his energy dream. *Is there significance?*

Snagov Lake was one of the deepest lakes in the country of Romania, and not only was it a source of fresh water but it also provided fish for food and was a natural defense against attack. As the author rowed peacefully, a sort of eerie feeling came over him as his mind replayed his dream at the bottom of the lagoon, and he kept his eyes and ears wide open for the slightest hint of interference. The foreigner's throat quivered as he continued to paddle his way whilst shaky breaths escaped through a set of pursed lips.

About halfway across, strong winds emerged out of nowhere and rummaged the deep waters. The Irishman was afraid they would push him back in the direction he started or, even worse, toss his boat over. Thus, he made haste and began to row almost wildly whilst the sky began to turn a dark, cloudy gray.

Legend claimed there was once a bridge that stretched to the island for Vlad himself took solace on the island frequently. According to Barbola, Dracula was said to have wreaked all sorts of havoc as well by building a jail with a special torture chamber where prisoners were killed by fire or iron and then thrown straight into the lake by a form of cannon. It was also believed when prisoners prayed in the medieval church to the icon of the Blessed Virgin, a trap opened up at the altar, dropping them onto sharp stakes below. It was during this time of Vlad's reign when it was suggested the bridge sank along with fifty-nine prison passengers. Throughout the following centuries and exhibitions, an unprecedented number of skeletons had been found with their skulls missing. This thought caused the bitterly cold water to appear stained crimson, and Bram's heart sank in his chest as he rowed onward.

Coupled in the reeling wind, the frightful—yet familiar— sound of a ringing bell filled the air, which originated from the old sunken church. They seemed to pay homage to the crimes, drama, and death that sent many to a watery grave.

"Oh, Mother of God! 'Tis all true!" Abraham exclaimed aloud.

He crossed his chest and said a silent prayer for them and rowed even harder to race against what seemed to be a terrible storm that was brewing. Suddenly, a sound of thunder shot through the air— much like the loud echo of gunfire—and beads of sweat formed and clung to the writer's brow as he quickened his pace even harder. Whether it 'twas thunder, actual gunfire, or his imagination, Stoker was uncertain, but an icy chill began to creep up his legs—a morose feeling that he liked not. And in an attempt to shake this unpleasant sensation, the journeyman began to recap important events the Hupnuff family shared regarding what 'twas supposedly the Count's final resting place.

The island of Snagov, one of several Vlad Tepes Dracul III had endowed in his role as prince of Wallachia and one he almost certainly fortified as an excellent strategic refuge at a time when war and invasion were the constants of life, was actually a small town in the Impaler's time with its own treasury, mint, and printing press. The bastions reaching to the water's edge gave comfort to boyar and peasant alike, both of whom could hide within the sanctuary of the Church.

According to Barbola, foundations of buildings, bones, and pottery shards indicated that the island had originally been a Bronze Age settlement; and evidence existed that Snagov was not only a monastery with its chapel, dormitories, cells, and chapter house but that it had been fortified against raving armies, with buttresses, trenches and thick walls.

The rolling clouds above Abraham Stoker turned a bleak, smoky overcast and almost blocked all sunlight. An occasional crash of thunder startled the Irishman, and he began to sense a feeling of coldness about the place that made him extremely nervous and overly anxious.

"For the love of God? How much bloody further is it?" he cried out in a voice broken by emotion, raising his head upward at the still-darkening sky as if in a remonstrance with the almighty. For the past several minutes, it seemed as if he were rowing in place and making no ground whatsoever.

And then, without any warning, the ripples in the lake being produced by the oars seemed to grow dim and take on queer shapes all around Bram. As he continued to row in an almost frantic pace to beat the oncoming storm, he watched what appeared to be an abyss or whirlpool that was rapidly surrounding the boat. Eyeballing the oncoming danger, the author began to paddle feverishly to get away from it—first to the left and then to the right—but still onward it came. For a lack of any other solution, he steered the boat in the opposite direction and began to row back to the landing from whence he came.

Stoker became overtaken by fear as a dark mass followed him under the rowboat and began to evolve. The journeyman felt the muscles of his abdomen close up on him like tapering coils. The sheer terror that possessed his body caused him to reel backward. He stumbled—almost falling headlong into the deep, cold, murky water—but recalling his reverie, he quickly reclaimed his balance as he watched in utter amazement. The abyss was coming to life—in ghostly human formations! They swarmed around the boat so fast that Abraham could barely make out the features of what seemed to be hundreds of lost souls swarming out of the original sunken church.

The constant and rapid swirling movement of the apparitions caused the boat to tremble and knock about wildly, and the quick integrated glimpses of endless arms, faces, and legs left him dumbfounded and terrorized with an unspeakable horror.

"As I stared into the water, the twisting movement almost slowed down to a crawl, and I began to make out detail of men, women—and God help us . . . even children! The features resembled those of Romanian, Turkish, and Moldavian Boyars, peasants, and Voivod stature of many age groups. And as a bolt of lightning streaked across the sky, the twisted faces began to scream all at once! How shall I even try to describe the harrowing wails in those faraway voices? They wrung my heart as would an innocent herd of cattle going to slaughter!" wrote the Irishman. Calling out to the voices, he answered, "I'm not here for Dracula's damned treasure! I'm here for your Master!"

Random ghostly figures began to change shape yet again, and within an instant, Abraham Stoker was able to quickly identify the innocent souls from the evildoers for the wretched specters quickly disintegrated into screeching corpses that actually took solid form and began to reach their skeletal hands out of the water and into the boat. Bram turned a greenish pallor as he saw that numerous phantoms were headless. And upon this realization, it donned on him what exactly they were after. Their ghastly purpose was resting on his *own* shoulders . . . thinking desperately what to do next.

With both oars in hand, Stoker began to attack back, thus knocking skeleton after skeleton off the side of the boat and back into the water. Suddenly, an idea came to him, and he began to loudly recite the burial service.

"I am the resurreccio and the life (sayth the Lorde): he that beleveth in me, yea though he were dead, yet shall he lieu. And whosoever lyueth and beleveth in me: shal not dye for ever" (John 11).

And pouring his entire soul into it, the foreigner began to row vigorously toward the island. Rain started to fall briskly from the sky, and as thunder rolled over the lake, the Irishman began to recite louder and row even faster, stopping every several seconds to cast an unwanted passenger back into a watery grave.

"I know that my redeme lyueth, and that I shall ryse out of the yearth in the last daye, and shalbe covered again with my skinne and shall see God in my flesh: yea and I myselfe shall beholde hym, not with other but with these same iyes" (Job 19).

The band of thieves, murderers, and rapists seemed to laugh a hideous noise in unison as one decapitated skeleton leapt totally out of the water and into the boat before Stoker could fight it off with one of his oars. Seeing something out of the corner of his eye, Bram spun around to see it come at him with outstretched arms. It began to claw and pull, aiming for Abraham's head, but the victim took one of the pieces of wood and struck the pile of bones in the center of its ribcage, knocking it back to its home with a heavy splash.

The absolute fear that swallowed the man's pounding heart sent a maddening shock of adrenaline to his brain and then outward through his entire body—as if a rush of electricity calibrated him to realize the true, grim reality of the situation. The journeyman's eyes were void, his gripping knuckles were intensely white, and extreme persistence that displayed in his jaw spoke silently of the understood danger at hand.

The severe downpour began to fall harder as the other fiends in the water seemed to grow angry and began to all reach for the boat at once, rocking it in an attempt to capsize their unwanted visitor. Upon seeing this, foreigner crossed his chest and began reciting the burial passage even louder and continued to row.

"We brought nothyng into this worlde, neyther may we carye anything out of this worlde. The Lorde geveth, and the Lorde taketh awaie. Even as it pleaseth the Lorde, so cummeth thynges to passé: blessed be the name of the Lorde" (Timothy 1:6; Job 1).

Through the rain, he could see the shore of the island less than a tenth of a mile in front of him, and he charged with arms as firm as steel.

Another headless remains came at Bram's throat again with a tearing motion that ripped at his collar, piercing his skin in the process. A small trickle of blood flowed down his shirt and neck that seemed to send the beheaded army of darkness into a frenzy of applause. This reaction of appeasement urged the thing on, and it reached for Stoker's head, seizing his jugular with both bony hands.

"For the love of God . . ." the Irishman shouted, gasping for breath. "Go back to hell you cursed heretic!" He then reached for the pickaxe that was lying on the floor of the boat. But to Abraham's disbelief, when he turned around, the rotting remains had up and disappeared.

The necklace! the writer thought. *It had touched the cross that hung around my throat!*

"What a kind, sweet, woman!" he said out loud of the lady on the train over to Transylvania. "God bless you for leaving it for me!"

Stoker was certain that the oncoming storm and ghouls of the deep were just another set of distractions in the Count's grand diabolical scheme of saving himself; however, this new sense of hope renewed Bram's commitment to stomp Dracula out. Drying the rain from his face with the sleeve of his left arm, he rowed like five men and faithfully began to recite the burial passage once more. The lurking skeletal mass yielded and quickly sank back into the depths of the lake as the boat struck land.

Standing tall amidst a dark sky of pouring rain was the bold, gothic building that sent shivers down Abraham Stoker's spine. Originally built in 1364 by Vlad's grandfather, Mircea cek Batron, it was a rustic cloister of generous architecture. Normal weathering and various earthquakes surely must have taken a toll on the brick building over the last four hundred years, but the exteriors were so neat and clean that he assumed they must have been renovated in the not too distant past. The multi-spired main chapel was unlike any church he had ever seen, and despite the horrible task at hand, the author was greatly impressed by the serene beauty of the place that managed to evoke feelings of an eerie peacefulness.

The original monastery was endowed in the fourteenth century, but the largest of its three chapels, that of the Annunciation, was built by Vladislav II of the Danesti family, the Impaler's enemy, in 1453. Tepes was supposedly responsible for the later fortifications of the island, although no documentary evidence for this has survived. The canonical statue of Dracula that stood in a courtyard in the center of the island sent an abundance of mixed emotions throughout Stoker's body.

To honor a man at the expense of cruelty of others is deserving of a home in eternal hell!

Through the blinding rain, Abraham caught a glimpse of a figure waving from a distance. The gesture belonged to a father who acted as the curator on the island, whom he seemed to be alarmed by the weather and even more surprised that Stoker was present, carrying a pickaxe and shovel. Calling out something in his native language, the priest pointed to the sky and then to the shore as if to suggest the Irishman was insane for setting foot on the island at such an inclement period of time. Waving the trespasser on, the father took shelter inside a small chapter house and closed the door behind him. The journeyman heard the door lock behind him but proceeded to shield off the rain somewhat by positioning himself against the structure. This stance gave Abraham an excellent view of the monastery, and his eyes felt an almost hypnotic aura originating from the place.

As the foreigner stood there captivated by its many mysteries, historical accounts of the incredible building resurfaced to his immediate memory.

Its architectural style followed the pattern that was characteristic of the monasteries that were situated on the Holy Mount Athos. The church was painted under the earnest care of Petru cel tanar (Peter the Young) Voivode in the year 1563, although bearing evident marks of reconditioning works. The present-day church building was constructed during the reign of Naegoe Basarb within the years of 1517 and 1521 and was referred to as Biseric Naegoe Basararb.

The structure itself had undergone several transformations since Tepes's time as part of the settlement burned toward the end of the 1462 campaign and storms and earthquakes had brought about the collapse of the Chapel of the Annunciation. The original door with carvings of saints from the fifteenth century was removed and put on display in the Bucharest Museum of Art when the country had gained a reputation in the seventeenth century as the center of culture and learning.

Beginning with 1840, many a people who had been persecuted by Romania's rulers were exiled, and therein the monastery died and interred within the sacred grounds. The holy establishment also played a significant cultural role, since, as was known, the print house set up by Antin Ivireanul functioned on the monastic premises after the monastery had undergone extensive repairs and restoration works during the reign on Constantine Brancoveanu Voivode.

Abraham Stoker began to feel spellbound, glaring at the remarkable construction that seemed to come alive and stare back in all its gothic proportions and medieval solemnity. He closed his eyes and turned away as in fear of slowly being driven to madness by its dismal appearance.

The rain continued to pelt down in sheets, and the raging wind was beginning to blow against the side of the chapter house. The Irishman was soaking wet and freezing by the time he reached the large gilded door of the monastery. Placing his tools down behind a large bush, he tried the door and found it unlocked. At this discovery, he took a deep breath and spoke out loud: "There are dark mysteries of old that age by centuries. Over time, they become monstrosities of suffering for all of humanity, and though every hundred years a piece of the puzzle is on the verge of being solved . . . alas, it is only to be lost in death or translation. The answer lies therein, and in God's holy name, give me strength to proceed and prevail!" Crossing himself, he swung open the door and walked inside the edifice.

* * * * *

The series of medieval wood sculpture in the building, combined with the Gothic portals from the chapel, inaugurated an atmosphere of weird beauty. Though the exteriors seemed newer, the main chapel's interior did not. The room was filled with fascinating frescoes that covered the walls. The paintings constituted the greatest mural complex to be found in all the Orthodox Church building of Romania. The chapel was the core of the medieval monastery, and tradition told that Dracula was buried in keeping with his rank and hour as Prince of Walachia, near the altar. The stone slab itself may once have borne inscriptions and frescoes typical of medieval Romanian tombs, but over the centuries the constant trampling my monks, soldiers, prisoners, and vandals had removed all trace. Inside many flickering candles lit up the rich gold and silver of a multitude of icons.

The great silvery number of cult objects of which supplied the foundations from Romanian Country, added to the ones given to the monasteries from other sides, typical to those from Athos Mountain, it presumed the existence at the end of the fifteenth century. Thus, the sixteenth century became prevalent to the ones inspired from Baroque or from Renaissance motifs. Abraham Stoker recalled Barbola as stating that the artistical activity came to its head in the periods of the ruling of Stefan the Great's epoch and signified not only the greatest constructive effort of Moldavian society, but above all the full maturation of what was called the Moldavian Style—the drawing up and the synthesizing of Moldavian church characteristics—and its primary features being the joining of a Byzantine plan executed by gothic hands and part gothic principles. The evolution of social structures and the changing from the conception of Romanian society favored new accumulations in architectural and artistic plans. To intensify the fond effort at the voivode's level, all art endeavors were correlated with esthetical sense. The Snagov Monastery certainly followed this plan of logic.

Abraham eyeballed a fast inventory of the chapel and quickly realized he was not alone. The Orthodox Church was operated by a nun that also took on the duty as guide, and aside from the priest, it appeared they were the only full-time residents that inhabited the island. She stood behind the altar and seemingly stared straight through Stoker. This sudden notice caught the writer off guard, and he instantly jumped back in a state of alarm. The nun gave no reply to his reaction or presence but appeared behind the altar, making strange signs over the grave, gesticulating and waving her arms as if in a trace.

Without notice, she sprung at him with a wild-eyed look and pointed toward the sky. Even from the thick walls of the old building, the sound of rolling thunder echoed throughout the monastery that would have interrupted one's silent moment of prayer with a loud burst or sudden boom. When the Irishman shook his head as a sign to relay a lack of understanding, the woman's face changed to an expression of fear and dread. She then stepped out in front of the altar and proceeded to draw his attention to Vlad's grave as if to signify a correlation between it and the storm. The nun then grew angry and walked up to Abraham, pointing her left index finger in a derogatory fashion, and began to shout a ranting stream of words dealing with revelation of evil curses. Indeed, Stoker could not make out any of what she was saying for the nun spoke way to fast for him to follow. Though he could tell by the sound of her tone that it was not complimentary, and he began to sense that a language barrier was cultivating the deeper he found himself into his journey.

As she walked toward the foreigner in an almost accusatory stride, he backed up with every pace she took until he found himself hemmed against the chapel door. With pointing finger she flung the door open, causing a strong wind to escape inside, which simultaneously blew in a mixture of rain and debris from the outside. Like the priest, she too was pointing in the direction of the shore, and it did not take long for him to translate the message that he was not welcomed on the island.

Having never struck a woman before—having decided Agatha Hupnuff was clearly not a "woman" by standard definition, let alone a figure of faith—once more the Irishman found himself in the elements as the bizarre nun closed the door behind him. The storm rushed overhead, and looking up, he could see the sky had formed a queer darkness that presaged a look of doom over the entire island. The great clouds wheeled in fury as the sheets of rain began to fall thicker and pound harder than of late.

Hitherto, he stood with hands in pockets, thinking about his plan of action until the sudden boisterous crack of thunder filled the air, followed by a long thread of lightning that streaked across the illuminated sky. It looked almost too close for comfort, thus he tried the door again. To the author's surprise, he found it unlocked and unguarded! The nun was nowhere in sight and presumably was in such a state of hysterics that she fled to seek deeper shelter without taking appropriate security measures.

Abraham found the tools he hid behind a nearby bush undisturbed, but as he retrieved them, a bolt of lightning shot from the sky, striking a neighboring willow in the center that split the trunk in half. The entire top of the tree caved in and fell in Bram's direction, almost barricading the door. Indeed, if he was any slower, reentering the monastery the huge limb could have proven a fatal blow.

The appearance of the chapel had not changed at all in his short duration outside; however, as Stoker was alone now, the reacquaintance of it proved to result in a total observation of the place. Though a religious structure in form and belief, never had the journeyman felt a more sense of grisly decay and presence of death. The haunting icons seemed to watch his every move, and the desolation of the chamber caused the slightest noise to stir a quick reaction of terror in Stoker that turned him a ghostly shade of white.

Indeed, the tomb was as silent as a long lost Egyptian pyramid, buried deeper century upon century by reoccurring sandstorms, thought the writer. *And its prolonged hush proved to be far more glum than could have existed had there been no remnants of a human occupancy, as even these dilapidated walls were evocative of what once had been, and the rapt tranquility which now pervaded them likewise incarcerated a depressive mood for the times of yore.*

The foreigner felt the bleak presence of the Count's dungeon—dampened and satiated of the most insalubrious exhalations—hidden well underneath the church. Thus, it looked as if in its excavations, the whole of the monastery had sunk in part due to the haughty weight of crushing death and forlorn souls.

The sediments of the Impaler's grave consisted of an Oriental rug that covered the great marble stone slab and an awful gaudy vase. Vlad's portrait, stenciled together with a sinister-looking chalice, rested at the head of the slab filled with an assorted bunch of wild roses that had wilted to ghastly shades of reddish-black and ashen purple.

Lying his pickaxe and shovel at the foot of the rock, he dried his face with his hands and thought, *Unclean snatcher . . .*

Listening to the storm carry on outside, he was able to establish a pattern: every twenty-two seconds a crash of thunder filled the chapel. Picking up the pickaxe, he quickly pushed away the rug and vase and began to strike at every interval. He smiled at this discovery as the breaking of the marble floor was masked and completely overshadowed by the raging storm.

Abraham was hard at it for what seemed to be over an hour pounding away and breaking pieces of stone, which proved to be mainly dry work. Stopping during the storm's period of silence, he wiped perspiration from his brow and thought about the purpose of his mission, which quickly rejuvenated his depleted strength. As the instrument swung down, it resembled a hammer of death striking what he hoped would be a powerful blow to the vampire's immortal heart.

"Show yourself, *Dracula!*"

Suddenly the floor began to shake—much like that of an earthquake—and the Irishman dropped his tools and then stumbled over them, falling face forward on the floor amidst the rubble. Smoke began to rise out of the half-dug-up pit, and the entire chapel began to tremble violently until the gyrations caused two candelabras on the wall to work their way loose and fall to the ground. The vase of flowers toppled over from the riveting vibrations, causing the portrait of Vlad the Impaler to be cracked down the center. The dead flowers likewise fell into the hole that seemed to project a domineering sensation of ferment heat.

Without notice, the grave exploded violently, throwing the author several feet across the floor. In his path Bram struck a large golden medallion that held a candle which stood adjacent to the marble slab. The ornately decorative object rolled with him until they both rested against the sidewall that was covered with fourteenth-century frescoes.

When the earth ceased shaking, Bram crawled over to the still-smoldering pit with a look of fruitless disappointment and of equal alarm. The hole was nothing more than a gaping grave that housed only fragments of pottery chards and the remains of animal bones. Disappointed, the final words of Agatha Hupnuff echoed in his ears: "Beware of the thieving cadaver and he who has more than one resting place!"

With tears rolling down his face, he said a prayer before God: "It is in the utmost depths of despair and tribulation that I turn my faltering faith and unwinding hope before my Father who art in heaven! Oh, do not forsake me now—for trusting in you is all the hope I have left and to live for to the end, and have mercy on me, Lord . . . to what end?"

As Stoker sat with his hands over his face, the chapel of the ancient church suddenly grew deathly dark. The candles flickered out by a sudden breeze—a quick, sudden movement that recalled Stoker's attention that originated from the gaping grave below him. The only light shined from a few loopholes in the masonry that dimly lit a few feet from the thick walls.

"Where art thou, Vlad Dracula? *Show yourself!*"

The man's hands turned clammy, and his throat dried out to that of a famished dog's bone. As the foreigner stood stock still—for he abruptly found himself unable to speak or move—he felt the sweat begin to drip from his limbs, which began to vibrate uncontrollably as his nerves contracted.

As if the creature Medusa had shown her grotesque cranium of snakes, the journeyman was scared stiff. To the Irishman's horror, the animal bones had gelled together and began to develop—to form veins, muscle, flesh, and skin—until it took shape and stood erect before him.

The pit began to smoke once more, and the black mass continued to grow and grow until it cast itself out of the grave and towered in front of Abraham Stoker with burning red eyes.

"Sometimes the laws of the universe are unexplainable, and the belief that the ways of man are all good merge into one harsh reality that is overrun by a fear of diabolical and unspeakable evil. It is during such times that your developed knowledge is misjudged and your senses become unusable. The heart and soul of the person you believe you have become are tested, and all hope seems to have been abandoned. This is the gut feeling of horror in the truest sense of the word in all of the tenses or meaning the definition can bring. You are utterly alone; you cannot move, and the overwhelming darkness envelops you until you are fixated by trepidation. I have felt this sensation many times but never in a way such as this. For the old chapel seemed to harbor the tap root of the ultimate enduring evil and the origin of the word *fear* itself." Abraham Stoker recalled in his journal.

"The figure that stood before me was of a creature of explicit ungodliness as old as time. It had red, leathery skin that seemed to burn into me and caused my own flesh to cringe and tighten to unnatural and unbearable proportions. The thing had talonlike hands that hovered like hungry beasts that snarled with drool, waiting impatiently for their master to give a command of attack."

As it stood there gazing at Stoker with a look of surprise, it seemed to know why he was there. And as Bram crouched in a corner of the room trembling at the preternatural sight before him, the immense thing spoke with a low, unearthly tone that made his blood run cold: "Thou seek the fact—the exact basis of the vampire's wrath—hence, the truth ye shall be given! But first recognize that the measure of a man shalt not be determined by his worldly possessions, or power over the land of which he liveth—for that be against God's will, but rather by his soul be judged by good deeds and the way he treated his fellow man," it said. The writer listened intently with colorless, quivering lips and an indescribable apprehension as the cunning tongue went on.

"Notwithstanding, Dracula used his earthly power to spill the blood of man for personal revenge, selfish greed, wealthy fortune, and perverse pleasure. This is the work of the dark angel, and it was I, God's fallen one, that claimed the Impaler's soul in exchange for immortality. 'Twas I that cursed Vlad Tepes to walk amongst the undead—shrouded in darkness, spilling more blood so that he might thrive and seek revenge on the human race that took his mortal life—whilst coveting mortal souls and crossing others over as his Children of the Night!"

Abraham was speechless and utterly engrossed by a total paralysis of consternation. He only looked on as Satan continued to address him.

"And just as Jesus Christ, the Son of God, was risen from his death by crucifixion by his father's power to promote eternal salvation, Dracula, the son of Lucifer, was risen from death by assassination by his maker to promote eternal damnation as the King of the Vampires! By multiplying his children of the damned, the Count's wicked circle continues to bring forth an evil death and promote unworldly destruction on behalf of *my* Kingdom!"

The powerful figure let out a diabolical, mechanical laugh that inoculated through Stoker like a painful malignant illness. And as the monster moved closer to the writer, it said with a stern look of accomplishment: "Vlad Tepes forsook the truth and the light and accepted darkness that will never enable him to rest in peace—not even within this blessed tomb. Nay, it did not seem right to know or try to understand in one's human brain how such an evil soul could live on after death."

The smiling tower of terror that looked down at Bram Stoker with demonic eyes somehow became intermingled with a third presence that suddenly haunted the chapel. When the author sensed this innocent and familiar feeling, he doubled over with fear and cried out in a world of mortal pain that wrung his heart and sent a shock of horror through the netherworld that would have caused the harshest of the sufferers to give sway. He felt his son, Noel, had somehow met this demon on at least two occasions.

"How dare you show yourself to my son when he had done nothing to deserve the pain and sorrow you seek to spread!" the Irishman sobbed.

The ruler of hell sneered and gave a low chuckle before making a reply that somehow carried an urgent sense of a warning. "Ahh . . . how could I ever lose sight of the very talent that connects you to the beyond! For this dark gift is what brought my son to you, but alas, I am afraid it is what will tear your soul apart! Your involvement in the Impaler's mortal life has gone beyond basic knowledge—it has gotten intrusive and your personal feelings have caused you to cast judgment. And now your trip to Draculaland—where his vampiric powers were formed and surged—had become a means to seek him out and destroy him! Clever devil, nevertheless, thou shan't deserve such a title—nay, not yet! Alas, how disappointing and what a tragic end to what could have been a most pleasant and rewarding relationship! For you, I am not surprised—however, I did not foresee your son getting involved as he serves no purpose in the mission.

Unfortunately, I am afraid the young one is about to go beyond his limit."

The journeyman's gut became full of fire.

"Leave him alone, ye cursed one—lest the light of God will surely strike you back to hell and disable you so that you never leave again! Pleasant? Rewarding? You speak pure folly . . . for what possible act of happiness could come out of a voyage that I was forced to make just to ensure the safety of my family and myself? I have surely witnessed nothing but horror, pain, and suffering, and I now feel it is crossing over to my family! How can I possibly trust Dracula will keep his promise? And how can I possibly be expected to write his terrible, savaged tale after knowing the sheer evil he has implicated upon others? Do you not know he beseeches you—that he wishes to end the curse you seeded within him?"

At this, the beastly thing lifted its right talonlike hand boldly as his snout sprouted sparks of hellfire.

"Silence! Your threats mean nothing to me and many a fine man with the purest of heart would give their soul to learn of the truth and walk though the ages as you have done! A bargain is a bargain – despite even if it were with the underworld—so heed your foolish tongue! The vampire beseeches no one but himself for thinking a foolish mortal such as you could carry out his desire!"

As those words, fell on the Irishman's overly anxious ears, he grew incredibly angry and torc the crucifix from around his neck and held it high above his head in the direction of the demon.

"May the power of Christ compel you!" he yelled as he cast the holy symbol into the gaping pit.

The dark thing before him let out a screech, and the entire chapel seemed to turn into a wild, spinning cyclone. Bram, holding on to the altar, closed his eyes in silent prayer as the fiend seemed to get caught in the middle of the whirlpool. The open grave then became a vacuum that sucked its ruler back into the mouth of Hades.

Within a few seconds, the thing was gone in one loud burst of wind and the sound of the marble slab fell back into place with a giant thud.

Along with his wherewithal, Abraham Stoker collapsed on the stone floor from total exhaustion as an eerie, dead silence dominated the chapel. Outside, the storm seemed to surrender upon itself and the sound of the rain striking against the church tapered off. As his mind began to stir again, the wicked wind began to howl insomuch like a pack of hungry wolves surrounded the edifice. The gloomy air inside whispered the foreigner's name repeatedly and moaned with acute solemnity. This weird chain of events repeated endlessly for sometime, and he soon feared it was the beginning of yet another nightmarish installment in this travesty of horrors.

CHAPTER 19

A Handbag of Horrors

Van Helsing, with his usual methodicalness
began taking the various contents from his bag
and placing them ready for use. To me, a doctor's
preparations for work of any kind are stimulating and bracing, but the effect of these things on
both Arthur and Quincey was to cause them a
sort of consternation.

—Dr. Seward's Diary

The origin of the vampire myth can be traced back to prehistory.
Indeed, the belief of such creatures preceded the introduction
of Christianity in southern and Eastern Europe. Experts believed the
folklore originated independently as a response to unexplained phe-
nomena that was common to most cultures. Ancient Greek writings
told of the *lamiai*, the *mormolykiai*, and other vampire-like forms,
and impartial accounts of vampires emerged and spread amongst
the Slavic people and were passed to their non-Slavic neighbors.
Naturally, the gypsies brought some belief in vampires from India
that contributed to the development of the myth; however, it was
not until 1047 that the first appearance in written form came as the
word *upir* (an early version of the word later to become "vampire")

was discovered in a document written by an unknown author that referred to a Russian prince as *Upir Lichy*, or "wicked vampire."

Noel Stoker's lack of adulthood did not prevent him from knowing that whatever was after his mother was, undoubtedly, wicked in every sense of the word. And even though he was sent away by Doctor Van Zant to live with his best friend, Jonathan Watts, whilst she recovered from illness, he did not let this interfere with his scheming. Nor did he fancy being left in the dark, especially when it came to his own mother; henceforth, he set out quickly to find out all he could about the evil that seemed to be enveloping the Stoker family like an immense legion of doom. Indeed, the days had been shaved away. It was time for action.

Noel came to his own conclusion that he could not believe in God without also believing in the devil. Thus, if the devil existed, vampires were its demons, unearthed from hell, and sent up to inflict pain amongst mortal man; whereas God's angels, whom were sent from heaven, were said to look after the innocent and pain-stricken of the Christian world. These two separate worlds have collided from the existence of time and could be traced back to account for most of the chaos and destruction that become what we refer to as "man's" history books.

As Christianity spread through the lands of the Mediterranean Basin and then northward across Europe, it encountered these vampire beliefs that had already arisen amongst the many pagan peoples. However, vampirism was never high on the Christian agenda and was thus rarely mentioned. Its continued presence was indicated by occasional documents such as an eleventh-century law promulgated by Charlemagne as emperor of the new Holy Roman Empire. The law condemned anyone who promoted the belief in the vampire, and who on account of that belief caused a person thought to be a vampire to be attacked or killed. Noel Stoker was prepared to break the law of the land, but first, he needed to find out exactly what he was dealing with. Therefore, once again, he and Jonathan paid Old Man Godalming a visit. Needless to say, he desperately wanted that mysterious black leather bag at all cause.

On a bright, early Saturday morning, the boys found the old man in a chipper mood and eager to talk whilst conducting business. Noel tossed the amulet on a table next to the man and said hurriedly, "Can you accept this for the twenty pounds we owe you?" Noel and Jonathan looked at their elder and waited for a reaction, yet the one they received was clearly not one they anticipated.

Godalming's eyes grew to the size of tea saucers as he stammered for words. The old man gingerly picked up the piece of jewelry in both hands like it was a living thing that suffered a serious injury. The friends watched in bewilderment as the necklace was inspected at every angle—top to bottom, front to back—with sudden gasps and nervous expletives with every turn.

"'ell . . ." Jonathan said at length. "Kin we 'ave th' bag?" Godalming looked at him curiously and found his voice again.

"Do you have any idea what you have brought me?" he asked excitedly, but with an edge to his voice. But without waiting for a reply, he went on, "Where . . . or should I say *how* did you procure this object?" The old man's voice and hands were trembling. Confusingly, Jonathan looked at Noel who parted his lips as if ready to speak.

"It was in Mum's hand the morning after those marks appeared on her throat," Noel answered.

"Amazing!" Godalming responded in disbelief.

"Kin we 'ave th' bag?" Jonathan repeated again but this time with a sense of authority in his voice.

"Oh yes . . . of course!" The old man said as he swept the amulet off the table and placed it in his trouser pocket. "But before I give you what you have come to claim, I think it best to prepare you. You need some background on those that have used the bag before you!"

The two boys quickly glanced at each other apprehensively. Though Noel could tell by the way his friend was sitting that Jonathan's patience was wearing thin.

"For starters," Godalming began, "it is worthy to note we are dealing with a creature that has had thousands of years to evolve and to spread its evil cunningly, and therefore, just from the nature of the beast, man has had centuries to misunderstand, deny, or question its existence in our world! By the end of the first Christian millennium, the Christian Church was still organizationally united in agreement upon the basic Christian affirmation—as contained in the Nicene Creed—but had already begun to differentiate itself into its primarily Greek Eastern Orthodox and Latin Roman Catholic branches. The Church formally broke in the year 1054, with each side excommunicating the other. The written reference to a vampire did not appear again until almost an entire century later, when Walter Map's *De Nagis Curialium* 1190 account told of vampire-like beings present in England, followed by a 1196 chronicle written by William of Newburgh that also recorded several stories of Nosferatu revenants in England."

Noel stopped the old man and said with an interested groan, "How did all this 'development' have an effect on the creation of Dracula?"

"Ah, you are using that boy brain of yours!" Godalming said, smiling from ear to ear. "Clever lad ye are!" he added, untidying the boy's reddish mass atop his small head. Then the old man continued, "During the second Christian millennium, the two churches completed their conquests through the remaining parts of Europe, especially Eastern Europe. Meanwhile, quite apart from the major doctrinal issues that had separated them in the eleventh century, the theology in the two churches began to develop numerous lesser differences! You see, children, these would become important especially in those areas where the boundaries of the two churches met and war brought people of one church under the control of political leaders of the other. Such a situation arose, for example, in the twelfth century when the predominantly Roman Catholic Hungarians conquered Transylvania, then populated by Romanians, the majority of whom were Eastern Orthodox. Slavic but Roman Catholic Poland was bounded on the east by Orthodox Russian states. In the Balkans, Roman Catholic Croatia existed beside predominantly Orthodox Serbia. For *our* Dracula, 1442 saw the year that Vlad Tepes was imprisoned by the Turks, which caused him to denounce his Roman Catholic faith for the Eastern Orthodox cause. This action was looked upon by his own people as a form of blasphemy and was the beginning of the Impaler's demise. It has been suspected that his own Wallachian peoples began to plot out his end as early as he first took the throne!"

"I'll give him a good whut for!" Jonathan said enthusiastically.

"But how art we supposed to bloody well find him durin' the day?"

"And what are we supposed to kill him with?" Noel added.

"Kin we 'ave somethin' in that black traps of yours?" Jonathan said, squirming on his bench.

At this point, Old Man Godalming went off to the forbidden "voo-doo" room toward the back of the shop and returned with the large leather bag the boys came to purchase. He looked at his visitors intently with his brow—wrinkled insomuch as a Chinese Shar-pei.

"Finding the resting place of a vampire takes skill, so we must learn from the master hunters of the ages. This bag belonged to one of them," the man said, patting the tote softly as he sat it down on the counter before them.

"Now where was I?" he asked himself aloud. "Oh, yes . . . in 1645, Leo Allatius wrote the first modern treatment of vampires, *De Graecorum hodie quirundam opinationabus*, and in it, he suggests that during the day, a vampire rests in the grave where its mortal body was buried. However, there is still much you need to know before you set off to locate and dispose of him. Alas, you need to know what you are looking for! In 1734, the word *vampyre* entered the English language in translations of German accounts of the European waves of vampire hysteria. Indeed, the identification, hunting down and disposing of vampires in all likelihood became a profession that was actually sought out—even by the most learned and nobleman!"

Noel and Jonathan looked at each other with expressions of surprise and then back to Old Man Godalming.

"Although the identification and disposal methods were different between certain religious beliefs, the need for hunters was actually a universal requirement! It has often been said that one divergence between the two churches frequently noted in vampire literature was their different understanding of the incorruptibility of dead bodies. In the east, if the soft tissue of a body did not decay quickly once placed in the ground, it was generally considered a sign of evil—that the body which refused to disintegrate meant that the earth would, for some supernatural reason, refuse to receive it! Most cultures contributed suicide to the creation of vampires, and a non-corrupting body became a candidate for vampirism—however, in the West, quite the opposite was true: the body of a dead saint often did not experience corruption like that of an ordinary body. Not only did it not decay, but frequently emitted a pleasant odor. It did not stink of putrefaction, and these differing understandings of incorruptibility explain in large part the demise of belief in vampires in the Catholic West, and the parallel survival of belief in Orthodox lands, even though the Greek Church officially tried to suppress the belief."

Jonathan looked puzzled and tilted his head as if deep in thought. As the old man paused, the lad spoke up. "Me chum's mum is feeling mighty poorly, an' she was fine afore that bite! So we need to know whut to look for and whut to do lest it all comes a cropper—"

Abruptly, Noel approached the black leather bag as if he were totally disengaged from the previous conversation. Next, he placed his hand on it and said, interrupting his mate, "Can we see what we have here to help us? I fear as though we do not have much time."

Godalming shook his head as if he understood perfectly and opened the large leather bag that was almost four feet in length and stood about a foot tall. He reached in and began to pull out object after object—lying articles of the most unusual sorts on the table: a bundle of garlic flowers, a vial of holy water, a small bag of poppy seeds; a envelope of Eucharistic wafers, a hatchet, a box of wolfsbane; a container of salt, a small mirror, and a pistol with a round of silver bullets; instruments for a blood transfusion, a wooden mallet, and a large Celtic crucifix that was pointed at the end.

A tempest seemed to fume through their now-frozen hearts, which were swiftly conjuring up a strong sense of an irrevocable mix of fear and dread. Indeed, the items placed out before them were meant to be afraid of, and Noel and Jonathan appeared to be dumbfounded and in complete awe over the contents of the bag. They were especially amazed at the cross that appeared to be made of sterling silver, with a base that had to be three feet deep.

"Do all these things actually work?" Noel inquired.

"Me don't want to argie, but we have been through the mill so don't want to be bothered up with bluff," said Jonathan. "Have you heerd everything in this biggo bag is artillery for a vampire?"

At this, the old man's eyes widened as he pulled up a chair next to where the two boys were standing. He pointed to the objects and said in the utmost serious tone he could muster: "These various objects have been used by the 'master slayers' as far back to ancient time to identify, deter, or dispose of a vampire. Many historical accounts of vampire sightings and their demise were documented by Cardinal Giuseppe Davanzatie when he published his treatise, *Dissertazione sopre I Vampiri* in 1744. This hysteria brought about the first modern vampire poem, "Der Vampir," that was published four years later by Heinrich August Ossenfelder."

As the man spoke, the two friends sat silently studying the articles that were placed on the table. The odd scene much appeared like a seasoned surgeon and his young apprentices praying before conducting an operation on a patient that was on the verge of death, and the sterilized objects being inventoried were the instruments of success.

"The works I describe openly mention such tools of the trade, and I, firsthand have seen these items in use during my younger years. True, many might find them to be bizarre or superstitious, but believe me, my dear friends, they all serve a purpose—a purpose that stands between life and death!"

As of late, the boys had never seen such a sad look of grave seriousness on the man's face. Scratching his reddish locks, Noel picked up the bag of seeds and asked, "What are these to be used for? How are they bloody well supposed to keep Dracula away from my mother?"

"Or help us to strikin' him daid?" interrupted Jonathan.

"The ancient Greeks believed scattering poppy seeds in the coffin of a troubled soul or around the tomb of a suspected or known vampire will keep the dead from materializing as superstition suggests vampires will count the seeds over and over again until sun rises," replied Old Man Godalming.

"We already know that Dracula is a vampire—however, your mother is probably in the transition phase," he said, continuing. Picking up the small pocket mirror encased in a gold leafing cover, he added, "As long as your mother continues to cast a reflection she is safe. However, the Count must be destroyed before he turns her completely!"

"And what if she doesn't cast a reflection?" Noel asked with a look of dismay upon his face. His heart was thumping so feverishly that at any moment he expected that it would drive through his chest walls. Jonathan stared on with a similar gaze, coupled with an aura of anticipation. The later dragged his left hand through his hair nervously as the shop owner finally answered in a direct but apathetic way that was also overshadowed with a feeling of cold fear.

"Then I am afraid it is too late to save her," the old man replied reluctantly. With a solemn expression, he finished his statement: "That means there will then be are *two* graves to dispose of."

Noel's face fell while his heart sank deep within his torso. The old man sadly watched as the two boys tried to maintain their composure whilst assembling the strength needed to carry on. Jonathan's throat felt tight and convulsed, but Godalming seemed to understand and made an attempt to sympathize with them and calm their fright.

"Ridding the earth of a vampire is no easy task—aye . . . even for an adult, it is difficult and dirty work. In fact, Maria Teresa, Arch Duchess of Austria and Queen of Hungary, issued a decree outlawing vampire hunts and the desecration of graves in 1755 because the killings became so vast and brutal the hysteria became too overwhelming for the families of the victims. Though killings continued underground, the heartbreak led to the 1798 writing of "Christabel," the first English vampire poem by Samuel Taylor Coleridge, about his love becoming one of the undead."

Godalming stood and picked up the empty bag and looked at the two frightened boys and said holding up the leather traps as if it was an ancient artifact stolen from the British Museum: "You will be pleased to know that both of you will be riding on the coattails of one of the greatest hunters of all time—for this bag and its contents belonged to William Newburgh! Amongst the famous case reports of vampires were those of Newburgh, who in the twelfth century collected a variety of accounts of vampires in England."

The lads' expressions turned to pleasing stares, and their interest in the bag grew to one of an alluring discomfort.

"For example, one incident that occurred in Newburgh's lifetime concerned a man who served the Lord of Alnwick Castle. An unfaithful wife plagued the man, who was himself known for his wicked ways. Now keep in mind universal vampiric superstition suggested that those who were evil in life were plagued with the curse of the vampire . . . well, having hidden on the roof above his bed to see her adulterous actions for himself, he fell to the ground and died the next day.

"However, following his burial, the bad man was seen by numerous townspeople after nightfall wondering through the village! People became so afraid of encountering him the entire town locked themselves in their houses after dark each day. Thenceforth, during this time, an epidemic of an unnamed disease broke out and a number of people died. The sickness was blamed on the 'vampire.' Finally, on Palm Sunday, Newburgh, the local priest, and a group of the more devout residents, including some of the leading citizens assembled and proceeded to the cemetery, and there they uncovered the body of the man, which appeared gorged with blood that gushed forth when it was struck with a spade! Having decided that the body had fed off the blood of its many victims, it was dragged out of town and burned. Soon thereafter, the epidemic ended, and the town returned to normal."

Upon hearing this, Noel turned a ghastly shade of white. Jonathan let out a low gasp and seemed to grow extremely restless, shifting his weight anxiously on his bench. They each looked around the room nervously, as if afraid there was a fourth presence of some kind lurking behind them. Godalming continued in his overly spooky tone: "It is important to understand that pagan myths and the religious belief that blood contained regenerative power linked unexplained sudden deaths or disappearances to vampirism. In the early- to mid-eighteenth century, the belief that the soul was powerful enough to return from the grave if it could not find peace spread all though Europe and even to America during the Revolution. At the same time, famine, floods, and various plagues wiped out part of Eastern Europe. Hitherto, it also gave witness to the birth of many vampires as bodies that did not decompose saw their hearts cut out and burned! Diseases that carried no known cause or cure provoked fear in the hearts of everyone and were linked to many premature burials whilst the victims were in coma-like states. Upon awakening, sheer panic would set in, followed by the sounds of shrieks and clawing. At the time, with the morgue and cemetery filled with the presence of Un-Dead souls, the work of the Vampire Hunter became a media event as so-called visits from previously buried townspeople began to pay homage to family and friends after nightfall. Meanwhile, reports of sheep being killed by having their jugular veins cut and their blood drained circulated through northern England, whilst similar reports from Ceven, Ireland, shared in this pandemonium."

"Disinterment of bodies became commonplace, and the revenant vampire was commonly identified by the plumpness of the body, long fingernails, and fresh blood on the mouth and clothing. Exhumed bodies that appeared to be quite complete. Undecayed or formed new skin were labeled as vampire creatures and were disposed of with a stake through the chest. Sometimes, hearts were cut out and burned, and the ashes of it were dissolved into medicine for those suffering from consumption. These practices continued everywhere until they were outlawed in the early twentieth century."

"So how we gwine to find where Dracula sleeps durin' the day?" asked Jonathan in a trembling voice.

"Well . . . John Polidori, who wrote the first vampire story published in English, suggested in his 1819 *The Vampyre* that the creatures sleep by day in their mortal place of rest. According to documented accounts, patterns of attack suggests vampires strike close to where they slumber out of fear of being caught by the sun lest they travel too far to feed. On the other hand, only a few years ago, Sheridan Le Fanu's 'Carmilla' suggested that some forms of vampires are able to rest in coffins that are not buried in the ground."

Godalming knew that finding the hidden resting place of a vampire was only half the challenge as he had once secretly witnessed the desecration of man's grave after he had been buried prematurely. There is scientific proof that a decomposing corpse can portray the appearance of an Un-Dead when it is impaled though the heart, creating gurgling and jerking movements due to the bodies lingering reflexes. These impulses have shocked many into mistakenly linking vampirism to a common death.

Thus he warned the boys of making the same mistake as he for that dreadful memory had haunted his nights for over fifty years and caused him to vow to never go on a vampire hunt again. The nightmarish sight of the blood-littered deck resembled a slaughterhouse that still troubled his mind. Notwithstanding, considering the ominous circumstance, the gentle man was beginning to rethink his vow. Having stepped away from his company, with many agonizing and grim thoughts to consider, he returned from the back room with a book on Romanian history. He flipped it open to a chapter that dealt with Vlad the Impaler's life and death.

"Many accounts claim that Vlad Dracula's body was taken to the monastery located on the tiny island of Snagnov, Romania," Godalming stated as he pointed to a picture of the burial chamber. "However, over the centuries, there has been tremendous controversy surrounding Vlad's gravesite. Some rumors suggested he was not buried there at all whilst others claimed his body was robbed or moved to a different tomb, possibly near the east entrance of the church."

"Papa is in Romania now, researching Vlad! If anyone could locate his grave, he could!" exclaimed Noel.

"An' he will gig the brute and not flicker an inch!" added Jonathan proudly.

Without saying a word, Godalming's facial cast turned hard and cold as he picked up a copy of a recent newspaper and opened it to a place he had marked. He then walked it over and placed it in front of the boys to study. After they read it over, he began to quiz them as if preparing them for sort of academic championship.

"Do you see anything odd about the murder outside of the Lyceum?"

"Jack decided to venture out of Whitechapel?" Noel suggested.

"What makes you think it is Jack?" challenged Godalming. "After all, the young woman was of the upper class. Moreover, as of late, he has been targeting prostitutes."

"'Tis true . . ." Jonathan added. "The bloke did not knuck 'er organs."

"I suppose it would be out of place for him to switch sides of town all of a sudden, but then perhaps he wants to throw off the investigators?" Noel guessed.

"If you are suggesting that Jack the Ripper did not murder her, then who did?"

Old Man Godalming put his hands up to his forehead for a moment and let out a prolonged sigh. And ever so calmly, he began to state his case—a plight that ended with the old man panting from a state of excitable ranting and wiping the perspiration off his shiny, balding head.

"Let us think hard about the facts . . . your dad claims Dracula visited him the night prior to his journey to Romania. Later, a woman is murdered outside the theatre whose throat was ripped apart and drained of blood. The Lyceum is only a few blocks away from South Hampton. Next, you claim you found a man that broke into your mother's room that resembled your dad's description of the Count. And then your mother is bitten by a large bat . . . are you beginning to get my drift?"

"Blimey!" shouted Jonathan. "I do believe the fiend has made him a home 'ere in *our* London!"

"I happen to have heard from an attendant at the medical examiner's office that the body of the woman murdered behind the theatre 'got up and walked off,' and though the old sot is off his rocker more times than not, I happen to believe him," said Old Man Godalming. "Children, do you see what this means? We are not dealing with one vampire here! There could be others we do not even know about! And the man that knows our fiend better than anyone in this world is out of the country on a wild goose chase!" The earnest gentleman covered his face in both his worn-out hands whilst resting his elbows on the tabletop. "Oh, woe what dire straits Dracula has cunningly created for us without our slightest suspicion!"

Noel suddenly fell to the floor, producing a despairing sound that came from his throat that signified the rages of the raw human soul. To nullify his uneasiness, he had been skimming a book of fourteenth-century paintings Godalming had also brought out, but it dropped from his hand abruptly and landed on the floor—opened up to a particular painting of a woman of voluptuous beauty.

Master Stoker's spirit was contracted in a polarized hand as a despairing cry fluttered in the air. A resonance of helpless terror overflowed his throat as his teeth champed in a condition of the most impotent fury.

"Great Scott! It's me mate's mum!" Jonathan said, picking up the book and showing it to Godalming. Underneath the painting were four simple words: "Countess Dracula—Artist Unknown."

Godalming's face turned a greenish shade, and he collapsed to his knees. Pummeling the deck, the man cursed himself for all the times he had thumbed through the publication, having never noted the striking resemblance before. Both friends began to comfort the sobbing Noel, whose alarming cries had chilled their blood. And at that moment, a harsh reality struck all three as if the devil himself had—up until that precise instant—trapped them between his horns. Not only was Abraham Stoker digging in the wrong place, for it was now obvious the vampire had relocated to London and was feeding and sleeping in their own backyard, but it was also apparent Bram was sent to Romania as a perishing tactic to get to Florence.

Their heartbeats quickened like three kettledrums that were rapidly approaching from a distance and beat profoundly in the center of their chests. The look on Noel's face especially was one of loss of hope and toiling tribulation that made the old man break the promise he made fifty years ago.

Old Man Godalming starred inquisitively at the various objects of horror displayed about the table whilst the two boys gazed at him for answers and reassurance. They were not sure what to do or say next. Here were two adolescent boys, still pure and innocent at heart, having no choice but to be imposed within a gruesome harsh reality—a situation that would cause even the strongest adult in complete control of his or her faculties to lose consciousness and swoon him- or herself into total shock and inflicting dismay.

Jonathan had slumped down next to his friend in silence, shuddering from fear and apprehension, whilst a traumatized Noel continued to sob in a fetal position, wedged against the corner of the table. They all three were silent and dealt with the situation in their own unique way, though they all were scatterbrained from the many thoughts and images that raced about after such a grim discovery.

Within a few seconds, Old Man Godalming rose to the occasion and reclaimed his role of adulthood. During the few minutes that seemed a lifetime of soundless agony, he began to lay out their plan of attack. Finally, the enticing mode was broken, and he was the first to speak.

"Noel, listen to me very closely. Jonathan, you too, as you should repeat it to our young friend anon for comprehension, as this is very important and concerns his mother. The theatre and your flat are only a few blocks apart. If my assumptions are correct, your mother is not rabid or suffering from consumption—she is 'becoming,' and it is during this stage she can be of instrumental value in locating Dracula's London lair! The vampire must be disposed of before she changes completely, but during the interim, she can be a sort of index to the comings and goings of the Count. And after we have some clues to lead us, I will join you on your search. However, we must split up as time is of the essence, and it is critical that we operate quickly—during the day, whilst we are out of the vampire's radar."

"Indeed, Dracula is clever, but if we are fast, we can outsmart his wits unnoticed and off guard. Likewise, it is crucial to forward word to your father, as I fear he is in grave danger and he needs to return home immediately without the Count's suspicion. During the next few days, you search every nook and cranny within a five-kilometer radius of South Hampton. Do you both understand?"

The boys, having never seen the man look so serious and earnest in their lives, nodded in acquiescence but chose not to quiz his methods or strategy in the slightest degree.

Godalming then picked up the silver stake that shared the shape of a cross in his right hand and grasped it firm, much like a son that had picked up his own mother's hand whilst on her deathbed. With a stern, grave expression, he looked Noel and Jonathan straight in the eyes and said, "Evil does not pass away by a natural death—it requires spiritual intervention!"

Placing the stake in Noel's hand, he took his own hand and wrapped it firm around his into a death grip. Jonathan followed suit as his mate looked up at him with a solemn expression that was too uncomfortable for words. Next, they all said a silent prayer. In an odd sort of way, the moment felt like a departure of friends, yet no one was quite sure who was leaving or what exactly the future had in store for their trio.

"Take this weapon," the man said, continuing, "and go with God's speed. May our faith not be in vain!"

CHAPTER 20

The Coming of the Count

> We waited in a suspense that made the seconds pass with nightmare slowness. The slow, careful steps came along the hall; the Count was evidently prepared for some surprise—at least he feared it. Suddenly, with a single bound he leaped into the room, winning a way past us before any of us could raise a hand to stay him. There was something so panther like in the movement—something so inhuman, that it seemed to sober us all from the shock of his coming.
>
> —Dr. Seward's Diary

After the malevolent demon absconded back into the gaping grave, Abraham Stoker was left utterly alone amidst the heap of rubble. Still recovering from the terrible shock of the wicked encounter, the sudden stillness had driven the man to a state of uneasiness and had left him quite faint. Stoker, lifting himself up from hands and knees, picked up the portrait of Vlad the Impaler that had once sat at the head of the grave. It lay a few feet from the explosive pit amongst the now-broken stenciled chalice containing the once euphoric flowers. Shattered pieces of glass were scattered amid the decayed wild roses—which in all purposes were placed there to ward off evil spirits.

What irony exists, Abraham thought, *in that it seemed the Romanian government might have discovered the vast secrets of the underworld and henceforth decided to hide them in the holiest of places!* However, as the journeyman stared at the portrait of Dracula, it was apparent to him that the sacred building had been corrupted and tainted by supernatural forces. "It is now up to the blood of an Irishman to re-sanctify it to God!" he exclaimed, though still shaking but reclaiming a vague rush of benevolence and the beginning of consciousness.

It only seemed practical that the man born to the mortal world as Vlad Dracul, the son of the devil, would grow up in the land beyond the forest to become known as one of the most evil and feared men of all ages. Thus, it was only perceived natural that he be assassinated by one of his own, just as in Shakespeare's *Macbeth*—only to be resurrected by the "unholy one"; after all, how could Satan allow something so amoral end with a proxy as trivial as death? The writer found himself impelled by the portrait—as if some sort of fascination came over him.

"There was something weird and uncanny about this image of Dracula, yet very familiar—almost as if I knew him somehow in the mortal sense," Abraham noted. "I could not shake this strange, dominating feeling, and all at once, I became overwhelmed with a state of weariness so extreme that my interior twisted into riveting cramps and my courage was racked from nervous tension. And I must have collapsed on the ground in front of the door of the tomb in a pure paroxysm of fright."

At this, the author had grown very pale and fell on the marble floor of the sepulcher in an alarmed grandeur of dreadfulness. By and by, the storm seemed to pass away, but the quiet was soon replaced by the sounds of yelps or barks that appeared to grow increasingly louder and closer to the monastery. Bram looked around in alarm and became very restless, and as he suspiciously sniffed the air, he began to shudder from a sudden cold wind that seemed to drift over the chapel.

Having found the Count's grave empty, and upon sterilizing it with a holy relic, the journeyman felt there was nothing more he could do but continue to search for his box of earth elsewhere. Since it was still daylight outside—though his misadventure was beginning to prove the raging blackness of storms merged with the light of day had yielded a never-ending nightmarish darkness—Stoker concluded it was best to find the creature whilst he was at his weakest. Indeed, the sole alternative was for the writer to wait for the vampire to come to *him* soon after the planet had taken its shadows from the sinking sun; however, this choice would surely bring the hunt to an unforgettable and tragic end.

But for whom?

In an agony of desperation, Bram's Irish blood rose as he reached for the door and found it would not yield. In an almost maddening spout of panic, Abraham leaned against the Doric mass, and pushing it with all his strength, he began to pummel the massive object for a matter of minutes. But to no avail; the exit remained fixed.

"My pursuit consumed the entire fiber of my being. Any amusement or pleasure in my purpose has long been discarded and all form of nourishment was somehow provided for me and sustained in minimal quantity, without my knowing," noted the foreigner. "Exercise was not for strength building but to escape from one horror into another!" The writer slumped to the ground with his back to the door, and with his hands upon his face, he began to sob like a helpless infantile. Having completely abounded himself, he commenced to shake with all the violence of extravagant emotion one man could possibly fabricate.

The cries of the wolves came in mysterious intervals outside the chapel. Their howling increased to an agonizing, eerie decibel and brought on a sense of solemnity and desolation that at times is pronounced in human life with the coming of death. Suddenly, an odd sort of rushing sound began to ring in the author's ears—a noise that muffled the calling of the wolves—and all at once the combination of the two began to lull him into a swoon of helpless slumber.

* * * * *

As Abraham Stoker dreamed, the riddles that had been rooted deep within the Transylvanian Alps for centuries seeming and abruptly manifested themselves before his very hollow eyes. And a visual representation of how Vlad the Impaler found his place in the underworld as the ruler of the vampires was unfolded like a diabolical map clandestinely distributed from the bowels of hell. And above all, the darkest secrets of the unholy legend were answered.

"I was drifting in a mass of snowy white clouds high above everything," Abraham recalled in his journal. "At first notice, I thought I was dead, but then, as the images below became more focused, it became apparent that I was alive and overlooking a great forest of trees deep within the Carpathian Mountains. As I could not understand the significance of this, I looked closer, doubting my judgement, when I noticed a spec in the center. As I concentrated on the image, it began to grow larger—or perhaps I was being drawn closer to it, for I was not certain—and then I was completely aware, it was a hidden door surrounded by a belt of trees. At this, I was in awe as the mountain looked like any other mountain, and the door, though unmarked, seemed to identify itself to me . . . and me *only*."

To Bram's complete amazement, the concealed entrance opened by itself and the Irishman instantly found himself inside what was a completely inhabited and furnished, though rustically archaic, residence of some kind. He continued to float along, only then at a slower pace, by many tables and chairs cluttered with books, dusty scrolls, antique charts, stone templates, iron axes, cloth bags, and other very queer objects he was unable to identify. The writer picked up a book that belonged to a Doctor Faustus that was written in elegant calligraphy with illuminations in gold and important letters in red.

The Black School! Bram thought to himself as he turned to a picture of witches flying on demons that took on the shape of horses.

Elements of magic potions, spells, charms, and incantations filled room after room in all kinds of boxes, jars, or bottles. Many of the containers were dust-ridden and/or broken. Nevertheless, others were newer and labeled with the various contents therein: eleoselunum, poplar leaves, mountain parsley, and soot; belladonna, water parsnip, sweet flag, and anquefoil; bat's blood, baby's fat, black cock's blood, and raven's gall—only to name a few that were legible.

As the foreigner's piercing gray eyes adjusted to the lighting—or more succinctly, the lack thereof—it became clear that the mountain was divided up into four sectors as by the directions of the compass: Urius, the Spirit of the East; Amaymon, the Spirit of the South; Paymon, the Spirit of the West; and Egin, the Spirit of the North. Each region contained their own distinguished rooms for these kings with a variation of stones, amulets, and garments to appease or contact them.

A dubious thought came to his mind: *'Twas this place some sort of institution of blasphemous learning?* Indeed, several of the larger quarters appeared to be set up for lecture whilst other areas resembled grand laboratories or apprenticeship-type environments. As he passed room after room, Stoker still had not seen one mortal soul; thus he was beginning to think the place was deserted. Nevertheless, as the journeyman crept along, his entire body pulsated in an uncontrollable condition of total distress brought on by a circumstance of harsh consternation. And even though the sockets in the back of his head had yet to identify a foreboding presence, this fraction of comfort in such an unnatural and blatantly paranormal surrounding failed neither to release any apprehension in his footing nor to ease up the anxiety in answering what the next step could bring forth.

"However, then the hidden hand that seemed to move my body along paused for a brief moment, and deep within the mountain came a kind of roaring sound that sent the blood surging up through my brain! At first, the noise appeared to be made by a grand motor of some sort, although, by and by, I concluded that there was more than one. And after realizing the tones were slightly different, I began to listen more closely, and with every instant, the panic in me rose to one of absolute scare. I became positive that the sounds were not machines at all but actually unearthly living beings communicating—actually calling out to one another!" he wrote.

Upon this startling conclusion, he was seized again in a giant grasp and dragged away deeper into the peak. Up to this point, the areas Abraham had witnessed were dimly lit by torches of various shapes and sizes that were mounted in every direction of the halls and rooms; although, this suddenly changed as he was plummeted into a darker area that seemed to lead toward the direction of the roars—sounds which grew louder as the author moved inward to what he believed was the center of the alp. Indeed, winding staircases seemed to be leading him further and further into the earth, sealed from the sunlight by giant, heavy iron doors.

"The light finally passed away, and it struck me that it was considerably colder than it had been at the commencement of my flight. Then I began to hear voices of several men! I could make out at least five distinct voices in all but could not make out enough words to understand any particular meaning of the muffled conversation."

As the Irishman moved closer to the dialogue, the structure of the mountain seemed to shift and he believed to be entering toward the core of the structure, as the ceiling was becoming a lofty dome, which stretched out high overhead. The occasional roars from the creatures became so loud they were stifled and caused his ears to react with an annoying ring.

"Traveling closer in the way of the voices, I felt my skin turn icy cold when by my surprised reaction I was able to identify the metallic Romanian voice of the Count!"

Soon the shadows of ten men were visible in the distance, and the temperature changed rapidly to one of ferment combustion. It only took a few minutes for Abraham Stoker's body to begin to suffer from the sweltering heat.

"The starting driving force placed me in a corner of the large room in which the men stood, and I remained in a state of fixed sated fear as I watched and listened as the scene before me—one that was already in action—which continued to unfold before my terrorized eyes."

Vlad Tepes looked identical to the portrait that graced the Snagov Monastery; only he was dressed differently than his princely attire. Along with the group of five men, he was clad in a black robe and appeared to be giving some kind of instruction to the group who stood around him in a state of enthrallment. Their garments were a wide assortment of black cloth or the skin of cat, bear, or wine.

And with a dark-handled ceremonial knife called an *arthame*, the smallest man drew a circle in the diameter of nine feet on the floor with a pentagram in its center. With a nod to the others, in unison, the group recited, "By virtue of Lucifer, we do clothe ourselves in Sabbath garments that so we fulfill, even unto their term, all things which we desire to affect through this Seal of Solomon!"

Vlad gave a look of acquiescence to the man closest to him and spoke something in his native Romanian language. The word *Scholomance* was mentioned several times, along with many queer phrases intermingled with all sorts of mysterious hand gestures.

"Dracula would recite what I hazarded to be part of a spell to the five onlooking dark-eyed men with bold foreheads. As he would pause, the group would then turn to a massive hole in the floor that seemed to be the core of the mountain.

"It was clear the monster was lighting the fires of hell up there!" Bram recalled. They each held strips of crimson-stained garments and approached a large rock that sat in front of the gaping pit. At this, they would imitate the Count in total unison, waving their arms in mechanical fashion while chanting: 'We knock this rag upon this lodestone to raise the wind in Lucifer's name . . . it shall not lye till we please thee again!'

"This went on for many minutes, and upon each occurrence, the unbearable roars would begin again as immense flames and offensive smoke leapt out of the horrid hole until the uncanny occurrence was repeated."

All five men, including Vlad, wore the same bags around their necks that looked to contain several items of importance that contributed to the appalling finale of whatever ritual was being performed. Then, as four other men soon joined dressed identical to the others, they all reached into the sacks and pulled out a bridle shaped from birch.

"I must have appeared invisible to the ghastly group because all ten of them walked directly by me as they gathered around the roaring furnace of heat and raised their instruments to what unleashed a sound and sight so terrible I quickly shut my eyes and screwed up my ears with my fingers in protest!" noted Stoker. "I started—my limbs grew extremely lethargic. And my muscles contracted to the degree whereas I could almost expect my brittle bones to snap at any given moment. All this transpired as the head of a fire-breathing dragon appeared from the pit, and it actually began to rain hailstones within the cavern!"

In disbelief, Bram gave a double take, only to discover his eyes and ears were not deceiving him. And at this second check, another familiar voice was heard.

"Scoala balaurilor!" sounded the great hall with a domineering echo, which proved to be a voice of gut-wrenching horror to the writer's ears. "Ye all hast mastered the skill of the Solomonari, and thus thou are to receive thy dark gift in which ye all hast eagerly awaited and respectfully earned."

Satan, grinning with delight, stepped out from behind what resembled a headmaster's throne as Vlad and the other pupils kneeled before him.

"Aye, the school of the Solomonari hast taught the secrets of nature and magic to ye—the original ten scholars! But before thy gift can be awarded, one of you must offer payment for being schooled by sacrificing thyself with a lifetime of service to me!"

The devil peered at them all as each man hesitated and looked at one another in awkward apprehension. And then Vlad Tepes stepped forward and bowed before him, kneeling downward as he kissed his master's feet. It was evident that Vlad was not yet a vampire, but neither was he alive. His eyes seemed empty, and he moved in a trance-like fashion as if he were a zombie or poltergeist. His body was in complete form, but his skin was chalky white. And then the devil replied, "Alas, the leader within my pupils hath come forward! So be it as it was to be destined: Behold . . . my *son*!"

The demon then gave all ten of the graduating apprenticeships their own book that resembled a stone talisman with nine mysterious letters in it. From a distance, Stoker watched and listened as Lucifer explained their significance and conducted the commencement ceremony.

"My faithful Solomanari, ye have all proven to change the weather through power over the dragons. With these tablets—knownst as the

'Key of Salomon' or 'The Book of Magical Instruction'—the magical instruments thou carry 'round thy necks are no longer necessary to operate your skills. The iron axes to break up the sky ice—thus producing hailstones—are now obsolete! Ye each have flawlessly captured a dragon, and thou magical books from which ye read the charts used to command the dragons are now antiquated!"

Smiles extended across the student's bloodless faces as they stood motionless, fixed upon their dark lord. They hung on to every word that was spoken to them as if their destiny depended upon it.

"Having surpassed a curriculum of a series of difficult physical tests and the mastery of nature, thou each has learned the language of the animals and the ability to shape shift into different forms," explained Satan. "So now . . . my dear disciples of the Scholomance, let these talismans provide revelation in any given situation and from it discern what he should do!"

At this, all sunshine passed away over the mountain and shady clouds drifted rapidly across the sky. All at once, the heavens were torn asunder by a vivid bolt of lightning that struck directly down the center of the crag, releasing three dragons from underneath. A combination of the bolting flashes and the powerful wind from the dragon's fierce wings caused Abraham to grow blind for a moment as he was hurled forcefully across the floor.

Meanwhile, with Satan in the center, all the men formed a circle around the Seal of Solomon, each raising their talismans to the middle until they all touched. At this, the sounds of the dragons seemed to scream from the mouth of the devil as he looked toward the sky and breathed fire—incredible flames that turned the heavens into a blazing pit of hell.

Still oblivious to any intrusion, the Sabbat continued with Lucifer taking a black chalice and cutting his left wrist with a talon from his right claw. Dark blood spurted from the wound that he drained into the cup as the others watched in breathtaking suspense. For several minutes, the cup was passed around the circle for each of Satan's minions to partake while reciting the refrain, "Lamac cahi achababe!"

Within seconds of drinking from the chalice, the black mass ended with the men reaching for the sky and growling in unison like a pack of wild, savage wolves. The Irishman looked on in breathtaking horror as he witnessed a frightful transformation in each and every pupil.

"As Jesus Christ is my witness . . . let me escape safely before God's wrath destroys them all!"

Claws grew from their fingers, and the ears on the men extended upward with puffs of hair that resembled those of a bat. Simultaneously, their eyes turned red as embers, and then from the roofs of the gaping mouths emerged long, canine fangs which sprouted to fine, pointed ends that protruded over their bottom lips like saber-toothed tigers.

Satan then leaned over and kissed them all on their foreheads while baptizing each with new names. Starting with Vlad the Impaler, he smiled a wily smile and said, "Prince Vlad Tepes Dracul is now to be known as Count Dracula, the Prince of Darkness!"

Abraham Stoker, now lying on the floor about fifty feet from the fiends, screamed out loud behind a smoldering boulder as the ten men continued to transform into hideous vampiric children of the night. But the disturbance was heard by the hounds of hell and stirred an immediate glance in his direction. Their sensitive doglike ears were now prevailing, thus his discovery was a travesty in the making—the foreigner's cover was blown. And not only had he been heard and seen, it was clear to the author that outside visitors were not welcome amongst their elite group.

When Bram discovered his invisibility had expired, he looked in all directions for a quick exit; however, five of the men had already surrounded him. Wit drooling mouths full of sharpened teeth, the other four soon followed their cohorts. All ready to make their first kill, they cornered the Irishman in a corner of the room where their fetid, acrid breath steamed over him, leaving him powerless, scared stiff, and quivering violently in a silent plight of terror.

Dracula stood next to Lucifer and said something that caused the devil to throw up his arm suddenly.

"Stop!" the demon commanded. "This man belongs to Dracula!"

A burst came from Satan's talon that immediately pushed the vampires away from Bram.

"The tremendous blow must have knocked me out for several minutes because when I awoke, the queer commencement ceremony was over, and the clout of the dragons seemed to have been passed on to the ten men, for they each, henceforth, began to levitate! The last I recall was seeing them pounce upward in flight—in a condition of shrill, morbid excitement, and as they sailed out from the top of the forbidden foothill, the blood-red sky was mottled . . . absolutely laden in what resembled to be an eclipse of the Un-Dead!"

* * * * *

Abraham awoke abruptly next to the shallow grave before the altar of the Snagov Monastery. It smoked as if it had just conjured up someone or something, and with beads of sweat dripping from his brow, Stoker wondered if that entity was *he*.

As the author rose in a perfect spasm of fear—white-faced, perspiring, trembling, and looking round him as if expecting that some dreadful presence would manifest its presence—he let out a blood-curdling scream of terror. It seemed as if his fantastic imagination had got hold of him or the lurid situation was all too real to fathom. Regardless of which may be, either would initiate a momentary lack of reasoning that questioned the man's level of sanity.

The Irishman had all too little time to react to his weird and disturbing dream as it was quickly curtailed by the still-reverberant howling of the wolves.

Have the blood hounds hunted me down? Has that hellish apprenticeship come to me . . . to relinquish more harrowing uninvited agony? However, the beasts' barks soon became a mere insignificant noise as a sort of bleak sighing sound drowned them out and quickly began to grip him by the heart.

Bram's gray eyes became wide alert and almost turned a solemn shade of lavender as he concentrated on a vague white moving mass that suddenly surfaced around the marble slab exactly underneath where he had moved. Traveling like a specter near the door of the church, the nightmarish mist seemed to circle and then close in on him, and as the concentration expanded, the yelping of the dogs grew louder and more violent. The hairs on the back of the Irishman's neck stood straight up, and the man leaned against the door of the tomb in complete awe and shock—unable to yield any movement from his own body, let alone the door—as the form of a tall, thin man stepped out of the mass. Abraham Stoker swallowed hard and attempted to gather all his learned philosophy and religious faith to face the Un-Dead—the glistening white teeth that had become the bane of his very existence.

From the spiritual center of the church, the slab underneath Stoker had somehow pushed itself back. It was exactly the same size as the one near the altar; however, a wooden coffin, all but rotted and wrapped in a pall, was revealed. Its purple plush and gold embroidery were still discernible and remarkable to look at despite their age of at least four hundred years.

Clad in yellow and brown silk brocade with sleeves of crimson, fastened with large silver buttons and cords typical of the fifteenth century, Count Dracula stepped forward with his right hand rested on the hilt of a sword. Upon his bosom was a plate of armor and a workaday harness, and atop his head was a crown with cloisonné inlay representing claws of terracotta color, each holding a turquoise jewel. With his right hand, he made a gesture of disappointment at the writer. Whilst Dracula's arm was extended, the journeyman's one opened eye noticed a gold ring on the vampire's right hand that signified the Order of the Dragon. The crest was the body of the dragon with its tail curling under to form a complete circle. Abraham studied him closely in silence and tautly waited in ticking suspense. The Impaler drew his sword and held it at the base of the foreigner's throat.

"Oh, you defiant man! How dare ye continue to test me! How quickly thou rob me of my patience! And now ye indirectly try me through thou offspring? If ye do not taketh control of thy son, then I must intervene and handle him according to my own terms and conditions, and rest assured ye will regret that I ever set foot in thy home! I will see to it you will be begging for mercy!"

The Irishman let out a forlorn groan as the sinister specter went on.

"Let no man defyeth a Prince; and any person who refuses to kneel before me will suffer a slow and painful death from *my* master. For I am your lord on earth and can buyeth any man a thousand times over . . . I can outmatch he who dares or has the gall to challenge me! The darkest things in life your fellow man fears I control in one hand! So, my dear friend Bram . . . I trusteth that ye get your house in order as I expect thou to uphold our deal. When ye produce a book I will leave you . . . never to return, however, until then, I will be watching ye and your family with an eagle eye!"

The author looked at the Count keenly but continued to shudder. Dracula then took a step closer to the man and bent down to where he was face to face with his captive spectator. The vile stench of the creature's breath filled the damp and stagnant air of the tomb and caused Abraham's stomach to churn in discontent.

With a powerful voice, the Impaler then said, "I am vampire. I am thine only God! With my animal instincts I am the ultimate predator that feedeth upon the life man worships, and through the powers of darkness, I work my magic! I am vampire . . . bow down before me!"

Bram did not react to this but instead looked at the coffin that was hidden under the stone slab in front of the entrance of the church. Dracula followed the writer's eyes and sneered offensively.

"Ha! Foolish, foolish man! Doest thou actually believeth this is my only place of refuge? I have made your earth my home for centuries, and to date, I have spread the soil of my homeland in so many places you could spend the remainder of your mortal life searching for only a few of these places I have taken up residence! Do not waste your time trying to thwart me!"

Dressed in death's ensemble, Dracula next proceeded to explain what his life was like after becoming a Solomanari. And speaking from a mouth that was previously gorged with fresh blood, he stated, "Upon being released from the school of the underworld into the realm of men, we were knownst as the 'original vampires' and spent the next several hundred years creating new and stronger breeds to please our maker and master! On Saint George's Day, sounds could be heard coming from the clay of the graves of men, women, and children. For that night was referred to by Romanian peoples as 'Walpurgis nacht,' and I saw that it became the night of the vampire—when the evil of the universe claimed full sway! The Un-Dead walked, rosy with life and their mouths tainted scarlet with blood! And so in haste to save their lives and their souls those who were left fled away to other places where the living lived and the dead were dead—but alas, where are we . . . somewhere between the living and the dead?"

As Vlad Dracula proceeded with his narration, he grew more and more animated. He then pointed the tip of his sword in the direction of a corner of the chapel. The Count smiled at the a brilliant cobweb and said, "Ah! Madame Spider has evidently been busy! Friend Bram, see it spin the web to trap her pray? Behold! The common spider must too feedeth on the blood of the living! Indeed, her masterpiece is compelling—as these insects would all agree! Ha! Doest thou see that all of nature has its place in the cycle of life? Beauty has its price, and just as her magnificent web attracteth many, she must feed, and ultimately, those that are less fortunate must meet their fate!"

At this, Dracula took his sword and swiftly brought the tip of the blade to the skin of Abraham Stoker's throat once more and hissed, "Why canst ye not be obedient like the rehabilitated Nicolae?"

The author's memory was flooded again with the accounts of the Slovak couple—the nice, helpful pair that assisted him whilst being trapped in Castle Dracula. And then he recalled the tragic ending and the last glimpse of the arachnid-like Nicolae making a meal on the contents of his wife's boiled, decapitated head. The journeyman trembled at the thought and returned his attention to the blade that was aimed at his throat—its pointy edge thrusted against the bottom of his neck, almost splicing into the delicate flesh.

Suddenly the vampire spotted the wound to the Irishman's throat that had occurred during his struggle across Lake Snagov. Immediately Dracula's eyes filled with rage, and his body seemed to surge and convulse with a wild, uncontrollable thirst for blood that caused him to leap upon the mortal like a savage animal. The attack from the vampire caused Abraham Stoker to fall backward, and the sting from the contact of the hard, tomb floor sent a shock of pain down his spine. The fiend was on top of the helpless man such as a common housecat upon encountering a mouse.

"It was as if the mere sight of blood reminded him instantly of the undying hunger that triggered his Un-Dead soul to react in the most carnal manner. His rage was like no other I had ever witnessed, and the look in his eyes jolted me back to consciousness of the awful truth and chilled me to the quick," described Abraham Stoker. "His sharp, white teeth gleamed in the gaping red mouth, and I could feel his steaming breath—fierce and acrid! A warm, rasping sensation was upon my throat as his razorlike claws tore at the collar of my shirt and pierced the skin around my neck. Though the horror of the moment seemed surreal to me, I subconsciously shielded myself with my only means of defense."

Whilst the writer's left hand guarded his jugular vein, Bram took his free right and searched Jonas's trouser pocket for the wolfsbane that he had acquired from the Hupnuff farm. When he found it, the victim displayed it freely like the foliage was an ancient spiritual relic of great import.

"The very sight of the plant provoked a sudden change in Dracula that was so remarkable that it almost made me wonder if I had imagined the entire assault. Upon the introduction to the wolfsbane, the vampire's eyes changed from a fiery red to black, and his grip around my throat went limp altogether. A look of helplessness fell over his face as his entire body left the ground and flew in the opposite direction," recalled the Irishman. "The cowering creature remained suspended above the door of the church, and for a brief moment, I felt a minute degree of pity for the wrongdoer. For somewhere deep within the brute's dark eyes was an element of a lost man that pleaded to be released from his own eternal hell."

As the two silently stared at each other intensely, Stoker could not help but notice the striking resemblance to the man in the broken portrait on the Impaler's empty grave and the hovering, helpless monster before him. Coincidentally he recalled his first encounter with the Count in England and how much older he seemed then.

"As of late, Vlad Dracula seems to have shaved off at least fifty years of age since he appeared in my study back in London! It was as if he had discovered the fountain of youth integrated within the blood that he steals from his victims," remembered the author.

At this thought, the look of pity disappeared from Abraham's face and the sight of his English home flashed inside the vampire's eyes like a vivid bolt of lightning.

Oh, Mother of God! the Irishman thought to himself. *I fear it is too late!*

The journeyman then glanced at the vampire with a look of quick pain and harrowing agony and asserted, "How dare you touch my family! What have you done to my dear wife?" he cried, clenching his fists 'til they turned white from a status of torturous despair. "Do what you wish with me, but keep Florence and Noel out of this diabolical madness! I will write what you wish, but I beg of you, please leave my loved ones alone! What has my household done to deserve such grief and sorrow?"

Abraham Stoker had hoped his cries and pleas would somehow find their way to that ounce of mortal hope remaining within the soul of the vampire.

May my words wring at his heart! However, Vlad Tepes's eyes were fixed on the wolfsbane that had dropped to the floor as the Irishman beat and shook his colorless fists together in dramatic fashion.

At this, Dracula returned to the floor, swooping down from the air like a hawk and crushed the plant by grinding it into the stone of the deck with the thickness of the heal of his leather boot.

"As I sayeth before, my friend Stoker, thou son's misbehavior is causing ye beloved Florence much grief, and any contact from you would only cause her more worry. Though their involvement in our deal—coupled with thy disobedience—has caused me a great amount of annoyance and would warrant drastic punishment by my own hand, I assure ye your family will not die. However, *you* will not returneth to them until thy part of our bargain has been hereby fulfilled. And as thou will see, the book ye will write will create such dividends thyself and your family will benefit financial independence long after thou leaveth this earth," stated the vampire.

With a hardened look upon his face, Dracula continued, "I will telegram them a short message simply stating ye are getting along well and that thou expect to returneth in three months. Thenceforth, Noel is to be the responsible man of the house as ye extend your stay in my homeland whilst you pen your manuscript."

As the writer did not have much choice in the matter at the time, he shook his head in agreement.

"I am afraid ye have done enough damage here," the Count added, placing the nail of his left index finger directly below Bram's right earlobe. "In fact, I ought to kill you here and now!" Dracula made a slow parallel-running motion across his neck to the left side as if slitting his throat. "However, I hath decided to spare you this final time and will surrender ye to my faithful Slovak who awaits you outside. He will taketh you back to my palace where thou are to commence your writing. I trust ye have learned enough and will see that you have the materials and comforts needed to complete your work."

The Count griped Stoker by the throat with his right hand, lifting the once-burly Irishman several inches off the floor.

"If there was ever a man contemplating murder and could provide a facial expression to accompany his thoughts, at that instant, Vlad Tepes gave me a look of death that left me on the cold chapel floor, shaking from utter fear and dismay," described Bram.

"I provideth fair warning that if ye slip again thyself and your family will suffer a fate like none you could ever begin to imagine in your darkest nightmares!"

A circle of mist suddenly enveloped Dracula, and then he was gone. Abraham was unsure if the Count became the cloud or if he created it to step into hiding his real exit. Like a man frantic with utmost purpose, he threw back the lid of the coffin that was well hidden under the entrance of the church. Like the gaping pit below the altar, it too was empty.

"Curses! Foiled again!" The man hung his head in disappointment and brushed both hands through the mane of his reddish beard. He paced the floor of the chapel over and over again whilst deep in thought.

To keep the vampire from ever making the monastery his home again, Stoker took the remaining wolfs bane he had upon his person and placed it in the coffin and repeated, "Blessed be he that causes the sun to rise on the evil and sends rain on the unrighteous!" The Irishman crossed himself and said a silent prayer before God.

Recalling that the vampire's powers weakened the farther it got from its homeland, Bram felt somewhat confident that he had shaken things up for his host in Transylvania, and though Dracula had every ounce of power within him to stop such intrusions, he only did so by minimal force and always spared his and his family's lives. It was obvious to him that the Count needed an author to write his chronicles, and to get this task accomplished, Dracula needed to keep his employee and his family —that is, if he is to remain hard at task—alive and unharmed. However, once the book was complete, Abraham Stoker feared for his life and those closest to him.

"I decided that if I could not kill the monster in his own homeland, I will instead drive him to London—where his powers are weaker and the land is less familiar to him—and there I will continue to hunt the wretch down to his real death," the journeyman wrote. "I will use myself as bait, his book as ammunition, and the Almighty as my protector!"

The last image the Irishman had before leaving the island was the portrait of Vlad the Impaler in complete royal attire, and his final thought was of how so many Romanian peasants and nobleman alike have gone to bed at night for the past four hundred years fearing for the notorious Prince's return to evil.

"Soon London, England, will know what it means to dread the night and to shudder at the howl of the wolf—to hide from the face that might appear in their bedroom window and to cling to their rosary like the life and soul depended upon it," recalled the author. "Alas, the coming of the Count is upon them, and if there are those that do not scare easily, in the end, they will learn that there *are* such things to elude which lurk beyond the breadth of death!"

CHAPTER 21

Hunting the Hungry

How then are we to begin our strike to destroy him? How shall we find his lair; and having found it, how can we destroy? My friends, this is much; it is a terrible task that we undertake, and there may be consequence to make the brave shudder. For if we fail in this our fight he must surely win; and then where end we? To fail here, is not mere life or death. It is that we become as him; that we henceforward become foul things of the night like him—without heart or conscience, preying on the bodies and the souls of those we love best. To us for ever are the gates of heaven shut; for who shall open them to us again?

—Mina Harker's journal

𝕿he nervous tension that manifested and consumed the air at David Godalming's shop was so thick that one needed a battle axe to cut through it. And when the old man mentioned there was one last item he had not exhumed from the large black leather bag, the two boys reeled back with sheepish expressions, creating another layer of suspense to the morbid aura of the event. Indeed, the solemn atmosphere of the place had peaked, that such adding to its existing level would construct a meltdown that no doubt would end with the chaotic outpour of frantic emotion. Nevertheless, the owner of the shop approached the last item as something of grave importance and proceeded to elucidate the significance as earnestly and carefully as with everything else he henceforth described.

"Ancient folklore suggests that Vlad Dracula was head pupil of the Scholomance—a school of black magic that was run by Satan himself—where the first vampires were said to had developed their powers from the medieval dragons that lived deep within the mountains," Godalming explained.

The old man reached inside the traps and pulled out a small dark book that was bound in the skin of swine and attached to a necklace made of ox hair. Noel and Jonathan eyeballed it suspiciously and then glanced back to Godalming as he continued his story: "Legend holds that every Solomonari received a copy of this dark book of spells from Lucifer—to which they used to practice black magic and perform mass rituals in underground churches where the dragons were worshipped and coveted as idols. It is believed that this book belonged to one of the original ten—possibly even Dracula himself—and may hold some clue to his lair, power, weakness, or means of destruction."

Jonathan let out a slight gasp as if some sort of mysterious foreboding reeked from it and gained possession of everyone and everything it came in contact with.

Noel shook his head, obviously pleased with this discovery, but then gave an expression as if he was not sure how this changed their witch-hunt scheme. "I have this overwhelming fear that something is happening to both my parents and I am next." The boy looked at the old man with bloodshot eyes. "Since time is sparse and you are used to dealing with translating old texts, can you study it while Jonathan and I begin our search?"

The three agreed that Godalming would analyze the book for clues and telegram Abraham Stoker to return to the country while Noel would quiz his mother in hopes she could provide some answers to where the vampire was sleeping during the day. Jonathan would also pay a visit to the mortuary where the murdered woman had been taken and interview the attendant that was on duty when the body turned up missing. Jonathan would also begin to search the surrounding blocks between Wellington, Exeter, and Burlegh streets. And finally, the group would reconvene at the shop in twenty-four hours to hold counsel.

It was approximately seven o'clock in the evening when an assembled handshake split up the team, but as they left the shop toward their various appointed destinations, nobody took notice to a group of twenty-four ravens that had perched themselves on the roof of the building.

As the flock sat perched, jerking their heads from left to right while pecking at smaller flying objects loose in the sky, the unusually large feathered creatures completely stood out from the others of their animal kingdom. The demonic birds of prey listened and looked on with malevolent purpose, hanging on to every word said and all movements made, and moved as like reincarnated gypsies with eyes made from crystal balls.

If only one of the three would have caught notion of the fowl tribe, it would have immediately raised suspicion amongst the group—if it had not otherwise sent the trio into an immediate status of alarm. For it could have distinctly been assumed that the wicked birds were plotting some grand method of perdition, sent up from their dark lord and master to spy on the just.

* * * * *

It had been several days since Noel Stoker had seen his mother. Dr. Van Zant was quite adamant that keeping Noel in the house would only upset the boy and prevent Florence from making a speedy recovery. Furthermore, the physician believed that his patient would feel obligated to get out of bed and take care of her son and the stress might lead to an outbreak that could infect the young Noel. The sun was sinking fast when the boy entered his house despite Dr. Van Zant's protest to do so.

"You do not disturb her sleep, eh? She is still infected, and I want her to be left alone . . ."

"Let me by," the angry son shouted. "I need to speak with her about something very important!"

When Noel found his mother soundly asleep on her bed, he cowered back in a terrorized look of agony. The young son let out a reeling gasp so breathtaking that the doctor jumped, thinking that his patient had gone into cardiac arrest. Noel put his hands over his mouth to withhold a scream, and his bloodshot eyes soon became a more distinguished red and filled with salty tears of grief. In disbelief, the boy could not imagine the almost unrecognizable shadow of a woman that was before him was actually human—let alone his own pitiful mother.

"It . . . it is Mum, correct? Is she alive?"

The doctor's stern look of territorial restriction fell from his face and nodded silently to the lad.

"What is happening to her?" the former moaned.

Florence's appearance had become one such as death. Her face was wan-looking, and her white lips were drawn back, displaying her gums that were crimson as fresh blood against her pale, waxen face. The two small white mangled wounds on her throat made him realize that the body was, indeed, his mother, and the sight sent a vivid reminder to his teenage brain of what he was dealing with. Her warm, soft, beautiful face had grown cold, hard, and ugly; her long, gorgeous hair was matted like a mangy dog and stank of the foul foam that drooled from the corners of her mouth as the stuttering breathing forced her diaphragm up and down underneath the sheets.

Noel reached out to take his mother's hand when the doctor jumped to balk. Not taking notice of Van Zant's objection, the boy took her right hand in his and cursed the Count.

"Dracula did this, Mum! But there is still hope! Believe me!"

Upon hearing these words, Florence Stoker's eyes flew open in a fit of terror. Simultaneously, she grabbed her son's right arm with both hands and pulled him down on top of her. She wailed like a banshee, masking Noel's sobs of grief—a sharp, disturbing call as a mad person makes in isolated captivity.

"Mother! It is I . . . Noel, your son . . . *your son!*"

"Did you bring me an ocean, boy? I see an ocean of bellowing blood!" she asked in a cruel voice, pushing his juvenile face to her breasts.

"Release him!" cried the doctor. "He is of your own flesh, Mrs. Florence!"

Van Zant rushed to Noel's rescue as Henry Irving suddenly sprung into the room. The sight almost seemed like the latter was lurking unnoticed for the opportunity to launch into action. But as queer as it was, nobody had time to ponder the issue, let alone discuss the matter.

"Come, Henry! Help me secure her hands! Her strength has become twofold!"

At this, the doctor motioned for Irving to intervene, grabbing her left arm as the actor seized her right. Master Stoker looked on in total shock as the men took leather belts and fastened each of her arms to loops in the iron headboard as if to suggest an evil spirit had gained possession of her body.

With an expression of fright still on his face, Noel's eyes followed his mother's toward the window where the large bat had visited her. How quickly the once beautiful, graceful, happy woman had come to this state of awful, ungraceful misery, how the buffeting at a windowpane could take a voluptuous person and destroy the body, heart, mind, and soul in only a matter of days, how in such a divine world we live in can a mere man enter into a family's life and reek such terror and havoc amongst one isolated household.

Florence's uneasiness called Noel's attention toward the drawing of the sunset—an event that seemed to have identified a peculiar freedom and internal struggle within her. The look of horror in her eyes lessened within a few minutes but remained fixed on Noel's face. In a voice that was weak but recognizable, she repeated, "The spell that I was sold is not the one that has been cast upon me!"

Noel saw that his mother was preparing to cry as her once bright-green eyes had become flooded with tears. Since her illness, they had grown dark and empty through endless days and nights of restless sleep.

The two men looked at Noel curiously as the boy took a step closer to where she whispered in his ear: "Look at me, my Noel, this is a fate far worse than death! He promised me the sweet bird of eternal youth! Yet see how my body suffers? Ah . . . and to what end? To *what* end?"

It was clear to Noel that Doctor Van Zant was flabbergasted that Florence was able to come down from such a long stupor and gain control of her reason so quickly and violently. It was almost like a physiological reaction to the moon, or perhaps it was Noel's presence that pulled her back to reality, but then again, maybe it had something to do with this person—rather, this Dracula—they kept referring to? At this thought, the doctor jumped in and pressed Noel for answers.

"Young boy, to whom is your mother speaking of, eh? And I also need to know of the man whom you refer to as Dracula . . . they are one and the same, no? And why does this man trouble you both so, eh?"

Noel nodded to acknowledge he and his mother were referring to the same man as the gentleman's entire countenance switched from one of absolute astonishment to wonder. Henry Irving began to pace the floor as if planning some grand scheme of rescue. Unsure how long his mother would remain conscious to answer his questions, Noel quickly took advantage of these few seconds to interrogate her about the creature that was transforming her once gorgeous body into a vile child of the night.

With Irish blood but of an English heart, the young lad placed his right hand against his mother's left cheek. It was an act of tenderness that made the uptight doctor smile slightly as it magically brought a small part of Florence's old self back for a brief moment. Despite her physical condition and state of bondage, her voice—though breaking occasionally with coughs and gasps for air—seemed to reclaim a sense of her otherwise graceful identity that Noel knew as his beloved mother. The actor continued to pace the floor as if preoccupied with other matters and totally unaware of any goings on.

"Mother," Noel began a with serious tone, "I need to know where Dracula is. Please think hard and tell me what you know or can see."

Lady Stoker looked at her son and seemed to understand the statement as she fell back in the bed, closing her eyes for a few seconds. After a slight pause, she looked up at him and replied, "The way to him is like no other—one must be entrenched by a bordello of blood! He talks to me in the night, but it all seems to be a multitude of lies, and during the day, he comes to me in restless dream sequences. I see events and places I do not understand . . . and his face—it seems to change from man to beast and then back to man again!"

"What does he tell you? What do you see . . . or hear?" asked the boy.

"I hear the wind rustling beyond these shroud-like ghostly curtains. I see his tall, dark figure fluttering in the breeze as he silently glides across the floor. He then begins to pledge me eternal beauty, wealth, and power . . . yet then I see the waxen pallor of his skin and the flashing darkness of his eyes—the hollow beneath that reminds me of death and sends my heart racing with utter fear! The vivid redness in his lips curls into a smile displaying his prominent canine teeth. Those . . . those fangs that sends an expression of undeniable melancholy! It diffuses a lonesome sadness deep inside of me . . ."

Noel pushed his mother further as the doctor, and Irving looked on in a state of suspended awe.

"Where is he now?" the son asked, almost in an imploring manner.

Noel Stoker was sitting down beside his mother on the bed, looking down at her bloodless face. He was in the process of stroking her fingers with his fingertips, but when the reply came, it rang like an echo as it passed her pale lips; it was as if his heart stopped.

The child's body became stationary, one firm, insensate mass of skin and blood. His pupils did not blink, his jaw was a stagnant line, and the progress of his breathing was so insignificant that it seemed to have ceased in total. With a grave expression, the reply to the question brought looks of announced fright that universally transcended upon all their faces: "He is here in this very room."

* * * * *

Dusk. A sunless hush covered the deserted streets as a disappointed Jonathan Watts walked swiftly away from the east-end morgue. The medical examiner that conducted an autopsy of the woman's body was away on call, and the attendant that was on duty when the body vanished had taken leave. According to the short, portly man that was currently on watch, he claimed, "Indubitably the ole drunkard was so overwrought by the ghastly ordeal that the poor bloke took holiday to get wallpapered and whitewashed! The chap was shaking all over, claiming that the body just 'rose up and mosey'd off' like she was just nappin'!"

Jonathan was beginning to believe the man whom he was speaking to was undoubtedly on the bottle himself as the pungent odor of alcohol filled the very air around him. Perhaps the mere occupation of these men pushed their unstable souls over the edge—the constant reminder of death that triggers a spiral of depression.

"Th' poor devil!" the boy replied.

"Lookie here, young fellow, I have enough horse sense to know a daid lass from a live 'un! And I tell you she was quite daid . . . daid as a wagon tire when she was brought in 'ere!"

After thanking the man, Jonathan decided to make his way to the place where the body of the woman was found, but not before asking one last question: "Did she have a name, mate?"

"Mary Alice Dickinson," the man politely answered. "But pray tell why you keer?"

As Jonathan made his way toward Burlegh Street, he thought about the woman's family and how they must have flown into absolute hysterics at the notion of her body missing. Indeed, the reaction to her gruesome and untimely death had to have been difficult enough, but coupled with the old sot's unbelievable story, well . . . no doubt a conquest will be pushed for and the investigation will be doubling their efforts.

The soft moonlight struck against Jonathan's blond hair, turning it a queer shade of white, transcending the freckles on his cheeks to jump out like fireflies. He was upset that Inspector Cotford was too tied up with business to supposedly entertain a "meddling fifteen-year-old boy who called on him with questions." So for all young Jonathan's good intentions, his efforts henceforth produced only a name of the vampire's victim. Though this did not seem important at the time, it was indeed a name he would never forget.

I'm afeared to go back to the others with nothin' more than a name! he thought to himself. Thus, the spunk in his adolescent brain sent him on a different quest. "If bloodsuckers only dander at night, 'eres my chance!"

Ghosts have been notoriously known to haunt the area closest to where their physical death occurred. This very thought caused the boy to shudder in his shoes, but perhaps putting this belief—as he did have faith in the concept—might be a clue to the mystery in itself and help turn up something of importance.

By hearing Godalming's summary of the police report, Jonathan was able to retrace Mary Dickinson's steps backward to the rear exit of the Lyceum Theatre. As he visually reenacted the murder in his mind, the lad's thoughts subconsciously kept drifting toward the well-nigh building. After numerous attempts of trying to shake this reoccurring feeling, his visit to the crime scene was overcome by a drastic case of the willies and, thus, cut short.

The bird-absent trees seemed to jump out abruptly. The breeze-less air began to choke Jonathan. And the longer Watts stood there, the more he found his body trembling until his palsied legs struggled to operate. For several minutes, the boy's body shuddered without end, one block completely of tension without self-power, bereft of will. Then, unexpectedly, it ceased, and with a throttled murmuring in his gullet, he tottered forward toward the theatre.

Whut godawful jitters . . .

The lad's thought was stifled as he glanced at the rear entrance again as a different thought came to mind: perchance someone at the theatre has seen someone suspicious lurking around hitherto or, henceforth, the murder? Thinking it would not hurt anyone to have a look around, he decided to give into his instinct. If nothing more, it would get him away of an spooky vicinity that appeared to be laden with unsettled spirits and bad memories.

To the boys' surprise, he found the door was unlocked and preceded to make his way inside. His eyes fastened dumbly to the darkness and the mystery of the night. And the gloomy serenity left him sagging against the back door. With shaking hands, he called out, "Ahoy!"

There was no answer.

The lights to the Lyceum were all off, and as there were no scheduled performances that evening, none of the cast or crew was presently rehearsing. Jonathan began to feel his way around a wall slowly.

"Anyone there?" he beckoned.

Only the dead silence of a cemetery answered. Within a brief moment, the boy began to doubt his decision to enter the place at all and resolved himself to the idea he would have been better off focusing on the crime scene.

Jonathan's stomach felt twice as intense as his earlier scare. And the glacial numbness of his flesh caused him to gulp in one giant, convulsive swallow as suddenly, the grand figure of a dark man reaching out startled the trespasser. The black image caused Watts's throat to throb with incredulity. With a quick gasp, he jumped and turned in the opposite direction to run; however, as the light of the full moon beamed its rays on the floor in front of him, the young lad realized he was frightened by his own shadow. He sighed a breath of relief and proceeded down the corridor, compressing his hands together—forcing the wet, quavering palms against each other, the jerking digits interweaving confoundedly.

Hell's bells, again! Th' jitters . . . damn 'em!

Within a few hundred feet, Jonathan discovered a room up ahead with a light peering out from under the doorway. As no one had answered his calls, he assumed the room had to be empty, yet the lad remained cautious all the same. The entrance was cracked, and looking through the gap, it appeared to be the dressing room of someone of importance. The quarters were in the status of a sort of disarray—such as someone who was in the process of changing clothing before leaving in a state of hurry. There were armor and regal robes strewn about the place.

After surveying through the open crack of the door for some time, Watts concluded the resident was away on some urgent business. Thus, the boy pushed against the entrance slowly and softly until it was ajar enough for his body to fit through. Quietly, Jonathan made a rapid inventory of the room, and from the few pictures that were hanging on the walls, he realized he was standing in the dressing room of a well-established actor.

All at once, the noise of the door closing behind him caused Jonathan to jump wildly and turn toward whence it came. This shocked the boy, as there appeared to be no living soul in the theatre—other than himself—and there were no open windows nearby to send a burst of air to trigger such movement. In a state of panic, the troubled lad bounded to what resembled to be the sole exit and found it would not yield. After numerous attempts of turning and twisting the knob, Jonathan accepted the reality that he was locked in.

Despite his youthful immaturity in such dire situations, by and by, the lad bottled his fear and decided he needed to either search the place for another exit or look for a spare key. Breaking the door down did cross his mind; however, this alternative could reap repercussions if reported and pursued by authorities. And then the ultimate prospecting hazard would have been to wait patiently for the coming of someone. Not only did this mean his visit would have been extended—probably until dawn for a caretaker or even Henry Irving to return—but also the likelihood of being discovered would be amply superior to the remaining courses of action.

In less than a few minutes, Watts concluded there were absolutely no other doors or windows in the room. Henceforth, he quickly began to take inventory of everything in the vicinity for any key ring or object that might unlock his sole means of escape.

With the exception of a few disorderly articles of wardrobe that was left out in plain view, the rest of the room was immaculately well kept and meticulously organized. On the dressing table were a multitude of makeup bottles in all sorts of sizes and varieties, lined up in orderly fashion. On each side of the table were three sets of drawers that each contained boxes of wigs of various styles and colors: brown, black, blond, white, red, and diversified two-toned degrees thereof.

A bookcase in the corner of the room contained stacks of outdated newspaper clippings, highlighting different performances at the theatre; a large stack of opened mail, all of which was addressed to the Lyceum Theatre; competitors' journals, and scripts by various playwrights, including Tennyson, Shakespeare, and Ibsen.

The other side of the room included an average-sized mahogany roll-top desk with matching chair. Hoping that a set of keys would be housed therein, the boy gently pushed away the cover, revealing several bottles of ink, pen quills, a small stack of post addressed to Abraham Stoker—all of which were recently dated and left unopened—and a heap of jewelry and coins. Amidst the other objects laid an address titled, "The Art of Acting by Henry Irving."

Recognizing the name as that of Noel's father's sometimes cold-natured and overdemanding employer, Jonathan's fit of urgency to find a way out magnified to that of the overzealous and egotistical owner of the space itself.

Of all the bloody 'ell, Watts thought to himself, *I'd have to get pickled in HIS room! Whut an uppity yahoo if there ever wus one!*

With an uprooted sense of insistence, the boy invaded the closet that stood as a grand-sized walk-in space off from the dressing table. It was larger than any average closet of a man, yet it was full up of elaborate costumes for all kinds of occasions. A shelf at the top contained many hatboxes, and to the left side of the closet, piled high from the floor to the ceiling, were smaller boxes filled with footwear—shoes of every kind and every color imaginable.

If the situation had been any different, the lad would have passed his time away in masquerade; however, he disliked Irving— not because he necessarily had personal reason to, but because Noel loathed him. As the seconds ticked by whilst Jonathan searched, he reminisced back to a period when Noel was several years younger, waiting in the theatre lobby with his mum whilst his father tallied up the books after a performance. The boy had grown impatient milling about, so he separated himself from his mother and roved off backstage, looking for his Pop. After finding himself lost and meandering around aimlessly for several minutes, he bumped into Irving who was still partially in makeup. The half human, half monster sight scared Noel, and when Bram found his son twenty minutes later, Henry had transformed him in full make up as the sinister Mephistopheles. Stoker scolded his employer as his boy was visually shaken from the morbid experience and feared it would have a traumatizing effect on his son. Irving simply laughed it off, claiming the author's notions were rubbish, and it was never brought up again. Although Jonathan knew well of the lasting impact regarding a man whom he already ostracized for taking advantage of Noel's father and monopolizing his time. Stoker summed up his truest feelings of the actor and fatherhood best by saying, "I could have another son, but there will never be another Henry Irving."

It was well past the witching hour when the young lad began to feel that his hopes of finding a key to Irving's dressing room had all but depleted. At this point, he had also gone through the pockets of every article of clothing, beginning with the garments that were left out in the open and concluding with the items hanging in the closet. Finally, Watts noticed a black waistcoat made of wool that was hanging on a hook adjacent to the bookcase. He mocked himself for not noticing this sooner, and praying it contained what he was looking for, the boy dug deep in the pockets. There was nothing in the front left pocket; however, the right turned out to be more promising—for there, the lad found a long brass key on a matching ring that was carved with the initials *HI* in brilliant calligraphy! With a half grin and eager aura of suspense, Jonathan approached the door and inserted the key. With a silent prayer, he turned the key.

Nothing.

"*No!*" he cried out loud. In a state of frustration, the adolescent bundle of nerves began to jerk the key back and forth—an option that proved to be no more successful than the first attempt. Finally, he returned the key to its rightful place and began to frantically grope the overcoat for other items.

Something in the inside left pocket struck Jonathan's attention. By the feel of it, he knew it was no key, but it dazzled his interest just the same. Despite his lack of maturity, it only took a moment for the reality of the situation to hit the boy on the head like a ton of bricks. Though the tales of the supernatural he, Noel, and Godalming had read and discussed were fascinating to Jonathan, he was not necessarily a part of them. And despite the fact that the horror that Noel and his family were facing was real, Watts felt more like a spectator. Likewise, the murder of Mary Alice Dickinson was of no direct interest to him, and in doing so only indirectly connected the Stoker family to the Count, that is, assuming Godalming's surmise that an association existed was correct. However, in a split second, the sandy-blond hairs on the back of Jonathan Watt's neck stood straight out as a soldier suddenly called to attention by a commanding authoritative.

In a mere second, he felt no rhythm in his chest—no heartbeat underneath his fingers. For the nucleus of his intellect seemed to have grown to stiffness, transmitting out uneven appearances of calcification 'til his cranium became as if it were made entirely of mineral. Jonathan removed what first appeared to be any old, crumpled Lyceum program from the inside pocket; however, his first impression was quickly abandoned for a much grimmer conclusion. Not only did the performance match that of the one Mary Alice Dickinson attended merely an hour prior to her murder, but also, it was autographed at the bottom by the actor. But when the boy saw that the playbill was smeared in blood, he knew he was no longer an oblique bystander. At that precise moment, he had become not only a trespasser but also an important holder of a piece of evidence to an unsolved crime.

"Sweet Mother of Jesus!" Jonathan cried out, dropping the crimson-splotched program to the deck.

The stakes had changed. The tide had turned. Indeed, he was now involved . . . whether he liked it or not!

* * * * *

The black spell book of the Scholomance took approximately eight hours for David Godalming to translate. Working right though

367

lunch and his afternoon tea break, he was just about to give up on finding anything that might help their situation—that is, until he made an important discovery in the last twenty pages of the text. The old man's eyes darted to the amulet Noel gave him which rested nearby on the table. Writing feverishly on a piece of parchment, the circulation in Godalming's toes gushed to his head as he jumped up and grabbed a light coat. Seizing the charm in his other hand, David bolted out the back door.

Alas, why did I not notice this sooner?

In fact, the old man had gotten so consumed by the black magic of the Solomonari that he had completely lost track of time. It was nightfall when he caught a cab at the corner of a late-night dive bar, where he quickly downed a spot of tea and a bran muffin and proceeded to Charles Street.

When Old Man Godalming arrived at the telegram office, a young fellow of about eighteen years of age had just hung a Closed sign on the window. As he did so, the youngster pointed to the sign with a look of sarcasm as a desperate-looking David Godalming approached. After a brief moment of door-banging and hand-signaling from both sides of the glass pane, Godalming waved a pound note in front of the boy. Within a few seconds, the old man found himself inside, ready to do business. Certainly, it is interesting and sometimes quite amusing how currency can alter policies and procedures, otherwise etched in stone, and influence the human mind— even in the noblest of gentlemen.

"My boss will not fancy the likes of me extending hours of operation for under the table profit, so let's make it quick, matey. "

"I need to send an urgent telegram to a Mr. Abraham Stoker in Transylvania who is staying with a Count . . ."

"Dracula?" interrupted the young fellow with a sort of odd look of surprise on his face.

Godalming's expression was of equal astonishment, and the two briefly exchanged a moment of awkward silence as they pondered what to say next. The old man spoke first, saying, "How on this sweet earth could you have known a name like that? You do not look like a gypsy with a traveling sideshow, and you do not carry a crystal ball either, so how—"

The boy cracked a smile and said, "I could never forget such an odd name, and it just so happens you are not the only person telegraphing the bloke at—now where was it—Poenari, Romania?"

The old man shook his head as if first confused and then slightly agitated.

"Now why did those boys not listen? I told them I would . . ."

"Boys?" the telegraph operator interjected again. "Pardon me, but it was a *man* that was in here a few days ago, wiring your same person at this . . . Castle Dracula."

Godalming's face fell. For a few seconds, he was speechless as if to guess who might have beaten him to the message. He then turned to the young man and asked with serious countenance, "Are you sure it was a message to Abraham Stoker?"

"Oh yes, indeed," the operator answered quickly. "I remember it all too well—believe me, I wish I did not, actually!"

Sensing that there was something eccentric about either the message or the messenger, Godalming drew him on.

"Could it be, my dear lad, that the person that stopped in to draft this wire was not a young man such as yourself?" Godalming asked, assuming the boy was mistaken. "And might so be only a few years his junior?"

Quickly the operator replied "Negative, sir, for not only do I recall such an unusual destination as Castle Dracula, but I vividly remember the man's visit as a peculiar experience." His teenage face turned a light shade of red as if he was blushing from embarrassment. "You see, I rarely have a customer get cross with me."

When the old man heard this, he realized he was on to something, but at the moment, Godalming was not sure exactly what it was. Clearly it was obvious the young man was retelling his story in earnest, but even though the old man appreciated his directness, more information was needed to place a finger on what had occurred.

"Can you tell me anything about the man who sent the wire?" Godalming asked.

The boy thought for a moment, looking up at the ceiling as if searching for some answer. "I suppose it would not be of any harm to say he was a tall, thin bloke with dark hair and pointed nose . . . possibly in his mid-fifties . . . slightly pale fellow . . ."

The description caused the old man's blood to freeze in his veins. Swallowing hard before answering the attendant, he replied, "It is very important that you answer this as truthfully as possible. Do you remember what he asked you? Can you tell me why he was unpleasant?"

The young man exchanged a look as though his customer was asking him to disclose too much information. Seeing this, Godalming handed the operator another bank note. The attendant took it and looked around to ensure that his boss did not notice the transaction prior to answering the question.

"I remember he seemed to be in some sort of hurry, but what really got the fellow upset was when I questioned his message."

"I'm afraid I do not understand," Godalming answered. "Why would you do such a thing or even take stock in such matters anyway?"

"Because it is not to be dispatched until tomorrow. You see, he postdated the wire, and I—assuming he forgot what day it was—called him on it. This is when he scolded me for questioning his intentions and reaffirmed he was adamant for it to go out as he directed. It all just seemed queer, considering the text of the message seemed of such urgent nature."

At this Godalming seemed to grow very nervous, and the operator could hear it in his voice as the old man began to pace the floor directly in front of the customer counter. He looked at the young man keenly but with an aura of discomfort and said, "I have my suspicions of who visited you that night, however, it is of utmost importance that I know for sure—"

"I don't remember his name offhand," the attendant interrupted sharply.

"Can you tell me what the message said?" asked the customer.

"I am sorry, sir, but we are closed, and I really need you to come back tomorrow morning when my supervisor—"

Godalming held his index finger up to the young man's mouth in a nonthreatening way and said softly in an honest but desperate tone, "Son, please listen to me carefully. I know you have a job to do, and be rest assured I will see to it that your boss is reminded of what an outstanding worker bee you are. However, I am afraid that a man and his family are in grave danger at the moment, and time is of the essence! The telegram you refer to is of dire, life-threatening urgency to me and could help save a boy's life, a woman's soul, and a good man's sanity. So I ask you now, in all honest intentions, will you please help me?"

Godalming then placed a wad of money in front of the teenager, who, in due course, seemed to be touched by the speech. The later could see the pain and deep sense of desperation in his patron's visage. With a face now full of sympathy and visible emotion, the young man pushed the money back. Having stepped away from the counter for a brief moment, he returned with a piece of paper he had secretly placed in his front shirt pocket. The operator handed it to Godalming and stood patiently by as his customer read it silently:

FLORENCE HAS TAKEN ILL. YOU ARE NEEDED AT HOME. RETURN TO LONDON ON THE NEXT TRAIN LEAVING BUDA-PESTH.
—HENRY

Vaguely, innate within the thrashing membranes of thought, the old man could not comprehend how he could remain standing still. He had to act. But as dejection trampled him to the earth, prostration failed him. He and time seemed to be trapped on a hook, and all stood set as if life and the world had jolted to an arrest.

There must be progress!

The reaction on David Godalming's face was of one of utter shock and disbelief. For a long while, he stood frozen. And then once more, he began to pace the floor speechless for several minutes. The old man began to talk to himself in short incoherent murmurs, but by and by, he turned to the attendant and said with a stern look in his eye, "The entire family must be warned!"

"Now it is *I* who does not understand," the youngster said, taken aback by his customer's new state of behavior. The glare in Godalming's eyes almost frightened the lad, who actually took several steps back from the counter.

The old man quickly filled out a wire submission slip, which read as follows:

BRAM, IT IS OF GRAVE IMPORTANCE YOU RETURN HOME IMMEDIATELY. TRUST NO ONE. WILL EXPLAIN IN PERSON.

—DG

Handing the request to the operator he explained, "This telegram must be delivered prior to—and I must stress *prior to*—the former and be dispatched during the day. I am in no position to explain such a strange request, but please understand I have very good reason. Know my intentions are with earnest purpose and utmost sincerity. Not only must the messenger deliver it during daylight hours but it must also be handed directly to Abraham Stoker—and only Mr. Stoker himself—understand?"

The young man nodded he understood as he wrote a series of directions on the transmission slip.

"It is critical that nobody else sees or intercepts this message!" Godalming added while sliding the pile of money over again in the attendant's direction.

"I will begin work on your request immediately," the lad said, handing back most of the money, "but sincerely, this is not all necessary."

His customer repocketed the bills and shook the operator's right hand proudly.

"Your friends are not the only people you are out to help tonight, for you have taught me a fine gentleman's lesson and have made a new confidant in the process!" the attendant added with a smile large enough to display the pearly whites of his front teeth.

"And indeed, you are a true gentleman's gentleman!" the old man said boisterously.

Leaving the telegraph office, David Godalming walked briskly to an awaiting cab that was parked across the street. The old man knew he needed to get in contact with Florence Stoker to warn her immediately, but foremost, he needed to call an emergency counsel meeting with the two boys to discuss his findings within the black book, and now . . .

A sudden and quick rustle startled the old man's ears. Simultaneously, without warning, the dark silhouette of a winged object cast its eerie reflection on the ground as it flew over the subject's head. Godalming jumped whilst entering the cab, and expecting the worst, he reached for the loaded pistol of silver bullets that was always carried on his side. The shaken fellow withdrew a sigh of relief to see it was only a large vulture scooping up a dead field mouse lying in the road.

"Cursed birds!" he said with a slight chuckle but sneering at the driver. "There is still a little life in me yet, so they will have to wait a while before making a meal out of this old buzzard!"

Driving home, Godalming thought over his newly found discoveries and henceforth decided that the vampire was cleverer than he had anticipated. *This only proves my theory. Vlad has spies to keep watch during the day, and if my senses are not failing me, his old powers of mind control have proven that the creature he has become is a mere reminder of what time alone cannot kill!* he thought to himself.

Pulling out his notebook containing the translation of the Scholomance, the old man underscored the name "Henry Irving" on the following page. Below it, he began to write, "Indeed, he was spawn from an evil as old as time yet it feeds off the up-to-date intelligences modern society has to offer. And so be it that he will be destroyed in this prevailing nineteenth century with a vengeance of the centuries before—to honor those bodies that he slaughtered and those souls that he raped forever! Thus for the sake of the Stoker family and Jonathan Watts, I pray there is granted time to inform them!"

CHAPTER 22

Confessions of a Madman

> All men are mad in some way or the other;
> and inasmuch as you dear discretely with your
> madmen, so deal with God's madmen, too the
> rest of the world.
>
> —Van Helsing to Dr. Seward

Noon. The door to the Snagov Monastery opened without indication and flooded the chapel with sunlight. After Abraham Stoker's near-death encounter with Vlad Dracula, a sort of breathless anxiety had consumed the former. The air in the church seemed to have grown shallow, almost all at once, and Bram found himself getting lightheaded and weary of the awful surroundings.

The bright rays streaming in from the world outside almost blinded the Irishman; however, he bounded for the door just the same—as if dreading that it would close again in the mere passing of seconds. The sheer sight of the broad daylight shocked the man, filling his mind with a whirlpool of mystifying thoughts.

Unless my sense of time and space are not deceiving me, I could swear to it that Count Dracula was just in this very room moments ago, yet . . .the sun is up in the sky! How can this be possible? Am I indeed going mad, or has the vampire found a new power or way to manipulate the ancient myth to where he can walk about during the day without harm? the author thought to himself.

By the position of the sun, Bram guessed that it was early afternoon. And due to the sight of visual evidence of a passing storm (overblown trees, random debris, and stagnant rainwater), it sent a mixed reaction to the free man: at least part of the horrible ordeal was not a distressing fabrication within the deep recesses of his mind. Could it have been the trip through the Carpathian Mountains and beyond into the school of the Scholomance had been a terrible nightmare—that the visit from the vampire was precipitated by his imagination running wild?

As Stoker pondered these thoughts, he collected his bags and began to walk toward the direction of the lake, stopping every few hundred yards to take in the scenery. He was hungry, thirsty, and coveted the desire to speak to a *real* human being. There was clearly no sight of either the father nor nun, and when Bram approached the chapter house to where he had recalled the priest had taken shelter during the storm, he found it bolted shut. After knocking several times had yielded no reply, it seemed to the Irishman that the only two caretakers had up and disappeared off the island. If this was true, Abraham was again . . . alone.

The raging storm of not so long ago had produced several puddles of fresh rainwater that had yet to be evaporated by the sunlight or heavily polluted by the various germs and sources of nature. The writer stopped at one of the larger random pools and proceeded to wash the dirt and grime off his face and beard—to which the latter was growing long and grisly since it was last trimmed at the Hupnuff vineyard. The journeyman then made his toilet behind a large willow tree whilst having spotted several bushes growing an assortment of wild berries: juniper, blue, and cloud—all to which he gathered and partook of whilst washing them down with rainwater.

It donned to the foreign alien of the country that one sure way to try his current state of mind would be at the dock for Vlad was certain that Nicolae, the groundskeeper that the vampire spared after helping Stoker escape from Castle Dracula, would be awaiting him. Hitherto there was no sign of any living soul on the small island—

neither man nor beast—and the calmness that enveloped the place was beginning to transcend a soothing, solitary state of tranquility over the author. In the distance, he saw the boat that he used to row his way over from the mainland docked several hundred yards from where he had abandoned it. Assuming that the ferocious storm tossed it about and washed it back up again, he was overjoyed to see its presence, despite its relocation and not-so-distant gruesome memories. Seeing that nobody was there to greet him, a cunning grin swept across his face, followed by a boisterous chuckle, both of which, coupled with the berries and water, acted like doses of a long overdue medicine.

Bram turned and looked back at the desolate medieval monastery that appeared to be sinking before his very eyes. The dreary willow trees hung over the towering, rustic edifice, and the faint sound of the ringing bells began to chime in his ears. Were they a signal of caution? Or perhaps they were meant as a tributary honor of respect to those that were held prisoner, tortured, and buried there? As the writer's eyes caught a last glimpse of the fourteenth-century foreboding portals, he believed the bells were ringing for him—the dead was thanking him for driving the evil off the island.

Notwithstanding, the dismal structure still seemed to be calling out to him in a grimmer sort of fashion, such as an unbeknownst supernatural force that was hard at toying jesters with his mind. The Irishman was beginning to feel its influence strongly when suddenly a loud, shrieking noise—like the sound an infant makes when in agony—came from the direction of the shore.

Reclaiming his traps, Abraham Stoker quickly set foot toward the coastline to investigate. Within a matter of seconds, the distraction came again; however, this time it was more distinct and prolonging to the man's troubled ears. It was clear that this time the noise was no human baby but rather that of a feline. Its cry was one of pain or torture, and from the sound of it, the animal was confronting death.

The clamor was almost too unbearable to withstand, so Bram hastened to the dock area to search for the cat, thinking that it might have gotten itself marred or caught up in some entangled predicament during the storm—perhaps trapped underneath a fallen tree or intertwined in a line. Then there came a low growl that lingered for several seconds, and finally . . . it ceased. Expecting an unfavorable fate, the writer's face fell, and he was saddened that in all probability, he arrived too late to save the poor animal.

All at once, a form resembling that of a medium-sized adult black feline was hurled into the lake. Before it made a splash in the water, the Irishman took notice that there was something unusual and mysterious about the incident. Indeed, Puss took flight from the sole rowboat—to where the man was headed for—and having his eyes already fixed on the small, wooden craft, he witnessed the bizarre whirl of the cat very clearly and its startling condition: It was headless.

As an astonished, wide-eyed Abraham stared at the reddening waters to which circled the bloodied remains, his sight and mind immediately reverted back to the boat. Approaching it slowly, the wild noise of a much larger savage beast digesting could be heard. There were sounds of bone snapping and flesh tearing, followed by the disturbing resonance of munching meat. This unsettling pattern of the partaking of food continued for a brief time, and Stoker concluded that whatever had trespassed upon his only means of departure was dangerous and could not be of human race. Quietly picking up a large rock from the ground nearby, the writer held it up in position to strike the thing.

As he walked softly, shaking from fears of the unknown, the author's muscles tensed from a prevailing nervous consternation. The tension only grew with each passing second. And then, taking one step closer, he kept his eyes fixed on the vessel . . . and waited.

When the ugly noises stopped, to the writer's surprise, the form of an aged brown hat appeared. And as it rose from the boat, he was flabbergasted to see the head of a man! He stood with his back toward the journeyman, grumbling something to himself, whilst he tossed what appeared to be pieces of the small animal's skull in the water.

The man was dressed in linen breeches of a beige color, of which were severely soiled, and a white shirt with wide sleeves. After discarding several more bone fragments, he proceeded to cleanse the feline's blood from his hands by wiping them on an apron that was tied about his waist.

The Irishman's circulation became impaired. He stood help-lessly by—paralyzed and dumb of thought—as the harrowing scene riveted his nerves and ravished his limbs with an inconsolable trepi-dation. The red hairs of Abraham's beard seemed to uncurl and prick into his skin as if in a means to awaken from a nightmare. His gray eyes bulged out of their sockets, withholding any signs of blinking.

The monster man had turned in the foreigner's direction. And as he did so, Bram was appalled to see the face of the Slovak, scratched in several places where Puss had evidently went on a war-path. The man's shirt was likewise clawed in several places, and his hob-nailed boots made of mule skin had traces of fresh blood splat-tered on the toes. Whether the droplets belonged to the man or the cat, the Irishman was not for certain, but one incontestable thought rang clear in Abraham's mind: the man had evolved into a maniacal psychopath.

Something horrible happened to his mind.

"If the blood feast that took place at the cave outside Poenari Mountain was of the mouth of hell, Nicolae has since regressed deep within the pit, forfeiting all power of reason that works the human soul! For if Vlad Dracula forced the Slovak to murder his own wife then, only the almighty espied him in the torture of the feline," the author wrote in his journal. "To look at him gave me deep pity for I could tell the Count's disturbing influence had a profound lasting effect on the Slovak. His once sanguine, calming, levelheaded nature had died out and was replaced by a mysterious, dangerous, morbidly excitable temperament. The later appears to have resulted in the man having hallucinations of gloomiest proportions and a carnivorous fixation I have yet to understand."

The lunatic stood staring at his audience with a wild look on his face as he gnawed the fresh blood away from underneath his finger-nails. Then with a swooping motion from his left hand, he welcomed Abraham Stoker aboard. The writer, having no other alternative but to swim across the lake, was forced to acquiesce. Recalling his terri-fying solo sail over to the island, Bram could not help noticing that the Slovak's physical strength, which seemed to had doubled from the way he remembered Nicolae at Castle Dracula, might work to his advantage.

At least I have one of Dracula's raving madman to protect me from harm's way, he thought to himself as he nodded politely and stepped on board. But secretly the man began to scheme—plotting and waiting patently for the right opportunity to separate himself from the half-wit servant and to plan his journey back to old England.

The two men did not speak for some time but, rather, studied each other with short, inconspicuous random glances. As Nicolae paddled their way across the cold, dismal lake, the writer sat as far away from the crazed driver as possible. Crowding the corner of the boat, he sat alert as a watchdog, almost as if he were prepared to dive into the pool of skeletons at any precise moment and swim to shore— that is, if a possible cannibalistic attack on him proved to be more fatal than the sleeping zombies of the deep.

Seeing the Slovak again only made Stoker cognizant of the fact that Vlad Dracula's visit to the monastery had to be true. This thought made the Irishman's core grow full of feelings mixed of terror, anxiety, and weariness; however, simultaneously, it calmed his fear that his mind was not conjuring up false hallucinations of horror. It was clear to Abraham that if there were any previous doubt that his own mind was becoming unhinged, observing Nicolae only reinforced that there was far worse out there and that hope was still available for the sane.

"He [the Slovak] gave me numerous sidelong glances that provoked chills equivalent to those of a murderer," recalled Bram. "I could not help but feel he was consumed by a profound problem that distressed him beyond his own scope of reason, and an aura of danger seemed to manifest all around him. A look of warning seemed to be rooted in his face, and all this unpleasantness made me watch him carefully and pray for my wellness."

Rowing the infested lake for the second time proved to be as uneventful as crossing the Thames on a clear, deserted day. All was calm and silent with the exception of the driver who hummed to himself softly. Keeping a discreet eye out for any menacing behavior, the author recalled his last visit from the Count and how folklore asserted that the undead were unable to cross water and detested holy symbols. For the remainder of the boat ride, he pondered this belief. *Is this why Vlad the Impaler was buried in a monastery surrounded by a lake?* Abraham Stoker thought to himself. If this was so, just as Dracula was able to move about during the daylight hours, Bram was confounded by the notion of how the vampire was able to come and go as if completely unaffected by the deep waters or religious relics that encompassed his tomb.

"There is a grand piece of this mystery still to be resolved. Think! Oh, what can it be?"

It took approximately twenty minutes to score dry land again. As the rowboat touched the dock, Nicolae took a burlap rope and tied the small vessel to the pier and brought Stoker's bags ashore. Parked alongside the narrow country road was the same coach that brought the Irishman from the Budapest train station to Vlad Tepes's birth palace in the town of Sighişoara, Transylvania. As Abraham approached the dark, gothic carriage, he sensed that his own spirit haunted it. Recalling his previous journey and everything that pro-ceeded it, the journeyman wished he could somehow reclaim his old soul and cast aside the horrific happenings—the stories of impale-ment, vampirism, and satanic rituals that kept him up at night in a state of terror and tried his sanity during the day.

Alas, *if. . .* only he could.

As the Slovak was placing the writer's traps in the caliche, the two reddish horses sniffed and snorted at the air like they sensed something only the animal kingdom could identify. And then, with no prior warning, they began to rear and kick wildly, to which Nicolae grabbed their reins and began to whisper to them like a sweet mother calming her young suffering from night terrors.

It only took a brief moment for both men to see a wild turkey that strutted its way in front of the horses. Having been frightened by the loud outbursts by the excited beasts, the bird began to stagger stupidly back and forth across the road in an aimless, foolish manner, much as an incarcerated sot would mill about a cell while liquored up on whiskey.

"The events that followed disgusted me in a way to the extent I had to lie down and trust that the Almighty would watch over me as my stomach churned from revolt," described Stoker in his diary. "Upon noticing the trajectory-challenged fowl, the man immediately dropped my luggage as a deranged look sparked within his eyes. I felt as if some unsettled scheme began to pan out in his demented mind. Quickly, the ignoramus began to chase down the poor game until at last, it was caught. And as if he had sufficient cause for his actions, the loon took the helpless creature by the neck, choking it in the process. Seeing this behavior as abnormally cruel, I called out, criticizing the man, and begged him to turn the fowl lose. My actions seemed to be in vain as my protest only made him break out in a blaze of fury. To my most nauseated disbelief, how shall I describe what the lunatic did next? With both hands around the poor creature's neck, the mad fellow placed the head of the entire bird inside his mouth and proceeded to make a meal of it—*alive and raw!* The mere sight of the heinous event, coupled with the pitiful squawking that followed, sent me into a panic of squeamish outrage and the horses into a status of untamed annoyance."

"Great heavens!" shouted the Irishman as Nicolae spit out a bloodcurdling shell on the ground and tossed the lifeless pile of feathers to the side of the road. Whatever fear had dwelled up in the Irishman's heart seemed to pay no heed to his overbearing brain that spurned out words of admonishment whilst scolding the man out of a sense of utmost revulsion.

"Oh, woe!" Stoker exclaimed. "To what purpose within your frail brain drove you to such an abominable act of brutality? To what level of lunacy can one man attain and still call himself a gentleman by his own right? How could anyone duly justify the diabolical madness you enacted afore my own eyes! Speak, man, of your colossal gall!"

The Slovak picked several feathers out of his teeth and approached Abraham as politely as any rational person would. And with a smile polluted with the harsh reeking of fresh blood, he said, "The bird was very succulent . . . wholesome to my wits! I already feel as though it has fed me new life and nourishment of knowledge!"

Stoker was entirely thunderstruck by this harrowing statement, and if he had developed a phobia regarding Nicolae hitherto, at this precise moment, his mere presence made his limbs shake in utter terror. Trying his best to not regurgitate his last meal, many different thoughts came to the forefront of his mind. It was clear the man had to be an underdeveloped homicidal maniac. And even though he was sent by the Count to take him back to Castle Dracula, what if he fancied a craving for dessert along the way?

The shock was invasive to the foreigner. His heart pounded like that of a drum, as he stood motionless in self-deprecating bones and skin.

It has been said that madman carry with them tremendous strength. Though the burly writer was several inches taller and larger than the Slovak, the former was weary, malnourished, and weakened by his travels abroad.

What am I to do now? the prisoner thought silently to himself. *An even grislier thought: What will HE—the monster man—do!* As the former watched the pathetic dupe unwind, Stoker realized that running would only get him lost and make the man agitated and more dangerous.

He will surely come after me.

"Come, Mr. Abraham Stoker," Nicolae said in an inviting manner. Sensing the terror in the Irishman's eyes, he smiled cunningly and said, "You are in my safekeeping, Mr. Stoker . . . my master needs you for your skill, so come, go write, take a ride on the devil's knee again, but I assure you, no harm will cross your path under my watch!"

"Augh! The thought of journeying anywhere with such a specimen of filth in a caliche of calamity causes my breath to gag in flagrancy!"

Fearing further protests at the present might trigger a spout of cannibalism, Bram quickly climbed into the coach and lay down to appease his unsettled stomach. But most of all, he stayed awake to think, watching the driver with an eagle eye.

The Slovak's grotesque actions and disturbing words dwelled on the writer like a traumatic episode on a frail, elderly woman. As he thought about them, the journeyman began to see a pattern in the Slovak's behavior. His wife—the feline . . . the wild turkey – it had become obvious to him here and now that the man had been systematically digesting the brains of other beings!

"To say he had a hunger for knowledge would be as ironic as comparing the Slovak to Dracula's undying thirst. For the method to his madness was of revolting equality," Abraham Stoker described. "Could his mad brain carry a thread of inferiority? And if so, could it be that by ingesting the brains of other creatures bring physiological satisfaction - inasmuch like a queer antidote to his shattered ego and swayed vanity? To combat his thread of sanity which sleeps in silence? And if size is of the relevance, how would he get on with the brain of a sperm whale?"

The carriage bounded over familiar territory as the foreigner began to organize his thoughts, notes, and journal to begin work on the ghastly tale that Vlad believed would set his spirit free from the eternal damnation of the Un-Dead. Using a combination of what he had read, dreamed, experienced, or heard—either from the lips of others or from the fanged mouth of the monster himself—the writer plotted out a spellbinding twenty-eight chapter outline, originally consisting of three books. From voivode to vampire, an early draft of the immortal work *Dracula* was born. However, as a madman drove the coach that took Bram Stoker across the twisting Transylvanian Alps, little did the Irishman know the macabre manuscript was not over; for the ending of his tale—as with the fate of the terrible Count he so loathed—rested in his own mortal hands.

* * * * *

As the caliche pulled up alongside the walkway that stood before Castle Dracula, Abraham Stoker's gut groaned whilst his body shuddered. According to his internal watch, it was early evening, and the rolling clouds had temporarily blocked the Poenari sun, which cooled the brisk air. When the Irishman finally mustered up enough willpower to step out of the coach and placed both feet on the ground, he noticed that the overcast sky had an eerie effect over the grand structure. Truly, it was like the man had stepped into someone else's bad dream—at the prelude of an unfortunate event that was preparing to unfold.

Seeing the immense boldness of the fortress now for the first time during the daylight hours, Bram was able to capture its true impact. The dramatic, ivy-clad ruin overlooked him with its intimidating five cylindrical towers consisting of platforms for cannon and angles for crossfire. Its walls, double-reinforced with stone and brick, were undoubtedly built to withstand a possible Turkish bombardment.

As the madman unloaded the writer's traps from the carriage, Stoker waited silently as an aura of doom and gloom overtook him like a death-like stillness that precedes a destructive storm.

"I have brought him, Master! We are here!" the Slovak shouted wildly. Surveying the area in an entire 360-degree radius, Abraham saw that he was utterly alone with Nicolae. The former looked upon the lunatic that seemed to have worked himself into a state of excitability the author could not understand. But within that precise instant, the foreign guest encountered a moment of truth so overwhelming he reeled back from the shock of reality. The single thought caused the journeyman's teeth to press together 'til they ached as his marbled gray eyes froze dumbly on the madman:

Both of us are prisoners of Dracula's Castle!

As the Irishman watched Vlad's irate, faithful follower mumble incoherent words to an unseen person, a vast degree of pity filled Abraham Stoker. Though the reality of the situation was grim, he realized the Slovak was completely under the Count's control, and much like a lab rat, the castle would be his ever-dying fate.

The crazed servant gave Bram a strange sideways look that disturbed the writer immensely and muttered his way up the front courtyard:

"Master, please hear me! The foreigner is here! I am free of this duty, so keep your oath to Nicolae!"

The Slovak uttered those words with a bloodthirsty tone—a manner that could only suggest murder on the horizon. The underlying hint caused the existing stress and fear within Stoker's heart to begin to thump terror throughout his entire body.

There was a strange sense of irony in the fact that the man before him, the gentle, sane Slovak that helped the Irishman escape, was now a raving psychopath inviting Abraham to his demise. Keeping his distance, Bram questioned Nicolae's importune words that seemed to have only been heard by himself and were thereafter lost in the bitterly cold wind that swirled throughout the Transylvanian Alps.

"Nicolae," the writer began, "you speak as if Dracula has promised you something of great value."

At hearing this, Slovak approached the great gothic door of the abode and grinned like a Cheshire Cat.

"Ay! The Master knows all!" he said, placing down the bags. "He has longed for a skillful writer whilst I crave for an exceptional brain!"

Abraham Stoker stood silent in a paralysis of unfathomable horror. Indeed, it is only in a moment of dire trepidation or alarm one can truly appreciate the bodily reaction and psychological condition that the living human form processes and its undistorted consequences of traumatic revelations.

His skin crawled. His blood polarized within his veins. And then a numb silence gained control as the gut-wrenching revelation consumed his soul:

The vampire was going to give Abraham Stoker over to the maniac after the novel was complete!

Attempting to hide his panic, Bram bottled his emotion and quickly began to scope out the surrounding area as the Slovak proceeded to hum a tune to himself whilst digging in his left trouser pocket—as if searching for a key to the front entrance of the castle.

"This sudden realization was clear: If I were to ever set foot in London again or have the opportunity to rejoin my family, I had to perform the *unthinkable*—there and then—or otherwise surrender myself by reentering the caliginous walls of the castle that would become my eternal tomb!"

Though the unattended carriage was in running distance, Stoker knew that the servant would become outraged and come after him if he made an attempt to overtake it. Thinking on his feet, his roving eyes caught a quick glimpse of some sort of tool that was partially covered up by ivy and wild weeds that were almost suffocating the side of the towering castle. Looking closer, he realized it was a kaiser blade that he assumed was left by a groundskeeper, possibly even the Slovak himself, used to thin out some of the overgrowth. The half-moon-like cutting edge was razor sharp on one side, dull on the other, and was attached to a long wooden handle of about four feet in length. As there were no signs of rust, the Irishman assumed it was recently used.

As Nicolae proceeded to inventory the contents of his right trouser pocket, with a wry face, Abraham discreetly took a few paces forward until he was within reach of the blade.

Sweet Mary, Mother of Jesus, do not forsake me now! he said to himself.

As the writer's arm extended to grab the handle, he heard a dreadful rasping noise—such as one attained by rubbing two objects together—followed by an intimidating hissing sound. Stoker immediately froze in his tracks as he saw two beady black eyes staring directly at him approximately twenty feet away. Bram recognized the creature as a long-nosed adder, roughly ninety centimeters long, and slowly began to back off from the poisonous snake. As he did so, the coiled gray and black mass continued to project a low rasp from chafing its scales, whilst it watched him intently through the dark stripes stamped behind each eye.

When Abraham felt he was out of striking range, his peripheral vision began to look for a large stick or some object he could use to wedge the kaiser blade without coming in direct contact with the viper. In less than a minute, he noticed a fallen limb that looked about ten feet long to his right.

Before he could act, all at once, there came a deafening foul hiss from the snake—a sudden noise that was more like a breathtaking shriek—as it lunged its entire body length directly at him. The Irishman cringed in an immobile position, and as mounds of perspiration collected on his face, he braced himself and prepared for a miserable end.

Out of nowhere, the quick image of an extended arm attached to a grasping hand came into plain view. And before the slithering serpent was upon him, the crazed Slovak had seized it as if it were an everyday inanimate object. The journeyman exhaled a lengthy sigh of relief as he looked on at the reptile being jerked away from the brush. Completely confounded by this rescue, the writer lost his balance and fell against the bank of the castle, amidst the overgrowth.

"*Vipera ammodytes!*" Nicolae said with a crooked smile as if talking directly to the Viper. "Behold! The Ancient Asp!"

"The wild man seemed to completely forget his purpose and became distracted of anything else but the hissing animal he griped tightly in his right hand," wrote Abraham Stoker. "In an inexplicable way, it almost appeared the two were communicating to each other, and for a brief moment, I actually believed this was so!"

The dark-brown marking that ran the length of the snake's back stood out boldly as it hung extended in midair, and the author could not help but wonder if the two had formed an alliance of the reptiles and were in the process of some grim purpose.

Whilst they were oblivious to his presence, Stoker's gut instinct communicated it was time to act. Seeing the kaiser blade lying on the bank, directly within arm's length of his left hand, he crossed himself and whispered out loud, "Lord, forgive me for what I am about to do!"

Mustering enough courage to complete an act he knew was beyond his scope of a gentleman, he apprehended the wooden handle with both hands in a deathlike grip and approached the Slovak from the side.

Just as it appeared Nicolae was about to make a meal of the serpent, the eccentric caught the glaring glimpse of the razor-sharp blade come at him and let out a bloodcurdling shriek as the metal shattered his neck bone and tore through the flesh, separating his head from his body.

"May God give you peace from your madness!" cried the journeyman with a flushed face dripping of sweat coupled with tears of compassion.

The decapitated head flew from the body amidst a fountain of spurting gore and rolled down the embankment far below. The body seemed to jerk and convulse for several seconds but finally staggered a few paces before falling upon the rocks in a bloody heap.

Having never killed a man before, Abraham Stoker fell to the cold, stony ground in complete exhaustion. Every ounce of color had escaped from his face, and he shook all over from nervous tension. The actual event—in its grim entirety—flashed before his murderous eyes in only mere seconds of the clock. Indeed, in all actuality, if the vital fluid was not on his hands, and the remains of the vampire's servant were not afore him, the instigator would have thought it was all a surreal crime.

Where exactly is one supposed to do when desolation has left him with only his faith to turn to? With heart in hand, the man prayed for the longest, begging for forgiveness and mercy. He sensed that his anatomy was turned completely inside out—that his naked conscience was being displayed in broad daylight. Twitching nervously from the traumatic aftereffects of shock, Stoker worked to comprehend the gripping terms of his actions and looked to God for a guiding hand.

The man's head ached from the loud panging of his pulsating arteries as the residue of stress dripped from his ravaged body. The dangling limbs were lifeless. Aloof. Without sensation. And the foreigner's widened eyes resembled broken saucers, unawares of all his surroundings, as he remained fixated on the dead monster man, whom he—as unimaginable as it seemed upon the registration of his mind—just murdered.

"Hark, when the cold, hard truth calls upon you so unexpectedly and the harshness of the objective phenomenon slaps one's face crudely, as if to lure its visitor out of oblivion, even a writer is at a loss for words."

He recoiled from the corpse with snuffed breath. And for several minutes, Bram muttered incoherently to himself.

Evening was at hand.

Holding himself rigidly, the author mustered enough willpower to stir. Next came a regaining of thought: first of Florence, then of Noel, and finally . . . the Count.

He had to take action.

I must somehow return home!

The viper was nowhere to be found, thus assuming that the Slovak lost his grip on the serpent whilst being struck by the kaiser blade, Bram resolved himself to believe that it slithered under a rock or back into the overgrowth alongside the castle walls. Regardless, before discarding the lifeless body of the victim into the Argnes River, the foreigner was careful where he stepped and placed his hands at all times.

The Irishman finally pulled the blood-soaked corpse past the awaiting coach and down the steep hillside to the river below. After repeating a silent prayer, he tossed the body over and shrunk to the ground in a sort of traumatic reverie. He sobbed uncontrollably for a long moment as the crystal clear mountain water turned crimson from the plasma that flowed freely from the wide-open wound at the neck of Nicolae's headless body.

By and by, his daydreaming was abruptly cut short. Without warning, a sharp sting shot through Stoker's body like a loud cannon that brought him to his feet. The horrible, blinding pain was inflicted by a quick bite wound in his left forearm, directly below the elbow. Stumbling backward and then again to his knees, the writer was shocked at what he witnessed before him:

"For there—there on the river bank, directly in front of my eyes—was the Slovak's head! His eyes were looking straight at me, burning red as hell fire, but . . . no! I counted four . . . actually *four* livid eyes! For slithering out of the mouth of the victim was the same ghastly gray and brown reptile that was no doubt the culprit of my injury hitherto!"

Abraham's head began to spin as the poisonous hemotoxic venom began to pollute his bloodstream. He heard the vile snake hiss and rasp whilst it struck terror in its victim with a deep, amber glowing beady stare that seemed to only suggest an evil act of vengeance not to be ignored.

Naturally, as the wicked pit viper crawled out of the mouth of madness, it was ironic to think that the two carnivores had switched places, for it was the lunatic's brain that was presently for the taking. Wishing he had the awful kaiser blade in hand, Bram watched the serpent sliver passed him and up the rocky slopes before collapsing on all fours. Knowing the massive tissue damage the deadly venom could cause to his body if medical aid was not administered soon, he began to summon for help.

Suddenly, snowflakes began to fall from the wide-open sky. As the Irishman lay helpless on his back atop the cold, jagged embankment, he looked up, groaning in agony as he held the flesh wound of his left arm, which smarted so. Simultaneously his vision begun to grow blurry, and it almost seemed the cold flakes that landed against his face were sent as a comfort or message of hope and faith by a higher power. For the white specks descending on the dark castle resembled thousands of angels transcending upon the bowels of hell.

"*Please . . . help me!*" the writer yelled again in a low, weak tone.

At the same precise moment, the voice of whom Abraham would become to know as the telegram dispatcher that saved his life also called out as he pounded on the castle door. Seeing Stoker's luggage, the awaiting coach, the kaiser blade, and the trail of blood, he became alarmed and decided to trust his intuition and investigate.

The last thoughts the writer could remember before fainting was a soft whisper that said "unclean snatcher," the same two words uttered by Barbola's Un-Dead mother as she blazed her way into an infernal vampiric death. However, this time, the words came from the ghost of Countess Dracula, who appeared in the Argnes directly to the right of Bram's head. Looking directly up through the snowy sky, he saw the tower window of her bedroom from whence she jumped. A tear rolled down Stoker's flushed face for her graceful presence and voice brought him comfort—almost like that of a guardian angel—who added, "Fear not, brave child . . . it is not your time to pass. Nay, it is *his*."

"The last visual I could recall before fainting was of the grotesque decapitated head of the mad Slovak, which rested on a large rock to the left of whence I laid. Even in the solitude of death, it seemed to still rant of wild confessions as Vlad's bride's reverent tone reinforced Agatha Hupnuff's dying words," Abraham Stoker remembered.

"As I closed my weary eyes to leave this queer and cruel world— for what I thought would be my last—my conclusive thought was of them and my family and how we were all five unique souls, from different worlds and passages of time, and that in our own peculiar way needed each other's restless spirits to free ourselves from the horror of Count Dracula."

CHAPTER 23

The Beefsteak Room

> This then was the Un-Dead home of the
> King-Vampire, to whom so many more were
> due. Its emptiness spoke eloquent to make cer-
> tain what I knew.
>
> —Professor Abraham Van Helsing's Journal

Florence Stoker once again uttered those three formidable words, which transformed the skin of everyone in the room into an irresolute pallor that was white as a sheet, "He is here!"

There was silence of the grave. Noel believed that if his mother's hands were not bound behind her, she would surely have leapt from the bed and absconded out of the room. She trembled like a leaf. A look of palpitation possessed her hollowed, haunted eyes, and the mattress beneath her quaked violently as she peered through the others as if sensing some inhuman presence of the supernatural underworld that only one experiencing a sort of transformation as herself could discern.

"Mother," Noel said aquiver as she looked reluctantly in the direction of the two men with eyes of glass, "we are all here to help you. Nobody in this room means to do you harm, understand? Dr. Van Zant, Henry Irving, and myself are all your friends."

A wry look came over her face as her son said these words. The latter kissed her on the forehead and then turned to look at the others with a confused glance that he purposely concealed from the one he loved. At first, it appeared Florence was staring at the doctor, who was crouched at the foot of her bed, observing everything that was taking place intently—occasionally writing something down in shorthand in a small notebook which he kept in the side pocket of his medical bag. But when the man got up and moved to the headboard of the bed to check the tightness of the belts that concealed her bound hands (as she was trying to wring them despite their entrapment), Noel was puzzled to see her eyes did not follow the physician. Instead, his mother's vision remained fixated—glued to the window where Irving stood—who was wearing away the floor like a worried horse afore a destructive storm. Noel looked at the man who seemed to be on pins and needles but said nothing of this observation as the doctor proceeded to calm his patient.

"Madame Florence, I am afraid this unpleasant talk is getting you all worked up in a frenzy, eh? You need your rest!"

Irving turned from the window, wiping the cold sweat from his forehead with the sleeve of his right arm and said, "If there was something waiting outside your room, I do believe we have frightened it away for I do not see anything at the present."

"Oh please!" the woman shrieked as in a state of faint heartedness. She pulled at her wrists vainly whilst her offspring clutched her right hand tightly in his. "I beg of you! Don't leave me! Great merciful God! Save my poor soul from this dark abyss and wretched beast who has indeed mated with Lucifer himself!" Florence's eyes were fixated with a glare of unspeakable horror.

"Kind woman, please clear your mind of all these weird thoughts you possess . . . for they will only alarm you further! Aye, I will wait near your bed all night to ensure that no harm is brought to you on my watch, eh?" Van Zant turned and looked at the boy crossly as if to change the subject. "Your son must be leaving now, but nay worry as he is in good hands until you recover from this illness that has toiled your body, mind, and spirit!"

Noel nodded but held up a finger as if to indicate he had one final question for his mother. "Mum, I need to know where this monster Dracula sleeps. Can you tell me? Think hard and tell me what you see . . . please! Can you answer this last request of me?"

Doctor Van Zant gave the boy a cynical, stern look as Irving backed away nervously from the window, displaying an ashen face that resembled the clear-cut profile of an alabaster statue.

Florence Stoker closed her eyes as if to swoon herself into a state of self-hypnosis. As she did so, not a soul spoke, and the sound of silence was only interrupted by the thumping of the occupants' hearts as each stood by with bated breath. A spine-chilling diffidence ransacked the trilogy of terror that all stood aghast in cowardice fashion. The passing minutes seemed an eternity to Noel, but suddenly, his mother opened her lips to speak: "I see a peculiar room . . . decked in gothic splendor, though it is anything but a primrose way. It is a chamber of somber oaken paneling with a hardwood floor. And there is an unusual gridiron suspended from the beamed ceiling. In the center of the room, there is a large antique dining table—complete with matching chairs that adorns a brilliant Oriental rug. The table is serviced of gold with pewter mugs of stout."

With her eyes closed, Florence paused, wincing momentarily, as if to note further observations, whilst the three caught each other's suspended glances, hanging like a group of children in story time.

"Go on, Mother . . . what else do you see?"

"One side of the room is lined with suits of armor, completely enveloped in a thick sheet of dust, whilst the wall on the opposite side is covered with a collection of medieval paintings of an odd assortment," she continued in a catalectic trance. "One end of the room contains a blazing baronial fireplace that contains a sign of some sort over a large cooking grate . . ."

The trio realized that whatever she was envisioning must be an actual place for her to imagine such detail would be highly unlikely if not completely impossible in her current state.

"What does it read, Mum? Can you look close and tell us what it says? Please . . . it is very important!" pleaded Noel.

Florence Stoker moved her head in several positions as if to focus in on what the object said as the others sat dangling in a macabre two-way conversation that was evolving into a witch hunt by way of an adolescent boy and his ailing mother. By and by, her voice cracked again, and she responded to the last question as if a thief in the night had stolen her breath:

"The Beefsteak Room . . . the small sign reads 'The Beefsteak Room.'"

The two men looked at each other frigidly as Noel hurriedly began to write down his mother's words with a quavering hand—a description of what was apparently the vampire's London lair.

"Is Count Dracula in the room? Can you hear anything? What do you smell, Mother?"

To this she replied, "There is a heavy, musty odor about the chamber that makes me extremely nauseous. It seems to be coming from the other end of the room, for there is a great wooden box, mounted on top of a stand, which resembles that of a funereal pyre."

Florence's harrowing voice began to shake with emotion as she described this last detail. She paused her speech and commenced to flail her limbs again to no avail.

"Is it *he*, mother? Is it *he*? *I have to know!*"

The two men began to show obvious signs in their posture and facial awareness that the terrible interrogation scene was getting to be too uncomfortable for everyone as this last question seemed to set the woman off into a fit of frenzy. She opened her eyes broadly and spoke in a tone that did not seem her own:

"The word *Dracula* is etched upon the coffin which is occupied with earth. It is empty—for *he* is amongst us!"

Florence began to excrete the fetid, vile odor of blood as she looked everyone in the eye, one by one, as if to resolve herself of the undying curse. She knocked Dr. Van Zant to the ground with a rash kick from her powerful left leg.

"Child, seize her feet tightly whilst I give her something to calm her down!" the doctor said, pushing himself up with hands and knees.

Whilst Noel and Van Zant were hard at it, Henry Irving approached Florence Stoker, preparing to ask the physician if he felt another transfusion of blood was in order. She appeared gaunt and bloodless, yet her skin seemed to be sweating what little blood she had left. But before he could speak the words, the wild woman turned her head in his direction and hissed, "You! Go save yourself! Nay . . . neither of us may rest in peace 'til the wicked thoughts we covet returns to the box! For it is only when the king is truly dead can his children reclaim freedom, and all these dreadful things which were bestowed on us are surrendered back—to pass with him into the Pandora's box—and entombed . . . ne'er to leave it thereafter!"

These bold words that came from Noel's mother's chapped and foaming lips did not seem to be her own words, yet they were spoken nonetheless through her and were directed to her husband's employer whilst sending a shock wave of newfound horror into the boy. Though his mother was not yet dead, he could interpret from the agony in her affrighting voice that she was not far from gone; thus, in due time, the devil would consume her heart, and she would soon take her place amongst the grisly ranks of the Un-Dead.

The local sedative Professor Van Zant administered worked quickly. Unable to ask his mother any questions regarding her plea to Irving, Noel turned to him and said, "Mister Irving, why did Mum ask you . . . ?"

Noel was startled when he turned and saw the actor was no longer standing there.

"Mister Irving?" the boy called out again, this time surveying the entire room in an attempt to locate his whereabouts. The physician immediately interrupted his search.

"I think it is your time to go too, eh? Your mother has had a tragic visit. Let's try not to have any more of these in the future . . . Hmmm? I will routinely inform Mister and Madame Watts of her condition, and you shall visit again thereafter she rests peacefully and reclaims some of her strength and former state of mental health, eh? Until then you have this—this Dracula to locate, no?" the professor stated in a cynical tone and with a halfhearted grin.

Noel Stoker nodded with a broken smile, for he felt it was neither the ideal time nor place for objections; after all, this was a man who would lay down his own life for his mother, and despite the fact he had misdiagnosed his patient, Van Zant would safely stand guard over her until the terrible Count could be destroyed.

As Noel kissed his mother's forehead, a teardrop welled up in the corner of his left eye and finally fell, splashing against the soiled pillowcase on which she lay. Indeed, one could never imagine what it might be like to see someone so dear, one so strong and beautiful as Florence Stoker, waste away to a frail, mere shadow of her former self—that is, until something of a higher power and beyond one's scope of control called upon them to do so. She was almost skeletal to him.

"I love you, Mum," Noel softly whispered into her right ear. Even whilst she slumbered soundly, he could almost sense an invisible force of rattling chains, which seemingly held her prisoner.

The lad made his exit quickly, and at an almost sprinting pace, he proceeded to make his way to the Watt's house to reflect on what his mother had disclosed. Despite the serene atmosphere of the night and cool breeze that traveled along his path, Noel was the antonym of the word *calm*. Placing his hand against the silver stake, which he discreetly wore at his side underneath his clothes, the symbol—as it likewise carried the distinguishing traits of a Celtic cross—appeared to transmit and convey a feeling of sweeping energy and everlasting faith. These sensations comforted the boy greatly and roused a much-needed state of renounced courage deep within him.

As the moonbeams shined on his reddish locks like twisted strands of virgin wool, the young son was thinking hard about the evil monster that had them all at such a precarious crossroad. Indeed, just as Dracula had awakened the dark side of his mother with the coagulated blood that glistened from the tiny bite wounds on her neck, the tears that streamed down Noel's face had awakened the sleeping giant inside himself. And almost like a wild dog barking at the full moon, he called out angrily, "Let the games begin!"

* * * * *

Jonathan Watts trembled as he took the bloodstained program and reluctantly placed it in his own pants pocket. Within seconds of doing so, the sound of approaching footsteps rang in his alert ears.

Similar to a child about to be caught red handed in the cookie jar, he let out a quick gasp and looked around in haste and decided upon a proper place to hide.

The steps became louder until they lapsed, almost as if they were directly outside the dressing room door. And then, in a brief moment, the sound of a key being inserted was heard, followed by a click of a lock and the turning of the knob. At this, Jonathan dodged for the closet and veiled his presence by positioning himself behind a wide assortment of costumes. And with heart in mouth . . . he waited.

With a slight creak, the boy heard the door open. Unable to see anything from his location, Jonathan did not know who had entered; however, he could hear everything loud and clear. First, there came the sounds of nearing footsteps, followed by the movement and rustling of various objects—one of the latter, which sounded like a key chain.

Suddenly, there came a groan from the person, much like a reaction one might expect after receiving bad news, followed by a louder and strung-out grumble—a sound which lasted for several seconds whilst an abundance of objects were tossed about the room.

Th' bloody program! Jonathan thought to himself. *Could it be whomever 'tis out there is a-lookin' for the bloody program?*

By and by, the distress taking place outside the wardrobe ceased. During this time, the youngster's form was frozen in the corner of the closet behind several racks of costumes, although he was finding it hard to remain completely still. His nerves were beginning to respond to the grisly thoughts that were racing though his brain: could this be a murderer . . . a hungry vampire . . . or perhaps Count Dracula himself?

The noise of nearing footsteps stopped directly outside the wardrobe. Jonathan held his breath as he could see the shadow of a tall, gaunt man in front of the floor, as if about to enter the closet. The former's heart stood still. And with an advancing step, the form of Henry Irving appeared, clad all in black, holding a single key in his right hand.

Unable to move or breathe, the boy's terrified eyes instantly recognized the key as the one he himself had tried in the dressing room door! This made Jonathan ever more afraid, for it only proved that Irving had taken inventory of his coat pocket in an effort to retrieve the key, only to find the program missing.

Whut could he be a doin' wif the key 'n 'ere?

At that moment, Irving's right arm extended and abruptly brushed several racks of clothes opposite the lad's direction. At this, Jonathan's throat tightened for his heart leapt from his chest, causing his entire body to tremble from fright. He clenched his teeth together to withhold any chatter, and again, he stalled with a sense of resolute helplessness. Bracing himself against the wardrobe, the boy's legs all but buckled underneath him whilst his breathing became irregular—short and laborious gasps. Dripping from perspiration, the brave juvenile said a silent prayer as he was assured that his next breath would be his last.

But to the boy's surprise, Henry Irving's eyes were not fixed in the intruder's direction at all but rather the actor seemed to be studying a bare wall that had been disclosed in the center of the space whence he occupied. There came a spell of silence; and then to the adolescent's astonishment, Irving placed the same key that Jonathan himself had tried, mere minutes before, into a small hole in the wall.

Blimey! Nary would I have thought . . . ah, bloody door!"

Indeed, looking very closely, the slight outline of a camouflaged entrance slapped the youngster in the face. As the door opened, all Jonathan could see beyond it was perfect blackness, into which a brutish Henry Irving entered, grumbling all the way, and then closed the door behind him.

For a nail-biting moment, the lad stood motionless, puzzled as to what was behind the door and unsure if and when the actor was going to return. After several seconds pondering this, Jonathan decided that there and then was his opportune chance to escape without notice. Quietly, he inched his way along the wall of the wardrobe and eventually into the dressing room—which Irving had left in a status of complete disarray. On tiptoe, the boy took several long steps across the middle of the floor, and without making a sound, he fled from the room and exited the theatre without looking back.

* * * * *

Dawn. An excitable and troubled Jonathan Watts met up with an equally weary and distressed Noel Stoker as the stillness of first light crept over the Watt's house. The two sat staring at one another awkwardly whilst Madame Watts prepared a breakfast that consisted of poached eggs, faggots, pastries, and freshly squeezed orange juice and who occasionally interrupted the silence by interjecting small talk about Noel's mother's condition: "Of all the blazes—to git bit by a bloody bat!" and "I'm sure that Doc of hers will hornswaggle this illness . . ."

Jonathan nodded at her silently, as if in full agreement, whilst Noel secretly thought to himself, *If only she knew the truth!*

Through the window sash of the kitchen, the brilliant morning rays of the rising sun coupled with the dull moonlight of the sinking disc seemed to communicate the reality of Florence Stoker's condition. Truly, every day that passed them by without making progress in their hunt to destroy Dracula was much like being stranded one step closer to a wanton wasteland consisting of an insatiable thirst for blood.

"Hush up, Mum!" Jonathan snapped at his mother, who was known to be the chatterbox of the Watts residence, as he could easily tell her words were only making Noel feel worse. She looked at her son crossly at first but then saw Noel's face, which spoke of agonizing despair.

"We's gwine Old Man Godalming's," Jonathan added. "His'n place will be op'n 'fore seven."

In the wee hours of the morning, David Godalming had previously sent word to Noel at the Watts flat that they were to converge at his shop around dawn. Unable to sleep, Noel personally received the message at approximately 4:00 a.m. without having to wake up Jonathan's parents. The two friends agreed that there had to have been good reason for the old man to bump their original meeting time up by twelve hours. It goes without saying they were equally enthralled and anxiously awaited his news.

As soon as both were clear of the Wattses' front walkway, lined with autumn flowers, they immediately begun to dazzle each other through their own stories from the previous evening.

"Do you think we should go to the police?" Noel asked, responding to Jonathan's tale of the blood smeared program. "You actually have it in your pocket?" he asked in disbelief.

"I dunno . . . yeah," his mate replied, wearily patting his right trouser pocket. "I shan't break it out 'ere but will when we git to Godalming's. I wonder whut ye mum meant by those things . . . an' why Irving acted so queer? An' pray tell—a room for beefsteaks!" said Jonathan with a perplexed look upon his face.

Noel shrugged his shoulders as they approached the old man's rustic boutique.

* * * * *

An enlivened David Godalming met the two boys at the front door of his shop. He immediately invited them in, and ensuring the CLOSED sign was clearly visible in the window, he shut the door. Carrying a cup of smoking tea to the center counter, the old man motioned them to take a seat on top while he gathered his stool.

For the next several hours, the three comrades took turns storytelling. Noel went first, who described his mother's horrid condition, her weird words, and Henry Irving's odd behavior, followed by Jonathan, who made an exhibit of the program and raved about his near encounter with the actor as he vanished in the hidden room. Godalming, who went last, told of the postdated telegram and finally read important fragments found in his translation of the dark book of the Scholomance:

"The black book of spells described the stone talisman, as 'upon being dismembered, its proprietor shall encounter a fleeting lapse of power—to which shall last for one-sixtieth of a degree, whilst your creator grieves amongst the underworld.'"

With inquisitive stares, the two adolescents looked at each other with stunned faces and then back to Godalming. Jonathan, who was sitting on the floor in front of the counter, appeared to be dumb-founded by the translation, whilst Noel, who sat on the edge of the counter with his legs dangling off the side like a fishing line, intently asked, "What does this mean?"

The old man leaned forward on his stool to where he was only mere inches from the boy's eyes, as the back legs came of the ground slightly.

"It means, dear friends, that we can fight the Count as Vlad the Impaler, as a mortal man, in human form . . . as opposed to Dracula, the King Vampire, for a short window of time after his talisman is shattered he will be rendered powerless," answered the man. "It is during these few passing and opportune seconds that we should look to as the greatest chance to beat him at his game—that is, whilst his vampiric powers are nonexistent!"

"Do we even know what it look like?" asked Noel.

Jonathan, who was listening with one eyebrow cocked like a ruffled bird, immediately interjected, "We's dunno whar' Dracula is—let alone 'ere stone!"

Somewhat disappointed by the lads' skepticism, Godalming stood up and squared off the corner of the countertop close to where Noel Stoker was sitting, resembling the parameters of an object approximately 220 cm (7 feet) in length and 113 cm (4 feet) in width.

"These dimensions sum up to the circumference of 666: the number of the beast, as described in the Holy Bible."

The old man paused. He observed the room was deathly quiet, as if the entire mood of the room had changed with his last statement. The youngsters seemed to be astonished that the old man knew this information; hence their faces fell with perplexed, silent stares. The odd tranquility of the room at such a dire and traumatic moment at hand made everyone extremely nervous. The ticking of an antique clock in the corner of the shop seemed to grow louder, and soon, the three were touched with a spout of paranoia. By and by, however, the surrealistic thoughts that the human mind uses as a self-defense tactic eventually followed and provoked from the long pause in com-munication was ended when David Godalming decided to go on, breaking the awkwardness of the cessation of sound: "I believe our vampire is hiding in the Beefsteak room and that the talisman is there as well." This single sentence could have made the most courageous man's straight hair curl into knots.

Noel came to life once again, kicking his legs wildly off the countertop like he was under a shark attack.

"So you really believe me Mum's talk of this room is real?"

"Indeed I do . . ." the man replied. "For it was here in London in the year 1709 that a group of great, wealthy men, who referred to themselves as The Steaks, formed and founded a secret organization known as the Beefsteak Club—a gluttonous society, of which it became to be, which dined and drank regularly in secluded places whilst telling off colored stories, lewd jokes, and participating in other ungentlemanly behavior. This new revolution only reconfirms that beyond a shadow of a doubt, Dracula is living amongst us!"

"But the measurements of the stone are colossal!" exclaimed Noel.

"Could the fiend've left it in Transylvania?" asked Jonathan.

The old man saw that their teenage brains were now operating like wheels in motion. Returning to his stool, he sat down with an audible sigh and addressed them both:

"I believe he brought the stone to London with him because he feeds off of the negative energy it projects. The dark book tells this. Nay, I don't think Florence overlooked it or withheld this during her inventory of Dracula's lair; nor do I believe the tablet is in an obvious, visible spot. It must be camouflaged in some strange sort of way."

"Perhaps, but what do you think Mum meant when she said Dracula was there in the room with us last night?"

"Righto, " the other added. "Yeah, if that was fact, the devil would surely have made itself known and put up 'un hell-of-ah fight!"

Godalming looked to the ceiling for several seconds and then down to his feet. "Yeah, that is probable, however, I believe the vampire is being overly cautious, for I can tell solely from Noel's description of his mother that she is changing rapidly and the Count is coming to Florence though her mind—a presence that she, indeed, must feel. The book of the Scholomance tells us that this supernatural phenomenon is strongest at the metamorphosis of nightfall."

"Should we not inform the authorities?" suggested Noel. "I mean . . . a woman is dead! And we have valuable evidence! And another will soon . . ." He paused there and sniffed to hold back tears. Jonathan kindly placed his hand on his friend's shoulder to comfort him and turned to look at the old man with a melancholy demeanor. With bated breath, he listened as their ringleader answered the former.

Returning to his feet, Godalming stated sympathetically but with indirect firmness, "Nay . . . not at the present. They will not believe talk of vampires and suggest that a young boy as yourself (he paused here and placed his right hand on Jonathan's head) was trespassing would open up all kinds of inquires we wish to avoid. Moreover, accusing a well-known actor of murder would indeed spark a whirlpool of scandalous controversy amongst the public the police would despise."

"So . . . we's on our own?" Jonathan asked, lowering his head like he was shamed.

"For now," the old man stated, scratching his balding white head. "We will bring the authorities in when the time is ado; but for now, I believe we need to be extremely careful of Irving and watch his behavior closely. He is somehow in the middle of this crisis, and the man seems to be an accomplice—some sort of strange index I cannot quite figure out to the comings and goings of the Count."

The two nodded at this last comment. All three agreed that the actor had turned dangerous and it was best to have him under surveillance at all times, especially when around Florence. More than ever, they needed Abraham Stoker's eyes around to help with this endeavor, as he knew the man best; however, Noel feared his father may experience some obstacles returning home if and when the vampire discovered his escape.

It was well into the afternoon when the group decided on the following action plan:

1. Noel would research the meeting locations of the Beefsteak Club at the British Library and search them during the

daylight hours for any similar place resembling his mother's description.

2. Jonathan would go to the London Station to find out if
    their cargo logs reflected any delivery of pickup of a large
    shipment or crate.

3. Godalming would go to the Whitby Harbor to see to it
    that a ship would be on standby to bring Stoker back from
    LeHarve, France.

Prior to going their own ways, Godalming embraced both Noel
and Jonathan separately. Noel thought this was an odd gesture, as
the old man had never done this before; however, respecting the wise
elder, he accepted his open display of affection and offered him a
slight smile, despite the horrid purpose of their mission.

On the other hand, Jonathan, who was more of the outspoken
of the two boys, looked at Godalming in a sort of curious way and
said, "Whut happened to 'ur fearless han'shake?"

The old man looked worn and woeful but grinned and replied,
"Indeed, our task is going to be a challenging, risky, and difficult one,
and sometimes one needs more than a simple handshake to gather
the valiancy to embark on such a deadly purpose as ours!"

The two boys immediately set aside their adolescent, anti-ho-
moerotic insecurities and formed a group embrace, on top of their
custom handshake, before setting on their individual missions that
collectively made up an amalgam of horror.

"As the two brave lads left my shop, I forced myself to hide
the tears that I felt welling up in the corners of mine eyes," David
Godalming wrote. "For the object of my affection was not truthfully
vocalized—surely out of a fear I dared my soul not to disclose! For I
felt deep within my heart that this momentous departure would be
the last time the three of us would ever be joined as one, and that an
inner voice foretold our trio would soon become a duo."

CHAPTER 24

A Web of Deceitful Discoveries

When, however, the conviction had come to me that I was helpless I sat down quietly—and began to think over what was best to be done. I am thinking still, and as yet have come to no definite conclusion. Of one thing only am I certain; that it is no use making my ideas known to the Count. He knows well that I am imprisoned as he has done it himself, and has doubtless his own motives for it. So far as I can see, my only plan will be to keep my knowledge and my fears to myself, and my eyes open. I am, I know, either being deceived like a baby, by my own fears, or else I am in desperate straits; and if the latter be so, I need, and shall need, all my brains to get through.

—Jonathan Harker's Journal

When Abraham Stoker awoke, he found himself being pulled in a carriage by several bolting horses. Indeed, it was the swift pace of the animals that had actually aroused him from his slumber as the coach had rolled over a rather large rock that caused the caliche to sway—almost capsizing down the lofty range of the Carpathian Mountains.

After opening his eyes, Bram sat still for a short while to gather his wits. His last recollection was being bitten by the poisonous snake and Castle Dracula; however, who actually found him or administered aid was a complete mystery insomuch as who placed him in a vehicle which appeared to be heading down the mountainous slopes. Noticing immediately that the coach was entirely empty—that is, with the exception of his luggage—the Irishman began to search his person with any clue to the abstruse rescue that saved his life.

It was instantly recognizable that the caliche he was in was not that of the Count's as the style of the coach was missing the gothic and luxury design that previously accompanied the writer on both of his trips to the castle. In contrast, however, the carriage he was in was lighter in color, rustic in nature, and was simpler in terms of console and structure.

Striking his head on the hard wood that was barely cushioned against the armrest, the fierce exertions from the galloping horses had caused the vehicle to sway with every twist and turn, resulting in a less-than-comfortable ride.

"Please, driver," the author called out to the coachman firmly. "Slow down!"

Stoker sat up to avoid further jolting to his head and proceeded to check out his outward appearance. The bite wound from the viper was not visible, as it was bandaged up and concealed by the long sleeve of his shirt. The journeyman was still in the same work clothes (those belonging to the late Jonas Hupnuff), although they did not appear to be as soiled as before his blackout from the serpent. Likewise, the foreigner's skin had been washed, and his hair and beard was recently groomed for he felt fresh and spruced up.

On the seat next to him was a piece of paper that resembled a handwritten note of some sort. Upon noticing this, he immediately seized it and read it to himself with the anxiety equal to a tot discovering Kris Kringle had visited on Christmas Eve. It read as follows:

Sir,

I was sent to Transylvania to dispatch an important telegram to you under strict orders that it be delivered personally. Having found you near death, I immediately took you to Bistritz where you were given medical treatment. Best of luck for a speedy recovery, and shall God keep you during your travels back home.

Sincerely,
R. N. Hawkins

P.S. You will find the urgent telegram in the left pocket of your shirt.

Marveling at the kindness of the man, who had apparently found him on the banks of the Argnes River, Abraham reached for the telegram, which was precisely where the note described it would be:

BRAM, IT IS OF GRAVE IMPORTANCE YOU RETURN HOME IMMEDIATELY. TRUST NO ONE. WILL EXPLAIN IN PERSON.

—DG

The Irishman was taken aback by this invidious message, and a vortex of unfortunate thoughts began racing through his oppressed brain: Was Florence ill? Was Noel in trouble? Had something dreadful happened at the Lyceum? Stoker thought about and agonized over all of these deplorable events, and in every situation he rose to the same conclusion: Why hadn't Henry Irving wired? Though the writer considered David Godalming a friend (though he knew Noel was quite fond of the man), it was very queer that he would be the bearer of any execrable news. True, he understood that his beloved would not have known the whats, whens, whys, and wheres of contacting him. The traveler also considered his son too young to engage in such matters of communication. Notwithstanding, the actor was well aware and able to comply.

Bram reread the telegram and pondered over the meaning of every word until the racing coach made a hard turn, causing the man to almost lose his seat. The paper dropped from his hand and upon the wood floor as he called out to the driver again, "Driver, can you please *slow it down*?"

Leaning forward, he pulled back the small fragment of drapery that covered the modest piece of glass that separated himself from the driver and was confounded by what he saw. A shrill quiver of hysteria bewitched the author like an abominable, vexatious impiety. His heart grew cold as the hairs on the back of his neck tingled as if being touched by an imperceptible hand.

"Everything that I woke up to seemed mysterious and far from comforting, yet when the driver did not seem to respond to my beckoning, I decided another approach—one which proved to be even more enigmatic!" wrote Abraham Stoker. "For it was to my disbelief to find that the very coach in whom I was riding in was without a driver!" The horror overcame the foreigner as he sank down unconsciously into his habitual state of loneliness.

The brown adult-sized horses seemed to be guided by some undetectable force as they continued to lunge forward at top speed. In total dismay, the writer fell back in his seat, overwrought by abhorrence. Frightened and unsure what to do, he looked a second time and reconfirmed his initial plight of terror.

He had now entered upon the outskirts of what appeared to be a major city, as the windows on both sides of the coach reflected passing images of all various sorts: a number of rafts and barges moored to the right bank of the Danube and long rows of clacking water mills to the left bank that sandwiched what seemed to be a modern rising town.

"I recognized the Danube from a Hungarian history book, and as the caliche passed a grand suspension bridge, that connected both sides near which the steamers were moored, I knew I was in Buda-Pesth," noted the author in his journal. "This comforted me as I confirmed I was far away from that castle of peccancy, although, on the other hand, the fact that the horses were not aimlessly darting down side streets or stopping occasionally to graze or fiddle about was baffling and quite disturbing, all the same, as if an apparition had them by the reins and were steering the charging animals to some predetermined destination that was undisclosed to me."

As the coach traveled past an abundance of picturesque images, the Irishman was reminded of the capital city's early history that had still shown visible traces of disaster. In fact, the scenes in the roads gave Stoker the mixed impression of splendor and semi-barbarism.

Several streets and squares had no marked features, except their size and width, and seemed disagreeably dusty, owing to the location of the town in a sandy plain. During and after the reign of Vlad the Impaler, the Turks invaded a total of five times, but the Duke of Lorraine finally rescued it in 1686 after the city was conquered lastly. Though it had since risen in prosperity and importance, its populous and commercial thrift were mainly due to its grain trade.

The horses stopped abruptly at the corner of Regent and Bond streets. Abraham Stoker saw that he was at the Buda-Pesth train platform, and in a state of rapture and excitable wit, he proceeded to collect his traps and make his way to the ticket counter.

It appeared to be early morning as there were not many passengers stirring, and the platforms were almost empty. Despite the ghost-town appearance of the place, seeing a human being manning a ticket counter all but brought Abraham Stoker to tears.

Luckily, the Hungarian spoke enough English for Bram to strike up a conversation with the man—indeed, one to which he would have a hard time forgetting. Though the gentleman seemed to protest being paid with British pound notes, Stoker was bent on purchasing a ticket for the next train heading to Vienna at all costs. It seemed the more the Irishman spoke, his horrible blight became increasingly more and more fantastic of ravings of malice, death, and peril. Misinterpreting the traveler's desperate straits as a sort of mental illness or mania, the attendant quickly made the transaction, and by pretending to not understand, he closed his window, refusing to converse further.

Ne' er-do-well . . .

The money Count Dracula had provided his journeyman the night prior to leaving London was no more than one-third of the way depleted. Henceforth, counting the remaining currency left

Abraham the confidence he had more than enough to make his way back homeward.

According to the clock at the station, he had a full hour before the train would arrive and another half hour before takeoff. About two blocks away, he found a telegraph office and hastily wired a message to Florence:

> FLORRIE, BE STRONG AND EXPECT
> MY ARRIVAL IN TWELVE DAYS. SEND
> MY LOVE TO NOEL. MISS YOU DEARLY,
> BRAM.

Upon leaving the establishment, the Irishman began to sneeze repeatedly and, making his way back to the platform, stumbled upon a bistro that was open for business. There he breakfasted on *palacsinta*, an international dish known as a stuffed crepe, spread with strawberry jam, rolled up and dusted with powdered sugar, and *ciganyszalonna*, a less commonly known recipe the cook described as "gypsy bacon."

"The pancake was heavenly thin and silky, and the smoked slab of pork, which was skewed with the rind and served on a stick, was quite settling to my stomach but rather thirsty. Seeing it was done up with paprika and chopped sweet onion, Abraham begun to wheeze and sneeze and prompted the handmaid for more egg coffee, to which she was more than willing to oblige."

"Ah," the waitress said, smiling upon noticing his condition, "you need *krumbumballe!*"

As Bram was finishing his breakfast, the Hungarian server, who was a respectable elderly woman of full bosom with salt-and-pepper hair dressed in a long dress, decorated with colorful embroidery, brought over a small glass of something she regarded as a sort of heirloom remedy for a cold. To Stoker, it tasted much like an integration of heated sugar water, a thinly sliced lemon, and a shot of whiskey.

"Having gone so long without seeing a human soul, I must have appeared too forward, for after taking the concoction, I reached out to thank the woman for her compassion and hospitality. However, her sense of merriment and pleasant demeanor seemed to disappear instantly when my hand touched hers, and a look of serenity quickly fell across her face," described the author.

And then the woman pulled back at once with a look of hair-raising scandal in her eyes and panic-stricken motions in all her limbs. Her once pleasant voice was replaced by a low gasp, as if overcome by fright. Taking several steps back from the table, she clutched her heart with both hands and whispered in a tone that was much different than she had used before—one that was unmistakably of doom and horror.

"The eye!" the old woman cried to Abraham with a glare of terror upon her visage. "The evil eye is upon you!"

Stoker coughed as he stood up in an attempt to reassure the old woman; however, any effort to calm her was in vain. Stigmatically, she pleaded.

"Don't you understand," she shuddered, "that the eye belongs to *him*! And *it* does not sleep? That it has marked you and his malevolence has full sway—even over the righteous?"

The elderly woman took several more steps backward as the foreigner approached her and then she let out a terrifying scream, stumbling over several chairs and striking the edge of another table.

"The gruesome event ended as the woman, who was reeling against the adjacent wall of the restaurant, crossed herself whilst mumbling a prayer and then fled from the room in a state of utter consternation," wrote Stoker in his diary.

As the man was left without a soul to wait on him further, payment for his meal was left on the table and he exited the café from whence he came resembling a loathed apostate—alarmed and uneasy at the lot of the world.

* * * * *

Feeling injured and slighted, Abraham Stoker made a hasty toilet before loading the train, only to discover it was delayed almost an hour before takeoff. As he tarried impatiently, he continued to cough and sneeze and looked around, noticing several of the few passengers gazed at him in repugnance as if he were the plague. To his surprise, several of them actually got up to move away from him.

Angrily, he continued to wait and checked the clock at the station and saw that a full hour had passed before the train steamed away from the platform. Fearing that any further untimeliness would throw his arrival in London off by as much as an extra day, he thought it would be best to send word home again from Le Havre, France—that is, if his assumptions proved to be correct. Though the autumn-like weather hinted it was mid-October, the Irishman was not sure of the day. Pulling out his ticket in an effort to confirm and calculate an extra twenty-four hours, he read the date that was printed on the thick stack of paper. At that defined flash, the vital, crushing blow alighted the author like a vile abomination. Again . . . a shock. Again . . . a dreadful discovery!

In that precise moment of time, the entire coach suddenly seemed to whirl around him, and if he had not already been sitting down, the writer would surely have fallen. Though people were talking nearby, their voices were muffled, masked with hopeless dejection. It was, by far, the darkest night of the soul.

"There was something so unexpected and unreal in seeing this date in conjunction with the lot of my implausible journey thus far—something so far-fetched and absurd, all the same. For the date in itself conjured up a reverie of doubt, fear, and bleakness that was almost too terrible to imagine," the man had scribed in handwriting so shaky it was almost not legible. Upon this startling revelation, the foreigner went into a mute shock that lasted a long while, though his mind raced with flurried thoughts and scathing images that seemed to offer their due diligence with his overwhelming level of despondency.

Abraham Stoker went numb at this latest development, and dropping the ticket from his hand, he sunk down in his chair as his limbs went limp. As if in a daze, the troubled man stared wearily at the piece of paper as it floated along. His mind became lost in a sea of wonders. And as the object struck the deck of the locomotive, it landed face up, revealing a date of October 17, 1896. Indeed, the Irishman had been held captive in Count Dracula's homeland and awful world for a full six years! The lovelorn malefactor had spread his envenom in such a deceitful way the abhorrence the journeyman felt was of such a degree of antipathy that if the vampire had chosen to reveal himself the man's exploding head of aversion would have sent him back to hell.

"I was almost overcome. The definite fixing of the time seemed like the voice of doom—when I think of it now, I can realize how a condemned man feels at his sentence, or at the last sounding of the hour he is to hear: poor atoms of earthly dust left to whirl in the wind."

Like a prisoner of war escaping after ages of imposing brutality, the escapee sat in the floor and sobbed, much like a lost child, pounding his fists in his chair and surrendered himself to all the excessive bottled emotion that had ballooned over innumerable wasted days and nights. The traveler's mobility was hindered by the aftermath of trauma. Though he beat his palms against the side of the coach as if in an angered fit of entrapment, the pain of the powerful blows failed to register in his mind, nor did the man seemed stunned by the sight of blood that resulted from his alarming reaction. As the passengers looked on in dismay, the author did not seem to care. Instead, his eyes seemed to calcify to two sunken orbs of hazed gray.

"This latest discovery burned into my brain like a red-hot iron. A whirlpool of inconceivable thoughts too adverse and outlandish for even the lowliest of peasants to imagine flooded my mind. The rat vampire involuntarily sucked away my years much like the blood he stole from his victims. Things were becoming clearer, and there grew on me a sense of my being in some queer way the sport of opposing forces—the scantily nebulous belief of which consumed my bones in a paragon of perfect horror! For I was certainly under some strange form of mysterious protection at times, and in certain situations, I could not resist thinking if Dracula was molesting me in an attempt to keep me in check whilst he and the underworld laughed mockingly at my own expense."

Seeing the scandalized foreigner fading fast, several passengers relocated their seats as the drawn man breathed faintly through a static countenance of snow. Indeed, the writer had spent six yearning and distressing years trapped in the vampire's demented mind. He sat docketly at the window for a long moment thinking—contemplating about what he should do to escape the evil force, the eye of Dracula, which seemingly followed him wherever and whenever he went and haunted his very existence to the point of blinding madness.

With tears streaming down his face, he screamed with detestation, "What day is it?" to what appeared to be a somewhat educated Hungarian man reading a newspaper that sat several seats over from whence Abraham was sitting. The man looked up at him stupidly as if he did not understand whilst the young woman positioned next to him cringed and grabbed hold of the gentleman as if consenting to protection.

Abraham then seized the newspaper, as the alarmed couple gathered their belongings and ventured to another coach on the train, staring back at Stoker with a sense of fright and pity.

The date on the newspaper reconfirmed that of the ticket, and once again, the author was utterly alone with a notebook of horrors and a mind that was becoming unraveled. All warmth in him had vanished with this latest account. And everything else occurring in the world—as surprising as it seemed to the journeyman—continued to coexist but rather became obsolete in nature. With no person to talk to and mindful that further outbursts could in fact expel him from his ride, he stole back to his seat and resolved to keep quiet by beginning the gruesome book as a testimonial of his misadventures.

"As I begin to write this horrid, repulsive tale which I helplessly am forced to comply with, I am still actively thinking about the monster's destruction, yet I have not come to any resolution about where to begin. I only know that my first step is to return home and hope and pray some answers come to me in a great leap of faith, but for now, may these first words express my feelings of infinite doom and somehow dislodge the suffering I so have so endured during my living nightmare of six long and ghastly years:

"When we started for our drive, the sun was shining brightly on Munich, and the air was full of the joyousness of early summer. Just as we were about to depart, Herr Delbruck (the maitre d'hotel of the Quatre Saisons, where I was staying) came down bareheaded to the carriage and, after wishing me a pleasant drive, said to the coachman, still holding his hand on the handle of the carriage door, "Remember you are back by nightfall . . ."

* * * * *

During Abraham Stoker's lengthy hiatus from humanity, the world around him had changed significantly: Utah became the forty-fifth state of the union, Nobel prizes were established, and Puccini composed *La Boheme*; the safety razor was invented by Gillette, Sears Roebuck Company opened a mail order business, and Sousa composed "The Stars and Stripes Forever." However, despite Bram's absences from these world events, he worked diligently, composing his own masterpiece of work.

Indeed, for the next forty-eight hours, he wrote feverishly describing the life and times of Vlad Tepes Dracul III and his metamorphosis to the Un-Dead. Only stopping to refuel and re-rail in Vienna, he wrote continuously, and if it was not already stated—and, henceforth validated—as if his life, soul, honor, and salvation depended upon it.

"Though my health seemed to be deteriorating after my escape from Castle Dracula, it was during the following twenty-four hours between take off in Buda-Pesth to Vienna that I underwent or encountered some sort of miraculous recovery!" the Irishman wrote. "It seemed the symptoms of my illness disappeared as I wrote, but whether my convalescence was attributed to the heirloom remedy or from time itself, I could not help but ponder upon the strangeness of it. For despite my starting condition, I wrote through the night—as sleep would not come to me. And it appeared as though with every line I composed, I could feel the fever and aching escape my body through the ink of the quill! If I decided to continue on scribing, I wondered if I could expect a similar revelation in terms with my mental health?"

Three days into his journey, the train steamed into familiar Munich for a two-hour layover, which consisted of a reboarding on an alternate railway. At the station the author refreshed himself, ate a hearty meal, consisting of lamb cutlet, mushrooms in butter and lentil pudding; and with a cup of tea and newspaper in hand, boarded what emerged to be a newer locomotive with a more pleasant coach. At approximately half an hour before take-off, the train began to fill up with different passengers of various nationalities: German, Hungarian, Austrian, French, Romanian, and Slovakian. The former three populating the car of ten travelers that would accompany Stoker on his departure to Le Havre, France.

Upon takeoff, Stoker took a few minutes to skim the headlines in the paper, but as it was written in German, he had to take what little of the language he knew, and coupled with the various images within the pages, he was able to translate that the first US Hockey League was organized and that it was announced that the first Modern Olympic Games were being held in Athens after a 1,500-year absence.

For several minutes henceforth, Bram chatted away with a German man sitting in the seat behind him, regarding the weather, which seemingly grew colder by the day; and next, he gazed at the hazy blue skies and lofty clouds that towered high above the fir and pine trees that made up the belts of forests amidst silvery springs and rocky mountainous peaks. It was mid-morning, and the brilliant sunlight escaping from the hovering disc shined through the thick transparent billows as a faithful reminder of God's supreme presence.

It was not even an hour after takeoff that the author took up writing again and was hard at it until his diligence was interrupted by a tremendous urge to sleep. Because he had eaten brunch at the Munich station, the Irishman had passed up lunch; nevertheless, he had stopped an attendant for afternoon tea and biscuits before deciding to finally fulfill his internal notion to nap.

"Far away from the aid of man, nothing could avail," recalled the foreigner. "I was mercilessly spared of the pain of ever hoping. All at once, the gates of sleep closed tightly."

The horrid evening dream, which soon followed his prolonged writing spree, began as a recap of the sermon the King Vampire gave whilst at the Snagov Monastery. This event lasted for some while, which proved to bring about spouts of restless thrashing and erratic cries that awoke him in a state of delirium.

Now broad awake, Abraham Stoker still tossed and turned, only to discover he could not free himself from a peculiar silky substance that stuck to both arms and legs. Though his head seemed to be positioned upright, he was unable to turn it, yet his eyes were wide open and were functioning as normal. The Irishman could see that he was in some antiquated underground church. The only light within the room came from a massive candelabrum, which hung across the way. This source of buoyancy was mounted to the decrypted bulwark, which happened to be to the immediate left of a large wooden crate that was nailed shut and rested propped up against the cracked wall.

The dust in the room was thick, as if it had been centuries undisturbed, and Abraham saw that he was in isolation. The atmosphere in the chapel gave off a sense of a caliginous, dormant stillness that at once unnerved the stranded man.

"I found the smell of the place to be almost a nauseating one, and consequent to noticing a segment of the room that at least once upon a time had been used as a crypt, as if all the vile odors of the remains buried of long ago had seeped into the air at once and clung to every loop hole in the crumbling cubes of ash-colored brick."

To no avail, Stoker tugged and pulled at the threadlike substance that adhesived him in a winged position. The room was dreadfully cold. And the eerie-like nature of the vault reminded him of a section of Castle Dracula yet to be explored.

God, please relinquish my mind of such an awful place of terror! thought the captive.

With the exception of the rustling and slight chirps from insects, not to dismiss the occasional squeak from a rat, the room was deathly still. However, soon the sound of Dracula's voice came to Bram. He was not sure if it was only in his mind or if in fact, the Count's thick, Romanian dialect actually filled the stagnant air. Nevertheless, the haunting words that followed rung true in his ears: "Behold the common spider . . . see it spin the web to trap her prey? All of nature has its place in the cycle of life . . . beauty has its price; and just as her magnificent web attracted many, she must feed—and ultimately, those that are less fortunate must meet their fate! Son of mortal, arise and cast thyself unto me in silence or dig thyself into the fiery abyss of hell!"

"Good God! Help me!" cried Abraham Stoker.

True, the reality that soon followed was a gruesome one. Now horrified, the victim once again tried to free himself, noticing numerous various insects of all sorts and sizes that encompassed him in what was a massive web.

"Forthwith my struggling came a grim whistling kind of sound that I knew could only mean the call of doom. How shall I ever describe in mere words that which I saw and felt next? For there—in the tangled web in which I fought in—appeared the largest Goliath tarantula any human eyes had ever witnessed! The woolly spider was crawling rapidly for me, and as every vibration I made in its bed of death only hastened the chase, I let out a piercing scream! Then I closed my eyes. And upon seeing that an attack was inevitable, I hung there in the arachnid's horrid home and helplessly waited my impending end."

The hostage realized in these last passing moments that he had been a victim of the paradox Dracula spoke of. As the living web of terror exploded in his veins, the writer could not help but ponder of the irony of his demise. For if he had the choice to pick between spending his remaining days tangled in the conceptual web that Vlad Tepes had spun or becoming dinner for a *Theraphosa blondi*, he would pick the latter and quickly make his peace with the Almighty.

Abraham Stoker's shriek seemed endless and almost appeared to shake the objects that had remained stationary for scores before. But then the rustling of the nailed box across from him caused Bram to reopen his eyes for it continued to wriggle violently, even minutes long after the outcry had cleared the air.

By and by, the nails in the wooden crate shot out like bullets being fired from a musket. And as the coarse hairs from the oversized grisly spider were becoming superimposed against his exposed skin, the lid of the box slid back and plummeted upon the dingy dirt floor. As it struck the ground with a low thud, Abraham gazed at the contents that caused his skin to crawl . . .

There lay the body of Florence Stoker.

"Afore me—here in the scantly made coffin, which was made of planks of oak—was my beloved Florie, yet she was not the same! She was a monster . . . one of those ghastly creatures of the Un-Dead— one that curdles the very blood in my veins to look upon!" wrote the author.

But just as the Goliath tarantula was about to champ down on Abraham's chest with its massive, snapping hooked incisors, Florence's resting body opened its eyes: "Her once-lovely green pupils were now a metallic color, such as of polished tin. The rosy cheeks I so adored were now pallid and settled in a face that was almost marble-looking and had lost all the voluptuousness which I had wed."

Again there came a low whistling sound, but this time the noise was louder—directly in Stoker's left ear. He could feel the legs of the spider upon him and the hairs of the arachnid tickled and pricked him with their rough ends and edges. Whilst this occurred, the journeyman cringed as he felt the silky stands getting tighter, and though his own eyes, he saw his beloved lean forward out of the coffin and actually take a step out of the burial case!

"She—or, shall I say, *it*—was dressed in the ghastly sediments of the grave: an antique-ish off-white gown that was soiled and wrinkled and contained splotches of blood that had presumably trickled from the horrid tusk-like teeth that protruded over her scarlet bottom lip!" the Irishman wrote in his diary. "Faugh! To think of it even now turns my blood cold and fills my soul with horror!"

Bram was surely in the toils, yet all he could do was lift his eyes up to the heavenly Father and pray. Finally, he bowed, closed his eyes, and mumbled an entreaty before God. As the two clawing creatures seemingly was about to fight over who should suck his blood first, the trapped man relinquished to his ugly fate or to the mercy of his maker.

And then a final shriek of terror—a shrill scream which echoed through the still darkness like a battle cry of an army of the dead.

* * * * *

Nightfall. Abraham Stoker waited in a state of horrifying anticipation until the suspense was overcome by madness. With clammy skin and a pool of sweat dripping from his forehead, he opened his eyes to an empty passenger car. The writer looked around deliriously and then turned to the sky.

Oh, thank you, dear Lord! My prayer has been answered! I pledge my allegiance and give you my oath to rid this world of the monster that has struck fear in the hearts of so many and has brought a world of such gruesome horrors upon myself and beloved ones! Cruel anguish, agony, and despair awoke me from my dismal abode only to weep further of sorrow. I sleep only to dream of frights of a man of incorrigible wretchedness and a demon worthy only of immortal damnation!

The coach was deathly still. The passengers had mysteriously vanished; thus the only sound was derived from the screeching of the locomotive's wheels as they bounded over the train tracks.

The overwhelming darkness struck him like a baby that suddenly awoke from night terrors to an empty room in total blackness. Even though the full orb outside projected glittery moonbeams from the sparse windows of the car, they also projected a variety of weird and eerie shadows on the deck that only exaggerated his overwhelming feelings of fright and loneliness.

Abraham looked down and saw that his work of the Un-Dead had been moved. Whether he repositioned it himself during his visit to the tomb of terror or if a phantasm had decided to partake before its midnight flight, he was not sure; however, one thing he was most positive of: Florence's life was in immediate jeopardy.

When Stoker glanced down to where he was sitting, he noticed a piece of paper lying in his lap. And as he recoiled from this startle, he cowered from another troubling consternation. He was also not alone after all. For sitting still on the aforementioned object was a deadly black widow.

Had I imagined this—this tiny, minute being for that monstrosity of a spider?

Even though the insect was slightly over an inch long, a bite could be fatal. Moreover, seeing any bread of spider; henceforth, his horrible ordeal in the tomb of dread instantly brought on a morbidly excitable state of arachnophobia that the Irishman could not shake.

As the man reeled, he quietly stood up, and giving sway to the paper, the note—and its eight-legged passenger—glided safely to the floor. Then the writer stood over it, peering down at the shape of an hourglass that marked the red spot on its abdomen. And in doing so, the sight resembled a cowardice giant towering over a mere fledgling of a threat. As "Goliath" Stoker took the toe of his left boot and swept the arachnid off the note, it seemingly mocked the writer's level of bravery and began to crawl away. However, before the pest was out of range, Abraham lifted his left foot and lowered his full weight on Miss Widow.

After a few seconds of sheer delight of grinding his boot against the brown wooden floor, he lifted his foot to a crumbled cluster of black and scarlet goo. Imaging the tragic closure of such a insignificant creature in a world of much greater intimidation or horrors, however foolish it might have seemed at the time, he looked upon the remains and secretly admired them as if they were those of Count Dracula himself and smiled deliciously.

"How droll! There, *there*! Take that . . . you devious brute! Hah!"

Returning to his seat, Stoker picked up the piece of paper and discovered it was a second telegram.

> FLORENCE HAS TAKEN ILL. YOU ARE NEEDED AT HOME. RETURN TO LONDON ON THE NEXT TRAIN LEAVING BUDA-PESTH.
>
> —HENRY

Realizing that his previous assumption was, indeed—as validated through the words of his employer —a correct one, a maelstrom of distressing questions filled his brain. How did it arrive in his lap? How did Henry Irving—and David Godalming too, for that matter—know who to go to or where to write? Likewise, he thought it was odd to hear from his own employer after receiving a telegram from Old Man Godalming; after all, his relationship with Irving justified a more immediate and sincere response. Though the telegram was welcome, the message was not, and the delivery was, by all general principles, suspect.

As Bram pondered these enigmas, the slight glimpse of something moving outside the boxcar caught his attention. Getting up, he approached the window and peered out into the darkness. And through the moonlight, he saw the figure of a tall man, clad completely in black, crawling away from the passenger car toward the front of the locomotive.

"Oh, God—oh, God! He has come again! The monster knows, hence, I am positively lame to consider myself a free man," the author wrote. "But rather I should succumb my spirit and serve as his puppet! The evil eye! Unclean snatcher! Why did I not heed to such now apparent warnings? Oh, woe! Barriers are surely abounding from all directions, and lest I do not take some kind of action, my fate and my family's well-being is left in this fiend's wicked hands!"

The Irishman trembled as he watched the thin, dark, and ghastly form of Vlad Dracula crawl sideways, in his own spiderlike fashion, down the edge of the train. A frightened and angry Abraham Stoker turned his head by the grotesque image and thought to himself,

Nay, I will ne'er be truly free of the burden of the Count until he has been properly disposed of. How foolish was I to believe his word that stormy night in the comforts of my own study! He knows full well I am returning to London, for he has left me Irving's telegram himself and has doubtless his own new scheme of villainy brewing in his Un-Dead, vampiric brain! Aughh! The sights and smells he leaves behind in the trail he blazes turns my stomach sour!

Indeed, the author needed to somehow decipher the vampire's motive reveal his plan of action and beat him at his game. However, this was much easier said than done, for how do you objectively psychoanalyze a supernatural being? What way can one outwit the son spawn from the oldest, most cunning, and irreverent adversary of God?

A melancholic stillness crept throughout the coach as a sort of presentiment feeling fell over the writer. It was an extreme foreboding sense of turmoil as if some evil or some dreadful event was about to occur to him—or perhaps worse—was happening in his native England, far beyond his scope of control: the House of London.

"Curse ye, Satan's foul child of the night! Hark! Hear ye this very hour that the more you try to control me, the more I want to free myself! Hence, the more you follow me, the further I run—even if it is to the depths of my despairing soul!" the irate man shouted out the open window.

"Damn you, you filthy bloodsucking leech! And cursed be that rock you crawl back under in the most wicked and nethermost hell! Bah! I could not loathe you any more! Prepare to meet thy God!"

At this, Abraham Stoker sank back into a state of utter insensibility on the moment. Again, he was helpless, still he was a prisoner, and if a person were available to pass a hand across his brow, no reaction would have been noted. For the Irishman trembled with numb fright and was of a deathlike paleness, and he altogether presented a perfect picture of colossal mental suffering.

CHAPTER 25

A Cold Voyage Home

> I found my dear one, oh so thin and pale
> and weak-looking. All the resolution has gone
> out of his dear eyes, and that quiet dignity which
> I told you was in his face has vanished. He is only
> a wreck of himself.
>
> —Letter, Mina Harker to Lucy Westenra

Oscar Whitman, a fifty-five-year-old sea captain, patiently awaited Abraham Stoker's arrival at St. Hebert's pier. The man was of a brawny and rugged sort, with a thick white beard and mustache that outwardly made him look brutish, despite his English gentlemanlike charm. Smoking a pipe and donning a skipper's pea coat and a cap with a gold braid that encompassed the brim, he stood at the pier, directing a group of steady fellow-looking Frenchmen loading an abundance of cargo onboard his ship.

"Take 'em all down to the hold below deck," he instructed a man who appeared to be the team leader of the group. "Follow my first mate down the companionway, will ye?"

As the commanding officer stole back to his port, puffing a cloud of smoke rings behind him, he recalled a phone conversation that he had several days ago. There was something about the dialogue that puzzled him, and although the commander tried his best not to dwell upon it, ever since the Whitby Bay guardsman contacted him that peaceful fall morning, an inexplicable impression of despondency and unnerved apprehension seemed to dwell upon his conscience. He could not explain this odd feeling, and though the anxiety seemed to grow on the captain daily, it appeared to peak as his ship docked at Le Havre. As the commanding officer reviewed his schedule for the next week in his cabin, the desperate words of David Godalming repeated over and over again in his ears:

"Though I cannot tell you more, as you will surely not understand—for aye, I too, as an educated gentleman, would find it too a fantastic story to comprehend—help me save a friend in desperate need! If the angels can spare him any further trouble, he will arrive by train at the Le Havre station around noon on the nineteenth of October. His destination will be to London by the means of Tate Hill Pier at Whitby Bay Harbor. Since I understand you have already a port call scheduled into Whitby this day, I implore your help! Oh, if you only knew the grave tale and horrible events this family has been trough and how imperative it is for this poor man to return back home! His deliverance is dependent upon it!"

The sea captain sat his pipe down on the side of his desk and looked out upon the dock. A partial grin faltered upon his worn, weather-chapped lips. Coming up the pier were his cracking crew: two hands men, his first mate, and a cook. Though the captain had thought about sharing his unusual conversation with a few of his people, he decided not to, for in spite of the fact that he had sailed over a hundred cruises with these same men, he was slightly disconcerted. Notwithstanding, these blokes were of typical sailor stereotype: boisterous and hard-nosed. To hear that their skipper, whom they admired and respected, nonetheless, was distraught over something so trivial as a phone call would assuredly result in a mares-tail and public humiliation. Upon reading a barometer, he returned to his bureau to sign the ship's manifest for the cargo brought on board.

Though the commanding officer was promised a large amount of money for his trouble—a sum that would apparently be awaiting his port arrival at Whitby Bay—he felt that currency, or sympathy alike, did not alter the facts of the matter: he sensed an impeccable, impending sentence over Abraham Stoker and David Godalming. And now the unpleasant lot was preparing to transcend over his ship, insomuch like a malignant plague.

Abraham Stoker? the captain thought to himself, scratching his head wearily. Unsure where any of these incomplete thoughts were leading to, he concluded that it was only distracting him from making the necessary preparations for getting underway. Therefore, the man purposely concluded his reverie of reflection and got up from his chair as calmly as he did anything in his entire life.

It was approximately 1:15 in the afternoon. Captain Oscar Whitman was amidships speaking to a cartographer regarding maps for a future voyage, when the first mate approached from the bow, carrying a worn-out bag and suitcase with a haggard-looking Irishman a few paces behind him.

"Cap'n," the man said interrupting their conversation, "this 'ere is the bloke who is to cruise wit' us into Whitby!"

"Ah, yes, Abraham Stoker, I presume," replied the skipper. "Welcome aboard the Citadel!"

The commanding officer's face fell when he saw who was standing before him. The former felt the tightness in his throat as he swallowed convulsively. For a short moment, both men were silent as the commander motioned to the other men to leave him be as he waved the writer, who responded acquiescently, to the fore of the ship and near the gunwale, where nothing was currently stirring.

"You! I thought your name was somehow familiar! Indeed, I recall you were a part of that tragic cruise into this port six years ago! Oh, Nigel Henley (here the sea captain crossed himself as he looks up toward the heavens), may he rest in peace!"

Stoker looked at the captain without saying a word and then to the mast near where the wolf had attacked the first mate. His heart leaped. And nervously shaking his head, he replied in a sorrowful tone, "Yes, who could forget such a savage carnal attack."

"You were the passenger heading to Transylvania! Aye, the Count contracted me to bring you to this port, and I believe you informed me you would be staying with him for a while at Castle Dracula? Is this not so?"

The author nodded his head again. "Yes, I am finally homeward bound—that is . . . what is left of me!" The journeyman's large gray eyes were visually etched with the long, lasting effects of mistrust, worry, and lonesomeness.

"Alas, I have been miserable due to separation from the ones I love but resentful and full of rage for being held prisoner by the villain who hasten my misery!"

The skipper paused and looked the man over for some time. Finally he said in a somewhat insensitive sort of way, "Indeed, you look like hell! But then I thought for sure you were being led into the jaws of doom! Don't you recall I warned ye?"

Again the Irishman nodded and both elapsed back into a momentary spell of awkward silence.

"So did your count hire you to misdirect my sail back to, say . . . Iceland?" asked the foreigner sarcastically.

"Oh! Nay, sir," the commanding officer quickly replied. "Though he contracts my services from occasion to occasion, he is not my only boss, and I do not think he has beckoned my use in . . . oh, 'bout three months or so, surely! It was actually a fretful crony of yours that cordially arranged your return home. However, you should know our conversation was anything remotely pleasant! In fact, he quite disturbed me, you know—ranting and raving like he was actually the one going to Castle Dracula!"

Abraham's face turned a sheepish color before asking, "And to whom did you speak to?"

"An old fellow by the name of David Godalming." And seeing the surprised expression on Stoker's face, he added, "But how odd it is that you did not know this!"

The two men continued to talk for some time. Though Old Man Godalming had warned Bram to not trust anyone, he could not help but answer Captain Whitman's questions regarding his travels abroad. Albeit he felt like it would not endanger him in any way—that is, since Godalming himself had hired the *Citadel* and the same skipper had previously provided him means of self-protection with a tiny vessel of holy water. Nevertheless, he crafted his answers to where they were lax and somewhat erroneous for cautionary reasons.

It was approximately 2:30 when one of the crewmembers called to the skipper from somewhere aft, and slightly embarrassed for losing track of time, he pardoned himself to see the ship underway.

At precisely 3:00, the boat pulled out of the harbor and proceeded to head northwestward and up the English Channel. The weather was clear and typical of that of an autumn day. The captain confirmed that unless they were to run into any inclement weather, the vessel was expected to reach Whitby around dawn on the twenty-ninth.

Having been invited to attend a late lunch with the crew on the mess decks, Abraham consumed a meal of fish and chips and retired to his cabin. There he took solitude in writing for many hours until the slight sweeping movement of the sea rocked him into an early evening siesta.

With all sails set, the *Citadel* made its way across the English Channel under a mass of splendidly colored clouds, fair winds, and following seas which remained unchanged until the evening of the third day. The ship's log noted that at approximately six o'clock, the air suddenly grew quite oppressive and a sort of sultry heat and stillness fell over the boat as if commonly felt before a raging storm. This condition lasted for several hours whilst the nervous crew stood by anxiously.

By nine o'clock, a dead calmness seemed to fall across the waters, which soon gave notice to the approach of thunder. The author, who was writing aggressively below deck, felt the sudden change of climate, and popped topside to make an inquiry.

The concerned captain took the helm and ordered two of the crew to seek shelter behind the deckhouse whilst ordering another to light several lanterns. One more was asked to confirm all the hatchways were closed.

The air began to carry a strange, faint, hollow booming as waves began to convulse in a growing fury. Within half an hour, they were overtopping the ship like a devouring monster, and the journeyman was ordered to go back below deck.

"She is on the verge of a maelstrom—a tempest wind is ahead us!" altered the skipper.

"Go back to your bunk, matey," shouted one of the hands men to the Irishman in a haughty tone. "Ye will only be in the way up 'ere!"

A downcast of rain quickly began to fall whilst the sky turned black as coal. One of the men assisted another in lowering the sails in an effort to protect them from being torn to shreds, resulting in the vessel being blown off course into the North Sea or into the Bay of Buscay. A stern commanding officer scowled when the cook returned after twenty minutes, carrying only one lantern.

"This is the sole lamp I could find!" he replied. "I don't understand how they all suddenly up and disappeared!" An intimidating growl came from the former. But seeing the cook was genuinely puzzled and almost distraught from an increasing onset of fear, he said nothing.

But when the second mate failed to return from closing all the hatchways, the commanding officer then sent the first mate to check on him.

He too did not return.

Indeed, all the prevailing signs of danger seemed to be revealing themselves like an unwelcome Armageddon of the sea, where life and soul were endangered.

"Holy Mary, mother of God!" said the commander silently, "Deliver me a vindication of my prayer for help!"

But for whatever reason, the mariner's prayer was left unanswered that night, and what transpired instead was what Abraham Stoker referred to in his diary as "a mammoth massacre of the macabre."

Indeed, it came.

* * * * *

Onward the stormed rushed, and frightful effects came close behind. The black darkness quickly overpowered the ship, surrendering itself to the only lamp and the sparse gleam of the moonlight that would arbitrarily break free from the great clouds that wheeled in fury.

For over half an hour, towering waves crashed against the side of Abraham Stoker's cabin like a presage of doom. The spew of the channel swept heavenward, drowning the weather decks from stem to stern and tossing the vessel about like a corked bottle in a hurricane.

The captain and one of his crewmates took turns manning the helm whilst the cook took shelter in the deckhouse. Though all their faces were panic-stricken, the blinding blackness hid their expressions from each other. The center of the storm—a flying, whirling, maddening path that brewed relentlessly into the night—was unnoticeable to them; however, if it had been subject to a ray of light, it surely would have doubled the tiny crew's fears into a groveling state of hopeless horror and desperation. In the meantime, however, the sole light source kept dry in the deckhouse flickered wildly displaying the ghastly silhouettes that rocked the shadow of the boat—living, dark gloom with extensions.

Below deck, a sudden noise aroused the author from his writing, which, due to the less than pleasant conditions, was becoming to be an unbearable and fruitless chore.

"The sound resembled that of someone fighting to get inside out of the cold—much like that of the scratching of one's hand. Notwithstanding, after examining the noise closely for several moments, I concluded that it was not the nails of a human hand but rather the claws of a creature or beast as it was accompanied by a low growl somewhat muffled by the squall of tempest," he recalled in his journal.

Unable to hear any of the crewmembers or progress being made topside, the Irishman flew aloft in a state of consternation, carrying the medium-sized candle that was adorned with an equally sized globe.

As Bram made his way to the port side of the vessel, he discovered a hatchway that was left ajar. All at once, the door flew open rendering a draft. The gust of wind produced was integrated with rain, and this mixture diffused the candle, leaving him in a secluded corridor—one totally absent of any light. Feeling his way slowly along the bulkhead, the passenger came to the hatchway and stopped for a slight moment in an effort to relight the wick. The journeyman spent endless minutes fumbling in the blackness to no avail—the dampness prevented his on-edge hands from resparking the candle.

There must had been something lodged in between the door and the adjacent stairwell as Bram tripped over an object, dropping the candle in the process into a pool of standing water. Searching for the waxen stick with his bare hands, he stole across and felt what appeared to be a boot. The foreigner's heart thudded nervously.

In a few laborious seconds, however, Stoker realized that the boot was not empty—that his candle was not resting in a puddle of water after all but upon a person! A warm being lying in a pool of blood! With bated breath and now scarlet-stained hands, he repositioned what was the leg of a dead man and gently pushed the door open enough for his own body to slip through.

The author found the captain inside the deckhouse, consulting with the cook, whilst a third crewmember proceeded to keep the boat under some sort of navigation until the terrible storm had settled. The former rushed in upon their conversation with a gaunt chest laboring to breathe.

"I tell you, Cap'n, it was him! I saw him with my own eyes!" stated the cook in a low whisper of utter fright. "I swear to you! But how can this be? How can *it* be?"

"There has been some kind of accident below," the Irishman said, interrupting. "I have discovered a corpse; though it was too dark for me to identify the body!"

"Hells bells! It is *he*! I tell you!" the cook said in a frantic state of gut-wrenching horror. "I implore you! Listen to me, please!"

Captain Whitman looked at the irate cook wearily and whispered something that apparently allayed him, for the man quieted down but still stood bruiting in undivided silence.

"We are missing two crewmembers," the captain stated calmly and earnestly. "And we are aimlessly navigating in the blind. Furthermore, all we have been able to locate is one lantern to keep eyes on the lookout. This maelstrom is a complete mystery to me; for there was no forewarning of such approaching weather by my barometer! May we pray all lighthouses be in operation! If this tempest continues through morning, we will need to signal for help!"

It was profoundly obvious that whatever scared the cook made him shudder to the extent that he cowered in the deckhouse and absolutely refused to leave until "it" was dealt with.

"What do you think happened to the crewman I stumbled upon?" directed Stoker to the cook. But before he could reply, the storm seemed to move southward. All three men gazed outside for the clouds gave way to the gleaming moonlight that seemed to illuminate the fore of the ship. This sudden change and additional light was hampered by the dread that followed.

Again, another shock.

All at once, the commanding officer's face dropped to the countenance of the dead when he saw the lifeless form of the navigator. The victim's head had been forced through one of the spokes of the steering column, and then the wheel was spun around until the helmsman's body collided with the deck, snapping the fellow's neck instantly.

"Help me move him!" ordered the captain quickly to the cook. "I must bring the ship back into course!"

The cook acquiesced, though shakily, with a face flushed of all color. The harsh rain and winds had apparently ceased, and the captain next ordered the cook to reset the sails, although it was during this time that another grisly encounter was discovered. As the Skipper proceeded to steer the ship back into their northwestward destination, the cook came bounding in their direction, screaming with bulging eyes and a facial expression which was contorted and convulsed with a look of sheer terror.

"It is all over! There is no hope for us now! Save yourselves from the curse whilst you still can!" cried the man as if in a state of complete mental and physical despair. His eyes rolled in a way that was almost too painful to watch.

"To my complete shock and dismay, the man crossed himself, and with terror-stricken flailing limbs, he hurled himself overboard," wrote Stoker. "And when I turned to look at the captain's reaction, I followed his eyes which was concentrated on the foremast, and then I realized what the cook had stumbled upon. For there, hanging high from the vertical wooden pole, was the first mate with a burlap noose around his neck!"

"We must cut him down if we are to ever reach shore!" shouted the captain.

"You steer," Abraham said. "I will cut him down . . . just tell me what I must do to set sails!"

After listening to a few directions and taking a large bowie knife from the Skipper, the writer bravely walked amidships to the foremast, making his way from the moonbeams that projected a ghostly glow on the upper deck. Despite the passing tempest, the eerie calmness that hung over the *Citadel* was an occasional haunting moan of the wind and the dead man striking the mast as he swayed back and forth with the movement of the schooner.

The writer got to the bow of the boat without further trouble. Finding that the bowie knife cut thought the rope easily; subsequently, he lowered the corpse without further ado. But finding that the man had been drained of all his blood, the journeyman could not help but question his own desire to exist onward in such a living nightmare. Dripping with perspiration, he crossed himself. Finally, with dull eyes of listless gray, the foreigner proceeded to raise the sails—looking tautly in every direction, dodging every slightest sight or sound.

"Within a moment of cutting the poor fellow down, the same sort of scraping noise I heard in my cabin rung in my ears again. And through the flapping cloth of the sails, I saw the immense, dreadful shadow of a lurking form with its talonlike fingers as they cut through the cloth like a razor blade!" wrote Abraham Stoker in his diary.

Something broke in the man's throat.

Bram stumbled backward to dodge the claws that were attached to two arms that were devoured in seaweed. The creature was dressed in what might have been a fantastic seagoing attire, such as that of a midshipman; however, the clothes had been eaten up with algae and plasma of the deep—such as a sunken chest that was brought up to man concluding centuries of containment in the dark and mysterious fathoms below sunshine.

Stoker's knees trembled as he backed away from the abomination with the bowie knife in hand. Concentrating on the monster's face, he could tell that it was of a mobile death for the pale, bloodless symptoms were prominent, although the vampire qualities were coupled with a bluish, clammy tinge that is often associated with victims of hypothermia. Any tissue deterioration seemed to be the result of aquatic life feasting upon its flesh as opposed to rigor mortis, and what was devoured appeared to heal itself or grow back to its grisly vampiric state.

Seeing the knife shake in Bram's frightened hand, the vampire smiled and growled with eyes blazing with diabolical glee.

"Do you want to knife me, matey? Be still, my unbeatin' heart!" it hissed. "You will need more than a sharpened blade to stop me from drinking gingerly from your veins!"

With the daggers on his right hand, he ripped away the tattered and soiled fragments of a water logged shirt that had become lodged with snails, crabs, and other small aquatic animals, and displayed the bleached blue skin that predominately revealed the underlying bones of its ribcage.

"'Ere then! Run it through me!" The fiend laughed as its fanged teeth drooled a murky greenish substance that made the Irishman grip the bowie even tighter. "Go ahead . . . take a stab, but if you miss—well, prepare to join me!" Its teeth bared in a throaty snarl.

The author quivered in a way like no other he had experienced before. The hideous being that was standing in front of him would have been a ghastly and frightening sight true dead; therefore, to look at it, Un-Dead was twice as appalling and twofold the degree of horror.

The facial features of the ghoul were most disturbing equality, for over a period they had become slightly distorted by other creatures of the deep. Its forehead and neck had become encrusted with a thick layer of moss. Many lacerations and abrasions existed due to the creature sharing its watery grave with other fierce animals of the sea, and the monster's long, stringy dark hair had become matted and entangled with vegetation or floating debris and had become home to many families of shellfish searching for a place to nest.

Abraham Stoker knew he could not falter, for missing his target would be a fatal move for his own livelihood. Henceforth, redoubling his efforts, he clutched the knife. And with harrowing numbness, he carefully took two paces forward, watching the leech gravely and closely, as the vampire smiled in return.

The bloodsucker positioned itself much like a tiger preparing to pounce upon its prey and gave the writer a glaring look which froze his body in a state of terror. It proceeded to drag its tongue across its mouth, slurping up the remnants of fresh blood—undoubtedly of the navigator—with its jaws snapping and popping with relish.

Then there came a loud bang from behind the journeyman that made him clutch his chest in a startled motion. The monster—with a look of pain-stricken anguish—looked down at its heart that consisted of a fresh bullet wound. Hobbling a few paces forward, it fell to its knees and pointed to the skipper who held a smoking gun on the poop deck above.

"Caaap . . . tainnn Whhhit . . . mannn," it called out in a low, gravelly voice. "Preparrre—to reunite . . . in hhhell!"

Finally, the Un-Dead fell face forward upon the deck, only inches away from his last and final victim.

"Blessed be the soul that created bullets of silver!" exclaimed the commanding officer as he made his approach from behind.

"Did you know this man?" asked the writer with an intense, wrinkled brow.

"Yes," answered the captain in a solemn tone. "Once again, meet my old first mate, Nigel Henley . . . alas, for it is twice his body be thrown to the sharks!"

* * * * *

The morning sun rose above the crystal waters of the English Channel like a resurgent force of vigor and energy and as an icon of hope for the two survivors of the *Citadel*. The picturesque sunrise was a welcoming sight to a long, dreadful dusk that was almost surreal to the men, and if the horrid events from the night before had not left four corpses to be properly disposed of, the two men would have passed their hideous plight off as an outlandish, horrific nightmare they somehow miraculously shared.

Likewise, the exemplary weather that shined its fantastic graces on the ship as it sailed onward to England acted as a rejuvenating factor much like a long terminally ill patient suddenly encountering the miracle of remission. Indeed, Abraham Stoker was so haunted by many troubling incidents, hellish fright mares, and formidable images over the course of the past six years that he had forgotten the name Nigel Henley—that is, until the captain reminded him.

"If you can recall, after he was fatally attacked by the wolf, we made a grave mistake!"

"And what was that?" asked the Irishman.

"We did not administer a proper burial! Consequently, I have learned that the wolf that attacked him that awful night was, in fact, Vlad Dracula! And because we did not dismember the head and remove his heart, he returned from the grave as one of his vampire children."

"But why us? And why last night?"

To this, the commander laughed and replied, "To feed! And I expect it was seeking his revenge on me! I hazard the Count rid him of my crew as a means of punishing me for warning you! And then last night—in all that horrible weather—we traveled over the very waters in which his body was cast!" answered the skipper in a stern tone.

"Now . . . *now* shall we do what is required to give the dead peace?"

Certainly, the bowie knife served its grisly purpose, though it was a few hours late of its original intent. The seaman Bram found dead in the stairwell below deck had, in fact, indisputable bite marks directly over the jugular vein and thus required to be disposed of in the same offensive fashion as Henley. Hence, along with the Un-Dead, the two men took turns in the mutilation process.

"How can a singular simple yet respectable man begin to fathom such an awful means of cruelty—such savage butchery—in any phase or place in life?" asked the bystander to his diary. "For no matter where my travels would take me in life, I have now certainly crossed over them all. The physical and spiritual world has collided today; and another piece of my soul has been killed. Indeed, I believe I have hit rock bottom, and when one finds himself digging his own grave, the only other direction left to go is up. However, I have proven to myself to withstand the brutal carnage that is required of me and feel I am ready for the ultimate task at hand. I only pray the fiend is not ready for me."

And when the harsh assignment was complete, all four bodies were thrown over the side of the ship like they were trivial fish bait. A moment of silence was also given for the cook who, no doubt, had become food for a great white.

Whether it was the downsized crew—as it was meant to be taken as another warning, instigated by the demonic forces at bay—or the simple fact that the at-sea period gave the author consumption of the hand, Abraham Stoker was reminded of his oath to the King Vampire and spent the next few days writing with endless vitality whilst the commanding officer steered them into Whitby Bay Harbor.

When the captain called the journeyman topside to assist in dropping sails, he politely asked, "Will someone be at port to great you for I understand your wife has taken ill?"

"I expect my employer, actor Henry Irving, will be standing by to see me back home," answered the writer.

Over the captain's visage stretched an odd reaction—one that signified that one's mind was suddenly being racked with queer information or intense thought. The Irishman could not make the expression out; but as the Skipper nodded, the idea was quickly dismissed as the ship landed at Tate Hill pier. Subsequently to securing the vessel in the harbor, Whitman shook his new shipmate's hand and wished him fair winds and following seas.

"Good luck with your treatise, mate!" he called out to the foreigner whilst touching the brim of his cap with his right hand. "May God keep and bless you and your family!" The serious tone was apparent but likewise discharged by the common anxious and nervous excitement generally associated with a sailor returning home after being lost at sea.

Stoker threw up a friendly hand as he departed the ship and never looked back. However, if he had turned to render a final salute to the quarterdeck, he would have seen the stern look of worry that was transparently fixed on the sea captain's face much like that of a death mask.

* * * * *

With baggage in hand, Abraham Stoker walked down the Tate Hill pier hunting for Henry Irving. However, it was an amazing blow to discover the man was not present. Indeed, it could certainly be implied that the Lord of the Lyceum owed the Irishman a favor for in the few years since Stoker saw the actor perform as Digby Grant, the writer had fulfilled his promise: Irving would become the talk of London.

It was said there were only two other men at whom pedestrians in the street turned to gaze: Prime Minister William Ewart Gladstone and Cardinal Henry Edward Manning. Henceforth, why had the journeyman's employer not returned the favor by greeting him home?

Contemplating this was rather easy. Control was vital to the actor, and he rarely let his guard down. And considering his manager's long absence—after all, a trip that was originally anticipated to last a few months turned into six years—the power factor in the man probably felt disappointed and harbored a degree of resentment toward his friendly employee.

Henry would not have left the theatre for a moment if 'twas to spend it with Helen of Troy! He is like Napoleon insomuch as the Lyceum is his army, and as its ruler, he is neither fool enough nor cruel enough to be an altruist. What he cares most for—that is, cares solely for—'tis the thing over which he can come to govern!

Moreover, it was an equally surprising reverence to find who awaited his arrival. For at the end of the pier, watching in intense anticipation, was an overjoyed David Godalming. The old man called out to him at first sight, stepping out of an awaiting cab that was illegally parked at the end of the ramp. He was dapperly dressed in a light-brown Gabardine suit with a blue bowtie and tweed hat. The Irishman almost did not recognize him as his hair had whitened considerably since he had seen him last. In like manner, Godalming all but passed the writer over for a flunky or homeless fisherman:

"The old fellow was haggard, lank, and wan-looking. The brawny spirit that was always captured in his gray eyes had vanished during his incredible journey. His outwardly appearance told he had been to hell and back again, whereas he had lost a considerable amount of weight and seemed to suffer from malnutrition. Likewise, the apparent toil of stress and turmoil had caused him to age beyond his true years. In sum, his departing robust middle-aged form had returned a poorly, devastated old man with no sense of hope or purpose, " noted the observer.

"Bram! Welcome home, old chap!" he said, waving him over to the car.

"Thank you so much for coming, David," the author said, holding out his right hand to greet his. "I assume Henry is preoccupied at the theatre?"

A grave and weary look immediately fell across Godalming's face upon hearing this question. The writer recognized the look but said nothing as the driver loaded his luggage in the back of the vehicle.

"We have much to talk about," sighed the old man finally.

The two men had about an hour to discuss the highlights of the past six years. Godalming learned of Stoker's captivity in Castle Dracula, his attempts to destroy the vampire and his struggles to escape, and Abraham learned of the murder outside the Lyceum, Florence's violent attack, and the morbid discoveries Noel, Jonathan, and the Old Man had uncovered.

"The liberating meeting was one that I will never forget until my dying day!" described the author. "For to be able to enter back into my own abode of old and to receive confirmation that the world I was leaving was, indeed, real—insomuch that my mind was healthy through it all was a remarkable feeling and an extreme weight off my shoulders! And even though the fearful facts were terrifying to accept, they were doubly horrifying combined with the negative feelings of guilt, doubt, and trust that empowers one to questions the associated knowledge and the stability of the human brain."

"To confide in someone—alas, with a man I knew and respected even prior to my six-year hiatus was a welcoming comfort!" continued the writer. "For here was a bloke who understood—one who had actually shared similar events of terror, from that same evil source! I was positively thunderstruck and bewildered beyond compare; nevertheless, our conversation yielded a miraculous recovery to my old inspiring self."

"Truly, sound sleep is a far-off cry for us at the present. Alas, the screams of any nightmares will be less terrifying and threatening at home. Ah, home . . . where I can form an alliance against the Un-Dead and antique mysteries can be unraveled as truths!"

This outpour of much-needed but all together dazzling information, overwhelmed Stoker to a state of utter silence the latter part of the ride. He dwelled on it all, and as intriguing as it was, tried his best to make some sort of sense of it.

No . . . not Florie! My dear, poor, beloved Florie!

When the cab pulled up to 7 South Hampton Street, both men uttered a silent prayer before God and looked upon the flat as if it were a funeral home. Wearily, they each mumbled a low "Lord be with us," and crossing themselves, the duo proceeded to climb out of the vehicle.

Whilst the old man exchanged money with the driver and as Bram's baggage was unloaded, Abraham Stoker stood like a statue, looking up at his apartment in a most unusual sort of way. It was almost like he was seeing it for the first time. Though its structure had not changed, it was different all the same, and an overpowering sense of brisk fullness ravaged his body all at once. And then the journeyman shuddered like a petite woman caught naked in a snowstorm as he proceeded up the drive. Even without yet facing whatever forces were lurking inside, the man was already aware of them. He felt them, and he knew they too felt his own coming. Indeed, he was being consumed with a devastating feeling that another chapter in his never-ending living nightmare was preparing to unfold.

A foreboding sense of gloom, death, and despair appeared to rally and cling to the air upon the duo's entry. As the Irishman stood silently in the foyer recalling his last memory of his home, Godalming slapped him in a friendly way on the shoulder and gravely said, "Take your time. She is directly upstairs in the master bedroom. She has been under the care of Dr. Van Zant ever since being bitten by that bat several weeks ago. It is my understanding he and Henry Irving have been alternating vigil watches throughout the night, but since you are here now—and for reasons I have already spoken of—I recommend relieving Irving of this duty."

The writer shook his head slightly to acknowledge the old man's suggestion but said nothing in return. His face was listless. His body seemed to have transformed into stone. And the weight of the journeyman's frail limbs appeared to bring him to his knees.

"As I mentioned previously, Noel has been staying with the Watt's family for Dr. Van Zant felt it best to not add any additional stress and worry upon the mother and the child," the former went on. "However, I am going to go send for him now as I know you both are eagerly awaiting to be reacquainted!"

Again, the writer nodded to indicate he understood. And then, pulling the author aside as if in a secret conference, Godalming whispered in Bram's ear softly, but in a most serious tone: "Understand she and your son have suffered their own shocks and battled their own unique spouts with illness, so please prepare yourself, and try to bottle any excessive appearance of alarm or emotional reaction. Indeed, Florence is brave, but the bite of the vampire has all but consumed her soul. Noel has been the man of the house, and though he has grown up nicely, however, the horrors of home are beginning to tell on his nerves. For example, he has begun to sleepwalk. But thank God for a good mate like Jonathan to keep him from harm's way!"

The bewildered traveler looked the old man softly in the eyes. And even under the dire circumstances, he attempted to communicate his own feelings of love, warmth, and utmost gratuity with a cordial smile. He was proud that the good people that surrounded him before his misadventures had likewise formed a tight circle to keep the dreadful evil at bay until he had returned. But as sad as it may be, what lies ahead? For he knew a million smiles of most sincere earnestness could not change anything. Ultimately, all the love and support friends and family can provide would not alter the horrid facts or the truth that awaited him upstairs.

Seeing his old friend had drifted away into a sort of deep state of reverie, he cleared his throat and said:

"I am off, and remember . . . approach her gently! And as I leave you alone with your beloved, go on now—go! Dr. Van Zant expects you! And your family needs you more than you will ever know!"

* * * * *

When Abraham Stoker struck up enough bravery to ascend the flight of stairs and to set foot in his bedroom of old, Florence Stoker was sleeping. To this the prodigal husband was grateful for her appearance was far worse than he ever could have imagined; henceforth, the journeyman immediately threw his hands up to his face to mute his shrieks of horror and wailing sadness:

"Her beautiful skin was ghastly pale; even her voluptuous lips were deathly white. They were slightly departed, revealing a trickle of some foam-like, vile-smelling substance that ran down her chin and onto the soiled nightgown that seemingly was spotted with traces of blood," wrote her husband. "Hitherto, her hair seemed to grow wild, and the graceful features of her youthful face had transformed into hard, cruel lines that resembled a livid mockery of its old self. Residing underneath, sunken in like those of a corpse, were the outlines of the dry bones that recognized the harsh and rude reality of her condition. Her circulation was languid, and she had a morbid resonance about her that brought me to a waterfall of tears."

After a brief "welcome home" and slight embrace, Van Zant pulled the Irishman over to the window that was drawn. Seeing that Abraham was curious that the room was so dark, he explained in a whisper, "She gets violent when any sunshine is let into the room— thus I keep the shades closed, eh?"

Sinking to his knees, Bram let out a low gasp and cried, "Dear God in heaven! My worst fears are unraveling before my very eyes! Alas! My nightmare has beaten me home!"

The doctor sighed and looked on sadly. True, he did not understand her husband's words, though he did recognize his pain and tried to comfort him with the tightening of his hand on the other's shoulder and a few reassuring statements: "She has been in this coma like state for several days now, and I am pleased she is resting with no further outbursts. This has been good for she and I, no? Yes, it has given me a chance to read up on her symptoms and document her case for others to examine."

The man of science then took on a look of awe and outstretched both arms to the ceiling as if reaching for the heavens. And then he continued, "As God is my witness, I have yet to see such a case of hydrophobia progress is such an odd neurological fashion! Indeed, I am quite baffled by her condition, eh?"

The writer looked at him, gnawing at his hands in a helpless state of worry and fear. In a low whisper, he replied in an almost intimidating manner, "You do not understand, Doctor—"

"No, I do not," Van Zant interrupted and then went on. "As I am having to provide her nourishment through her veins, it is almost as if her body is rejecting it and finding nourishment by some outside source! Yes, it is so strange—so mindboggling to medical science— for I have not seen any case like hers in all my days of practice, eh? She subconsciously rips out the needle! And when she is awake, she does the same—only in a more defiant way! And she violently protests by yelling mysterious, incoherent phrases!"

"Such as what?" Stoker asked.

"'The blood is the existence now' or 'Food no longer matters'! Eh? Indeed, I believe I have discovered a new form of *Rhabdovirus*, and with your position, of course, I am suggesting getting a second opinion from the medical industry. I have already informed two of my colleagues regarding a new classification, and I have been waiting for your return to seek your approval, eh?"

Abraham walked over and took his beloved's hand as she continued to lie sleeping. He found it cold to the touch—almost as if the stutteringly breathing woman before him was actually a corpse instead of that of a living being. Indeed, he had to contest this very notion by confirming a vital sign himself. Her circulation was positively indolent; thus, he began chafing her limbs in a loving effort to regain some warmth and sign of life to her body.

Although, at the instant he leaned over and kissed her cheek, her eyes flew open wide, and her hot, pestiferous breath fell upon his face. Florence Stoker looked upon her husband with untamed eyes and a cunning grin. And with outstretched hands, she screamed, "Behold! The coming of a bride is amongst us! Beware, for the King is at neigh! You—*you*, my husband, now of unclean spirit! Hah! How blind mortal man can be whence darkness falls and rids your land of all sunshine! Hark! Nay, nothing of this world can prevail the dark lord, the promise of a new day is at hand, and man shall feel his power once again! And dusk will reign . . . forever!"

A shock of mortal terror stretched across the physician's facade as he stumbled clumsily over the contents of the room. The journeyman's skin tingled and tightened in a manner that spoke of a horror of the most threatening import.

"As I looked upon the dreadful swoon that laid on our bed come to foul life and, consequently, hearing the queer, blasphemous words spoken in a distant and foreign voice, I had to assert myself that my Florie was somewhere helplessly lost deep inside the ghastly creature she had become. My legs gave full sway resembling the same terrible paralysis I suffered as a child," Stoker wrote.

Van Zant reacted in a typical, logical way of his by offering a philosophical explanation filled with scientific commentary that annoyed the Irishman even beyond his present rank of affairs.

"This religious mania baffles me for it seems to come and go! Her dreams likewise disturb me that I am considering giving her a PCEC shot," stressed the doctor. "Though the drug is still experimental and highly dangerous, I believe her current state warrants such a risk, eh? Do you, by any chance, know of the meanings of such ravings? She has not a history of such spasms, no?"

The two men were silent as Florence returned to a semiconscious, passive condition. Though her eyes turned black as onyx, they remained partially open and attentive. And still unable to walk, the author lay completely sprawled out on the floor, thinking over a courteous way to answer his wife's physician.

"I believe, dear sir," the Irishman began kindly, "that you will have all the answers in due time."

For Abraham Stoker there was much to be done, yet he was not sure where to start—he needed to consult with the doctor in private, he needed to be alone with Florence, and he needed to strategically plot out his vampiric plan of destruction. He needed to send Noel on a few errands of his own, and he needed to pay Irving an unchecked visit, but firstly, he wanted to talk it all over with himself whilst he drew a long, warm bath.

"Please wait on the shot, Doctor," Abraham stated. "There are some things I want to tell you that I believe will turn many a myth to fact, but it is neither the time nor place. For now, may I have some time alone with my beloved?"

Though the doctor hesitated at first, he admitted being tired, and thinking that perhaps the affection and support of her spouse might do Florence some good, he acquiesced by saying, "As you wish. She seems to have settled again. As Noel is on his way here, please send for me at the office immediately—and I stress *immediately*—if anything unusual happens, eh? Otherwise, I will be back at dusk."

And then Doctor Van Zant was gone in an instant.

Within a few moments, Stoker regained mobility. Kneeling over his half-conscious wife, he imagined her as the way she looked when they met many long years ago. And then with a healing hand, Bram whispered to his wife, "Alas, sometimes you have to lose so you can win, and at times the rose pricks the hand that prunes it. Indeed, I may have lost the battle in Dracula's country, but I am prepared to win the war at home!"

As he said those words, her half-snarl seemed less cruel and the glare of her eyes softened. She lay calm and placid and seemingly drifted back into a less frightful sleep.

"As certain as you are the flower, my dear," he said as he continued, "the thorns do not ultimately matter!" And though his rose was fading fast, so were the days of the monster that had ravished her external beauty, toyed with her precious life, and unpurified her fragile mind.

"Aye, I am back now; and I will be damned to let Vlad steal your soul! Nay . . . we will never be torn apart again!"

CHAPTER 26

The Turn of the Tide

I do believe that under God's providence I have made a discovery . . . I am more than ever sure that I am right. My new conclusion is ready, so I shall get our party together and read it. They can judge it; it is well to be accurate, and every minute is precious.

—Mina Harker's Journal

James Dickens, a rugged, industrious man who was the customs inspector and overseen imported shipments into the Whitby Bay Harbor, was an acquaintance of David Godalming. They met in 1870 when the shop owner took up fishing off of Tate Hill Pier. As Dickens likewise enjoyed catching his own catfish for lunch, the two men naturally shared tall tails describing the "one that got away." Needless to say, when Old Man Godalming called upon Mr. Dickens to help track down the arrival of several large crates, he was more than obliged to assist.

Having worked the job for over thirty years, the man had the shipping inventory process down to a precise art form, and though looking at him outwardly would suggest him as a disorderly ignoramus, the man was actually quite methodical in nature and kept strict records. And despite his long and hard number of years on earth, he was blessed with the memory of an elephant. In sum, nothing could get by him.

About an hour after celebrating Abraham Stoker's return to London, David found the elderly boor in his small shack, which was located a few hundred feet adjacent to Tate Hill pier. He was wearing what resembled to be a combination of fisherman's attire and naval anima: a dark-colored shirt with anchored buttons, a pair of common fishing pants tucked in a set of large rubber goulashes, and an officer's cap. His face was red-splotched, and the skin, which hung loosely from his neck, appeared clammy and resembled the wattle of a turkey. Having been in the habit of nipping the brandy late into the evening hours, Godalming found the man leaning backward in a small wooden chair behind an antique mahogany desk with a strong whiff of spirits on his breath.

"Shiver me! How are ye mate?" called out the old salt in a stentorian voice as he removed his feet off his desk. His eyes spoke of feverish excitement.

"I am getting along well, " Godalming replied sincerely. The mariner, who had quite the ruddy complexion, was now standing and reached out his hand and replied, "Business is slow these days; but by Jove, I shan't complain, matey . . . now what brought ye here? I don't think it's fishin' for I don't see your gear, right?"

"Do you have any recollection of—say, two medium-sized crates being shipped from Transylvania?" asked Godalming inquisitively.

Mr. Dickens threw his head back and scratched his snow-white beard.

"Nay . . . blimey, I don't recall anything of the sort as of late," he replied earnestly. "Do ye happen to know when approximately they were shipped? Care for a grog?" The brutish man placed his hand on a bottle of whisky he kept in his desk drawer and smiled genially at his guest.

"I'm 'fraid not—on both accounts," he answered regretfully. "I hazard to guess they were shipped anywhere between six months to a year ago, but I honestly don't have an inkling. And I am afraid I cannot stay long enough for a drink today, but I appreciate your offer all the same."

"Aye, aye! Well, do you know who shipped them?" asked the record keeper in a blaring voice as he took a swig from the bottle and wiped his nose with the palm of his rough left hand.

"Does the name *Vlad Dracula* ring a bell?" answered Godalming.

Mr. Dickens scratched his head as if deep in thought and moved over to a sort of rusty filing cabinet that contained several drawers—apparently filled to the rims with an assortment of papers. Placing a thick pair of round spectacles over his bumpy nose, the man began to thumb through the records, mumbling and grumbling incoherent words along the way.

As the seafarer diligently inspected the accounts, Godalming whiled away the minutes by listening to the diverse sounds of the harbor: the squeaking of the pier, the calling of seagulls, the dashing of water, the fleeting wind, the articulation of voyagers, and the various fanfare of incoming and outgoing boats. In lieu of past odious events, witnessing the peaceful tones as they were brought to life by the sightseeing window, the tranquil, picturesque images almost seemed unlawful and uncompassionate.

Indeed, it is a sometimes callous and inharmonious world we live in! he concluded despondently in his own mind.

By and by, Mr. Dickens cleared his voice as if he discovered something of usage. Pulling out a scrap of paper that resembled a ledger from April 15, 1889, he motioned Godalming to come and take a look. In a boisterous manner, the inspector bristly replied, "Well, ole lubber . . . I only show one shipment that arrived from such a destination—brought in port on a Schooner, nonetheless."

"Are you sure of the date?" asked the Old Man, aghast. "Why, that was seven years ago!"

"Ay, most certainly," replied the record keeper noisily. "The *Citadel* was the ship, all right . . . see 'ere? It says she delivered a cargo inventoried as 'two wooden boxes full of soil' and some kind of 'large, adamantine-like object'—whatever the hell that is, matey! Labeled as a 'religious artifact.'"

Godalming's face fell instantly as he recognized the name of the very ship that returned Stoker to England. The inside of his head shrieked in mortal terror as the outside resembled a nadir of frustrated despair. Indeed, if he were of a weak heart, he would surely have fainted then and there without hesitation.

"My God!" he exclaimed in a grating rasp as if completely thunderstruck. "What have I done? Have I delivered my friend into the lair of the beast without even the slightest clue—but with all good intentions? Oh, woe is me!" he said, wringing his hands and beating his fists together in a deep state of regret and consternation. "But then . . . how was I to know?"

David Godalming's unexpected outburst caught the abrasive man off guard, and for a moment, he was lost for words. The latter looked on in prostration as the former seemed to encroach himself deeper into that of an abhorred image.

"Shiver me timbers! Is everything all right, mate?" asked Mr. Dickens as he snorted and took another nip of whiskey. "Are ye sure its not some 'en the ole tar water won't make do?" Here he held out the bottle of booze to Godalming gallantly but with a wiry face.

His guest shook his head with a distorted expression whilst motioning the liquor away. Still reeling from the latest apoplexy, the Old Man sat down on the edge of the desk in an effort to recover his wits and replied, "It is all too weird and far too complicated for me to even begin to explain!" he replied earnestly but with galvanized bluntness. "However, it is even more crucial that I know the last piece of information I have come for, which is, can you please let me know exactly where the shipment was taken?"

"Nay—not precisely," replied Mr. Dickens, shaking his head repeatedly. There is only a note that the inventory was ported to Whitby Station by Nigel Henley."

A look of hope and excitement flashed across Godalming's face as he asked rather gleefully, "Do you have an address for this man?"

"Aye, only that he was the first mate onboard the *Citadel*, but I am afraid it will not do you much good."

"Why?"

"I regret to say the ole sot died six years ago."

Godalming summoned his hands high over his head as if appealing to the entire universe.

"But by Jove," continued James Dickens, "they were signed for by Captain Oscar Whitman!"

Once more, a look of exasperation sweltered o'er David Godalming's troubled face.

"Yes, I am afraid I had to speak to him on a different matter, and shall I dare say . . . I am still quite distressed over it," recalled the old man with an implacable countenance of vulgarity contortions.

The record keeper was silent for some spell. And for a fellow who was normally quite talky, lest he was sleeping, to which, in turn, he snored clamorously, Godalming knew the man was deadly serious about something. But then, as he took another swallow of drink, the inspector pointed out the shack's sightseeing window at a schooner docked several hundred feet in front of them.

"Aye, aye! You're in luck, the *Citadel* is in port . . . and Whitman 'tis, ole lubber, still her skipper!"

* * * * *

It was unorthodox for Captain Oscar Whitman to fret or appear perturbed—or even openly disquiet by anything for that matter. It just was not in his ancient mariner nature. However, ever since the day Abraham Stoker left the *Citadel*, the skipper had many vague, foreboding thoughts that haunted the back of his mind like skeletons in an assassin's closet. He believed they concerned his passenger in some queer way, but it was the last statement that Stoker made whilst stepping off the gangplank that seemed to intrude upon and trouble his mind endlessly. Indeed, it was as if the mere words "I expect my employer, actor Henry Irving, will be standing by to see me back home" challenged his inner conscience.

If this mysterious life was a chess game, Bram proved to the commanding officer to be a good omen—a human soul playing against a force of evil. And even though he was confident that the enemy Count Dracula would be properly reckoned with, the commander of the vessel could not shrink from the idea there was something more to his passenger's incredible story.

Indeed, if karma were like a boomerang, then Abraham Stoker shall find himself home, sitting in his study amidst a cozy fire alongside his family; whereas the evil vampire will be extinct of this earth and cast into the eternal damnation of hellfire.

After the ship docked at Tate Hill pier, the crew took twenty-four-hour liberties and then began to prepare for a voyage to Varna. It was during liberty call that the captain found himself onboard alone and began to look over the details of the upcoming at sea period in his cabin when his mind was again flooded with the same despairing thoughts: the moment on the gangplank, the fantastic story, the unsettling phone call, and the opprobrious events at sea.

What does it all mean? What was missing?

Unexpectedly, the air around him became miserably cold, dank, and dark. Consequently, within a short while, his limbs turned polar, yet his forehead began to perspire profusely all the same. And unable to concentrate on his work, the skipper got up and began to move about his cabin in an uneasy sort of fashion. A rancorous temblor gained power over his mind and body whilst his final conversation with the writer surfaced again and replayed over and over until he felt as if he were in a world of monotonous horror. Even though the weather outside the skin of the ship did not call for it, the sea captain put on his pea coat and began to pace the floor wildly, shivering with his hands deep inside his warm pockets.

"What in the bloody hell is happening here?" he cried out loud, notwithstanding knowing full well that there was no person onboard to hear his interjections.

He pondered for several minutes, and then a clear, complete thought came to his brain.

By Jove! I think I have found something here!

He went to a shelf where he stored cruise reports, logs, and manifests of the *Citadel* and began to search abrasively. After several minutes of increasing excitability, he stopped at a page and exclaimed, "A-ha! The missing piece!"

As he read to himself the total stillness and solitude of the ship seemed to continue to agitate his nerves. It was dreadfully dismal, eerie, and quiet on board, and the slightest sound or creaking on deck caused him to hesitate and look over his shoulder.

A quick snap echoed behind him. The man jolted away from the collection of data and shouted in a rough voice filled with disapprobation: "Who goes there?"

No one could be seen.

He paused from his study of the document and waited for a short moment, frozen in utter suspense before slowly walking to his cabin door. When he saw nothing stirring through the window and only eyeballed the same mundane objects he otherwise expected to be there, he smiled and chuckled slightly to himself.

My fear is helping me imagination run amuck!

But then another creak froze his ears whilst the man remained stock-still. A mortal dread began to flow in his veins. And then an abrupt faint rush of wind swept passed him so quickly that he wondered if it even happened at all.

My bureau is becoming an assemblage of terror! I must get out!

Though as he was walking toward the door, the captain felt a cold, hard hand come up behind him and clutch his shoulder. With a fright-stricken heart, the sea-goer turned to face his malice with the highest level of contention any traumatic event would allow.

"*You!*" Whitman bellowed in a pitch packed with emotion of succeeded narcosis and astonishment.

Before the mariner had the chance to defend himself, there came a sharp blow to the back of his head. As he desperately tried to strike the figure back, his vision quickly became out of focus, and then stumbling to keep his balance, he soon dropped to the deck with a paltry countenance etched upon his visage.

For the next few seconds, the room spun all around Captain Whitman as a bright light blinded him. At length, he rolled over on his stomach and became succumbed to the total darkness that unconsciousness conveys in its victims.

* * * * *

Jonathan Watt's patience had never been tested inasmuch as that day cueing outside London's stationmaster's office. An hour went by, and then two, but before a third one rolled over, he began to stew. At last the impatient boy commenced to banging on the door wildly in a disrepute way. The old lady that was in front of him, who had previously entered the office at least a half hour thereto, as so the middle-aged gentleman that had been awaiting behind him all of an hour, seemed to cover there faces from embarrassment.

"Great mother of Jesus!" the lad exploded. "One would think I was in cue to visit the likes of the Queen of England herself rather than ask the bloody bookkeeper of the railway a blooming question!"

A man with a conductor's hat quickly appeared in the window and gave him an uncompromising look. Seeing that the youth was not going to budge but rather would probably dive into similar or even further extravagant hysterics, he threw up his hand in gesture as if signifying "one moment please."

With a look of discontent still on his face, the flustered juvenile resolutely rejoined his place in line and continued to play out the waiting game, sulking in the process. Nevertheless, his devouring anxiety reaped its benefits when the door opened approximately two minutes henceforth.

"What say you?" asked the stationmaster laconically.

Seeing that the man was not amused by his hurried nature, Jonathan thought out his words carefully. Upon leaving Whitby Harbor, Old Man Godalming had telegrammed him a man's name and a date. Therefore, ascertain that this information would help in the narrowing down of delivery invoices, he answered the man accordingly.

"A Mr. Nigel Henley boarded a shipment of three parcels on April 15, 1889. I need to know—"

"Sorry, tyke, 'fraid I can't help you there," interrupted the man rudely.

"Shan't or can't?" asked the boy in the same obnoxious manner.

"Don't get sassy with me, aye, kid! I don't even believe our manifest records go back that far, and besides . . . even if they did, why should I disclose such private information to a buggering boy as yourself? Hmmm? Whom, by the way, I don't even know from Adam!"

"Lookie 'ere, guvna'," Jonathan began, changing his tone to one of most earnest empathy. "I am sorry for a-causin' a scene, but it is

454

very important that I know where those boxes were taken," the lad said in an infallible kind of disposition. "Jist all I will disturb you with, really. I don't keer whut they 'ere or how much was paid to ship 'em."

The youth read the man's countenance and could see his words had a positive effect on him. The station master looked at him keenly and came back a few minutes later with a stack of invoices with a thick piece of paper on top that read in large bold letters, APRIL 15, 1889.

"Well, kid, you're in luck, but you still have not told me why I need to tell you anything."

Though Jonathan Watts was normally a very demonstrative and polite youngster, the shadow of dread he had been operating under as of late had seemingly banished all sense of patience and therewith invoked his hostile side.

With a no-nonsense or false impression, he answered the stationmaster by ejaculating, "Cause if'n ye chose not to, I will stand outside your'n office 'til ye change your mind! It be Sat'day, is it? An I's don't fancy a break, neitha' . . . an' so be it as it may, I could be too full up of conniption to goes back to school come Monday morn!"

The teenager watched the man's eyes signify a look of astonishment and then worry. Next, they rolled slightly as if fearing a full-blown fit was brewing inside his customer. Finally, the man gave in and said, "All right, I am making an exception with this query, but I stand firm that future inquiries must follow proper protocol!"

The boy stood there silently in a somewhat excitable state to which the man thought of as a hungry dog playfully panting for a bone from its master.

"I believe this is what you are looking for," the worker added, pulling out a marked-up invoice apparently aged with wrinkles.

A lump formed in Master Watt's throat, as the man not only told where they were shipped but also who signed for them. A nonpareil look of impotence descended upon the formers waning visage. And as a lugubrious expression cut across Jonathan's face like a sharpened blade, he held back a shrill shriek before staggering out the man's office without even thanking the stationmaster whom looked on in complete wonder.

"They were signed for at the Piccadilly Station by actor Henry Irving . . . then delivered to the Lyceum Theatre by coach."

* * * * *

Noel Stoker was waiting eagerly at the British Library when it opened the following Saturday morning. Though he had not quite reached adulthood, he stood at the front steps of the archive patiently with the urge and devotion of an adult with important purpose and the wit and zeal of a mature man.

As he anxiously awaited with a look of forbearance etched upon his adolescent façade, he thought about the people he was closest to: his mother, who was gravely ill; Jonathan, his best mate; and Old Man Godalming, who had become a second father. Though a prestigious wall of doom seemed to be closing in on their tight circle, Noel said a humbling prayer for his cohorts before his mind drifted over to his father, whom he missed dearly and was overly distraught to see again.

My dad is hardy, and I am sure he will return with an appetite for destruction! Certainly, the wealth of knowledge that he brings back could be used against the vampire, and four minds against one is better than three!

As an attendant unlocked the door, he then thought about Henry Irving and his unusual and questionable placement in everything that was uncovered thus far. And 'twas not the first time that the actor had been the subject of controversy or shrouded in mystery.

Indeed, the Lord of the Lyceum had once married Florence O'Callaghan, statuesque daughter of Surgeon-General Daniel O'Callaghan of her Majesty's Indian Army, King of Munster. And together they bore a son they named Henry. However, her harmonious dread of a close marriage was overshadowed by her husband's attachment to the theatre and his cold, macabre nature. There was a breach, and Irving found bachelor quarters once again.

As the doors of the library opened and the youth was let in, he recalled the public scandal that occurred on the night of the actor's greatest victory: the opening of *The Bells*. Florence Irving watched reticently as her husband captivated the audience. And after the curtain fell, each present—from the pit to the balcony—sat in stunned stillness, convalescing from their partaking in the sadistic departure of a beleaguered soul. The proud actor stepped before the drape to receive sequence upon sequence of ovation. And on their way homeward, an euphoric Irving placed his hand on Florence's arm and beamed his opinion: "Well, my dear, we too shall have our carriage and pair," reciting an earlier vow of Edmund Kean concluding his conquest as Shylock.

But as the story goes, his spouse lashed out in discontent. "Are you going on making a fool of yourself like this all of your life?" The Lyceum Lord abruptly ordered the brougham to halt. The actor than dismounted, closed the door behind him, and walked off into the night. He never returned home and never again spoke to Florence, then expectant with their second child.

Subsequent to the adolescent digging up these bones, an overwhelming sense of grief captured the youth. Even though Noel did not care for the man, he knew his father respected and trusted him immensely, and because of their long friendship, coupled with their employer-employee relationship, perhaps their assessment of the man was taken out of context?

Could the actor have been framed? he thought to himself. *Perhaps by a disgruntled actor at the theatre?*

Whatever the case may be, Noel knew his Pop would find out sooner than any of them probably could. And then the former looked up from the table whence he was sitting. *Hark! A young lass!*

It is sometimes worth mentioning that charming looks can produce positive results, for within an hour of darting inside the building, the young, alluring female librarian who had been eyeballing the handsome Noel secretly, made certain that her customer was properly taken care of in a sort of flirtatious way. Indeed, in less than fifteen minutes, Noel had every possible book and publication that addressed the Beefsteak Club. And with a returned smile, he researched what he came there for.

In sum, the Beefsteak Club was founded in 1709 with actor Richard Estcourt as steward. Of this the chief wits and great men of the nation were members; however, its fame was entirely eclipsed in 1735 when the Sublime Society of Steaks was established by John Rich as Covent Garden theatre, of which he was then manager. It was further said that Lord Peterborough, supping one night with Rich in his private room, was so delighted with the steak the latter grilled him, that he suggested a repetition of the meal the next week. From this started the Club, and a secret society was born. Amongst the many celebrities were Hogarth, Garrick, Wilkes, and Bubb Doddington. In 1785, the Prince of Wales joined, and later his brothers, the dukes of Clarence and Sussex, became members. The rendezvous was the Covent Garden theatre till the fire in 1808, when the club moved first to the Bedford Coffee House, and the next year to the Old Lyceum.

The boy's heart went racing out of control.

On the burning of the Lyceum, the Steaks met again in the Bedford Coffee House till 1838, when the New Lyceum was opened, and a large room there was allotted the club. These secret meeting were held there till the club ceased to exist in 1867.

Noel's reaction to this information was one of complete shock and awe. His eyes bulged out at the book whose sentences then seemingly whirled around him. His hands began to shake violently as he dropped the text upon the table as it landed with a slight thud. Master Stoker fell back into his chair overcome with emotion.

The boy was so amazed by what he had just read that he could not all together accept their true and horrific import. However, after pausing a short moment, he closed his eyes and attempted to clear his mind of all the fears and terrible events that encompassed him. A moment later, he reread the text and found that the type written words were, indeed, true for not only did this gruesome discovery prove that the mysterious dream his mother had of a Beefsteak room was horrifically real but that such an awful room existed at the Lyceum.

The booming sound of the heavy book falling to the table caused the young female Liberian to stop her activity and cast a startling glance over to Noel. Though his breathing became laborious, short, broken gasps, he tried his best to conceal this in an attempt to not attract any attention to him. He smiled slightly at the woman and consequently nodded as if to say everything was okay. And after the sudden spout of panic subsided within him, he assembled the grit necessary to take himself home expeditiously to face the terror that was spreading within.

* * * * *

Abraham Stoker had worn an unclean, unpressed suit for so long that getting out of it made him feel temporarily like a man born again. He had also bathed while Florence rested and afterward changed into a crisp seersucker suit. When he returned from the washroom and discovered he was still alone with Florence, the unusual stillness of the flat made him wish that Noel would hurry.

What in God's name could be keeping him? Bram thought to himself.

"The flat seemingly projected and overpowering aura of doom and gloom that, presumably, froze my blood to an almost unmovable state of consciousness," the Irishman described. "Clearly the longer I remained in the house, the worse the feeling became, and though it was not yet the season for splitting wood, it was as if a supernatural force drove me into the study, where I shuddered from the cold and lit a blazing fire! Seeing my familiar desk before me—though slightly covered with a film of dust—I grew incredibly weak and weary of everything. And as my mind became twisted and spiraled like a great cyclone, I sat down and frantically began to write. To work, yes, to work . . ."

A few hours later, the sound of Noel's approaching footsteps echoed up the stairwell and then down the hall. Indeed, the teenager was frightened enough by his mother's condition that when he returned home to find his bleak father glued to his desk like a madman held captive in his cell with a strait waistcoat, the sight was almost too much for him to handle. Even though he had forewarned himself—as he feared his father's state of mind and health must have been in the toils—the shock of reality that awaited him brought the horror to an entirely different level.

The author was writing at such a frenzied pace and endless vigor that he did not even see his own son enter the apartment.

"Father!" Noel called to him ecstatically but with a foreboding sense of alarm.

The man did not look up but kept writing without taking any pause. By the looks of the amount of paper, if he had not known Abraham had just returned home that morning, Noel would have guessed he had been glued to the desk for at least a week, writing endlessly without food nor rest.

"*Pop!*"

A dazed expression fell on the journeyman's face, and after a short instant, he seemed to shake himself out of his writer's trance. And then his look changed to one of astonishment, and a wide grin swept across his physiognomy from ear to ear.

"Noel!" he cried as he clutched his boy tightly and held him in both arms like a vice.

"My son! My dear, dear, Noel!"

The Irishman's tears flowed like a waterfall, and at that moment neither angel nor demon could have separated the two. Finally, Bram pulled back and, with both hands on the boy's shoulders said gleefully as he gazed at his face, "You have grown into a handsome, well-built young man! Oh, woe . . . have I ever missed you so!"

For a while, it appeared whatever cloud of evil that had befell on the Stoker residence had lifted with the reunion of father and son. Though Florence continued to sleep in her half Un-Dead trance, the pair talked for several hours. The conversation drifted from more pleasant things—such as Noel's splendid grades in school—but soon evolved into the inevitable horror story that divided and terrorized the family and whose originating force was still at bay.

As they talked over the terrible events, Bram's beaming facial expression shrunk to one of solemnity when Noel told him of Henry Irving's behavior, Jonathan's discovery of the bloodstained program, and the Beefsteak room. He seemed bewildered and somewhat disturbed and slightly angry by it all and shook his head as if denouncing it as untrue.

"I need to pay him a visit and find out what is going on. I am sure the whole of this—though very queer and fantastic as it may be—can be explained in a logical context. Perhaps our minds have been so overwrought with such tragic circumstances with Count Dracula that we are having a difficult time rationalizing fact from fiction and fantasy from reality. I am certain his involvement in these matters were simply mere misunderstandings, and although I do have some questions for him myself, his purpose in all of this was to help your mother get better."

Noel, though slightly disappointed with his father's reaction, was partially prepared for this type of reasoning; however, he was left discontented, nonetheless. Notwithstanding, it was his Papa's homecoming; therefore, he decided to save face and let his father find out the bitter truth in his own time—whatever that turns out to be. In the meantime, however, the conversation moved on to another topic: Florence's ailing condition.

Noel had already tried to provide hints to Doctor Van Zant that his mother was attacked by the supernatural world of a vampire rather the rabid bite of a bat. When this concept was indirectly rejected, Noel continued to pursue his plight without the physician's say in it.

"I suppose he will find out soon enough," Noel stated wearily though forcefully.

"I concur," agreed his father. "However, for now, I need your help ridding this evil—this . . . this bane of my existence—that is trapped in our home! Until we can rid Dracula of this earth, we must deter him from setting foot in this house again!"

Noel nodded in agreement but said nothing. The shock of having his periodical parent back after so long, coupled with the nerve-wracking ordeal of his ailing mother was almost too much for the youth to digest.

"Listen to me closely, son—I need you to go to market and pick up several batches of fresh garlic flowers. Waste no time!" shouted Stoker through a whisper. "After you return, I will laden our room whilst you go to St. Joseph's and bring back some Eucharistic wafer that has been blessed by Father Fletcher—*go!*"

After taking a wad of money from Abraham, Noel descended the steps and Bram could hear the door slam. Soon the awful brisk-ness returned to the room, and he began to shudder once more. As he did so, Florence, who was sleeping soundly in the bedroom, began to grow restless, and he could hear her despairing, incoherent, and agonizing cries all the way into the study. Quickly, he began to walk to her room to see about her when his legs buckled underneath him. And then, the ultimate of all harrowing events happened.

A tantalizing glare of consternation pulsated from the onlook-er's bulging eyes. To his complete disbelief, his writing chair moved across the floor, only there was no visible entity in the room, other than himself, that could have controlled its position! As it relocated, the screeching of its legs across the hardwood floor panged so loudly that it could have driven the dead from their grave.

"The painful sound was like a symphony of glasses of blood where their ghastly rims were being chimed against with many a mon-strous hand!" described the author. "And as it played out, I feared I was on the verge of falling apart at the seams! I closed my eyes tightly and screwed up my ears with my fingers and simply screamed like a horrified child."

"I called out helplessly, for that terrible infancy curse struck its cord out of nowhere—again!" wrote the Irishman. "But when the paralysis attacked, I realized that Noel was too far away from the house and that the doctor would not return until dusk, I became absolutely terrorized. For I was left utterly alone with Florence—or should I say, what was left of her—wailing in the other room, yet I could not go to her. And as my writing chair slid out from under my desk, on its own accord, I felt the absolute lack of physical sensation dart though my lower body like the onset of rigor mortis. And the emotional effects of blinding dismay anesthetized my brain to the degree I questioned my own subsistence. How I wished I had my father's bell to ring! Perhaps someone—or something—would come to my desperate rescue! Yet I was unable to move. I was one bulky, unyielding slab of flesh and bone—categorically immobile from a atrocious scare."

But as he crawled toward the chair, which seemed to announce his presence—much like a piano stool being pulled back for its musician at a concerto—a dreadful, evil-pitched voice echoed five words through the grim, clammy study which initiated a howl from Abraham far worse than his beloved's enduring cries:

"The quill is the life!"

CHAPTER 27

To Hell and Back

> The battle has but begun; and in the end
> we shall win. So sure as that God sits on high to
> watch over his children.
> —Professor Abraham Van Helsing

L ate afternoon. When Noel Stoker returned home with several bushels of garlic blossoms and consecrated bread, he was again appalled with his father's abnormal behavior. Abraham was in the same position he was discovered in earlier that day—that is, hunched over at his writing table, scribbling energetically, presumably in a trancelike state.

"I could tell from the position in which he was sitting that his legs were numb or immobile. They were in an awkward kink, and it seemed he had crawled his way up to his desk from the marks left on the floor," Noel recalled years later. "Though I had learned of his long spout with paralysis as a child, it was only from Mum as he never spoke of it. Truly, I believe he was quite traumatized and ashamed by his childhood disability, nonetheless, discussing it during adulthood might have been a superstitious move to which he psychologically feared would revert to those painful years and begin to regress and suffer from apathy of the legs."

As he had done earlier, the apprehensive son called to his father several times before Bram finally broke free from his concentration and started back as a cat does when taken unawares. Whether it was his voice or the strong odor of fresh garlic, Noel was never sure, but he was beginning to worry about his dad's queer spouts of mystic abstraction—especially at such a time of need. Indeed, with Count Dracula at large and his mother's ailing condition, he needed the man to be alert and strong. With listless eyes, the tired writer lifted a hand leisurely to his beard and strummed, befuddled.

But after seeing the garlic wreaths and sacred wafer in hand, the Irishman smiled and attempted to stand, but to no avail. With a look of worry and embarrassment on his face, the eldest said nothing. Yet his mannerisms and visage spoke of one of deep consternation. Thus, the youngest broke the awkward moment through trivial conversation.

"I did not tell Father Fletcher the real reason behind my request for the sacred loaf but simply stated Mum was very sick—that she had mentioned it would do her well to take communion," the boy explained. "When I told him we were all down in our spirits, he gave me these after blessing them," the teenager added holding up five beautiful rosaries.

At this realization, Stoker absolutely beamed ecstatically and said, "We must each wear one; and you shall deliver the remaining to that fine friend Jonathan and Mr. Godalming!" Placing a crucifix around his neck as he watched his son do the same, the author motioned in the direction of the bedroom where Florence Stoker had lapsed back into a deathly, desolate slumber. Noel took the silent suggestion and went to hang one around his mother's painfully thin throat, which still revealed the two tiny bite wounds that appeared pale and jagged around the edges as if inflamed from a sort of infection.

"Her cheeks were sunken, her collarbone stuck out like a clothes hanger. And her knees resembled doorknobs," recalled the son. "Her fragile, pale skin was dry and flaky, with a skeletal weight of approximately seventy-five pounds! She refuses to eat. Moreover, her thinning hair is falling out, her gums appear swollen are separating from her loosening teeth."

When Noel saw this, he shrunk back with a gasp. He blinked one time only as the taut flesh contracted over his features. Indeed, the adolescent was debilitated with terror. With a pain-stricken voice, the son called to his father in the study, "It is time to take action! I must go to the others now!"

Without alarming Noel of his failing legs, the latter answered, "I must stay with your mother until Van Zant returns. However, before you go, please take the wreaths and deck them about the bedroom. And then crumble the Eucharist all along the window sash and edges of the door!"

The lad assented but suspiciously looked back at his father, who sat peering over the pile of papers before him in a state of desperation. Seeing his son's concern out of his peripheral vision, he cleared his throat and said with slight hesitation,

"Please understand my reasons for not joining you, as too I gather Van Zant has not given you much time with her; hitherto, I believe my spell with her today has had a draining effect on my nerves. Nevertheless, I must try to make some sense of my notes from my travels abroad—I have been putting them in chronological order, hoping that they provide some clue to where the vampire's lair could be!"

When the eccentric décor was in its proper and rather unusual places, Noel made a hasty toilet, grabbed a change of clothes, and bid his father goodbye. When the two embraced, the boy could not conceal the impeding feeling that something was not quite right with his dad and that there was an incoherent, impending danger ahead for them all.

* * * * *

Evening. Whilst Bram was in the study fervently writing another sequence of Vlad's chronicles, Florence Stoker mysteriously managed to leave her bed and sleepwalk her way out of the house. Like a moth to a flame, she followed a fixed beam of light as if being pulled by a cable. Though she was heavy with slumber when Noel hung the rosary around her neck, whereas the sympathetic son had unbound his mother's hands and repositioned them lovingly to her sides, the ailing mother grew unusually restless as dusk approached, and this cosmic effect whereas the sun and the moon exchanged places in the universe's playground had an alluring and almost supernatural reaction to her mind, body, and spirit. Her tortured breathing aided in a remarkable transformation as her face transcended into an overwrought appearance, which became twisted and gnarled with fright.

As of late, the minutes around dusk and dawn had become increasingly and painfully problematic for the woman; they seemed to open up a passage—a great unknown tunnel of endless darkness—to which was filled with all sorts of queer noises and mean images that left her trembling relentlessly beneath the sheets. This was likewise true this day; although past periods of thrashing were stifled by Dr. Van Zant administering a mild sleeping draft. Notwithstanding, if violent exertions occurred, as past instances had proven, her physician would restrain her until the fit had subsided. This evening, however, was the worse case yet, and Abraham, was too consumed with his writing to take notice, failed to react to the commotion that was taking place albeit 'twas only a few rooms away or to witness his wife's twilight stroll.

When Florence became aware she was out of bed, she was taken aback with awe and surprise. She looked around aimlessly in gawking wonderment as her jaw went slack. Upon noticing that she was in her own backyard, she stood staring at the almost foreign scenery for a long, breathless moment. The sudden realization and change of surroundings startled her to the point of tears for it had been months since she had walked the pathway of their English garden that celebrated nature's beauty within its own secluded gated fortress. Bewildered, she eyed the radiant colors of the fall flowers, trees, and shrubs sadly fade away and eventually darken under the moonlit sky. There she remained frozen like a porcelain statue as the splendor of the day became suffocated with the shadows of the twilight, which simultaneously released its own family of darker things: the owl, bat, and wolf. And to this she smiled—though unwillingly at first—and at length realized she was, indeed, home.

Now recognizing the path before her, she began to walk only to be stifled by the sensation of the soft ground beneath her feet as it sank deep into every crevice of flesh and gelled between her toes. Truly, she forgot to put on her house slippers. As she continued to glide toward the back porch the cool wind felt clammy against her body and seemed to blow entirely though her nightgown, chilling her tiny frame to the bone. Quickly, she set off toward the back door and hastened her way up the real stairwell and onward to the cozy fire that her husband kept pumping full of life.

She shuffled her feet into the study where her husband sat amidst and consumed by the mound of papers. Indeed, he did not see her enter; however, as she called his name whilst standing at the fireplace with her back toward him, Bram sat down his quill and turned in her direction.

"Florie!" he called in a half astonished and partially worried tone. Though his legs had not fully regain their strength, he slowly stood, and by holding on to the side of his desk he made his way over in her direction using a varied assortment of objects for support. She stood motionless and did not answer.

"You must be back to your old self again, my love?" he smiled as he held out one of his arms for her to take in an effort to refrain him from falling. She again remained silent but continued warming herself by the hearth.

With a puzzled look on his face, the author asked thoughtfully, "Can you talk to me, love?" And looking down, he took alarm to the trail of earth that was evidently tracked across the room from Florence's bare, muddy feet.

"Good heavens!" the Irishman explained. "You have been outside—but how? When? No wonder you stand warming yourself . . . you have taken a terrible chill!"

At this, she finally turned around, exposing her face. And offering her hand to keep him stable on his feet, she said in a low, soft tone, "Warm me, Abraham . . . I am cold as death itself."

Stoker froze momentarily at the sight in front of him with bobbing head and a strained neck. His eyes widened and almost bulged out of their sockets as he took one, two, and at length, three paces backward, whereas he ultimately slipped on the wet mud and fell completely on his back. His tongue felt stilted. His mind declined to operate with clarity. As he lay resembling a helpless insect trapped in a poisonous compound, kicking its way to its stomach and supreme freedom, his mouth fell open wide and his lips drew back to a tight and hideous set of mind-boggling horror. And as with a most terrifying, life-threatening nightmare, he finally screamed without sound.

Seeing her husband's unsettling behavior toward her, Florence shed a tear and absconded from the room—as if a bird in flight—and proceeded down the corridor in the direction of her own secluded quarters. Directly outside her chamber was a mirror that adorned a highly decorative wall. As she passed it by, she abruptly stopped and was equally horrified at what she saw.

The gleaming whiteness of her face was, in fact, not skin at all but rather fleshless bone that was neatly articulated to the bare pebbly skeletal fragments of the neck, which were connected to discs that adjoined the spinal column. At this harrowing revelation, there came a blood-curdling shriek from the hollowed skeleton, followed by a similar answer from the study, which in unison, filled the Stoker residence with a brooding atmosphere that only a sepulture could compare.

The animated anatomy, which was loosely bound by frayed strings of ligament, took hold of what was left of the fluttering shreds and began to roll herself up in the death robe in a desperate measure to conceal as much of the visual signs that accompanies the crude nature of demise. The act of consternation closely resembled that on an ancient Egyptian princess preparing herself for the ghastly act of mummification. Then, escaping to her bed, she plummeted despairingly into the sarcophagus that had kept her prisoner for so long and moaned until the darkness of nothingness swallowed her whole once again.

* * * * *

When Doctor Van Zant returned to the Stoker household, he stumbled upon a scene, which provoked discouraging thoughts and regret of leaving Abraham alone with his wife. As the physician crossed the threshold, he immediately became overwhelmed by the strong stench of garlic—a scent that was so rank that combined with the unpleasant odor that accompanies a bedridden adult diseased by a nervous disorder, the marrying of the two was a dreadful combination. In fact, the smell was so vulgar and vile that the doctor became sickened by it and was practically knocked off his feet—insomuch as he made a beeline toward the washroom before addressing the writer, who was positioned at his wife's side softly whispering words of comfort whilst stroking her feeble, trembling hands.

"My goodness! What in heaven's name happened here?" Van Zant asked in a shocked but almost derogatory way. "Why is my patient not restrained? Why is there mud on her feet and the floor? And for the love of the Almighty, what is that ghastly, horrid smell, eh? It is quite unsettling, and from the look of Madame Florence, it evidently has upset her too! Hmm?"

With fair going, it seemed whatever evil had invaded Florence's sleep had departed for her colorless complexion and lethargic condition had returned. And although the paleness and languid form was, indeed, a reminder that all was not well, for the present moment, it was surely a comforting and welcome sight as opposed to the more horrifying postmortem resemblance that terrorized the couple less than an hour hitherto.

"She was sleeping soundly . . . so deeply," began Stoker, "that I asked Noel to free her hands for I was fearful the constraints were restricting what little blood supply she still has—"

"Foolish, foolish measure!" Van Zant said interrupting, shaking his head in disappointment whilst restraining her hands and checking her vital signs.

"She then had a night terror so fearful she actually got out of bed and began to sleepwalk!" continued Bram. "I think it distressed her very severely for she got as far as the backyard . . ." Here he paused as he was afraid of how the man might react to his carelessness of letting her get up on her free will, much less leave the house and reenter without his knowing. Therefore, he thought it be best to speak the partial truth in a vague sort of way and beg for forgiveness in the process.

"Pardon me," the Irishman continued in an imploring manner, "for I was unable to contain her, and it has taken me almost half an hour to get her calm," explained Stoker.

At the present, Florence was in a semiconscious state—half alert but in a dreamy kind of fashion—blurting out random words such as *burial*, *death*, and *cold*.

"Did she tell you what the nightmare was about? No?" the physician asked while he mixed up a draft of something that he quickly pressed to Florence's lips in a small flask.

"I gather that she awoke from her unconsciousness to find that she had been buried alive," the writer explained, withholding the fact that it was no dream at all and that her temporary zombie-like countenance had driven them both into a state of hysterics. "I believe she mistakenly accepted the mud on her feet to be that of her grave!"

Abraham appeared to be choking on these words and paused as the doctor sat down the empty container that held the concoction. Van Zant looked at his pocket watch and nodded before saying sternly. "Ah, she will be resting peacefully in a few minutes. However, we need to talk about her condition and what evidently occurred tonight for I fear she has had a setback. Madame Florence appears to be bitterly cold and frightened, nonetheless, eh?"

The physician stood and motioned for Stoker to follow him to the window, where he continued to speak in a soft but firm tone. The author, who had since recovered full movement in both legs, acquiesced. "I have known your beloved for many years—even before you two were married, hmmm? And as I accepted and celebrated her choice in holy matrimony. Consequently, I have learned to appreciate your work in the theatre and your writings, though I fancy them not. However, I cannot for the life of me begin to understand what your son has been driving at these past few months! And from the events of this evening, it seems you have joined him in his abstruse folly!" Van Zant picked up a wreath of garlic that hung from the sash and put it up to his nose and said hotly, "Garlic, eh? Really! Such pungent odor would swoon even the healthiest creature into a lurid state of restless agony!"

Abraham's reaction to the doctor was one of equal coldness and hostility. The tears that had been building up in his eyes faded and a look of resentment filled his entire cavity until words began to pour out of his mouth all at once: "Folly, you say? You have not a clue, man, what it is like to have wasted six years of your life held captive in an unknown land whilst being haunted every second by unspeakable horrors!" reputed he. "You know not what it is to loathe the actual monster that you fear is spreading its evil across your land whilst invading your own home! Folly, you say? No, dear Doctor, it is madness in the worse but truest form! Indeed, I was cast into the innermost depths of hell, and the crux of this horrid irony is that I failed to resolve myself of it whilst I was away—yet I have known the truth all the while!"

Van Zant looked at him with a puzzled glare and stood quietly.

"Nay, you know not," ranted the writer, "absolutely nothing of the horror that my family and I are facing! And to dismiss their import with a lack of faith is an insult to injury!"

Though the physician continued to listen, Bram could tell the former's patience was being tested as his face was set with a stern expression.

"Forgive me for speaking harshly, Doctor," Stoker went on, "but the real folly rest in your hands, for, in contrast, you chose to discard every trace or piece of evidence and mock the warnings my beloved, Noel, and now I have provided! Case in point: you continue to misdiagnose Florie's condition as a new form of rabies!"

The physician held up his hand with an annoyed look on his face and said, "Speak plainly, man for I truly do not get your drift!"

"Don't you see? There!" he motioned to his poor beloved's neck. "The wounds on the throat, the appearance of death, the supernatural dreams, the loss of blood, the fear of sunlight, and now the garlic flowers?" Stoker asked in a frustrated tone, attempting to keep his voice down while his wife rested across the way.

"Do you not know what they all mean?" shouted he with an underlying weariness full of desperation.

The physician looked cross and folded his arms defiantly in a state of protest.

"Do you forget, Mr. Stoker, that I am a man of science? Thus, I search for visual signs and symptoms, then I take that proof and match it to root causes written out in the world's most respected and modern medical journals! Only then can I prescribe a proper diagnosis, accept it as truth, and offer a remedy to treat an illness," he said somewhat angrily. "And nowhere in my field do I go to witch doctors and crystal balls for answers! The fact of the matter is she was bit by a bat carrying an unique form of hydrophobia."

"I am afraid this is not so," the Irishman said earnestly, "and though I respect your profession and ability as a learned man, I am afraid your prejudice to have an open mind is clouding your sense of reason."

"Well, perhaps it is the garlic, eh?" Van Zant said sarcastically, almost shouting in rebuttal. Looking out the window, he stared for a moment at a sheet of dust that sparkled like stars before his contesting eyes. This bizarre sight took him off guard, and he closed his lids for an instant. When he opened them again, the spectacle was gone. Looking back at the Irishman, he went on in a more settling and calm tone.

"I too respect you—but as a writer!" he replied hotly. "Therefore, I do not see what qualifies you the right to diagnose a patient or offer medical advice! Notwithstanding, I will hear you out. Please, tell me what you believe to be true."

"As I previously mentioned, the truth is so fantastic and remarkably wild you will find it to be unbelievable and an insult against your intelligence. I speak from past experience as I too felt this same way, as did Noel. All I ask you is to hear me out and keep an open mind. I promise you if you cannot accept my hypothesis as first, the underlying proof will come in due time."

"In God's holy name, out with it then!"

"Indeed, she was bitten," answered Stoker. "And true, it came to her in the form of a bat! But alas, the wounds derived from what the old country refers to as the land beyond the forest. And this very strange place from whence I only scarcely returned, labeled my beloved's aggressor Nosferatu . . . or the Un-Dead! And this terrible devil has a name: one I have come to know and hate to well, and one that has struck fear and horror in the hearts of men, women, and children for hundreds of years! Sir, he is none other than Count Vlad Tepes Dracul."

"Stop! This is insurmountable!" Van Zant said, throwing up both arms in protest. "'Tis that the essence, eh? You must think I'm off my bloomin' head to believe such an idea! Is this the foretelling of a script you are taking to the stage? Or is this some terrible joke you are trying out as a chapter in your next book? Indeed, your misadventure must have caused your brain to come undone!"

"Nay," Stoker answered. "For I have journeyed to the homeland of the beast that consumed Florence's life blood and have learned of his legend! Likewise, I have witnessed his power firsthand, and moreover, the most important piece to the chronicles I have sworn to put to paper will reveal my prudent discovery: the means that will lead to the vampire's destruction!"

At this the doctor's back arched, and he stood firm and proud. His facial expression resembled a man who was in the process of being mocked and whose profession was being made a laughingstock.

"Alas! It is true! You *are* off your head, eh?" the doctor stormed. "What you speak of is an outrage against common and scientific sense!"

The writer looked at the physician sadly. And for some time, the conversation was the perfect picture of two professions struggling to join forces—going to and fro like a badminton match—unable to see the other's point of view.

Though neither party saw it (as they were too preoccupied with each other's plight and keeping the sleeping sick at bay), the sheet of twinkling specs of dust reappeared and hovered directly outside of Florence's window. At last, Abraham realized there was nothing more he could do at the moment and decided it was best to leave the man to digest what he had just been told and proceed to the Lyceum to confront yet another person, actor Henry Irving.

After kissing his wife on the cheek, Abraham turned to the doctor and said politely but wearily, "In time, my friend . . . as sure as the sun will rise on such a miserable house, you will surely have your evidence. But for the sake of you and your own family, I just pray that it will not be too late!"

And as Stoker walked out of the house and proceeded to make his way down the drive, it did not occur to him that the proof was actually at hand: for lurking directly outside, impatiently awaiting his exit remained the spooky layer of sparkling particles beyond a pale, silvery moon.

* * * * *

Florence Stoker began to show signs of restlessness again mere minutes after her husband left. As her seemingly uncomfortable status seemed to be focused or concentrated around the area of her throat, Doctor Van Zant concluded that the beads of the rosary was somehow irritating the two puncture wounds that were still very prominent and jagged-looking around the edges. Thus, he removed the icon and tucked it away in her nightstand. Upon watching her several minutes more, the woman's anxiety seemed to increase, and at last she sat up in bed—as if broad awake, with her eyes wide and glassy, pointing directly at the windowsill. She made a vague but uneasy sound in her throat as her terrified eyes grew larger and larger until one expected them to explode out of their sockets with any passing second.

The physician, who could not make any sense out of this—as she refused to speak coherently and was still in a half-swoon—pondered over it. He was beginning to get somewhat used to the odor of the wild garlic; however, thinking that she was pointing to the batch that was hung on the sash, he decided the vile stench was contributing to her uneasiness.

Quickly, Van Zant transported the strong-smelling wreaths of flowers to the kitchen and then opened the sash to let some fresh air into Florence's bedroom. As he did so, the doctor's eyes became fixed upon the thick sheet of particles—the same enigmatic observation that he noticed earlier but had since far forgotten, as they seemingly whirled about as though performing a strange midnight dance around the windowsill. The moonlight was bright enough for him to see the fine transparent powdery-like matter wheel, and as his eyes gazed upon the mass, they began to grow weary and tired.

Van Zant's reaction to dozing was quite a shock to him as there was no known cause for it. Indeed, he had slept soundly all afternoon before gathering up several medical journals regarding peculiar disorders of the blood and nervous systems.

A low, prolonged moan from Florence Stoker provoked the doctor from his daze. And next, he witnessed the sheet of particles as it picked itself up and floated like a raincloud into the room! If the physician had not known better, he would have fancied the idea that the particles must have had a remarkable purpose of their own—as if every twinkle was some form of question or answer that ended with the mass shifting shape and moving closer to its decided destination.

Indeed, Van Zant was stunned by this unusual experience, and he was quite dumbfounded over what to do about it. His uncertain nerves jerked violently. Without thinking, he began to wave his hands about, much as a policeman directing traffic, in hopes that the matter would venture its way back outside. But to no avail—the sparkling substance remained fixed in a grim position of systematic intent.

The sheet then seemed to expand once it stole its way into the middle of the bedroom and continued to glow insomuch that the chamber was lit up with millions of tiny Yuletide-like lamps. However, by and by, they begun to darken, and the doctor felt an incredible sinking feeling in his chest as Florence let out a terrifying shriek.

Without warning, the now dim mass collapsed on the man and pushed him against the adjacent wall. And before he tumbled headlong, he saw a dark, thin man step out of the matter as if every twinkle suddenly formed into a cell of his body.

"Greetings," the voice said to the doctor in a thick Romanian accent, "I am Dracula—and I hast an undying hunger only thou patient can applaud or help restoreth." The message of revelation was spoken in a callous, forlorn voice that had misplaced all parallelism with humanity.

Florence twisted wildly on the mattress as Van Zant, who lay cowering on the floor recovered from the collision. The Count turned to the latter with an intent look, and his eyes began to glow a piercing red. Finally, within less than a minute, the physician was lying in a heap, snoring as if in a stupor.

With a haunting, malicious smile, the vampire approached the bed and looked upon the trembling woman, who resembled a helpless newborn struggling for its senses.

"Ah, my love," the nocturnal nemesis snarled as he seized her throat, "thy veins will quench my thirst once more, but prepare to bid thou mortal life ado as I welcome ye to the immoral ranks of my army of darkness!"

The ghoul's red lips pulled back, revealing the bared canine teeth that were sharp like the ice of a glacier. And resembling a leech attaching itself to its prey, he champed down a final time onto Florence's jugular and drank his way to merriment.

A sharp ping shot though the woman's system, and for a long moment, she lay quaking with convulsions. In an instant, the monster pulled back, revealing a renewed stamp of the fiend's grim appetite. The victim's body agitated for a short moment and produced a morose groan that came from the depths of her fearing, apprehensive soul that was struggling its best to do battle against the horror that had once more invaded her body. As the brute wiped her smeared blood from his lips, he said to her, "Drink from my blood and become my immortal love. We become one flesh and will reign the centuries together!"

A petrified look of sheer terror spread across her face as Vlad tore open his shirt, exposing his naked chest. And using the pointed nail of his right index finger as a blade, he made an incision across his left breast. Almost instantly, the crimson flow trickled down his torso, and taking Florence by the bulk of her hair, he pressed her face to the wound.

"Drink—drink, my bride! And soon ye will become blood of my blood, flesh of my flesh, kin of my kin, and all the memories, knowledge, and experiences though the centuries—both great and small or of gayety or pain—will become thy own to know. Thou thirst for eternal lasting youth will be fulfilled in exchange for thy obedience to me. For ye will abideth with me and walk where I walketh. You will feedeth as I feed and will surrender thou self to my father—the master of the heretic forces. And as ye and I become joined, ye will be faithful to my bidding and protecteth me from the infidels that wish to interfere and come between us—even if this means death to thou mortal family!"

The harrowing conviction was then upon Florence as she was too weak to fight it. And though his diabolically cold blood seemingly iced her veins, there was some grim pulsation that sent a shock of life through her lethargic condition and insensibility. It took control of her and seized all sense of reason. A sudden apathy came to her limbs, and her heart began to beat like the powerful blows of a hammer. The terrorizing sense of horror that surged though her was replaced by looks of contorted and distorted ecstasy followed by a sinful, succulent stare that fell across her face like an inviting whore.

And then came a loud knock at the front door—such as one would give in dire emergency—which prompted the Count away from the bed. The sound of smashing glass echoed throughout the house, and the rapid movement of climbing footsteps quickly followed. With a wily grin on his face and dark burning eyes, Dracula spoke to the door: "May thou heaven bid ye welcome, for I bid thee not!"

* * * * *

Jonathan Watts could not sleep. Not only had the thought of the shipments arriving from Transylvania being delivered to Henry Irving left him thunderstruck, he was anxiously awaiting word from Old Man Godalming regarding their next group meeting. As he lay in bed with his arms folded behind his head and between his pillow, he stared at the shadows that stretched their way across the ceiling of his room. The house was deathly quiet, and his parents slept soundly in their chamber crosswise his own.

The morose atmosphere left him chilled, uneasy, and scared. And all his senses seemed to mock his wearied countenance in exaggerated extremes of alertness. Though peaceful solitude of the night would have normally lulled him to sleep the events of the past few months had left him dreading nightfall, and sleep was beginning to become a chore for him.

It was 5:30 a.m., and there was still no word from David Godalming. A combination of the waiting to hear from him and

Noel's return from the library at such a suspenseful time was clearly keeping him readily attentive and on edge.

Why have I not heerd from the Old Man? An' whut in the bloody blazes is a-keepin' Noel?

All at once, there came a thud that caused the boy to jump up in alarm. With bursting heart, he lit a piece of candle. Then he stammered out of bed and looked about the room in an attempt to identify the source of the noise. Finding everything in order, next, he darted to the window and peered out into the night; however, again his effort was in vain for he could not see anything that looked out of the ordinary. Keeping his ears and eyes fully open, he finally decided to creep throughout the house.

Thinking one of his parents had gotten up to make his or her toilet, it was likely that one of them might have dropped something in the dark. Nevertheless, he found the pair soundly still as if they had not heard the noise at all.

Upon venturing downstairs, he gritted his teeth in intense apprehension. He paroled the kitchen, living room, and dining quarters to no avail. However, just as he began to think his insomniac mind was finally beginning to play tricks on him, the noise came again. This time it was louder—perhaps closer even—and he stood stark still. Listening . . .

The piece of candle he was holding was very small; therefore, he was frightened that the wick would soon burn out. Some of the hot wax dripped against his right hand, and he started up in pain but withheld any audible sign of agony. The quick sting only alluded that the frightful moment was, indeed, real.

Too real! thought he.

For over a minute, he watched and listened with puissance similar to that of a night owl. And at length, he decided to redirect his position to a bloodhound and bravely proceeded to outsmart the fox.

Quickly but silently, he scrambled around the kitchen, looking for another form of light, when he heard a faint whisper: "Jon-a-than!"

The teenager swallowed hard as the candle flickered and then went out all together. A blast of wind blew against the flat producing a melancholic, eerie effect, which on any other occasion would have passed him by as the other noises of the night invited him join the Sandman in his quest for sleepers. However, for the moment, never had a rustle or bustle struck such a powerful cord of reverence in the boy. And never had the absence of light or disquiet manifested such feelings of dread, solicitude, and expectation of harm.

His heart stood still as he shuddered in total darkness. For several seconds, which in anticipation seemed like an eternity, the lad remained motionless, trying to pinpoint the direction of the voice. Watts began to feel the increasing thud in his chest. But when the call failed to come again, he began to feel his way toward the front of the house where a fire had been lit hours before. As he did so, he stumbled upon an object in the corridor that almost produced a crashing fall. Still, with the collision there came an abrupt rustle, and the lad was afraid he had just made his presence known to the unwanted visitor. Indeed, immediately after the impact, there came again the same voice, only this time slightly louder in volume:

"*Jon . . . a . . . than!*"

Watts felt his stomach contract. The lad cringed as he rose up and placed his left hand on what was the front door and was quickly overcome with the alarming apprehension of a complete state of fear. True, whatever he had been searching for was standing directly outside, and *it* did not take the called but a horrifying second to realize that the only object coming between "it" and him was a common door—a mere piece of wood that suddenly seemed insignificant now, knowing the horrors that have been.

Deciding it best to arm himself with something more substantial, he quickly grabbed a poker from the fire and felt his way back to the door by the aid of the moonlight, which refracted all sorts of queer shadows and images on the floor in front of him. And with panting breath and trembling hands, he called out in a broken voice, lacking the sternness he strived too desperately to assemble: "Wh-wh-who's th-th-there?"

Only the wind answered with a blustering howl. As he waited with beads of sweat collecting on his brow, he called out again, "Wh-wh-whut s-s-say y-y-ou?"

Still there was no reply.

A branch from a nearby overgrown tree scratched its gnarly limb against the window as a moonbeam cast the resemblance of a dangerous burglar on the adjacent wall. Watts bent over with a gasp, recoiled alongside the door, and then continued to wait in the desperation of darkness.

After a long pause of hearing nothing more than chirping crickets, taking his clammy left hand with poker clenched in his right, Jonathan slowly unlatched the door and quietly turned the knob until it was slightly ajar, leaving a gap wide enough for him to look out but little enough to latch again swiftly if need be.

The tension in his body seemed to be lifted away when he saw nobody standing there. Several seconds passed. Opening the door wider, he quickly noticed the front porch was stark empty. Stepping out on the porch, he took a deep breath and gazed out over the horizon. The coming of the dawn was slowly approaching, yet he was even more alert and anxious than ever. It seemed almost surreal that the majority of the city—or half the world for that matter—could be asleep with such evil abroad.

To Jonathan's shock and dismay, his teeth clenched in a state of complete consternation as two arms suddenly came up behind his back and grabbed him about the waist like a python. Lifting the poker as if preparing to strike, a familiar voice shouted, "Jonathan! It's me!"

There stood the form of Noel Stoker.

"For the lov' of Christ, mate! Are ye daft?" said Jonathan, recovering from the sudden fright.

"Did you not hear me call you?"

The two soon turned and simultaneously noticed that someone else had recently been on the porch. Indeed, for there—pinned to the frame of the door—was a telegram that read:

N & J
    MEET ME HALF PAST MIDNIGHT AT
THE STOKER HOUSE. THERE IS MUCH
TO DISCUSS WITH THE OTHERS.
                                        —G

"Half past midnight? My God!" replied Noel afraid for the worse, "It will be morning in an hour! How long has this telegram been here?"

"I dunno, but the dispatcher must've been a-sleepin' on the job!" answered Jonathan. "Me parents are still nappin' so be quiet—I will leave 'em a note, and tally ho we'z go . . ."

The flight of stairs and corridor leading to Jonathan's room was still very dark, so using a glowing ember from the hearth as a means for light, the poker led the pair to Noel's room. Closing the door behind them, Jonathan, with poker in hand, searched for a piece of parchment and quickly scribed a note.

As they were several hours late, Jonathan knew they needed to hasten. And as he wrote with his back toward Noel, he could not help but notice his friend's heavy breathing.

"Ye better catch your breath, mate as we'z a headin' back from whence ye came—"

"Me?" Noel interrupted immediately. "I thought it was you breathing so shallow after a-runnin' into you below!"

At the same instant, the two identified the mirrored look of terror that flared in both sets of eyes as they each slowly turned in unison to look behind them. In mammoth horror, their teeth bit convulsively against their pursed bottom lips.

Blocking the door, breathing heavily with arms stretched out to her sides, stood the figure of a harrowing creature that might once have been a beautiful woman in her early forties. Her light shoulder-length hair fell against an alluring ashen face with catlike eyes. She was dressed in an elegant royal-blue corset with shoes of equal appeal, although her sensual red lips pulled back, revealing a fierce set of ivory white teeth with long incisors that were pointed like daggers at the tips.

Indeed, it was the Lyceum victim, and she smacked her cruel mouth and moved her tongue to and fro much like a hungry, wild beast as a pool of fresh blood dripped from her nasty reddened chin.

The boys' hearts sank instantly upon seeing the vital fluid. And as the two stood congealed in a perfect seizure of consternation, the thing spoke as if reading their minds in a harsh, sinister tone.

"Yes, boy," addressing Jonathan. "Your parents are dead! So do not fear—any scream you or your friend makes will not cause them to stir! But I am afraid my hunger has only just begun!"

The vampire reached out for Noel, as he was positioned closest to where it stood, whilst Jonathan swallowed his grief and took the poker and placed it in the hearth on the opposite side of the bedroom. How he wished the black leather bag Noel had purchased from Old Man Godalming was within reach.

The strength of the woman was tremendous, and though Noel tried his best to push her off and take a violent swing, she had already seized both his arms in one of hers and laughed mockingly, "How quickly death causes your thirst to rise! I believe young boys will make for a splendid dessert! And you will be my first refreshment!"

The fiend quickly went for his jugular, and Noel could feel her hot, corrupt breath that smelled of the bitter odor of newly looted gore against the sensitive skin. The diabolical stare of the vampire had a sudden hypnotic effect on the adolescent for his body went limp in her clutched arm upon pulling his throat to her fanged mouth.

As commonly described by those who have walked away from near-death experiences, in the passing seconds, Noel's life seemed to flash before his eyes: Every fond memory of his parents, family and friends jetted like a living montage of moving experiences. The future was totally disabled, and the reflections of the past left no room for present active thought.

Nevertheless, as he felt the indentions of the spiked teeth against his neck, there came an abrupt pause. For just a mere second before the monster pierced the prudent vein, she cowered back as if a cat had pounced on a mouse preparing to feast on a piece of cheese.

The beads of the rosary, which hung around Noel's neck, had singed into the side of the creature's face much like a heifer being branded for slaughter. In that precise moment, she let go of her victim—dropping him to the floor—and as she towered over him with fixed, devilish eyes and a bloodthirsty mouth, Noel watched as the tips of the ghoul's ears grew to a fine point with coarse hairs, resembling those of a savage tiger.

"You—you with you idolatrous icons! Hah!" it said, spitting droplets of blood into Noel's face in a threatening, scornful sort of way. "I command you to remove it at once! Otherwise, witness your friend's throat as it is ripped to shreds like his parents!"

This latest development and evil words outraged Jonathan, who had ventured to the dwindling hearth in a discreet manner. He stood with his mouth partly open, gaping at the horror before him. And upon forking a large, glowing ember of wood to the end of the poker, he charged at the fiend full throttle. The vampire's brow became wrinkled with rows of angry beet-red flesh, which caused its eyebrows to meet in the middle, producing a bat-like appearance over its burning, hellish eyes.

As Jonathan attempted to urge the creature on toward the corner of the room, he touched the edge of its corset with the glowing piece of wood. Within a few seconds, the garment began to smoke. In reaction, the monster became even angrier and growled like a wild bear, attempting to seize the iron rod with her left hand whilst putting out the fire with her right.

Noel, who was recovering from his hypnotic fall, slowly regained consciousness and quickly became cognizant of the situation. As he did so, his heart raced wildly, and his visage became ransacked with the contorted countenance of fear.

"Your mother and I will soon share the same master, boy!" she sneered at Noel. "And we all despise naughty children! Say your prayers if you've got any left!"

In his front trouser pocket, the former removed a piece of the altar bread that he happened to save and came at the brute from the opposite direction, trapping it like an escaped convict. And seeing the signs of dawn coming in through the bedroom window, Noel gave his friend a quick sidelong look that was acknowledged with a nod. Apparently, the vampire saw it too, for a flash of apprehension crossed her face. And then the duo was on her faster than she had the time to react.

The two boys pushed harder as the vampire's corset was now ablaze. In the distance, a cock crew and a priceless look of defeat fell upon the monster that both friends would never forget to their dying days. With a direct, rapid stab, Jonathan plunged the poker in the heart of the vampire, which welled and spurted like a fountain of blood. The thing wailed and flailed its arms as the two pressed onward, forcing the undead intruder out the window.

With sacred wafer in hand, Jonathan took the final step forward, which cornered the bloodsucker of darkness until at last it broke through the glass pane with a loud crash. Upon impact, his friend ran the dowel even harder into its chest.

"In the name of the Father, Son, and of the Holy Ghost . . ." Noel began.

"Go back from whence ye came—never to return of this earth!" continued Jonathan. "Back to 'ell with ye!"

The child of the night sprung from the window like a raging inferno, screaming in agony, with both hands, clutching the iron rod to no avail. The two mates watched with pleased expressions as it hit the ground just as the morning sun began to spread its rays over the dew-covered grass. In an instant, the Un-Dead and the sun seemed to catch sight of one another, and the ghastly form quickly wasted away to a heap of dust and then blew into the morning breeze as if it had failed to ever exist.

"Here," Noel said with almost a smile on his face. "I believe it be best that you put this on!"

And tossing the extra rosary Father Fletcher had given him from his pocket, Jonathan caught it in midair and actually laughed manically until he cried.

CHAPTER 28

Setbacks of Sorrow

We did not know whence, or how, or when
the bolt would come; but I think we all expected
that something strange would happen. None
the less, however, was it a surprise. I suppose
that nature works on such a hopeful basis that
we believe against ourselves that things will be
as they ought to be, not as we should know that
they will be.

—Dr. Seward's Diary

Dusk. Prior to Abraham Stoker leaving London to embark upon his traumatic six-year tour of Transylvania, the writer had ventured on a research trip with the Royal Scottish Academy to aid in the Lyceum's production of *Macbeth*. This initiative consisted of a walking tour of Scotland's own Cruden Bay, a quiet fishing village north of Aberdeen, overshadowed by Slains Castle on a precarious headland overlooking the North Sea.

Its isolation, contorted rocks, and caves were irresistible to Bram, and the sandhills, meadows, and the distant Bralmar Mountain fancied his interests as so did the rows of fishermen cottages with their red-tile-drying sheds. There he hiked over the two-hundred-foot cliffs to Slains Castle and took solitude and inspiration from the sheer beauty of the landscape. Indeed, the admission of what he saw changed his entire world.

However, as Stoker left Dr. Van Zant to watch over his wife and departed from his own abode, the landscape he was off to research was far from one of tranquility: it was a murder site. As the Irishman waited patiently at the back of the Lyceum Theatre to speak to Henry Irving—for he had given his sole key to the actor prior to his trip to Romania—he thought about the eccentric man and the relationship that put a strain on his own marriage and family life.

In pondering over his employer's potential and mysterious involvement in the horror at hand, feelings of empathy and compassion regarding his unconventional friendship clouded the writer's reality. *Perhaps all uncertainty pertaining to the actor's contribution in this macabre of events is simply a failure to understand the man behind the strangeness,* the journeyman thought to himself. For indeed someone with such an unusual talent in theatrics—yet whose unfortunate upbringing formed a quirky personality, which at times overshadowed his ability to act—resulted in gossip or false impressions. Here Bram's mind raced to images of various mortuaries he and his employer frequented when on tour with a Lyceum production. To while away their free time, the couple amused themselves by studying the condition of the corpse and placing bets on the manner of death before confirming the real cause against its toe tag. Though this morbid pastime caused the theatrical crew to shudder, the Lyceum manager did manage to audit his employer's weaknesses: "Irving is in face and form of a type of strongly expressed individuality such as Hogarth has touched upon in his comparison of character and caricature. Irving's physical appearance sets him at once above his fellows as no common man, but his physique is somewhat too weak for the heavy work, which he has to go through. Thus at times there is a variance between voice and gesture or expression, which is manifestly due to want of physical power . . . the voice lacks power to be strong in some tones, and in moments of passion, the speech loses its clarity and becomes somewhat inarticulate."

Unmoving, the returning prodigal man waited in a sea of wonderment. His thoughts next drifted onward to his active imagination of how his partner might react to the controversy, questions, and allegations set before the table. Without question, it would evolve into a story of grandeur told with increasing frenzy!

He saw the Lord of the Lyceum become afire and went on and on. *Till at last he was a living flame,* thought he. *His eyes shined like jewels as the firelight flashed. We sat quite still. We fear to interrupt him. The end of his story leaves us fired and exalted too.*

Images of old danced before the visitor's weary pupils—performances that left the audience sometimes disturbed and children quite scared. A particular reaction from the Flying Dutchman came to memory: "Like embers of glowing red from out of the marble face." Stoker recalled being captivated by Irving's presence. "In his eyes shines the wild glamour of the lost—in his every tone and action there is the stamp of death."

Nonetheless, the theatre manager remained . . . waiting anxiously for such a man. The seconds slowly ticked away; these lapsed into minutes, which in spite of their dire import crept into hours.

For the time of day, the air was unusually still and abnormally quiet. And the desolation of the abounding blackness caused him to forsake his prior thought to ones of brighter equality. But as he lingered the author's thoughts kept returning to the attraction he felt toward the quaint village and how desperately he and his family needed such a change of pace. All three members were being sucked into the horror of Dracula, and the likelihood of getting out prior to death, insanity, or something worse was beginning to look slim. It was a world of confusion. The framework of his life was collapsing around the Stokers, and Scotland seemed to be the key to unlock the malice.

"During my brief tour of Cruden Bay," the author recalled, "I heeded to the earthly smells of my invalid days, whilst nestled amongst grasses and flowers, I inhaled the great outdoors—whither wild rabbits scampered through the dunes as the sun rose over the North Sea."

Yes, this was the furious contentment Stoker was longing for. It was the answer. And still no Irving.

In due time, it was apparent that the theatre was completely deserted: for all the doors and windows were locked, the inside was dark and silent, and not a soul answered to the loud knocks Abraham administered time and time again. Indeed, the pursuer felt as if he was trapped in an abyss of misery and disappointment only he could understand. Not even the pursued could comprehend the greatness of his agony despite the fact their lives have been somewhat adjoined at the hip.

After a long while pacing around the theatre, a sort of grim reality took hold of Bram such as an uncomforting shock one feels when suspected bad news suddenly becomes validated. Though he had countless reasons to question Henry Irving's involvement in many of the situations surrounding the Count's sightings and carnal matters, coming to terms with the suspicions were much harder than he ever thought. Indeed, there was something at work which he failed to comprehend, and the fine line between fact and fancy was becoming more clouded by the day—hanging by a mere thread.

Why did I not keep a spare key to the building? the journeyman thought, scolding himself.

Abraham decided that continuing to scope the place out into the night would lead into unwanted run-ins with law enforcement, especially after an unsolved murder occurred, and as of late, was still very fresh on people's minds. Likewise, breaking in would more than likely bring his excursion to a close; for having not acted as manager for six years, any suspicions officials would have of him would presumably not be positively conceived. Therefore, as opposed to approaching and confronting Irving as originally intended, Bram decided to stake him out in an act of surveillance instead.

Since the actor was a man of habit, the writer assumed the Lyceum Lord would enter the theatre by the back door. Though Stoker did not know when this would occur—as the actor had been notorious for coming and going at strange hours—he positioned himself across the alley and hid in an archway to a neighboring building that was partially concealed by a large lamppost.

There the journeyman remained all during the night, awaiting Irving's arrival. It was a disciplined endeavor; however, the perfect desolation conjured up reminders of the frenetic terror that was to be. Thus, whenever these feelings began to creep on, the author drove his mind to brighter things: pleasant images of his family and the warm atmosphere of Cruden Bay. It was that moment that Abraham began to contemplate about escaping with his family to the quiet, homey suburban village in contrast to restricting them to the turbulent, perilous home that accompanies the hustle and bustle of urban London.

The seconds seemingly ticked away like hours, and with every passing minute, the Irishman wondered if the theatre had in fact been abandoned—only that the people closest to him had not the heart to communicate the unfortunate news. Indeed, other pressing priorities—such as his family's safety—were at hand, and work naturally was not the foremost of concerns.

At length, the man began to feel like a trespasser. His internal instinct told him his cat-and-mouse game was not going to play out *that* night, and he decided to pay Henry a surprise visit at his home in Sheffield instead. Hence, he collected himself and proceeded to walk westward. Though the streets were desolate, he kept on the main strip in an effort to signal a cab driver on an all-night patrol.

The air became unusually dense. And as he walked, the briskness of his stride seemed to be weighted by a mist that settled along his path like an eerie carpet.

"The mist appeared out of nowhere and wheeled about like a family of phantoms. However, it was like no other substance that I had ever seen before. Pray tell, being a citizen of London, I have seen my fair share of foggy and misty streets," described Stoker. "I was completely baffled for it positively centered itself around the path in which I pursued! Indeed, it was almost like the road before me was split up in four directions: north, south, east, and west. And in my case, it was clearly the westward that became the 'mystified' one—that is, oppressive with air fully engulfed in the weird substance. Yet all the other avenues were full of clarity and unmistakably normal!"

Despite the challenge of finding a ride in such an unsightly condition, Bram persisted onward. However, a quarter of a mile away, the obscurity became so abundant, and his entire vision grew severely impaired: to the extreme, he quickly became lost in the thick of it.

My security of reason is ebbing to and fro like the North Sea tide!

For some time, he wandered aimlessly about, walking in the direction of any sounds or faint sightings of streetlights, until at last, the mist suddenly and completely melted away—much like a large gloved hand of a magician had quickly unveiled a trick of illusion.

"When I stepped out of the cloud, I had to recheck myself for I could not believe my eyes," wrote the author. And as he stood at the end of his *own* drive, the very pathway leading up to his *own* house, the feeling that something was very wrong and different quickly overpowered the shock of arriving at an alternative destination than he sought after. Normally, the sight of his flat brought forth the feeling of joy, peace, and comfort, yet looking upon the structure, this unsettled night caused the smooth column of his throat to contract in complete consternation.

The spectacle left me tongue-tied and twisted, and there was no doubt about it: this deceitful act was yet another merciless atrocity the Count had plotted out in his demoniacal blueprint of lies! The sounds of bells sounded in the journeyman's ears—bells such as a church would ring in the times of old when evil was spotted abroad.

For God's sake! Go in!

Upon approaching the front door, he began to trample upon pieces of what sounded like broken bits of glass. Consequently, he noticed the front windowpane had been busted out by force followed by a tormenting tactility, which sailed through him like rapid gunfire: a vague whisper of the paranormal communicated to him that something dark and sinister lurked inside.

"*Florence!*"

The man ascended the stairs quickly but with extreme caution, by a coal oil lamp that was left in the foyer.

"I had horrible fears and moaned in terror as I crossed myself and hurried up the steps to my beloved's room, preparing for the worse but praying it was not too late," Stoker wrote. "But the horrors that awaited me curdled my blood and knocked the wind out of my body. What progress we had gained seemed to have been lost in that moment, and any hope of triumph I had felt as of late had slipped through my fingers like dirtied water. For the first time, I gravely felt the end was truly upon us. Whether it would be Dracula's end or the end of mankind as we knew it, I was not certain, but one thing I was for sure of: I was afraid—terribly afraid!"

Florence Stoker was collapsed toward the edge of the bed with her head, left shoulder, and both arms partially dangling off the side as if attempting to flee from danger. A look of extreme dismay was etched upon her face—a pale stone look of lethargy coupled with swelling eyes that remained fixed upon some grim and horrid sight that only she could see. Perhaps the terrible source of shock had come and gone. But whatever the case, it vividly continued to chill her to the quick and terrorized her brain. The dressing gown she lain in and bedsheets were spotted with the remnant of fresh blood, and the tiny wounds on her neck looked finer, serrated, and distended—oozing a sanguineous foam that continued to drip, producing an expert puddle of hemoglobin on the floor.

The appalling sight quickened the beating of Abraham Stoker's heart, and as he rushed madly to her side, his veins pulsated and pounded wildly to the level where his face was flushed with disquiet and his head became faint.

"Florrie! My beloved!"

In the corner of the room, not far from the window, lay Dr. Van Zant as if in a stupor. Bram found him all in a heap in sort of a half swoon. The back of his head and upper back were bruised. And though his breathing seemed difficult, he was alive, nonetheless.

Praise the Almighty—neither has left me yet!

"Doctor!" the writer shouted in a tone of instating passion and alarm. "Up with you! She still has a pulse!"

Slapping the doctor in the face repeatedly, the man slowly began to stir, opened his eyes, and looked around. At first glance, he seemed confused and dazed, but within a few seconds, his glare became one of dread, dismay, and worry.

The physician could not remember anything that occurred; however, consequently, he was far less skeptical of what he had called the author's outlandish plight.

"She is still alive but slipping quickly! I am going to administer a PCEC shot and she needs a transfusion fast! You roll up your sleeve, eh? Quick! There is no time to lose!"

After the operation, Florence seemed to regain some of her natural color. Notwithstanding, it was as if she was fighting for every living breath—that was taking every ounce of her heart and soul to denounce the evil that seemed destined she was cursed to become. Though she slept, it did not appear to be a restful sleep, nor did it seem she was at peace with herself.

"The air around me turned absolutely stagnant, and I knew at that point some internal tug-of-war was occurring, which was out of her control. She was like a tortured beast that had been gunned down by a fierce hunter," wrote the journeyman. "And though the gravity of death hung over her like a shrill, coldness, she fought feverishly to stay alive. Truly, that hole in her heart made her wilder—and even stranger at times—but simultaneously, the peaceful rest that once nested within and streamed happiness from her eyes had disappeared. Yes, in body and in spirit, she was disappearing too, and the creature was emerging fast. Indeed, I stood pining for the cruel mockery of her once blissful and youthful beauty, yet it was the thought of her old self that shocked me back into the harsh reality of my resolve. God save us all!"

In that harsh moment, if there was a dance of exorcism either one of the men could have prescribed, one would have been granted without question, sparing no expense. And if Florence's love could have performed one himself, he would have danced until his legs wavered until he collapsed on the floor—no matter how outlandish it would have appeared to others.

Bram took the tip of his right index finger and pushed back the upper lip of his spouse's cruel-looking mouth. Almost instantly, he let out a woeful wail and shuddered at what he revealed. The husband's throat moved violently. Her ghostly gums were shrunken back, and there was no mistaking it: her teeth were longer and sharper. The former's spine tingled all over from aquiver that left him ravished with fear.

"See!" Stoker explained to Van Zant in a state of nervous apprehension. "There is your proof! Her new freedom is at hand! We must do something *now!*"

The doctor was clearly thunderstruck. He said nothing at first but finally let out a gasp so prolonged it sounded as if his chest would explode from the exertion. For the first time in his profession, the man of modern science was at a complete loss for words. He stood watching her sleep, with his hands on top of his head as if in a state of complete awe and wonder whilst the man of the house wandered into the study in a deep, active state of thought. But as the physician's thoughts recoiled within the dark shadows and recesses of his mind, a hoarse cry echoed from the study: 'twas the scream of the journeyman, and the horrible wail ripped open the silent calamity that possessed the house.

Alas . . . another shock.

There, lying on the floor, directly in front of the hearth, was the body of a dead man sprawled out in a pool of blood. Abraham was left without a choice but to identify the body by its clothes for the victim's head had been placed directly in the fire and was terribly burned beyond recognition.

Indeed, it was David Godalming.

It was like the gates of hell were flung wide open upon this house! This blow crushed my spirit, draining any reverence out of my flesh and bones!

It was evident he had been dead for some time for the fire had completely burned out, and even the coals were ashen gray. Oh, but the smell! The awful, vile smell! The pungent odor of cooked flesh almost keeled even the most burly of men off his stockinged feet! The duo had to sit down; the writer actually *fell* into his desk chair transporting a fright-twisted face.

Consequently, the tarn of sanguine substance did not come from the facial damage, as any vital fluid became food for the fire, but rather from a grand sword that protruded from his middle back.

"In God's holy name!" the Irishman cried. "How could such a fiend continue to walk this earth—to reek such havoc and continue to invoke terrible turmoil amongst common men and remain to go scot-free? Damn you! Damn you to hell and back again! Lord, tell me! What do you do with such a monster?"

The end of the powerful sword spoke volume: the image of a circular dragon with its tail coiled around its throat. On its back, from the base of its neck to its tail, was the red cross of St. George on the background of a silver shield . . . the Order of the Dragon.

On the author's desk, lying on the top of the heap of notes and papers that was being chronicled into the book, the Count dictated him to write was a grim reminder of his own order. Written in the Old Man's blood, in the evil hand of the vampire, were these beseeching words: "Let the world see where I have been and where my fruit lay! Remember thy vow! D."

* * * * *

Jonathan Watts wept when he entered his parents' quarters. A later inquest suggested that they had been dead for several hours—even as early as several minutes before the strange noise that alerted the boy from bed. Indeed, the vampire was not lying: for their throats had been torn open—much like the Lyceum victim—and the discovery was a blatant reminder of the grotesque peril that disintegrated into the morning breeze by the rising sun. The bodies were completely bathed in blood—that is, from head to feet in one perfect, sadistic crimson stain.

Like being submerged into a bath of iced water, Watts twitched from the distressed conditions of shock. First it brought about numbness; next, came listless eyes. Then the long macabre spell of mute sadness and hopelessness. It took a while before the grief-stricken son realized that his breath had stopped.

Noel nursed his emotional friend for several minutes but said nothing. For he too was engulfed in melancholy and feared this heinous act was only the prelude of what was to come. He was scared for his own sake, as the two families had become closely connected, supporting each other through endless sorrow and peril. By and by, Jonathan must have read his mate's mind and said in broken, despairing sobs: "Ye go on an' jaw wif' Godalming! An' yeens humbug the Sam Hill that started all this—put some lead pills in him!"

"Are you certain?" asked Noel in a guilty tone, looking in the direction of the red-stained sheet that covered his friend's murdered parents.

Will this savage act of carnage go unavenged? Noel was quite positive—nay, rather hell-bent that revenge was, in fact, the only thread of hope and certainty that kept him motivated. Vengeance was now his pose in life: it had become his sole means of existence.

"For as of late, I have not given up on the Almighty and feel He has not forsaken me. But God save us all when the sinful are called to justice! For when heaven forsakes the unrighteous on earth and hell runneth over with evil, those fears beyond the grave are arisen—to walk in blackness, amongst the undead—in an immortal state, with an insatiable thirst for human blood!"

The former looked at the latter with swollen, tear-reddened eyes and replied, "Yes'm—I will stay richeer. My uncle will be 'ere an' we'z will alert a Bobby an' sort out th'—" Here he stopped and could not go on. But waving Noel onward, he finally repeated the word "*Go!*"

And like the old vampiric legend of a nude virgin girl boldly mounting a great mare, Noel too set forward to sniff out the Lord of the Undead with nothing more than a heavy heart and the loving icon of Christ's passion.

* * * * *

A half hour later, Noel Stoker returned home. As he raced up the stairs to his parents' bedroom to the sound of his mother screaming, his ears rang until they hurt. It was not a normal open display of fear, such as one would hear a lady give upon being startled by a mouse or large insect, but rather, it was one driven out of anger. And it reeked of rudeness and disgust. Following the outburst, there came a crashing noise and a woeful cry that chilled his heart with horror.

"Did you not see it? Florence asked her husband with bulging eyes. "My reflection in the mirror is fading! Soon it will cast not!"

The doctor gazed in dumbfounded terror with shards of looking glass all around him. Seeing Noel had entered, Bram addressed Van Zant and then his son with a façade set as steel.

"God's will be done. There is nothing more you can do for her. Only I can save her now, and if she is to become a vampire, I am ascertain it will not happen in this cursed house!"

As the doctor looked on in amazement, the writer packed up several changes of clothes for himself and his wife whilst Noel followed suit. Then the husband changed his wife into a clean dress and placed a large cartwheel hat with a veil on her head as a means to hide the sunlight and conceal her haggard appearance. Finally, he tied a scarf around her neck to shroud the mark of the vampire.

"The body, eh?" Van Zant shouted, holding up a finger in alarm.

At this point, Noel was so overwhelmed by everything else that he did not even take notice of Godalming's body when he ran passed the study. Upon seeing it, he wept inconsolably and clung to his father like a helpless child.

"Nobody will believe the truth," the Irishman said to the doctor. "However, call the authorities and say that a burglar broke in during the night, and you awoke to find everything in this condition. Wire us at the Kilmarnock Arms Hotel if need be."

"Hark! And where might this place reside, eh?"

Before he answered the physician, Bram had already picked up his wife and rushed his family out of the flat. The journeyman then returned to the horrid house and paused outside the study one last time. The man hesitated a moment but ultimately grabbed the lot of papers on his desk. He then wrote two words on a piece of paper for only the physician to see and then shredded it into a hundred fragments. It read, "Cruden Bay."

* * * * *

Dawn. Translated, Cruden Bay means "Blood of the Danes" and is a constant reminder of when blood flowed as Celt and Dane slaughtered each other in the days of Malcolm and Macbeth. Hence, this aforementioned history provoked Stoker's original interest for a walking tour several years earlier. Dominated by Slains Castle, ancestral home of the Errolls, one of Britain's most ancient families—the village was more feudal than Victorian.

And in a fighting tone, the Londoner screamed as he absconded out of the city he just recently returned to. *Oh, Lord, emancipate me from the shackles of hell! For at the foot of the cross, a man can sleep as a child of God as opposed to being under the diabolical influence of a demon!*

Though slightly shadowed, the 667-km rail ride to the broken embattlements of the village, long since inhabited by the crimson lust of the dead, was a far cry from the horrors that actively and brutally haunted them back home. And feeling he was unable to persuade or change the outcome there, the author settled his family into a gabled suite of the Kilmarnock Arms overlooking the river of Cruden Bay.

On the passenger train ride over, Noel told his father of the gruesome encounter with the vampire and what she did to Jonathan's parents. His son's description of the female creature caused him to swallow hard, and as the locomotive steamed along in the daylight hours, the two could not help but notice Florence's skin had become extended and tight as she slept. Her fingernails were unusually long, and the harsh lines and caustic cheeks made them both very uneasy. And they liked it not.

"My bleeding heart beats for you," Abraham whispered.

And for a long moment, the writer stared out of the window, stroking his wife's hair, mumbling things to people Noel could neither see nor hear. This incoherent chatting and grumbling continued for the remaining duration of the trip, which lasted well over two hours.

Though Noel was extremely puzzled by his father's odd behavior, Noel did not want to upset him any more than he already was; and by his own accord, he did not have the wherewithal to question him about it. However, as the boy reclined back in his chair to lose himself to slumber, he was in a half doze when he thought his father muttered something that sounded like "The quill is the life."

* * * * *

Neither Jonathan Watts nor Dr. Van Zant knew about the other's murderous incident until after the police had found out. It just so happened the officials interviewed both of them as character witnesses at the same time, and oddly enough, it was not until all three bodies turned up at the same funeral home that the revelation was made. However, the police was on it sooner; and Inspector Cotford was once again backing the investigation.

Both the doctor and the Watts boy described the intruder as being a tall, gaunt, somber man clad all in black with pale skin and dark hair. This was all the doctor could recall of the unfortunate episode, but he guessed the burglar entered from braking the window downstairs. He literally had no idea how the Old Man came into the picture other than the fact that he must have been coming by to check on Stoker's wife, saw the broken window, and caught the thief off guard. When asked why the Stoker's were not available for questioning, the physician politely answered, "Abraham feared for his family's safety and fled until the murderer had been caught." He added that he knew where they were staying in the event he was needed for questioning.

Indeed, Jonathan did not give an accurate description of the creature that killed his parents for several reasons: first and foremost, the female vampire was destroyed, and secondly, if he did tell the truth, he would have to explain what happened to the body. Furthermore, they simply would not believe such an outlandish vampire story. So upon weighing the consequences of either the inspectors becoming angry at a teenage boy, who seemed off his head, wasting their time by making up monster tales—or collaborating on the search of Count Dracula—he and his Uncle Tom decided it was best to go with the latter choice. Though Tom Watts thought his nephew's account of the incident was the most outrageous story he had heard in his life, he did not think Jonathan had reason to lie at such a time of grief. Furthermore, he had an open mind and the boy appeared earnest as ever about it in vivid, lurid detail. To conjure up such a tall tale on such a short timeframe would have been a mammoth chore and masterpiece for even the greatest epic novelist.

It was clear to Inspector Cotford that the murders at the Watts home were almost identical to the woman outside the Lyceum Theatre: extensive mutilations and lacerations to the face and throat, severed carotid arteries and internal jugular veins, crushed carpal bones and perforations of the esophagus. Likewise, there were two bite wounds on the neck of each victim with frayed tissue borders. Because the victims were killed in their sleep, there was no evidence of struggle and no tissue or hair samples found of the intruder. Like the Stoker house, a broken window—albeit on the top floor—'twas made by the intruder for a means of a hasty escape.

Though the corpse of David Godalming was found in a different manner, it was equally deranged. Likewise, it was evident that the Old Man saw the killer coming and made some attempt to defend himself for a dark hair follicle of the assassin was in the dead man's hand and 'twas later matched to the one found at the Lyceum.

It was striking to the detective, who was still on the hunt for the murderer of the theatergoer, that all three victims were somehow directly or indirectly connected with the Stokers or the theatre in which he cooperated with Henry Irving. Furthermore, Inspector Cotford realized that the tall, gaunt, somber description matched that of Henry Irving perfectly. Moreover, he had dark hair; however, at the time of his previous inquest with the actor, he did not have enough evidence to trigger the warrant of a hair sample.

The latter statement would soon change.

The funeral services for both David Godalming and Mr. and Mrs. Watts were scheduled three days from discovery of the bodies and were set only a few hours apart: the Old Man's being in the late morning and the Watts' service residing in the early afternoon.

Though Dr. Van Zant did not personally know David Godalming; nevertheless, out of proper courtesy—not to mention the odd circumstances that a man was murdered two rooms away from his own blackout—he respectfully attended the service. And whereas the Old Man did not have any immediate family, a group of about twenty-five friends and customers of his unique shop came to honor his memory and to pray for his good-hearted soul.

Jonathan, who literally ran directly into the family physician in the front lobby, was astonished to see the doctor that was presumably taking care of his best mate's mother.

"Whut are ye doin' 'ere?" Jonathan asked in a quiet but surprised tone.

"There was an accident at the Stoker's residence . . ." he began, but seeing the wild looks that immediately swept across the boy's face, he quickly corrected himself. "No, it is not what it seems—the boy is fine, and so is his father. And his mother—well, she is as good as can be expected, eh?"

The doctor's reply eased his worst fears, although the lad was not fully satisfied with the man's answer.

"Well . . . then *who* are ye 'ere for?"

"An old man—one that the Stokers knew quite well—was murdered a few nights back."

The doctor's laconic words did not sit well with Jonathan, and his head began to whirl with suspicious doubt.

"Whut old man . . . to *whom* are ye referrin' to?" pressed the boy with a sad and impatient look on his face.

The physician's countenance plunged, and there was a long, uncomfortable pause. He did not have to say the words for there was only one "old man" that came to mind, and the boy immediately became light headed at the mere suggestion. Indeed, Watts would have fallen if the doctor had not caught him in his arms.

"I was there while it happened, son," Van Zant said. "And since the Stokers could not be here for the funeral, I decided it would be appropriate to attend on their behalf. I am glad I did, for I thought you knew. Come . . . let me walk you in to view his casket."

Without a doubt, the delivery of the grim and sad news hit the already troubled boy like a brick and caused him to suffer from additional stress and confusion. For not only had he abruptly lost his parents at such a perilous time, for the past forty-eight hours, he had been worried sick about the old man.

To learn of Godalming's death only mere minutes before the service began was a dreadful blow, indeed, but to discover the body was directly down the hall from his late parents' remains left him fully aghast. And if the strangeness and crudeness of the situation was not already at full sway, the morbidity continued to escalate. The adolescent still did not know how the man died, and Van Zant did not feel it was the time or place to discuss it.

The first service was unique in the sense that it was a closed casket ceremony. This seemed to shock and bewilder Jonathan but he sat quiet in his seat, shifting his weight nervously every few minutes like the angel of death was calling for another volunteer and all eyes were upon him.

The undertaker could do little with the deceased's face. The extent of the burns were so severe, a decision to alter the traditional viewing practice had been made the evening prior. However, at short notice, a few loyal and faithful customers contributed and decked the top of the casket with a beautiful assortment of bouquets that resembled a field of wild flowers that was almost identical to the lot of blossoms behind his odd boutique. The bittersweet atmosphere almost moved the doctor to tears; but seeing the boy cry only tug harder at his heartstrings. Thus, he too wept. And though nobody seemed to question why the Stokers were not present, somehow he and Jonathan knew the Old Man understood and felt they were there in spirit.

The second service was also unique in the sense that there were two coffins, placed side by side, as if the house of pain was mocking the mourning crowd by suggesting one was near enough. As a harpsichord echoed its sweet and morbid notes of funereal gloom, the doctor and the boy found sitting through yet another service harder and more arduous than ever they could have imagined. "Alas, 'twas indubitably spooky!" remembered the physician.

Surely there had never been, and there will never be to come, such a sad look—such a blank, melancholic gaze of sorrow and despair—in Jonathan Watts's eyes than the moment he placed one . . . and then a *second* long stem rose in the caskets and kissed both his mother and father goodbye.

Unlike the previous service for the old man, the second service was an open casket ceremony. Truly, the lacerations to their faces proved to be a laborious challenge to the undertaker's line of work, howbeit he was able to clean and treat the wounds, and apply makeup to conceal their cruel visibility. On the other hand, an assortment of clothing was needed to hide the severe wounds to the throat of each victim. And though this was kept from Jonathan, the mortician, who was known for having quite an ego, was overheard making the following laconic statement:

"I have never been tasked with attending to the cover-up of such a savage act of carnal cruelty in all my years of work. Notwithstanding, I believe I have done the old couple justice—my effort was far from being pleasurable and 'twas certainly not something I could be proud of . . . I hope to Jesus I never have to do anything of this magnitude again!"

If angels safeguarded acts of mercy, then their presence was surely manifested that unhappy afternoon, for words cannot describe the grief-stricken scene that would naturally stay in everyone's memory thereafter—an event that brought even the strongest man to tears that day.

The audience, which consisted of about seventy-five family members and friends of both decedents coupled with a handful employment acquaintances of Mr. Watts, was given a final viewing of the couple prior to the conduction of the burial service. As Jonathan was the most immediate family member, he walked last. At first he held back his sobs, and then he continued to do so whilst he began to wring his hands. Next, he started to pound his fists together, and finally—but positively—broke down into an alarming entreaty of question: "Why, God . . . why them? Not Mum *and* me dad too! Ye can't take both away! No! It can't be!" The adolescent's chest commenced to pulsate at a level of severity that every beating of his heart resembled fists pounding from within his own coffin—bleeding fists belonging to another victim—a helpless child, who would one day awake to the horror, a part of himself went in the ground with his parents.

Seizing his mother's left hand in his left and his father's right hand in his right, the poor boy began to weep, moan, and wail and then completely rendered himself to the most extravagant empathy that death can bring. As Watts clutched his mother, he buried his head in her bosom. When he did so, the teenager inadvertently halfway tore back the scarf that hid the mangled neck. Several gasps were heard in the audience, and several elderly women actually fainted by the disturbing scene and were quickly removed outside for revival in fresh air.

Drowning in pain himself, his Uncle Tom stood up to remove the boy. Doctor Van Zant, who had seated himself directly behind Jonathan, helped the man, and they each took an arm and whispered words of comfort to the lad as they gently eased him away from the depressing scene. Two men, who almost appeared out of nowhere, immediately stepped up and closed the caskets while the boy let out a last helpless and despairing cry, reaching outwardly as the men prepared their removal and finally covered his face in an ultimate state of lamentation as the funeral procession was prepared.

The reading of the burial service at the gravesite seemed to be a comforting memorial for everyone.

But thank the Lord almighty it was only read once! thought Tom Watts.

As Dr. Van Zant walked away from the double grave, he thought he would try to cheer the boy up as best he could by commending him of his thoughtful gesture.

"They were lucky to have a son like you, eh? It was very loving what you did—placing a rose in both . . ." Here he paused for a moment, stammering over his choice of words. "Anyway, my child, I know they were comforted, eh?"

"But they were no ordinary roses," he answered.

"Pardon me?"

"Aye, they were wild roses," replied Jonathan. "An' they are meant to revoke th' vampiric curse that 'tis up'n 'em."

The doctor seemed surprised by this statement but said nothing. He towered like a grand monument—still . . . astonished . . . and with a façade of perplexing peculiarity. And as his Uncle Tom approached from behind to bid them homeward, the former let out a protracted sigh as if he had been holding his breath.

"There is much to do, boy," the man said as if directing his comment to Jonathan whilst looking at the physician. "An attorney of Godalming's found me before the service and requested to meet us back at the house in about an hour. We better go . . ."

They all exchanged pleasantries in their own unique way, and then they departed to their own destinations. Van Zant went home and anticipated to sleep like a giant, yet he was awakened numerous times to sensationally unpleasant dreams. Prior to sleep, he had been thinking about Jonathan's troubling, parting words; and for whatever reason, he left the funerals actually feeling guilty and rather unclean.

Why did I not listen to them, eh? Land sakes, I took the garlic down! Oh, why did I fail to heed their warnings? he scolded himself with genuine regret.

The uncle took Jonathan to his own house to meet with the Old Man's attorney. For not only was the boy's home currently overrun by an assortment of crime scene officials, but Tom figured it would be a while before his nephew would feel like returning to the very place where he found his parents murdered. Uncle Tom seemingly walked away in a state of ignorant sadness, almost as if the moment were unreal. Van Zant took it as the passing happened so quickly and unexpectedly, and it would take a while for the freshness to wear off before his emotions settled.

On the other hand, Jonathan's overwhelming grief seemed to have all been emptied whilst in the service. And as he spoke of the "curse" to the doctor, the man saw a glare in the boy's eyes that seemed to have unleashed a darker side of him yet to be revealed to anyone. Indeed, it carried the mute form of anger. And as he nodded his farewell to the doctor, a devastating feeling vengeance seemed to hover over the boy that made Van Zant fearful of what was to be.

* * * * *

Afternoon. The attorney spent all of tea break and several hours thereafter with Jonathan Watts and his uncle. And if it had not been for the ravenous feeling of hunger that hit the businessperson around 6:30 p.m., Jonathan thought the smart gentleman would have chatted until midnight.

Though most of his talk was very serious and was directed to Tom Watts, all matters pertained to Jonathan. Because the old man had no immediate family, he had it in his will that everything was to be split between Noel Stoker and Jonathan Watts. And in the event they were minors at the time, his house contents of his store and all his personal possessions—excluding those that were specifically directed otherwise in will or by note—would be put up for auction, and the monies were to be split into trust accounts, on the minors' behalf, with their fathers as trustees. However, in Jonathan's sake, his Uncle Tom would monitor his portion until the lad reached legal age.

Johnathan sat aghast. Though he picked up and comprehended bits and pieces of the matter, the legality of it all failed to fully register in his adolescent mind. He seemed like a listless doll along for the party. And undoubtedly, even the uncle had difficulty digesting the import of the conversation until hours afterwards.

"Are you positive of the facts?" Tom Watts asked nervously. "Are you certain that I am the person to take control of what must be a large sum of money?"

"Indeed, I am the one who helped David Godalming draw up his will, and excuse me for if this sounds egotistical, but the details are quite clear to me. Insomuch as it was less than six months ago, he asked me for my services! I recall vividly that there was a sort of rushed quality about him, you know . . . to finish—on his part, a feeling of being pushed to complete the transaction. I remember I did not like it, and please forgive me if this seems harsh, but I felt as if he *knew* . . ."

"Thank you for your time," Tom said, recognizing that the conversation was beginning to stir Jonathan's emotions.

"I will commence the paperwork this corresponding week, but keep in mind nothing will be made official until the police has ruled out any concerned parties as being a suspect."

Both men noticed that Jonathan seemed alarmed and somewhat insulted by this statement.

"I understand," Tom answered as the man stood and shook hands with them both as if in preparing to exit.

"Oh, one final thing that I almost forgot!"

Jonathan had not seen him sit down the large black leather bag in the foyer when he entered, but he immediately recognized it. Watts recoiled back in his chair with a shudder and expression of apprehension as if it were alive. Handing it directly to the lad the attorney explained, "Mr. Godalming left specific instructions that this bag go to either you or Noel Stoker; and since the Stokers are on holiday at present, I am turning the property over to you."

Holiday? the adolescent thought to himself. *If he only . . .*

Jonathan nodded and attempted to exchange a smile as his Uncle Tom saw the lawyer to the door.

If only he knew!

* * * * *

It was an extremely strange and solemn evening.

Jonathan and his uncle spoke few words over dinner for they both were exhausted and too overwrought for conversation. After clearing the table, Tom Watts sat down in the living room and proceeded to read the newspapers from the previous two days as Jonathan retired to the guest chamber that was located two rooms down the hall. His uncle, who was only in his late twenties, was a successful farmer. And though he inherited the small farmhouse from his grandmother, Tom never seemed interested in having a woman around the house. Thus, the dishes would go dirty until they were needed again. Young Watts found this concept rather amusing. Though Tom called on young lasses frequently, he did not fancy being tied down, and Jonathan could never stay abreast with whom he was seeing at any moment in time. The latter too found this idea humorous. And such random thoughts at a time or sore trial and uncertainty were welcomed.

"Are ye goin' to wait for Annie to call and scrub up these 'ere dishes?" the nephew joked. "Or . . . wait . . . is it Mary?"

"*Bah!*" the uncle said without looking up from the paper.

"Me dad called ye fickle," Jonathan joked, going to the guestroom with the bag in hand. "I think he was righto!"

"Bugger off!" Uncle Tom yelled back with a half laugh in his voice.

The small iron bed creaked as Jonathan sat down and boldly but, sadly, began to open the bag. As expected, it contained the same superstitious, eccentric vampiric deterrents and objects of their destruction: holy water, wolfsbane, a box of salt, a mirror, a pistol loaded with silver bullets, amongst others similar tools of the supernatural. The only item that was missing was the large silver Celtic crucifix that was pointed at the base, for he had given that object to Noel. However, there were two items that had not been placed there originally.

The first was a small envelope of money, which—in the old man's handwriting—'twas labeled, "For Noel Stoker and Jonathan Watts." It was precisely twenty-five pounds.

"Th' loot wez got from th' bloody jewel of sev'n stars!" the boy said aloud.

Shoving the money in his pocket, he picked up the second item: a sort of notebook or diary that was bounded to the dark book of the Solomonari. Flipping through it, at first glance, it appeared to be a word-by-word translation of the latter. However, after the lad reclined back and began to read it cover to cover, it was clearly something more. Indeed, it was an account of everything the three of them had researched and discovered up to the night of his murder.

Watts began to choke on his own saliva, and for several hours, he was spellbound and riveted by the document. And as Jonathan finished a partial thought came to his head. He pondered on it for several minutes, over and over, and then flipped back to Godalming's account at the Tate Pier. And as he recalled the last conversation he had with Noel, the thought became *complete.*

Several minutes henceforth, he failed to discover his lungs were without oxygen. "As Sam Hill 'tis me witness! I've been blind as a bat!" he shouted as he shot up in bed with a look of complete astonishment on his face.

"Vlad egged Irvin' to port his coffin to the Lyceum, an' then he hid it n' th' bloomin' Beef Steak room—th' spot behind his bloody closet! Blimey, that's wheere th' scoundrel sleeps durin' th' day!"

CHAPTER 29

Servants to the Undead

He called the Count "lord and master," and
he may want to get out to help him in some diabolical way. That horrid thing has the wolves and
the rats and his own kind to help him . . .
—Jonathan Harker's Journal

From Jonathan Watts's point of view, having the Stokers suddenly up and leave London with no prior warning was a complete shock. Just hearing of the dreadful news caused his adolescent
nerves to squirm in feral trepidation. True, not only was it a peculiar
transit at a grave and tragic time, but it also seemed Count Dracula
had mockingly evoked his influence and guided the family away in
an devious effort to further stifle the intrepid alliance that Jonathan,
Godalming, and Noel had strived so diligently to form and combat
him. Did the vampire know their newfound purpose in life was to
seek out and destroy him by impalement—as he had executed four
centuries prior to?

Nevertheless, using the majority of the remaining funds Count
Dracula had given Abraham, the Stokers settled in a family suite at
the Kilmarnock Arms Hotel. The establishment was a respectable
middle- to upper-class abode with its name deriving from a son of
the Earl of Kilmarnock, who in 1724 married into the Errol family

of Slains Castle, whose title became that of the eldest son of the Earl of Erroll. It advertised sea bathing, let bicycles and provided facilities for fishing and shooting.

"When I first saw the place I fell in love with it," Stoker once recalled. "Had it been possible, I should have spent my summer there in a house of my own, but the want of any place in which to live forbade such an opportunity. So I stayed in the little hotel, the Kilmarnock Arms."

Noel, who was still freshly grieving over the loss of Jonathan's parents and Old Man Godalming's death, wanted nothing more than a few peaceful days to morn. In conjunction, he hoped for the opportunity to reconnect with his father and the time to talk over a strategic move on how to destroy Dracula without the fear of other interference. However, it was quickly noticeable that the underlying cloud of primal fear seemed to follow the family onward to Cruden Bay.

Here was a respectable man—a writer, theatre manager, husband, and father—who appeared to be so horribly affected by the terrible events hitherto that at times he seemed to be a completely different person, anything he wrote was full of appalling nightmares, Florence's health woes were toiling on his nerves, his behavior toward his estranged son had been queer and suspicious, and his future with Henry Irving and the theatre was questionable and seemed to be linked somehow with the evil Count. In sum, Dracula was everywhere. There was no way of escaping him. And the King Vampire was a poison that went beyond the consideration of human life

"Father sat down at a table that he positioned by the window and gazed out at the ruined castle for long moments without saying a word to anyone with a blank stare that troubled me deeply," described Noel. "While I attended to Mum, who began to somewhat regain her pre-illness appearance, though her lethargy seemed to worsen during the day, Dad seemingly began to fall into a state of hypnotic trance that only increased in intensity the longer he sat by the window. I called him away from it in the early hours of our arrival only to find him right back in his previous spot a moment later. In due time, he became unresponsive all together. And though I did not understand what was happening to him, I made a dreadful realization: what if we were not fleeing from the Count—rather, we were going *to* him. And somehow Slains's forbidden past was taking possession of Pop."

Slains Castle was a large imposing ruin fronting directly onto the south facing cliffs about a kilometer east of Cruden Bay. It was one of the most famous ruins in Scotland erected by the ninth Earl of Erroll in 1597—the year he returned from exile after making his peace with James VI for blowing up the successor edifice. After connecting his father's odd behavior to the castle, Noel began to pry information out of the hotel employees regarding its history and its present condition.

"Slains Castle has always been an unsettling place," explained the booking attendant. "You'd be hard pressed to call it attractive, even on the brightest of days, but it is most certainly an interesting study."

"What do you mean by interesting?" Noel asked with an inquisitive stare. The man, who resembled a banker, dressed in a suit, tie, and swept-back hairdo, paused for a brief moment to cordially exchange some money from a guest for a room key, and sat back in his chair and began like he was preaching a lesson to a roomful of pupils: "Well, sir . . . the original castle was built in the 1200s as a fortress. However, in 1594, the owner, the Earl of Erroll, backed a plot by the Earl of Huntly against King James VI. James responded by blowing up Old Slains castle, which was overwrought by an unspoken history of bloodlust. Rather than trying to rebuild it, the ninth Earl used a tower house at Bowness as the basis for a new home; the tower was extended and ranges of buildings were added around a courtyard. In 1664, the castle was again expanded and altered, and a corridor was built across the tract. Whispers of carnal acts of bloodletting began to resurface over the years! The final major change came in 1836 when further wings were added and the underlying castle was given granite facing. Subsequent earls rebuilt and added to the castle with its last great reconstruction being completed in 1837. But the sins of the past caught up with the godforsaken place for death duties forced the twentieth earl to sell the castle, and Slains was allowed to fall into an utter and decrepit state of disrepair."

"So nobody lives there now?" asked Noel.

"Heavens, no," the attendant responded hurriedly with an amazed look. "And we caution vacationers who fancy the notion to scamper over the rocks to have a closer look! Slains Castle is dangerous and distinctly different from others!"

"What do you mean by *different?*"

Here the man paused and pointed his finger as if giving a warning.

"Well, sir . . . it is a testament of God's way of omitting the bloodshed that occurred here long ago! See what happens to ruins when nature has just been left to get on with it?" He pointed in the direction of the great cliff, which housed the massive ruined structure. "There have been reports of people who embarked on good spirit to tour the place only to never be heard from again. Whilst others have spoken of strange noises or sights that could not be confirmed! Indeed, if you are thinking of visiting the castle, I strongly warn you for the cleft is way high! And when you are out there with only the sound of waves crashing on the rocks far below, I hope that the good Lord leads you to safety lest thou be surrendered to your active imagination! For your mind can play tricks, and the slightest scream can send part of the building down on top of you!"

Noel thanked the man earnestly and returned to his family's room to find his mother sitting up in bed, brood awake, pointing to the window that was wide open. His father did not seem to notice the brisk fall wind stealing in, even though he was positioned directly under it.

"Dad, did you open the sash? Mum must be freezing!" he said, closing the window promptly with a look of perplexing concern. Abraham Stoker said nothing as if he failed to recognize his son's loud voice and did not look up from the table.

"*Father!*"

Indeed, Bram had begun to write again, but it was unlike any style that Noel had witnessed before. It was almost like his dad were asleep—though a glassy and unflinching look chilled his eyes—and a preternatural being had taken control of his faculties. The Irishman was hard at it, writing as if his life was dependent upon the completion of the deplorable tale. His right hand seemed to be responding to an unseen militant dictator whilst the rest of his body was frozen in a catatonic condition, slowly drifting into insanity.

Though Noel could not get a response or reaction from his father, he had better luck with his mother; for she rambled off strange, incoherent words and phrases that seemed to waken her with a sense of lassitude and melancholy.

"She was clearly in a status of alarm or distress, and in an unreal, distant voice, I heard all sorts of strange things that did not make sense. Notwithstanding, I distinctly heard the words *unearth*, *Messiah*, and *take wing*. Next I splashed some water in her face, and she popped to almost instantly." The ordeal left the son in his own state of shock, much like a momentary glare of madness had snapped within him.

Lord Jesus! Is this a malignant sign that a case of schizophrenia is at hand?

Indeed, Noel arrived at a crossroad where his craving for sensations went beyond what a teenage boy could provide. Soon something about his chambers seemed not quite right, and the impression that eyes watched him from inside the walls turned to the rustlings and scalings—and worst of all, the click of teeth. The minutes of waiting were a foretaste for the future.

This odd behavior in both his parents continued and seemed to worsen by the day. His mother languor weighed upon her during sunlight hours with distressing dreams that made her sleep restless and were painful to watch. However, her midnight suffering seemed to be even more severe. She claimed she had no desire to sleep and she needed fresh air—for her breathing was irregular, strenuous, and shallow. Noel would awaken astounded numerous times in the night to find his mother wide awake, either sitting up in bed looking oddly at him and her husband or standing docketly at the window. On several occasions, she would stare into the darkness at the top of the steep hill and then open the window wide, sending in a wild gush of brisk air that caused Noel and Bram to stir out of bed. But whoever got up to close the sash, Florence's reaction was always the same: she had to be drug away by force, protest, and almost under violent revolt. Indeed, it appeared she was reaching out to Slains. Or perhaps *it* was reaching out *for her!*

Abraham Stoker's vigorous writing spells typically began around noon and lasted until sunset. During this time, he was a man not to be reckoned with; thus, Noel bothered him not—for he seemed to pour his entire heart and soul into the creative process and rarely stopped for anything. Necessities such as food and personal hygiene seemed trivial when he would lapse into one of these frenzied moments, and it almost seemed like he forgot his family was even present. Noel caught him on several occasions writing without looking at the paper with his right hand, pointing out the window with his left.

Again, that castle! What in the blazes does all this mean? Noel thought to himself. After several days and nights of Noel attempting to keep both his mother and his father settled, he began to wish he were back in London. At least there he had the doctor and Jonathan to confide in and keep matters under control without second-guessing himself. Although, unknowingly, the unexpected was about to occur—the unknown key that would unlock the horror at hand and that would provide him with additional foresight he so utterly prayed for.

The third night at the hotel began like the previous two: shortly after sunset, allegorically Bram's writing ambition played out in a form of cringe-induced vigor that coursed though his veins until nightfall—which ended in abrupt exasperation and profound sleep. Whereas Florence's restless slumber transitioned to her being stark alert in a circumstance of perverse excitability. When Noel saw that his dad seemed shocked at the amount of material he had written, he asked him point blank, "Why? Why kill yourself like this, Pop? Mum needs you . . . I need you! How long must we carry on like so?" The youth's graphic voice was loaded of sick apprehension and genuine sadness.

"Do you not like it here?" Abraham asked as if surprised by his son's questioning.

"No," the teenager replied honestly, seeing that his father was falling back to his old self. "I do not like it here after all! You are losing your spirit in this book, you are, and you pursue it whilst Mum and I suffer! Can't you see it? Her eyes appear to have blackened, and the vampire's curse will soon be upon her! I have a very bad feeling about this place! I want to leave immediately—right now, even! Don't you remember we have our own work to do? Now that Godalming is dead, we must make sure the same thing does not happen to Jonathan or Van Zant!"

"I have an oath—"

"Bother—to hell with your oath!"

The Irishman let out a long sigh and, after a brief moment, looked lovingly into his son's aching eyes. Shaking his head despairingly, he said gravely, "I cannot afford to lose either you or your mother! And as long as I keep my oath to the vampire, I have his promise we shall be kept safe. I *must* finish the book! And when this is done, I swear on your mother's life we will return to London! If Dracula keeps his word, everything should be back to normal after his chronicles are complete."

Noel scowled silently. And seeing he was unable to change his father's mind, he turned around and reproached his mother.

"I feel so alive in the night!" she exclaimed excitedly. "It is like a resurgence of endless energy!" Her son's throat contracted in a wrench of despair.

"And what do you feel during the day?" Noel asked hesitantly with a fearful tone.

"It is a possessive, sinking feeling that causes my heartbeat to pound faster," she began intently. "Though the sensation resembles an induction by the spirit of sadness, it is bitterly sweet all the same. My breathing grows rapidly—until it is full drawn—followed by a morose sobbing that exculpates to the terrible feeling of strangulation! This develops into a horrific convulsion in which all senses give full sway, and ultimately, unconsciousness becomes my final desolation!"

This candid look into his mother's condition chilled Noel's blood to the marrow. He looked at his mother with an immense sentiment of fear and pity. Indeed, he did not know what to say. The boy's body stiffened to that resembling a week-old corpse as his lips pressed together tightly. A sort of wild state next came from her eyes—one that would go on to terrorize his dreams. She then continued: "Though my soul takes acquiesce in this bizarre pleasure, there is a part of me that is fearful of letting go. I see people, but their faces are hid in the darkness, and I hear voices that are garbled beyond recognition. They all cry out at once—in a sharp, deafening fusillade of screams—and then I cry with them, forcing myself wide awake . . . and next, I look around this room in dread and I realize where I am at and what I have done!" The youth's eyes were riveted on the ungainly form, and heartfelt tears began to stream down his smooth cheeks.

"It was that precise flash," Noel Stoker described, "that I could see the dramatic changes in her. The vampire's curse had begun its metamorphosis of evil, and the visible traits were breathtaking: her piercing black eyes looked at me almost vindictively and appeared catlike in appearance. Her unusual stern brow and high fierce nose spoke volume, resting above a nasty chin that insinuated the pointed eye teeth that had now hung over her bottom lip. Oh, the bloodless face!" Her ears also struck a chord with him as they had begun to grow an unusual amount of dark hair around them, and whenever she brushed her long locks away, Noel could see the particularity of the tips: they were beginning to resemble those of the nocturnal bat.

Saint Joseph, pray for us! Lord, please help her! How could my own mother—a creature so made in heaven—tolerate so monstrous an indulgence of the lusts and the malignity of hell? God only knows how she crossed that span! Jesus, give me the strength to pull her out of the darkness!

By then, Noel's father was sound asleep, and neither the nudging from his son nor the disturbing cries from his wife would release him from his deep stupor. As Florence seemed to be in a foreign, talkative mood, the teenager began to drill her, thinking that somehow she might reveal more information regarding the Count's diabolical scheme or daytime lair.

"Is Vlad coming for you? Where is he now?"

"Yes," she said, "when the moment is at hand! He is flying, watching, waiting . . ."

His mother pointed to the foreboding window. The moon's fitful beams were full and sat high above the ruined castle whose imposing embattlements seemed even eerier and intimidating than in the daytime. All of a sudden, Noel could see the shape of a large, winged object flay open the night. It came from out of the blackness of the highest tower, and as it flew, it flapped its way westward, crossing the scope of the brilliant orb that revealed its true entity: a repulsive vampire bat. When Noel got glimpse of the writhing fiend, his own body jerked with a convulsive shudder. He then rushed back to his mother and shook her madly but with the most earnest and protective intent.

"Why does he wait?" Noel cried to her angrily with a reddened face. His teeth gritted together as he waited impatiently for an answer. "Why not come now—this very night, even? He hovers outside like a weak coward!"

His mother let out a sort of chuckle he had never heard before and then turned and looked at him resolutely with an almost devilish grin and said, "Darling, son . . . alas, you hasten so, but the earth is not yet prepared for my coming. The time is nigh."

"Mum, you look at me so strangely! Please fight it!" Noel pleaded desperately with labored breath. The youth could see the lurid changes in her that seemingly continued to transform real time before his very troubled eyes. It was if she turned into a wasp and was preparing to sting. He took several steps backward, trembling in an aghast of horror.

"For the love of the Almighty and for the sake of this family . . . do not let him win!"

* * * * *

The following morning proved to be a difficult time for Noel. He had sat up all night with his mother, and just like the previous mornings, as the sun rose his mum elapsed into a deep sleep, as willingly as a drained newborn baby does. Bram began to stir and finally arose, wondering why his son, who was in the process of filling up a canteen with water, was already dressed. As he secured the top on the jug, Master Stoker thought the odd scene occurring between his two parents would have him laughing one day when his tears had all dried out. Indeed, it was as if the Sandman had jumped from one bed to the other, unable to work his magic simultaneously. Truly, as sure as one rose from his or her mattress, the other fell back onto theirs in an inexplicable siesta.

"Are you going somewhere, Noel?" his father questioned placidly.

"Yes, but I can't tell you where," the teenager retorted firmly. "Look after Mum, and keep the window closed. I will be back before nightfall!" And armed to the teeth, with the rosary around his neck and the silver Celtic stake in hand, he left the hotel and began to proceed toward Slains Castle.

The edifice, perched high on the steep south cliff, took longer to reach than Noel had expected for he was unaided by any roads or guideposts. Though a main access road once existed, it had long been out of use and did not provide a direct route to the top of the mountain. Indelibly, it only went precisely halfway where it evolved into a grown-up winding trail that proved to be equally as dangerous and risky as any other path that Noel chose to make on his own.

The climb up the treacherous perpendicular rocks quickly took their toil on the lad's already weary body. With the slightest misstep, the boy could have tumbled off the gorge leading to the North Sea. However, he refused to falter. And he did not give up. Whenever the youth felt like his body was caving in, he thought about what the malicious, blood-hungry Count had done to his loved ones: his parents, friends—not to mention himself. Subsequently, a mad gust of rushing violence went soaring through his body like a missile, and this adrenaline pushed the teenager to climb harder than ever.

Every few minutes, Noel rested on segments of the mountainous range that could hold his weight, and then he would continue on, drinking small sips of water when he began to feel parched. And then, after about a one and a half hour hike, his determination paid off.

The front of the castle lay literally along the edge of the steep cliffs, whilst its rear, beyond what were once its gardens, was protected from unwanted guests by a deep cleft that cut into the precipice as far as the overgrown main access road. Noel stood in front of the towering mass of stone for several minutes as if in awe and spellbound by the brick and mortar. The lofty spire—that is, the one the giant bat sailed out of the previous night—sat high above all the rest, though seemingly empty and still. With a hint of hesitation and fear, the teenager crossed himself, and holding the Celtic stake tightly, cautiously approached the structure.

Internally, the castle was a collection of mostly brick-built intersecting corridors wrapped around rooms now deeply in nettles. In the heart of the castle was the courtyard, though it took some time for Noel to meander and work out which were outside areas in the original design and which were inside.

How in the devil do I get in? Noel asked himself and began to carefully survey the grounds for doors or stairwells.

Slains's general air of creepiness was not helped by the wind that seemed to constantly blow and, at certain times, unleash a gust so shrill and fierce that it escaped into the core of the stone ruins with the brutal alarm of a screaming banshee. When this would happen, Noel almost jumped out of his skin and cursed himself until he settled back down and the next blast came, thus repeating the endless cycle of nerve bashing.

Though the teenager was unsure where to go—not to mention slightly uncertain what he was even looking for—in less than half an hour, the adolescent discovered a hidden passage which revealed a dark opening. His chest shuddered as he gazed upon it with a countenance of dismay.

"Th-this . . . this is for you, Mum!"

Lighting a match from his pocket, the youth saw that no steps were present but rather a muddy slide descended into what appeared to be a vaulted room that was probably once a kitchen storage compartment with large stone cargo bins all the way around the walls. *Unless . . .* he began to wonder peering round in the near total darkness, *it was some sort of crypt . . .*

The screeching cry of a passing gull took Noel off guard and startled the boy causing him to almost lose his balance and topple head long into the mysterious hole. His heart raced wildly. Catching hold of the surface edges, he sent numerous clumps of dirt and debris down the chute. Then out of nowhere there came another sound—a slight rustle, which originated from the hole rather the sky. Next, the ray of an approaching light appeared, and the youth felt a torrential sinking sensation in the pit of his abdomen.

Noel Stoker was not alone.

Quietly, the boy made a hasty exit. As he jumped out of the opening and concealed himself behind part of a jagged, broken wall nearby, he heard movement. And then as he hid watching in a façade of utter fear, the shadow of a man slowly appeared.

"A tall, narrow-chested fellow peered out of the passage. He was covered in black from head to toe. And as he stood in a stooped position looking all around for the source of the distraction, I was somewhat drawn to the high shoulders. There was something strange and oddly familiar about them, but at the moment, I could not seem to distinguish why," the lad recalled.

However, it was clear that the man was not Vlad. For it was broad daylight, and according to the Old Man, full-blown vampires are rendered powerless during the day and are restricted to only move about in the confinements of their own crypt or areas away from direct sunlight.

"Disappointingly, the queer man's back was toward me—like-wise, his face was hidden by an oddly shaped hat with a broad leaf. He stepped out into the clearing, looking around and listening atten-tively for several seconds. Staring through a hole in the brick wall, I watched him carefully. He walked slowly with an odd, shambling gait that was also keen to me, and then he darted back down into the hole from whence he came."

A minute later, Master Stoker heard him pick up a shovel or tool of some sort and began to break the ground or rock in a constant scratching fashion that quickly grated on Noel's nerves much like ones fingernails being drug across a chalkboard. The youth pressed his adolescent fingers in until the curved nails dug into his dirty, sweaty palms.

Who is this strange character, and what in the blazes is he up to?

Noel was not prepared to answer these questions at the time, and part of him did not care to. For an internal voice told him to run without looking back, but another voice—the voice that spoke from his heart—told him that he needed to find these answers if he was to save his family. Moreover, it was this love that made him swallow hard in secret prayer and quietly slide his way down into the hole, creeping up on his mysterious stranger.

The digging and scraping grew louder as he descended whilst the light of a lantern began to flood the ugly walls and low ceiling. And as the teenager made his way to the end of the tunnel, the morbid shadows the man's long, swinging arms working a shovel refracted and bounced off the clearing surfaces. Likewise, the strong smell of freshly turned molded earth jarred his gullible senses as if to slap him aback into the harsh reality of the grotesque encounter.

Noel secretly peered around the corner and watched the man dig what appeared to be a new grave. However, when the man backed away from the gaping pit to put on a pair of soiled black gloves, the lantern identified the uncheerful man had been extremely busy. Indeed, 'twas his *second*—for another newly dug heinous hole was beyond his immediate left! The lad covered his mouth in a feeble attempt to restrict the bottled outburst that was on the verge of exploding inside his teenage chest.

When the man had covered his lank hands, he picked up where he left off and continued to swing his long arms as he dug and gesticulated in utter abstraction. The ghastly sight was much like watching a grave robber in operation; only, Noel was not inclined to believe them to be existing graves. And this important fact reached him like a thunderbolt.

Whom were they meant for?

Noel was absolutely positive Vlad Dracula had been at the castle the evening prior. He felt it like he knew he was on the verge of losing his mother forever. There was no doubt about that, and since the castle was uninhibited, the vampire must have ordered that these graves be dug. And if his mother knew that the Count was lingering, it was only logical to assume that the monster knew of the Stoker's arrival. Why else would he leave London?

The adolescent continued to ponder over these specifics when the man completed the second grave and stood back from them flashing a perpetual smile that sent shivers down the boy's spine. But at that grim, awkward moment, when the stranger took off his left gloved hand to wipe the perspiration from his brow, his hat was pushed back, and the grisly horrors of the universe seemed to cave in on the teenager all at once, leaving him unable to speak, scream, or breathe.

The vivid facial features of the man hit young Stoker in the head like a massive brick as he gasped internally, almost collapsing backward against the muddy surface of the hole. Too frightened to remain yet too scared to flee, Noel instantaneously transformed into a congealing pillar of astonishment. The man's entire demeanor was laced with malice, which caused the unearthed room to plummet in temperature and readily distorted the spectator's flesh into a clammy dimension of skin. The terrified youth looked on with an unblinking stare as he branded the man as the one notorious Henry Irving!

This gruesome discovery would not later prove to be a case of mistaken identity: the actor's eccentric features and unique facial expressions were illuminated in a way that no trickery of lighting or masterpiece makeup application could alter.

With his liberated profile, brunette wavy locks, keenly engraved features, and an inquisitively cut coat with lithe collar and shirt, Irving was an unconventional character indeed. And while the scared adolescent remained absolutely still, seeing Irving again only reminded the former of the morbid memory at the theatre—when he was a small, impressionable child and was introduced to the Lord of the Lyceum's artistry of disguise by force as opposed to pleasure.

There was no doubt that Henry Irving's self-developed makeup technique was partially to blame for the actor's tremendous success. Designed during the gaslight era, he always preferred to apply his own in solitude. And being the self-absorbed actor he was, he disliked the thought of anyone learning his secrets to triumph at the scare of thinking he would be carbon-copied into someone else's persona or production. To him, there would only be one Henry Irving in the spotlight. He detested imposters. And he loathed being spied on.

The man with the shovel was once again in the spotlight today, and as in the past, 'twas an infamous spot Noel would remember long into adulthood: "It was usually these limelight shots that best portrayed Irving, whose acting methodology was heavily supported by facial expression," Noel noted. "This skill would become an advanced step toward cinematic close-ups, but for now, I found such an intimate encounter to be a far cry from any pleasantry." True, some critics debated if he was an overrated actor commendable of inheriting the veneer of Garrick and Kean. Whilst other detractors labeled him as merely a fine-oiled, satisfactory made-up over-the-top villain, superior with playhouse grimaces than with unadulterated phrases of Shakespeare.

Noel Stoker agreed with both crushing statements.

Henry Irving turned completely around as if he were about to bow before a packed crowd at the end of an award-winning performance. And as the gas lantern shined over him, his sole audience could not help but notice the startling differences between the effects of gaslight versus electricity.

As the face of the man tilted his head into the ray of the lamp, his pallor—free of any makeup—appeared drained of color. His burgundy lips was a striking contrast against the deathly countenance and caused the boy to flinch in fright. On the other hand, the alternate affects electricity would have provided in the darkened hole would have been rather misleading—the cool light of the electric arc would have shown Noel a complexion of a slightly different shade, including purple lips and a softer face.

Indeed, Irving himself had explained to Abraham Stoker's only child how scenery usually painted with a gaslight—that is, in the usual predominance of blue—did not pass scrutiny. 'Twas that same dreadful occurrence whilst Noel sat unwillingly in the actor's guest chair of his dressing room. And the lad grudgingly recalled his own transformation to Mephistopheles.

"The shady, explicit lines were applied to my innocent face almost as if they were a striking death mask than a labor of love," regurgitated the boy. "And each step of the way Irving gave creepy commentary—to which I was too young to understand—that I found to be equally frightening as the horrific colors.

"Embrace the thick softness with the lovely specks and motes in it," said he in a deep tone of intimidation. "Like natural light, it gives illusion to many a scene!"

As Noel wished that the spooked moment in the actor's dressing room were an illusion, he closed his dried-out eyes for a split second and prayed he would open them to a different place and time. However, when he did so, Irving remained, as so did the gaping graves, and the teenager was transported back to the horrifying memory when the actor stepped back to admire his artistic talent: a satanic child casting its grim reflection in the dark pupil's of the Lyceum's lord.

"Alas, perfection!"

Even years before there were a tint of disturbance in the actor's voice, but hearing these words again alerted Master Stoker from his reflection and warned him there was a presence of evil.

Alas, perfection!

Noel watched the culprit step back after Irving restated those two disturbing words and admire his toils of terror with a savory smile that was equally menacing. Although barely perceptual, gaslight actually moves, giving verve and profundity to flats, as carpenters would tap quietly on the foliage cloths to augment this shifting. However, there was no need for such exaggeration this day. Indeed, the man standing before young Stoker was a chameleon—one instant extraordinarily mesmeric, stylish yet uncomfortable, frequently glum, from time to time, mischievous. In sum, the actor defiled delineation.

Noel had seen far enough.

Demented watchdog of the Un-Dead! he cursed to himself.

Master Stoker's mind began to play on him like a symphony of horrors that ran wild of endless implacable surmises. He first concluded that Dracula was making plans to relocate his grave. After all, the old man had mentioned that vampires had to rest in unhallowed ground.

Mum was right! During her sleep, she saw darkness and digging! But if this were the case, why would he need two graves? Unless . . . dear God! Could the other be for me, Mum?

Now blind-sighted, his mind continued to belt and whirl. Perhaps the vampire had knowledge that he, Jonathan, and Godalming were hot on his trail? Correction—his brain solemnly reminded himself that Godalming was gone . . .

Sweet Jesus! Please tell me I have not willingly invited myself to this hellish spot to stare down my own demise and that of Jonathan's too!

For regardless of the intent, the family needed to return to London quickly—if not for the purposes to prolong the chase and burial of the ones he loved, it was to corner the vampire before he relocated his lair.

Noel fled from the crypt in a flight of sheer terror, praying to the divine Father that all hope was not lost.

* * * * *

When Noel returned to the hotel, the same booking attendant that had spoken to him the day before regarding Slains Castle greeted him unexpectedly. The man had a weighty, unsmiling, shifty look upon his face as if he were bothered by some uneasy business. And at that moment, Noel's visage fell, wishing desperately that he had heeded the gentleman's warning. The lad was almost entirely out of breath from his speedy return from the hill—though he did speak of his outing—but asked in a shaky, ominous voice: "Is everything okay?"

"Well, sir . . . whilst you were away, an Inspector Cotford called upon a Mister Abraham Stoker; however, your father refused to open the door! I say this implying no disrespect, but I am quite certain he was in the room for I heard queer noises, such as low whispering coming from the inside. Indeed, there could be no way Mr. Stoker could not have heard the knocking for the Inspector's pounding and calling rose to a level that began to agitate the other guests.!"

The usual somber-like man tried diligently to fall back into his gentlemanly façade. But after a slight pause and a clearing of his throat, the attendant started up again with the son asking, "Where is Cotford?"

"Well, sir . . . I finally had to ask the man to leave unless he had a warrant of some kind. He angrily asked me to fetch a key, and I refused without the proper consideration. Although, after the man absconded from the premises, an overwhelming feeling of dread came over me regarding the event; and fearing something was terribly wrong, I took the liberty of letting myself into the room."

Here the man stopped with an aura of self-humiliation as he said wearily, "I apologize for the intrusion! Please, you will forgive me . . . will you not, Lad?" By then, his stern expression grew to one of a deeper pose of desperation.

"Yes, I certainly do! But please, go on!" exclaimed Noel hurriedly, almost in a frantic state of alarm.

"Dear boy, it is the most puzzling thing. I tried every skeleton key we have in the place, but the door would simply not budge! It is like an unseen force had welded the door shut—"

Without letting the man finish his story, Noel raced up to his family's room. And with palsied hands and spasmodic fingers, the youth approached the closed entrance. The teenager found the door unlocked, and as he swung open the portal, he found his father sitting at the table with his hands folded over a large stack of papers, gently rocking back and forth in his chair, staring blankly out at the cliff whence Noel had just returned. The elder seemed to be in a mid-concentrated state of entreaty. Insomuch as every few seconds, he would ramble off some half-coherent whispers. And as his son burst into the room and confronted him, Noel overheard Abraham's words: "Master, I implore you! Keep your oath and free me of my duty. Spare my life and that of my family . . ."

"Pop!" Noel said, sharply interrupting. "Are you okay? Why did you not open the doorway for Detective Cotford?"

His father did not flinch from his precarious position. Thus, Noel ran over and began to shake him uncontrollably. At this moment, the staid booking attendant appeared in the entrance and looked upon the scene with the countenance of utmost confusion and wonderment.

"Father! It's me, Noel. Wake up!"

Finally, Bram turned his head and gazed at his son with empty eyes. And with a haggard stare, he said: "'Tis done!"

"What do you mean?" his son replied, sick-eyed with worry. And looking around, the lad quickly noticed his mother was not in her bed.

"It's all over!" the author said with a wild glare in his eyes.

"Father, what on earth are you referring to? What is done? And where in the blazes is Mum?"

As he questioned his father, the attendant surveyed every nook and cranny in the suite where someone could possibly hide and returned, shaking his head solemnly. Based on the man's unsettled posture, Master Stoker began to deject his father's words with a different meaning—a grisly translation that caused his pulse to raise, his bones to turn polar, and his mind and spirit to become engulfed with dismal consternation.

"There are no others present at this time, sir."

"Pop! Answer me!" Noel said hotly with an increasingly reddened face. "Where is Mother?"

To this, Stoker simply replied, "The book is finished. Can't you see, son?" he said calmly, placing his hands on the mound of papers in front of him. "It is all over now."

The boy did not like the direction of the conversation one bit. Young Stoker was not sure if he was more shocked to find his mother missing or that his father seemed totally oblivious and unconcerned by the peril at hand.

Outside the room, a voice down the corridor called the attendant away briefly. Soon he returned carrying a piece of parchment. Slightly embarrassed by the confrontation taking place, he cleared his voice.

"Ahem . . ."

Noel quickly took notice and acquiesced to the hint, retrieving what was a telegram from Jonathan.

NOEL
    I KNOW WHERE *HE* IS.

—J

I believe I do too, old chum, but one of us must be wrong. For how can he be in two places at once?

It was less than five hours before sunset when Abraham Stoker returned to a state of normalcy. Noel told his father of his mysterious encounter with Henry Irving, and Bram lowered his head in an absolute state of peril. They both agreed that a second trip to the castle was warranted, for what if Dracula had planned to kidnap Florence—who was almost a full-blown vampire—with the intention of bringing her to that forsaken place?

"It is possible Vlad is planning on using those graves for himself and—" muttered the Irishman, unable to finish the sentence.

"Mum," replied Noel gloomily. "We simply cannot take any chances!"

The seventeen-year-old recalled that he had secretly retrieved the knife that the Old Man had sold him. Florence Stoker had hidden it high in the kitchen cupboard years ago; nevertheless, the adolescent reclaimed it without his parents' knowledge and placed it in his traps.

"Smart thinking, son," the writer said as Noel son held up the impressive blade. "We must each be armed against man or beast."

The trek up the steep, mountainous range was less of a struggle for Noel the second time as his previous steps were fresh. Therefore, he led the way, calling out to his father where *to* and where *not* to step. Indeed, the youth's exertions would normally have outperformed his elder. But today, they labored together, hiking side-by-side in equal diminutive, cycled breaths of anticipation.

In about an hour, they found themselves before the eluding edifice, and they both stood in complete silence—each shuddering in the dark, overwhelming thoughts of what might be prowling inside. Without words, Noel handed his father the Celtic Cross made of silver, which doubled as a stake, and gripping the large sharp knife in his own right hand, with a small candle in his left, he motioned by a sideward glance the direction of the gruesome hole.

The crypt was exactly as Noel had witnessed it; however, there was one significant difference: Henry Irving was nowhere in sight. On the other hand, neither was Dracula or Florence Stoker. A sense of baffling surprise coupled with sighs of relief spawned from their bodies, as they stood motionless for several seconds. But then a signal came from the eldest.

"Come, there is instrumental work to be done here!"

Removing the rosaries from their necks, they each placed one on top of the unhallowed graves and sanctified them to God. Next, at the entrance of the crypt, Noel crumbled up the last holy wafer.

"Where in the bloody hell could she be?" Noel asked his father in an astounded state of expression.

"As she does not know anyone in the village or her way around Cruden Bay, I don't think she would have ventured out on her own. Especially in her frail condition," answered Bram worriedly.

On the way back down the steep precipice, Noel thought about the situation further and posed another question: "Do you think she could have found her way to the train station—that is if, for whatever reason, she took a strange notion to return home?"

A crazed look came in Abraham's eyes, and they both seemed to be thinking the same alarming thought: What if Florence awoke to the hostile sound of a mysterious man banging on the door—only then to look around and see her son was missing? And finally, she realized her husband was unable to aid her as he was in a hypnotic state of penmanship?

"In retrospect, she was probably frightened for me and set out looking for you," replied the journeyman, short of breath. "And while she was out she probably lapsed into one of her hallucinations or spells of paranoia. Thus, being the train station was newly familiar to her, she probably headed there in a state of confusion!" Whatever the case may be, they planned to talk with someone who was on duty at the ticket counter in the afternoon. If she were not recalled as being seen there, they would check the nearest hospital, and if all else failed, the next one would telegram Dr. Van Zant whilst the other would finally file a missing persons report with the local officials.

However, when the duo returned to the hotel, reverberating shocks of terror filled their hearts. The helpful attendant had already confirmed that a lady that fit Florence's description was seen with a tall, somber-looking man at approximately 3:00 p.m.

Both the elder and younger Stoker were thunderstruck. Mutters of consternation escaped the journeyman's throat as the youth dug his nails furiously into the flesh of his hot palms.

"The man purchased two tickets leaving for Piccadilly Station at 3:30," began the booker, "but don't fret, sirs . . . I also took the liberty of purchasing both your tickets—that is, under the assumption you each wish to leave toward the same destination on the next train out."

Both their faces lit up like living flames.

"Well, sirs . . . that would be on the midnight special," said the gentleman. "If you hurry and gather your luggage, you should be able to make in due time!"

"Good man!" whispered Stoker in a croaking voice.

After gathering all their belongings and settling with the front desk, the pair was well on their way. And as they started back home to London, Noel began to wonder if his friend had found out that Dracula had made a claim to Slains Castle. So afraid that Jonathan might be making plans to meet up with the Stokers in Cruden Bay, Noel quickly wired him to stay put until he arrived early morning for they had much to discuss.

As the train steamed away from its platform, father and son looked up at the horrid mountain and ominous structure, praying they would never have to set eyes on them again. And in the not-so-far-off distance, the eerie howling of dogs commenced, which evolved into an endless series of echoes that continued to fill their ears well far beyond what Abraham Stoker had once considered a peaceful village.

The vow of solitude was broken. Its tamed nature had turned savage. And the tranquility the Stokers came for rescued them not. Alas, it turned against the trio. The family now returned as a duo.

* * * * *

Late afternoon. Jonathan and Tom Watts had eaten an early dinner at around 3:00 p.m., and as there was work to be done on the farm, the uncle left his nephew to his own devices at around 4:30. It was no surprise that the adolescent could not wait for Noel to return before making arrangements to confront the vampire. After all, the vengeance that he had against Count Dracula was far more personal and darker than human consideration might allow. Furthermore, now that the boy believed he knew where the lurid monster was hiding—not to mention who was protecting him during the daylight hours—Jonathan took another inventory of the large black leather bag and planned a surprise visit.

Word was out—new evidence regarding the Lyceum murder had made Henry Irving a suspect: for the purse of the victim was caught by a fisherman working the Thames River, and consequently, after it was turned over to the police, the actor's fingerprints opened up a new line of inquiry. Since there were strong similarities between the first murder and the subsequent murders of David Godalming and Mr. and Mrs. Watts, officials realized that there were lose ends connecting Irving to the heinous crimes in an indexed sort of way.

However, according to reliable sources, Irving was unavailable for questioning for he had up and vanished. And though nobody had seen him since the late afternoon prior to the slaying of the Old Man, Jonathan wanted to take precaution. Thus, removing the loaded pistol with silver bullets out of the handbag of horrors, he hid it on his person and, with the leather traps in hand, walked a quarter of a mile to catch a cab to the Lyceum Theatre.

The normal twenty-minute ride to the dreadful building took over an hour due to complications. Several roads were blocked off because of structural damage and political events, which caused the driver to take several back roads that were notorious for being congested with heavy traffic and pedestrians. As the minutes ticked away, Jonathan was apprehensive of the time and grew very nervous and grave; he had only a few hours remaining before nightfall. And though he knew his way around the theatre, he was even more fearful of making a second visit to the horrid place. Indeed, he was aware now of Irving's plight, but nothing could prepare him for the evil that was lurking inside the Beefsteak room.

"Park 'er ovah there, mate," the lad told the driver in a voice that was shaking, full of nerves and tenseness. The cab idled its engine a block from the large 1,500-seat edifice, and taking part of the twenty-five pounds the Old Man had returned to the two boys, the cabbie touched his right hand to the brim of his hat and drove away.

Jonathan walked toward the back of the theatre like a seasoned burglar. As expected, he found the door lock. Consequently, when there was no one in sight, he took the black leather bag and knocked it against a glass window. The breaking sound was muffled by the evening sounds of the street, and once he broke off enough of the fragments for the bag to fit through, he lowered it onto the floor. Carefully removing all the sharp fragments, he soon followed by pushing himself through the small opening, stepping over shards of glass.

The inside was exactly as he had remembered: dark and desolate. By the use of a match, he found his way easily to Irving's dressing room. Quietly, the teenager pressed his right ear up to the door and waited for almost a full minute, listening for any sign of life behind it. And when the youth concluded that neither living nor Un-Dead presences were stirring, he turned the door handle and found it as he had expected: locked tight.

Nevertheless, Jonathan was prepared for this discovery as well. Indeed, his previous entrapment was a learning experience and his since proactive approach of lock picking would certainly save the day. True, if Jonathan's knowledge during his second unwelcome visit had been intact during his first, he would surely have burglared his way in, staked the loathsome creature, and escaped undetected. But as he solemnly pulled a tension wrench out of the black bag, he knew retrospective worry was to no avail. Though time would lessen but never fully heal his wounds, it was the integration of death and trouble the foul vampire instigated which tripled his efforts and his vigor to destroy him that much more intense.

With intrepid ease, Jonathan inserted the tool into the keyhole and turned it in the same direction that he would have turned the key, if he so had one. He watched the movement offset the plug to where 'twas slightly balanced from the housing around it, exposing the slight ledge in the pin shafts.

Me Uncle Tom taught me well . . . 'tis a bloody cascade type! he thought to himself.

Wiping the perspiration from his brow, the teenager hesitated a moment and looked around in a stance of apprehension.

A noise.

Pausing from his unlawful form of trespassing, Watts stood rigid in a complete block of fear. But after identifying the source of the sound, he cursed himself with a taste of humorous relief and proceeded with his systematic scheme of entry.

'Tis a G-damn cah! Hah!

Young Watts then pulled a particular pick—for there were several he had placed in the bag—and whilst applying pressure on the plug, the juvenile locksmith inserted the special tool into the keyhole and began lifting the pins inside. And while still applying pressure with the wrench, he carefully proceeded to feel his way with the instrument. Jonathan listened closely as he hoisted each pin pair upward to the extent at which the top fastening moved completely into the housing, as if it were being pushed by the correct key.

And with a smile on his face, he felt and heard a click.

Jonathan found the dressing room in total disarray—much like as if someone was in a great hurry to leave. Likewise, there was a morbid pattern—one that resembled to be a trail of blood—which, for all intense purposes, began toward the center of the room and winded in the direction of the actor's wardrobe. Interestingly enough, the path, with its randomly sized crimson splashes, stopped directly at the hidden door to the Beefsteak room.

It too was secured.

Touching his trembling right index finger to the cold wooden floor, he sensed that the blood was still fairly fresh and that maybe it had originated there some four hours ago. With chilled soul and quickened heart, Master Watts slowly and gently approached the closet and ensued to unveil the hidden passage. With all miscellaneous garments, various articles and costumed objects pushed aside, Jonathan could hear no movement beyond the door. Yet there was a degree of coldness and sense of danger about the area that made him uneasy just the same. His body was writhing like a dying soldier on a battlefield. Though the teenager's mind begged him to run, his heart prayed for him to remain and stand firm.

Bother me not . . . this is for me mum and pop . . . for Old G1!
the youth thought to himself as he took a deep breath and began to
squint, peering into the lock.

Suddenly, Jonathan's blood turned to ice as his nerves began to
tremble froze as he felt the cold metal barrel of a revolver press upon
the back of his skull.

"Give me one reason I should not blow yer brains out!" an
equally alarming voice said hotly. "Stand up slowly and turn 'round!
And don't try and play games with me, boy!"

As Jonathan remained on his hand and knees with his head
fixed directly in front of the keyhole, he did his best to identify the
voice. Though he had seen Henry Irving on numerous occasions,
it dawned on him he had never heard the man speak; therefore, he
would not be able to recognize his speech. Even during the previous close encounter with the actor, no dialogue took place, and the
lad only had the recollections of several grumbles of irritability and
utmost disgust to go on. Disappointingly, the lad felt his own pistol
being removed from his rear gig line with a wily laugh.

"Bullets don't kill vampires, son . . . leave that line of business
for the men of your world!" he said in a derogative tone filled with
sarcasm.

Luckily, the black bag that Old Man Godalming had provided
Jonathan and Noel sat opened within reach. Obviously, the assailant
did not pay any notice to the bag, for if he had, he would have at least
pushed it away with his foot.

"By Jove, up with ye, I said!" the man yelled with lesser patience
and increased harshness than before. Slowly, Jonathan began to rise.
Watts's adrenaline, heart rate, and mind were racing like the most
powerful locomotive. He was almost lightheaded from the palpitat-
ing sensation. But he swallowed with a noisy gulp and did as the
man ordered. Though stricken with fright, the youth had little time
to dwell on the utter terror that pumped through his small frame full
throttle.

"Hold 'em high, 'n' back off from the bloody door! *Now!*"

Jonathan seemed to acquiesce, but as he stepped away from the
portal preparing to stand in the upright position, he only raised his

left hand. Thus, with his right hand, he reached under and to the side, seizing the handle of the wooden mallet that was intended to splatter the vampire's flesh with silver.

Though the boy could not see the face of his aggressor, he could behold his legs from his peripheral vision, and with dire quickness and complete strength, Jonathan came at him with a tremendous swing.

The hard blow took the man off guard, and Watts quickly heard the stunning effect. As the mallet hit the scoundrel on the side of his right leg, he let out a moan filled with agony and bent over slightly, as if about to double up in gut-wrenching soreness, and dropping the gun level to the smartness of the blow, he held his right leg in harsh pain.

Not giving the man a chance to recover, the teenager immediately turned around and came at him a second time, this strike aiming for his stomach, knocking the wind out of him without warning. As the man dropped to the floor, vainly gasping for breath, Jonathan got a clear first look at the man's face as the gun fell from his hand.

Indeed, it was *not* actor Henry Irving.

The assaulter—or rather the intruder's intruder—was a startlingly odd-looking Englishman: he walked hunchbacked, with sharp brutish features and wore a pointed white beard. He reeked of the stale mixture of smoke and gore and was dressed in color, ebony, and mandarin red, and crossed with more straps and belts than Jonathan could count, from which hung all manner of things: a small lantern, a jar filled with live amphibians, a smoking pipe, the filleted vestiges of a variety of different mammals, a revolver holster (which now held Jonathan's pistol), and a vast skin—the unique combination of a numerous defunct creatures all dried and neatly stitched into one . . .

The terror of the event left the boy trembling in horror, breathing ineptly as if he was the one that had the sails knocked out of him instead of the mysterious heap on the floor. Quickly, young Watts kicked the gun away, which produced such a heartless, demented glare in the man that communicated an unspoken look of evil that did not sit well with Jonathan. Indeed, a look of defiance twisted the berserker's visage until a sudden rage came over the lad, and without hesitation, the adolescent kicked the man in his face with the thick heel of his right boot, breaking his nose on contact. With a despairing groan, the man passed out as Jonathan stood over him in a weary state of victory. He watched the trickles of blood seep out the holes of his warped nose, and dropping the mallet from his hand, he imagined how young David felt when he conquered the giant Goliath.

"Vic'try!"

To no avail, Jonathan quickly searched the man for any form of identification. And as an aura of stillness settled over the boy, he recalled himself to the present time: he had but an hour before dusk. He shuddered in fear and hastily returned to the concealed door of the Beefsteak room. Master Watts stood there looking at the secluded entrance for several seconds, staring at the lock like it was the opening to the bowels of hell. Yet his body was too wary and too desensitized to understand the true import of the moment at bay: he had very little time, and being afraid was not going to hold him back . . . alas, it would not work to his advantage.

And before grabbing his locksmith tools, he gathered up the rosary that hung around his neck and praised thanks for his best mate for giving it to him. Indeed, it was a welcomed feeling of comfort at a time he needed it most. And as he shoved a wrench in the door, a particular line from *Macbeth* fell upon his ears. Whether ghosts of the theatre materialized or Abraham Stoker was commending the boy's bravery from afar, he repeated them with the heartfelt bravado of an inspiring actor—and in a manner that Henry Irving would have been envious of:

"It were done when 'tis done . . ."

CHAPTER 30

The Terrorizing Truth

> You think you have left me without a place
> to rest, but I have more. My revenge has just
> begun. I spread it over centuries, and time is on
> my side.
>
> —Count Dracula

𝕴t was well into the night that Abraham and Noel Stoker were awakened by a loud pang, which resembled the alarming sound of a gunshot. They each looked at the other in a surprised sort of way; and then turning to the other few passengers onboard—most of whom were asleep—they arrived at the same perplexing conclusion: no one else on board had heard it.

It was not until dawn, however, that the two consulted about the strange incident, when they made the astonishing discovery that the noise had actually come to them in a queer dream they essentially shared.

"I dreamt that I was levitating aimlessly in a thick fog, and peering through it, I saw what I believed to be Vlad Dracula reading the wretched book I was commissioned to write," began Bram, describing the reverie to his son. And hanging his head in a look of utter despair, he continued unsuccessfully: "Followed by an image of Fl-Flo-Flor . . ."

"Mum," answered Noel. The Irishman nodded solemnly in agreement.

"Yet she looked terrifying and more amoral than ever before, as if she had fully transformed into one of *his* kind," added Noel.

"And with a scathing chuckle, he closed the book—" continued the writer.

"To the sound of a gunshot!" further exclaimed Noel with a tone of amazement. The writer, too, concurred.

"And simultaneously, there appeared a great blinding light that originated from on high—such as the glory of heaven had flooded the pandemonium of the vampiric netherworld with all its righteousness . . ." Stoker went on.

The two were silent for a long spell, pondering over the common vision with the unspoken attitude as if there were something more but puzzled over its meaning or interpretation. They each sat in their own gothic gloom of prolific introspection. By and by, the adolescent broke the silence by posing the question: "When the gunfire and the light woke you, did you open your eyes to the sights of the train?" asked Noel.

"Nay," the author replied gravely.

"Neither did I," the teenager said in a serious overtone. His dulled eyes suddenly grew fever-lit with dire interest. For without even speaking, the words they both realized each had seen the same familiar building.

"Indeed, I believe Countess Dracula has again intervened in our quest by providing direction whence we need it and to heed a sharp warning. Alas, the book is finished, but the curse has not been lifted! And with Florence missing, I fear for the worse! Truly the real author of the endless sufferings we have endured seems to continue to distress our days and haunts our nights!" The journeyman sunk back in his chair in a complete plight of misery. His wary head rolled slightly as he further stated, "Aye, we were both told where our misadventure is to continue next, and who am I to disagree with a four-century-year-old ghost that has steered me away from death time and time again, hmmm?"

"To the Lyceum," Noel said laconically.

"Yes," repeated Abraham. "To the Lyceum."

Visible signs of nervous apprehension must have been painted on the faces of father and son for the morning crowd seemed to peel back from the platform resembling the almighty guiding Moses and his people whilst God's holy hand divided the Red Sea. Hurriedly, Abraham and Noel caught an awaiting cab and was in front of the Lyceum at precisely 8:08 a.m.

Walking toward the back of the theatre, Noel stepped on a piece of broken glass, and calling their attention to the shattered window, they each looked at one another with solemn and cautious expressions.

"A burglar?" Noel suggested.

"We shall see," the eldest responded, unsmiling. As it was still early in the morn, there were few passers-by and even less frequent was the occasional policeman on patrol. And with casual poise and purpose, the Irishman waited until the area was free of any onlookers and then reached through the gaping pane with his left arm. With little effort, the length of his limb fumbled with the lock of the adjacent door until each heard an audible click. And armed solely with the Celtic stake and hunters' knife, they replicated the universal sign of the cross over their chests and, in a melancholic fashion, pushed open the door. But almost instantly, a founding wave of swelling fear was unleashed upon the dueling duo.

Jonathan Watts was discovered lying facedown in a pool of blood directly in front of the hidden passage to the Beefsteak room. Noel's face fell as his father rushed to his mate's side and checked his pulse. A raging storm began to break in the youth's heart as the journeyman jumped like a child's novelty toy and sprung into action.

"He is still alive, though his breathing is very shallow!" cried the writer. "He has been shot in the shoulder. Quick! Bring me something from the closet and I will form a tourniquet to stop the bleeding!"

The tenseness in the youth's body had increased at such a dramatic level that he was practically to stiff to move a muscle. However, further urging from his elder sent him into emergency action mode with adrenaline coursing through his body.

Whilst Noel grabbed a ruffled poet's shirt from Irving's closet, his father seized a decanter of brandy from a drawer in the dressing table and moistened the boy's lips, elevating him slightly. A bubbling groan passed Watt's mouth. Upon pouring a generous amount over the wound, Jonathan opened his eyes to forming clouds and began to writhe in pain. And then he let out a cry of agony. Next, ripping the garment into, Abraham made a tight circling band underneath the victim's left arm. The latter's graying lips were powdery dry and twitched slightly. His eyes then fluttered from absolute shock.

Noel and his father lifted Jonathan and carefully propped himself up against the inner wall of the closet. Watts coughed weakly. The increased blood flow made the pain billow up and swallow him whole for a moment. Though the injured one could not speak, his vision began to clear, but upon the realization of suffering, his eyes became stark with pain. When his sight focused on his company, his look softened as though he pleased to see the two of them were there. A frail, tortured smile flitted over his lips as the swelling throbbed with spasmodic stings.

"Hang on, mate!" Noel said reassuringly. "We will get you some help soon!"

It was evident to father and son that the young lad was in the process of picking the lock of the concealed passage—for various locksmith instruments were scattered round the floor—when someone approached and fired from behind. Resurveying the room more closely, Noel asked angrily to his father: "Who could have done this?" and "Where is the weapon?"

"We shall see . . ." was again Stoker's laconic response.

Jonathan coughed again, and each could tell the boy was trying hard to communicate by cautioning them as to what was behind the door.

"We have no time to lose . . . let's break it down!" shouted the writer.

On the count of three, the two rammed the door, forcing their entire weight upon the mysterious portal. When it did not yield, they repeated the process again. It gave in slightly, and upon the third attempt, the object split into pieces, resembling kindling or a feeble structure that was smashed in my inclement weather.

In shrinking horror, the two reeled aback in a gasp—as so did Jonathan—as they peered into the dark abyss. Thus, holding a candelabrum, Bram confiscated from Irving's desk in his left hand and the Celtic cross in his right, he stepped into the doorway repeating an invocation. Noel followed close behind with his forbidden knife, trembling every step of the way. The adjacent Watts agonized in breathless terror and grimaced as the pain filled is upper cavity. Looking onward, it appeared the courageous duo was stepping upon a tightrope of meager survival across an infinite maw of demise.

* * * * *

The air enveloping the Beefsteak room was the same strong, earthly odor that nearly choked Noel whilst visiting Slains Castle and the description of the inexplicable place was exactly as Florence Stoker had described it in her dreamlike state:

"The gothic chamber was decked in gloomy oaken paneling with a hardwood floor," wrote Abraham. "A curious gridiron was hanging from the beamed ceiling, and in the core of the room, there was a grand, antiquated dining table with marching chairs that sat atop a gleaming Oriental floor covering. The table was serviced with a gold place setting, complete with pewter mugs of stout. Alongside the wall fronting us was an immense aggregation of grotesque paintings, seemingly covered in dust. The right end of the room contained a baronial hearth, absent of life, containing a small sign and housed with a massive cooking grate. And on the other side of the room, there was a large, darkly decorated wooden coffin held by an elaborate stand." Indeed, the moment on its own terms was almost implausible to fully comprehend. They each looked upon the box with faces that spoke of endless, nerve-clinching dismay.

The flames from the candelabrum shook wildly and were an apparent visible sign of the Irishman's iron nerves were giving sway to the ghastly place. Pointing to the coffin, the writer exclaimed, "See! There is only one! Perhaps we are still not too late to save your mother!" To Noel, Abraham's almost excitable conduct seemed misplaced, yet he nodded with a partial translucent smile just the same. Truly, 'twas no time to relax. And to let one's guard down at such a dire moment would surely envelop him completely in a state of consternation.

Sitting the candelabra down on the center table, the father turned and faced his son, who was standing on the opposite side of the Beefsteak room, which was lined with several suits of armor intermingled with cobwebs, and said, pointing to the crude crate, "That must be where the monster resides during the daylight hours! We have to move forward quickly with our dirty work—however, it looks like we still need to look for Flor—"

Noel saw his father's face transform from a look of half triumph to one overthrown with timorous defeat. In a state of perfect narcosis, the Celtic cross fell from his trembling hand as he muttered in a broken voice, "Watch out, Noel!"

The boy spun around swiftly with the knife in hand and saw the shadow of a savagely hunchbacked figure as it stepped out from amongst the armory.

"Drop the knife!" the brute bellowed in an English accent, and upon seeing the man was aiming a gun at him and his father, Noel quickly acquiesced.

The man's pointed snowy beard was doused in blood, which looked as though to have seeped from his broken nose. He gave off an almost smoky stench coupled with sanguine fluid. And colliding with the earthly odor of the freshly turned molded dirt, Noel began to empty his stomach into his mouth, only to reswallow from apprehension. Amidst the dangling strips and belts before him, the wearer displayed a scathing sneer. It was evident the man was not always hunched, but rather, he recently received a nasty blow to his back, resulting in a compromising injury that explained his eccentric hobble. The youth's heart skipped a beat and then began to thud like a kettledrum as it sank deep within his chest.

The pallor of the writer's face turned from an ashen color to almost a sickly greenish tint when he identified the voice of Captain Oscar Whitman. But oh, how the man had changed! There was something diabolical and savage-like in the man's tone and demeanor that stamped out any previous countenance of kindheartedness and purity. Indeed, the Skipper's grace had sailed and a demented, soulless wreck of the former was stranded in his place.

"Alas, I was no longer looking at the brave man that carried the Citadel through a terrible storm and fought for his crew," recalled Stoker. "Nay . . . that evil monster which was holding my son and me at bay was not the same fellow I confided in at sea, but rather, he had been transformed into one of the founds from hell! And this servant of the Uun-Dead should be dealt with on equal unholy carnal terms."

It was likewise clear to both father and son that the scathing brute that held them at gunpoint was probably the same fiend that shot poor Jonathan. And for a full half minute, the villain held his hostages with a devious snarl that made Abraham and Noel's blood rush to their heads in statuses of neurotic consternation. The awkward silence was an unbearable aching void that seemed like an eternity, but then a groan from Jonathan echoed within the room and reinforced the purpose of the grim encounter. Indeed, the sharp pain dug through Watts like a rusty razor.

Now I lay me down to sleep . . .

"Ah," the captain said coldly to Noel, "your chum regrets his burglarous nature. How sad, indeed,"—he laughed under his breath—"but I am afraid the King has spoken, his demise was henceforth determined!"

I pray me Lord my soul to keep . . .

The fear in Noel's heart quickly evolved into an obstinate state of loathing anger. And as he grasped the hunting knife tightly in his right hand, the boy felt the blood that rushed to his head had transformed into a boiling, fuming time bomb.

And if I die before I wake . . .

"How could you do such a thing? Damn you, animal! You and Dracula can go to hell!" cried Noel, charging at the captain whilst aiming the point of the blade at his chest.

I pray me Lord my soul to take . . .

"No, Noel!" cried his father. "Watch out!"

Amen!

In a flight of bone-crushing horror, a barreling gunshot echoed through the desolate chamber like a mountain slide in a cavern. Noel fell to the floor with a grunt as his father let out a wail of sorrow from the other side of the vastness. A grief-stricken Abraham threw his hands up to his face in a despairing act of awe as the captain slowly approached the coffin. His lips were drawn back in a soundless snarl. And with the smoking gun pointed directly at the Irishman, hell's newest member spoke with a stern forked tongue: "So we meet again, Abraham Stoker; yet I see that your bravery is beginning to fail you! I suggest you remain still. Do not make the same fatal mistake that these foolish boys made!" Here he stopped and pointed to Noel who lay in a heap, writhing on the floor with Jonathan moaning only a short distance behind him in the doorway.

Bram looked on with a numbing, helpless stare, and with tears flowing down his face, the author addressed the captain: "What on earth have you done? Do you not understand? *He* had driven you to this! I have resolved myself to everything that Count Dracula has asked me to do! I have went abroad for him, I have written his cursed book, and I have forfeited six years of my life whilst humbly being engulfed in a multitude of horrors that have terrorized the very heart and soul of my family! What more can he expect? I do not have anything more to give!" The man was on his dignity, yet his misery and sobs did not seem to affect the captain at all. On the contrary, he was short of being argumentative.

The captain's face gleamed as he let out a hellish chuckle and said, "Nay, you are wrong! There is something else that the King needs. It is the next step . . ." And flinging open the lid to the horrid coffin, he pleaded forcefully, "Join us!"

And then a vast blizzard of wintry air sent an aloof, arctic aware-ness—a grim sensation that hardened his flesh and crept into his bones. For with that very instant, the words of the captain seemed to echo over and over in the Irishman's ears until it produced a muffled roar which became the soundtrack to the haunting image of Noel falling to his death. The author's feat became undeniably racked with pain as he looked upon the dreaded contents of the box.

"I could not move them," the author wrote. "My legs became numb, followed by an icy feeling at the back of my neck that shot fully down my spine. And my ears, henceforth, became like my feet: dead yet in torment, and there came an overwhelming sense of coldness in my breast, which was by comparison far worse than any memory of being an invalid and doubly terrorizing than any nightmare Vlad Dracula had tested me with. And if there have ever been an event of trepidation that struck both one's physical and mental cord beyond reason, it was at the unveiling of that vile coffin."

The terrible sight scourged out his eyes, for there—together in all their unnatural and revolting glory —lay the bodies of Florence Stoker and Henry Irving.

Indeed, it was a bad dream—a physical and mental phantasm that toppled a ponderous weight on Stoker's chest. With the disclosure of the casket, the manifested emanation of the two bodies mixed with the moldy soil beneath them flooded the already reeking air. This rejuvenation brought about an aggrandized offensive emanation, which clung to the vastness, making it impossible for him to breathe. He could not think. Truly, for the first moment in his life, Abraham Stoker was absolutely at a loss for words.

The two shared the cruel box like a wicked bride and groom from the innermost depths of Hades. They rested in complete stillness but with dark eyes that were wide open, which mocked the author's on look of shock and dismay. Though the bodies could not be denied as those of his beloved and employer, they were remarkably deviant: their facial features appeared harshly distorted and mean-looking. To Stoker's eyes, they were unreal jackals that somehow took on their forms whilst misplacing their souls. As his footing gave sway, the poor man collapsed, hanging on to the lower lid of the sarcophagus sobbing uncontrollably.

"Listen closely, matey," the Skipper scowled. "It is not too late to save these two mites if you do as I say and join *his* fold! But time is fleeting! You must make your decision now!"

God forgive me! But I need thee this very hour!

A confused and troubled Abraham Stoker looked at him with a tear-stricken gaze and finally replied in a broken, solemn voice, "Tell me . . . what am I to do?"

The commander of the Beefsteak room smiled wryly and stepped toward the center of the leeway. But as he did so, the weary and distinct voice of Jonathan Watts cried, "Stop!" and both the Irishman and the captain turned and looked in the boy's direction with the attitude of surprise.

A whirling hatchet sailed through the air at top speed. And before Oscar Whitman had a second to react, the object lodged itself in the center of his forehead, splitting the skull like a ravine as he dropped to the floor. The author reeled back in amazement as he saw the eyes of the corpse turn back in his head with an expression of defeat as it toppled over, painting the floor crimson as the aggressive color seeped freely from the fatal serrated wound.

Hitherto, Jonathan was sinking fast, but in a last-ditch effort to conquer evil, he had secretly been reaching for the small axe that Godalming had inventoried when explaining the contents of the black leather bag. Ideally, 'twas meant to be used to decapitate Dracula. However, in such a frantic insufficiency, it was prudent that urgency superseded foregoing plans.

Upon witnessing this last ordeal of horror, Abraham's fingers grated down the bottom lid of the coffin—literally splitting his nails and tearing his cubicles apart in an agony of turmoil and desperation. But as he did so, the body of Florence Stoker began to wriggle, and then she finally sat up, looking at him intensely with extended arms and said, "Abraham, my husband! It *is* your voice! I knew you could come to me!"

It shan't be! Nay! In God's holy name, what vile remorseless villain would carry out such a deliberate, evil act of cruelty?

The sight was too much for the writer to withstand. He tremored violently. And as he cowered back, he let go of the coffin and fell to the cold wood floor in a state of perfect exasperation.

"Don't you want me anymore, Abraham?" she asked in a soft, sinful faraway voice. The Irishman saw the long, cruel pointed teeth, the voluptuous red mouth, the alluring sinister stare. He shuddered in fright, but with his last ounce of courage, he addressed the thing in the box that resembled his wife.

"Why? Explain why, my beloved? And him—of all people, why did you choose him? Ohhh . . . and your eyes! They look at me so strangely!"

"Nay, you are wrong, my husband. Come! Join me, darling, and be my first! So Noel shall live!"

In a miserable state of helpless grief, Abraham Stoker reluctantly held out his hand to Florence as an assembly of gut-wrenching terrors crowded upon his troubled brain.

"Ohhh! Florie!"

Suddenly an extended arm seized the journeyman by the right leg. Indeed, it belonged to Noel Stoker. The youth reached out to his father, handing him the Celtic cross that he retrieved after the hostile encounter with the captain.

"Don't listen to her!" the boy said in a low but strong voice. "She lies! Just like *he* does!"

The author's face actually beamed upon seeing his son, and taking the silver stake from him, exclaimed, "But . . . you are not shot?"

"Nay," said he in agreement. "Blessed be, I lost my footing on this bloody rug a mere second before the captain fired! Alas, I am fine . . . just a twisted ankle . . ."

The gruesome but seductive thing in the coffin caught sight of the holy relic and recoiled with a contorted look of the most absolute hate and depravity. Her eyes flashed with the immoral flames of hellfire, hissing the inhuman backlash of a loathsome serpent as he raised the stake directly over her heart.

"Forgive me, my beloved! Oh, mighty God in heaven! Have mercy upon me, Lord! Jesus, please save us all and grant me the courage and where with all to go through with my awful task!" The journeyman pleaded with extravagant emotion as he prepared to plunge the silver Celtic crucifix deep into his wife's bosom. His visage remained a taut, lined front of resistance to the sorrow. Noel Stoker wept as he looked on in terror as his father proceeded with the dirty deed. Whilst Jonathan Watts sunk further into death, somewhere, he heard an angel moan. And if there was ever a moment of hell on earth for Abraham Stoker, it was that pivotal moment of primal fear.

* * * * *

"I am afraid Jesus did not come here," said a devious and familiar voice boldly interrupting the Irishman's entreaty. "And it looks like God hath forgotten thee and thy loved ones . . ."

As the disturbing words echoed uncannily throughout the Beefsteak room, an unseen force snatched the icon from the writer's hand just as he was about to free his wife of the vampiric curse.

And then the ultimate twist of the supernatural occurred before Abraham and Noel's bewildered eyes: the form of Dracula actually rose out of the body of Henry Irving! The Count spoke as he towered over the author with a commanding presence, much like an unworthy sinner praying for forgiveness before the son of Dues.

"How could you . . . how did you . . . ?" a thunderstruck Abraham Stoker stammered out in disbelief.

"Ah, so the words Agatha Hupnuff called out to ye as her Un-Dead heart were burned to a cinder did not transliterate upon thou ears?"

Unclean snatcher? Abraham thought to himself. And then the meaning and the two words, married up with the weird events involving Henry Irving and Vlad, whirled turbulently in his head. How was Dracula able to move about during the day? Why were there so many odd connections linking the actor to the crimes of the vampire? All these questions suddenly took on new, deeper, and even darker translation.

The Count has secretly been merging into Irving's body when need be to carry out his demoniacal drudgery whilst misleading those inclined to believe it was Dracula! thought the writer. *That is how he crossed the water at the monastery, how he kidnapped Florence in Cruden Bay and attacked the captain during daylight hours . . .*

Noel Stoker's mind was aloof as well for he too had similar clues that his mother had given him, and if he had connected the two together, he might have saved his mother and realized the location of the Beefsteak room sooner. Father and son were confounded to states of stuttering silence, as the shell of Henry Irving remained lifeless in the oppressive crate. The vampires mocked the human's stupidity and muteness.

Hark, go there not . . . for that way, madness waits!

"Why Henry?" the Irishman asked in an astounded way. "Of all the people you could have chosen, you looted an actor's body?"

"Alas, but I needed to get close to ye, did I not? I needed a writer to complete my chronicles—is this not so? And after careful observation, I hast decided it was Henry whom I want to portray me in the ultimate theatrical version of my story!" And holding up the completed text in his hand, he said, "Splendid work, may I add! However, now I require a bold playwright . . ." And seeing Captain Whitman on the floor, he let out a laconic sigh and added, "And from the state of affairs, a new bulwark too! First Nicolae and now the captain! Once more, thou are testing my patience!"

The author was absolutely dumbfounded.

"Theatrical version? You want to turn this horrid story into a play? The world must never see such a relentless act of carnage!" Bram asserted. "And to think you are insisting to use Henry in *our* theatre to do so! Nay! I will not stand for it! Not on my life!" Stoker said in protest. "Have you forgotten? You told me in the beginning that by me writing this book, you would be released of the vampiric—;is this not true? Hark the herald! Remember your oath!"

Vlad Dracula simply laughed in response as Noel discreetly began to crawl across the floorboards closer toward the debate.

"I am sorry to disappoint ye, my gullible friend, for only *real* death will release me of the spell of the Un-Dead! And likewise, I am not finished with you! For now, friend Stoker, thou hath a momentous decision to make. I needeth a new disciple—ay, someone to see out my Theatre of the Vampires to its fullest capability! Thus, inviting new blood into my family—or rather, I say *our* family—for alas, why not let this person be you? After all, who else could possibly be greater qualified? Thou hath studied me well. You know this city— the people, this theatre—and more importantly, what an exemplary play needest! I trust ye will join me. But alas, I ask you to think hard and think quickly. If thou sayeth no, ye forsake your family forever. However, if thou agreeth, it is not too late to save the ones ye love!"

The soulless fiend that resembled the shape of Florence Stoker stirred again in the loathsome box and ultimately tossed the actor's body out of the unhallowed earth and upon the deck like an undesired pawn or prototype. Bram saw that Henry was not a vampire, but rather he was in a deep hypnotic stupor that Dracula evidently enchanted upon him.

The journeyman did not know what to say or do. He stood frozen in a confused state of fright. His eyes were stricken with grief. His throat and mouth felt dry as sanding paper. And his limbs trembled helplessly in terror.

With wanton lips, Florence called her husband again in the same illusory and ghostly voice, "Shall you join me, my husband? Why do you wait? It has been six long years . . ."

"Oh, Florie!"

She summoned him over in a state of exotic levitation and began to caress his hair and lapped at his earlobes with a snakelike tongue that brought shivers down Noel's spine and clabbered his veins. By and by, she moved close to his jugular whilst exposing the long canine teeth that she yet had a chance to explore. And just as the tips of the hideous fangs made their dents on his father's throat, a defiant voice came from behind the table.

"You are not my mother! I warned you once—don't you dare touch him!"

Noel sounded, again presenting the crucifix. "Back away, you jackal!"

Florence let go of Abraham and darted behind the King Vampire like a helpless child. And for a brief moment, the gruesome twosome stood there, exchanging grinding looks of malice toward their mortal audience like conflicting forces on a battlefield.

"So it is the righteous father and child of the world versus the unrighteous creator and offspring of the underworld, eh? My fortitude is quickly wearing thin for you, boy, I should bash thy brains in here and now!"

"I beseech you, Dracula!" Stoker bellowed with heartfelt emotion. "Please leave him out of this!"

"Hah!" answered the Un-Dead. "I predicted this would happen, but undoubtedly disappointed all the same. But both of ye can join thou holy relics in the very graves at Slains you so ignorantly marked! For they belongst to you! I have my earth, and I have other places of rest! And most importantly, I have all the time in the world! On the other hand, yours hast just runneth out!"

By raising of his left hand, the evil Count extended his long index finger in a bolt of opposition. The horrid, razor-sharp nail seemed to cut into Bram as the vampire's dark eyes began to glow like red-hot coals. All at once, they captivated the Irishman, and he felt his limbs began to react unwillingly. Then his entire body lifted itself off the floor, despite the aching numbness that hindered his mobility.

"Rise . . . I commandeth you . . ." ordered Dracula as his finger spelled Stoker's movement—guiding him much like a dancing marionette. And with a glare of heartless cruelty, he delivered the two words that made Noel's heart sink deep within his chest.

"Kill him!"

Noel recoiled and continued to guard himself with the crucifix, but seeing the changed look upon his father's face, he soon realized it was no protection against a zombie of Lucifer. A gaze of horror fell over the boy, and he began to pray loudly, pressing the cross tightly to his chest and unconsciously started to cry.

"Father, stop! It's Noel! Your only child! Remember *our* oath!"

A look of extreme coldness pulsated out of the Irishman's piercing eyes. As he hobbled slowly toward his son with outstretched arms and wanton gripping hands, there was an overwhelming presence of unjust possession about him as if—in a matter of a few seconds—his entire universe had come undone before his very eyes. And as he was about to reach for his son's neck in a chokehold, the last mothering instinct within Florence Stoker manifested itself as she called out to him in an entreaty of opposition, "Abraham! Please . . . *no!*"

"Silence, wretch!" the King Vampire scowled hotly. As she jumped from behind Vlad, the latter lifted his other hand, and with a slight sweep of his arm, he viciously cast her to the ground like a ragdoll. Florence struck the hard flooring with a giant thud and lay there motionless, groaning and sobbing in unreserved misery.

The writer's attention was distracted by this outburst, and he looked at both his beloved and possessor with tears streaming down his glassy eyes. Hitherto, Noel had covertly positioned his hunting knife behind his back and gripped it with iron nerve. With an impeccable demonstration of love and forthright, he caught his father off guard and sliced into his right ankle with the sharp blade.

"Come back to us!" the boy cried out desperately. "He must not win!"

Abraham Stoker bellowed out in a state of agony and flattered to the parterre, reeling from pain. His trancelike state was broken by the act, and he looked around in awe as in an attempt to somehow recap what happened during his brief hiatus. He held his ankle whilst the blood flowed through his fingers.

The vampire was incensed.

His long, pointed teeth champed down hard over the bottom lip of his cruel mouth, emitting a stream of fresh blood that trickled down his chin, staining his white shirt. The extreme contrast between the aggressive color of the life's fluid and the gleaming pearliness of his teeth was an ironic reminder of the ongoing battle between good and evil and the underlying relationship between life and death.

Truly, the situation within the walls of the Beefsteak room was one terrifying consequence: to the left of Noel was the dead captain, his body still warm and his grisly purpose and demise still fresh in the adolescent's mind; to his right sat his inured father, fighting for his soul and freedom, and in front of Bram lay his beloved wife, all in a heap and almost fully changed. The dreadful moans of Jonathan Watt's life quickly slipping away from mortality echoed in Noel's ears whilst the stupefaction of Henry Irving was positioned directly to the right of the coffin. Indeed, he was completely unaware of anything that had taken place, yet what an ironic thought if the actor were in tune with the off-pitch energy of the supernatural forces around him and the evil that had invaded his theatre . . . his quarters . . . his Beefsteak room . . .

The room—as it was upon entrance and when shrouded in darkness—had looked merciless and frightening enough, but now, after all the death and consternation that had come to pass in only bare minutes of a person's entire lifetime, left the teenager bewildered in a complete state of absolute terror. For when the unfeeling wooden floor had been bathed in warm gore, when the sound of silence was broken by the wails of sadness, when the shadow of the sleeping sarcophagus gave way to a scream of horror, and when the moans of pain preempted the tremulous flame of the dying candle, the consequence was more dreary and squalid than he could ever imagined. It offered the irreparable notion that life—bestial, physical life—was not the only existence that could die.

"As for meself," Master Stoker recalled later, "I was utterly mortified and, for the first time, in my life was at a complete loss of hope. But then the strange, sweet voice of an old long-lost soul whispered to me, 'The talisman!' and I recalled what the old man had told our small alliance about the tablet of the Scholomance. It must be here somewhere!" Noel thought to himself. "In this very room!" Thus, the young lad began to discreetly survey everything in sight closely, eyeballing every scope—every nook and cranny that he could make out.

Dracula's expression beamed of one of utter loathsomeness and evil atonement. The folds of his morose face seemingly to pulsate of heartless cruelty. The glare in his eyes jettisoned sparks of hellfire and foul images of the blazing pit from whence he came. His aquiline nose appeared to flare out dispensing immense heat and wrath that would have blown everyone to his or her feet—that is, if they weren't already lying helpless on the ground. The coarse stands on the vampire's batlike ears stuck straight out like the hairs of an angered feline, ready to pounce upon and claw its prey to a mauled death. The bushy dark eyebrows came together and met in a way that announced danger and provoked a new level of terror in anyone or anything that had enough courage to look. The dark, flowing cape that adorned the monster seemed to wrap around the malignancy in an ominous sort of way—almost suggesting that it worked as a dike or barrier that held back his vehemence to loading point, and now the dam was ready to burst. And then suddenly, the fiend spread his cloak wide and spoke in a harrowing voice that will go down in mankind as one of the most demonic equality.

"Fools! All of you!" Count Dracula cursed at them in a ferine voice. "I am infinite! I am immortal! And no creature under heaven or hell can defeat me! Nay, the most powerful regime cannot strike me down. I can be neither bought 'ere sold, and those that cross my path or standeth in my way will know what it is like to come to pass with their darkest thoughts and worst fears! I see death in all your eyes! And I welcome ye to your most horrifying nightmare! Hah! Thou hast had your fun and folly during this battle . . . but now the war is mine!"

CHAPTER 31

A Requiem of the Vampire or the Final Battle

Coming close to Arthur, he said, "My friend Arthur, you have had a sore trial, but after, when you look back, you will see how it was necessary. You are now in the bitter waters, my child. By this time tomorrow you will, please God, have passed them, and have drunk of the sweet waters. So do not mourn over-much. Till then I shall not ask you to forgive me."
—Dr. Van Helsing to Arthur Holmwood

Count Dracula's power was at its strongest when feeding on the fears of others. Indeed, victims that became overwhelmed with uncontrollable fright triggered confusion, and this weakened state often produced a level of fogginess that can cause the brain to react in bad judgement. During this condition of vulnerability—when a frozen feeling evolved within the limbs, producing a state of immobility—was when the vampire reached into the minds of Abraham and Noel Stoker and found the most susceptible place and struck to the core of their consternations. Consequently, each of them grew terribly afraid but reacted in their own unique physical, spiritual, and mental way.

Bram's mind had long been feeding fears from his youthful years as an invalid, and there he kept them hidden. In the deep, dark recesses of his heart and soul, they nagged steadfast and invited the notion that if they were brought out into the light of day, they would become true and destroy him—much like a vampire being trapped in the sun and saturated by its beams.

Dracula's relentless evil had undoubtedly breached the brave Irishman's stronghold, and the strain on the man's weakened mind had hardened his spirit, giving sway to possession.

On the other hand, Noel's youthful body was absent of the horrors the author suffered abroad. And with a grimacing face, Noel eyed Vlad the Impaler with an undeniable anxiety in his heart that made his stomach churn with the utmost repulsion. His father's fresh blood dripped from the edge of the hunting knife, which the boy still held in his right hand; and when he took his sight off Dracula long enough to realize what had just occurred, he shuddered in sheer horror.

"Indeed, the grim reality of it all flashed before me like soaring seconds of frightfulness, but the loathsome minutes of the dreadful events came back to me in awful nightmares that enabled me to relive the horrid experience over and over again as if it were part of the vampire's vile, sordid story that needed to be retold," recalled Master Stoker.

And at that moment of absolute fear, it donned on his adolescent brain that consternation did not play fair in their dreadful quest—it preyed on their minds; and their harrowing thoughts fed the fiend's hunger when they were in the greatest amount of pain.

Then it were done quickly, the boy thought with a level of sharp clarity.

Much like a beacon, the Irishman exchanged a discreet wink at his son, and a spark of hope swelled up in the lad that numbed the madness of the moment. Without question, the invoking pain of the knife wound intercepted the Count's spell and all of the writer's hope and faith had become renewed. Abraham kept applying pressure with his right hand, and with his free left, he seized the silver crucifix that had once again fallen to the floor.

Though the son had caught sight of his father's reclaimed freedom, he withheld all emotion, and gripping the dagger tighter than ever, he lunged forward with his father at his side in the direction of Vlad Tepes.

Seeing the two come toward him with such a level of undying faith and everlasting vigor made the fiend feel not as haughty as before. Though the ghoul sneered at them in disbelief, the journeyman recalled a slight hesitation and touch of urgency in his voice that seemed to remind himself that he was not completely safe. After all, it was broad daylight outside and his supernatural powers were not at full sway. In all sense of the phrase, Count Dracula was—though if only pursued with complete faith and gallant vigor—at his hunter's disposal.

"Ye both hath chosen unwisely, and thou each will pay with ye lives!" the vampire scoffed. Tossing his enveloping black cape to the floor, Vlad reached for a ponderous sword that was harbored by the most grandeur of the suits of armor that stood erect on the far side of the Beefsteak room.

The massive weapon seemingly came to life and sprung to his call like a king calling his troops to attention. It sailed through the air with such swiftness that would have knocked Noel off his feet; however, it was intercepted by the least expected.

For out of nowhere, Florence Stoker leapt off the ground like a fierce lion and attacked the vampire. She jumped on Dracula's back with the barbaric savageness as Attila the Hun and gorged both her thumbs in the sockets of her creator's monstrous eyes. Her talonlike nails blinded the Count and he almost stumbled backward in complete surprise. Simultaneously, the long uncaught blade struck the wooden floor with a thunderous clang as the vampire felt him being cornered from every angle.

Dracula cursed at the temporary blindness as Florence held on, riding him as if he were the devil's steed. The grotesque image was like witnessing a bizarre conflict between two opposing demonic forces shot up from hell whilst God's brave soldiers marched onward.

Bram, who approached from the right, reached the grisly calamity first and pressed the Celtic symbol against the vampire's right leg. In reaction, the Un-Dead ruler howled in agony as the immediate area smoked and became filled with the revolting, sizzling scent of singed flesh.

Noel, who next advanced from the left, plunged his dagger into the Count's stomach as he concurrently rotated his wrist, turning and thrusting the knife deeper and deeper into the horrific flesh. From the fiend there came a long, wailing canine cry—much like that of a ferocious wolf caught in a deathtrap.

"Indeed, the contenting sight of the vampire's prey turning on him in conquest was a familiar irony in that Vlad Tepes was said to have been slain in battle by his own men," wrote Bram Stoker. "What a paradoxical and fortifying spectacle to witness, and oh . . . what I would have gladly given to behold the thoughts and images that must have raced through the berserker's diabolical brain that rancorous hour!"

Vlad then seized Florence with his left hand and, lifting her high in the air, whirled her into the casket where he pushed on the lid to where it collapsed in on itself. Though the thing inside was not totally human, the small part of Florence Stoker that remained appeared to call out to Abraham and Noel as it beat and pounded its fists against the wooden frame of the sarcophagus.

Bram cringed in his skin as the unrelenting affair almost ridiculed the hideous nightmare that his wife had during her sleepwalking incident: being buried alive and clawing her way to an erroneous liberation. Seeing that his father was too taken up with his beloved to grab the sword Dracula so desperately yearned for, Noel dove for the vacancy head-on.

The Irishman feasted his eyes on the evil sight of the rampageous King Vampire just long enough to defy his narcotic stare. At first, Dracula's eye's resembled the gory hollow sockets of a corpse after vultures and buzzards have had their way with them. However, by and by the mangled damage to his visage reverted itself, as so did the gaping wound to his stomach and the burn on his leg. Notwithstanding, the vampire appeared somewhat distraught from the combat, and the scars that remained on his cadaver spoke eloquently of his weakened state.

"How dare thee! How dare thee defy me!" the Prince scathed hotly.

Noel had seized the sword by both hands and was just about to raise the grand weapon up for engagement when the Count struck him with an angered fist across the jaw and then pelted him in the chest with a powerful blow. Noel stumbled back, slipping in a pool of his father's blood, and sailed across the floor, striking the back of his head against the base of the large table.

As Dracula finally seized the sword, he turned back and smiled at the Irishman who was then kneeling over Henry Irving's unconscious body. The ghoul laughed and said, "Hah! He is mine—ye are all mine! Thou canst earnestly attempt to try your wits against mine, ye will lose every time! Why challenge me? Thy fruitless efforts only leaves ye that much weaker and hopeless. Nay, you hath no understanding of what prolonged suffering can bringeth!"

The vampire approached with the mighty implement of war in hand which carried the eccentric seal of the Order of the Dragon. With his back still to the monster, the writer listened on as Dracula raised the sword and spoke with a stern but discouraged voice that echoed throughout the tiny room like the ripples of a stone tossed into a lake.

"This is your final opportunity to save thyself! Join me, as the actor has already done, and we will create a Theatre of the Vampires—a gothic performance which will surely go down in history and prevail forever!"

With the utmost zest and zeal-like form, Abraham lifted himself up with hands and knees and turned to the bloodsucker. And in a proud but laconic voice, he answered Count Dracula saying, "I have saved myself . . . and Henry is no longer yours, and I will now take back my wife—even if it means I have to fight you to the bitter end!"

As Bram took a step toward the vampire, the monster recoiled. Stoker was wearing a wreath of wolfsbane around his neck, and as the author moved away from Irving's body, the Count could see the edge of the black leather bag that Jonathan Watts, who was scarcely respiring at the veer of the wardrobe, had carried into the Lyceum.

The leech scowled and made numerous attempts to slip around Stoker as if in a plight to merge again into the actor's vulnerable body.

Perhaps it was in a feeble effort to escape into the daylight or in retrospect, Bram thought. *Dracula believed I would have a harder time assassinating Henry Irving's form over his own. Nevertheless, upon seeing Henry Irving was too wearing a wreath of the strong herb, a grave and angered expression fell upon the monster's acutely agitated face.*

The fiend's mouth fell open like a gaping, fiery pit displaying the gleaming saber-toothed incisors that dominated the crimson aperture. He unleashed a prolonged forked tongue that darted in and out like a slithering serpent, which hissed like the coils of Medusa's head as the benevolent form announced its full fury.

"Hark! I dare ye to further defy my wishes!" the creature said hotly. "Yay, do not cometh any closer . . . or I will surely strike him down before thy very eyes!"

Stoker continued to walk toward the parasite with the Celtic cross in hand. Noel, who was lying under the table, had since emerged from the fall and had been preoccupied with a mysterious object that had caught his eye. For when he had slipped, a section of the massive Oriental rug, which rested below the colossal dining table, had been peeled back. And without the Count noticing, Noel nictitated reassuringly at his father. The writer directed a discreet gesture back to his son, as if to say he understood, but continued to push Dracula in the same direction with the silver crucifix in hand.

As Dracula reluctantly cowered back, the vile villain raised the sword high and positioned it to slay Noel in executor-style, saying crossly, "When the bowls of hell runneth over, when the heavens are empty of every angel, and when the Un-Dead inherit the earth, ye will then—and only then—fully understandeth the true import of what thou each forsaketh this day!"

"Let the redeemed say so!" yelled Stoker as the sharp-edged metal swung down at a mighty force.

Noel quickly rolled out of its imposed path, exposing the talisman of the Scholomance, which Dracula cleverly kept hidden under the rug the table rested upon. As it made contact with the powerful blade, the mystical object was entirely shattered. An immediate glare of consternation pervaded the Count's twitching, dark sockets. Simultaneously there came an unearthly yowl, followed by a sort of windstorm, which lasted for several seconds. Next an idiom of outright shock sweltered across the Un-Dead's visage, which began to suspire and emit an unseen energy or force for half a minute.

The room then turned deathly quiet, and as if Father Time had peeled back the calendar four hundred years, behold! For there stood Prince Vlad Tepes Dracula—as a man stripped of any supernatural powers! And for the first time ever, Abraham Stoker detected a sense of encumbrance swelling inside his beast of burden that made his long sparse hands and gangly legs shiver with apprehension, divergent of that of a commanding Voivode. With a look of hate in the Prince's shady eyes, the fallen warrior tried to lift his sword out of the floor to no avail.

"Hurry Pop! Godalming said once the talisman has been destroyed, Dracula returns to human form for only one minute!"

At the same instant, Vlad's vampiric powers were lost, the writer miraculously regained full use of his legs, and despite the injury to his ankle and with the Celtic stake in hand, he charged at the war Prince like a fearless mercenary. In a defensive move to shield his chest, Vlad Tepes raised both arms, crossing his breast in the form of an *X*. Bram collided head-on with the Prince and was greeted with a powerful swing of Dracula's right fist, which struck the left side of the Irishman's face as if he rammed into a brick wall. The author let out a moan but immediately punched the Impaler in his left side. Expecting his opponent would fall in defeat, the Prince was completely caught off guard by the colossal blow and winced, producing a loud gasp whilst staring down his rival with a look of shock and awe.

Underneath the table, Noel was nervously counting to sixty with blood, sweat, and tears rolling down his face. And as Dracula took a step forward to have another shot at his father, the boy lunged his body forward and seized the enemies' legs with the stronghold of a vice.

The Prince lost his balance and rocked like a towering tree caught in the midst of a brutal hurricane. And then, with the fleeting of a few agonizing seconds—which seemingly advanced like the torturous ephemeral of the infinite boundaries of hell—he fell face forward upon the hardwood floor.

"Thy time is up, Abraham Stoker," the Impaler said as he landed facedown with a thud that echoed against the chamber walls like rolling thunder. "Prepare to joineth ye wife in the darkest place of the human soul!"

But as the Prince turned over to reclaim his footing, the writer threw himself on top of Vlad Tepes and plunged the silver stake deep into his chest, saying, "In the name of the Almighty—of the holiest of symbols—through this cross may the evil spirit be cast out until the end of time! Free . . . free forever! I implore for sovereignty for all those stricken by your evil, may they take up in the light of the living and forever step out of the shadows of the Un-Dead!"

A look of crucifixion swept across the vampire's facade as a prolonged, caterwauling shriek escaped his canine-like mouth. The monster's stare was filled with the baneful wrath of Satan. Though it was in vain, he gyrated and flailed his limbs in agony in an attempt to remove the Celtic crucifix and snatch the author by the throat.

Noel Stoker quickly followed up by rescuing the wooden mallet off the floor of Irving's dressing room and proceeded to drive the icon even deeper into the fiend's cavity. As he did so, the young vampire slayer continued the strange requiem by crying out, "Be lifted, unholy curse, and might thy confined body—that has been long Un-Dead enforcing demise and destruction throughout the ages—be exorcised and liberated from thy dark and unholy master!"

The call of a wild wolf sounded far off from the distant busy streets of London. And over the course of a short spell several more joined in until an entire pack of baying dogs emerged into a complete symphony of hounds, which appeared to surround and stake out their territory on the outer walls of the theatre.

The deep hole in Count Dracula's chest spurted like a geyser as thick crimson foam flowed from the corners of the fiend's mouth. The torrent of frothing gore that gushed from the vampire's heart drenched the entire floor of the Beefsteak room as if the vital fluid of every life Vlad had taken as a living man or as an Un-Dead monster was, at that very moment, returned in the ghastly excretion of blood. The writhing ghoul squirmed and wriggled wildly as it continued to scream and wail, twisting from the agonizing pain.

"This prolonged suffering lasted for some time during a period where his features became contorted and twisted much like the victim of a raging fire," described Stoker. As the Un-Dead curse left Vlad's body, his flesh collided straightway with Mother Nature and instantaneously caught up to its real age.

The creature's eyes bulged and then sunk back into its head, and its dark hair grew to a long, peculiar length, changing its color to an ashen gray and then a snowy white. Finally, it fell off the body altogether as the Count again desperately yanked at the cross buried deep within his chest, whilst burning the palms of his hands to the bare bone. As a grisly metamorphosis of the true dead took place, the kinky limbs appeared to cast out apparitions in all directions.

"Indeed, souls that were long forgotten by God were once again resurrected and remembered. The lost and the eternally damned to a vampiric hell were all at once freed, and every righteous victim finally found his or her path to heaven amongst the other angels on high," remembered Noel.

At length, resting in a contorted position, on the scarlet floor of the Beefsteak room, was the brittle remains of the skeleton of a man—clad all in black—and holding the silver Celtic crucifix that remained deep in his bosom was the skeletal hands of a long-forgotten Prince.

Abraham and Noel Stoker looked on at this transformation, dazed and bewildered. Indeed, their awestruck and amazed stares suggested that they had witnessed a divine miracle or the revelation of the afterlife in a way that nobody else could grasp, appreciate, or possibly understand but themselves.

By and by, the awful screaming ceased, as so did the soaring ghosts and the howling of the dogs. The room was so eerily quiet that the two jumped affright when a meek cry came from the coffin on the other side of the room.

"Mum!"

Noel looked around for something to pry open the top of the horrid box. The body of the captain truly had vanished, yet the bloody hatchet that lingered where it lay bluntly reinforced his tragic memory. The boy quickly picked it up and broke into the lid of the casket, hearing a loud, prolonged gasp of air escape the hole. And upon dislodging the lid, he threw open the sarcophagus with life-saving haste.

"Never has there been such a renewal of hope and love when out of that dreadful box emerged the most beautiful sight of all God's creations!" recalled Bram. For there sat a renewed Florence Stoker, who had reverted back to her youthful and graceful self.

"The marks," exclaimed the boy, "they are gone!"

Father and son let out a sigh of relief as they inspected her throat. Indeed, it was absent of the vampire's heinous stamp of ownership, and all color and voluptuousness had been restored.

"Florie!" the husband cried passionately. "My beloved!" And he embraced and kissed her repeatedly; and for a moment, it seemed as if time stood still for them until the married couple tired themselves into a lovers' oblivion.

The importance was abruptly ended by a loud pang that was made by the heavy sword that had been lodged in the fragmented talisman that had since crumbled to dust such as the fine particles of the native soil that filled the bottom of the monster's coffin.

Quickly, the Irishman took Dracula's sword and decapitated the Prince's remains. Then, taking some of the dried garlic blossoms from the large leather bag, he proceeded to stuff the vampire's mouth with the smelly flowers. And in a final resolution, the family towered over the appalling carcass and recited together the queer words of a vampire's interment.

"Hark! To the laws of heaven and hell, to the guardians of the flames and the nether pit—for the sake of mankind—permit this body to be forever incarcerated, consumed, and expurgated by the separation of head and body! May all baleful specters that threaten the souls of man be banished of all wicked words by the filling of these herb blossoms. Amen!"

* * * * *

In his unconscious state, Henry Irving was dreaming how old age had proven to be a wicked passage into a dark, unknown land where one is steadily astound by the impracticable. Hitherto, as a gentleman mortally staked, he realized his star was declining. Thus, the weary actor woke with an expression of intense perplexity upon his face. As he looked around at length, he became aware of the string of wolfsbane that hung around his neck and soon voiced his astonishment to Bram who, in turn, lifted him up from his dumbfounded predicament.

"What in God's name has happened here?" he exclaimed, eyeballing every corner of the room and then to himself. "Yech! What is this revolting festoon around my neck?"

"Here," the writer said, throwing his employer the thick text lying on the table. "I suggest you read it! It will explain everything!"

Doctor Van Zant next arrived on the scene, and after reviving Jonathan Watts with somewhat vigorous effort, said, "It is a true miracle of God that the bullet dislodged itself!" And after dressing Bram's knife wound, he added, "And we are blessed that gangrene did begin to fester on you both, eh?" The others nodded thankfully at the physician and shook his hand with valiant appreciation and respect.

"Indeed, you are a fine gentleman, valiant doctor, and a true friend!" said the Irishman gratefully. This Van Zant acknowledged by blushing and tipped his head in a pleased obliging sort of way.

The dreadful room resembled a place destroyed by the furious path of a tornado. Though the spilled blood had vanished with all traces of vampirism, the true impeding horrors were still fresh and vivid in everyone's minds.

Though Henry Irving could not remember any of the events whilst he was in a trance or hexed with Dracula's being, waking to the ghastly sight of an impaled, decapitated fleshless carcass was, by far, a vision to remember and a sure testament of what he would soon read about in Abraham's novel.

"Hitherto, I have titled it *The Un-Dead*," stated Stoker. "Now the next step is to decide where to go from here."

As all of the adults consulted about what to do with Vlad's remains, Noel commended his young friend for his great bravery at such a pinnacle of death.

"Ay, I never hurled any hatchet!" Jonathan answered. But he described the same glowing presence that Abraham had felt in the underground cavern and Noel and his father had experienced on the train back to London.

"Countess Dracula struck again!" they blurted out in unison. "She is at last in peaceful rest!"

Certainly, there was a odd calmness about the room and everyone surely felt it without saying the words: the soul that had been adrift for four hundred years had finally found her true home in a moment of sublime excretion. And after the group piled the Count's bones back in the coffin, they repeated a burial service for his true love and offered an entreaty swearing to not forsake her kindness for as long as they lived.

And then suddenly, with a look of surprise as if he were about to forget something of utmost importance, Jonathan reached in his pocket and pulled out the ruby necklace he and Noel pawned to Godalming for the money to take claim of the black leather bag. He handed it to Madame Stoker who embraced the boy with the same graceful charm and loveliness of old.

But as Jonathan shared the research, the old man left behind in his notebook found in the handbag of horrors, unhinged pieces of their incredible story were sewn together.

"The Jewel of the Seven Stars was owned and used by Pamela Coleman Smith and was the very means that summoned Dracula the night I attended a séance that was meant to speak to the Egyptian Sorceress, Queen Tera," explained Bram. "Henry was there in secrecy; for it was St. George's Eve, and he wished to remain anonymous— thereby, fervently requested his name to be left off the docket. Nevertheless, it was the spirit of Vlad the Impaler that was reached, and this was when the vampire made his first contact with Irving and began using his form for his bidding."

Each silently turned from the writer and looked at the actor in their own unique way, displaying unspoken forms of surprise, pity, and sadness. In response, Henry shrugged his shoulders with an appearance of alarm across his face but almost immediately fell back into his proud state by sitting up straight, as a man on his dignity, and cleared his voice to speak. However, Bram held up his finger in a warning-like manner, and the Lyceum owner realized his place in the situation and fell back quietly. Jonathan actually let out a chuckle as everyone looked on in amazement and back to Florence who was studying the jewel.

"Thank you, dear," she responded to Watts politely as she continued to inspect the beautiful object seriously as if deciding if she was holding a gift or a curse.

Noel smiled and griped his friend's uninjured shoulder tightly as his mother continued to look at the scarlet jewel with a weird, standoffish glare—almost like it was completely foreign to her. Finally, she broke her silence by uttering a brief statement of aversion in an eloquent style that only her ladylike demeanor could have relayed.

"Hmmm . . . I do not think I fancy the color in the same manner as I have hitherto," she added laconically. "As a matter of fact, I have lost all stock in the offensive hue."

They were all silent for a spell, as her mind seemed to drift into a daytime reverie. And placing her right hand on the large box, she changed the subject by making an unexpected suggestion.

"Perhaps we should send Vlad's remains to the Romanian government?" Everyone eyed her with a look of astonishment.

"Although I want to board up this room," replied Irving. "I do not feel comfortable sealing up—that is, what you claim to be—an infamous corpse!" he added.

"Nay," Abraham answered. "We need to get these bones as far away from here as possible!"

"Righto!" interjected Watts weakly. "Ye would be bonkers not to!"

The decision was unanimous: Count Dracula's remains would be drifting across the North Sea by noon the following day.

Upon heading back to his uncle's house, Jonathan expressed his unwillingness to keep the "handbag of horrors" despite Godalming's or Noel's wishful thinking.

"I shan't need it anymore," the blond lad said, handing the traps to his friend as if it were a ticking time bomb. "It would only give me nightmares of all that has been!"

At this, Van Zant shook his head sympathetically and said with grave earnest and deepest empathy, "Indeed, this intrepid group of heroes has been through a painful ordeal, eh? However, we have finally reached the long-awaited bitter end, and we praise God we can finally see its ray of light. This fantastic journey into a blackened abyss has caused all of us to grow stronger, to treasure our friends and loved ones that much more; and it has renewed our faith in the Almighty! Notwithstanding, and most importantly, it has proven to us that in a world full of evil predators in the end the power of good and the righteous always prevails!"

The physician's encouraging words touched everyone and moved him or her all in his or her personal and individual fashion. As Florence Stoker swept her long mahogany locks out of her face, everyone could see her eyes began to well up with tears. The actor acknowledged by shaking his head in a solemn kind of way. Noel Stoker looked at everyone one at a time whilst Jonathan Watts let out a loud "Amen!" and then fell silent, concentrating his sight on the floor as if paying his respect toward the dead. A melancholic Abraham Stoker brushed out his reddish beard with the fingers on his right hand, and after crossing himself, solicited a hail from everyone.

By and by, the doctor saw Jonathan to the farm and left his mate, the writer, and the actor to remove the sarcophagus and other items of importance from the Beefsteak room. After it was decided the Prince's remains should, in fact, go back to the Snagov Monastery, they all shared the same stunning and disconcerting feeling that if they had not shared so much of that grim misadventure together—that if they had not attained such strange testimony and weird evidence to support their harrowing story—that they would all surely have been mistaken for the insane. Noel left the Lyceum hugging his mother, saying, "Welcome back, Mum!" And returning the embrace, they laughed fabulously until they cried.

Then the actor and the writer soon followed, but before Irving nailed up the passage to the hidden chamber, Bram Stoker hung a sign over the blackened hearth that read these words:

It were done when 'tis done, then it were
done quickly.
—Macbeth

At last, Abraham followed his family home where they ultimately fell to pieces on one another, and when the realization of the end slowly began to numb the sorrow, the ultimate gleam of peace was soon ceded through the publishing of the greatest psychological gothic horror tale—not just of the Victorian era—but of all time. And with that delivery, a legend was resurrected, and a King Vampire would begin to haunt the dreams of millions . . . and to what end?

Consequently, after experiencing such a lengthy reign of an anathematic terror, the journeyman looked at the population of the earth differently. At times, he wondered if he even belonged to it. The soulless plight of the new age seemed to support a loss of faith in the Almighty while scientists, political figures, and demented men played God. Truly, angels were far in between. And after Countess Dracula's spirit joined the others on high, 'twas as if an invisible shield was put into place—to give restriction as a barrier between earth and the heavens, which sealed all visitation rights. Indeed, the air was absent of angelic beauty. But the cries of the sick, the wails of the criminals, and the screams of the murder's victims could be heard loud and clear.

Though an old horror was exterminated from this earth, a new dismay was born in death: Count Dracula—a novel fallacy entering the unattainable stronghold without end.

Epilogue

Molded into the likeness of Le Fanus's *Carmilla, Dracula* was published in 1897, the same year William McKinley was inaugurated as the US president Johannes Brahms was born, Queen Victoria's Diamond Jubilee was held and the first practical subway was completed in Boston. Though the original commissioning by Dracula was to exploit his evil and recruit new blood, the final concept of the manuscript could almost have been interpreted as a warning to the world and that only through hope, faith, and love might humanity truly conquer darkness. Key characters and the storyline was changed to protect the identity of those who dies or otherwise outlived the true consternation; however, the underlying plot of physiological terror remained the same: to beat down and destroy the monster to defend the ones you love—to free the world of his horror while shielding one's own sanity and personal faith.

Despite the public's mixed reviews and meager sales that foreshadowed a sad story of financial distress to come, Bram continued to write occasionally and managed the Lyceum until fire forced Irving to sell the theatre shortly before ill-health shed its ugly face. Abraham Stoker's melancholy seemed to grow to that much like Irving's, and in reaction to the actor's passing, the writer's own health began to decline. In humble tribute to the man he gave so much of his life to, the author noted, "It was all so desolate and lonely—as so much of his life had been. So lonely that in the midst of my own sorrow, I could not but rejoice at one thing: for him, there was now peace and rest. In my own speaking to the dead man, I can find an analogue in the words of heartbreaking sincerity (of Elizabeth Barrett Browning):

Stand up on the jasper sea
And be witness I have given
All the gifts required of me!

Indeed, the legacy of terror that appeared to follow the Irishman seemingly produced a shroud of darkness over his remaining years of life. Though the author would have liked to believe he was released of the monster's horror and that he would never have to return to the disturbing account again, fate assumed to have a different spin on his senior years. For example, with this hushed rumors of estrangement from Florence began to circulate among his friends and colleagues: could the grotesque memory of his beloved as an Un-Dead being driven him away in fearful disassociation, or was it Irving's own nefarious control that subconsciously drove him into a desolate world that manifested his captivity as that of the vampire's?

Certainly, Abraham Stoker wished that his eyes could have forgotten what they had seen, that his ears should have not retained what they had heard, and more importantly, that his brain would heave ceased to remind him of Count Dracula's horrors in the following days, weeks, months, and years to come. Nevertheless, the world seemed to be free of the fiend's evil, but its dark spirit looked to live on through the writer.

On the other hand, the remains of Vlad Tepes Dracula never did reach the officials of the Romanian government. Whether a body thief intercepted the cargo or one of the vampire's watchdogs had stolen the carcass, or perhaps, if it was a simple case of international shipping gone bad, was to be known. Notwithstanding, a return to Transylvania years later was meant to close that tragic chapter of his life:

"In the ages to come, terrible convulsions of the earth caused Castle Dracula to rock to and fro until the horrid structure at last fell to its knees," Bram recalled. "And with each moment, there came a roar from the very heavens—noises that shook the whole appalling structure, the colossal rock and even the hideous hill on which it stood. On each occurrence, a mighty cloud of black and yellow smoke would rise hazily into the air and, over time, scatter fragments of the edifice. Volume upon volume, until finally, in a rolling grandeur, was shot upward with unconceivable rapidity as of one fierce volcano burst would satisfy the needs of nature and that the fortress and the frightful structure of the hill had sunk into the void."

Although, in the author's last days, a reoccurring vision began to wake him with eyes filled of terror: that underneath the ruins, in a deep crypt lain an empty leaden coffin, lavishly detailed, and with a single word etched in brilliant Romanesque letters:

𝔇𝔯𝔞𝔠𝔲𝔩𝔞.

Like the infamous vampire, who drew much strength from his sustained absence in Stoker's legendary tale, Bram chose that the world would be a better place if he forgot about the character and never wrote of him again. And perhaps the world once agreed. Perhaps.

Onward, my life should have taken me to encounter distinct people and explore diverse themes; however, here at the conclusion, where the secrets and the true anecdotes of my life are learned, I revisit the fiber of my life work and say somberly and without assurance, "Finis."

Acknowledgments

First and foremost, I thank God for giving me the ability to express myself on paper. And when my writing is not of merit, I thank Him for the humble attitude to recognize this, seek and accept constructive criticism, and the patience to rewrite, rewrite, and rewrite without losing enthusiasm for the cause.

Secondly I would like to thank my ex-wife, Lisa Diane Cherry, for her love, time, patience, and support while this book was being written. For not only did she act as my editor, she was also the beacon that kept me focused. I owe her for the utmost courage and unselfishness in dealing with the insanity she must have experienced during its creation. Words cannot thank her enough for her continuous understanding.

I want to express my undiminished gratitude to the families and estates of the late Bram Stoker and Sir Henry Irving for the latitude to complete this vision. Without their approval, this book would not have been possible.

Thanks, Dad, for buying me that Dracula comic book in 1977. Who would have thought . . . ?

To the Dracula audience for keeping the genre alive—it is this fanbase that has enabled me to find my niche in the marketplace.

Finally, I want to acknowledge Michael Logan and Katie Hale for their friendships, inspiration, and feedback that remained intact though out the creative process.

About the Author

C alvin H. Cherry was born and raised in Marietta, Georgia, and relocated to rural Red Boiling Springs, Tennessee, at age seventeen. In 1988, he joined the navy as a radioman where he spent a year in San Diego, two years in Sicily, and twelve months onboard the USS *Thorn* (DD-988) during the commission of Operation Desert Storm.

When his enlistment ended in 1992, he moved back to Marietta where he met his first spouse, Lisa, whom he married in 1994, and relocated to Kennesaw, Georgia. At this time, he began a twelve-year career with the Canada Life Assurance Company, holding various positions within the Claims and Technology departments. During his tenure there, he acted as publisher and/or contributing writer for several firm newsletters and worked as a technical writer for creating procedure and system manuals.

In 2002, he earned an undergraduate degree in business management from Kennesaw State University and celebrated with Lisa the birth of their only child, Jacob Parker Cherry.

In 2005, Calvin joined ZC Sterling (now known as QBE) Insurance Agency in Atlanta as a business analyst. In 2009, he earned a project management professional (PMP) and Six Sigma Green Belt certifications, and retired from the Navy Reserve as an information technician first-class petty officer.

Calvin divorced and remarried in 2015 and is a member of the City of Light Church in Atlanta, Georgia, where he is a member of their choir. Calvin's hobbies include music, movies, literature, hiking, and traveling. He currently lives in Hiram, Georgia, with his spouse, Kevin Scott Bilbrey, and their cat Moses and now works as a business systems analyst for Assurant in Marietta. This is his first novel.

CPSIA information can be obtained
at www.ICGtesting.com
Printed in the USA
BVHW04s1730220418
514107BV00001B/26/P